PRAISE

"Richard Seward ⟨...⟩ ordinary feat of fantasy an⟨...⟩ the all-too real and vexed ⟨...⟩ ⟨w⟩hale." – *Philip Hoare, autho⟨r⟩ ⟨...⟩ ⟨S⟩amuel Johnson Prizewinner) and* The ⟨...⟩

"A magnificent, brilliant ⟨...⟩." – *Peter Wagstaffe*

"Richard Seward Newton writes with a clear engaging voice as he takes the reader into a very unexpected world." – *Emma Craigie, author of* What Was Never Said *and* Chocolate Cake With Hitler

"Tisala exudes warmth and a profound vision of love for nature and humanity." – *Christopher Cheung*

"A powerful commentary on our civilisation." – *Peter Parks*

"*Tisala* is written in clear, flowing prose that dwells perceptively and imaginatively on the big questions of sentient life and human society. The story couples meticulous attention to detail with an overflowing love of wisdom. It is a thought-provoking and romantic read that is sorely needed in a tired modern age." – *Liki Ng*

"An astonishing achievement." – *Judy Newbury*

"I was awed by the scope of the novel, and moved by the ending." – *Simon Loveday, author of* The Romances of John Fowles

"An intellectual tour de force, and a compelling story about the inhumane barbarity of humans. Newton gently encourages us to re-think what it means to live ethically." – *Professor Chris Palmer, author of* Shooting in the Wild

A NOTE ON THE AUTHOR

Richard Seward Newton was educated at Trinity College, Dublin, and Oxford where he studied history and English literature. He has, over many years, researched the biology and history of whales and whaling.

The whales' story, together with his life-long interest in history, literature and the natural sciences, have come togther in *Tisala*, his first novel.

www.richardsewardnewton.com
www.tisala.com

Tisala

Richard Seward Newton

*To Martin
With Best Wishes
Richard Newton*

Ⓜ
BLUE MARK BOOKS

First published in Great Britain by
Blue Mark Books Limited in 2015

This paperback edition published by
Blue Mark Books Limited in 2015

www.bluemarkbooks.com

© Richard Seward Newton 2015

The moral rights of the author have been asserted

This is a work of fiction. All characters in this publication
(save historical figures) are fictitious and any resemblance to real
persons either living or dead is purely coincidental

A catalogue record for this book is
available from the British Library

ISBN 978-1-910369-06-7

All rights reserved. No part of this publication may be reproduced, stored
in any retrieval system or electronic system, or transmitted, in any form or
by any means without the prior written permission of the publisher, nor
be lent, resold, hired out or otherwise circulated in any form of binding or
cover other than that in which is it published and without a similar
condition being imposed on the subsequent purchaser

Blue Mark Books Limited supports the Forest Stewardship Council®. The
FSC® promotes the responsible management of the world's forests.
All our books carrying the FSC® logo are printed on FSC®-certified paper

MIX
Paper from
responsible sources
FSC® C013604

Typeset in Minion Pro by Blue Mark Books Limited

Printed and bound by CPI Group (UK) Ltd, CR0 4YY

For Sally

'I desire only to know the truth and live as worthily as I can.'
Socrates

'Think for yourself, and let others enjoy the privilege of doing so too.'
Voltaire

'The ink of wise men is worth more than the blood of martyrs.'
The Prophet Mohammed

'History becomes more and more a race between education and catastrophe.'
H G Wells

'If at first the idea is not absurd then there is no hope for it.'
Albert Einstein

'Truths go through three stages: first they are ridiculed; then they are hated; and then they are declared entirely obvious.'
Schopenhauer

Contents

	Prologue	1
1	My Aunt Jane	4
2	In the Scottish Islands	10
3	The Meeting	16
4	In London	28
5	The Return	34
6	Robert Thompson	40
7	The Party	46
8	Progress	51
9	A Visit to Wiltshire	60
10	Retrospect	65
11	The Future	73
12	Three Years: A New Education	81
13	At Fieldbanks House	89
14	Tisala's World	94
15	The Legend of Tisano	101
16	The Coming of Whaling	109
17	Siana	117
18	The Antarctic Opened – 1904-1914	127
19	Saba	133
20	The Great Death – 1928-1939	139
21	Ellie's Day	148
22	A New Life	155
23	Consumer Products	159
24	In the Image of God	166
25	The Advance of Death	174
26	The Beginning of the End?	181

27	The Struggle	190
28	A Glimmer of Dawn	202
29	On Evolution	208
30	The Coming of Darkness	221
31	Alone	227
32	Will and Penny	232
33	On the Origins of Belief	237
34	On Religions	243
35	Against Exclusivity	255
36	On Power and Hell	265
37	Whaling 1964-75	276
38	The Russian Trawler	286
39	On War and Peace	295
40	The Nuclear Threat	306
41	Eric and Family	314
42	Illicit Whaling and the Moratorium	326
43	On Population	332
44	Human Numbers and Restraint	340
45	Economic Resources	348
46	A Visit to the Tropics	356
47	Music	372
48	Eric	380
49	On Education	392
50	Aspects of Learning	401
51	Guinevere's Grief, and Susannah	414
52	The Terrible Event	423
53	Aftermath	435

54	London, 1983 and Ethics	445
55	On the Origin of Christianity	460
56	Vancouver	473
57	London and Susannah	480
58	On Inis Cuan Again	488
59	On Happiness	493
60	A Wedding	505
61	On Meaning and Value in Life	511
62	Whaling: 1980's and the Japanese	519
63	Families	527
64	The Nation State, War and Peace	533
65	Hopes and Peace	544
66	Europe – a new Beginning?	553
67	The Parliament of the World	566
68	On Modern Whaling and the Future	570
69	Guinevere and Heaven	582
70	Changing Beliefs	596
71	Final Days	604
72	Valete	619

Tisala

Prologue

This is the story of Tisala. I have come to believe that the animals most to be revered in all the Earth are the Blue Whales. I say 'in' Earth because Tisala has shifted my perspective. As whales live in the top of the Earth's water oceans, so we humans live confined to the bottom of the next layer out, the ocean of air. The real boundary of Earth is beyond that – beyond the stratosphere and delicate ionosphere, the thin but vital sheltering layers of outer atmosphere. You may feel it more on cloudy days, especially if you are on the hills, when the clouds lie just above you like a ceiling. But those who live under blue skies may miss this awareness, for the blue expanse above seems limitless, though in reality we know the atmosphere exists for only a few miles above us, thinning rapidly. A mere five miles above sea level the air is so thin and the cold so great that oxygen-dependent animals can hardly survive; and our localised comfort in a big jet aircraft flying serenely above the clouds is wholly misleading. We all live within, and outside is the vast unfriendly emptiness of space. And 'revered', for though we humans dominate the world with our activities, many of them are bad and unworthy, and the Blue Whales are wise and full of goodwill and inflict no harm on the world. And I learned this from Tisala, whom I loved greatly.

If you find this history strange, I ask you to remember my experience. It has had a startling effect on the judgement I make of human affairs, and is part of my justification for finding them often foolish or cruel.

Throughout our history until recently we have been like crabs, living at the bottom of our element, only mobile to the small extent that our legs can carry us before exhaustion. We have of course developed props, such as the use of horses on land, or boats on water, to relieve our disability. With these it became possible to scuttle a little faster and further on our known bit of land or sea at the bottom of our ocean of air. Even the extent of our planetary home was not known to mankind for nearly the whole of our existence. Only in the last few hundred years was the surface – the oceans and continents – revealed to all by the explorers: Diaz, Columbus, Magellan and a line of others to Cook and later explorers. Thus the humans of different lands discovered each other, for though all the continents except the last-found had human inhabitants, some of them did not know of each other's existence. But this last-found continent, Antarctica, discovered by men only in the nineteenth century had, for thousands of years, been known to the non-human inhabitants of the high latitudes.

Meanwhile, the astronomers, from Copernicus onwards found we inhabited a planet that with others circled the sun. Thus the parts of the Earth and its place in the solar system came into our consciousness. But much of the topography of the ocean beds became known to humans only in the twentieth century, and the waters of deep oceans themselves remain largely unknown; though both have been familiar to whales for many thousands of years. And whales in the seas and birds in the air have long ago learnt to migrate in the layers of water or air across oceans and continents; they, not men, have had the freedom of the Earth.

Only now with air travel and submarines have we caught up with our animal cousins by being able to swim down in the water or rise away from the ground into the higher reaches of the air. And similarly, only with the understanding of electricity and radio waves have our powers of communication arrived at, and outstretched, those used for some millions of years – long before men existed – by the Blue Whales.

Yet there is a human prejudice that thinks all other animals inferior to ourselves. This is a prejudice of recent vintage – it did not exist for our myth-spinning forebears but was a development of semi-educated man. The argument ran: while we think and build palaces the other animals merely breed, feed and die. But palaces may be of two kinds, of stone and of the mind. This is the story of a palace of the mind.

But when I put that down it was unsatisfactory. It did not reflect the magnificent mind I have been privileged to know. For a palace is full of gilt and opulent proud ornaments, yet may be devoid of wisdom. I thought then to parallel other architectural edifices. But when I came to holy places, 'temples' echoed a line of strange or false gods, 'churches' wealth and cruel intolerance, 'mosques' fatalism and fundamentalism, 'synagogues' a localised self-righteousness. And whichever you use you immediately confront the fractured nature of man's religions, each contradicting and giving offence to the others; none of which remotely resembled the mind of Tisala. Perhaps, I thought, a parliament, or great hall, but they did not do, the one too full of personal ambition and disputation, the other empty but for feasting; or court of justice – indeed law and justice are necessary to order the lives of men – but in Tisala passing judgement went only so far as necessary for enlightenment and truth. Perhaps a university where, under intellectual discipline, the mind is free and encouraged to roam; but not like dusty, narrow or idle academies, or ones which are all assessment, and wealth obsessive.

I concluded that no institution of men measured the mind of Tisala. You may wonder at this, but first read my story, then judge. Only I am afraid I may not do justice to my subject. Tisala's story has set me a daunting task and I ask for the patience and goodwill of any who read this book. For I believe that what happened, and what came out of it, is of wide importance. And it led to my taking up the huge responsibility for knowledge of which I, with a few others, have been guardian for many years; but in which at the same time we delighted. In all those years, secrecy, as my history will unhappily show, has been a life-and-death priority, and I have previously been unable to open our knowledge to the world. But now I hope to discharge this onerous responsibility.

David Somerset, October 2004

CHAPTER 1

My Aunt Jane

My Aunt Jane died in 1956, but no one would then have believed how her death and what followed might lead to a more enlightened understanding of the world among a significant part of humanity. She left me nearly £9,000. Not a vast sum – although in those days you could buy a pleasant house and garden for half that – but as it turned out, enough. She gave me my freedom. By her gift she continued after her death the happy influence she had in her lifetime. Without her this history would probably not have come about.

Supported by her legacy, three years later, when I had completed my degree, I found myself spending a summer on an island in the Hebrides, off the west coast of Scotland. And there occurred the event that was to shape my life; though that is like pointing to one star in a galaxy of consequences.

I had been to The Hebrides once before, in the summer of 1955. That year, in the late autumn of my final year at school, I paid my last visit to Aunt Jane. She now looked ill and feeble and when she had let me in, sat on her sofa and did not get up, asking me to get the tea, before patting the cushion next to her for me to sit. But she retained her mind completely, and with it her sense of fun.

'I no longer bake,' she said 'but as I presume schools still starve young men, you see I have got in a cake. You must cut it – here.' She indicated the knife. She insisted her slice should be tiny. 'Give me just a sliver. No, no – really. I have no appetite.'

I do not know if she then realised how little time she had left. Perhaps it was this that made her want to move my perception of her out of childhood.

'Aunt Jane – '

'David,' she interrupted, 'as you are now a young man, shall I be just Jane? I would like that.' It was put as a question because she would not impose her wish on me, but as she rightly anticipated, I saw it as an enlargement, an advancement of friendship between us.

We talked all afternoon. She wanted to know about my life and goings on at school – sports and friends, but most of all about my mind; what was of interest, what I was thinking. I was full of my recent summer expedition to the Hebrides and the wonder and freedom of the experience. She laughed at my intensity and enthusiasm. I told her how a group of us from school had mounted an expedition to one of the remote Hebridean islands, taking with us camping gear and food for three weeks; how we had planned it, gathered stores, tents and equipment, written dozens of letters, and had been rewarded by manufacturers with various staples of life – cases of chicken supreme, beer, soup and condensed milk.

'How disgusting!' said Aunt Jane laughing, and to encourage me.

I told her how we had hired a small trawler and its skipper for the day, set out across the Hebridean sea and disembarked on the uninhabited island. How we waded ashore like so many invaders in the little bay with the beautiful beach and the stone ruins of a nineteenth century pre-clearance cottage, where a stream came down. How we nearly smashed our little outboard boat, and heaved all our kit and stores over the edge of the trawler, and how we shouted and laughed and tried not to drop tents in the water.

'No one had been there for years. We put up a small marquee for our living quarters. The beach and nearby coves were full of driftwood and we built a big communal table and benches in the marquee and a cooking range for the gas burners. We used the bottom of the stream – the water was freezing – as a larder for keeping meat, weighed down with stone. We used the stream for all our water.' Jane made a slightly dubious face. 'Above the larder,' I laughed. 'It's perfectly pure,' I said, showing off my new-found knowledge. 'There are no sheep on the Island only deer, and deer don't carry liver flukes.'

I chatted on about the freedom of that place – living on a wild coast with lochs and the mountains behind where we climbed and studied the mosses, the shoreline, the rocks and the bird life, and combated the midges. And how one day, when three of us were out at sea in the little outboard boat we had suddenly been aware of a great black shape, and then another, in the dark water beside the boat, and

'Dolphins!' had given way to an awed 'They're huge! What are they – whales?' as fifteen feet of black back had slid past us in the water and returned and shot under the boat and come by again two or three times before finally making off, blowing in salute.

'Goodness me, weren't you terrified?' asked Jane.

'No, not at all,' I said, truthfully. 'It was just exhilarating and exciting, like meeting people from outer space. I am sure they were saying "Hello". They could easily have tipped the boat over, but were careful not to. They were pilot whales – with blunt heads – we had a book in camp. I want to go back there and maybe do research into wildlife.'

She questioned me on the geology and later history of the island, and what area of knowledge I might add to by animal research. To the last, she was engaged in life. We discussed my forthcoming Oxford entrance exams, my plans to read biology and my reluctance to give up English literature. She said Jane Austen was one of her favourite friends and that one must always make friends among the best minds, for they enable you to be the most alive in your own life. Only once, having glanced out of the window at a red streak in the sky, did she sigh, when she observed the afternoon was getting on.

Three months later Jane was dead of cancer. My family lost a dear aunt, and I, a good friend as well. But I discovered when my mother told me about her will that she continued to be my benefactor.

My mother said that in a way she was relieved that Jane had died. For the last year she had found it wretched to watch her dying, often in pain. She said one day when she was with her and there had been no more to say she had put her arms round Jane and in tears they had put their heads together in a gesture of unity in Jane's lonely battle. I thought of my last visit and my chatting on about sport and school and felt very uncomfortable that I had not acknowledged the main reality taking place in Jane's sitting room. But years later what pleased me most about that afternoon was that she had lived to know the opening chapter and direction of my adult life, which her legacy was to support through difficult times. And I remember how she smiled at me, for she knew she was dying and was somehow passing on her life to me.

Her funeral service was in her church in Wimbledon. We were all there, my mother, my younger sister Susan, Jane's sister, Aunt Laura, and her two children and a few relatives by marriage. My mother, when I glanced sideways, was calm but with tears in her eyes. Susan was pale and quiet. We sat in the front pews. There were sounds behind us of people coming in. In a hush the coffin arrived. One of the undertaker's men looked old and unsteady, and I wondered how long before he would be in a box himself. Jane's coffin looked too narrow to fit her in, and I tried to imagine her face inside, but couldn't, for I'd never seen a corpse, and remembered her face when it was animated. The Vicar appeared to know little of Jane's views on religion but said kind things about her and made everyone laugh a couple of times. We sang the hymns, and as the service proceeded I found myself enjoying it, as sadness gave way to relief that she was out of her troubles, and that I was alive.

There was a surprising number of people in the church and at the end of the service I heard snippets of condolences, and names, some of which I knew from things Jane had said, but others not. A few older people introduced themselves, and I shook various hands, but then as people left I was aware of that little nexus of society breaking and dissolving.

After the service the family members went to the crematorium. I did not enjoy the mechanical nature of that place, the neat little curtains and cheapened solemnity masking its purpose of getting rid of bodies. But Jane had said firmly she wished to be cremated. She had once said, 'There are too many bodies cluttering up London. There soon won't be room for anyone to live.'

I was glad to get out in the January sunshine afterwards. The air was cool, but it was a bright sunny day, which seemed appropriate. As I walked down the path my mind went back to my last afternoon with Jane; to our talk about the Hebrides and my idea to return there to research wildlife. At that moment, I decided my future.

That Summer I passed my school-leaving exams just well enough to secure a place at Oxford, where I started in October. After some initial bemusement at College and University life, I found like minds, made friends, chased girls, got drunk and very soon loved the place. The core of my studies was biology, but I had friends reading history, English, politics and philosophy. We had long arguments and discussions into the early hours on such topics – and on religion, evolution and economic systems, social injustice and everything from the fate of Dr. Faustus to the price of beer. I felt my mind expanding under all these influences, and had an insatiable eagerness to read and experience widely. I took up geology, initially as a framework for the history of biology, but afterwards in its own right. I joined the Union, argued politics, debated, and even decided, briefly, to become a politician. In short, Oxford continued what genes, home and school had begun, but on a wider canvas.

A group of us wrote articles and pamphlets and became embroiled in various political causes of the day. Behind all of them loomed the ever-present threat of the Cold War – of mankind running mad in a nuclear holocaust. It hung over everything. We argued long whether global destruction would come within five years, or whether it could be delayed for ten, or whether it could possibly be avoided, at least for a generation. But that issue was for the most part too big and intangible to grasp – certainly to resolve – although we did devise a scheme for worldwide nuclear disarmament. The great powers were to divest themselves of nuclear bombs except for six each – sufficient to deter surprise attacks, but not enough, even if the worst happened, to annihilate the world. The UN was to hold a residual nuclear armoury controlled by an international committee of Swedes, Turks and New Zealanders. The Swedes were neutral and would be sensible. The Turks would not allow Soviet expansion, but having fought against Britain in the First World War would be seen as independent, and the New Zealanders ensured British common-sense and stability at an acceptable remove. In reply to our paper, The Ministry of Defence, on behalf of the Minister, was polite but infinitely non-committal. We thought it might be because of the Turks or possibly the Swedes, though we began to suspect after further fruitless letters that inertia, love of influence and lack of wider altruism was stronger in the British Government than fear of catastrophe. Those who hold nuclear arms always think it needful and wise to do so, and that no one else should.

But the nuclear threat did not stop me punting, writing romantic poetry, discovering sixteenth century sacred music in the College chapel, jazz in pubs and college rooms (wafting in from America), and falling for one girl simply by sitting behind her in a concert and admiring her beautiful hair and neck.

By the end of my three years at Oxford I had a group of good friends, a mind teeming with ideas and enthusiasms, and in certain departments a reasonable amount of knowledge; but little idea of what career to follow.

My time and studies at Oxford and my summer student travels together confirmed and consolidated in me one of the greatest gifts: a love of learning. This was to be of crucial value in my strange, and then unimagined, career, such as it became.

I was accepted to do a doctorate at University College, London. This would return me to the Hebrides, where I was to study animal communications in British feral mammals with particular reference to red deer. The purpose of this was somewhat obscure, but it was to do with the conservation of animal species in a world of increasing human encroachment on the natural habitats of many mammals. At any rate, the project found me writing to various landowners in the western Highlands and Islands seeking permission to carry out field studies on their estates. The response was almost uniformly open-handed and generous, their letters usually starting, 'Dear David', as if they already knew me. And that is how in the early summer of 1959 I came to be studying in an island deer forest. The term 'deer forest' is a quirk of Scottish usage. It does not denote the presence of trees: far from it. The Hebrides are islands of wild moorlands and coasts, where the deer make their home. Any small patches of woodland are confined to sheltered areas, often around sparse habitations, or on a lee shore, or in gullies. Such were the islands where I found myself.

And that is where it all started, and where my life was irrevocably changed.

CHAPTER 2

In The Scottish Islands

The estate was owned by Eric and Guinevere Sullivan. It comprised two islands, both with small deer populations, and was ideal for my intended studies. The two islands lay off a much bigger one known locally as the Great Island. The Sullivans' invitation was warm and pragmatic. They lived in the farmhouse on the sheltered landward side of Eilean Mòr, the larger island. It was settled that I could use the two rooms above the stone barn across the yard from their house. The rooms had been converted into a simple bedsitting unit. I was also given the use of an empty crofting cottage on the smaller island. This island was uninhabited and lay, at the nearest part, about two hundred yards across a narrow sheltered channel. It was called Inis Cuan, which means, rather strangely, 'the island of the sea'. When I arrived on Eilean Mòr I walked up a stony track lined with a few stunted and weather-beaten beech trees. The house was of solid stone and in need of some repair, but it was a charming place and I soon discovered that its owners were kindness itself. They were, I supposed, in their early sixties, grey haired but fit and sprightly. We rapidly became good friends. They lived alone on the island except for the MacLeods, who lived in the farm cottage and helped on the estate. Father MacLeod was elderly, and now only did odd jobs, as did his wife, for Guinevere. Their son, Jimmy, who was by training both a mechanic and a forester, was Eric's main helper on the estate.

I was due to spend eight weeks of the summer up there. Eric knew a great deal about the deer including some of the characteristics of individual animals, and his preliminary briefings were invaluable in my work. My first exercise was to monitor the number and location of the deer. It soon became clear that they followed a progression in their grazing habits, moving from one area to the next. My task was to investigate how this was determined within the different groups, particularly with reference to any apparent vocal communication between them. The University had provided me with a parabolic reflector and a tape recorder. These let me eavesdrop on their communicating sounds with some ease from a range of quarter of a mile or so.

Eilean Mòr was about four miles long and had a rocky coastline, except for two small bays on the northern side, where there were silver sand beaches. The rocks at one end of the island were ancient, worn pink granite, but much of the rest was a mix of old sandstone overlaid in places by dark crystalline basalt. The basalt – from volcanic activity about sixty million years ago – was the newcomer in this land of ancient rocks. On the eastern side, around the area of Eric and Guinevere's house, there were glacial deposits of stony soil left behind by the last ice age. And here stood a remnant of woodland, perhaps two or three acres in total. Otherwise, apart from the planting of stunted beeches near the house, the island at first sight seemed treeless. But as I explored I noticed short birches and elder growing in some of the more sheltered gullies. Where there were trees there were small birds – blue tits, coal tits, robins and everywhere tiny brown wrens.

On windless days in such sheltered places, and among the peat bogs, there were hundreds of tiny midges. Sometimes they formed undulating swarming patterns in the air above the vegetation. Initially, I thought their pinprick bites would drive me mad. Eric said, laughing at me, that they were the origin of the Highland Fling. But somehow as the days went by I became stoical or immune. In some way anyway, they ceased to concern me much – partly perhaps because I avoided the worst places on midgy days. There was little soil – a few inches at the foot of declivities and in pockets in the rocks – but everywhere the pale gleam of bedrock showed through the broken blanket of peat bog, and in drier places as outcrops above the rough grass and heather. Higher up, on the shoulder of the hills, the peat was crusty and wind-sculpted, with a scattering of white sand and feldspar from ancient decayed rocks. The island rose to a rocky summit over a thousand feet high. I grew to love the high bogs with their yellow bog asphodel, insect-eating sundews and tiny red tipped grey-green lichens, all with their busy insect life. Here too were pale yellow maroon-topped sphagnum mosses in spongy tussocks yielding iodine – used, Jimmy MacLeod told me, for treating wounded soldiers in the First World

War. These islands induced in me, as such islands have always done in humankind, a feeling of wellbeing and happiness, for they provide a world complete in themselves, where all is in place and balanced, and man is of very little consequence.

I spent the days exploring the island thoroughly. My olive green jersey and stone coloured trousers enabled me to merge into the landscape, so I could more easily track and live among the deer. The red deer were very shy, but beautiful in their movements and in the way they held their heads and ears, listening and interpreting the messages on the breeze. After one or two false starts, I quickly learned to come at them from down wind, and began to recognise the groupings. Sometimes, lying in the heather for quite long periods, just down from the tops of ridges so as not to show against the skyline, I became aware of the closer world. The heather was alive with bees, flies and many different small-winged moths. I noticed too the flitting flight of small birds – meadow pipits and stonechats – half hidden amongst the rocks and vegetation.

After nearly two weeks on Eilean Mòr, Eric took me across to Inis Cuan, transporting me in his inboard boat, with my kit, a few books and papers, portable recording equipment, and food for a week. We towed a little outboard boat, lent for my use. We landed on a small arm of rocks, which passed for a jetty. He showed me the spring near the old cottage. It welled out of a tiny patch of green grass and was incredibly clear. Inis Cuan was similar to its bigger sister but it rose to only five hundred feet or so. Round its cottage there were obvious signs of earlier cultivation, including some broken dry-stone walls and two or three areas of green grass, gradually being encroached upon by small patches of bracken, but kept close cropped by the deer and some rabbits. Its coast, though not spectacular, was full of interest. In places the rocks were broken open and coloured, showing the constituents of the Earth's crust. But below the high waterline they were black where they met the sea in an ancient partnership. The island had two sheltered inlets, one on the north coast and one on the south. The southern inlet was almost landlocked and formed a natural hidden harbour.

Eric said these islands might have seen the crude sails of the early Christians following Columba from Ireland, and had certainly seen the fierce swift sails of the Viking raiders. Many of the hills of the islands have Viking names, and traces of their fortifications remain among defendable vantage points.

I spent three days exploring the island. The weather was fine and I had an exhilarating sense of freedom, scrambling up rocky outcrops and walking the sea cliffs. I found myself continually drawn to the coast, as I have always been since my first family seaside holiday.

That was after the War when my mother had little enough money for holidays. I was nine and my sister Susan was seven. I discovered then the powerful human affinity with the littoral region – perhaps it raises ancient ancestral memories. From the moment we walked down the little Devon path through the butterfly-filled scrub and hedges, and first met the smell and sound of the sea, and then came out on the beach and saw the sunlit surf, sand, rocks and cliffs, it was as if I were coming back to my own long-forgotten country. It is a common experience, at least I believe among seaboard peoples, and endures within us.

I loved the seaside from those first moments. We paddled in the water's edge wondering at the great sea beyond, Susan running a few steps into the shallow water and timidly back again as the remains of the next wave hissed, with its little foam edge, up the sand. Soon we found rock pools and with their clear little worlds – darkened sea anemones, little purple-flecked sea snails moving slowly across the rocky bed and occasional tiny darting fishes and shrimp-like creatures. And always there was the sea – the tide slowly but inexorably pushing forward amongst the rock pools and running out again before the next wave came in causing seaweed to flow first one way and then the other. Towards the end of the beach there was a little rocky islet which you could only reach when the tide was out. I used to lead Susan up there to sit near the summit among the tufts of soft sea grass and thrift. The topmost rocks grew lichen, silver-green and bright yellow, and were streaked with great splashes of gull droppings. Seashore debris littered the cracks and crannies – bits of broken egg, empty limpet shells, a few little bones. We poked about and sat in a sort of sibling unity inspecting and prising apart our various finds. The sea shushed quietly against the rocks below and the gulls mewed above almost unnoticed; but the seashore entered our dreams forever. Later, when I read that one of the key developments of early man was his use of an opposing thumb and fingers, and that he had first made this adaptation on the seashore prising open shellfish, the idea surprised me not at all.

Now on Inis Cuan I was drawn again to the sounds of the sea and mewing of the hundreds of wheeling seabirds – fulmars, gulls and occasional terns. On the foreshore red-billed oystercatchers ran about searching for food with their haunting cries. And further out was the spectacle of gleaming white gannets plunging vertically into the sea with half-folded wings as they fished. There were cliffs, rock-falls and bays to inspect. I came across raised beaches with their rounded stones now half hidden in the long sea grass fifty feet above the present beach levels. Whether the land had risen or the sea fallen was an intriguing mystery. Time lay before me in the rocks in untold thousands of years.

My fourth day on Inis Cuan was a lovely sunny day with a light breeze, and the sky and sea blue upon blue into the distance. I was sitting on some rocks at the seaward end of the southern inlet that formed the hidden natural harbour. I felt at one with the world. At that moment, a couple of seals poked their heads inquisitively out of the sea about fifty yards off shore. I had the parabolic reflector and tape recorder with me. Although the seals appeared to be looking at me silently, when I began recording, I discovered they were making soft noises to each other. It was fanciful, but I wondered if they were commenting on my presence, and then, what they would think of such a land animal, crouching on the rocks. I stood up slowly, spreading my arms out and spoke to the seals, wishing them well. Words that meant nothing to them. But my idea was to experiment with gesture and tone of voice to gain their confidence sufficiently for them to recognise my peaceful intentions towards them, and so in a small and rudimentary way cross a species barrier.

I said I was honoured to meet them in their beautiful world. After about a minute they submerged, but a few seconds later surfaced some yards closer. This happened a couple of times and from nowhere two more heads emerged making an audience of four. To hold their attention and see what would happen I started to sing –

the first thing that came into my head – the tunes of a couple of arias from Mozart – *Don Giovanni*. I had the impression that a sort of excitement ran amongst the seals. During this operatic excerpt three more seals appeared; by the end of the concert, there were nine or ten. Afterwards, playing back the tape I discovered that their original soft noises to each other had turned to higher pitched sounds, but I did not pick that up at the time. I am no great singer and soon reverted to speech, asking the seals – voicing a sudden notion that came to me – whether they heard in music a universal language for all creatures. I sought to convey a calm and benevolent tone, for all the world like St Francis of Assisi. Eventually something disturbed them and with little surges and ripples they were gone.

I stood on the rocks looking out to sea and have rarely felt so at peace. It was as if I were standing on the edge of a new and precious world, one quite different from the troubled world of men. Suddenly and unexpectedly, I felt a surge of anger that Russians and Americans, at that time at the height of their cold war stand-off, both holding huge nuclear arsenals, could threaten the destruction of the planet for a mere ideological argument.

CHAPTER 3

The Meeting

The next day I took the outboard round the coast to the southern inlet. Eric called it Cala Bearn, though it was not named on any map. As I approached I cut the engine and rowed, hoping to see the seals, but the inlet, though calm, was empty. Leaving the boat on the shore, intending to return later in the day, I walked back across the island to the cottage – a distance of less than two miles – and spent the afternoon sitting outside the cottage writing up my notes.

That evening I walked back over to the southern harbour and sat on a rock on the edge of the sea, wondering if the seals would come back. It was a serene evening with not a breath of even the lightest breeze. The sea was a silver-pale reflection of the evening sky and was flat calm, the great Atlantic producing a tiny swell only three or four inches high when it reached the rocks, rising silently before falling back with a little sighing sound. In the quiet of evening I had a sense of oneness between land and sea, and after a few minutes felt a strong urge to be out on the water. I went round to the tiny beach, launched the boat, leaving the outboard raised, and rowed as silently as possible out between the little rocky headlands which formed the harbour entrance. As the boat drew away from the land the island's low hills seemed to rise higher out of the water, while the shrinking sea cliffs grew smaller and seemed to creep into the sea. A small seabird was dabbling on the water and ducked underneath with a little plop, which I could clearly hear at thirty yards. Behind it to the east the evening light was on the hills of Eilean Mòr and, fainter in the distance, there rose the hills of the Great Island. The pale blue sky dropping towards the horizon turned pinkish lilac, and where the sky, hills and sea merged, shaded into a twilight mauve. Away from the sun, the sky was a cool greenish turquoise. 'Viridian green for evening light' I had found scribbled on one of my father's half-finished watercolours.

The whole scene was like a great painting. Here in all its

magnificence was the original of the sublime in watercolours and oil paintings of the early nineteenth century, and the latter awe-inspiring scenes recorded by American artists pressing westward across their unknown continent. I too felt like a pioneer, feeling awe and wonder in the natural world. The painting image put me in mind of the contrast with the stricken fractured imagery of chaos and distortion I had seen in the London galleries – and in so much of the art of our own century. Perhaps it reflected the dislocation of our times, but here it struck me suddenly that such art only worked in a metropolitan context, and might signal to later ages an alien viewpoint. All around me was a whole and beautiful world.

I looked over my shoulder to the south and saw a disturbance on the surface of the water about fifty yards off like a current welling up. But as I watched it seemed to elongate and I thought it might be a shoal of fish. I rowed a few yards towards it, shipped oars and stood up facing the bow as the boat glided a little way onwards towards the disturbance. And then I saw a stronger eddy and suddenly a break in the water and the slight curve of something that became part of a huge back. For a moment I thought it was a basking shark, but there was no fin and the back went on and on like a great wheel, slowly revolving. I saw a glint of slate blue and was transfixed by the majestic calm of it; and suddenly knew with a wild certainty that it was a Blue Whale. After what seemed forever, the back revealed a disproportionately small fin with a ragged nick in it, before that too slid under the water and disappeared leaving only a little eddy. I stared after it, once or twice thinking I saw new eddies, but there was nothing.

But a minute or two later I saw a whale's back again, considerably closer this time, heading in the same direction as previously. I thought it must be another whale, following the first, but when his fin showed I saw the same nick, and realised with a start of disbelief and awe that this huge creature must have deliberately circled me. He disappeared. It was very strange that he had come round again – my mind raced – but I could only think he was curious.

I stared at the water all round the boat for several minutes, but there was no sign of the whale. I had nearly given up when a slight noise behind me made me turn my head, and there was the great back shining and sliding through the water – this time closer still – coming past me the other way. I caught my breath in excitement and a shiver went right down me. As he went past I involuntarily called out in a loud voice 'Whale! Welcome!' but he went on and on.

This time he did not reappear, although I waited for half an hour peering in all directions. By now the sun had dipped below the horizon. But when at length I noticed the evening light and colours – the reds, yellows and pinks of these high latitudes – they seemed even more beautiful than before.

Eventually I rowed slowly back to the harbour in the falling dusk. The encounter had replaced my earlier peace with exultant happiness and I squeezed the oars as if I expected them to respond in some way. Three times! He had come three times: that was extraordinary. What did it mean? What if he wanted to make contact? The thought stopped me dead, oars in mid air; but the idea was absurd, and so I rowed on.

Back at the cottage I consulted the only relevant book I had with me – on marine mammals. I spent the evening looking up whales, with increasing frustration. The information seemed sketchy and irrelevant – nothing about contact with man, or intelligence – but mainly anatomical descriptions with some comments about whaling for Right Whales, Bowhead and Sperm Whales. There was little about Blue Whales except mention of their enormous size and their abundance in Antarctic waters; but I found one short reference to the existence of an Arctic stock and occasional sightings in British waters. I recalled from my boyhood pictures of huge whales ferociously thrashing their tails and flicking tormenting whalers, both men and boats, into the air. It occurred to me that I had not been in the least frightened by my encounter, having sensed he intended no harm. I could not help laughing at myself for addressing the whale, yet found myself delighted that I had, and determined to do so again, if the chance arose.

The next day was fine and calm. I spent most of the day out in the boat scanning the water for renewed signs of the whale, getting further out to sea. But in the end I ran out of drinking water and got a headache from squinting against the bright light on the water.

In the evening I went out again. There was a little breeze just ruffling the surface of the water, which made it more difficult to see any possible underlying disturbance. After a while I began to get downhearted. It will be two hundred miles away heading for the

Arctic, I argued, and tried to console myself with the thought that I should be grateful ever to have seen such a magnificent animal. But despite the logic of my argument felt disappointed, and found I was hoping for something more.

Then suddenly, there he was, coming at a slant straight towards me. I stood up in the boat and shaded my eyes for he was coming half out of the sun. He passed slowly and colossally within a few yards of me. 'Hello whale!' I cried out, 'Welcome back!'

He went a little way off, but now I believed he would come back again. There was a small flurry of broken water like waves breaking a sandbank in the sea and I saw him heading towards me, with the bow wave in front of his head. He came very slowly and for the first time, I was aware of the true immensity of his bulk. He started to pass no more than twenty feet from me. He rolled slightly, and in disbelief, I saw his eye and realised at once he was gazing at me. I could scarcely breathe, for somehow I knew with that look we were entering each other's world. I waved an arm slowly by way of greeting and so as not to alarm him, and called out again, 'Welcome the whale!'

That evening we consolidated our first real contact. He circled the boat five or six times and each time I stood up. I think he realised this was a signal of my vulnerability and that I trusted him not to upset my cockleshell boat. Yet he too was taking a risk, for he brought his vulnerable eye within a few feet of my boat; and as he passed I marvelled at the smoothness with which he could trouble the water so little. Just in his wake the boat gave a little tug towards him.

Instinctively, I knew I must make further contact and had an intimation, without knowing clearly why, that I was encountering an extraordinary and intelligent being. It struck me forcibly that here was an invitation to the unknown, if I could only know how to use it. The idea made me dry in the throat with excitement.

On his sixth circle of the boat, he drew further away and seemed to speed up – as if he were preparing to depart. Then his back dipped down, and on and on the slate pale-flecked back slid downwards into the deep until suddenly there rose out of the water a huge pair of flukes – twenty feet across – up into the sky, the water cascading from them, before they too slid with a rush under the water and he was gone. I sat dumbfounded, full of whirling thoughts and emotions for countless minutes, before at last turning the boat shoreward. But I believed in my heart that he had saluted me.

I left the boat in the inlet and walked back in the twilight to the cottage. That evening I conceived the idea of testing the whale's capacity to receive information and communicate. I was exultant with the audacity of the thought, and spent half the night thinking of ideas and plans. His return and his methodical circling of the boat continued to amaze me. I tried to deflate my excitement rationally. He was merely spending a day or two in these waters before passing on, and was curious – possibly a young whale; but I could not suppress for long the thought that he had returned deliberately to seek me out for some purpose. Then I was dismayed by the recurring thought of migration: that his pause in the Hebrides was over, that even now he was heading into the dark sea for the Arctic, and our brief contact was an end.

It was therefore with an uncomfortable mixture of hope and dread that I took the boat out next day. The weather remained fine and calm. The sea stayed empty through a long morning and hot afternoon. Then, in the late afternoon and to my delight, he appeared once more. This time he circled the boat very slowly and then drew a little way off and stopped. I waited for him to come close again but he did not, though neither did he move away. To start with it puzzled me. Then I realised he might want me to go to him. Very quietly, so as not to disturb him, I rowed towards him. He was lying sideways on to me. The boat came up alongside him. We bobbed closer and closer and he did not move. I suddenly had a great urge to make physical contact. I leant out and patted him. He seemed motionless. I called out quietly – 'Welcome, Whale! Welcome! I have come to talk to you. Let us be friends.' Though to him the words would be meaningless, I hoped he would, like the seals, catch something of my tone. I knew I had to seize my chance to let him know that men have rational minds. I patted him once, not hard, but deliberately and called out 'One.' After a pause I patted him twice and called out 'Two,' and the same for three.

Initially, there was no reaction. The great body lay still, the water lapping over the slate blue expanse of back on which I could now see the variations of colour – a few lighter markings of almost a milky blue. Then something remarkable happened. He blew spray with a hiss from his blowhole. I afterwards realised it was only a token spout but it startled me with its loudness. A jet of spray and moisture rose a dozen feet in the air. It subsided, and I was just wondering what to do next when he blew again – this time twice in quick succession and after a pause, three in quick succession. He was counting. I was electrified: he was telling me of another intelligence residing in our planet. I felt the world begin to change. I leant out of the boat and with my open hand slapped him lightly but firmly in a steady rhythm – once; twice; three times and so on up to a group of five. There was a pause – as if he was waiting to see if I had finished. This time the answer came as a sound, halfway between a grunt and a squeak, steady and deliberate, one, one two, and so on up to five. His skin was smooth and for the first time I smelt the pungent sweet odour of whale on my hand. Afterwards it became so familiar that when I was away from the sea for long I yearned for it. At that moment I felt nothing but pure excitement at our meeting and knew I must communicate it to him. I sat in the boat and sang a tune from *The Marriage of Figaro*. I do not know why that particular song came into my mind, except perhaps that it is very beautiful. After the last note there was complete stillness for two or three seconds.

Then there was a great suction in of air at his blowhole and slowly he raised his head so that his eye emerged, and the huge lid of his mouth, with the water pouring off until the last streams formed a runnel rather like a gutter where the lid sank into the protruding massive lower jaw bone. He seemed to be able to hold this position with ease. I pushed the boat away from him a few feet, so he could more readily see me, and stood up facing him. So we looked at each other; two creatures of the same planet but vastly separated worlds, meeting in potential friendship.

I spoke to him quietly, saying how greatly privileged I was to be visited by him out of the ocean, indicating this with my arms. I said there should be no more destruction of whales by men and that I wished peace for the whales in all the oceans. In the silence that followed he slowly submerged and came up again. I did not know what else to do except to secure further meetings, so I said, 'I will come back tomorrow. Tomorrow,' and I pointed at the setting sun and very slowly dragged my arm to the north-western horizon and traced the journey of the sun round under the Earth to the eastern horizon and with both hands made hand bursts in the air to try to indicate the sunrise, and, with arms and fingers stretched out as if carrying the orb, brought them round to the sun. 'The sun. The sun, tomorrow.' I repeated the round diurnal motion of the sun with my arms.

Then I began to row slowly towards the shore. An evening breeze had sprung up and there was movement on the face of the water. He swam slowly in a circle round the boat, and I watched, bursting with happiness. Then he headed out to sea.

On shore that evening, thinking over our meeting, I suddenly became dismayed, realising I had repeated the semaphore of 'the sun, tomorrow'. He will not come tomorrow – he will think I meant in two day's time; and if the weather breaks I will not be able to go out. If I fail to appear he will think me untrustworthy, and not return. My happiness drained away and I waited for an hour with a dry mouth for the weather forecast. The crackling voice came through on the wireless: the weather tomorrow and the next day would be fine. I was startled by the strength of my feeling of relief. Relief quickly gave way to speculation. If he could count, he had a rational brain. Could he understand words and even language? It was suspected that whales and dolphins had their own language. Could he understand ours? Had he understood my gestures and accompanying words concerning the sun and coming tomorrow? I wondered if he would be able to understand numbers and letters. Might he be able to learn a human language? I determined to try.

The following day I woke early to a bright sunny morning and after a hurried breakfast walked over to Cala Bearn, took the boat down the inlet and round the coast to Eilean Mòr. I wanted to see Eric and Guinevere. When I arrived they insisted I must stay for lunch, and would not hear otherwise. They were full of an incident about a deer which had become so entangled in a bramble patch that he could not escape.

'Godfathers, how he wanted to live,' said Eric. 'He bucked like a bronco.'

'You should have talked to him,' I laughed.

'I did, I did,' said Eric, 'and in the end he calmed down enough for me to cut a few big brambles, and he was able to break free. Do you know, he stood on the ridge and looked back at me afterwards to say

"Thank you". He saw Guinevere looking at him with a quizzical smile. 'He did, he certainly did, old girl.'

'You're a silly old fool,' said Guinevere smiling. 'You'll think you're St Francis next.'

'That'll be two of us,' I said, and told them of my concert with the seals. But of the whale, I kept quiet.

'Yes,' said Eric, 'I once sung to the seals, only I gave them hymns, which probably put them off. And I got such a coughing fit that they were pretty alarmed and shot away. I don't suppose they thought they'd got their money's worth. Anyway,' he said, 'I want a footnote in your thesis for my deer story.' I promised it to him with pleasure.

After some chat, when I enthused about Inis Cuan and the glorious weather, I asked Eric if he had some paint. He looked at me, yes, he had some white paint, and yes, some thin board. I hedged, saying I had an idea for marking out areas on the moors, for the deer. We went out to one of the byres where he had some plywood offcuts which we sawed into pieces about a foot square. Back at the house, I mentioned casually that I had seen a whale, and did he have any books on whales that I could borrow. He had a good number of books and found one entitled *The Great Whales of the Seven Seas*. I held it carefully with a tingling sense of anticipation, like a child with an unopened birthday present. They gave me lunch, and Guinevere afterwards fussed round insisting that I take more food. I set off back with my rucksack heavy with paint, boards, food, a bottle of whisky ('to keep your throat oiled for singing,' said Eric), and the precious book.

I crossed back to my cottage on Inis Cuan, and unpacked. Then I painted five of the boards with numerals 1 to 5. The paint seemed to take an age to dry. In the evening I went over to the southern inlet and with a mixture of apprehension and anticipation took the outboard out to sea. About half a mile beyond the little headlands, I cut the engine and waited in the silence that followed, the water slip-slopping against the boat. A long and anxious half-hour passed, my eyes constantly searching the sea all around for the whale. Then, without warning, he suddenly surfaced very close by, almost underneath me, startling me greatly, for he had approached completely undetected. He made a sound, mid-range to the human ear, that rose towards the end, which he repeated, and which I came to recognise as his greeting. He lay at a slight upward angle with his eye above the water and his head half out. I welcomed him back delightedly, manoeuvring the boat right up to him and leaning over, thumping him lightly with my fists in a drum beat of sheer pleasure at his return. Then I pulled the boat away, stood up and held the board bearing the number one. 'One,' I said pointing to it, 'one,' and leaning over smacked the stern of the boat with my hand 'One.' And so we progressed, up to five, and he responded with the appropriate groups of sounds. But then to my astonishment he continued – a group of six sounds, then seven and on up to ten – with me calling out at each stage the new numbers, six, seven, eight, nine, ten. I believe he could tell my excitement from my reaction. Afterwards I sang for him again. After the encounter had lasted about an hour, I signalled that I was returning to the island, but would come back next day, and started to row towards the shore. He circled the boat twice before heading out to the open sea.

In the following days I knew with increasing certainty that he would come back. He did, and we met every day. Thus began our friendship. I discovered he was able to lie with his eye above water level for considerable periods, occasionally submerging, to keep his skin wet. I painted the numerals 6 to 10 on the backs of the plywood squares and held them up for him to see while calling out their names and counting the number by slapping the boat. Similarly I painted most of an alphabet (using torn up cardboard boxes to supplement my boards) and showed to him letter by letter, calling out the letters, 'A, B, C,' and so on. Then I picked out the vowels, 'A, E, I, O, U,' held up the boards and repeated the sound. Then said loudly and deliberately, 'Letters – make – words,' and held up clumsily – THE – and then – SEA. Then I scooped seawater up in my hands and let it run through my fingers. 'The sea' I said and indicated the vast expanse. So too, THE – SKY, and pointed and gestured to the blue sky above. So we went on, day by day, with single words and gestures, but other than by occasional little snorts from his blowhole, and a series of sounds which meant nothing to me, I got little discernible reaction.

After several days and many repetitions, for his patience seemed unlimited, I decided to speak in complete sentences, not expecting that they would be understood, but to demonstrate to him that language existed by stringing together letters to make words, and words to make sentences. I said, holding up the letters, 'You are a WHAL,' (the E defeated me for I could only hold up four letters).

'You live in the SEA.' I waved with an arm towards the horizon and dropped the A, nearly losing it overboard. 'I am a MAN.' I held up MAN, then put it down and pointed with both hands to my chest: 'Man.' Then I pointed to the hills behind me. 'I live on the LAND.' LAND came up in a somewhat uneven line.

I recorded his responses – small squeaks and grunts – on the tape recorder, but when played back I could make nothing of them.

After a few days I became gloomy and depressed and did not know how to proceed or whether what I was saying was simply incomprehensible to him. Remarkably, the calm fine weather lasted for over a week, but then one day the sky became overcast and a steady breeze of three or four knots blew up from the south-west. The fatuousness of the situation was borne in on me. Although he came and lay motionless as before, I could not keep the boat still. There was now a foot or two of water rising and falling between him and me. I was afraid both of lurching into him or upsetting the boat. I tried to progress with one or two more words but began to get queasy with the irregular motion of the boat. I realised how stupid it was even to think in terms of making real contact. Besides, how could a creature that had no idea of anything other than swimming round in the murk of the oceans have any idea of the life of mankind with our houses, cities, mountains and forests and deserts. And anyway, he had no possible means of communicating with me. Eventually I called out above the breeze and the noise of the water slapping against the boat, 'Goodbye Whale, I am going home now.'

I started to row towards the harbour inlet which was then about quarter of a mile off. But I had not gone many yards when I realised that the distance between us was not increasing. I rowed on a bit further and then knew from the slap, slap of his bow wave that he was following me. I felt a stab of fear, the ancient fear of being hunted, and wondered whether my going had angered this great creature. I knew he could smash my tiny boat to oblivion with a flick of his tail. But a calm voice inside said, he is your friend, and I was ashamed of my fear. He kept about thirty yards off and came steadily after me. Then I thought with a rush, he is coming to see where I go. By this time we were coming towards the little islets that guarded the mouth of Cala Bearn. My first sense of fright was replaced by wonder that he was coming with me – Blue Whales are ocean dwellers and rarely come close to land – and then by the fear that he might damage himself on the underwater rocks. For the channel into the loch, though deep, became quite narrow, before opening up into the inlet itself. It was a natural haven about four hundred yards long and nearly two hundred yards wide at its widest point. To my amazement he followed me into the harbour, which was sheltered and quite calm. I stayed in the middle and he floated alongside me. I could scarcely believe what was happening, but even then recognised the possibility of developing a more permanent contact, not wholly dependent on the weather and a bobbing little boat on the edge of the ocean. I called out, 'Welcome to my harbour,' and gestured all round: 'Harbour!' He swam carefully round the inlet, as if he were exploring it and noting its geography, for he paused in places, and two or three times dipped under the water completely. I stayed in the middle, and eventually he came back to me. After a few minutes, he headed down the inlet and out to sea.

The next day the sea was choppy and I walked out to the little promontory at the end of the inlet to see how the sea was running. I saw him about three hundred yards off, circling slowly as if he were waiting. I cupped my hands and shouted for him to come in. My voice was lost on the wind and he did not come. By now it was quite rough and though I hesitated to take the boat out, I was afraid he would think I had abandoned him. So I went out, tossing and pitching as the boat got out between the islets into open water. We made contact. It was windy and quite rough. I shouted and pointed back to the harbour. To my delight he followed. I wanted to make him understand that he was safe, but guessed he would not come into the harbour without me leading him, and supposed he might fear the confined space. But when he followed me in that second time I was exultant for he seemed to trust me, and I renewed my word lessons with growing confidence.

After that he came in several times when the weather was not good; but when the weather was calm he stayed outside in the sea. On one or two occasions we missed each other for a day, and I was always then in a state of apprehension. But he always reappeared. Other thoughts and fears came to me ashore at night, as I lay awake in bed. What might happen if other men discovered a great whale was coming into such a place? Our meetings went on for about three weeks.

Then one day in late May I sensed a difference in his behaviour. We were out in the sea. He came up to me as usual but instead of lying quiescent, after a minute or two when we had exchanged greetings – me with my normal calls of welcome and he with what had become his signal – he started to move off and circle the boat. He swam in a complete circle three times. I slowly grasped what I did not want – that he was saying goodbye. He was about to migrate. I felt a strong sense of impending loss, but knew it was the time of year when he should, before now, have been heading for the feeding grounds in the Arctic. I stood up in the boat and pointed to the north and made an undulating swimming motion with my arms and pointed to the north again. As he came close he rolled and I saw his eye looking at me, and I waved, a sort of half frozen wave. Then, as he came past me again, the front part of him dipped and the great wheel of his back arched more than normally out of the sea until his great flukes rose slowly out the water with their attendant shining waterfall. I knew it was his farewell. His head came up again and he gave a great spout from his blowhole, and a long low call, like the boom of a foghorn. Then he headed north-west without turning back.

CHAPTER 4

In London

For the first two or three days I kept a fairly constant lookout, but became increasingly sure he had gone. I resumed work on the deer, though without much enthusiasm. I stayed on the islands for another two weeks, then started to close down the cottage and pack my belongings for the return to London. As I worked my mind was constantly occupied by events and images of the previous weeks. I knew with certainty that the whale had intelligence. But was it compatible with ours? I wondered whether he had deliberately sought me out, but that seemed preposterous. I thought with some pleasure of my rudimentary attempts to make contact by signs and language, but always came up against the blank wall of his inability to respond in a recognisable way. I was enough of a biologist to know that his larynx, tongue and lips could not articulate sound in the same way as humans. But I was aware of speculation suggesting that whales have a language of their own. And it was clear they could – perhaps by a different mechanism – produce a wide range of sounds. My mind kept coming back to the persistence with which he had returned over the four-week period. Had I been stupid not to regard more closely his blowhole responses and the peculiar varied sounds he often made? Were these signal patterns or some sort of code? I resolved to get into the Natural History Museum at the first opportunity to research what was known, and enlist expert help. I ordered my papers and looked through my work on red deer. It had not got as far as it should have done. But somehow it now seemed flat and dull.

Each evening I went out on the promontory at the seaward end of the inlet and scanned the sea ceaselessly, initially with binoculars, though I soon gave this up – straining my eyes over the expanse of middle distance water was pointless; either he would come close enough in to be seen or he was not there. The sea on those evenings seemed empty and desolate, but I was always reluctant to leave.

I felt the same on leaving Inis Cuan. Twice I crossed to Eilean Mòr, ferrying my kit. Eric sent Jimmy MacLeod with the tractor and trailer to pick me up, as I had too much to carry. We bumped and lurched our way along the track across the island to the ancient private ferry. This was a former fishing boat, small but sturdy with a handsome inboard engine. I said warm goodbyes to Eric and Guinevere, promising to come back in the spring. They had come down to the jetty, and we waved as the boat pulled out. On the far side Jimmy picked up the dilapidated lorry, which was full of oil drums, some fencing posts, and coils of wire. He drove the twenty miles to the public ferry. We shook hands and I boarded the ferry for the mainland. And so came to the railhead for the overnight sleeper south.

I spent a fretful noisy night on the train and woke up in a different world. The train was passing through English countryside, full of enormous trees, green and fresh in their June foliage. The houses were red brick and so neat they looked unreal, like dolls' houses. The train entered the unending eruption of houses and buildings that is London. From the noisy concourse of the station I took a taxi to the university. My rooms in college seemed small and cramped, but after a day or two I got used to them again, although I frequently found myself miles away in the Hebrides on the edge of the great ocean in the company of the whale.

As soon as I had dealt with various administrative tasks and social visits, I went to the Natural History Museum. They issued me with a reader's ticket and I found my way down to the cavernous basement below the public galleries; great spaces full of the skeletons of whales of various species, reassembled with wire and hanging from the ceiling; and jawbones standing fifteen feet high, leaning against the walls. Everywhere in these silent ill-lit caverns dust lay thick and a strange musty smell of whales pervaded everything. At one end through a glass door was the whaling library, which was housed in a more pleasant 'L'-shaped room with good lighting, and mahogany desks and tables with black leather tops and worn gold tooling round the edges. All round the sides stood tall Victorian bookcases, full of books containing the sum of man's knowledge about whales. For some reason many of them were bound in black cloth.

I spent most of my time for the next two months in that place. Initially I consulted various books and indexes, but things that interested me, like eyesight, intelligence, sound communication and so on were sparsely alluded to. Early on I asked one of the curators there for help, saying I wanted to study Blue Whales. He looked up and asked, 'Why Blue Whales particularly? They are pretty well fished out, I'm afraid. You should study Sperm Whales – they are the future of whaling.' He peered at me. 'What are you looking for? What angle?' I sensed danger and did not intend to confide in him.

'I am interested in methods of navigation in dolphins and whales.' That was general enough not to invite more specific enquiries.

'Ah,' he said, 'yes, if only we knew that. You are welcome to try, but I don't think we have much.' He mentioned a few books and reports where I might start.

Gradually I discovered why it was difficult to find my information: it simply was not known. And nearly everything that was known had been learnt through the activities of the whaling industries. It was they who very largely provided such facilities as there were for research scientists and often paid them to do their work, which was aimed at understanding the growth, feeding and migratory habits of the species of great whales, precisely in the order of importance of each species to commercial whaling, the better to hunt and kill them. There was much concern over the decline in availability of favourite catches – in turn Right Whales, (Black, Greenland and Bow Heads), Sperm Whales, Humpbacks and Gray Whales, and then the rorquals – Blue Whales, Fin and Sei. But the concern appeared to arise almost solely from fears that whaling would become uneconomic if the 'stocks' of great whales were too depleted. The whales were to be studied to discover their maximum sustainable yield. They were otherwise to be 'cropped', 'harvested' and 'fished', relentlessly.

Slowly over the weeks in that room below the museum the horror of whaling history was revealed to me. I discovered commercial greed and unbelievable cruelty were the norm in man's relationship with the whales. Much was known about certain aspects of whale anatomy – various dimensions and the sizes of foetuses; the measurements of parts – jawbones, baleen, flukes, fins, penises, eyes, the weight of blubber, oil yield, stomach contents, and the number of laminations of ear plugs (showing longevity, like rings in trees). Virtually all was derived from inspecting and cutting up carcasses as a by-product of the slaughter carried out by commercial whaling. And virtually nothing was known of the character of living whales, their attributes or capabilities, or their society. Hardly anything appeared to be known of their intelligence, communicative powers, or methods of finding their way round the oceans. It was known that they migrated to and from their summer feeding grounds in the Arctic and Antarctic, but the rest was veiled in mystery. The brains of dead whales had been weighed and measured. 'The brain is very large with an extensive and highly developed cortex', it was reported. But no one seemed to ask, other than in the most cursory manner, why they are so, or what whales do with their hugely developed brains. Similarly, they are known to emit sounds, I read. The latest research, using microphones lowered in water, produced sounds recorded on gramophone discs: whistles, clicks, squeaks and low frequency booms. Possibly these were navigational aids or call signs for mating purposes. But these were only surmises, or in scientific terms, as the researchers soberly reported, they were 'not yet fully understood'.

My reading in the museum gave me a number of ideas. One day, not long after I started my studies, I was looking at a photograph of a dead female Blue Whale on the slipway at the whaling station in South Georgia – that remote snow-covered Antarctic island. The photograph had a caption that drew attention to the whale's long throat grooves and genital slit. It reminded me that although I had always mentally referred to 'my' whale as 'he', I had no idea what sex he or she was, or what age. The idea that the whale patiently making contact with me might be a young female charmed and delighted me. At once I felt very protective towards her. But then another thought struck me – what if 'she' were a grandfather whale, the possessor of who knows what ancient wisdom? I did not know the answer to these questions, but over the weeks that followed my habit of thinking of 'him' tended to re-assert itself. The calm inquisitive bravery of the great animal somehow struck me as male. But he was large. I now knew the largest Blue Whales could occasionally grow to over a hundred feet long, and the largest known whale ever caught was female. I thought mine might be eighty feet in length. The questions remained unresolved.

Bizarrely, the pictures of the whaling sheds of South Georgia, the scene of mass butchery of dead whales, gave me another idea. My idea was to build a shed on the shore of the inlet, immediately above a place where the whale could berth. The shed would give me shelter, and a base to set up recording equipment. Communication would become much easier. This basic idea soon gathered improvements.

If I could build a big rack for letters, say on a ledge on the rocks immediately up from deep water, I could display long words. The whale could learn our language. With various aids – texts, pictures, a globe (yes, definitely a globe), maps and the like – he might learn to read, and understand our land world. I became elated. If only he could be taught to communicate… But the more I thought about that the more the obstacles seemed insurmountable and I became low and discouraged. Besides, always at the back of my mind was the fear that he might never come back again, or worse, might end up dead on a whaler's slipway, hauled up prior to being cut into strips by flensers in their thigh-high rubber boots and overalls, wading in blood and gore, and wielding their devastating long-handled flensing knives; a great mammal being reduced to bloody piles of flesh and blubber, dismembered, and rendered down for oil and bone meal. I tried not to dwell on that possibility, though it formed an underlying anxiety.

But when I thought again about my own extraordinary encounters, it brightened my mind and set me seeking new solutions. I continued to study and plan and started to consider electronic communication. If he were moored by the shed, which in my mind's eye suddenly acquired electric power, some sort of communication system could be set up, perhaps solving the problem of a totally different sound reproduction system from our own. If spoken sounds could be reduced to electronic impulses in a telephone and back again into sound, why not words translated into whale sounds and vice versa? That idea immediately raised two connected problems. I was not electronically competent. The exploration of such possibilities would mean finding and confiding in such a person. And after reading about the ruthless exploration and greed associated with the international slaughter of whales, I suddenly felt afraid, inadequate, and isolated; nearly all those knowledgeable about whales were implicated in their destruction. I needed an altruistic physicist who could be trusted, and I had no idea how to proceed.

To generate some action I returned to the shed idea. As a first step I wrote to Eric about the shed, saying my research would be much assisted if I had a sort of shed shelter over by the southern inlet, and asked if I could erect one. About ten days later he replied. He sounded puzzled, but of course I could, though regretfully it would have to be at my expense, and the shed would eventually have to be dismantled, or left for the benefit of the island. Jimmy MacLeod would be able to help me build it, his fencing and other estate duties permitting. And he himself was a dab hand with hammer and nails, having once built a cabin in Canada, though it had cost him a thumbnail.

Letters and telephone calls to builders' suppliers on the West Coast followed, concerning posts, boarding, corrugated iron, ribbing, bolts and cement. The idea was feasible, but the cost including delivery rather appalled me. I thanked them for their estimates, but said any order must first await site development. I had in mind two possible spots in the southern inlet. But 'first' in reality hung on whether or not the whale reappeared in the autumn. I was haunted by the fear that he might never return, and that my dreams of the last months would come to nothing.

CHAPTER 5

The Return

It was with trepidation therefore, that in early October, I set off back to the Hebrides. I calculated, from what was known about the migratory habits of Arctic Blue Whales, that the summer feeding would end sometime in October and the journey south to warmer winter seas would commence. If my whale came back he would probably be passing through the Hebrides between mid-October and early November. I had decided to call him Rorq, after his kind, as he was one of the rorqual species.

Back on Eilean Mòr, I was met by Eric. We walked up the drive to his house past the stunted beech trees. Their crowns were already nearly bare of leaves, with just a thin scattering of leaves, gold turning copper, fluttering among the lower branches. After some cheerful talk he asked me about the projected 'shack', as he called it. He found it difficult to understand the purpose, as Cala Bearn – the south inlet – was only a couple of miles across the island from the cottage. 'Well,' I said 'you may be right – it may not be strictly necessary – but I do find myself over that side pretty frequently, and bringing the equipment around is a problem.'

He looked at me closely: 'It is not to do with your seals is it?' he asked.

I wanted to tell him the truth but had decided that, although I trusted him and Guinevere completely, I would not say anything unless the whale came back. 'Now that's an idea,' I said, half-mockingly. 'If we could wire the place up we could broadcast concerts to the seals.'

He rubbed his chin and grinned. 'Half-mad Englishman!' But added after a pause, 'What about Beethoven? That'd stir 'em up.'

I installed myself in the cottage on Inis Cuan. For over a week I kept a daily lookout from the southern promontory and in the evenings took the boat out, except for two days when a storm blew up. Then, on about the tenth day I was out in the boat in a choppy sea and thought I saw, two or three hundred yards away, a dark shape. My heart went to my throat, but I could not be sure, and the shape seemed to disappear. It was a day with scudding clouds and intermittent sunshine. When the sun went in, the dark shadows of the waves were confusing. But then I saw unmistakably the great back break the water and head towards me. The whale! My heart surged – he had returned! I sent the boat dancing towards him in showers of spray. The symphony of the Earth thundered in my mind. I shouted to him 'Rorq! Hello Rorq! Welcome! Welcome back!' And did a triumphal circle round him at full throttle, in some danger of swamping the boat on the tight circle, and then came in, cut the engine and wallowed towards him.

The sun came out. As I came near, his huge flank rolled in the sea, slate-indigo and living, and lapped in the water, accompanied by its trails of bubbles sparkling in the sunlight. He raised his head and looked at me. I was pulsating with the triumph of life – that he had thrust his huge form from the iceberg seas of the far Arctic through two thousand miles of northerly waters – to return to this exact spot. As we came together I leaned overboard and slapped him delightedly on the flank. He gave and repeated his welcome sound and suddenly spouted. The wind took the spray and soaked me in it. 'Hey!' I laughed.

Those were ecstatic moments, welcoming back this great animal. After a bit I calmed down and indicated to him, because of the choppiness of the sea, I wanted to go into the harbour. We went towards the inlet side by side, and then I opened the throttle and led him in.

So began three weeks of learning and constant attempts to communicate. I found a site suitable for the shack – where the rocks went vertically into deep water and he could come close in with no difficulty. This became his regular berth. I built a rudimentary letter rack on the rocks and so could use longer words. I told him my name was David and that I had called him Rorq. Increasingly I was coming to recognise the tone of various sounds he made. While using the repetition of numbers I came to recognise his reactions when he had done enough and I was able to ask him whether he wanted to do more or not. By dint of practice we established by this means a code for 'yes' and 'no.' Now I might be able to discover his age and sex. I made two large drawings – one of a whale with a baby whale, and one of a whale with its penis hanging out. He gave me 'yes' to the picture of the male whale. Then I showed him a picture of six whales, each of increasing size, with a number over each – 10, 20, 30, 40, 50, 60 – by which I hoped to indicate age. By demonstrating to him the story of his seasonal migrations to the arctic and the tropics I tried to establish that one, two and upwards to 10 and 20 and so on represented years on my pictures. He chose the fourth whale. I repeated the options, but still he chose the fourth; and so it was I learned that Rorq was an adult male about forty years old. I drew him a picture of a naked woman standing, with a baby and then one of a naked man and pointed to that and then to me; then I took off my clothes, and stood facing him so he should know what humans are like without their borrowed covering.

I noticed during our sessions with words that he was using streams of sounds, which, becoming more familiar, could be picked up quite readily. By use of the parabolic reflector and the tape recorder I recorded sequences of these and played them back to myself in the evenings, trying to match the sound responses to the words we had been exploring. After two weeks we managed to establish that he would leave in six days time and that he was heading south towards the warm seas. I showed him a map of the Hebrides, brightly coloured, and our islands, with the inlet; and with a globe traced routes from the north, (showing him a picture of an iceberg strewn sea) to the Hebrides and south to equatorial seas (with another picture of tropical islands in blue seas). He emitted strings of sounds in response and I had the feeling he was amazed that I knew of these things and could reproduce them. With these and like aids he showed he understood not only the concept of a year, but its division into seasons and twelfths, and he told me by elimination and a 'yes' that he would return in April.

This put me in mind again of the outside world. So far our meeting had remained undiscovered because of the loneliness of Eilean Mòr and Inis Cuan, and the existence of the almost secret harbour of Cala Bearn. But I began to fear for the future. Who knew how long – how many seasons of the whale coming and going – would be needed to work this miracle, if it could be done at all? And what fishing boats or other vessels might sight him and raise the news? And what talk might be aroused along the coast by reports of scientists and equipment arriving on the islands? I concluded that the full involvement of

Eric and Guinevere would be a vital pre-requisite to keep the islands inviolate and give any chance of success. I did not for a single second doubt their assent and commitment.

I told Rorq by word and drawings about my human friends, and that they should meet. So, four days before he was due to depart, when he had left the inlet in the afternoon to go back to sea, I set out across the islands to speak to Eric and Guinevere. We sat in their kitchen with large mugs of tea and slices of Guinevere's fruitcake. 'You know the shack?' I said to Eric, 'Well, I did have another idea in mind.' Then I told them the whole story of my encounters with the whale, ending up with my hopes for the future and dread of discovery by outsiders – boats arriving, curiosity and interference – Rorq being put in danger, and the whole chance of communication with another intelligence being lost for ever. When I finished there was a silence.

'Godfathers alive!' said Eric quietly. 'My dear,' he said to Guinevere, 'young David has fallen upon a great wonder.'

'What do you want us to do, David?' asked Guinevere. There was an unspoken assumption between them of immediate support.

'We must secure the islands from casual visitors,' said Eric. He paused. 'I wonder how he chose our islands?'

'He chose David,' said Guinevere, smiling at me. 'Whales, you know, can recognise a genius!'

I blushed at her teasing, but was pleased, for I sensed in her expression of fondness for me a declaration of commitment; and that is especially welcome when it is needed and comes from friendship. We talked into the evening.

The next morning they came over with me to Inis Cuan and down to the inlet. I went out in the boat and met Rorq as usual and brought him back to the harbour while they waited on the rocks. As we came towards them I called out to Rorq, 'My friends,' and indicated where they were standing on the rocks. He came to his station close in. I clambered ashore, went up to Guinevere and called out 'Guinevere,' and hugged her to show we were friends. Then I put an arm round Eric's shoulder and called out 'Eric'. And held out my arm to Rorq and called out his name.

Eric called out, 'Hello Rorq, you are most welcome here. We are much honoured.' Then he turned to me and said, 'This is utterly astonishing. I've never...' he trailed away.

That day and the following days they watched the word lessons, Guinevere making suggestions now and then. On the second day, Eric came out in the boat with me to meet Rorq. I think Eric thought of what was happening in terms of a biblical epic. As we approached he called out in sonorous tones, 'Hello, oh whale of the deep! Welcome back to Inis Cuan!'

I thought, any minute now he's going to conjure up Neptune and his sea horses, and started laughing. He saw I was laughing and his face broke into a great grin. 'This is wonderful,' he said.

On the final day, when Rorq was due to depart, we all three went out in the boat to say goodbye. He circled the boat three times as we waved and called to him, and he gave his resounding farewell. Then as he headed past us he dipped and we saw his great flukes rise into the air before he headed away southwards.

I remained on the islands two more days, staying with Eric and Guinevere. We talked for hours. I told them about my ideas for electronic communication and said I would try to find someone who could help back in London. Eric pulled out charts and we pored over them trying to work out why Rorq had come to these islands in the first place. We thought it could be related to the deep-water passages that lay off these coasts, but it did not really make any particular sense. We considered the shack, and briefly the alternative of using a site on Eilean Mòr, which would make a supply of electricity easier, but this idea was abandoned as there was no very suitable sheltered spot. And anyway, Eric said the occasional fishing boat did go up that water between the islands, though it was still remote. He said he had been thinking of buying a small generator to put in the cottage on Inis Cuan. We even wondered about the feasibility and cost of getting mains electricity across. Eric said that over the winter he would put his mind to building a proper letter rack system, and more letters to cope with sentences. And so the talk and planning went on.

'I have a feeling,' said Eric on the morning I was leaving, 'that the red deer on these islands are not going to miss you much.'

I had done some work in between times, but confessed that the future of my doctorate did not look altogether certain. Guinevere, who had begun to treat me like a favourite nephew, said, 'We will miss you, David. Come back soon.'

As I came south in the train I thought over in my mind of our attempts – Rorq's and mine – to communicate. The first conclusion – which was startling, though I was now used to it – was that he quite plainly had a thinking mind capable of understanding language. But I came back constantly to the next question: how two animals with physically different sound – making apparatuses developed over long periods of evolution could find a common language. I believed the answer might lie in the electronic analysis of sound, and hoped it was only my ignorance that masked a solution. But I did not know where to start.

CHAPTER 6

Robert Thompson

It is strange how problems in life are solved. One day not long after my return to London I met two or three of my friends in a pub at lunchtime. One of them, Mike Walsh, had graduated in electronic engineering at Southampton. He was now working in the defence industry. I had never taken much interest in the subject matter of his discipline, but now I started questioning him abut the workings of telephonic impulses and their conversion into language. He was mildly surprised, but gratified, by my sudden engagement in the subject, and launched into it. Eventually I was able to ask some questions about sound in water and related matters, from which it soon transpired, even from my amateur probings, that Mike's expertise was in areas that were unlikely to assist.

But then he said, almost as the last words in the conversation, 'Of course, the real expert in marine acoustics is my prof – Robert Thompson – international reputation, way out in front. You'd never know it – he's extremely modest – not in the least interested in plaudits. Got me my job, though he distrusts the military. When I asked him he said, "The things I do – you want me to recommend you to a post where you may employ your skill to kill people?" He meant it, too. He used to work for the Navy on secret stuff – sonar and so on – but became very disillusioned. He might be willing to help you. I shouldn't mention my name, I wasn't a star pupil.'

I wrote: 'Dear Professor Thompson, a former pupil of yours, Michael Walsh, who said it would be better if I did not mention his name, told me you might be able to help me.' I then outlined a communications project, with some sample problems to do with recording sound communications between marine mammals, while remaining fairly vague on the real reason for raising the questions. He replied more or less by return: 'I remember Michael Walsh. A fitful student, but a charming man who will I am sure have a most successful career in industry, though I hope he doesn't kill people. Please send him my best wishes. I may be able to help you if I know a little more of your intentions. As it happens, I shall be in London the week after next. Perhaps we could meet at the Institute.'

He set out details and a time, if I would confirm it. I felt a lifting excitement and was gratified by his response, which in addition to offering his expertise gave me hope of finding an ally. Then I noticed the test he had inserted in 'your intentions', which after careful rereading I realised covered not only my ideas, but my motivation. I became momentarily anxious; but then determined: I must pass his test; and he, if he were the right man, must pass mine.

We met at the Institute of Electrical Engineers, on the Embankment, a late Victorian building with a surprisingly modern feel to it. There were busts of Faraday and Kelvin in the entrance hall. I was shown up to the library, a light airy room overlooking the Thames. Professor Thompson was sitting at a table. He rose on seeing me.

'Ah, Mr Somerset. How do you do?' He held out a hand. 'Kind of you to come.'

'Very kind of you to see me.'

He had a firm handshake and was agile in his movements, though I guessed from his general appearance he was approaching sixty. He led me out of the library. 'We can talk in here,' he said, indicating and opening a door that led into a reading room with about half a dozen armchairs. No one else was in the room.

We sat and we talked. He was friendly, and interested. He wanted to know about my project. I told him something of the background to my work on communications among red deer and how I was now expanding that study to the cetaceans. When I mentioned dolphins in particular, for I was being cautious about whales, I sensed a tightening in his attitude. We plunged into technicalities about sound waves in water and the possibilities of recording and monitoring. After a bit I became aware that my vagueness as to my aims probably told him I was holding something back. But, my eagerness to explore knowledge of the natural world seemed to satisfy him that I had no unacceptable agenda or intent.

He suddenly smiled and said, with a gesture of his hand, 'Tell me about yourself.'

He had decided that my ideas, though indirectly set out, were of interest, and he was embarking on a new stage – an assessment of me. I already liked the man and found myself pleased that he was being thorough – somehow it made me feel I could trust him. I told him something of my background, and my academic career, such as it was. He approved of my enthusiasm for the living world and concern at the destruction of it. I mentioned my experiences of recent months uncovering the melancholy history of whaling, which we discussed for a few minutes. He too was oppressed by it, and made clear he had no whaling connection, which encouraged me.

As I asked about his work and why he did it, there flitted through my mind dismay that he might take offence at such questions from an unknown young man, refuse me, and terminate his interest. But I believe it never crossed his mind – he treated me throughout with the courtesy of an equal whose personal questions should receive his best answers. And in his replies, although he did not directly say so, the answer came back loud and clear – he did his work because he loved knowledge and increasing the boundaries of man's understanding of the natural world. Yet a shadow emerged as we talked: the shadow of science put to appalling uses. He knew some of the team who had worked on atomic fission at the Alamo eighteen or more years before. The ever-growing destructive power of nuclear arms had increasingly alarmed him.

'Of course,' he said 'you start off by arming your own people against a regime like Hitler's, but once the knowledge is out and that enemy is beaten, you find the whole thing is unstoppable. One protective measure begets an offensive countermeasure and so on. And in our nuclear age, this world has changed utterly – we face a potential planetary disaster. And where is it now? Who trusts the Soviet military, or ultimately for that matter, the American? Both have their fanatics – we may believe our American friends are better motivated, but they are as capable of catastrophic error of judgement as anyone else.'

In his own field he had seen advances in sonar used in submarine warfare. He said, for instance, that it was known that the Americans were experimenting with training dolphins to deliver tactical nuclear warheads. Then I understood his reaction to my mention of dolphins.

The co-operative trusting dolphin would, unknowingly, be sent on a mission to kill large numbers of people, and would itself be blown to atoms. He thought it profoundly immoral, and a breach of trust. He was pleased when I agreed strongly with this position and made clear my interest had nothing whatsoever to do with the military; and that on the contrary official misuse of scientific information was one of my major worries. But as I did not explain the matter any further we reached a natural pause. He looked at his watch. I looked at mine. We had been talking nearly two hours.

'Would you like some lunch? he asked. 'It's quite good upstairs.'

Our conversation at lunch was general, but relevant; the mutual assessment continued.

Afterwards we returned to the reading room with coffee. There was a moment's silence. He tapped his fingers twice on the arm of the chair as if giving a signal to himself. He looked at me and said with a slight smile, 'I believe I can help you. If you would like me to, you had better tell me what it's really about.'

My heart jumped and I felt a surge of exhilaration. But I told him there was first a vital question of confidentiality of knowledge, which I hoped he would not find presumptuous. I said I was afraid of revealing to anyone my discovery, for fear of the knowledge ending up in the wrong hands; that I had been very relieved to find he had no connection with the whaling industry or research in it, as that would have constituted an impossible stumbling block; and, after initial concern at his connection with the defence industry, reassured by his views on that. I would only be able to confide in him if he would promise and undertake to me that it would remain entirely confidential. I sought his eyes and he could see that I was slightly frightened, but wholly serious.

He said, 'I approve of your caution. I promise that what you tell me will remain entirely confidential, with one proviso.' He made a gesture with his hand. 'There must be one proviso. It is a question of ethics. If what you tell me contains a danger to the world or humanity that outweighs the value, in my best moral judgement, of the confidentiality you impart to me, or if it seeks for wrong purposes to impose silence on the development of true and valuable science, then I reserve the right to speak out.' He added quietly, as if by way of a layman's explanation, 'Otherwise, if I am to help you, you will have to trust me.'

So I told him everything, barring the exact location, and the identity of Eric and Guinevere. I believe he could feel the excitement in my story as I recounted the detail of my meetings with the great whale, and my hope of creating a language between us, for when I finished he said, 'How utterly fascinating,' and I saw that his eyes were shining.

After a pause, he said, 'By the way, you are quite right – I entirely approve of your caution in relation to the whaling industry and officialdom. It is imperative that this is kept secret – if anything can be worked it will take time – two or three years, perhaps more. Let me see. I think…' In his mind's eye he was already gauging requirements. He looked up 'What about the landowners? Where is this exactly? You did not say.'

I looked at him. He laughed, 'Ah, yes. No, no, don't tell me; that can wait.'

We smiled at each other. I had found an ally.

And I swear that money was never once mentioned. But money quickly came into it. After that first meeting we had three or four others, two of them at his laboratory. While he would be able to supply a certain amount of basic equipment on loan it rapidly became clear that his ideas on the electronic systems necessary would involve some initial and probably increasing investment. It also became obvious that I should need at the very least a storm-proof building of some sort to set up and store the equipment down by the harbour inlet. The 'shack' began to change shape and grow.

I was faced with a dilemma; I had no money or savings other than my inheritance from Aunt Jane. Sometimes when I thought about it the whole scheme seemed harebrained, and I imagined a visitor to the south harbour on Inis Cuan in thirty years time looking at the battered remains of a shack and peering in finding one or two rusting pieces of old fashioned electronic equipment and wondering, 'What on earth was somebody trying to do here?' I started to backtrack. Better first to go back in the spring and see whether it was really necessary, and even whether Rorq reappeared again. But then I chided myself for lack of faith and courage, and argued that the whole endeavour would anyway open up new areas of learning and experience. Even if it ultimately failed, it must be done. And in a strange way I then felt quite calmly that it was right, and Jane would have approved. That, having stumbled on a unique discovery, I had the privilege and duty to respond to the limit of my power and ability, and that is what my inheritance was for.

So I resolved to go ahead. The West Coast builders' merchants were rung again, this time for the requirements of the storm proof shack. Numerous calls followed, to them and to Eric. Eventually everything was organised. The components were to be delivered to the mainland pier-head for onward shipment to Eilean Mòr. I contacted Robert Thompson and said I expected to be able to house his equipment. He told me he would need £200 to purchase electrical equipment and components. He would be able to make do to some extent, and supply some elements from his department. He could get some of it cheaply – an inverter and other bits – from the government surplus shop in Lisle Street. And he would make his own way to Scotland. The question of payment for his time and effort was raised with some dread by me, only to be dismissed. He would come up some time at about the beginning of May, when I told him things were ready, or ready enough, and that would be part of his contribution, as well as his holiday. I was to go up in advance at the beginning of April. My planning proceeded with increasing enthusiasm and excitement. I acquired a large-scale Admiralty chart of the area and got together various teaching aids, though the book I bought on 'Teaching English to Foreigners' left me momentarily flat and depressed. Ten percent of my inheritance was already committed.

By the middle of March, my plans to return to Scotland were well advanced. At that critical juncture I fell in love.

CHAPTER 7

The Party

It happened like this. Anthony Ainsley and his flatmates, who lived just off the Fulham Road, gave a party. Mike Walsh and his crowd, who were part of our overlapping social circles, were going, as were several girls I knew from Oxford. But though the origins of these friendships were Oxford, our Oxford had largely moved to London. The London element too was growing, as the young of many universities and none were drawn to the capital and to careers: medical students and nurses, articled clerks and barristers, city hopefuls dealing in money and management, student teachers, a few in publishing and broadcasting; and a smattering of flatmates of both sexes, sisters of brothers, brothers of sisters and friends of both. In short a mixture of the young and educated with a full quota of hormones, ambitions and doubts. Everybody was looking for enjoyment, and most for sexual experience; but also, sometimes contradictorily, for innocence and romantic marriage. This last consideration, which we watched at work at such parties, gave the timid, plainer and conventional girls a chance to establish their often kind and competent qualities, and some were quickly married. The natural party-goers, their more beautiful, confident or adventurous sisters were quite often clever or lucky enough to marry for love, to wealth and with family approbation. But others of them, after a few years, having played the game too long or with too much looseness, choosiness or pride, remained unmarried, would come to feel the strain of unfulfilled expectation, and on party nights apply more make-up with creeping apprehension.

But that evening as I walked down Fulham Road we were all young and confident. In those days, that part of London retained something of a village feel. Sometimes on Saturday mornings in the shops I would see the same people, with the same dogs tied by their leads to the display of fruit and veg boxes spread across the pavement. There were greengrocers, butchers, one fishmonger and an ironmonger; nearly all within twenty years destined to disappear, their trade destroyed, subsumed into one or two conglomerate supermarkets. Soon smart antique shops would proliferate where rhubarb and cabbages had been stacked. The first of a spreading number of wine shops had already appeared. I stopped in one to buy a bottle of wine for the party.

I arrived quite late and the two rooms in use were full of people, loud chatter and cigarette smoke. Anthony was in the kitchen amid a sea of bottles.

'Arm yourself,' he said, handing me a glass of wine, 'The house is full of those of whom Cicero would have approved.'

This was a phrase of his variously applied to anything good or civilised, but mainly to beautiful women.

'Rose has brought two or three of her friends from college,' he said. 'Delightful. And Alison's new flatmate is here.' He looked at me in mock solemnity. 'Could be a source of disloyalty: she's gorgeous, but alas attached.'

Rose was his younger sister, reading English at Oxford, and Alison was a colleague from work (publishing) and now his girlfriend. Glass in hand, I went through to join the party and to look for the beautiful women.

But the first person I met was my sister, Susan. 'Hi sis.' We kissed. 'Hoped you'd be here.'

We caught up on each other's news and on family matters. Since coming to London we had both taken renewed pleasure in our relationship, in its new setting, and growing equality. We saw each other quite frequently, at my rooms or her flat, when we encouraged and comforted each other as the vagaries of life demanded. She had become fond of Anthony, but Alison had appeared on the scene, and briefly I became the experienced older brother again, recommending her course of action.

'Who is that talking to Rose?' Susan asked. I looked up and saw a young man.

'Don't know.'

But my eye fell on the third person in that group, a lovely looking girl with shoulder-length hair. She was looking from the young man to Rose and back as they talked, smiling. Susan asked someone else who the young man was, and another guest spoke to me. I looked again. The girl was still there. She appeared not to be fully engaged in the conversation. Her gaze left the little group and she looked across the room. Our eyes met. I felt my heart go thump. She smiled, and her eyes and smile said, 'Where've you been, I've been looking for you.'

And apparently she had. When I went over with Susan and we introduced ourselves, she said she had been primed by Rose's talk of her brother's handsome friend, the English-loving biologist. She said the words 'English-loving biologist' with a beautiful smile, but a hint of mockery, as if she wanted to confer an accolade, but wanted to know if it were deserved. I felt a flicker of pleasure, but at the same moment, apprehension. Such prior recommendations raise expectations which may be disappointed by the reality. But as we talked, her questions and reactions revealed a shy pleasure in my person and company. And all the time I couldn't believe how beautiful she was. Her name was Elizabeth Rowlandson, but she was called Ellie. She came from Salisbury where her father was a GP. She had read English at Exeter, had a brother, was training to be a teacher and loved children. She wore no make-up except a little blue eye shadow. It was applied in such a way that I guessed she didn't usually wear it but had been persuaded into it by her flatmates on party night, and had put it on with self-deprecating humour. She had an aura of outdoor health about her and a lively intelligence balanced by a certain social reticence. When she spoke of her family home in the country I imagined her there at once, a slim figure in jeans standing in a field of long grass in Wiltshire, a country girl.

Susan was talking to the young man who had caught her eye. He was called Daniel and was working in a solicitor's office in the City, but didn't know if he could stand it after the freedom of university. Susan and Ellie found they had girlfriends in common, and I saw with pleasure that they liked each other.

By the end of two hours I was in love. At the end of the party, a group of us went for a Chinese meal. After that, on the pavement outside while one of her flatmates, Vanessa, waited, we spoke our first words alone together. I was trembling. But she gave me her telephone number and a quiet 'Yes, I'd like to,' when I asked if we could meet again. Even now I can remember the flood of happiness she released within me.

After that my days and nights were in turmoil. We met several times and though outwardly she liked me, I tried to force down the intensity of my feelings, for she was at first a little wary and kept me at arm's length. I heard that she had a sort of boyfriend and Vanessa let it out that she was still involved. If I rang and one of her flatmates answered saying she was out, I was plunged in agitation not far from panic. My clumsy enquiries of Vanessa resulted only in a loyal pretence of ignorance. I did not know how to question Ellie directly – it seemed too presumptuous – and so had to endure the development of events. But my determination to win her love grew fiercely, and if I managed to seem carefree it was a triumph of appearance over real feeling. Inside I felt that without her life would be misery and pointless. The joint force of biological and imaginative love had caught me in its wonderful plunging recklessness, and life and exhilaration were flowing in me. I could not see beyond it, and did not want to.

While all this was going on, I was supposed to be working – studying and making arrangements to go back to the Hebrides. I had told Ellie of my deer researches. She laughed at my seriousness, and made me laugh at it; but underneath I felt she approved. The story of my meetings with the whale remained a secret. My feverish plan was that if Rorq did not return, I should abandon deer researches and get an academic job at a southern university, marry this girl, buy a cottage in the country and live happily ever after. At times I did not want to go back to the islands, and the whole project sometimes seemed to be verging on the farcical, condemning me to an outcast existence when everything in the world was now in London. Losing her would be unbearable. I was to be away ten weeks: the boyfriend might find his opportunity, or worse, she knew or could meet any number of young men in London more eligible than me. I suddenly wished my career and prospects were more settled, and for the first time understood and envied the confident suavity of lawyers and accountants. When I voiced my unwillingness to go away, to my dismay she did not seem to mind my going, but took it quite calmly as something that had been previously arranged, and said it would not be for long.

I left for the Hebrides only a little comforted by our last evening together. She seemed a bit low and by her small signs of affection perhaps indicated a reluctance to part. 'Write to me, David.'

'Of course I will. But I don't suppose there'll be much to report – red deer and empty mountains. I shall miss you, Ellie.'

'No you won't, you'll love it – your desolate mountains and sea lochs – it's your idea of heaven.'

I smiled. 'Yes, but – '

'Anyway, I've got masses I want to do and sort out. Not to mention work.'

She gave me a light goodbye kiss, looked into my eyes, and said with a slight smile, 'But don't you forget to write.'

CHAPTER 8

Progress

The weather in the Hebrides in late March can be distinctly cool; but because the Gulf Stream, turning into the North Atlantic Drift, brings warm water from the Caribbean to northern Europe, the islands are never gripped by icy winters appropriate to their latitude. Sometimes the temperature drops below freezing and occasionally there is some modest snowfall on the coast. It increases markedly on the hills and further eastwards, over the Great Island and the mainland beyond. When I arrived back on Eric and Guinevere's little islands the air was quite cold, but we had sunny days and spring had clearly arrived. There were little groups of daffodils on the sheltered eastern side of Eilean Mòr. The bright spring yellow made a fine contrast with the vivid blue sky and the towering white cumulus clouds above. I longed to bring Ellie to share this place with me, to add her beauty to its own beauty and freedom.

But the boat with all the components for the shack was due in four days and there was much preparatory work to be done at the site, measuring, marking out, clearing peat and broken stone for the foundations, and I was soon absorbed in the task, with the help of Jimmy MacLeod.

We took delivery of the materials for the shack and Eric's generator, on the western side of Eilean Mòr, facing Inis Cuan. The depth of water at the jetty was sufficient for the draught of the old converted trawler which now did service as a small freighter in those parts. The decision not to deliver to Cala Bearn cost us a great deal of hard work in the following days, but it meant that the location of the shack remained a secret. The generator – petrol not diesel for lightness and compactness – nevertheless weighed half a hundredweight and took some manoeuvring onto the boat. We transported it, and the posts, boarding, window frames, doors, sand and cement by seaward journeys round the coast to the southern inlet. Eric, Jimmy MacLeod and I spent a week hard at work. Once the foundations and concrete work were done, the shack itself soon began to take shape. We were interrupted by four days of cold, wet weather, the rain driving in from the Atlantic and making it impossible to work. Eric and Jimmy went back to Eilean Mòr. I stayed in the cottage on Inis Cuan.

In the evening, after the work of the previous days, I thought of Ellie in London. But when I tried to write to her, after some enthusiastic description of the island and work on the shack, hoping she was well, and asking what she had been doing, I found it difficult to convey my thoughts openly. I sensed this letter could be important and fretted over it for a long time. But I could not refer to the whale project, though I dearly wanted to tell her. And as yet being unable to say 'I love you' for fear of being too forward, eventually ended after several trial versions, 'With my love, David'. Guinevere was going over to the Great Island and took my much-amended hopes of happiness with her. For the moment the die was cast and almost with relief I turned back to work.

After four days the weather cleared. It turned bright and warm and we resumed construction. A week after that the shack, though not finished, was waterproof and serviceable. It had one room for a bed and storage and a larger one for working, with a big sliding window and a door opening onto a platform overlooking the water. The generator was installed in a tiny shed of its own, a little way inland, behind a slight rise in the rocks. This was Robert Thompson's idea, to minimise possible noise interference with his acoustic equipment.

The shack itself with its protruding platform was perched right on the edge of the water just above high tide mark on rocks that fell away vertically into the sheltered inlet. My idea was to get our working station as close to the great whale as possible. He could come right alongside with ease in the deep calm water.

At first glance this natural harbour appeared to be landlocked. The entrance from the sea was through a narrow gap, guarded at the seaward end by a rocky islet and beyond that some rocks. From the sea it was almost impossible to know that a natural harbour lay behind the islet and the low cliffs. Just behind the shack was a small hill, usable as a viewpoint, with a good view of the sea to the south. To the east about two miles away lay the south-western tip of Eilean Mòr. And westward the sea stretched away into the distance.

When the shack was well advanced I wrote a steadier and more informative letter to Ellie, but without mentioning my excitement, which was rising by the day, over the hoped-for return of Rorq. Instead, I wrote about the red deer project, to lend me credibility in her eyes, but attempted to atone for that untruth by hinting at work on another idea. I wrote that she must come up here one day – I meant as my wife and so imagined it, but didn't say so – and tried to describe the magnificence of the place and the exhilaration of living in it. Yet I was somehow relieved that her academic term would anyway prevent her coming. It was too early. This was not yet her world, and I would be a tangle of emotional complications, and be distracted. Somehow even then I felt a profound responsibility to fulfil my encounter with the great whale. For deep down I believed that this might be a pivotal moment. If another species proved to have both powerful intelligence and the capacity for language, that discovery might lead to the greatest adjustment in the understanding of man and his place in nature since Darwin himself. In my more confident moments I believed with a surging certainty that I could pursue this destiny, and win my love too.

On 5th April I crossed onto the Great Island to post the letter. I was to collect Eric's mail. To my delight there was a letter from Ellie waiting for me. The letter was not long but I pored over it looking for signs of affection, interpreting her words as favourably as I could. On the reverse side of the paper near the bottom she had written 'I miss you'. I was momentarily delirious; but then afraid to build too much on a few words. I decided to telephone her to say I loved her, but changed my mind three times, for fear of being rejected when so far away. Better, I concluded, to declare my love and hopes when with her, and able to fight for her love.

So in the end, and as she would have my letter in a couple of days, the only person I telephoned was the prof – Robert Thompson – confirming that the shack was built and would be ready for his equipment. His kit was assembled and he was looking forward to coming with keen anticipation. He would be with us in a week.

He arrived on 12th April. Eric, Guinevere and I went down to the quay on Eilean Mòr to meet him. We waved hello as the little boat came in. We could see it was full of boxes. He came ashore and I made the introductions. Yes, he had had a good journey, and was delighted to be here. Eric and Guinevere immediately made a great fuss of him, treating his boxes of electrical equipment as if they contained priceless treasures, so that no man could have been other than completely charmed.

The next day we ferried the equipment round to Cala Bearn and set to work to install it in the shack. He had brought with him two large lead acid back-up batteries together with a power converter, a multi-speed tape recorder, an oscilloscope, a frequency shifter kit and various other pieces of electrical equipment, much of which then bemused me, but afterwards became familiar. As we worked he discussed the problem which, from our earlier conversations in London, I knew to exist concerning the passage of sound waves between air and water. Sound travels well through air, but it travels more than five times better through water. The difficulty is the discontinuity between air and water where sound refracts. A sound travelling through the air is very difficult to hear underwater, and a sound made underwater very difficult to pick up in the air. Although this could be overcome by use of a hydrophone, or a double hydrophone for speaking and listening, he had concluded that air-to-air communication might be preferable, if it proved possible. He had taken careful note during our meetings in London of my description of Rorq's ability to lie with his head half out of the water exposing his eyes and ears. I had initially panicked when ears were mentioned, as I had previously simply taken his hearing for granted; but further research at the National History Museum had confirmed that all was well. A whale's ears lie a short distance behind the eyes, and both of these organs in the Blue Whale lie high up in the head – only some eighteen inches below its flattish top. When Rorq lay with his head tilted up and his eyes out of the water, his ears were also in the air. Of course this was not immediately obvious as, through millions of years of streamlining, whales have no visible external pinna or ear flap. Although I knew from my research that the whale's eyes and ears are very well adapted for life under water, I was soon to learn – and had already suspected despite silence in the whale books – that both are perfectly serviceable for the reception of sight and sound in the air above water. Nevertheless, Robert had also concluded that we must set up equipment for underwater working, not least because that is the whale's natural environment for communication; and although we knew he could operate with his head out of water, clearly confining our work to those occasions would be limiting. And underwater, helped by the properties of sound, we believed some longer communication might be established.

Over the course of three or four days Robert installed his equipment, including sound measuring and recording devices. I had previously lent him my own earlier tapes. He said he would need to discover what spectrum of sound frequencies and decibel levels the whale both employed and could hear. He hoped, by recording Rorq's sound responses, he would be able to translate these and see whether, as seemed very likely from what I had already told him, the whale was capable of thought in a manner that was compatible with our own. Beyond that the question of a possible response communication lay as yet undiscovered. He was concerned that Rorq's sound production would mainly lie in the low range of the spectrum, necessitating, for easy human hearing, raising the pitch; but that, he worried, might in turn give rise to distortion – either too much relative pitch or underwater speed distortion. He went about his work in those days with a deceptive air of calm, but underneath I learned to recognise a high level of suppressed excitement.

In the evenings we cooked supper and talked or read, and I tried to keep up observations in my journal. On two occasions we took the boat across to Eilean Mòr and walked over to share an evening with Eric and Guinevere. I learned much from Robert. He was very engaged by the conflict between the advancement of scientific knowledge and the political use to which it might be put. He regarded most political power with suspicion. He was deeply concerned that this time of greatest advancement for mankind might result in horrendous abuse of the world both economically and militarily; but above all that the great experiment of life on Earth might be grotesquely distorted or even destroyed by nuclear war. He thought that in the worst case intelligent life, civilisation, the higher animals and much else besides might be wiped out, and the planet be left a silent wreck. In odd places, plants and lower forms of animal life might survive, probably mainly insects but possibly fish and marine mammals. Intelligent life might be put back a hundred million years or more. Even if pockets of humanity survived, and might slowly spread again over the face of the Earth, perhaps the knowledge to recreate civilisation would be too fragmented and be lost. In such conversations I felt a yearning for something lying beyond the reach of my thought, yet already familiar.

But Robert's mind ranged across many subjects. He was fond of the cinema, jazz and modern art, and we passed easy evenings chatting about this and that. I found myself questioning him about his family life with an interest that would not have existed before I met Ellie. His wife was Scottish and they had met at Scottish dancing in London. She lectured part-time in French and they often holidayed in France or Switzerland. They had two grown up children, a son who was a hospital doctor in Leeds, and a married daughter, by training a research chemist, who he thought ought to be producing grandchildren for them.

On the evenings when we joined Eric and Guinevere we had convivial times. The whisky came out and Eric regaled us with tall stories from his early life. He had spent two years as a young man in Canada gold panning in the Yukon, canoeing in Alaska, near misses with black bears, and all sorts of tales told with a wonderful relish. One evening the talk turned to children. They had one child, a daughter called Mary who lived in Vancouver. She was married to a Canadian engineer and had a son and a daughter. They had hoped originally that she might come back to live on the islands, but now Eric's hopes for an heir and successor were rather more pinned on his young grandson. Robert asked some questions about Canadian schooling, and when they went on to talk about that, I found myself thinking in a strangely protective way about Ellie and what might be between us. And when it came out that I had hopes with her, in the teasing that followed, I was surprised by an intense pleasure.

By day our work continued, and eventually our preparations for Rorq's arrival were complete. One day Robert said, 'All I need now is your whale.'

For some days I had been becoming somewhat anxious about his return and had been much out on the promontory and in the boat, all without result. Despite my attempts to rationalise his non-appearance, my anxiety was growing.

One evening I was watching the sea from the promontory with my binoculars. The water was choppy. Twice – a glimpse – was it his back? – came and went in the waves. I tucked my elbows into my sides for steadiness and gripped the binoculars tightly – yes, yes! There was the now familiar back breaking water about four hundred yards out to sea. I ran back towards the little inlet beach to launch the boat and shouted to Robert, who was in the shack. I jumped in the boat, started the outboard and headed down the inlet. Robert came out of the shack and I gesticulated excitedly towards the sea, before heading out past the islet and the rocks. Rorq was waiting for me to go out to him. As the boat came near him I cut the engine and called out a welcome. He gave a low blast in return, raising his head out of the water, and I bobbed alongside to leeward and thumped him in exhilarated greeting, welcoming him back. Then we headed back to the inlet. I beached the boat and went round to the shack. Rorq lay almost submerged in the middle of the inlet, but when I appeared at the shack and called him he came slowly over to the berth position. He raised his colossal head out of the water, and, sixty feet behind his flukes caused a stir in the water.

Robert, who was standing beside me, breathed 'Good God!'

I introduced them by using my arms and calling their names out. Robert at once entered into things, and told Rorq in a firm loud voice how greatly honoured he was to meet him. I said that Robert was a friend who had come to help us to talk.

In the next day or two, we introduced Rorq to the workings of the equipment. So far as I could tell from his reactions, the ever-patient whale was intrigued by our new ability, via the two-way-hydrophones, to listen and speak underwater, and to play back our speech and his sounds. We began to record a steady flow of responses.

In the weeks that followed we made good progress. The hydrophone enabled us to pick up Rorq's responses from under water. Robert worked out, with the help of his instruments, that Rorq had a truly astonishing range of sound production.

'I don't know how low he can go,' he said one day, 'he is way off the end of my machine and that goes down to 30 hertz – about the sound produced by the biggest organ pipe in a Cathedral. His low notes are so low that they are beyond our hearing – you can just get a *feel* that there is some lower vibration happening. And astonishingly, he is also way off the top of the scale: bat-like frequencies. He makes us humans look extremely poorly equipped.'

While I continued my language lessons, Robert monitored Rorq's responses, recorded them and analysed them. We erected what became known as 'the listening post' on which microphones were wired up and mounted. It was a duplex system which worked really something like a telephone. If Rorq could learn language, as we hoped, he should be able to respond via his sound system, which when decoded could be unscrambled, as the electronic signals on a telephone wire could be converted into audible speech.

It was long and painstaking work as the days and then weeks went by. Sometimes one of us would become discouraged, but we kept at it and were always sustained by a belief that it could work. For one thing, we argued, why on earth would Rorq keep coming back and submitting himself to long hours of teaching if it all meant nothing? Robert was convinced that there was no logical reason, in terms of physics, why a whale could not learn to speak. On the biological side it was already clear that he had the brain, and it soon became apparent from our recordings that Rorq could deliver strings of different sounds despite his aquatic vocal apparatus. Robert tried varying the pitch and speed of the recorder, and played these variations back to him. Gradually his tone tended to centre on sounds that approximated to human speech pitch – roughly between 200 and 3,000 hertz, and normally at about 800. The shifter gradually fell into disuse. Moreover, as Robert pointed out after some weeks, the pattern of sounds we were recording was changing. The grouping was different and becoming much more variable, more like a language. He produced clicks and pings audibly like T, D or B. Increasingly his responses sometimes sounded quite like words, but at one remove as if obscured by a curtain of distortion. We became convinced that the whale was trying to communicate, if only we could find the code.

But at the end of the season, when Rorq was showing signs of restlessness and we knew he must head north to the feeding grounds, we still had not achieved a breakthrough. We wanted to meet again in mid October when he would be returning from the Arctic summer. We put the question to him electronically, but used the old letter rack system to gather his reply. By elimination, mid October was fixed on. We wondered anxiously as we prepared to disperse whether some unforeseen development or accident would prevent the fulfilment of our endeavour.

Such was my involvement with Rorq that I had only intermittently had time to look forward to seeing my beloved Ellie again. Over the preceding weeks our letters hinted at a mutual deepening of feeling –

or so I convinced myself – but contained no declaration of love.

I had sent her also two poems, mainly about nature, but with some personal references and allusions. A love poem I had kept to myself, for it was full of vulnerable hope and explicit desire. Increasingly as our letters passed I had felt it wrong, and somehow deceptive, to mislead her by silence about Rorq. But I wanted to tell her everything in person. So in one of my later letters I hinted broadly about my engagement on an important confidential project other than the deer. Her letter in response was puzzled and unhappy, and I guessed she had been hurt by the realisation that I had not taken her into my confidence. Perhaps that had made her unsure of where she stood with me. I cursed myself and wrote my most open letter promising to explain all and saying how much I was looking forward to seeing her. But as the day to return to England approached I became increasingly anxious. Her letters had been charming – even affectionate – and reassuring. But when I re-read them, she seemed to be more involved with the people and goings on down there. She seemed always out to supper with friends, had seen several films, been to two or three theatres and a couple of 'late night raves' with Rose and Anthony and the gang, with the dance floor full of sweaty young men and incredibly loud music, but 'quite exciting'. Her life and mine suddenly felt separate and apart. What did that half-admitted 'quite exciting' mean? I would soon find out.

On the 28th May we escorted the great whale down the inlet and said our farewells. As he left for the Arctic I felt flat and dispirited. The next day Robert left, taking our sound recordings with him for analysis. We would meet in London. I closed down the shack, spending my last day on Eilean Mòr with Eric and Guinevere, and then headed south.

CHAPTER 9

A Visit to Wiltshire

As I walked down the platform at King's Cross, I saw Ellie coming towards me. We had not arranged to meet and I felt a surge of joy. It was quickly followed by panic. I was not ready to meet her now, my clothes were filthy and smelly and this dirty and noisy station was not the meeting time or place I had dreamed of for weeks. But a moment later she saw me and her anxious face was transformed by a beautiful smile. She broke into a run for a pace or two and in that moment I glimpsed that my love was returned. We embraced and clung together, intertwined. After a while, the railway station came back again. My rucksack and kit bag were lying disregarded on the platform. Ellie wanted to help carry something and we set off laughing and chatting, eager to know what the other had felt and thought about each other's letters, being apart and our intervening lives.

That evening at supper in my room, she wanted to know in detail about my time in the islands. From her questions, it was clear she had been trying to envisage my life there. So I told her the whole story of the great whale. I was ablaze with love and excitement: for her, the whale, the islands, life and the future – intoxicated with it all. She was at first taken aback, perhaps by my passion and the realisation that there was this strange new burgeoning element and being in my life of which she had been unaware. But she knew already I loved the wild places of the Earth and she was in sympathy with that. Besides, I swore, though I shouldn't have done, that I would have nothing more to do with the whale unless she was with me.

'No, you must go on with it,' she said quietly. She looked down and then in my eyes, almost frightened. 'Will you let me help you?'

Her fear was of being excluded. I held out my hands and she took them, 'Ellie, please, please will you help me?'

Then we talked and talked. She told me how she too had found her love growing when we were apart; and of the London to which I had feared to lose her turning into a cage. Eventually, we spoke too of the strange, epic task of teaching the whale a way of finding human language. A third person with shining eyes. And we were changed and united in a new and subtle way.

At the end of the evening I longed for her to stay. I could see that she wanted to, but hesitated. Whether it was the strangeness of my revelations, or the newness of our being together again, I am not sure, but we were shy of making love. Partly no doubt it was the mores of the time and our upbringing – we were of a generation brought up strictly in social morals, though about to break into the new world of the sixties and the pill. But somehow also my love for her had a sense of sanctity – I wanted to do nothing that she might reject or find wrong, and I believe she felt the same. Besides, there was something profoundly touching – and loving – in our circling closer, like a slow-motion rite, until we were ready, while we longed for each other.

So I said she should sleep in my bed whilst I made up a makeshift bed in the living room. When she was in bed I went in and knelt on the floor and we kissed and clung together in her sweet warm smell. We eventually kissed goodnight, and love and rightness were gratified, but longing and desire were not. I lay in the makeshift bed, my mind in an ecstatic turmoil, and could not sleep for hours.

In the following days we were constantly together. We met after her lectures, and between my academic commitments. We frequented sandwich bars and cafés near the university. The sunlit parks and gardens of London, where we sat and lay became corners of paradise, made perfect by the presence of her always astonishing beauty. We talked for hours, and grew to know each other. I remember how she blushed when forced to admit her wish to teach rose from her love of children. When I asked her if she would like to have children she blushed again and looked down and picked blades of grass. But when she looked up, smiled, and said 'Yes,' I thought my heart would stop.

A month after my return from Scotland, Ellie was due to visit her family for the weekend. She asked me to go. A little smile: 'They know a bit about you. They want to meet you and I want you to meet them!' We caught the train on a sunny Saturday morning and passed through summer England going down to Wiltshire. Her father met us at Salisbury station with an old but well-kept Rover. He was a good-looking man of about fifty, clearly delighted to see his daughter, and by extension pleased to see her young man. I knew before we arrived at the house that it would be a pleasant English home. There was a short, rather bare and uneven gravel drive, and as we came round a yew hedge I saw a pretty Regency house.

In the hall, Dr. Rowlandson called out, 'Penelope, we're home!' Ellie's mother appeared smiling. It was immediately clear where her daughter's beauty had come from. Ellie and her mother hugged each other, and I was introduced. We went through into a drawing room and out of open French windows into a large garden. It must have been about an acre, with a long lawn stretching down to some trees, with fields beyond. We sat in the garden. I suppose I wanted to like her family, but from those first moments I certainly did. Ellie's nineteen-year-old brother Philip came in. They greeted each other with obvious affection. I took to him at once.

Mrs Rowlandson said, 'Edmund, are you going to bring us some drinks?'

'I certainly am. David, will white wine suit you?'

'Definitely.'

Dr. Rowlandson went in and returned with a tray of glasses and a couple of bottles of white wine on which condensation was already forming.

'What a beautiful day! Lunch out of doors, I think?' he said to his wife.

So we sat and talked of medicine and biology, village things, and the state of the country. They asked me about the Hebrides and we talked of their own holiday visits to Scotland. Ellie's mother asked about my mother and sister: a gentle probing, but done with such straightforwardness and interest that I was pleased to describe my family's modest circumstances, and felt my loyalty well received. I told them how we had moved to our small West Country village after my father's death at El Alamein – I was four and Susan two at the time – and how our mother had brought us up, and supported us by teaching at the village school.

When it was lunchtime, we brought things through from the kitchen, everyone helping. Going through the rooms I noticed the décor was comfortably old, with some elegant furniture, a scattering of rather worn Persian rugs, and various bookcases quite untidily filled, with some books pushed in flat on top of the others. A house where books were accumulated, and read.

Towards the end of the meal, Philip went into the house to get the coffee.

'We're going to have trouble with that boy,' his father confided in me. 'He wants to be a politician. Do you think you can persuade him otherwise?' He was clearly proud of his son, and I sensed his including me in such family matters was a sign at least of willingness to approve of me.

After coffee, Dr. Rowlandson waved an arm at the garden, 'It's all too much. It'll cripple me trying to keep this place from becoming a jungle. Now you're all here we can have a working party in the paddock.' He glanced at us mischievously, but was mocked by his children for being a slave driver.

'No way,' said Philip, laughing. 'I'd rather go canvassing.'

'Medical help is available for extreme conditions,' teased Ellie.

'Someone's got to do it.'

'And someone's got to do the weeding.'

'Oh, Dad,' said Ellie, 'we've come here to relax not pull nettles.'

But we did spend part of the afternoon pulling nettles and cutting down docks in the paddock 'before they seed,' as Dr. Rowlandson said. It was a warm drowsy June day. We chatted and joked as we worked, and I found a pleasure in the unity of this family. I caught myself looking at Dr. Rowlandson trying to see what likeness and affinity he had with Ellie, and found a fascination in odd moments of recognition. But when I looked at Philip, who was clearly recognisable as Ellie's sibling, I caught myself wondering what a son of mine aged twenty would look like.

Later she showed me round the house. In the sitting room there was a writing desk with family photos on it. Her grandparents – her grandfather was also a doctor – standing by a 1920s car, her parents' wedding photo, two or three family groups, a portrait of Ellie and one of Philip, and a few others. One was of a great aunt Enid, who had hitched her skirts up and gone trekking in the Himalayas with her surveyor husband. She showed me a glass-topped display table with her grandfather's First World War medals, some silver objects and an onyx box. 'Yes, Great Aunt Enid's.' A collection of things and people who had led to this home, and to Ellie.

Upstairs, her own room was light and airy, pastel greens and white, with blue and yellow flowered curtains and cushions. There was a picture of a group of New Forest ponies, and another of a ballet class. There was a brightly painted daub of Montmartre, Paris, and a breezy sunlit seascape with sailing boats. Above a chest of drawers hung a framed photograph of Michelangelo's David. She saw me glancing at it. 'You see I've got a David.'

'Classical competition is unfair!'

'My David,' she said ambiguously, smiling.

She had a large white painted bookcase, the inside painted turquoise blue. Her childhood books were neatly ordered, but now much outnumbered by the less tidy literature of a growing mind, and familiar bulky student files and textbooks. And projecting into the centre of the room her bed, simple, somehow innocent, where she had slept, I supposed, since a little girl.

By the end of the weekend it was clear that I was accepted in the family as Ellie's boyfriend, and I saw that acceptance gave her great pleasure. That was the first of several visits to the little village outside Salisbury that summer.

We knew on the train going back to London that we would become lovers that night. Back in my rooms after supper, as we were finishing the washing up, she saw me looking at her.

'Ellie, please stay the night with me.'

She came up to me and said, 'Oh David, I so want to be loved by you.' She stretched her arms over my shoulders, smiled and said, 'My beautiful David, I want to love you for ever and ever.'

When we undressed it somehow seemed quite pre-ordained and natural to be revealing our nakedness together. She wore a pretty pair of knickers and when she took them off, leaning forward, the light caught the underside of her soft pendulous breasts above the concave curve of her stomach, like a crescent moon. I was trembling for the loveliness of her. 'I've got some cond...'

'No need,' she said, 'I've got a Dutch cap.'

'You mean... How did – '

She smiled, 'It's for you.'

We kissed tenderly, my hands on her waist. She drew me to her and down onto the bed. We lay in the sheets and gently folded into each other's lives.

That was in the summer of 1961. My poor, beautiful, beloved Ellie.

CHAPTER 10

Retrospect

That first visit to Salisbury, and the visit shortly afterwards to my mother's home, seemed to draw us into a new understanding: we advanced our sense of belonging to one another. My mother and Ellie found each other's company congenial and Ellie loved my mother's West Country cottage; I wanted to show Ellie my boyhood countryside.

I have always had a sense of freedom which partly comes from living in the countryside. Our village backed onto a line of small hills running irregularly east and west. Below them to the south lay meadowlands. So from almost my earliest days I was brought up in this English farming countryside, a scruffy, cows-and-sheep, grassy part of the country, where grass and wildflowers grew undisturbed out of the stone walls and there were always corners with nettles and foxgloves and rusting old bits of farm machinery.

Down in the meadows I would trail through the long grass at pollen time or when the myriad of seed heads were full and heavy. I thought the grassland was the Earth's most beautiful dress, like a gorgeous Elizabethan silk cloak. And among the delicate green and golden grass threads the jewels, like so many sapphires, topazes and amethysts, were the blue, yellow, purple, pink wild flowers of the meadow and the diamond flashes of reflected light. Sometimes when we were small, my mother would take us on picnics down by the little river which ran through the meadow. We had an old navy and green tartan rug to spread on the grass, and you had to crawl about on it pushing with your hands to flatten the grass underneath. But afterwards, when you took it up, the grass was all broken and spoiled. We would wade in the river where it was shallow and peer into the clear pools under the banks amid the ash tree roots that ran along the banks like great snakes. Later I would play with friends from the village, sometimes rowdily, fighting splashy battles and fording the river on imaginary horseback. Or I would go fishing with a friend or on my own. Then I would explore the pools in a different way, carefully, secretly, so as to find and live with the fish and disturb nothing amid the dancing insects. Then, perhaps as I waited for a fish to bite on lazy afternoons, that unconscious early synthesis between culture and nature would take place, when the images from nursery history books and the riverbank joined forces. The steep-banked track that led down to where the sun shone on our little river became the friendly gap where Xenophon and the Greeks came through the passes to the sea. The little clay riverbanks opposite where we sat, some four feet high, became the Heights of Abraham; and I imagined the tiny redcoats picking their way up the goat track to reach the top, and win the whole of Canada.

By that stream I was introduced on a small scale to the underwater world. I knew nothing then of its oceanic counterpart nor of its influence on my own future life. But I knew the deep pools and curved underwater gravel banks on the undulating riverbed, even particular stones, and where the trout and minnows lived. And although on occasion we did catch a trout and bear it home triumphantly for supper, I entered their world in my mind and imagined young trout having adventures, like Peter Rabbit, and escaping the fishermen. I learned too that under those placid waters was a world of eat and be eaten, of ceaseless competitive effort, but also a beautiful world of balanced nature. In time I stopped fishing, for the pleasure of it became outweighed by the feeling that it was not for me to disturb or destroy it. Similarly, I learned too that you did not break a spider's web gratuitously, but carefully altered your path and went round it. For although it was a trap for insects, that was between the spiders and the insects, and not a reason for human interference. Nor did you cut an earthworm when digging. You put him on one side and broke the ground a bit so that he could go back in again. Woodlice and spiders you put carefully out of the house; but swarming woodlouse colonies and slugs, under the stones in the rockery, when their numbers destroyed my mother's newly planted flowers, could be massacred. Living in the country you came to know that nature was a whole and that you were part of it.

Out of the village to the north there were two lanes that led uncertainly up the hills. They had once been tarmacked by a forward-looking Council. But I remember them slowly decaying with the tar dried out, bits of grass appearing in the middle, the edges getting broken gradually by occasional small open-engined tractors; but mainly by the little runnels of water forging channels down the sides, and the frost breaking off bits in winter. There were hardly any cars, and anyway they didn't go up there. The lanes in winter and early spring were awash with stones, twigs, gravel and the debris of heavy rain coming down the hill. The lane between the hedges was full of grass and flowers, and if you turned left into an unmade narrow track that rose diagonally upwards, you came out on Butler's Hill – another world. In the tussocky long grass of the steep slopes, where no improvers or cutting machinery came, dotted with the occasional bramble patch and little hawthorn trees a few feet high, was a world where you could lie facing south in the hot sun and daydream all sorts of boyish scenes high above the meadows.

I was often a Red Indian guarding the sanctity of our forefathers' lands against the ignorant, foul-mouthed and never-ending stream of white invaders. Sometimes I was a young Greek spying the advancing dust and glitter of the Persian hosts; or a young Briton in King Arthur's time alerted of the threat to his kingdom by the slowing winding column of knights through the meadows below, the sun flashing on their armour. I did not know it consciously at the time, but there was often a theme of threat to the order and stability of the world in these stories, which theme afterwards loomed in the adult world in more urgent and grotesque forms.

With puberty, the foreign armies faded and were replaced by images of girls, and sometimes when you were lucky a real one. I remember my first love and our mix of shyness and desire as we sat in a grassy vantage point near the top of a hill, she gazing out into the distance, and me looking at her sideways, the breeze and sun in her hair. The grassy hollows where then we kissed became secret places searched out to be safe from any interruption of tender moments. And always above there was the sky – the deep blue sky of spring cutting the edge of whitish yellow grass against the skyline, or the pale blue skies of the summer with lines of bright white and lavender summer clouds bobbling away to the horizon. Always too there was bird song – larks and linnets, the cawing of crows and sometimes the wild cry of the sky-floating buzzard.

This was the countryside I wanted to show to Ellie. We strolled down to the meadows. The little river had somehow shrunk and become more ordinary; a stream through a field, though pretty still. We climbed up Butler's Hill and lay in the grass, gazing at the view far to the south and listening to the birds on the breeze. We made love there, lying on the lip of the hill in a grassy dip under that great sky. My youthful yearnings and daydreams of love had become reality.

At the end of our visit, when my mother and Ellie kissed goodbye, it was already with affection, and promises to come again.

On the train back to London Ellie was full of the visit. She wanted to know about my fatherless childhood, and how we had managed. She had seen the photographs of my father, and several of his watercolours that hung on the walls. 'And the house is full of books – that's where you got your bug, isn't it?' she laughed. 'And now geology?'

I nodded and told her it had been a good life, although we did not have much money. In winter we scrimped on heating, as did many in those days. In cold spells sometimes our feet and fingers were frozen and we got chilblains. One of my duties as the only male of the house was to go out to the coal shed on freezing winter nights to fill the coal scuttle by torchlight, breaking up the bigger lumps of coal with a little hand pickaxe and shovelling the scuttle full, with a bit of slack to use it up. Sometimes the coal I broke open had lovely shiny black surfaces and very occasionally an imprint of something like a leaf. Then I forgot the cold and found myself in ancient swampy forests. I wondered at the impression of a leaf surviving millions of years from deep down inside the Earth – there in my frozen fingers. The knowledge of it made the whole world seem different. I remember the acrid smell of the coal, and the dust and my condensed breath hanging in the torchlight. By the time I got back into the house, my hands were numb with cold from the icy iron latch on the coal shed door, handling the pick and shovel, and the brass handle of the scuttle; but my body was warm from the exertion and my mind was full of exhilaration. Coal was preferred to logs – it lasted better, gave out more heat, and did not tar up the chimney. But it involved hard work, dirt, and ashes to be cleared. Smokeless zones, oil, natural gas and central heating would see the end of it. But then, from its red-hot caves that glowed and pulsed as you watched, the fire gave a cosy radiated heat – hot in front, if chilly round the back; but warm enough for my mother on winter evenings to open up to us the world of books, of which we had large numbers in the house.

'This one was your father's when he was a boy,' or 'this was one of your father's favourites,' said my mother as we settled in the sofa. So Susan and I inherited stories and history and new worlds. And although we had no father, I knew from things she said how real he was to my mother, and by degrees over the years I got to know him. There were photographs of him as a boy and a young man and sometimes I would strangely see myself in him. He had painted watercolours. My mother kept boxes of these in a cupboard behind a curtain in the sitting room. When as a teenager I went through them I learned that he had loved trees, wide open moors, the coast and the sea, and he had a great feeling for light in nature.

'And stamp collecting?' asked Ellie with a quizzical smile.

'That was Aunt Jane. And ethics too.'

'Tell me about Aunt Jane.'

So I gave her an account of Jane, which took me back to those years. I told her that she was one of six children – two girls and four boys – but only she, her sister Laura, and my father, William (who was the youngest) had survived early adulthood. One boy, Stanley, had died of typhoid at school in 1912 owing to the carelessness of the regime there, which had never been brought to book. When as a schoolboy I was having tea with Aunt Jane in her flat in Wimbledon, I remember sensing that the event still bought sadness to her. She also had to bear the loss of two brothers, Alfred and Geoffrey, in the murderous slaughter of Flanders. She never referred to it as that. When she was a girl, King, country and service were a framework of life, and one which she never afterwards abandoned. But I could tell from the way she spoke when she showed me her girlhood photographs, how sunny Edwardian times had been before that catastrophe. Yet she was never bitter. She was well read and felt the wider loss. She remembered her dear Alfred (she seemed to have been particularly close to him) and Geoffrey, 'Killed along with half the young men of Europe, including all those poor German boys.'

I told Ellie about my schoolboy visits to Jane's home in Wimbledon, approaching sunlit Victorian villas with long thin gardens and dark green shady places, contrasting the yellow London stock brick and the white painted features of the houses. Jane still had a sense of beauty about her, especially when she smiled, and she had a light sparkling laugh. Her grey hair was done elegantly but with a degree of untidiness that indicated there were more important things in life than personal neatness. She had an enquiring mind, and although it took me some years fully to realise it, she was one of those radical spirits who constantly strove to construct good things out of her experience of life and make them available to the young. She had no children herself, which was a matter of sadness to her, her fiancé too having been killed in the Great War. But in retrospect I think this intensified the efforts she made to encourage and guide her nephews and nieces.

When I went there on visits from school I always came away with a steady view of the world, and a feeling of wellbeing, even when I had received the reprimands which she was quite capable of giving. On one occasion, after I had demonstrated a continuing interest in my own stamp collection, which she had started me on, she produced Uncle Alfred's collection. She had it in the drawer of her display cabinet, and she gave me that schoolboy treasure, a penny black. Thereafter the drawer with its little brass handles had a sort of fascination for me, a typically acquisitive schoolboy. On the following visit, a few weeks later, she started a discussion on gratefulness. During this, as she cut me a large piece of chocolate cake, she somehow got it across without saying so, that I had not written a thank-you letter for the penny black; that Aunts liked to get thank-you letters when they had been kind; that kindnesses in life should be acknowledged and reciprocated; that we should be grateful for friends; and that friends should not be misused. I remember going red and feeling hot. In such small ways she taught me ethics. And I always left her house happy. It was not just the teas – she took the trouble to know and provide favourite foods – but the enjoyment she showed in having you there, and her relish of the whole occasion and the liveliness of her enquiries and observations.

On my last visit before Jane's death, she had returned to the topic of stamps.

'Now,' she had said, 'do you still collect stamps and if so why?'

'Yes.' I thought for a moment. 'Well, they teach me things like

Arab numerals and about Palestine under the League of Nations, and the amazing calligraphy of the Middle East – like the signature of Suleyman the Magnificent. I visit the world,' I said in mock solemnity – 'salt raking in the Turks and Caicos, parliament buildings in Ottawa, native canoes and huts in the Cook Islands and Fiji. I meet the Kings and Queens and rulers of the world: King Farouk of Egypt in his fez, Wilhelmina of the Netherlands, Dr. Sun Yat Sen, Kemal Ataturk – and how would I otherwise know the likeness of Simon Bolivar in his military collar, and some of the American presidents like Adams, or Jackson? Besides,' I said, 'I like their quiet order; stamps are never cross with me because I haven't made my bed or done some chore.'

She smiled. 'You must help your mother, and I'm sure you do.' She seemed pleased with my explanation. 'Well,' she said, having cleared the decks, 'I think I should give you Alfred's collection. Will you look after it? I... I would not want it sold.' She put her hand on my arm, 'unless you really needed to.'

'No, no,' I said as she took the album out of the drawer. I glimpsed her thought: she was giving me part of her past and that of her dead brother of which she was trustee. 'I would love to have it, and keep it in the family.'

She gave it to me.

I did not know it, but stamp collecting was nearly past for me, and after initially poring over the pages and transferring a few stamps from a number of countries to my own collection to make up sets, most of the stamps stayed in the album, which then lay in a drawer until a later generation.

'I do like your family,' said Ellie, holding my hand. And as the train left the West Country behind, I thought that all our lives we live in a pool of social history, though we mostly don't recognise it.

There were practical things to organise that summer. Ellie passed her exams; she and her friends threw a celebratory party. There was much talk of summer travel and beyond that, teaching posts. Among all the smiling faces, I remember enthusiasm and idealism, which I supposed would be much called upon. Ellie and one or two of the others had been in a dilemma over job applications and were considering another year's study for a masters degree. In the end, Ellie decided to do so and obtained a place at University College, London to study the history and philosophy of education. She would be not far from me. Her term started towards the end of October. I was delighted: she was free to come up to the Hebrides, in my mind's eye the nub of everything.

Progress on my own doctorate was in trouble. After consultation with Robert Thompson, I negotiated with my professor, saying I wanted to change direction to include communication work on marine mammals, citing work I had already done in conjunction with Robert. This aroused interest, but also a number of objections on what I took to be absurdly narrow grounds. I was in effect given an academic ultimatum: to finish the red deer project or the university would withdraw their support for my doctorate. I argued in frustration against this, but in vain, like a worm on a hook, twisting and turning to no avail, and felt the cold fear of abandoning the safe academic and career framework of the PhD. I fretted about providing for Ellie and the concerns that would be raised in her family over her possible future with a biologist of very uncertain prospects. But I knew with iron certainty that I would not abandon my work with Rorq.

Fortunately, before I had to make the fatal decision, the matter was temporarily resolved by Robert Thompson representing to my department that he would very much value my further help by way of secondment, and I received a two-term extension to my timetable. Decisions were deferred, and I thought with relief of the coming autumn return to the Western Isles.

CHAPTER 11

The Future

On the 8th September, Ellie and I went north. Robert was to follow ten days later. I was pleased we would have some time on our own. I could hardly wait to introduce her to the islands – the bays, the hills, the wild intricate mantle of the moorland and coastal flora and its denizens.

The weather was kind: we sailed into an Indian summer. We lent on the railing of the inter-island ferry as it slid out of the mainland harbour with its following of gulls and headed out towards the Great Island. I had the feeling of returning to another world beyond the edge of the normal one: that out there, though storms blow, a deep peace resides. I looked at Ellie sideways watching her lovely profile and marvelling at the soft perfection of the hair at her temple. She caught me gazing, turned her head and smiled, her eyes fresh and clear. I gripped the ship's rail and surveyed the world from its highest vantage point.

The sea was calm for the crossing and the Great Island was dappled in sunlight and increasing colour as we headed west. We landed and crossed the island. Jimmy MacLeod met us at the little ferry and fetched us across the arm of the sea that made up the last leg of our journey. He was bashful towards Ellie, as islanders and men from small communities can be towards young and pretty outsiders from beyond. As we turned into the breeze spray came up and sparkled in the air, wetting the gunwale. We shifted our bags.

'The next one'll get you,' said Jimmy and we laughed and looked towards the island.

Eric and Guinevere's welcome was like a homecoming. They fussed over Ellie and me like long-lost children. They insisted that we stay with them for three or four days, 'To shake off London,' as Guinevere said, 'before you start work.'

In the following days the weather stayed fine and we walked the island. I showed Ellie my favourite places. We took food and water for the day. We scrambled in rocky areas and pushed through the sometimes knee deep heather and tussocks, for there were no paths, other than the occasional lengths of deer track which petered out or divided, or veered steeply up hillsides. No one came to these places. We lay in the heather and the sea cliff grass and made love in remote and beautiful spots. Ellie, laughing, said they would have to be named or renamed. She sat in the grass above the sea with my map on her knees, and tucking her hair behind her ear she wrote in her neat handwriting. I still have the map, battered, and furry with paper fibres at the corners, and split along one or two of the folds. The ink is faded, but perfectly legible. The names she wrote still vividly evoke for me those scenes, and even bring back her voice.

In between our explorations, we helped Eric and Guinevere about the house and demesne. One morning I helped Eric repair a drystone wall while Ellie gave Guinevere a hand in the kitchen. At one point they brought out some coffee and I could hear them talking. Guinevere was saying, 'Don't take any notice of those men, Ellie dear,' and they laughed.

'Ah, shortbread,' said Eric eying the plate.

'Just one for you. He's terrible,' Guinevere said to Ellie, 'if I'd let him, he'd look like a seal.' But she let him have two. Eric was fit and wiry.

'No bad thing, a bit of blubber,' said Eric. 'The seals will last longer than us if the Russians come.' He told us that Russian trawlers, 'antennae everywhere,' had several times been spotted in the islands that summer.

He talked about the navy's use of the deep water hereabouts for exercises for our nuclear submarines up from the Clyde bases. The Russians watched them, and the navy had a corvette keeping an eye on the Russians.

'I had an encounter with one of our nuclear subs about a year ago,' he said. 'I was out in the boat. It was a grey, still day and this huge black shape rose out of the water not three hundred yards from me. It was colossal – made even your Blue Whale look like a tiddler. It was… menacing. Do you remember, old girl,' he said to Guinevere, 'I said at the time it felt almost evil, even if it was ours. When you think it has missiles in its belly that could pretty well blow the world apart.'

There was a silence and my notion of peace residing in the islands was invaded by a layer of unwelcome knowledge.

I thought of Cala Bearn and Rorq. 'We ought to go over to Inis Cuan tomorrow.'

'Oh yes,' said Eric, 'that reminds me. I had an idea.' He went into an outhouse and came back with a large piece of cardboard. Sketched on it was a notice in large capital letters headed by a skull and crossbones. The wording read:

> GOVERNMENT RESEARCH STATION AREA
> KEEP OUT – ENTRY STRICTLY FORBIDDEN
> BY ORDER

'For the entrance of Cala Bearn. You never know what stray boats may come snooping.'

Eric's idea met with general approval, but the wording gave rise to discussion. In the end it was thought that 'Station' might excite curiosity, and 'Government' official enquiries, if by any ill luck the notice should be seen by anyone in officialdom. So those words were deleted, rather to Eric's disappointment. 'Less painting to do I suppose,' he said. A red background with white lettering was chosen. We kept the skull and crossbones but it afterwards gave Eric so much trouble to get right that he painted it out. 'Don't like the red eyes, anyway,' he conceded. The notice was to be sited so that it could not be seen from the sea, but would confront anyone trying to enter the inlet.

Two days later Eric took us across to the cottage on Inis Cuan where Ellie and I were to be based. We dumped our kit and stores off in the cottage and climbed back into the boat with Eric to go round to Cala Bearn. In the boat was the newly painted signboard – plywood four foot by three – and two stout posts. Just inside the inlet we clambered ashore with some difficulty and found a suitable position to erect the notice where there was sufficient depth of peat to drive the stakes in securely. The notice board was nailed to them and support stays put in place. We stood back to admire it:

RESEARCH AREA
KEEP OUT
ENTRY STRICTLY FORBIDDEN
BY ORDER

'There,' said Eric proudly, slapping the top of a post. He looked round. 'What we ought to have is a cannon. Anybody disobeying should be blown out of the water.'

We climbed back into the boat and Eric dropped us off further up the inlet near the shack. Ellie and I waved him goodbye and he set off seawards to return to Eilean Mòr.

For days, I had been becoming increasingly impatient to show Ellie the inlet and the shack, so she could see in reality what she knew from my description. I felt the familiar tightening of excitement in my chest. Here at last was going to be the test of my long held hopes and theories. I believed that in this spot we should find men not to be the sole advanced intelligence in the solar system. Here at our feet, from the seas of the Earth might be revealed another – perhaps greater – intelligence. Over the previous weeks, Ellie and I had talked into the night about the implications of this, and how it might happen. I was strangely calm and felt deep down that unique events were converging. We looked over the shack and the apparatus, which I was relieved to find in good order. Ellie asked me to explain the equipment. When we had finished, we went out onto the edge of the rock overlooking Rorq's empty berth.

'Do you think he will come back?' asked Ellie, and her tone on the word 'will' told me she was anxious on my behalf that it should be soon.

'Soon,' I said. 'Unless he is prevented.' I did not allow myself to say, or even think, unless he has been killed. And to steer away from that said: 'You know, it will be very painstaking work.'

'I know,' and then with a smile, 'I'm a teacher too.'

And she started to scold the empty berth where Rorq would come, like a teacher chiding children she loved, pretending to be cross.

We walked back across the island to the cottage. As we arrived, a squall blew up and it started to rain. We went in. It was cold inside and cheerless and more tatty than I had previously noticed.

But Ellie seemed pleased. 'It needs to be lived in,' she said.

I did not know it then but that cottage was to be our seasonal home for five years.

A few days later Robert Thompson joined us. He was very excited. He had been working during the summer analysing sequences of Rorq's recorded sound patterns. He said he now believed Rorq was responding in a language form, and was working his way towards sound sequences that would make sense to us but which we had not yet recognised because of technical discrepancies and 'filters' which required alteration. Robert installed a new bit of kit and made two or three modifications, we tested the adjusted equipment. Ellie was made familiar with the working of it. Her voice came across as gentle and calm. Initially there was plenty to do, but in reality we were soon waiting.

As the days went by tension mounted. It was absurd, but I felt responsible for Rorq's reappearance, for I had built so much on it. Ellie and I used to go out on the headland. We scanned the sea. One day we saw some dolphins, but the sea otherwise remained empty.

But on the 26th September, Ellie was looking through the binoculars at a choppy sea. 'David, look…! Is that…?'

I grabbed the binoculars.

'Yes! Yes, it's Rorq!' I saw the familiar dark shape in the water. We looked at each other wildly and hugged. We ran to the boat and called to Robert. His head appeared above the rocks over by the generator shed, and as Ellie and I climbed into the boat and set off, he strode towards the shack.

I headed the boat impatiently down the inlet and out round the islet and rocks. As usual, Rorq waited in the sea to be met. We manoeuvred the boat towards him and he raised part of his great head out of the water and greeted us. I tried to stand in the boat, my hand on Ellie's shoulder for steadiness and called out, 'Rorq – this is Ellie,' and found myself adding, to my own surprise, 'whom I love.' I called out my declaration to the whale and to the winds and the seas and the whole world. The boat lurched and I grabbed Ellie and had to crouch down. Balance regained, I saw she was blushing and laughing, 'Stupid boy!' Rorq looked at us and spouted. I don't know how, but I had the impression he was pleased.

We came close. Ellie was awed.

'David… he's absolutely colossal.'

But as we edged up to him she showed no fear at all. We tried to pat him but the sea was quite choppy and it was not easy. After a minute he started to swim slowly towards the island, not waiting for me to lead. He seemed keen to come in. We overtook him and slipped into the calm waters of the inlet in line ahead. He swam straight to his position at the berth.

Back in the shack we crouched tensely over the equipment. We waited to see whether Robert was right, and whether his modifications would provide the conduit between two worlds. Robert had warned us that, even if he got the technicalities right to interpret Rorq's signals, speech itself depended completely on Rorq's ability to comprehend and then reproduce language.

'Hello, Rorq, welcome back!'

His first discernable response syllables came through. 'Epo.' 'Flow.' 'Tapit.' There was a pause then Rorq repeated with an exhalation of sound and a long 'f', 'Fello,' and the other word with the same strange exhalation at the beginning, 'Tavit.'

Robert said suddenly, 'He's saying "Hello!" Good God! He's saying "Hello David!" Answer him, answer him!'

I said, though I could scarcely get it out for the choke in my throat, 'Hello Rorq. I understand you.'

More syllables came from Rorq. After five minutes we had pieced together, 'I have come back' and 'to see you again.'

And then, as if from a long way back, out of the deep, his voice came quite clearly: 'I am Tisala.'

It was spoken with a sort of nobility, as if we were strangers meeting for the first time. There was some emphasis on the second syllable. The 'i' was short as in 'tissue' and the 'a' was as in 'car'.

'My name is Tisala.'

The words came steadily with something of an exhalation. So the great whale we had called Rorq was revealed to be Tisala. We shot glances at each other. We realised its significance at once: Blue Whales must have a form of developed society. New doors were opening.

'You speak with me.'

And we did, Ellie, Robert and I, heads bowed over the speakers in concentration, whispering interpretations and clarifications to each other before we responded to Tisala. Slowly, phrases and simple responses passed between us. We were entering a new-found land.

We spent three days deciphering and remodelling his words. Ellie was wonderful with her clear vowels and consonants and endless patience. The doubts and troubles of two years fell away. We worked excitedly and with unstoppable determination. Once Tisala had found the key to speech, two-way communication could commence.

Eric and Guinevere came over and shared in the excitement. They listened intently to the sounds coming from the equipment. 'Godfathers,' said Eric quietly, 'a talking whale.'

It was an odd moment. We all looked at each other. No one had previously articulated the thought out loud, and the enormity of it struck us all anew.

Within two weeks we were able to hold our first simple but rational exchanges. Ellie and I took it in turns to teach him. The language lessons took off, for now he could ask questions, or stop us and ask for explanations. He seemed to be able to absorb and learn hour after hour effortlessly. Occasionally he would take himself out to sea, hardly disturbing the waters of the inlet as he went. I was not sure whether it was to give us a rest, or for his own recreation. After an hour or two at sea he took to returning to the berth without being led in. In the evenings when we finished work, he would go to sea for the night.

In a sense the rest was easy. What at first was extraordinary was his apparent understanding of the structure of English, but it afterwards transpired that learning the basic language gave him little trouble: the difficulty had been reproduction of sound in a form recognisable by humans. As we subsequently learned, Tisala's development of his range and mastery of sound, practised all summer in the high arctic, provided the breakthrough.

By the end of three weeks Ellie and I were exhausted. Robert taught us how to work the equipment, even fine tuning, but he did most of the monitoring. We lived from day to day. We all three shared the cooking duties and whoever was to cook in the evening would set off across the island to the cottage in advance to start preparing. Sometimes after supper we were so tired that the talk was desultory and we often went to bed early, Ellie and I in the one bedroom and Robert, uncomplainingly, in the living room. We arose with the light to get back over to the inlet to make the most of the teaching day. Eric came over as necessary with fresh bread and other provisions.

Four weeks after Tisala's return, Ellie was due to go south before the start of her academic course. She refused point blank to go and arrangements were made via several telephone calls for her to commence her studies a week late; Dr. Rowlandson confirming to the authorities what he was shamefully led to believe, on the strength of a one day headache, that his daughter had been unwell. Even then, she was only persuaded to go because we were all aware that the time for Tisala's departure was approaching and that Robert and I would be following her south in a week or two. In the meantime we worked even longer hours, as we urgently wanted to maximise progress.

Eric came over again to collect Ellie. She had been near to tears as she said her goodbyes over the microphone to Tisala, and had then sat down by him on the rocks for a while. I found myself wondering with a pang whether our own goodbyes would be a lesser thing. But it was a foolish thought soon corrected by our kisses, and her tearful waving from the boat.

By early November we were beginning to converse with Tisala in the true sense of the word. It had very rapidly become apparent that progress did not depend on the ability of the learner, but of the speed and quality of the information we could impart. He appeared to understand grammar and reasoned argument with no difficulty at all. Words and pieces of information once imparted seemed never to be forgotten and his questioning was never ending.

But we knew it was time for him to depart to the southerly winter latitudes. We spoke of his return in the spring, and said our goodbyes. When he departed Robert and I went down and stood on the low cliffs above the inlet entrance, waving and calling to him as he swam slowly through the gap and out into the sea and towards the vast ocean beyond. When we could see him no longer, Robert turned to me and said, 'This has been the most extraordinary six weeks my entire life.'

CHAPTER 12

Three Years: A New Education

So began an intensive three-year period of work, governed by the seasons. Ellie and I, and to a lesser extent Robert, followed Tisala in becoming migratory. He migrated to the polar regions in the early summer, returning to Inis Cuan in the autumn before wintering in southern seas. In the spring he came back to the island before continuing north. Ellie and I fell into the same seasonal rhythm between the south of England and the Hebrides. Eric and Guinevere of course stayed on. They were our indispensable base, and between seasons were the guardians of the whole enterprise.

One spring Eric spotted Tisala first, who had arrived a fortnight or so earlier than usual. I received a telephone call from Eric. He sounded very conspiratorial. 'Our friend... you know... he's an early bird...' Then in a completely changed tone of voice he said, as if speaking publicly, 'Guinevere and I would be delighted if you could come up as soon as possible. The weather up here is beautiful.'

I could not help smiling – Eric was fiercely protective of Tisala. Three days later I was on Eilean Mòr. Eric said to me rather apologetically, 'Sorry about the cloak and dagger, but you know the West Coast telephone operators...'

'Quite right Eric,' I said, but added to tease him, 'They're probably linked up to the Russian Embassy.'

Nevertheless, we decided it would be sensible to have code words to cover future situations, and Eric went away in great glee to work something out. At supper he produced a piece of paper.

'What about "The wandering albatross has returned,"' he started proudly. His enthusiasm for Tisala's magnificence had sent him to the most spectacular of birds. 'What do you think?' he asked.

'But Eric, when was a wandering albatross last seen in Scotland? We might have dozens of fanatical bird watchers descending on us. And less congenial enquirers.'

His solution was to go to the other end of the scale. So, 'The wrens are nesting early' and 'The wrens are nesting late' were adopted to mean Tisala had returned, or not returned.

'Ah,' said Eric 'that will only work in the spring. In the autumn what about "the deer are rutting" or "not yet rutting?" Completely different,' he said, pleased. 'Good to ring the changes. That'll fox our telephone ladies, and any listening Bolsheviks.'

Our work with Tisala continued. Weeks slowly stretched into seasons. To start with we concentrated on English language, its syntax, usage and endless riches of vocabulary. Ellie was in her element. But before he could properly comprehend much of the language itself, he had first to acquire a whole range of concepts previously undreamed of in the world of whales.

Just by the shack, near Tisala's berthing place, we built a viewing chamber on a shelf in where the rocks dropped vertically into deep water at low tide. The chamber's outside wall was perched on the edge of the natural drop and we inserted into it a small plate glass window thirty inches square. Tisala could therefore nose his way right up to these rocks, like a great liner docking. We fixed car-tyre fenders along the rock face to prevent him chafing against it. So twice a day for almost two hours as the tide rose, we had an underwater viewing window. Tisala was able to bring his eye close to the window. We acquired thereby a means of underwater visual communication. We wired up the microphone and used the window to show him all manner of pictures, maps and small artefacts. Though these learning periods were restricted by the tides, they were invaluable.

So we did a great deal with pictures and picture books, familiarising him with scenes and naming the objects in them, very much as children are taught. We showed him the varied geography of the land-world – its cities, forests, mountains and deserts, its animals, and a whole range of human activities and artefacts, and the words that describe them. We showed him houses, cars, tractors, trains, tools and weapons and a thousand things of everyday human life, and illustrated their use. He always wanted to know how we built such things, from our simple beginning to our palaces and skyscrapers, ships, aircraft and many another. His linguistic progress became astonishing. And he seemed to understand concepts, like perspective and representing the Earth's surface by maps, with commanding ease.

He was fascinated, and initially astonished, by the maps of the seabed that were then being produced.

Of course, as soon as we had established good conversational communication I was impatient to question him about the nature of whales and their society. But the full story emerged slowly over two or three years.

About a year after he had first spoken, he told me, on my pressing him to do so, how he had come to single me out. He said he had been seeking out a human contact for about four seasons. As he plied his seasonal migratory route across a quarter of the globe's surface, he varied his routes, to bring him nearer into land.

'You will understand,' he said, 'that as your species is slaughtering mine, we normally do our best to avoid humankind.'

They knew however that the 'slaughter-ships' operate in their feeding grounds. There were some parts of the sea where they felt safe. Even when humans in their ships passed, they did not disturb them or seem interested beyond a mild curiosity. He noticed also that the people who live on islands seemed to have an affinity with the sea, and ventured onto its surface in their small boats. So he started to look in these places. First, among some islands in the warm seas, he found a man in a small boat who started to talk to him. But after two or three encounters, he concluded he was not a man of wisdom. 'He treated me as some strange being.' It became clear from his entreaties that he wanted Tisala to show him where to catch fish. He realised that this man knew nothing of the humans who destroyed Blue Whales – those men 'who came in powerful ships out of the land in the colder northern waters, tracking us across the world to the farthest north and to the southernmost oceans, to kill us all.'

'And eventually you found me,' I said, slightly aghast at his mission, but rather proudly.

'After two other false starts, yes. I saw you first standing on the edge of the land making strange rhythmic noises to the seals, as if you were trying to communicate. This immediately aroused my interest. So I watched for you and recognised you when you came out in your boat. And when you stood up and met me and tried to talk to me, I overcame my distrust and became excited, though I was for a while wary of a trap.'

'But why,' I asked on reflection, 'were you trying to contact us humans in the first place?' There was a long pause before he said,

'It is the last chance to save our race.'

There was a silence. I realised with dismay that I had been chosen as the representative of a genocidal species of killers. I knew the history of whaling sufficiently well to be ashamed for humanity, and did not then question him further.

But he said: 'We, the Blue Whales, who have long known ourselves to be the most advanced form of life in the seas of the Earth, are nearing extinction by – of all things – a ferocious little land animal. We are mystified as to why humans are hunting us to the end with such relentless determination. If we are of use, either for food, or as we guessed, some other purpose, how could they gain from killing us all? They would simply destroy what they wanted.'

The slaughter appeared to them barbaric and illogical. They knew from other contacts with mankind that not all humans are murderous, and that some are peaceable and even honoured them. They knew too that men had language – they picked up snatches and incidences of it at sea.

Tisala said, 'I came to believe that, if humans only knew more of whales, they might stop killing us. But I saw that the only possibility of saving our species is by men stopping men. I realised that I had somehow to make contact with good men – if they could be found – to appeal against our genocide. So I began to look. And so, at length, I found you.'

He was silent.

At first, I felt pleasure and honour in being chosen, though reason told me it was mainly chance. Then I felt, far off, the beginnings of a huge responsibility gathering, coming towards me from all the oceans of the world, to settle here on this tiny Scottish island. But I was young and with the overwhelming challenge came a blazing hope. What I did not see was the benefit to mankind that might lie in the discharge of such responsibility. That I only saw much later.

Over the months we learned more about Tisala and his kind. For, despite the detailed whaling records, vital characteristics remained unknown, or unreported, and some repeated assertions were simply guesses, which once made tended to reappear in subsequent writings.

Many were wrong. For instance, I saw stated categorically in more than one whale book, that whales' vision is two-dimensional. The widest part of the Blue Whale's head is at the point where the eyes are mounted and I quickly discovered that they have a highly developed ability to swivel their eyes, allowing forward-looking three-dimensional focus, quite close beyond the great forward-thrusting jaws. They have reasonable long-distance vision, which Tisala later said he assumed his forebears had developed to assist them in iceberg and island-strewn seas. Initially I thought he could not see in three-dimensional vision sideways, as of course sideways on he viewed with his nearside eye alone. However, close to, I noticed that he made almost imperceptively small eye movements, and I afterwards realised he was in effect creating his own stereoscope. That movement was sufficient for his brain to synthesise a three-dimensional image. I soon discovered also that he had colour vision, again contrary to the belief of the very few whale researchers who troubled to ask themselves the question. It was only years later that I saw in scientific writing the assertion that dissection of a dead whale's eye showed it had cones as well as rods, indicating the possession of colour vision.

As time passed, we made additions and improvements to the physical arrangements at the shack. A lean-to was built on. The storeroom became a bedroom, and in the main room, basic washing and cooking facilities were provided by a header tank, a sink and a small bottled- gas cooker. The water came from a small stream, but in dry weather sometimes had to be supplemented by plastic containers brought by boat.

From the beginning, Tisala liked music. He was curious about our 'songs'. I answered him initially with a rather complacent account of music as evidencing our higher qualities, and explained that often we did not sing but used instruments, singly, or in a group, up to the full-blown symphony orchestra.

Within a year we installed a record player and loudspeaker. On calm evenings, our inlet would be transformed into a natural amphitheatre. As the sun went down, the pool of water became lighter, reflecting the sky, as the surrounding rocks fell into twilight shadow, and the light lingered long in the north-west. Then, out across the still water would float some of the most beautiful music ever created by man. I was usually by the shack, to change the records and talk with Tisala in between – explaining the music and exchanging comments. When I joined Ellie again, sitting on the rocks, the music seemed to flood into the universe. It felt as if we were linked by some higher harmony of life, as if behind the sounds lay silent depths of love. Sometimes Ellie would take the boat on the water to be with Tisala and I would watch their shapes darkening as the light faded. And we were still as one. When a piece was finished, Tisala would sometimes stir his great flukes causing a rippling movement of evening light to spread across the water, as if the inlet itself was affected by the music. Sometimes we would gather additional listeners, seals and the occasional sea otter.

So Tisala got to know my 1950s conventional western experience, starting with the Baroque and ending up in the early twentieth century with some traditional jazz. In time he was to demand a wider repertoire. But he did not like all music. He admired Bach but found him often too busy, and he disliked the bombast and thick opaque sounds of later nineteenth- century music. And as time went on I found that there was much music that disturbed him. He loved, as befitted his form and temperament, the slow and graceful and the purity and clarity of sound dropping out of the quiet nights. He said it awakened beauty in the stillness of the mind and that such sounds opened passageways and connections in the brain. He once remarked, 'Music must give you humans hope about yourselves, for it shows the desire to live on a higher plane.' In the love songs of Mozart, through which we had met, he found some of his most loved music; as he did in many of the slow movements of classical concertos and symphonies, with their underlying rhythmic vitality – the heartbeat – which he recognised as common to all animals – the pulse of life which sustained the melodic song. One of his favourite pieces was the serene undulating current of Beethoven's last symphonic adagio, which he thought carried something of eternal hope in it. He found Beethoven's music fascinating, though he did not like all of it. He was wary of the fierceness, but attracted by the determination and morality that somehow pulsated through it.

I concluded that the attraction of music was universal and speculated whether, although composers 'made' the music, they were releasing what was already there.

'Like the music of the spheres,' said Robert once, laughing at me. 'But you are right that it depends on physics that exists whether or not man is in the universe.' And he said the length and shortness of vibrations producing pitch would be exactly the same on a planet on the other side of the universe inhabited by giant aria-singing crabs.

'But it's not just that,' said Ellie. 'How do you explain the expression of love in music, or moral force, or a sense of the spiritual? Was that in the music before it was written? Or was it in the composer?'

So we got into such things. But I did not then understand what remarkable shifts in ideas might be made of them in Tisala's mind; though I should have guessed more than I did, knowing something of the importance of songs among whales.

About two years after the beginning we erected an outdoor cinema. It may sound bizarre – it seemed bizarre – but we did. At the landward side of Tisala's berthing place we built and plastered a breezeblock wall, facing the water, and painted it white. We acquired a film projector. It was rather cumbersome. We had to lug it across the rocks and set it up with a sound system on fine nights. We joked that it was the only cinema in the world where the stalls audience was in the sea, whilst we humans were confined to the slips on the rock ledge at the side. In the early days we mainly used it for travelogues but it became used increasingly for a wide range of documentaries, feature films and visual aids. Some of the feature films, even historical ones, Tisala thought did mankind no credit at all, for they showed our taste for murder and death. He thought it astonishing that we fed on them for entertainment. And he found almost painful the tinny sound reproduction of Hollywood violins and dramatic crescendos. But the cinema was a useful means of envisaging life on Earth and bringing him to places and ideas which would have been otherwise difficult to describe. In later years it was replaced altogether by more modern technology.

Over the seasons, as his learning proceeded, our work with Tisala changed. And the synthesising way his mind worked resulted in we ourselves understanding many topics and their relatedness with a new clarity. His mind could simultaneously retain thoughts and concepts parallel and behind each other with an awe-inspiring transparency and ease. Our lessons became increasingly advanced studies. I became a teacher of the development of civilisation and history, geography, astronomy, evolutionary biology, religion, philosophy and an ever-expanding range of topics. By inclination, my curiosity equipped me well for much of this, but I soon found my state of knowledge fell lamentably short of what Tisala required. In the periods when we returned to London, I increasingly spent the time studying. Ellie, in addition to helping me with all this, gave him, amongst other topics, social history, art and music. Robert taught him physics and an understanding of chemistry. He found the electromagnetic spectrum and the reality of radio and television waves particularly engrossing.

Later Robert did not need to come up so long or so often, which was as well, as initially he had only been able to do so with great difficulty by rearranging his timetable and duties at the university. He insisted, however, in coming up to the island at least once during every season, even if on occasion only for a few days. In the third spring he had a sabbatical and stayed for six weeks, when much progress was made. In time, with the help of further refinements to the equipment, Tisala's speech and reproduction of sound improved to the point where we hardly thought about it as we conversed.

But I am getting ahead of the story. For in the spring of 1962 my life changed again, when I asked Ellie to marry me.

CHAPTER 13

At Fieldbanks House

I remember the morning at Fieldbanks House. I woke early, and being unable to sleep, came downstairs. It was a lovely April morning, bright and fresh. I was standing by the bookcase in the sitting room, thumbing nervously through a book on Alpine climbs, but not taking anything in – the black and white photographs of various peaks and glaciers all looked remote and somehow hostile, and the text seemed wordy and impenetrable.

We were visiting Ellie's parents for the weekend. On the train coming down, as we passed through the green sunlit countryside I had decided this was the weekend, this was the moment, to ask her to marry me. I imagined the scene – her acceptance and her family gathering round to congratulate us – and I rehearsed it two or three times with pleasure, adding touches each time.

I looked at Ellie sitting opposite me, gazing out of the compartment window. Her face was serious: she was thinking of other things. She looked at me and said, 'Have you written that letter to the university?'

'About the doctorate? No. I was going to.' My dream faded in the reality of the railway carriage, and the problems beyond.

'You must, you really must.'

'Yes I will.' I patted her knee and smiled, but her returning smile was strained.

A doubt flickered in my mind. Was she worrying about our financial position and future?

'I will do it on Monday, first thing. Yes, it needs sorting out.'

I felt momentarily reassured by my own words. But we fell silent and I began to think uncomfortable thoughts. Suddenly and unexpectedly I felt doubtful. Should I sort out the next stages of my career before asking her to marry me? Down here she was surrounded by the comfort and certainty of her own home and family. It was not that they were wealthy, or even materialistic; they were a country doctor's family, hardworking and conscientious, but by the standards of the day, having sufficient income to live with a sense of untroubled security which pervades a happy family in such circumstances. Soon, as I thought about my position, my stomach began to churn. I thought, You are a fool – what can you offer her? – no proper job, few prospects, a widowed mother, a single sister living in London with enough troubles of her own. Once again, as I often had when a boy, I wished I had a father. The photograph of his smiling face in the desert in Eighth Army shorts came back to me vividly. Why was he killed – Montgomery was careful of his soldiers – killed so long ago? Often I had been alone across the years, trying to build to a new generation. And now – maybe – failure. What if she rejects me? What if she says no, in that family setting, or even that she is not sure, not ready, and will I understand? Then would follow weeks of nightmares, doubts and sickening awakenings each morning.

This is dreadful, I thought. But then anger stirred in me. My inner voice said, come on, come on – these are night fears unworthy of you and her love – dismiss them; you know she loves you. And gradually a sort of calm returned.

And when she next spoke, she had forgotten the letter and turned her mind to the coming weekend. She was my same warm and loving Ellie. Then, as we talked, the bad moments retreated and passed.

And our welcome at her parents' house was as cheerful, affectionate and kind as any young man could wish. By bedtime, I had again decided to ask her. So here was the morning. My tongue felt dry as I flicked through the pages, waiting for Ellie to come down, but I was almost trembling in anticipation.

I heard a sound behind me. Ellie stood in the doorway in jeans and a t-shirt, her feet bare. Everything stopped. There was a double thump in my chest.

'You're up early,' she said coming forward.

My brain said, Ask her, now. Ask her. But then countermanded me urgently, no, no, not now – in a –

She kissed me. 'Are you all right?' She looked at me doubtfully.

'Yes, fine. Let's go outside.' It was not quite true, but those few words, and the action of opening the door and going outside somehow reassured me and I remember saying to myself, ask her in the garden and she will accept you, for she loves you.

We walked down the path and sat on a wooden bench, a little way from the house in the warmth of the sun. 'You're very serious this morning,' she teased. But holding my hands fell silent and looked down, fingering them.

And in that place and in her silence I found my courage.

'Ellie, will you... Will you marry me?'

Her hands stopped moving. There was a slight pause and I saw her colour rising. She looked up at me and our eyes met deep inside.

'Yes,' she said, 'Yes I will.' And then she whispered, 'Will you really have me?'

'Oh, Ellie, I love you so much.'

We burned with a new but ancient fire that we both recognised. We kissed and it was like the first kiss of Adam and Eve. We walked hand in hand – now differently together, down to the fields at the end of the garden, stood under the trees and embraced, gently and forever.

Eventually I said, smiling, 'You've shrunk.'

'No shoes,' she laughed.

Her feet were wet with dew. I picked her up and sat her on a beech log, took off my shirt and dried her feet with it.

She smiled, her hand on my shoulder and protested softly, 'Silly boy. They'll just get wet again.'

But she knew it was an offering. We longed for each other but didn't need to rush. She helped me put my shirt back on. We started to talk, and the future belonged to us.

'When shall we tell them?' she said, looking up at the house.

And soon we were chattering and laughing and contradicting ourselves in a sea of happiness.

At breakfast, I think they knew that something was afoot. Ellie was flushed and beautiful. I didn't answer questions properly, and grinned inappropriately. I saw Penelope looking at Ellie, a little smile playing around her lips. But we said nothing, for we wanted for a while to enjoy our own news together. After breakfast we went for a walk. The shadows flickeringly returned. 'Do you think your family will really approve?'

'They love you, David.'

'And my career... well – it isn't... I...'

'I can teach, you'll get established. I know you will.'

'I... yes I will.' And I suddenly felt a surge of certainty that I would succeed.

We made our announcement before lunch, sitting under the sunshades in the garden.

'Ellie and I have something to tell you. We want to get married.' We looked at each other, 'And we hope you will…' I can't remember the rest. We were all standing up hugging and laughing.

'Oh Ellie! Lovely! Delighted!' Mother and daughter in each other's arms, a few tears brushed away laughingly.

Her father hugged her, and holding her out from him said, 'You're a lucky girl, Ellie. And so are you,' he said, smiling broadly and clapping a hand on me. 'By God you are.'

And I glimpsed briefly the ancient lament of a father passing his daughter to another man, which would presage his own decline. I thought, yes but you have a new son, and I have a father again at last. I determined to love this couple forever. When Edmund could no longer cope with the garden, I would come and deal with it. Whatever was necessary to be done would be done.

'Edmund,' said Penelope eventually, 'we need – '

'A celebration – at once,' and he disappeared inside.

We sat down. Ellie and I held hands. Penelope smiled at us. 'Well, you two. When did you know?'

Well, when was it? I asked myself. Perhaps the first night we ever met, at the Fulham Road party. Maybe to say that would sound presumptuous or shallow. Or did it accumulate by unseen degrees in waking and sleeping hours. And when for her? – I glanced at her.

'Oh, Mummy, what a question!' she said. And in that slight defensiveness she signalled that it was something we had not yet ourselves explored, and that it was ours to discover first.

So I just replied, 'More or less forever, I think,' and grinned at Ellie. Edmund returned with the drinks.

'Not cold enough. Ice in the glasses, I'm afraid. Dreadful thing to do, but the occasion demands the real stuff, immediately. My dear,' he said to Penelope, 'Let us have a toast. To Ellie and David, our lovely daughter and our new son David, long years and every happiness.'

Penelope echoed, 'Long years and every happiness.'

It was decided to keep the news secret for a week before telling Ellie's brother or anyone else, so that we could go down to tell my mother first.

'I will give you a letter for your mother, David, to say how pleased we are, and to ask her to come and stay.' So my future mother-in-law took care to add to my happiness. There was talk of a possible late July wedding, but as Ellie and I wanted to be in the islands until June, and as it was thought Ellie should be at home for a few weeks beforehand, nothing was fixed.

Two weeks later Ellie and I were back in the cottage on Inis Cuan.

CHAPTER 14

Tisala's World

The island was already the place in the whole world where Ellie and I were most free, most ourselves, and very soon where we felt we most belonged. Life was simple in this place of always astonishing beauty, and though sometimes basic or short of this or that, we laughed and made do.

And when Tisala returned, as he did a week later in a day of sun and flying spray and oiled wool jerseys; and when the teaching and learning recommenced; and when Ellie, as I looked at her in her tender seriousness towards her great sea child, was beyond description beautiful; then this little island of the sea – which nursed the sea in its bays and inlets – became a unique and wonderful paradise. For in this sea-garden we found the beginnings of a knowledge and love new to mankind.

We gradually entered into Tisala's unknown marine world, and he into ours. We learned from him in numerous conversations over a long period. I will try to put what he told us in some sort of order. Our language does not easily give the feeling of the whale's world.

This is what he told us, of how the great whales live in the oceans, almost wholly beyond human sight and knowledge. They spend their lives swim-flying peaceably on the top of the water layer, the world's best protected and most life abundant region, the globe-encompassing sea. Below them lies the security of the dense deep, resting on the rocky core, except where the crust protrudes as continents and islands into the air layer. Above them enveloping the outer Earth is the thin haze of the atmosphere. As mammals, of course they must rise to the air layer to breathe, and on hot sunny days they delight to float in the top of the waters, to laze at the bottom of the sky. But they regard the air as too thin and volatile, too near the emptiness beyond and too prone to violent storms and extremes of heat and cold, to be a proper place to live.

We learned early on that whales have always known we live in a revolving sphere. They know it from the sun, the stars, from echoes off the curvature of the oceans and from the Earth's magnetic field. Whales in their present form have existed for some twenty-five million years. Tisala found it difficult to believe that men – through explorers like Magellan – only discovered that the world is round a few hundred years ago. I tried to excuse our ignorance by explaining that the Greeks, as developers of one of our foremost civilisations, had worked it out two thousand years ago; and not only worked it out, but (Erastosthenes it was) measured accurately the Earth's circumference by means of the sun and the shadow angles of poles placed in the ground along the North African coast between Alexandria and Cyrene. But I had to admit that the Greeks had destroyed themselves and their civilisation by fighting, and that the knowledge was lost.

I asked him about sea monsters and the denizens of the deep, saying with a laugh that ill-informed men in early days had believed in all sorts of fantastic creatures, but now we believed that there was little life beyond the shallows except creatures such as giant squid and a few strange fish, and that the deep oceans are cold and lifeless. I said we knew Sperm Whales could dive three thousand feet to catch giant squid, but even that was less than ten percent of the deepest ocean trenches. He was surprised by our modern beliefs and said that life is vastly more potent and varied and invasive of all kinds of environments. He told me the deep sea in general was seething with creatures of strange shapes and forms, some with internal sources of light and electric power, which passed up and down from the depths to the surface in their rituals of living. Whales know this partly because of the amount of sound arising from the inner depths of the water.

He said whales can 'see' through the entire depths of the ocean. They do not need light to see the dark deep – they can see it in their minds, through sound. The great diapason booms of the Blue Whale send sound waves down to the ocean bed. Where they hit impediments – the sea floor or undersea mountains and ridges – sound is reflected back to give the whale a mental image of the topography of the sea basins. For more immediate sound reflection, for instance among icebergs or among island waters, they use a higher frequency, which though of a shorter range, gives a more detailed picture.

When Robert Thompson worked these matters out, it was in the knowledge that sound in air is a poor relation: in water, it travels a mile a second, five times its speed in air. Robert concluded, for instance, that in the relatively shallow island-scattered sea of the Hebrides the picture of the sea-bed vertically below and in front of Tisala, revealed from differentiated returned sounds, would be formed almost instantaneously. Even beyond the islands, over the edge of the continental shelf where the seabed dropped to the deep Atlantic basin, the returned sounds would take only a few seconds. We thought this mental image must work something like a photographic negative, gaps in reflected sound indicating clear water. Diagonal or horizontal sounds, bounced back, say, from an island five miles in front, would clearly take a number of seconds to return. We concluded that to form a coherent picture-map the co-ordinating and imaging power of the whale's brain must be prodigious.

We afterwards learned that Tisala had stored in his memory, recallable at will, the images of sea basins and features on the various routes of his seasonal migrations. We were filled with awe. Imagine then, our feelings when we eventually realised he could describe quite accurately, so that it could be picked up on detailed maps of the seabed, places he had been to only once or twice in his life – in the Indian Ocean and Pacific. And how silent we were when we finally realised he could describe parts of the ocean floor stretching under the polar ice cap. As a biologist I was having rapidly to revise my understanding of evolutionary development.

And he was fascinated by the theory of evolution. I explained, rather triumphantly, that he was a mammal, and described the place of mammals in the scheme of things. I said that he, like us, was one of the highest forms of life. For some reason, he did not much like the comparison between whales and men. I told him the fossil record showed that whales had developed from a four-legged land mammal.

He said, 'We have a story that tells us we once lived above the water, but we found it an inhospitable place and our forebears wisely took us back to the oceans.' I asked him whether this history had to do with that strange phenomenon when whales beach themselves on the land, where they die. But he said that it was caused by a breakdown of their ability to use what he called the 'ring auras' by which they navigated. I was much puzzled by this initially, but eventually understood that they have developed a sophisticated system for navigation using the Earth's magnetic field.

It emerged from our talks that whales thought that the function of the Earth's crust was largely to form a bedrock which would support the water strata. The water kept the crust within bounds except where it broke through as continents and islands. He described how the rocky layer of the planet was subject to huge disruptive forces from within that made it erupt and buckle and in places break through its proper confines below the oceans, rising into the air, to form the upper land. He told me to my astonishment of undersea volcanoes and the red-hot cracks in the seabed. I could scarcely believe such things, which were only later discovered by scientists; nor how he could know, for most of them lay at the bottom of deep oceans far below the level to which whales could dive. He said there were places where rivers of red-hot rock came quite near the surface, but that they knew it mostly by sound and the rising of gases. I listened in amazement as he told me, not only of the noise of underwater volcanoes and fiery fissures in the Earth's surface, but of the daily tidal noise of creaking and groaning of the Earth's rock layer being pulled by the moon. When I protested, he insisted this was certainly so, and found it difficult to comprehend my lack of knowledge, particularly when I had to admit we knew perfectly well of the water strata being pulled by the moon. He put it down to the fact that most of the crust above the water was silent and dead, being far from the centre of the globe's activities. I said rather feebly that we had our own volcanoes and earthquakes; but that served only to underline our ignorance of the diurnal rock movements.

In the years when even plate tectonics were still a rudimentary notion, I attended several geological meetings in London, Boston and Baltimore, and dropped some of these ideas into the conversation. Who knows what knowledge of Tisala's, floated in these hotels and conference centres, and afterwards remembered in other times and places, led to academic hunches and connections, which were gradually turned by research into acceptable knowledge? When I told Tisala of these occasions, he made the low rumble that indicated amusement.

I asked him how deep Blue Whales could dive. He said long-breath depth, but only the curiosity of young whales took them so far down, for there was no need. We afterwards discovered by experiment that Tisala could descend two thousand feet, which is deeper than scientists then, or even in modern times, allow. But he said they would not normally go down much more than half that. I asked him why they should dive at all, for their food is near the surface. He said the most common purpose was to sink below the turbulence of storms – a mere hundred or two hundred feet. Their deep dives were he said, for two reasons: the first, for the pleasure and freedom of it, and the second, to enter what he called the sound zone.

He said whales could communicate through the sea at large distances. He told me how Blue Whales use their great size and resultant ability to produce huge, very low, long-wave sound to send signals through the deep ocean. These messages could be heard and recognised, in good conditions, thousands of miles away. Robert muttered that it did not seem possible. But when he went back to London he took the problem with him, and worked on it periodically. For a few years we did not understand the mechanism. It turned out that, because of the different density of water at depth and a temperature 'ceiling' near the surface, the deep oceans act as a sounding funnel. Travelling obliquely, the sound waves bounce off the dense deep water and the shallow temperature ceilings, so that the sound is not dissipated by breaking the surface, or by being absorbed by the seabed. The low pulses of sound can travel along the funnel for enormous distances, bending within the water layer round the curve of the Earth without losing their quality. Tisala told me that a Blue Whale in the tropical seas could send a signal of his whereabouts, identity and wellbeing to members of his family in either the Arctic or the Antarctic. For normal purposes however he said they would communicate over shorter distances, starting at perhaps twelve or fifteen hundred miles, and communicating more or less freely from six hundred miles and closer.

I began to discover how whales have evolved their large brains. It was commonly confirmed in whaling literature that Blue Whales have very large brains. But there was little detailed record. This was initially surprising as in the heyday of whaling for Blue Whales, in the first half of the twentieth century, whaling nations had provided innumerable specimens for their researchers to measure when disposing of the slaughtered carcasses; and indeed there were detailed measurements of all parts of whale anatomy. But it appeared they had not much bothered with brains, for these are about the only part of the animal of no use or value commercially. Nearly the whole of man's painstaking whale research had been directed at discovering the whales' life and reproductive cycles, so as many as possible could be killed without undermining the sustainability of the whaling industry. As to intrinsic interest in whales themselves, in all the literature up to that time in the 1960s, there was virtually none.

When I did eventually unearth a few statistics, it was recorded that a Blue whale's brain weighed about fifteen pounds. Moreover, the whale's cerebral cortex was said to be highly developed and convoluted, characteristics believed to denote intelligence. I sat with my mind in a state of excited conjecture. For I knew our own brains weigh only about three pounds.

Now every biologist knows that brain weight has a relationship to body size: a large animal such as a whale or an elephant, owes part of its brain size to the need to co-ordinate its large body. But when I researched further, I concluded that this element could in no way account for the whale's brain. Some large animals, famously dinosaurs, had tiny brains. And there were a host of other anomalies in other animals. Moreover, it was becoming clear from advances in knowledge, even in those days, and within twenty years it had become plain, that once a higher animal develops the structure of the brain evolutionarily, its use is not confined to the reasons which gave rise to that development. Human consciousness, the development of language, reasoning power, the ability to envisage future events, and organise past ones – and so create art, writing, buildings and machines – all arose as by-products of more humble though often skilful survival functions. The implications of the existence of an animal with a brain more developed than our own began to sink in.

I began to have an inkling that man's view of himself as a uniquely created being, apart from, and superior to nature, a delusion fostered among much of humanity down the centuries since early civilisations and religions, might at last be banished.

Originally my idea had been an unformed aspiration of talking with whales, not knowing what might be revealed or achieved. Increasingly, as I lived with Tisala's responses, I began to contemplate the idea of shared intelligence being used to view the world from a less exclusively human angle. If whales' brains – the hardware – were more developed than human brains, what powers might be released by advanced education – the software – in creating wise minds? Perhaps Blue Whales, free as they are of such activities of mankind as fighting, killing, enslaving, stealing and exploiting, could become repositories of reason, philosophy and ethics; in short the qualities so desperately needed by humanity. These ideas grew slowly in my mind while we were finding out more of Tisala's world. Here might be an opportunity to help save us from ourselves and from our increasing destruction of the world.

CHAPTER 15

The Legend of Tisano

But long before such ideas took shape, I had first discovered from Tisala with increasingly awed understanding much about Blue Whales and their society in the oceans. He in turn constantly enquired about life on the dry land.

At the beginning, he thought it a handicap that we were confined by our little twin legs to scrambling about on the surface of the crust. He thought we were of strange design, and that the four-footed mammals were better conceived – if they damaged a leg they could go on three, whereas a man with one useless leg was immobilised. He found it hard to believe we could only walk twenty miles in a day and so could not migrate or use other than very small areas of the Earth where we happened to find ourselves. I had to concede this, but claimed that things were now very different with our mastery of transport; although the result of artificial aids was that our practical ability to walk was becoming curtailed, and that many people at least in advanced economies could seemingly not walk more than a mile or two without discomfort. Blue Whales on the other hand thought little of swimming four thousand miles each season between the tropics and the Arctic or Antarctic.

Tisala told me the Blue Whales, except when they congregated in the Arctic or Antarctic regions in summer to feed, when they used to be present in large numbers, travelled on their migrations in small family groups; typically, a mother and father with their offspring, perhaps a three year old, and a newborn, and often with an adult aunt and young nephew or niece. But in the days before they were hunted, families migrated in extended unison. A small family unit would keep in contact with similar families a few miles apart. The less attached members, such as the young – nephews, nieces, or sometimes friends – would often swap groups for part of the journey. It became clear from what Tisala said that Blue Whales were sociable beings. Their migrations were family and social events. In the old days hundreds of these family groups, though separated, moved through the oceans together, linked by steady streams of sound messages, and the arrival and departures of individuals between groups. The very young whales listened, but kept by their mothers; the youngsters played, sometimes dashing ahead in the exhilaration of the journey; and adolescents tentatively met. The parents oversaw the armada, keeping it at a steady speed for the benefit of the youngest and oldest whales.

In the north Atlantic these family groups would go north in early summer, off the edge of the continental shelf, which acted as a sounding board to funnel up the signals of more distant groups. So the travelling whales gathered in the feeding grounds in the high latitudes in summer, and returned south to one of the equatorial breeding grounds in winter. In the southern hemisphere the seasons are of course at opposite times of year – high summer being in January – but the pattern is the same. I asked him whether the whale populations of the hemispheres mixed. He said very often they did not, or did not for several seasons, but they could travel the whole world at will, and since the Great Death, had done so more frequently. He told me there was an ancient story of the discovery of the southern hemisphere by the Blue Whales.

One day Tisala told us the legend – the legend of Tisano. 'In distant times, the story goes, we Blue Whales were small. Fully grown we were about as long as our newborns today. We lived only in the northern sea. It was closed to the north by the ice and to the south by the hot ocean where there was no food. Life was hard – in those times there were great storms, and huge toothed predators twice our own size. The storms took their toll and drained our strength. Even in the summer, the gales often whipped up the water dispersing the krill and it was difficult to find enough to eat. We spent our time and energy hunting for food.

'Tisano, who was a young whale approaching adulthood, noticed that larger whales did better and won partners more easily. But big whales ate more food and there was not enough. For the smaller ones, life became even more difficult. As a young leader of the smaller whales, Tisano, who had fallen in love with a beautiful large young female, and wanted to win her, began to search his mind for a solution. He could see the advantage lay with the bigger whales – they could ride out the storms more easily, survive without food longer, and defend themselves more easily against their enemies. For a year Tisano thought about this, and gradually formed a plan. He knew from the curve of the sea that the planet was a sphere. In his mind's eye he worked out that they must inhabit only a section of it. What, he asked himself, lies in the other parts of the globe – perhaps there are new and bountiful seas elsewhere. Tisano asked the adults, but they all said, "No, the land to the north closes in and is blocked by the ice. To the south, the sea gets hotter and hotter and contains no food, and the land closes in there too." But they were vague about this, and he could not find anyone who had been all the way. He said to himself, "Suppose the world is balanced. If there is ice in the north and hot seas in the middle, will not the seas beyond be cold? For the sun comes to the north in the summer, so in the south, without the sun, there must be cold regions." But for a while no-one would listen and some of the grown-ups said, "He is only a small whale, don't listen to him."

'But his ideas spread among the young whales. The young female whom he loved became attracted to him and grew to love him. Her parents said, "Find yourself a bigger partner." But she said, "Tisano is bigger than any of them." And she loved him the more. She thought, if he is right this may be a new future for our kind, and she desired his children. In the end she said that she would go with him. To mark her commitment to him she asked her friends and family to call her Tisani. Eventually, a group of their friends were also persuaded to swim into the unknown. They were fourteen in number. They did not tell the older whales and they spent that summer in secret excitement, eating as much food as they could find to give them strength for the intended journey.

'When they came south in autumn to the intermediate waters, they did not stop. Some of the older whales called after them and were distressed when they found out the plan, as they thought they would die in the hot seas and never be seen again. But the little group pressed steadily south. The water got warmer and warmer. They came to some islands where there was an upwelling of cool water and with it some food. Some of them said, "This is a beautiful place, why not stop here? These are good breeding grounds, and from here we could still return to the north."

'But Tisano said they should go on, and reminded them of the plan to go to the further end of the globe. In the end, six of them refused, but eight went on. The warm sea became still warmer and the land began to close in and push their course towards the afternoon sun. They began to fear that what the elders had said was true.

'But Tisano said, "Have you not noticed from the distant echoes that the deep is extending in the same direction, and the great spine mountains also?" The warm sea got hotter, but Tisano said to encourage them, "Our blubber layer is thinner now, and we can survive the heat. Besides, we must be near the middle of the globe, and if I am right, before long the water will start to cool." After two more days it was hotter than ever and a number of the whales were frightened. But Tisani swam in unison with him, and as she was the biggest whale, the others followed. Then they noticed that the land had ceased to push them to the west and they felt the ocean opening out before them. In another day or two, they began to notice the water was becoming a little less hot, and in a day or two after that the trend was clear. They entered a noticeably cooler current flowing from the south. They began to get excited. One or two of them started to rush ahead but Tisano said, "There is a long way to go – we should go steadily."

'As they went further south, the land, far from closing in, shrank away, and the open seas became ever more open and increasingly cold, until at last they found the southern ice. And that was how they discovered the Great South Ocean – the Blue Whales' paradise. There they found, in the cold currents that circled the ice-continent, krill in countless billions carpeting the surface of the ocean pink and red.

'"Now," said Tisano to Tisani, "our young, and in turn their young, will never be short of food. They will grow to great size and be untroubled by storms and enemies and have the endurance to swim through all the oceans at will." And that is what happened, owing to the foresight and courage of Tisano and Tisani.'

'That is a lovely story, Tisala,' said Ellie, 'How old do you think it is?'

'Who knows?' he said, 'Five hundred generations?'

'From time immemorial,' I said, and had a strange sense of the story coming down the generations of whales from before the last ice age, before men recorded histories.

Later, Tisala made me explain 'time immemorial'. I told him that in England it means before 1189, the accession of King Richard I. The phrase is a legal one relating to the development of the Common Law of England in the thirteenth century. Any long-standing custom found to have existed in an area 'since time immemorial' could be regarded as a local law that might be incorporated into the Common Law of England. But in everyday use it came to mean – longer ago than anyone can remember.

Tisala was at first amused by the shortness of our collective memory and then intrigued by the way men allow time to close up behind them.

'If you lose the past so easily, you lose its experience and wisdom, and since the present is gone as you breathe you have little to look to but the future; and since the future in your land-world is largely unknowable you remain prey to fear, ignorance and superstition, and constantly have to relearn what should be known.'

He contrasted this, before the coming of the whalers, with the life they had led passing down from generation to generation their accumulated stories, wisdom, geographical and navigational skills, in the almost unchanging sanctity of the Earth's water mantle.

Sometimes when he spoke, I could tell he was recalling a golden age, when the great Blue Whales lived and moved through wide clear seas as they had for countless thousands of years, swim-flying freely and superbly in harmony with each other, their environment, and the seasons of the water planet; and in calm summer seas tisurfing in the sparkling blue expanse. Tisurfing is the term they use for slow-cruising and exhaling at the surface, so as to feel on their backs the pleasure of the warm sun and gently breaking waters. For the Blue Whales as they evolved, because of their size and speed, were without fear and totally without enemies. They came to consider themselves as the most fortunate beneficiaries of earthly creation.

'You cannot have a golden age,' he said once when I raised it with him, 'without a system of knowledge and a structured society. We had developed knowledge and a living wisdom – experienced on an everyday basis by all our kind – while we were making our seasonal journeys between the tropics and the icefields. Our swimming was full of joy and fulfilment and we were united in our community by song and speech. We could hold in our mind's eye images of the tropics, the Arctic and Antarctic regions and the underlying topography of the ocean beds, and picture our friends and relatives foregathering in different oceans of the world. We could send and receive messages from around the globe – in slow motion as it were, though that was of no consequence, as time was ours – with a three-hour lapse for sound to travel from the Antarctica to the Arctic. Of course, even in those times there were occasional accidents, deaths of children, disease and suffering, but these were few and infrequent and largely individual tragedies, and accepted as such. The community of Blue Whales itself was as near balanced perfection as may be in the world. That was before men came.'

I knew what he meant. From my knowledge of whaling history I was deeply ashamed for humanity. I said bitterly: 'Before men started slaughtering you.'

'And now we are nearly gone, and the oceans are filled instead with a ceaseless noise from the engines and propellers of your countless ships. Yes, the killing was the beginning of the end.' He was silent. But in his silence he returned in his mind to the golden days and after a while said, 'And it was much more. What made it so wonderful was that we ourselves had consciously assisted in the development of that world.'

I thought this was a startling claim. I had argued without much refinement the standard Darwinian theory of development through initial chance mutation of the genes which when successful became the norm and led to adaptations allowing a better chance of survival, and over vast periods of time, further development.

'You have told me,' he said, 'of numerous incidences of such things – the predator-deterring eye patterns on the wings of a butterfly, the sandy disguise of a flat fish – and that these are everywhere to be seen. But they merely preserve life, and do not much enhance it. Who remembers which fish bred which fifty years ago, let alone a thousand? Hundreds of generations pass, waiting for something to evolve, some change in an individual to enable a species to break into new developments. The ultimate advance,' he said, 'is into conscious intelligence. We found our way into it from advancing our survival skills, through the complexities of interpreting sound, our navigational ability and our need to develop communication in the vast oceans. Along the way, we increasingly employed thought and reason, and developed language, to influence the direction of our advancement. Long, long ago, some of our number preferred not to fight and kill for food. A more reliable and peaceable method of preservation was found to be better. We gradually adopted our seasonal cropping of surface-carpeting food produced in the cold icy regions, and so evolved as we are, without teeth. In matters of procreation we abandoned the method of maximum reproduction, by a dominant, aggressive individual with a blind urge to procreate at every opportunity. Such characteristics came to be regarded as misdeveloped and not those of the best whales. Physical beauty was nearly universal amongst us and attractiveness between whales tended to become centred on other qualities.'

'As Tisani felt for Tisano,' intervened Ellie.

'Yes,' said Tisala, 'physical qualities but also qualities of the mind – fortitude, foresight, and capacity for thought and expression. The best singers of our songs were admired and emulated. Education of our young, in our ways and attitudes – and what you would call ethics – required more years of parental and close family instruction. We long ago concluded that quality not quantity in reproduction was the key. We therefore consciously reinforced our natural tendency to avoid conflict and enhance harmony by altering our social behaviour. We became monogamous, and on occasion refrained from having children, substituting delight in the children of others, and adjusting our responses to ensure that as a community we did not outrun our food supply. This in turn freed us from a constant competitive search for food: we have for many generations been able to take this for granted, so releasing us from that tyranny, as our great size released us from fear of enemies. We became free. Our greatest aim and delight was to devote ourselves to the contemplation and enjoyment of the world, the improvement of our minds and our social excellence. We developed a skein of peaceable and reasoned harmony around the globe.'

During the period when Tisala was telling us all these things, we questioned him and learned much that was previously unknown to men; and at the same time he continued avidly to question us about our world.

Quite early on, he had noticed and remarked on our reliance on fresh water. He thought we were ill adapted, only being able to use the 'land water'. But given our dependence on it, he was puzzled as to why some parts of mankind choose to live in desert places, using what trickles of water there are to hang on to life. He thought that these were places to which rational beings would attach little or no value, and would seek to escape. I assured him that he was wrong and that such places have been the scene of recurrent fighting for possession and repossession, and many deaths, the enthusiasm of the population to live in such places being so great. He concluded that the people there must have created strange myths in their own minds to enhance the land's arid value, and that the slaughter by related people of each other for the possession of barren rocks was otherwise inexplicable.

As we taught him, with the aid of books and maps, pictures, and later films, he gradually learned of our condition and ways; of our advances and triumphs, the rise and fall of our civilisations, and our long lamentable history of killing each other and our fellow animals.

But from the beginning, the killings I knew we would have to address were those of his own kind. He would want to know the history and reasons for mankind's centuries-long slaughter of the whales. And I dreaded telling him.

CHAPTER 16

The Coming of Whaling

The more I learned of the Blue Whales' advanced nature, the more appalling the history of whaling appeared. The whalers had almost totally destroyed their wonderfully wrought society. And some whalers – at the time Tisala came to me in 1960 – were still hunting and killing the few remaining Blues wherever they could be found. By then it was increasingly clear that extinction must be near; and even that it might already be too late to halt. And I knew why Tisala had come: to reason with the enemy, and somehow fight against the enclosing oblivion.

There are good accounts of the destruction of the whales by the cruelty and greed of the whalers, ship owners and their complicit governments, and I will not set out any full history of it here. But an outline is necessary, certainly so far as the Blue Whales are concerned, so that what happened to Tisala and his family can be understood. As I learnt and then recounted the shameful history to him, I started to loathe some of my own species. I knew and could see the misery it caused him, but he always insisted on the full account. He wanted to know the truth.

'It is to understand that I have come to you out of the sea, for we are few and scattered. If we are to survive in the oceans of the Earth I know we have to understand men.'

On a later occasion, when he had learnt more of human ways, he said, 'I see now the enormity of my task. You humans can be clever and noble, but also savage and malign; you can use your consciousness, reason and skills for good, but you can wreak destruction on all the life in the Earth. Men's power has outrun their wisdom.'

The underlying pattern of whaling has been constant: when men turned to whaling, they did so in a fatal combination of ignorance and greed. In the early days, whales were seen as an inexhaustible God-given supply of whale oil and other useful and profitable substances.

The oceans were regarded as alive and seething with leviathans of all kinds, widely regarded as fish. Gradually, when faced with the evidence of emptying seas, but only statistically by the mid twentieth century, did men finally acknowledge that whales have always been – in terms of numbers in each species – members of relatively small populations, scarce and precious. At their greatest extent Blue Whales probably numbered about three hundred thousand: the number of humans in one smallish city. Their development as fellow higher mammals, their rare and wonderful qualities, though sometimes partially glimpsed, remained almost unknown. And whalers remained totally indifferent.

What follows is an outline of what I told Tisala. The beginning of it was really the Right Whale fishery – the first commercial whaling. It grew from whaling learned from the Norsemen. During the dark ages, they came from Norway with their skill in boats and spread the practice of whaling in the western North Atlantic from Norway to Iceland, and south to Biscay in northern Spain. But it really flourished, if that is not too obscene a word, for over three centuries from the sixteenth century.

I recounted to him the technique, which he had heard from his grandfather, of catching the Right Whales by the use of swift rowing boats from the mother sailing ship; how the harpooner standing in the bows hurled cruelly barbed harpoons with ropes attached that anchored in the living flesh; and how, when the whales tried to escape, they merely pulled their tormentors after them until more barbarous harpoons could be plunged in the suffering whales, though they sometimes took several hours to be exhausted and die. How, when the savage little hunters brought the carcases alongside the mother ship they would be cut up and the blubber hauled on board for rendering down into oil by use of the furnaces on board. I found myself almost pleased to recount that occasionally the thrashing agony of the whales smashed the chasing boats, and that whalers drowned, though it was a fearful enough death for those men.

The remorseless hunting pattern was this: whatever species that could profitably be caught was slaughtered. The peaceable baleen whales of several species (the Biscayan Right, Greenland Right, or Bowhead, and later the Southern Right) were first. They were lumped by the whalers under the term 'Right Whales,' for they were slow swimmers and easy to catch and kill. They had thick oily blubber, and when dead conveniently floated, and so could be easily recovered. By the 1500s, the local Biscayan Right Whales had been exterminated. The hunters moved on across the Atlantic. The Greenland Right Whales, found off Newfoundland, were next. The Dutch, with their superior shipping, joined the hunt. Towards the end of the sixteenth century, the English joined in, having captured Newfoundland from the French. By 1600 the Right Whales off Newfoundland had been virtually destroyed. Greed turned the whalers north, and in the icy waters of Greenland, and Spitsbergen they found abundant killing. The scale of whaling rapidly increased, as did the number and size of ships. The Dutch alone, by 1700, had two hundred whaling ships.

Another pattern recurred: when a new area was opened up, and later when new species were hunted, the lust to kill the maximum number of whales, driven by the lure of rich profits, and bounties for the crews, soon resulted in a gross oversupply in the market and prices and profits tumbled. So, many thousands of whales were destroyed needlessly and, even from the whalers' point of view wastefully, in reckless and uncontrolled orgies of killing.

Tisala questioned me closely on these matters. That required me to explore and afterwards explain the economic theory of trade, supply and demand, and price, as developed by the classical economists. This initially gave me much work over a period of a year or two. Tisala's questioning was methodical and persistent. I was never able to fob him off, but had to come to a thorough understanding of economics myself, which gradually I did with growing fascination.

By the early eighteenth century, I told him, the numbers of Right Whales in traditional areas had almost vanished. The whalers responded, not by moderating their hunting to allow recovery, but by opening new areas, pressing further towards the Arctic ice pack in the Davis Straight between Canada and Greenland, and down into the southern hemisphere.

At this stage, I told Tisala, the hunt widened dramatically. Men from the New World, where people had gone to escape from the iniquities of the Old, joined in the hunt. American settlers in the eighteenth century exploited the lucrative whale oil trade for export. The whale populations were to be systematically destroyed, for money. The American whalers hunted the whales out to sea from Nantucket, Martha's Vineyard and New Bedford, quickening the pace of the extermination of the Right Whales. The resulting shortage was an ominous turn of events for a new species of whale: the Americans turned to killing Sperm Whales, and discovered their unique and highly profitable payload of spermaceti oil. As the Right Whales disappeared, the Sperm Whales became the main target, notwithstanding their larger size and speed. So too the size, speed and number of whaling ships grew. By the time of the American War of Independence, New Bedford alone boasted sixty whalers, which rivalled the number out of Nantucket.

Here another pattern emerged, but this time one of the very few to help the whales: war. When men turn to killing men, they kill fewer whales. In the American War of Independence, the British fleet severely corralled and restricted the American whalers for several years; the presence of the French Revolutionary and Napoleonic fleets in turn likewise led to the decline of the English and Dutch whaling fleets; and in the Anglo-American War of 1812 the British fleet destroyed or severely blockaded the American whaling fleet. The whales thereby benefited from a respite in the remorseless killing. But it was only temporary, and after the war of 1812, the scarcity of whale products raised their price. The lure of resultant profits led to the rapid rebuilding and enlargement of the whaling fleets. The scale and areas of destruction grew. The American boats rounded Cape Horn and spread out as far as New Zealand and up the length of South America to the Galapagos Islands searching for Right Whales and Sperm Whales.

By 1820, the English whaling fleet had risen to over two hundred ships, and the Scots had joined in with over thirty ships. In the southern oceans, English convict ships deporting criminals and unfortunates to Australia were fitted out as whalers: convicts on the way out, slaughtered whales and whale oil on the way back via the Cape of Good Hope. The shipmasters and owners were pleased with this excellent and economical use of shipping. In 1857, the Californian gold rush, like war, led to a decline in whaling. The alternative labour market in the gold fields for the greedy and desperate drew away many would-be whaling recruits. But that occurrence came too late to save the Right Whales; though for a brief period it brought some respite to the Sperm Whales.

Another recurring pattern could be seen in each decimated area.

The elimination of a whale population speeds up towards the end. As the Right Whales became increasingly hard to find, the ship owners became increasingly anxious for their profits; and so younger whales, calves and even newborns, which previously had been left as scarcely worthwhile, for they had scant blubber and oil, were targeted and killed. The fate of the remaining population was rapidly sealed, for if you kill the children, you kill the future. In response to scarcity the American whalers spread their search across the huge Pacific to Japanese waters and into the Indian Ocean.

By 1850, the American whaling fleet was over seven hundred sailing ships strong – three times the size of the rest of the world's fleets put together. But that was the peak. The catchable whales – the Right Whales and then the Sperm Whales – in many areas of the world had been decimated. Still men did not learn. The destruction continued even further afield: whales were taken off Australia, and, at the other end of the world, from the Bering Straits and off the Californian coast. But the supply inexorably diminished. By 1860, the whaling fleets all over the world were searching in vain for their quarry. Even the Sperm Whales were becoming hard to find. The several species of Right Whales throughout the world were on the verge of extinction. But there was one more part of the Right whaling history to be told.

The Japanese, I told Tisala, would figure largely in later whaling developments, but in the nineteenth century, they were not advanced; indeed, they were backward. Tisala questioned me on what I meant by 'advanced' and 'backward.' I told him the Japanese had not had our western technology. 'You mean they were less efficient killers?' asked Tisala.

'Yes, at that time,' I said. For many centuries they had been inshore whalers on a small scale, using hand thrown harpoons. I had to concede that they used whalemeat for food while other forms of food were sometimes scarce, though the eyes and mammary glands were regarded as special delicacies, and commanded luxury goods prices. I recounted how in the seventeenth century the Japanese developed whaling by netting across channels between islands. When caught and entangled, the whales were attacked by swordsmen who attempted to stab them to death, and although this sometimes took an hour or two, the whales eventually succumbed. When a whale was sufficiently weakened from loss of blood, a hunter climbed on top and carved a hole through the nasal septum between the nostrils, while the whale was still alive, so that a rope could be run through it to stop the whale sinking when it died. Another technique was to hammer wooden pegs into the wounded whale's blowhole, so suffocating it. This was one of the occasions when Tisala fell silent, and then swam slowly down the inlet and out to sea and did not return for several hours.

Sometimes he himself would add to the history, which had come down to him from his father and grandfather. 'It took us a long time to grow wary of your hunting ships. Some of our gentle cousins, among what you call the Right Whales, never did learn to get away, and were anyway slow and vulnerable. Gradually over two or three generations we Blue Whales became more aware of the advancing catastrophe. This itself took time because we spent most of our lives in either the higher latitudes or the open oceans of the winter seas and were not often in the areas where the Right Whales lived and were hunted.'

He said that although different species of whale have an overlapping affinity in language, some are little developed and are not readily understandable to others. But they learned enough from the Right Whales to know eventually of the carnage. Their reaction was to avoid, even more than normal, the areas where the hunting took place. They learned to recognise all the signs of whaling ships and their accompanying flotillas of oared little 'chasing-boats', and could swiftly take themselves out of their vicinity where they came across them. There were times when they witnessed the terrible bloodletting and cries of their wounded and dying cousins as they were attacked. At night they would pass silently, away from the black-hulled ships sitting on the sea with their hanging square sails lit with the glow of furnaces in their bowels and black acrid smoke drifting across the sea. They could not imagine what the whalers did with their dead kinsfolk, but they knew it was very bad.

'And when you turned to killing Sperm Whales, who are a less peaceable race,' said Tisala, 'the whalers often provoked anger and deliberate retaliation. We heard tales of Sperm Whales turning on their tormentors. My grandfather told me once how he had been near a Sperm Whale hunt when one of the little boats had been smashed, and how he was surprised that their virulent little attackers with their death-filled darts were apparently so ill-adapted to the sea that they could not, when thrown in it, survive more than a few minutes, and then floated downwards through the water, still and harmless looking.

'We heard tales occasionally of the bravest or angriest Sperm Whales attacking the mother ships themselves, but mainly this was seen as futile for ramming ships usually caused dreadful injuries and there were always more whaling ships, coming over the horizon and bearing down with their weapons of death. Escape, where that could be achieved, became the Sperm Whales' only real defence.'

The gruesome history of whaling has some strange turns. For those species of whales still left intact by the middle of the nineteenth century – the swift and powerful rorqual species – the Sei, the Fin, and swiftest and most powerful of all, the Blue – the threat had not yet materialised. The existing form of sailing ships, though much improved since the earlier days, could not catch the rorquals. So the whaling fleets began their steep decline. Moreover, the discovery of oil in the ground in 1859 in America, and the resultant development of oil products, including petrol, paraffin and lubricating oil meant that for the first time there was a cheaper replacement for whale oil which was used for lighting and running machinery. For it was the demand for whale oil, despite the numerous other products from whaling, that was at the heart of the industry.

But, in another recurring pattern, technology came to the aid of the whalers. In the very same year, 1859, the English launched the first steam-driven whaling ship. The future of whaling hung in the balance. New and more deadly forms of whaling were emerging. Steam driven ships were faster and not at the mercy of the winds. They could chase at greater speed and more easily direct their hunting. But at this critical juncture the Americans, with their huge whaling fleet, turned from killing whales, to killing each other. Between 1861 and 1865 more than ten times the number of Americans killed in the Vietnam War were killed by their fellow countrymen, or died as a result of the war. For the whales, war again came to their aid, and the effect was dramatic. The whaling fleets belonged to the northern Union States. Their whaling ships were burned and smashed in large numbers by the Confederate navy, and what remained could not put to sea for fear of destruction. The destroyers were largely destroyed. The small remnants of the Right Whales were spared. Moreover, after the Civil War, the whaling fleets did not recover. The decline in whaling continued, for there were scarcely any catchable whales left, and the hazards and costs of whaling outweighed the profits. It looked for a few years as if the remaining societies of whale species – the rorqual whales – might survive to live and swim in the oceans as they had for millions of years. There was a lull of twenty years before the storm, but it was a deceptive lull.

Less than eighty years after that storm broke, mankind's attitude to the great whales at last began to change. An idea of the nobleness and wonder of these beings began to replace ignorance and indifference, leading gradually to protests against their being hunted to extinction for the mere profit of a few by an unnecessary industry. This change was just beginning to happen by the time Tisala came to me. But eighty years was too long: in that period the rorquals were largely destroyed, and the Blue Whales themselves driven to the edge of extinction.

CHAPTER 17

Siana

'So,' said Tisala one day, 'why are you delaying?' For two or three weeks I had been making excuses, saying I needed to re-read parts of the history to get it in order in my mind.

'I am afraid.'

'You have no need. I know it is the history of our destruction.'

'I am afraid when you hear how and why that destruction took place, you will be so repulsed you will abandon us and never come back again.'

'Do not impute to me your own doubtful nature. I have come to learn.'

So over three days I told him the dreadful history, stopping only for food and sleep when we needed it. During our meals Ellie sometimes sat with me on the rocks at the water's edge. Her presence and the quiet beauty of that inlet from the sea comforted me. I remember days of high spring tides. The inlet was flat calm, but full, as if the water too was creeping in to listen.

We proceeded by ellipses and diversions, for Tisala always questioned me closely and demanded explanations when I mentioned unfamiliar things. To try and rationalise the shameful annals of modern whaling I remember saying that, looked at from a human point of view, the destruction of the Blue Whales was a small item in the history of industrialisation; and afterwards I burned with guilt, though Tisala never condemned me.

'Tell me about industrialisation,' he said. It was another of his simple requests, which eventually gave me months of work. Initially, I gave him a sketch of that extraordinary outburst of inventive ingenuity, the industrial revolution. I told him about the capture of kinetic power, eighteenth century steam engines pumping out mines, and the transfer of the steam engine into the hulls of ships to drive them through the seas.

'Yes, the screw-ships with their ceaseless churning and thumping engines. My grandfather said to start with they were merely an occasional irritant. But their numbers grew year by year and their noise increasingly filled the oceans, disrupting our ancient long distance call signals. The harmonious unity of our ocean sound world began to be broken and distorted.'

I remembered that sound travels much quicker and more efficiently in water and I imagined the disruptive power of thousands of ships.

'For sheer noise, the North Atlantic was worst,' said Tisala. 'For a good number of years, my grandfather said the traffic in most of the seas was tolerable. And because our groups were numerous and usually communicating over short distances – perhaps two or three hundred miles – we could still easily converse. Besides, in our Arctic and Antarctic feeding grounds there was scarcely any shipping. But we adjusted the routes to our love-seas to avoid shipping; though for the most part our warm water haunts were distant from the main shipping lanes.'

I asked him about his description of their breeding areas as love-seas, for nobody knew where the Blue Whales went. He told me that to humans they would be areas of the sea indistinguishable from any others, but to the whales they were like inverted tropical islands. The whales floated, caressed, made love and passed their days in peace above familiar seamounts and undulations on the sea floor, various groups having favourite places to which they returned.

'But eventually the screw-driven ships came hunting us,' said Tisala. 'And they came with a new form of death.'

'Yes,' I said, 'the Norwegians invented the harpoon gun. And, as you know, within ten years, everything changed.'

I told him what happened. Just at the time when steam-driven ships were first being built for whaling, a Norwegian called Svend Foyn, after several attempts, succeeded in designing three revolutionary weapons. The curse of technological advance was about to descend on the rorquals.

All through the nineteenth century, attempts had been made to produce a whaling gun. I assured Tisala that this particular branch of industrial ingenuity was not limited to whale guns. Men were busy inventing, improving and perfecting a wide range of weaponry, mainly for use against other men. By the end of that century, I told him, they were spectacularly successful.

Tisala said, 'You have a strange measure of success.'

I could sense that he was about to plunge off in a whole new area of enquiry, so I said, 'Anyway, the result of Foyn's invention was the bow-mounted harpoon cannon – 1863.'

I recounted how initially the new weapon was mounted on the old sailing ships, with their limited manoeuvrability. But a decade later, the harpoon guns were being mounted on steam whalers. The cannons were mounted by means of heavy steel bolts onto the specially constructed bows of the new whaling ships.

Foyn's second invention was the cannon's harpoon; not only a heavy steel spear, but one with an exploding head. I explained – though Tisala knew its outline only too well – that the shaft was of solid steel, about four feet long, with a heavy hemp line fixed to the back end. A barbed steel head about eighteen inches long was attached to the front of the shaft and on to that was screwed a sharp-ended shrapnel explosive. The whole thing was like a solid steel arrow, but one that weighed a hundred and sixty pounds. It took two or three men to load the cannon; and, unlike an arrow the barbed head had four heavy hinged flanges that opened on impact, lodging the whole weapon firmly in the whale's body, so that it could not be pulled out or lost. As a result, when a harpooned whale tried to escape, it would have to pull the whaling ship after it: no longer an open boat as in the old whaling days, but a hundred-ton steel ship, which could play the whale like a giant fishing rod. The harpoon, despite its weight, did not usually kill. That was left to the explosive head – a massive shrapnel grenade.

The exploding head at first gave Foyn much difficulty. I recounted how he enlisted the help of a Protestant pastor, a friend of his, who was good at fireworks. The priest perfected the bomb. Tisala queried why a pastor, a man of God, should have done this. I told him that Foyn too was a devout Protestant Christian. Both believed that God had put the whales in the sea precisely so that men like Svend Foyn should be able to fish them out and increase their wealth. The Bible taught them that all creation is at man's disposal. That is how God looks after his children. Foyn wanted profit, and was justified in his method of getting it by the teaching of his religion. He piously marked his logbook with suitable biblical quotations. Once, during an early experimental firing of the harpoon at sea, the line from the harpoon got wrapped around his ankle, and he was whipped overboard. He was almost miraculously saved, and at once put it down to the tender mercy of God who wanted him to prosper. His wealth, and his religious mindset, gave him the means to persevere.

Tisala asked me many questions about religion and ethics. I could see he was considering the conflict that arises when faith and morality collide. 'We must return to these issues,' he said, 'but go on.'

I told him the explosive bomb was supposed to go off deep inside the whale's body, although one of the drawbacks was that sometimes the firing was not very accurate and two, three or more harpoons were needed, for instance if one penetrated in an awkward place, or skidded off the whale's body, merely gouging a wound a few feet long as it went; or struck with an impact sufficient only to set off the shrapnel explosive externally. Such common occurrences caused hideous wounds, but failed to secure the whale, which, though it would probably die anyway, would be lost to the whalers. The result of these drawbacks was that the considerable effort and expense of harpooning was wasted. Sometimes half a dozen or more exploding harpoons were needed to finish off a whale. This slowed down the rate of killing and was not very efficient. But the missile was effective, despite the hemp rope, at up to fifty yards. It was a truly murderous weapon, though I had to recount that Foyn was praised by his fellow Norwegians for his 'most wonderful invention'. Tisala exhaled but said nothing.

I went on. The gun and the exploding harpoon would themselves have been of limited use without Foyn's third innovation, the hollow steel inflation lance. This was a sharp lance attached to an air-pipe. The lance was driven into the body cavity of the whale immediately it was dead and compressed air pumped in so that the whale floated. Until this development the Blue Whale had not been hunted because their speed and strength made them difficult to catch – impossible in the days of the sailing ships – but also because they sank when dead. Hunting them had previously been pointless. At a stroke this vital safeguard was removed. And their former advantages of strength and speed were in turn being eroded by the increased speed and size of the steam whalers. For the first time they could be hunted and recovered. And their huge size now became a deadly liability: they became the greatest prize.

So the scene was set for the Norwegians to dominate whaling around the world for the next seventy years. But Foyn, and then the Norwegian whaling industry, first deployed these weapons in their home waters of the North Atlantic. Even in Foyn's first year of operation, 1868, thirty rorquals, mainly Fin Whales – the nearest relatives to the Blues – were killed in Norwegian water.

Within twenty years the local Fin Whales off the Norwegian coast were becoming scarce. At that point, Foyn's activities nearly failed. The Norwegian fishermen believed the Fin Whales chased the herring and cod into the fjords where the fishermen could catch them. With the decline in the local whales, the fishermen said the fish no longer came into the fjords. The fishing industry suffered, and that powerful interest group persuaded their government to ban whaling off the coast. The old pattern repeated itself: the whalers turned to exploiting new areas. That was the beginning of the hunt for the Blue Whales. By the end of the 1890s the Norwegian whaling had spread to the Shetland, Orkney and Faeroe Islands, and the Hebrides. And for the first time, Blue Whales too were hunted and killed.

'It began before that for us,' said Tisala. 'My immediate family lived at that time in the North Atlantic. My grandfather, Saba, who was head of my family, had been concerned about the noise and disruption from shipping traffic, on our spring and autumn migration routes. Then, in the years just before my father was born, the hunting began. The first alarms for us as a family were killings off the Wrinkled Coast by the new and newly armed steam whalers. Long afterwards my grandfather told me they knew then that our ancient, beautiful and peaceful world was threatened. But we had no understanding of what was to follow. We were swift and strong and the whaling ships were few in number.'

From various things Tisala said and by questioning him I established that he was talking of the north Norwegian coast in the 1880s and 1890s. I worked out that Tisala's father, Tarba, had been born in about 1890.

Tisala continued his account. 'All along that coast, my grandfather told me, while we were migrating north to the feeding grounds, and in the autumn coming south, the incidences and reports of hunting grew. In those days, the first to suffer were our Humpback cousins, who are slower than us and tended to travel in larger groups and nearer the coast. Next, further from the coast, swam the Fin Whales. We travelled further out, over the edge of the deep. But this did not save us. We heard first the grief of groups of Fin Whales. We were appalled for them, who are big and swift like ourselves. But soon enough we heard the distress calls of Blue Whales. My grandfather said he could always remember those first cries and how his heart grew cold, for he knew death had reached even us, and he felt the dull pain of foreboding. After that, on our journeys north and south, he told me we heard and came to dread the cries that told of more deaths, and their aftermath of mourning. When the groups of families met after our migrations, each time a few more members were missing. We heard tales of terrible deaths. Occasionally a wounded whale struggled exhausted to the feeding grounds. The senior females of the families gathered round, mothering the victim. The inquisitive young were chased away and forbidden to eat krill – no one did – in the area of an injured whale, to give it more chance.

'Each season the losses grew worse. My father was born in one of those seasons, and after that my grandfather avoided the Wrinkled Coast, and our journeys skirted the east coast of the Fire Island – what you call Iceland – and the west side of the Northern Spine. In the far north we knew we were still safe. The killing ships did not come there, and our summer feeding seas were left as in the old days.

'But everything changed the year my grandmother was killed. She was called Siana, which means sky-whale, for she was of unusually light blue colouring with extensive mottling. She was killed twenty years before I was born.'

Later I worked out from various things Tisala had told me that Siana was probably killed in 1901 or 1902 when his father was about ten years old.

'I have always been sad that I never knew her,' continued Tisala. 'My grandfather, Saba used to tell me about her. At forty-five, she was still capable of bearing children, though she and my grandfather had last had a child five years before, when my father's last sister was born. In those days, the older whales who had offspring often decided to rest from child making. For the young too should have offspring and they believed that the population of families should stay stable, so as not to outrun the balance of life in the oceans. Besides, having a Blue

Whale child is a great undertaking and there are other roles that older whales should fulfil.'

Tisala told us what happened that summer. The family group was swimming north, on the edge of the deep water off the Icelandic shelf. They heard a ship's engine, but initially were not concerned, for until then, those waters had been safe. But then they realised the ship, instead of going across and fading away behind them, or diverging at an angle away from them, as usually happened, was coming up behind them and getting closer. They started to swim faster and veered off to the west. The ship veered with them. Within a minute or two, and before they knew what was happening, the ship was amongst them and nearest Siana. Suddenly my grandfather heard Siana give a choking squeal as she leapt ahead and slowed and he saw the heavy end of a fearsome harpoon protruding out of her head near the front of her jaws, its line trailing up to the surface. As he looked he felt and heard an underwater explosion and saw the front of her head blown open and for an instant part of her upper jaw at right angles to her body. Then there was blood welling everywhere. He saw her head start to dip and he rushed to put himself beneath her and push her up. But he already knew: how could she swim with such injuries, how breathe, how live?

The light-filled sea became opaque with dark clouds of blood. They enveloped him and he could no longer see. But he could feel her soft underbelly on his back, and how when she tried to breathe, instead of a great steady intake, all she took were stuttering, shuddering little gasps, interspersed with tiny screams of exhalation. His mind was numb with horror and helplessness. They hung there, she in her gasping agony, he transfixed. Then he became aware of the ship's engine, coming very close and he thought that death was coming to him. He waited for the blow, but did not move. He heard a thump above him and Siana jerked and let out a great groan. There was a small space of almost silence, almost calm. Then there was a huge eruption deep in Siana's body. He felt splinters of pain in his own back. She shuddered along her whole length and juddered and shook and screamed for the minutes it took her to die. He felt the life going from her, his beloved Siana, and found himself begging her to die. Then she released her remaining air and was still. He shook with horror, but also with relief that her ordeal was finished.

His sense of preservation and leadership gradually returned and he rolled away and looked above the murky water. He saw the killing ship close by and a man in the upper part shouting at two men at the front, and gesticulating towards him. The two were busy lifting one of the heavy death spears into its thrower. He rolled, and dived into the friendly deep. When he surfaced again the ship was a small thing a long way off. He thought of Siana, and wanted to go back to her, but he knew that she was dead and he could do nothing. And then the pity of it swelled in his mind and he shook with loss, not for himself, but in comprehension of what had happened, and for Siana. They had swum together for nearly forty years and had six children.

A day later, the family group reassembled further north. They were all badly shaken, and when they first met, swam milling together, rubbing and nursing each other for comfort.

'My grandfather was marked for life,' said Tisala. 'Though he had many years left and resolutely led our family, he never wholly recovered his previous joy of life.' Tisala was silent when he had finished. I glanced at Ellie. She was very pale. I started to say, 'Do you want to...' but she shook her head vehemently.

'Later that same summer,' Tisala continued, 'we came to know that Siana's death had been relatively quick. As the family was heading south in early autumn, my father's cousin, a young male, a few years older than himself, on the edge of adulthood, who was swimming as an outrider, about half a mile away from the main group, was chased and harpooned. The harpoon missed his heart and lungs and lodged towards his tail, the explosion tearing a terrible wound in him. He let out a great bellow of surprise and pain, which the whole group heard. My father, who was close friends with this cousin, turned towards him. My grandfather rushed at him, cut him off, and forbade him to leave the group. He knew he must lead the group away from the catcher boat. The cousin pulled that steam whaler for nearly a mile, for twenty minutes, trying desperately to get away, the extended flanges of the harpoon taking the weight, until it finally ripped out of his flesh and he was free. For some reason the ship did not chase him. He tried to swim away from his tormentors, leaving an ever-widening stream of blood behind him, and in agony. Soon it became clear that the whaler had not given chase, and it eventually disappeared to the east. The cousin instinctively sought the family group, sending out distress signals. My grandfather and his brother – my cousin's father – swam urgently towards him in great plunging dives, leaving the rest of the group with strict instructions to swim south. My father was to stand off and guard the group.

'When the two reached him he was in a pitiful state, his swimming reduced almost to a wallow. He was in a state of terror both as to what had happened and what would now happen. The loss of blood continued. My grandfather and his brother swam each side of him and buoyed him up so that he could partially rest, for initially in his terror he would not stop trying to swim away. The flow of blood as the hours went by began to lessen, but it was clear he was becoming weaker and they knew he was dying. And he cried for the life he should have had, but knew he was losing. They stayed with him propping him up a day and a night through his long agony. At one point, at dawn, there was an alarm, for a ship was heard some way off. The little party lay as one, low in the water, and eventually the noise of the propellers grew fainter. The dying whale saw the sun come up, but it was for the last time, and by mid morning he was very weak and slipped mercifully into unconsciousness. The two continued to hold him. About half an hour later he gave a long exhalation, and gave up his life. They were loath to let him go but snuggled him for a while. Then they slipped away from him so he could start the long dive.'

When I looked at Ellie again, there were silent tears running down her face. I put an arm round her. She said through her tears, 'I want to hug Tisala.'

'That may be difficult,' said Tisala, with a shaft of humour lightening the moment, and to comfort her. Ellie sniffed and managed a weak smile.

We talked some more, and I said inadequate things about the bravery of whales. Tisala said that after that time, fear lived with them in the seas. The whales learned that few escaped the chasing whale boats and their death-bringing harpoons. Across the North Atlantic community, the stories were similar. And although no more members of Tisala's family were killed in the two years that followed, the stories of death among other whale families multiplied each summer.

When I checked the history of the North Atlantic whaling, it was clear that steam whalers from Norway armed with the new explosive harpoon began the modern revolution in whaling there. Over the twenty years from 1880, Blue, Fin, Sei and Humpback whales were taken by these Norwegian based whalers, spreading out across the whole of the North Atlantic, the number of kills rising to a thousand whales a year.

'Yes,' confirmed Tisala, 'But that was not all. In the summer when my father was about twelve years old, a big new ship appeared off the ice pack of the Happy Isles – our name for what you call Spitsbergen and the Svalbards. It soon became apparent that it was a mother ship to the hunter-chasers. The hunting had extended to our feeding grounds. We knew at once that the big ship, to which the bodies of our friends and relatives were dragged tail-first by the hunting ships, was new and bad. Whatever they did with our bodies could now be done at sea, and quickly freed the catchers to kill again. The following year was a black one for my family – a cousin and an aunt were both killed. My uncle, who followed them to the mother ship, saw them hauled up, dead and lifeless, against the side of the big ship before they disappeared. That summer, my grandfather decided to leave our home waters and take our family to the Southern Ocean.'

I worked out that this was in 1903. I felt sick in the pit of my stomach. I knew what was coming. For in the following year, the Norwegians sent the first properly equipped whaling expedition to Antarctica.

CHAPTER 18

The Antarctic Opened – 1904-1914

The history was this. A decade earlier in 1893, Foyn had sent a whaling ship to the Southern Ocean to hunt for any remaining Right Whales, and Sperm Whales. This expedition revealed, for the first time, the large numbers of Blue and Fin Whales in the southernmost regions. There had, of course, been previous reports of rorquals in the Southern Ocean, but in the days of the Right Whale hunts, the rorquals, being uncatchable, were of little interest. Besides, the Humpbacks had been hunted further north, not in the highest latitude round Antarctica itself, but on the migratory routes to South Africa, Australia and New Zealand. The far south was largely unknown and the very existence of the Antarctic continent had at that time only been known for fifty years. Though Captain Cook thought he saw land through terrible weather, he probably saw one of the groups of outlying islands. Not until 1822 did Captain Weddell discover the South Orkneys. And the existence of the icebound Antarctic continent itself was not established until 1839. Thus the ancient inviolate world of the Blue Whale lost its precious isolation from man.

After Foyn's 1893 expedition it took only ten years for the Norwegians to adjust and improve their whaling armoury specifically to target rorquals. In 1904 the first real expedition, though mainly to catch Humpbacks, was sent. A whaling station was built on South Georgia, which formed a perfect land base with its ice-free waters. The full horror of modern whaling was transferred to the southern hemisphere.

Tisala remembered his father, Tarba, who was then coming into adulthood, telling him of their arrival. It was the first time Tarba had been to the Southern Ocean. They relived the story of Tisana on the journey south, but they swam confidently through the warm tropics, knowing what lay beyond. When they arrived, he was overwhelmed by the wonder of the place. There were many more Blues than he had ever seen before. Some of the older whales knew each other, or were related. In the weeks that followed, the group from the North Atlantic was welcomed with excitement and much calling and counter-calling of greetings, meetings and reunions, sometimes after a gap of years. But almost best of all, for a whale who had not seen it before, was the majesty of the setting.

The Blue Whales, more than any other species, went further south, to the edge of the icepack, and in places, to the vast white continent itself. Here great ice cliffs, in places hundreds of feet high, marked the end of mighty glaciers that had flowed imperceptibly for thousands of years from the interior of the continent to crash eventually into the summer sea. On calm sunny days against the blue sky, the towering ice was blindingly white, with its blue shadows and the green blue of the sea lending fantastic shades of turquoise and aquamarine to the bases of the cliffs, icebergs and floes. The sea itself, welling up nitrate-rich from the continental basins, was in summer as the ice retreated a marine paradise of minute plant life – of algae in their billions – turning the water green. Then the animal plankton burst into life, feeding on the algae, and in turn the streaming concentrations of krill stained the ocean meadows red for miles. All were swept by the circumpolar currents round the continent, spreading out from it like the arms of a spiral galaxy. Teeming life was everywhere. Even the whales themselves, during the course of the summer, acquired a yellow sheen from diatoms that coated their undersides – hence the Blue Whales' nickname of 'Sulphur Bottomed Whale'.

The water was alive with the sound of whale talk – the Blues themselves, and some miles further out the Fin Whales and the Humpbacks. For the young Tarba everything was exciting and exhilarating, but awe-inspiring, and he kept close to his family. He saw for the first time upright flightless birds, standing on the ice. Above was the more familiar sight and sound of countless seabirds wheeling in the bright blue air. For a few brief seasons Tarba knew the world of the Blue Whales as it had been for thousands of years.

But slowly the whales became aware, even in the vastness of the Southern Oceans, that the deadly hunting ships had arrived, though initially the target was the slower Humpbacks.

I looked up the figures: 1910 to 1912 was the turning point – the Humpback catch reached new peaks, but by this time the species, which was never numerous in Antarctica, had been decimated, and their numbers rapidly declined. The whalers meanwhile had already turned their attention and tuned their equipment to the Blues. I told Tisala it was hardly surprising: they had only to kill two Blues to obtain the same quantity of whale oil as was produced from five Humpbacks. So it began again – a few hundred Blues killed in 1910 rising steadily by a thousand or more each Antarctic summer season to five thousand in 1914.

The thickest concentration of krill, and therefore whales, at the summer feeding was at the exit of the Weddell Sea where the great hooked arm of the Antarctic volcanic peninsula curves eastwards and the most productive cold current in the world laden with all forms of planktonic life flows out to circle the continent, passing first the South Orkney and South Sandwich Islands. Those two groups of islands lie so far south that in winter they are frozen into the pack ice surrounding the continent, but in the summer the ice breaks up and the seas amid the floes release the astonishing abundance of life that Tisala had described. Between these two groups of islands, further to the north, beyond the grip of the ice at all times of year, lies South Georgia.

Here the Norwegians set up their Southern Ocean whaling operations, at a place they called Grytviken. The initial whaling company involved was run by a whaling captain and entrepreneur called Larsen. To this place his whalers towed the slaughtered Blue Whales, more and more each year, dragged behind the whalers with ropes attached round their fluked tails. First they were towed in singularly or in pairs, but by 1912 the whole operation was becoming so efficient that whalers could be seen coming into harbour towing as many as nine Blue Whales. Winched up the slipways of the shore factories the huge whales were cut up and the blubber rendered down for oil. The whalers did not bother at this period with the meat or bones, but tipped the carcasses into the margins of the bay, which became full of rotting bodies. Skeletons littered the shoreline and in a few years huge stacks of bones built up along it.

The profits were equally enormous. It was rumoured that in its first year, Larsen's company paid dividends of forty percent of capital invested, and in years after that the dividend exceeded one hundred percent. Norwegians were becoming wealthy on the blood of whales.

By 1912, with the Antarctic whaling rapidly predominating, there were sixty Norwegian companies whaling all over the world. Virtually the entire worldwide industry was in their hands.

At Grytviken, the wealth created was reflected in Larsen's establishment. He had planted palm trees and exotic flowering plants, as if to demonstrate his success in life and to defy the natural world. He had a large conservatory attached to the house, inside which were more luxuriant plants, and the house was complete with caged singing canaries and a piano. Being a patriotic man, he hung a large portrait of King Haakon of Norway. On occasions he provided eight course dinners, served by a butler and finished off with cigars. Appropriately for a good Christian, he built a little Lutheran church, where no doubt he and his men could give thanks to God for His bounty; and doubtless too thought of the monetary rewards that would follow.

Larsen had a fleet of whaling ships producing huge quantities of whale oil which was shipped back to his base in Argentina, for transport onwards to Europe and America. Within a few years there were whaling stations in half a dozen of the bays on South Georgia. There seems to have been no thought at all for what they were doing to the natural world. Whaling was to be indulged in to the maximum possible degree of killing without any moral scruple to hold it back.

Much later on, Tisala drew a parallel between Grytviken and Auschwitz. He said of course that the motivation was different, in that at Grytviken, they did not set out to exterminate the Blue Whales, but were merely criminally indifferent; and though the driving force in one case was greed and the accumulation of wealth, and in the other fear and hatred, he said the common element was the exercise of untrammelled power without any effective restraints of morals or ethics. He cited the Old Testament doctrine, readily adopted by the Christians, that God had made all creatures for the use and service of man. He thought it ironic that the justification of genocidal slaughter of whales should have such Jewish roots.

'It makes you question some of the basics of religion,' I said, keen to show I understood. But Tisala was deep in his own thought and did not answer.

At the time, I went on with history. By the 1914 season, I told him, the Norwegians were killing over five thousand Blue Whales each season in Antarctica.

'Those are your figures,' said Tisala, 'but we knew it as family and friends who were hunted and slaughtered. In those years three more members of our family were killed, and many more amongst other groups known to us. Hardly a single family escaped deaths among them. One of the three was my father's eldest sister. She was much loved by three generations for her wisdom and serenity. She had a child less than a year old – only a few months finished weaning. She was hunted down trying to lead a group of three youngsters, including her own young child, away from danger. When the whaling ship outran the exhausted youngsters, she shielded them with her body. So they escaped and she died. The young child cried out for her for a month.' Tisala sighed as he remembered the story.

'My father told me that soon after,' Tisala resumed, 'I think about a year later, the hunting suddenly and eerily ceased. We waited hardly daring to hope. But the seas remained clear. We did not at first understand.'

'War again', I said. 'The Emperor of Germany came to your rescue.'

'Without intending to?' asked Tisala perceptively.

'Yes.'

'He was not a good man?'

'He was one of a small group of men largely instrumental in starting a war that killed twenty-five million people.' I told Tisala about the First World War and he listened in disbelief, questioning me at length about my explanation of it. I told him how by then warfare had come to mean, in addition to the carnage of several million soldiers being killed, millions of civilians dying from dislocation, disease and starvation, such was the power of patriotic war.

Tisala was silent for a minute, then he said: 'I have much to learn. You make me very sad that respite for us was brought about by such an event, and by so much brutal death and misery. I remember my father telling me something of this war from occasional sightings of exploding and sinking ships and a scattering of human bodies in the surrounding sea, but nothing on the scale of death you have described. The land must be a dreadful place.'

I explained why the whaling had ceased. Norway was neutral in that war. But as the sea was a dangerous place to be, and the ship owners valued their vessels and their investments, whaling was virtually suspended for four years. That interminable time in Europe was four short seasons for Norwegians, and the whales.

But after the War, there were massive shortages, and con-sequently price rises, including in whale products. The whaling fleets had been kept safe in harbour. Profits beckoned, and they soon commenced action again. But now they were increasingly joined by whaling ships from other nations, led, I had to admit, by the British. The slaughter recommenced.

CHAPTER 19

Saba

After the First World War, I told Tisala, the price of whale oil rose with the demands of peace. Whales became yet more valuable, and even more profitable to hunt and kill. Further ominous advances in technology resulted in the widespread use of converted merchantmen as factory ships. Whales no longer had to be caught within range of South Georgia and dragged back by the tail to a base there, but could be processed at sea or in the shelter of other islands and bays around Antarctica. And the factory ships in the summer months went closer and closer to the permanent ice, and the edge of the continent itself. Then, from 1925, the first vast 20,000-ton purpose-built factory ships appeared. They boasted huge maw-like slipways running up from the bows or the stern of the ship, with twin funnels, and engines set either side of the slipway, so that the carcasses of dead whales could be winched into the ship, swallowed up and processed – stripped, dismembered, rendered down and disposed of. And all with much greater speed and capacity than previously. In the same period, bigger and faster catcher ships were being built. Industrial whaling was about to make a leap in scale undreamed of in the whole history of whaling. The result was catastrophic for the Blue Whales.

By 1922, after the wartime lull, the pre-war seasonal figure of 5,000 Blue Whales killed was again reached, but this time it did not stop. By 1927-28 the slaughter had reached the huge figure of 10,000 Blue Whales per season.

'But even that appalling number became much worse.' said Tisala intervening. 'There came a time when 10,000 deaths among us in a season was greeted with relief. We called those years, "The Great Death".' He told Ellie and me the story. 'I was born at the start of them. It was a terrible time, and my childhood was spent with death all around me. In those years my family – all our families – were decimated. Groups of us, spread out over large areas of the Southern

Ocean, would be found, sometimes by two or three catcher ships, slicing into the middle of us, picking their victims and firing their deadly harpoons. We tried to escape the approaching thump and churning sounds. I remember my mother used to put herself between me and any ship, and our group learned to scatter to confuse the hunters. But always we heard the terrible cries when someone was hit, and the ghastly wait – it seemed time was suspended, but it was only a few seconds – before the dull crump of explosion, and we knew that one of our number was destroyed or maimed. Often there would be a second or third explosion signifying a dreadful, drawn out death. Sometimes we heard six or more explosions from the same quarter, and we shuddered and cried out at the hideousness of it.

'And after the chase, the explosions and screams, eventually the catcher ships' engines would fade and we would send out frantic signals of enquiry, straining for the answering messages. Sometimes there was relief when a familiar and loved voice was heard in reply, but there was too often fear and rising distress when it was recognised that this voice or that voice – a parent, a child, brother, sister, uncle, aunt or cousin – was missing and silent, and would never be heard again. Each time this happened, as we re-gathered again, we slowly came to know that our families and the great community itself were being torn apart. The structure of thousands of years was being destroyed. The losses were heaviest among the older generations – they were the biggest and therefore, we came to recognise, the most prized – and the old were slower and less ready or able to abandon the old ways. They had lived all their lives steadily and calmly, without enemies, and some of them scorned to run or flee or even to fear. Older generations were disappearing before their time, and among the young there were increasing gaps. Suddenly they were no more, and we began to realise that many of the future generations would never be.

'It seemed uncanny how they could find us, for we would dive and be safe deep in the sea for twenty minutes or longer, but when we resurfaced, too often they would find us and the chase would continue again – '

'It was the spouts – the spouts gave you away,' I said, envisaging the scene miserably. 'They watched out for your spouts.'

'Yes, we learned that. But we have to breathe, and that giveaway we could not change, except that we also learned, when the catcher ships' engines were first heard, to slow our swimming and breathe shallowly; but we were slow to adopt this attempt to hide, for it takes courage to do that, knowing you are thereby allowing the hunters to come closer. And once we were found and chased, we had to swim and dive full out; and for that we had to spout when we surfaced.

'My grandfather, the head of our family, was one of the leaders of our wider community. "Let's ask Saba" was often heard. But over these years he became increasingly anguished, though my father said he rarely showed it. He had a strong sense of duty. He had lived his life in the days when the Blue Whale society was the glory of the oceans. He found himself, as he got older, presiding over a worsening horror, with responsibility for trying to save generations of the family. Our ever-increasing losses and the failure to prevent them weighed heavily on him. It is one of the penalties of a large mind: to be able to remember too many things with too much clarity. But it is also one of the blessings. He told my father that he thought more and more of Siana, his lost love of thirty years before. He could revisit in his mind the sky blue days of summer in the far Arctic with Siana, her lovely body tisurfing through the ice-strewn sea in unison with his; or accompanying her as she carried another child to the warm seas to be born, sliding together for the pleasure of touching each other.

'But the family noticed that his age was telling and he was getting slower. He had instructed my father in leading the family, and impressed on him his duty to survive as long as possible. In those years, any might be called on to be the family leaders, and all sought to learn how to survive the deadly hunting.'

'He said to me, "Tisala, watch your father and learn, for you too will have to lead, and perhaps sooner than you should."

'I was five at the time, which in our terms is more advanced than humans; it was my boyhood. Saba was particularly fond of me, perhaps because I carried some of my grandmother's lighter blue markings, or perhaps because he saw something of his character in me even at that young age. But I was old enough to be independent of my mother which was as well, for she was killed soon after. My poor little sister was only two and was left bereft, though we afterwards developed the closeness of orphans.'

Tisala followed this with one of his silences, which he sometimes did when considering his thoughts. Then he continued, 'In the worst season of the Great Death, the slaughter was a catastrophe. In my family alone we lost twenty members – my grandfather's two remaining sisters and only surviving brother – nearly all of our wise leaders – eight of the next generation, and a similar number of younger members. Of my grandfather's generation, only he was left. The chill of fear was constantly among us. Those twenty represented a quarter of all our remaining family – all killed and vanished in a six-month season. It became obvious, even to us young ones, that we might be slaughtered to extinction. And all across the Southern Ocean the story was the same.

'But the next year a miracle happened. Suddenly most of the whaling ships were gone. Some few remained, and there were too many deaths, but only a fraction of those of the preceding year. My father said he was glad my grandfather lived to see that year, for it gave him hope, which had fast been disappearing, that our world might not be totally destroyed.

'In the following year the family decided to move further round the great ice continent to a new part of the ocean. Although the krill there were somewhat less plentiful, we knew few whaling ships had penetrated that region. For a period near the beginning of the summer season we had peace. But then we heard again the dreaded propellers of an approaching whale-catcher. We lay low and breathed quietly, but it was soon clear that somehow the hunters were heading straight for us, and Saba gave the signal to scatter. We veered and dived. I stayed close to my mother. Saba was with us. My father led the other members of the family away from us, as it was now our rule that the family leaders must divide so one at least might escape. In our group also were my sister and two of my cousins. Suddenly, we heard another ship in front of us, and from the rapidly closing gap realised we were heading for each other. In alarm, it flashed through my mind that we were trapped and we might all die. I was very frightened and I could hear the little sounds of panic from my young cousins. My grandfather signalled in a steady voice that we were all to make a big dive, and keep straight on. He was directing us to go under the oncoming hunting ship. As I came up for my diving breath, I became aware that he himself was turning – I saw him in front of me to the right, turning in a great arc and lifting himself high out of the water as he went. He was immense and magnificent. For a moment I couldn't understand why he had so obviously shown himself, and then I knew. He had turned and headed back, across the first whaling ship. In our deep dive we passed under the catcher ship in front of us. Both whalers must have seen him at about the same time, for we heard the change in engine tone as both put on speed and altered course towards him. They raced each other for him. Then I heard their engines change and slow – we knew he must have dived – and I hoped he would dive deep and long. But in only two or three minutes we heard the engines roar again. Twice more this happened, the sounds becoming further away. Then I heard a dull explosion and cried out, for we all knew what it meant. But some minutes later there was a second explosion further away, and then after what seemed a long time later, and fainter, a third. We heard no more.

'We young ones cried for him for days. But I kept running my mind back over the events, and questioning my mother. She said that he was very brave, and loving, and old, and he knew he was near the end of his life. Later, she told me what my father had seen. Having shepherded his group beyond the danger area, my father turned back, on an instinct to help his own father. He saw Saba with the taut, thick rope protruding from him, pulling the catcher ship away from us with all his strength, blood pouring from his flank, mutilated by the first harpoon. The second catcher ship was nearby and he could see men watching. When the second harpoon struck Saba, the men on the second catcher cheered and waved. Yet still he pulled the ship through the water, away from his family, wallowing in his own blood. They thought he would die, so it seemed they did not bother for a while to load the third harpoon. But when he did not die, they began to shout and drew the ship right up to him. And when the third harpoon exploded my father turned away for he knew that was the end. He knew too that the second catcher would now leave the spectacle and search for another kill, and that he must survive and lead the family.'

When Tisala finished this part of his story, Ellie and I were silent. Then Ellie burst out, 'The Norwegians are disgusting. They're not human. They're animals.' She saw me looking down – 'Well, aren't they?' she said angrily.

I said: 'Ellie, at the time we're talking about, though it is true that by far the biggest part of the whaling fleet was still Norwegian, we

– the British – were increasingly involved. And other nations were joining the carnage.'

'Animals?' said Tisala, 'The problem is they are humans – a species, it seems, by virtue of their brains, more vicious and malign than any other on the planet. Though you are right to differentiate between your nations, to us it was always the animal called man who relentlessly pursues our destruction by all means.'

'It is stupid men with weapons, and arrogance, and greed,' said Ellie, distressed. 'Always stupid, stupid men. Fighting and killing.' Then remembering again she said, 'How could they kill Saba like... he was eighty years old... with those... horrible.' There were tears in her eyes. 'I don't want to hear any more.' She got up and walked off.

I turned back to Tisala. 'The figures are quite appalling – '

'David, David, the figures can wait – go and comfort her,' said Tisala. 'I am going out into the sea.'

I felt a momentary prick of anger with Ellie for the disruption, and for causing Tisala to rebuke me, but I went after her. When I looked back over my shoulder I saw Tisala swimming slowly and majestically down the inlet. Then I realised that my anger was really at being found wanting, being found less caring than Ellie and Tisala.

I came on Ellie sitting on a rock looking out to sea, and sat beside her. She was still crying quietly.

'Look – '

'Don't talk to me... it's... it's just too cruel. I hate it. Always the same – men – like those half-witted Russians and Americans in Cuba last year.' Her tears started to well again. 'They were going to let loose hundreds of nuclear bombs at each other. Millions of people were going to die, we were all going to die, all the children – '

'But they avoided – '

'This time,' – and now she was angry – 'They'll do it next year, or soon, or sometime. They'll blow up the whole world. I don't want to have children. I'm not going to have children. It's not... I can't.'

I put an arm round her and stared at the sea alarmed at her vehemence and run of thought. I suddenly felt our whole future threatened – our lives, our unborn children, everybody's lives and children, the whole world – threatened by the complete bloody idiocy of mankind.

CHAPTER 20

The Great Death – 1928-1939

'You were going to give us some figures,' said Tisala the next day when we had reassembled, 'if Ellie will allow it,' he added, mischievously.

'Oh Tisala, I'm very sorry. I was – '

'Do not apologise. You revealed an aspect of humanity I was pleased to see.'

I looked at Ellie. The black threats of the previous day were distanced by the morning sunshine. My feelings were now of pleasure and pride in her reaction.

So I continued with the appalling history of what was done by commercial whalers to the Blue Whales. At the start of the Great Death, the Antarctic annual slaughter had risen to a dreadful 10,000 Blue Whales. But in 1928-29, 15,000 individuals were slaughtered, 20,000 the next season, and 30,000 in 1930-31. Thirty thousand masterpieces of nature. It was a disaster unprecedented since men first trod the Earth. Before that terrible year, the accumulated slaughter had halved the original population. That year alone resulted in the death of nearly a quarter of the remainder.

Tisala said quietly, 'There were so many members of my family, and all the others.' Eventually he questioned me on the figures. I was obliged to confess that they related to recorded catches.

'So it was even worse than that,' said Tisala, 'when you add the hundreds of our wounded and mutilated. Some recovered, but many died slowly and painfully, sometimes over several weeks, as wounds festered and blood turned bad.'

'Septicaemia,' I said. I told him of a technique the Norwegians had earlier developed back in their home waters. In the days of hand harpoons they had sometimes driven whales into fjords, closed off the entrances, and then harpooned the trapped whales, deliberately using rusty old harpoons. One was sufficient in each whale as it was found that after a few days or a week or two disease took hold, and though the whale died a horrible death of septicaemia, it saved the trouble of a full-scale hunt of a healthy whale. I had earlier been too ashamed to mention this, though Tisala always wanted to know everything.

Tisala did not comment on this bit of history, but I know he stored the knowledge.

'Sometimes,' he continued, reverting to Antarctica, 'the injuries were such that the victims could not feed, and slowly through a combination of their wounds and starvation weakened and died.'

He paused remembering. 'I witnessed some pitiful scenes, both for the dying and bereaved,' he said, but did not enlarge. 'There were orphans too. Sometimes the nursing young whose mothers were killed could not survive without their milk to the weaning stage, despite the efforts of some of the other females.'

'They were not supposed to kill nursing mothers,' I said bitterly.

'But they did,' he said. 'Though not always.'

Then he said, 'I would like to know what happened in the Miracle Year – as we called it – when the ships didn't come.'

I explained what had happened; that in the madness of 1930-31, forty-one factory ships and over two-hundred whale-catching ships had been active in Antarctic waters; and that the frenzy of competitive slaughter had produced such a glut of oil that the market collapsed – from £35 to £10 a barrel. The Norwegians saw their vast profits about to disappear. To diminish the glut, restore prices and avoid costs they simply closed the whole whaling fleet down for a year. It did not sail. The British, I told him, continued to hunt, but without the Norwegians the killing in that next season fell from 30,000 to 6,000. The whaling industry had given itself such a financial fright that it at last tried to reach some agreement to limit catches: not through any altruistic motive, but out of fear for further markets and profits.

There had been, prior to this, desultory attempts, mainly by various governments, to bring some rudimentary discipline to the anarchic industrial fishery (for so it was euphemistically termed and regarded). South Georgia was part of the Falkland Island Dependencies, administered by the British Colonial Office. The British were uneasy about the scale of Norwegian exploitation of 'their' Antarctic waters. Licenses to operate were required with some minimal rules to prevent indiscriminate slaughter. Nursing mothers accompanying calves were not meant to be harpooned, limits were put on the number of catcher ships, and a tax was levied per barrel of oil. Some at least of this money was to be used for whale research. For even then it was realised that the woeful state of ignorance about the life cycle of the great whales might result in the collapse of the whale stocks (for so again they were regarded), and destroy the industry. The warning from the fate of other species of whales was stark.

Old patterns re-emerged. Attempts to regulate even the most brutish, cruel and greedy stupidity resulted in the whalers developing ways round the restrictions. The tax on whale oil landed or processed in British dependencies – principally South Georgia – simply resulted in the faster development of factory ships. These could operate outside the territorial waters and transfer their oil direct to tankers, so avoiding the tax. And the factory ships greatly opened up the areas of the Southern Ocean that could be exploited. Restrictions on the numbers of catcher ships led to them being built bigger and faster, so more whales could be caught despite the restrictions. If suckling mother whales with calves were not to be killed, the death of a calf would mean the mother could then be targeted. It became known that the mother would not leave the dead child, and would so present a sitting target. So child killing became a useful technique. And in merry evening discussions over cheap whisky, the whalers soon learned that it was even better to fire a harpoon to mutilate a calf before killing it – its resultant distress cries would bring in other female whales, which could then be slaughtered with ease.

Most of the whalers were young – for the work was physically hard – who would reckon on a profitable career for a limited number of seasons. They gave no thought beyond that, but did their killing and cutting up of carcasses day by day. Their furthest horizon was the end of the season with their pay and bonuses in their pockets to spend back home, too much of it on alcohol. It was a stinking, miserable and sometimes dangerous employment. Although the working whalers were complicit in the crime, the Blue Whales were being destroyed not for them, but for the ruthless pursuit of profit among the older, shrewder people involved – the captains, managers, ship owners, and investors: the respectable of Norwegian society, and their counterparts in Britain and the other whaling industries.

After the near financial ruination of the 1930-31 season, and the consequent suspension of most whaling the next season, the whaling interests of the leading countries agreed between themselves to put a ceiling figure on the total catch. But such was their individual greed that the figure was set only a little below the horrendous level of 1930-31. And it was done in such a way that it would remain preferable to catch Blue Whales rather than any other species. The whaling nations would race each other to take as many Blue Whales as they each could, merely making up with other species. When they reached the huge cut-off figure, they were supposed to stop, so that the oil market would not be swamped and prices tumble. There was, of course, no method of enforcement whatsoever.

The result was that after the lull of the 1931-32 season, the Great Death continued. But to the destructive competition between the British and Norwegians was added a new and ominous factor: the Japanese and then the Germans joined in Antarctic whaling. They all relentlessly hunted the remaining Blue Whales. The figures for the slaughter soared again: 20,000 recorded in the first resumed season, and similar though gradually falling numbers over the next six seasons to 15,000, and then a more sudden drop to 10,000 in the two seasons up to 1939-40. Each year the quota the whalers set themselves was set above what could be caught. The truth was the Blue Whales were being slaughtered out of existence. Whole families were devastated and destroyed, each death bringing another individual trauma and horror; among them Tarba's: Tisala lost his father only three years after his grandfather's death. But only much later did he tell me the circumstances.

Another pattern re-emerged – as the numbers of Blue Whales declined, the whalers turned their attention to another species – in this case the Fin Whale, which although large, contained only half the oil of a Blue Whale. Once again the destructiveness of the whalers was boosted by technological developments. The catcher ships were now eight hundred tons or more, diesel powered and capable of 18 knots, rather than the 14 knots of the whalers up to that time. The difference in speed was fatal. A Blue Whale can sustain swimming at 15 knots for several hours, and can sprint for a short while at 20 knots, but a prolonged chase at 18 knots runs even a Blue Whale to exhaustion. More and more, in the effort to catch the rapidly diminishing number of Blues, the whalers abandoned any pretence of stalking and simply ran down their prey. Chases of twelve hours are recorded. In the end the whale becomes so exhausted it can no longer dive. Its fate is sealed, and the possibility of escape lost. That is how the whalers of the 1930s continued to prosper.

Through this explanation, Tisala had raised many questions, but when I reached this point, he exhaled heavily as if he was giving a great sigh.

'It was those years that destroyed our families and our society,' he said. 'Even after the worst year – 1931 – though gravely damaged and diminished, our society itself still had a structure. But a few years later, by the end of the Great Death, when the years of peace came, eight out of ten of the remainder of us had been killed, and our society was broken into a remnant of scattered surviving groups.'

His expression surprised me for a moment, but I realised almost at once that 'the years of peace' referred to the Second World War. For in those years there was virtually no whaling at all. Once more, when men turned to killing men, whales were the unintended beneficiaries.

'But I understand, from what you said earlier, that we helped fuel that war,' said Tisala. I told him that Imperial Japan and Nazi Germany entered whaling, firstly and quite literally, to oil the war machines they were rapidly building; and secondly because whale oil was a vital source of glycerine for the manufacture of nitro-glycerine for explosive weapons and munitions. I discovered that in 1935, when over-production had again resulted in the collapse of oil prices, the Norwegian, and to some extent the British, whaling industries saved themselves by large sales of whale oil to the German government. The significance of this was not lost on Tisala: that the British and Norwegians killed whales for profit, and to maintain those profits helped to launch a war that resulted in the German invasion of Norway, and the killing of great numbers of British people.

'Truly, these profits are glittering things,' said Tisala. He asked, 'Where were the democratic governments – the governments of the people you were telling me about?'

Later I could have answered him, but my attempted reply then was feeble, and dried up. But I sensed he did not expect a proper answer and had a strange inkling that somehow he already knew it.

'But for us,' resumed Tisala, 'your World War marked an end to the Great Death. For five years the killing stopped, and we swam in the oceans in relative peace. It was only relative, for we guessed that when whatever conflict was going on ended, the hunting would resume. Initially, our society was so shattered, and some of our young females so terrified by the killings that there was a reluctance to have children. For we all knew of those who had been hunted to death while heavily pregnant: doubly distressed and handicapped in trying to save themselves and their unborn child. But others, including me, said that, more than ever, we should procreate to save our kind, and rebuild our society. We were already dispersed in the oceans and many families decided that avoiding the old favourite feeding grounds was the only way to stay alive, though at the cost of further scattering, and losing our great annual meetings.

'What happened to you, Tisala?' asked Ellie. She always wanted to know about the individuals – what happened to Tisala's brothers and sisters and the cousins they swam with – who were part of the changing family groups; and whether they became partners and parents. She learned much by this informal personal approach, and afterwards wrote an account which throws more light on Blue Whale relationships and social behaviour than any subsequent scientific study I have seen.

Tisala told us his story: 'I swam into the adult part of my life when I was twelve, which for us is into young adulthood. I had always been of a bold and enquiring nature and now I was fully formed and bursting with life. But I swam less joyously than before. Though I was the fifth child all my elder brothers and sisters had been killed, one by one, in the preceding dreadful years.

'I was left with my young sister, Shumi. Though I swam with her and two remaining female cousins I was looking past them for my lifetime partner with a hunger to find her. But the oceans were too often empty, or the groups we met were small and damaged by death and trauma. There were few young females, and one or two I did meet were still following their mothers' bubble water.

'One day we heard a new group quite close by – about three hundred of your miles – emerging from behind the curve of the great ice continent. They seemed to be talkative and lively and I could hear young voices among them.

'Life stirred in me and I somehow knew it was important to meet this group. My young sister Shumi, who was looking for a husband, also felt this urgency of expectation, for young males too were few.

As the young are, I was agitated by the sense of opportunity, and the trepidation of it passing by.

'But it soon became apparent that our two groups, though they would pass within a hundred miles, would not converge. We were heading for a particular krill-clouded ice-bay and there was reluctance in our group to diverge. One of the aunts, who was thinking of the old days said, "There will be plenty of other groups, further along."

But we said, "There may not be, not now."

'There was counter discussion until eventually I spoke up: "I, Tisala, say this is my time and Shumi's time and we are to make this meeting." So it was agreed, and the urge of nature won. We altered our course a few degrees, sending out signals of recognition as we went. The new group slowed its pace for us to converge.

'We met and mingled with greetings and pleasure. There were no less than three young females in this group (two sisters and a cousin), one boy cousin, two youngsters, and five adults. We swam together and they came with us to our krill-clouded bay, which they did not know of. This was a time of plenty, for we were so few to harvest the food, and the other species had not yet filled the gap. I spent my time with the young females.'

'Were they all lovely?' asked Ellie teasingly.

'Each of the three was lovely,' said Tisala making his smiling sound, for whales smile in their minds, and communicate their smiles by sound. 'But all whales are beautiful: we have had beauty and symmetry and our serenity passed into us down the ages.'

Twenty seven million years, I thought, and wondered about the future beauty of mankind, who had struggled out of the caves a mere twelve thousand years ago, grim faced and fearful.

'Yes, I found them all beautiful,' said Tisala. And my sister Shumi found one of the young male cousins so. He was the same age as me. But as the days went by I knew the one who I would court. She was very young – only nine years old – the younger of the two sisters. She was of a beautiful mid slate, blue, unusually consistent and bright, with small darker markings above, and some lighter mottling towards her underside. She was called Sayli. Though she was gentle I found she was brave and there was about her a constant brightness of spirit that attracted me to her. And as I was drawn to her I saw that she was drawn to me.

'She would come up unexpectedly and nudge me before diving shyly away, and I would follow her sideways and down, slipping along her flank, drawing her in protectively with my wing along her back before powering away. After a few weeks I knew I had found my life's companion. For three months we swam together, and when the time was right, we came together in love.

'In due time we had our first child. I watched him slipping out of Sayli's body tail first into the warm tropical sea, and I rejoiced, and thought how my grandfather Saba would have been pleased.

'Two years later, our second child was born. She was beautiful, like her mother.

'When we could forget the threatening world and swim, feed, migrate and make love as in earlier days, we were happy. But the thud of ships' screws when we came across them always re-awakened our fear – which we deliberately taught to our children, for fear is better than death, though it is against our nature to be fearful. We sought to contain our danger by allowing controlled fear in our minds.

'Some had argued that fear was unacceptable, and not to be admitted to our minds at all; that for thousands of years we had by our size and way of life lived fear-free without external enemies, mastering internal competition by our ethics and social restraint, so eliminating want or overpopulation and bringing peace; that admitting fear would be a betrayal of our being; and that our vicious little four-limbed predators were a temporary phenomenon which would disappear again.'

To start with, when Tisala talked of fear as unknown to them, I found it difficult to comprehend that the Blue Whales had developed such an advanced fear-free society. I tried to envisage a human society without fear, but could find it only in representations of heaven presented by religions. I concluded this indicated that such a society was not possible on Earth, but had been aspired to by men longing to escape from reality.

And it oppressed me heavily that the real achievement of whale society, developed over many millennia, had been sickeningly destroyed by a relatively small number of men – a group of cruel, ignorant, mercenary destroyers. But then I thought of all in the world we humans had destroyed, and still were; and looked gloomily into the future. But at the time I kept such thoughts to myself.

'Tell us about Sayli, and your children,' said Ellie. She asked it confidently, almost excitedly, as if she were about to make new friends, but then hesitated towards the end. And I felt a flicker of fear as to what would be told. And a protective apprehension for Ellie, and our own unborn children, for we were to be married that summer.

CHAPTER 21

Ellie's Day

The history and stories of the whales emerged slowly over a period. In that time, Tisala's command of language developed strongly and his ability to absorb learning remained astonishing. When back in London, Ellie, Robert, and I spent weeks researching and looking out material on the whole gamut of knowledge to feed Tisala.

At Tisala's request, Robert explored some aspects of world religion – he called it '*Terra incognita* for us physicists' – and afterwards remarked, 'We think we're teaching Tisala, but in reality he's teaching us.'

There was a great deal more of terra incognita to come for all of us. The transport of books, pictures, films and the rest to the island became a logistical problem. When two years later Robert retired, the position was somewhat eased. He and his wife lived in London – at Richmond near the edge of the Great Park. He willingly took on the ferreting out of books and materials in London while Ellie and I were on the island and on two or three important occasions brought up a carload and stayed with Eric and Guinevere, where he was unfailingly welcome.

But before that, much had changed also for Ellie and me. We were engaged in spring 1962 and were to be married at the end of that July. To the disappointment of her mother, Ellie did not spend the whole period prior to the wedding at home. She was immersed in the dissertation for her masters degree. She was determined to do well and finish it before the wedding. So, after we came back from the islands, she went down to her parents' house in Wiltshire for two weeks in June.

When Ellie arrived at Fieldbanks House, she and her mother plunged into wedding activities. Ellie recounted the happenings to me in our long, nightly telephone calls. The wedding dress and bridesmaid's dresses were fitted, with minor crises, lots of pins, injunctions to the bridesmaids – 'Don't eat too much, there's not much give.' The feet of one of the bridesmaids appeared to be growing out of control. 'She'll never get into those shoes, and they haven't got a larger pair in that colour – we'll have to spray the black ones – and for goodness sake keep that child away from the cakes.'

And on fitting the bride's dress, Penelope badgered her daughter – 'Ellie, you must eat properly. Do eat, dear, we don't want it to sag!' Edmund, tell her.'

'We don't want a ghost at this wedding,' laughed Edmund.

'Don't be stupid, Edmund,' said Penelope sharply.

'Poor Daddy had to retreat,' giggled Ellie down the phone to me.

Lists were drawn up, marked, deleted, redrawn, lost. Electricity was found to be inadequate – perfectly good wires and lamps were suddenly discovered to be without earths or mysteriously to have gone completely phut.

'That boy's an idiot,' said Edmund of Mrs Taylor's son Tom from the village, who had rashly been volunteered to help, and proved to be an expert at blowing fuses. And when Penelope tactfully put him to work in the garden, he managed to destroy half a flower bed of Edmund's prize seedlings before he was stopped. 'A complete thoroughgoing menace,' said Edmund morosely.

'It's a madhouse,' Ellie reported, laughing, as Edmund's telephone bill mounted.

But after a week it was clear that stress levels were rising, even for her. I listened, and tried to make sensible comments, but someone being calm and rational outside the fray can be very irritating. 'Yes, but you don't have to... She's ... no, I already told her... it's ridiculous.'

'Ellie,' I said, 'It's only a wedding.' There was a silence. 'Ellie?'

'What do you mean?' I heard the dismay in her voice. I was suddenly frightened of my stupid clumsiness. An abyss had suddenly opened up and we each, listening down the telephone, stood on different sides. And then, with relief, I heard the dismay turn to indignation – 'What do you mean?'

'Ellie, I only meant... don't get things out of... I wish I was down there to help.' Then, calling us both to order, I said, 'Hey, you know how much I love you, you silly thing. Very, very much.'

'I love you too.' I could hear the relief in her voice, and we spoke to assure and reassure each other.

By the end of the second week a certain calm descended on the household, as arrangements gradually fell into place and jobs were completed. Ellie came back to London at the end of June for the last four weeks before the wedding to finish her work. Even my time with her was rationed, which I met with initial protest. But I admired her stance on the matter, and when as a result I got thoroughly immersed in my own work, I noticed an unexpected feeling of relief.

'Anyway,' she said, 'we spend lots of hours together when we are asleep.'

'But I can't... It's completely useless when I'm unconscious.'

'Well,' she said, with a little smile, 'your unconscious seems to lead a pretty independent life.'

We went down to Fieldbanks House two days before the wedding. As we got nearer, I could feel a sense of tension and excitement rising, and I could see from Ellie's face that she felt the same – it was as if we were coming to a new place, where we had never been before. When we drove up to the house, we saw new gravel had been put on the drive. As we got out of the car, Ellie's father came out of the front door. They embraced. 'Dad!' Ellie protested, indicating the new gravel.

'It needed doing anyway,' he said, and Ellie kissed him laughing. Philip came out of the house and greeted us.

'Hi, beautiful,' he said to Ellie. Sister and brother hugged. When they clung together it seemed in that moment as though they recognised an alteration – a departure – was taking place in their familiar childhood relationship. Penelope came out of the house and greeted us.

'Hello David.' I kissed her on both cheeks. 'At last,' she said. 'Lovely to see you both.'

'Come in, come in,' said Edmund. 'Philip – Ellie's suitcase and bags – ' indicating to the rear of the car.

'Slave,' said Ellie, grinning at him affectionately as he carried them into the house.

'You'll have to watch out for her, David,' he said over his shoulder, 'she's pretty demanding.'

'Look at that rose,' said Ellie. The normally rather wild climbing rose to the left of the doorway had been trimmed and tied back onto the house and was full of pink blooms. 'Have you spent ages on the garden, Dad?'

'No, no... Well, we wanted the place to look good for you.'

Penelope took me by the arm and led me into the house. 'He's been slaving away for weeks!' she said.

Some presents had arrived and there was a stack of brightly papered parcels on the hall sideboard. Out in the garden, there was a marquee on the lawn, and the garden was looking splendid. We did a tour of inspection of both, talking and chattering as we went, and admiring the flowers. At one place there was half a bed full of flowers which looked somehow as if they had arrived in full bloom and had not taken the trouble to grow. 'Ah,' I said to Edmund, 'is this the miracle bed?' Edmund looked at me sideways.

'Don't remind me,' he said.

At lunch the talk went on. Bridesmaids, the church flowers, the vicar – rehearsal tomorrow afternoon – speeches, the best man – he won't be too rude will he? – this arrangement, that arrangement, who was coming, who couldn't – cousin Sheila – no, Mrs Turner's nephew, not her son – funny old trout... At one point my mind withdrew and I ceased to hear. I looked around the table in a state of almost ecstatic excitement – my beloved Ellie and her family. My mind said I don't believe it. It's too wonderful. And when I looked at Ellie I wanted her and somehow drifted off and found myself lying with her on a vast bed with billowy white sails, and a blue sky beyond. We lay our limbs and bodies cool and free, and turned to each other, our eyes drawing us in –

'Don't you think so, David?'

'I, um – '

'He's miles away,' laughed Ellie.

'Bring him back, someone,' said Edmund.

'I'm sorry, I missed what you said,' and added, rather sheepishly, 'Well, I was with Ellie.'

'I should hope so!' said Philip amid the merriment, and Ellie caught my eye and blushed as she laughed. The rest of the day passed in a haze of happiness.

The next morning almost dragged. My various offers of help were not needed – 'That's very kind, but we'll manage,' or, 'We've done that.' I felt in the way as Ellie and her mother dealt with remaining tasks – part of the hem of the wedding dress needed attention.

I was ready, and having nothing to do, yet feeling vaguely that I ought to have, began to feel edgy. I went over my speech again. The two jokes that had originally seemed funny, now felt flat. Tinkering began to make things worse, and after a while I crossed out most of the amendments and put it away, reassuring myself that everyone would be in congenial mood and my speech was really only an extended thank-you anyway.

In the afternoon my best man, Mike Walsh, arrived, as did the two bridesmaids and their mothers. We went down to the church and were taken through the service. The vicar was kind and reassuring, for by this time a certain nervousness had set in, and we were all quiet and serious.

Later in the afternoon my mother arrived with Susan. 'Certainly they are staying with us,' Penelope had said some weeks earlier when the arrangements were made. 'You David, and your best man, can go and stay the night with the Smithsons.' The tradition of the groom not seeing his bride on the wedding day until she gets to church was to be upheld. After the greetings and welcoming, I went for a walk round the garden with my mother.

My mother said, smiling, 'Well, my young man's getting married: I can hardly believe it.'

'Do you blame me?'

She laughed, 'No – she's a lovely person – you're very fortunate. But she's fortunate too.'

'Thanks Mum.'

'I hope you will be very happy. You are not overawed by the prospect?'

'No, it's what I want more than anything.' And suddenly I saw the trail of my tendency to diffidence, that impoverisher of lives, leading back into my childhood and in that recognition knew I had grown beyond it.

My mother said, 'And I think Susan will soon be engaged, and then that will be both of you.'

We sat and talked and I slowly realised there was an element of fulfilment in her mind: that sitting in this established old garden she was comforted to know that years of struggle to bring up two children decently was nearly over. She could pass the baton. She was fond of Ellie and approved of her family, and she could pass it with pleasurable release and anticipation.

Ellie and I were married the next day. I felt a sense of stability provided by an English country wedding in the parish church, where for four hundred years, since the Reformation ushered in the modern world in Europe, the same form of words has been used, instituted by our sovereign lady, Elizabeth. Elizabeth of England, pale faced and of jewel-bedecked gowns, like our flower-strewn meadow. And here was my Elizabeth standing beside me, our arms just touching.

'Dearly beloved, we are gathered together in the sight of God to join together this man and this woman…'

I glanced at Ellie, and accepted my new life with gratitude. The words rolled on, 'For richer, for poorer, in sickness and in health, to love and to cherish, till death do us part.'

I remember saying, 'I, David, take you Elizabeth – '

And she said, 'I, Elizabeth, take you David.'

And when she looked at me there was such a light in her eyes. There was sunlight in the church and splashes of colour about our heads from the stained glass windows and the stands of flowers.

So we entered the estate of matrimony, an honourable estate. And afterwards we had a reception in the garden and the marquee. The day was warm and sunny and there was champagne and endless trays of food.

There was the buzz of conversation across the generations, and eyeing up of those who looked older since they last met, and those who had blossomed or grown up – a pretty dress or hat turning heads, and marking the transition between a girl and young woman. A few people had too much to drink, but only to the stage of tiddliness, except one young boy who had evaded his mother's eye and was led away to be sick behind some bushes, everyone amused and asking, 'Is he all right?'

One old doctor got too hot and had to be sat down with his coat off and a glass of iced water.

The afternoon went by in a blur. Ellie and I went round the guests, showered with greetings and goodwill. Everyone wanted to kiss Ellie – my lovely bride – my wife! Yes – my wife: Ellie, the clear centre of all my memories that day. So, though I kissed – the young and perfumed, laughing to get under hats – and laid my cheek against old cheeks, known and unknown, powdered and painted, soft and prickly, wrinkled and smooth, they merged and blended indistinctly in the periphery of my recollection. And there were speeches and laughter and telegrams, and all went off happily. But at the centre of everything was Ellie.

CHAPTER 22

A New Life

So we began our married life. We bought a small flat in Battersea with Aunt Jane's money, and Ellie found a job as a teacher, crossing the Thames each day to her primary school in Pimlico, so as to complete her qualification by a year's teaching. She loved the job and the children, but for that year her time in the islands was very curtailed – a half term in October, and a three-week period in the following Easter holidays. I was up there for six or eight weeks at a time. We were like identical twins when parted, incomplete and searching for our other half.

In the early summer of the year following our marriage, we decided to abandon contraception.

'I want to make your babies,' said Ellie looking down with an almost shy blush. When her eyes looked in mine, they told of her yearning desire to be filled with my seed, and to be the creator and guardian of new life that is motherhood. And when we came together I felt a sense of wonder, almost sacredness; it was as if we were new to each other and this was our first union; a freedom, like first swimming naked in the sea. When we made love it was with the most complete life-yearning openness of our bodies, one to the other, and she drew me in lovingly as the ultimate carer of me, and our seeds.

Three months later on Inis Cuan on a warm, sunny August morning full of blue sky and tumbling white clouds, and the bracken by the cottage just turning gold, Ellie said to me, putting her hands in mine, 'I think I'm pregnant.'

And she was. In the following March, our baby son was born. And a year later – in April – our little girl. We called our son William Edmund after his grandfathers, and our daughter Penny Elizabeth. From the beginning we took them up to the islands. Will first went when he was four weeks old. Initially, when they were each very young, Ellie stayed with Eric and Guinevere. Guinevere insisted on turning one bedroom into a nursery and fussed about organising it as if it were for her own grandchild. 'Mine are in Canada – so far away,' she said.

The little crofting cottage on Inis Cuan became for parts of the year our real home: it was not ours, though Eric and Guinevere insisted that we treated it as such, and I built shelves for books, and a cupboard in the kitchen. Ellie bought a roll of red wallpaper and put it up behind the shelves near the fireplace. One of the bookshelves was soon filled with seashells and coloured pebbles and strangely shaped driftwood. And soon a little pile of children's books, at first with thick cardboard picture pages, began to accumulate. On rainy days, or when it was cold, we lit a fire, and the children knew the huddle of warmth and the flicker of fire in the evenings, and stories with the wind outside – scenes I suppose, that go back to the cave dwellers emerging from the ice age. In our second year, I dug turf, and we dried it on the heather before stacking it under the little lean-to roof against the cottage. It burned less well and more quickly than wood, but the smell of a turf fire conjures up a whole world. I've always been glad that we managed to extend the fireplaces of my own boyhood to the next generation, for the central heating of modern living trades in much for convenience.

We collected driftwood from the shore for the fires. In those days what was thrown up on the little beaches and rocks as evidence of human maritime activity was wood – boards of various sizes, the wood weathered silver, and almost silky to the touch, lengths of square-cut, occasional spars and beams and battered wooden pallets – the detritus that might have been brought ashore in the days of wooden hulls and sailing ships. Sometimes there was the occasional green glass ball, lost from fishing nets. Initially, when I found a broken one, the sharp glass amongst the rocks seemed an abuse of nature, but I noticed the glass soon acquired rounded frosted edges; and then somehow it seemed like a natural process of recycling: sand into glass into sand, one day to be rolled back into the fiery tectonic interior of the Earth. Even the aluminium fish floats we sometimes found, though not as attractive as the glass ones, had that charm; the silvery aluminium beginning to oxidise to a whitish powdery surface. The tide of brightly coloured imperishable plastic bottles, containers, nylon nets and any number of artefacts of later years had not then commenced.

As Will grew – to two and three – our work with Tisala progressed into advanced studies of all kinds that stretched our ability to keep up. At the same time, with Will, and then with Penny, we reverted in our own lives to the beginning: the learning of first words and putting together of language. Tisala took a great interest in this. At first I thought it was a casual interest, but he regularly used to ask what Will had said as he pronounced first words, and then linked words to words, used phrases and produced first sentences; and I soon realised he was watching and exploring the growth of a human mind. In other circumstances, being asked to consider and share this family intimacy might have felt intrusive, but his careful interest had the opposite effect. We trusted his good will towards us absolutely, and from very early we became more conscious and attentive to the effect our speech and behaviour would have on the developing mind and temperament of a child.

This would later result in a view of educational theory which recognised that too much of the behaviour of parents and schools was often inadequate, if not counter-productive. How often have children taken years of adult life to compensate for their early verbal starvation and unlearn the conduct, ideas and inhibitions wrongly taught in childhood and only painfully – if ever – rectified in the light of their own experience of living?

But this was far away from those early happy days when Ellie dangled Penny from her hip as she did tasks around the cottage, or squatted with Will between her knees peering at the bubbling of our little spring and watching the green grass moving in the upwelling water; or taught the children to feed our robin who hopped into the doorway of the cottage cocking his head; or stood holding Will by the hand on the edge of the inlet by the shack as Tisala slid once more into his berth. From the beginning, Will knew Tisala as our special friend, and he had not the slightest fear of this colossal creature, but regarded him as an extension of some of his picture book friends, or as a kindly relative, which though distant, it turned out he was.

And then one day, a year or two later, when Will was four, he came to me with a picture book of whaling he had found, very upset, with tears in his eyes, and asked, 'Why are they killing the whales?' I sat him on my lap and told him there were bad men in the world who killed things, and did other things they shouldn't; but that there were lots of people who were trying to stop it happening any more, including Mummy and me. He allowed himself to be comforted in my arms; but years later he recounted the incident to me, still remembering the dismay and desolation he had felt at the time.

And I did not then tell him what I had already told Tisala.

CHAPTER 23

Consumer Products

From early on, Tisala had asked us repeatedly why the different species of whale including his own had been so ruthlessly hunted. He knew that in the early days at least it was not for meat, because everywhere the whalers went the bodies of whales, stripped of their blubber, were discarded and abandoned both at sea and in festering piles of corpses round bays of the land bases. And many a whale had seen with dismayed incomprehension the body of a family member stripped to the flesh and bone, bleeding and flukeless, but had not recognised in that mutilated lump their parent, partner or child.

The history of whaling is full of horror. But I had gradually realised not only that whaling is itself cruel and barbarous, but that it revealed, in the connivance of large sections of society, some deeply unattractive attributes of humanity in general. People are often indifferent to suffering not their own, especially when it is out of sight and they are enjoying its products. Our drive to exploit and consume, reckless of consequences, increasingly appalled me.

Initially, I had told him about the use of whale oil, from Right Whales, and of the special oil from Sperm Whales; that whale oil lamps were an advance on candles, and lit domestic winter evenings in the Northern Hemisphere before the advent of gaslight and electricity; that it was important as a lubricating oil for the machinery of the industrial revolution, which drove much of the advance of nineteenth century society; and that both for lubrication and illumination, whale oil had no real substitute before the discovery of oil in the ground and its processing for machine oil and kerosene lighting. But Tisala soon learnt that the need for whale oil for those purposes was nearly over by the time the Norwegians' hunting techniques had improved sufficiently to enable them to hunt and kill Blue and Fin Whales.

'So why have we been hunted – and continue in some quarters still to be hunted?' he asked.

'Because men are cruel and greedy.' said Ellie.

I told him that the oil was only part of the story. Even in the eighteenth and nineteenth centuries, the most valuable part of the whale was baleen, often called whalebone – the curtains of flexible brownish black plates hanging down from the whale's upper jaws, used by the baleen whales in place of teeth for sieving plankton and small fish.

'They killed us for our mouth-sieves?' asked Tisala.

I told him with some trepidation that the whalebone was used in fashions that led the way in the civilised world of Europe and America. It was used for strengthening and shaping bodices, bonnets, hooped skirts, stays and bustles. The more preposterous the fashions, the more whalebone was needed. The whole look of women in polite society in those two centuries depended upon the whalebone industry, and could not have come about without it. In the eighteenth century, a single Greenland Right Whale's baleen was at one time worth £3,000, when an artisan's cottage at the time cost about £100. Such was the sartorial vanity of the elegant, well-educated ladies of Europe and the Americas.

'It cannot be right that we died for this.' said Tisala incredulously.

I said, 'I'm ashamed to say it is, but not only that – '

'He blames the women, Tisala,' Ellie interrupted, 'but then in our society men almost obliged women to adopt those fashions.'

'Ellie, that's rub – nonsense. What do you mean?'

'No, it's not. It was partly caused by a dreadful male dominance,' she explained to Tisala. 'Women were wholly dependent on men for their lives and livelihoods – men had a monopoly on assets and wealth – where woman had any, the law (all passed by men) took all our money. We had to dress in those absurd fashions to survive by pleasing men.'

I was slightly startled by this heated feminism from Ellie. 'You've caught the modern infection,' I said, grinning at her to bait her a bit more. Ellie flushed red in her cheeks. When angry she was absolutely beautiful.

'Don't grin at me,' she said. 'Well, you even got God, who was of course a man, to lay down things in the Bible about obedience to husbands – women were trapped.'

'Come on,' I said, 'you're emancipated now, but you're still wiping out leopards and ocelots for fur coats.'

'I am not saying women were blameless – of course they were vain – but I'm just giving Tisala another angle. And there are still many human societies where women are downtrodden chattels.' She looked at me pointedly – 'Unlike the Blue Whale society.'

Tisala said: 'I should like to hear more of Ellie's side of history. I learn that men not only kill other animals and men on any pretext, but now that they oppress their own women. Their belligerence for survival comes at a great price.' He paused. 'But was whalebone used also in men's fashions?'

I had to admit to him that it was – for strengthening men's hats and helmet frames amongst other things.

'All for men,' said Ellie smiling at me.

Tisala said, 'But most whalebone fashions went out, as I understand it, before we Blue Whales were hunted. You still have not explained why we were so hunted.'

'Well,' I said, 'for one thing the baleen was used for other things – and it went on being used – such as brushes, shoe horns, fishing rods, riding crops, umbrella ribs, covers for telescopes and such like.' And when I explained what these things were, and how entirely essential to the survival of mankind, Tisala was silent. Ellie looked chastened.

'I didn't know – so many unnecessary things. It's awful.'

I told Tisala that luckily whale skin is thin and useless for leather, so that was not a source of demand; although the skin of Blue Whales' penises, cut around the base, was used to make golf bags, which were sought after in America, where the whitish flecked colour went rather well with smart golfing shoes, and where, luckily for their peace of mind, Americans had never yet discovered the meaning of the word vulgar. I explained that golf is a game played with metal-ended sticks and a small white ball which you try and hit into a hole; and that some people, when they had finished their years of work, devoted much of their lives to it, using golf as a diversion to mask the passage of time, so wasting their lives without noticing it until time wastes them.

'I find it difficult to believe,' said Tisala, 'that after four billion years of evolution, members of perhaps the most intelligent species yet to evolve should be satisfied by such a way of spending their remaining years.'

But I assured him that it was true and that we had invented many other diversions to shelter us from reality instead of doing anything useful.

'I suppose,' said Tisala, 'it is at least harmless.'

I conceded that hitting little white balls was better than killing things, though in some poor countries, much land and water is given over the production of golf courses. This is especially true in dry countries, because people like to play in the sun and on green grass, so dams have to be built, pipes laid, and water diverted from local uses.

In the twentieth century, I told Tisala, whale oil was also used in more modern fashions when it was discovered that chemical modification enabled it to be widely used in cosmetics.

I explained to Tisala that cosmetics were chemicals that women put on their faces to enhance their beauty, add colour, highlight or disguise their features, and eradicate wrinkles; that they are much favoured by ageing women, who, with great expenditure of time and money, and sometimes several layers of the stuff, manage temporarily to transform their faces in the hope of running time backwards; in which they are much influenced by women's magazines, which are issued for the purpose every week in their millions, and at great profit to their owners.

Human numbers, and the scale of our consumption, I had come to see, were also at the heart of the problem. At the time of the whalebone fashions and subsequently, the industrial revolution and medical advances in Europe and America led to a great increase in both population and disposable wealth which could be spent on non-essentials. The huge and growing demand for whale products destroyed the whales. At the beginning of the nineteenth century, for instance, the population of the United States and Britain together was less than 15 million, but by 1950 the figure was 200 million. The Blue Whales were caught up in this. Their relatively tiny population – at about 300,000 – was sacrificed unthinkingly to ours.

'But reverting to whale oil,' I said, 'another reason the trade continued, and grew despite the coming of petroleum substitutes, was that technology again found further uses for it. Large quantities went into the manufacture of cheap soap. And it was the production of cheap soap in the nineteenth century industrialised world that led to a dramatic fall in the death rate, and thereby a dramatic increase in the human populations.'

'Which in turn increased the demand for our oil,' said Tisala.

'Yes. But other uses were also found. As you know, the Germans and the Japanese wanted to secure supplies of glycerine for the manufacture of explosives. And – in 1930 – the year before the greatest ever slaughter of you Blue Whales, a brand new use was discovered: a new method of hydrogenation, which could turn whale oil into margarine.' I explained that margarine was a cheap butter substitute. 'This led to a great increase in whale oil demand just at the time when the slaughter of you Blue Whales was reaching its height.'

Tisala considered this, and I think he thought of all his family who had been killed.

'So you tell me that the Great Death amongst us was caused in part to spread fat on bread for an ever-increasing human population.' He sighed heavily, then added: 'That is at least better than cosmetics – people being fed. But was there no substitute that could have saved us?'

'Oh yes, plenty: various fish and vegetable oils – peanut, palm and coconut oil are all suitable. There was no need to kill whales. But everything depended on money. If the whalers could make money, they would kill anything. Whales in the sea were free, so each whaling fleet set out to maximise its catch, regardless of the consequences to whales. They were even more reckless than they might have been, for fear of competitive substitute markets developing. As always, it was greed and ignorance.'

Tisala said: 'I see that the understanding and practice of ethical behaviour is not spread throughout mankind. I fear for the world, for you have immense capacity to do ill.'

From somewhere the words of Edmund Burke came into my mind, and I quoted: '"All that is necessary for the triumph of evil is that good men do nothing."'

'We must return to the idea of good and evil,' he said, 'Human development has been bedevilled – I note the word itself – by false premises and superstition.'

He reverted to the question of why whales have been slaughtered by men: 'So is that the end of your miserable catalogue?'

'Not yet,' I said, 'You were too useful – with technological advances your oil was used for many other things in the textile and leather industries, for the manufacture of oil paints, linoleum, oil cloth and I don't know what. And the invention of refrigeration meant that your flesh could be prepared on factory ships and chilled or frozen and transported all over the world.'

'Ah. So you did kill us to eat us. That at least must have meant hungry people fed.'

'Not really. Apart from small-scale consumption by Norwegians and Icelanders, the only real whale meat-eating nation is Japan. I explained that in earlier centuries the religious authorities in Japan had forbidden meat eating, but fish was allowed, so they categorised whale as fish and continued to do so long after they knew it was untrue, and still to this day do so, telling lies about it to enable it to continue.'

'But what really did for you was not meat, but animal feed and fertiliser.'

'Go on,' said Tisala heavily.

I explained the processing that took place on the factory ships: that after the whalers had extracted the oil, which came from all parts, pre-eminently the blubber, but also flesh and bones, they boiled up everything – flesh, bones, brains, eyes, blood, guts, even stomach contents. After twelve hours, the boilers were opened and the residues were shovelled out and taken to the driers – large rotating cylinders specially constructed – and dried into a grey powder. This was turned into either animal feed – cattle cake and suchlike – or fertiliser.

'Did the Germans do this with Jews?'

I laughed tightly, thinking it a bitter joke. 'No, even the Nazis were not evil enough for that.'

'Yet those Germans are thought of as more evil than the Norwegians, the Icelanders, the Russians and the Japanese, who as we speak, continue the process of turning us into grey powder for profit when they can find us.'

'Yes, they hide from themselves the truth that you are intelligent beings, and claim to regard you as an expendable free commodity.'

Tisala said, 'Your human morality, such as it is, seems to be little developed and extends for the most part just to yourselves.'

He asked: 'What is cattle cake?'

I explained that farmers fed dead whales to cows so the cows grew better before being killed and eaten by us.

'But cows are herbivorous.'

'Yes. We make them behave unnaturally.'

When pressed again by Tisala, I had to confirm that cattle cake from whales was wholly unnecessary, there being many non-animal substitutes, but that it provided another element of profit which kept the whole whaling industry alive. I mentioned too that some of the animal feed was bought by the Russians and fed to mink – a ferocious little animal farmed for its fur – for turning into expensive fashionable coats. The leaders of the people's revolution gave them to their wives – they were useful in winter in their second homes – but otherwise they were exported to the capitalist West for money and worn for show – the women to indulge their vanity, and the men their pleasure in flaunting wealth.

Throughout these discussions, Tisala had pursued at various times many other questions and subjects relating both to whaling and the human world. By this time I knew he was thinking beyond his original impulse to learn about men in order to save his own kind. I think he saw clearly that, if the Blue Whales could survive, they could influence humanity for the better – even help in saving humanity from itself. *If* they could first survive, for they were on the edge of extinction. But neither the urgency of the threat to his species nor the vastness of that emerging undertaking seemed to dismay him at all. He wanted to know the true nature of our world, what we believed and why, and how we reconciled our conduct as savage killers with our higher aspirations. We had by then talked of our philosophies and religions. And I knew he was storing the knowledge to consider in his own mind while he was away each season in the Artic summer or among the winter trade-wind seas.

CHAPTER 24

In the Image of God

Among human subjects of belief, I had introduced and explained the Christian religion to Tisala, with some anticipation, as I thought this would be a startling revelation in his world. I said that Christians, of whom by upbringing I was one, believed it to be the true religion, revealed to mankind though Christ, the Son of God, as the underlying reality behind the world. This we had been taught through the Bible stories when young, and like many had been caught up in its wonders. I had therefore assumed, without at first knowing much about them, that the other religions, though no doubt worthy attempts to find God, were misdirected. But increasingly as I grew up, like most people, I found aspects of my religion that did not fit other realities in the world. Questions and doubts arose. Later, I had read about other religions, and in my education and in science found other ways of looking at the world.

The idea of God as portrayed in our religions was at first new to Tisala, and he questioned me closely. What was the nature of God? Where did such ideas come from? What was the purpose of worship and why should it exist? How did men come to believe you could foretell the future? Always the questions came, and so Ellie and I often found ourselves talking about these things. We were all exploring, old texts and assumptions, new interpretations, new ideas, new connections. But Tisala's conclusions only emerged gradually, sometimes much later. And each time, in a strange way, it seemed to me he grew nearer the truth of human existence. And the pattern was the same – I came to recognise the process – in whichever aspect of humanity's affairs we explored. Tisala had over several years, through our conversations, readings and discussions, studied and considered carefully our main religions. But in answering his wide-ranging enquiries, and confronting my own beliefs, the anomalies and difficulties had mounted.

For instance, initially because of the slaughter of the whales by Christian nations, but later on a wider basis, I had grown to loathe the pernicious doctrine, which Christians got from Judaism, that all animals and plants were created by God for the benefit and use of men. Men, moreover, said to be made in the image of God. We counted ourselves different and superior to the animal kingdom – and thereby justified all manner of capricious and barbaric destruction of animals. The doctrine of Islam, that mankind is a part of nature, seemed in that superior, though their ethics in the treatment of animals appeared cruel and inferior to the Buddhist belief. But in turn the Buddhist sensitivity to animals is offset by superstition, as is the otherwise admirable toleration of the Hindus. In short, I found the doctrines of all religions on other animals to be defective.

One day, when we were discussing these things, Tisala said, 'The notion of man made in the image of God has caused much trouble. The idea seems to come from your creation myths. We whales, of course, have our legends of the beginning. For all animals live within time, and when the consciousness of any animal develops sufficiently, it seeks to explore the world of past time. We too, in our minds, created a story god. He was, as you may imagine, a Blue Whale. He, greatest of all the whales, swam far out amongst the stars, accompanied by a myriad of other life, and spread his seed streaming through the universe – in our story that is what the stars are, the remnant of his seed. He saw the ocean world, and circled it lovingly. And when the stars fell into the sea, we whales were created, and the host of other life came from the shimmering star dust. There are many versions and variations of our legends. Some dealt with the coming of death from the jealousy of other creatures, and the silent demands of the unborn, who should have their turn; and how the balance of life and death was settled. Some stories told of an afterlife, when we would swim out amongst the stars. We delighted in constructing intricate tales of our journeys to find love and wisdom. Such stories give pleasure, and practical ethical guidance. But we never made the mistake that humans have of believing and relying on legends. They foster beliefs that your histories show have led to terrible aberrations. The realities of the ocean world taught us differently. We know that our time-life is in the oceans – life which, until the coming of men, was a thing of wonder.' He paused. 'It was easier for us. The marine environment is simpler for us, and safer, because of our huge size and speed. Unlike some of the smaller or slower whales, we had no enemies who could harm us, until the coming of twentieth century man. We didn't have your land-based material wants and demands to contend with and were not prey to the many fears of humanity.'

He said that he had thought about the discoveries of twentieth century biology in relation to our religions. He questioned, if it is true that a chimpanzee's genes are nearly the same as a man's, how the religions would then view God, and man made in God's image? For he supposed religious people would not like much an image of God based on chimpanzee genes. Only a few years after this discussion, research into DNA showed irrefutably that genes common between men and chimpanzees are 98.4 percent, and that the species of chimpanzees and men began to separate and diverge from a common ancestry a mere seven million or so years ago. He understood that Jews, Christians and Muslims might be horrified to find that man, who has the genes of apes, resembles God. But that finding poses a fundamental question about their God, and should tell them that their concept is mistaken and untrue; though they may argue that God does not have genes, that he was before genes were, and so for a period seek to escape the consequences of the illogicality of their own belief.

Instead, they should ask, Tisala argued, if they believe such a God exists, why should he have created and run a universe for 14 billion years without creating anything remotely like himself before, and then creating an ape-man, but then only, so far as we know, on one planet near one little star of one galaxy out of billions.

I said, joining the trail of these ideas: 'Which apes then claim for themselves that they are made in the likeness of God. And really, why should God be like us, one of several hominoid species with ape genes and characteristics, the rest of which became extinct like millions of other species which developed and flourished more or less briefly and then died out? And maybe *Homo sapiens* was neither the most intelligent nor the "best" of the hominoid groups which have lived on Earth, though undoubtedly the most successful. It has been suggested that we may indeed be of mixed descent – some of the spacious aspects of men's minds may come from interbreeding with the bigger-brained Neanderthal man. Is it to be argued that the god-figure is in part Neanderthal?'

'So why should we whales believe that any God of the universe is like your chance – produced and often-vicious species? Should men any more believe in a god who is like a whale, or some other animal? If they did – as they did, and do, in some of your religions – would that not merely mark the inadequacy of their belief?'

So Tisala quietly questioned the true standing of the religious conviction dating back only two or three thousand years, that the God of the whole universe existed in man-like form for billions of years and that men are made in His image. He thought it so unlikely as to be wholly unbelievable. 'It runs counter to all reason. Any rational being would conclude this: that man made God in the image of man.

'And that,' he went on, 'is even before you apply coherent understanding of the way your astronomers, chemists and biologists have shown how the world evolved; knowledge, we should remember, that those who formulated your great religions had no opportunity or possibility of understanding.'

Tisala thought it a sign of advancement that at last our creation stories were becoming widely unbelievable. Belief in them had presumably survived so long for two reasons. First, because the scriptures were regarded as endowed with mystical supernatural authority, while having intertwined in them valuable stories, lessons and ethics making them attractive repositories of wisdom and guides to living in an often perplexing and savage world. Second, because of the prevalence of ignorance which is still widespread in our century: a degree of effort and learning is required to understand the evolution of the stars, chemistry and life; while childhood teaching, culture, busy lives and vested interests prop up belief in the various religious legends. He said that what I had told him about humans showed they have often believed their imaginations, rather than reason, in the brief recorded period of man's consciousness.

Tisala said: 'Thus men found gods in fire or in the sun, in thunder, or in woods, in streams, in mountains or in household shrines, and gods of love or war or death – and built societies of messengers and angels round them. The Egyptians, Greeks and Romans thought it best to keep the gods divided. The desert-moulded Jews, groping their way to monotheistic absolutes, condensed their power in one omnipotent God. And Christ and Paul and Constantine, and then

Mohammed thus unleashed a fearsome force for good and ill upon the world; not just your world of men; but through your mastery of much that lies between the quiet poles, trampling on the wonders of the Earth, destroying miracles you do not even see.'

The chain of explanation brought me up sharply. But something else tugged at my mind. There was a strange and compelling power in the way Tisala spoke. Then I realised with a start what it was, and I asked disbelievingly: 'Tisala, are you talking in verse?'

He rumbled his pleasure and said he found he sometimes slipped into it for the pure delight of it. He said an interesting study would be – rather like exploring the fossil record in the Earth's sedimentary rocks – to assess the flowering and use of language to chart the development of higher civilisations; and conversely to consider whether poor use and currency of language would throw light on their decline and fall.

Tisala observed that danger often starts with something good: as with printing presses, which released learning from the ever-present risk of being lost – learning that until then had been precariously preserved by the few, scratching by doubtful candlelight across the centuries. But now the printing presses have multiplied a thousandfold and the airways opened up. And though when we first spoke of this television seemed relatively innocent, and domestic computers hardly existed, the possible decay of language could be seen as a coming danger that might challenge the survival of hard-won learning by the spread of overwhelming trivia, prejudice and ignorance.

Too often, he thought, it seems that men take a lifetime to sift knowledge from information and wisdom from knowledge; and too often they are then past the time of action and so fail to pass on that wisdom.

He instanced some parts of academic philosophy. The point of philosophy, he said, is to fit us better for living, not to burden our students in the bright days of their minds by obliging them to study at inordinate length the history and byways of philosophical exploration. So we bog them down in what this or that minor Greek or Roman thought, or misthought, and half of it in contradiction of any sense, because of some strange belief in the nature of fire, or water, or the gods; or in the more modern convoluted musings and thin obsessions of what we label modernism and post-modernism seeking to define and enshrine their abstract notions as if life and larger issues did not exist.

Tisala held that the main use of philosophy is to enable us to analyse and distinguish reality and value with clarity, and to apply ethics and morals to life and the issues of our times. I remember the impact on my mind when he first said of racism, that if philosophy were properly taught, racism in the future should increasingly decline. For racism, which he called 'your age-old inter-human scourge,' arises out of biological ignorance, and the state of our biological knowledge is such that it is impossible for any man still to be a racist, unless he is ignorant. And the philosophers should master sufficient biology to clarify such ethical truths, so teachers can pass them on to the world.

Tisala said that he found similar obstacles in many subjects: that our way of dividing knowledge to aid learning too often merely fragmented it; that in close focus the amount of information studied is out of all proportion to the knowledge won; and that the blind alleys of past beliefs and gropings for knowledge are like an endless maze, which when finally followed land us near the beginning, but worn out, like many children at the end of schooling.

But I said, rather indignantly, that we valued learning highly. It distinguished us from other animals. The loss of learning was to be deplored, like the sad instance of a great house, where the lead roofs had gone, so rain ran down the inside walls and the backs of bookcases turning the old leather-bound books of a former bishop into pulp, fit only to be shovelled into wheelbarrows.

But Tisala said: 'You rightly lament the loss of knowledge. But what was lost? From what you told me previously much would be the long agonies of holy men in the frightened confines of medieval minds, in fear of a god of wrath, of judgement and everlasting hellfire, countering these inventions by desperate belief in intervention by supernatural power, dead saints or holy relics. Faith and superstition, without knowledge, are too close allies; and without wisdom will still unleash much misery in the world, through the cruel callousness of your species.'

Scholars he thought must re-state for their own times such parts of earlier works as may still hold value. Otherwise, the accumulation will grow endlessly, the useful buried and lost in the dusty museum of time, till the young, coming into it, are put off or shut out from whole rooms of history and experience. From my descriptions of our sometimes troubled societies, he knew that many young people reject learning and wider knowledge in favour of what is immediate, and so are condemned to live in small worlds, often of urban decay within our sprawling cities.

Beware ignorance from within, I thought; we are the barbarians. Perhaps this is how civilisations decline before breaking up. For many, life is raw, of immediate sensations, whether of drudgery, violence, or sex, or from some new fragmentary creed, or cult of music, drugs or drink, which can become the limit of their world.

Tisala said: 'It seems obvious to me as an outsider that the necessary conditions for the preservation of civilised human society are sufficient peace, wealth, knowledge and wisdom, and the freedom and means to spread them.'

He saw that mankind should value learning from the past, but that it must be interpreted and sifted. 'Nor is it sufficient for the young to cling to the limitations of their parents' culture. Wise teachers and interpreters are required, linking not dividing, knowledge. And such teachers where they exist should be much honoured in your society.'

He said, 'Education should be like one of your well kept gardens, which are conceived by vision but only created, maintained and extended by hard-working gardeners. In your societies everyone, in one way or another, should feel they can contribute to the garden.'

I noticed that Tisala, when he wanted to impart some order and wholeness to human affairs, often used the imagery of gardens, which he said, in a lighter moment, might compensate us in a very limited way for our lack of oceanic freedom. For with their sonic view Blue Whales live in and can visualise the gardens of the sea across hundreds of miles, and even round the curvature of the Earth.

When Tisala spoke about education, I saw across the ages the bright hope of civilisations, and afterwards their later confusion, decay and overthrow. In our century, I thought of the endless political and economic tracts, the ranting bile of racism and envy of nationalists, communists and fascists – sometimes whole nations in thrall to dogmatic, grotesque stupidity; and of the purges, executions, mass murders and wars that followed, the folly of men in power leading to colossal ruin and destruction. In the twentieth century it has taken decades and many millions of lives, among them those of my father and two uncles, to rescue freedom and peace.

And still, in the early 1960s, as Ellie and I worked with Tisala on that rocky island shore on the ocean-edge of Europe, the future for a world armed with nuclear weapons looked more dangerous than ever. Though the immediate crisis, in Cuba that time, had passed, the dire threat of nuclear obliteration hung over the world. But for the moment we lived, and could strive to understand our existence.

CHAPTER 25

The Advance of Death

But before anything else I should say what happened in whaling and to Tisala and his family from the Second World War to the time that Tisala came to me.

I knew from him that the years of peace to 1945 had been a good time for the whales. Tisala's life companion Sayli had been pregnant with her first child in 1939 – they had decided in the face of all the slaughter of the proceeding years that there must be new life. By the time of the birth in April 1940, though they did not know it, the years of peace had begun. A few months later they took the new child south from the subtropics to the Antarctic summer. They found the seas empty of whaling ships. Slowly, as the months went by, their apprehension dissolved into the joy of a family free to live without fear and see the growth of their child as in the old days. They had a second child immediately: that is to say two years later (for the cycle of birth and nursing takes about two years), and a third in 1944.

Across the oceans the Blue Whales heard reassuring messages from each other, of parents and young who lived. And their numbers very slowly began to grow. It was a time of hope and young parenthood. They did not know that huge armies were closing in on Berlin, or that bombs of painstaking and ingenious iniquity would soon be dropped on two cities in Japan, and that the peace would soon be over.

I told Tisala that, in 1944, in anticipation of the end of the War, there was a meeting of the allied whaling nations. After the War, the fourteen competing whaling nations met in Washington. They eyed each other suspiciously for they feared that the resumption of whaling would result in the return of the competitive destruction of what they called 'stocks' – the number of whales available to be killed – and with it their investments. Their meeting, tellingly called the International Convention for the Regulation of Whaling, set up the International Whaling Commission to prevent all the whales being killed at once, in the interest of the continuation of whaling. Their aim was to control the free-for-all slaughter of the pre-war years to preserve enough whales each year 'to make possible the orderly development of the industry.'

'So no conservation,' said Tisala, 'but regulation of killing. But to us there didn't even appear to be any regulation, because when the whalers reappeared in 1946, and even more in the following year, we remaining Blue Whales were hunted with renewed single-minded efficiency.'

He remembered several occasions when the hunters went straight past groups of Fin Whales – who were much more numerous than they – and deliberately singled them out. The small increase in their numbers during the peace years was quickly destroyed and with it many young hopes and families.

I explained to Tisala that any hope for conservation had been falsified. The truth is that the International Whaling Commission, the IWC, was the forum of a gang of whalers. And for many years afterwards they ran it so that the letters 'IWC' became dreaded by all who knew the real position.

In 1945, as after previous wars, there were great food shortages. The demand for edible oil for margarine soared. There were large profits to be made. The whaling fleets were rebuilt and more nations joined in. There was no attempt to conserve specific species, even the most hard-pressed – the Blues and the Humpbacks. And the Blues were the biggest and most profitable. They therefore remained the most desirable to be hunted and killed.

The Commission simply applied an overall quota of whales to be 'taken' annually. This was measured in the infamous 'Blue Whale unit'. The Blue Whale unit measured all whales thus: a Blue was 'worth' two Fins, two-and-a-half Humpbacks, and so on according to the size of other species. There was no limit within that total for any particular species. Everyone therefore wanted to hunt Blues as the quickest and easiest way to fulfil their catch before the quota total was reached. There was no enforcement even of this total: the only sanction was that fear of everyone else cheating would keep the cheats within bounds. The quotas themselves, as earlier, were set at absurdly high levels.

But in addition some countries, led by the USA, insisted on having a right of objection to even these quotas. If a country objected, the quotas did not apply to the objecting country. The free-for-all could continue under the guise of regulation. Year after year, in the face of information of ever-increased scarcity of the Blue Whales, the Commission scientists suggested caution in quota setting. Year after year, the members overruled them. They consistently took the view that they would assume there were plenty until the contrary was proved; and even then they were not in the slightest bit concerned with the fate of any particular species, let alone the whales – families or individuals – themselves. They supported research programmes, but only to support their greedy hope that enough whales would be left to reproduce sufficiently to sustain their killing programme. If not, they shrugged their shoulders and moved on to other species. As usual, the Norwegians took the lead in all this. But they were to be increasingly challenged and eventually overtaken in the coming years by newer whaling nations.

'This competitive killing,' I told Tisala, 'is why you Blue Whales are being hunted to extinction.'

I looked up the 'official' figures for this period and Ellie made a graph. In 1947, to my dismay, the Commission recorded about 9,000 Blues killed. Thereafter the figures show a steepening downward curve: a decade later – in 1957 – the catch, despite all their efforts, was about 1,700. The dreadful truth was clear: the end of the Blue Whales was rapidly approaching. But, as before, the virtual elimination of one species did not mean the end of whaling: the whalers simply turned their attention to the next most convenient species. So the Fin Whales, and afterwards the Sperm Whales and then the Sei Whales, increasingly bore the brunt of the slaughter. By that means the whaling ships kept whaling, and where they could find Blues, they killed them.

Tisala said: 'It was the beginning of the end years to which we have come. Within that decade five sixths of our numbers had gone. And still they chased us – and do still chase us – although the number of deaths now is small, for in all the world's oceans there are less than 2,000 of us left, scattered and hiding where we can.'

'So few?' I said, appalled. And I felt in my mind that something was wrong; that there should have been more; and then I knew that the whalers were even more evil than I had supposed. The final figures will never be known, but I came to believe that about 10,000

Blues in those years were taken unrecorded, to disguise the grossness of the whalers' crime against them. Total genocide stared at us from the graph.

But Tisala said, 'All that is left is about 1,000 of us in the Southern Ocean, and a few hundred in each of the North Pacific and the North Atlantic. In the last years there has been some transmigration. We realised there was much less whaling in the north, and though the families were few, some left the south for the north. But these were now lonely journeys, full of the unknown. And wherever we hide they know we have to go to the feeding grounds, and they lie in wait.'

I thought of the vast oceans of the world. I saw in my inward eye the empty seas and the desolation in my friend's mind. And I hated the cruel folly of men.

After a pause, Ellie asked, 'What happened to your three children?'

Tisala was silent. Then he said, 'Our eldest son, whose birth gave us such pleasure, died a terrible death over a day and a night. His blood coloured the sea for fifteen miles.' He paused. I saw he was reliving that loss. He did not enlarge, and it was some years before I heard the full story.

He said: 'Our daughter had the light markings of our family. I never knew what happened to her – how she died. We had scattered in an alarm. After a while I thought we had all escaped. We heard her calls from about twenty miles off, when the danger should have passed, and we began to swim in a long arc which would bring us together some sixty miles on. But then we heard four explosions from her direction. We heard her call after the first two, but then she ceased to call. We continued to call her hoping she had fallen silent as a stratagem. But we all knew. We swam in a great circle still trying to hope. Sayli continued to call her for several hours. But then I told her to stop because she was simply distressing herself. We never heard from our daughter again.

We were left with our little one. He was killed the next year. Mercifully his death was quick – they chased him for about three miles. He was in mid-call when there was a single explosion, and immediate silence.' Tisala sighed again, 'He was a lovely child, cheerful and mischievous. We were distraught – we swam close together for comfort of each other. We had lost all of our children, one after the other. None of them reached ten years old. Each time we had a child we thought they would reach adulthood and take our place, and each time they were blown apart; and I, who would have died for any of them, could not save them or die in their place.

After that Sayli lost heart and would have no more children. She could not face the anguish of more birth and death. For four years I did not trouble her. But eventually I argued for hope, that something might change, that more peace years might come, and if there were children there was hope. Otherwise there was none. And then, in answer to my wish, about eight years ago she became pregnant once more and we had a boy child.'

Ellie looked at me, but neither of us wanted to ask the question.

'Yes, he is alive. He is my future.'

'But where... when you are here?' asked Ellie.

'He swims with his cousin. It is to secure their future that I have come to you.'

Ellie said gently, 'And Sayli?'

'Five years ago we were swimming south after a summer in the Arctic. Sayli was carrying our fifth child and was near to delivery. We should have been out of the danger zone, but a lone boat came across us further south, hunting for Fin whales. We split and dived. She was to turn and head back under the oncoming whaler. I determined to show myself further south to divert them. I knew that they would chase me and try and kill me and I remembered my grandfather. But I was determined not to die. I surfaced to show myself clearly, and then headed away at full plunge. But then I heard the ship's engine slow, and when I curved to the surface I saw it heading back towards where Sayli would surface after her long dive. I felt a stab of horror, and turned and plunged back towards her. How had they known that she had gone under them?'

'Sonar,' I said. 'By now they had sonar.'

Tisala said: 'Yes, but then it was new and we did not know. Afterwards we came to recognise their sound and knew they had copied our echo-bouncing technique. They had located Sayli and knew where she would surface. She never had time to recover. They gave chase at full speed. I was still a little way off, but tried to come in close to offer myself. Before I could get there they caught Sayli. I think that they could see she was labouring. I saw the harpoon on its snaking line hit her on the side behind her head just by her wing. I heard the thump of the explosion and saw her side explode out in a shower of red. "No!" I bellowed, distraught.

'But still she swam with all her might, her great flukes driving her forward. She must have heard my bellow through her agony, for as I came up with her, she cried out in distress "No! no! – go!". She knew she was doomed, yet even at that moment wanted above all that I should live. But I would not go. Then I heard a second ship approaching. It flashed through my mind that this was the end for us all – Sayli, me, our unborn child, and the future generations who would not be.

'But then a strange thing happened. The hunting boat changed course and started to head away still going at speed. The second ship changed course to keep towards the whaler. I saw that the second ship was long and grey, not like a whaler. The noise of the propellers grew further away. Sayli had slowed to a crawl. A plume of blood flowed from her ruined side where her wing had been – gone except for a trailing remnant. The harpoon had hit it and gone through, but only partly penetrated her body. I rested against and underneath her to support her. She was giving little shuddering movements. And then I felt our child twisting and jerking. Our child was alive! Alive! I felt a second of hope. But as the jerking and writhing continued, I knew it was wrong. And realised that our little one must have been hit by pieces of shrapnel, and was dying in agony, trapped in the body of her mother before any chance of birth, for it was not yet her time.

'The engines of the ships went away and we were left wallowing in the sea. Our child lived for about an hour, but the movements became weaker, then she was still. Sayli gave a great groan. But she did not die then. She had to wait to die of loss of blood. I changed positions several times and sought to comfort her, but I was crying inside. For several hours – I don't know how long – the blood continued to pour from her ghastly wounds, but gradually she got weaker, and the worst pain gave way to creeping numbness and she was calm in approaching death. She told me she couldn't feel her left side. She said, "I'm sorry, sorry. You have lost your child. I couldn't get away. I tried. I tried."

'"Ssh, ssh. You are my beloved, and I am with you."

'A little later she said, "When I am gone, go far away and live where we were happy." Near the end she said, "How strange not to be with you. I shall rest, and the sea will carry me down on the long dive. But after a while you must not be sad." And then: "I think I am going."

'Soon after, she stopped breathing. I could not hold her, and she started on her journey into the deep. For two weeks I swam south in a desultory way, crying for my love and half hoping that a whaling ship would come across me and release me from my misery so I need do no more. But I saw no ship.

'I spent that winter alone in the warm seas. It was the first time in my life I had been all alone. But gradually into my grieving came other thoughts and the flicker of the will to live. And anger. Why should these savage little humans exterminate our kind and peaceful race from the oceans? What is their purpose? Why?

'And gradually, I began to form a plan. I knew from my contacts with men, and from what I had heard, that not all humans hunted whales. And I began to think what could be done – what new thing could be done – to save our small remaining numbers. I thought, my son must have our children now that Sayli is gone; and that I was released from that responsibility. A different responsibility began to seep into my thoughts.'

Tisala paused in his story. 'Well, you know what I eventually concluded, and what happened.'

'You found David,' said Ellie in a thin voice. Although she was very quiet, she had now heard so much of death, she didn't weep.

But in bed that night, as we spoke of Tisala's story and clung together for comfort there were tears in her eyes when she said, 'We have got to stop the killing, David. I don't know how, but we must.' And as I held her, I felt the gathering of huge responsibilities, winging their way through the night from all the oceans of the world towards our little cottage on Inis Cuan. And the strange thing was, I was not afraid or overawed, but welcomed them with a sort of fierce determination, even exhilaration.

That was in 1963. In the next two years the survival of the Blue Whales hung in the balance.

CHAPTER 26

The Beginning of the End?

First I had to arm myself with knowledge of the International Whaling Commission's activities. Back in London I began to research and read the IWC reports. In their own terms – bringing some semblance of regulation to the slaughter of whales – there was discussion, especially from their scientific advisors, of conservation, lowering quotas, shortening hunting seasons, and designating protected areas for Blue Whales. There was an air of reasonableness about their whale 'management', though their aim was only to preserve the whalers' own future.

But all this was in glaring contradiction of Tisala's damning account of a continuing genocide of Blue Whales up to that time – 1963. Soon, even from the Commission's own reports and figures, a different picture began to emerge. From the standpoint of real conservation, I became convinced that the Commission's activity since the war had been a charade.

At the beginning, in 1946, the Commission set the overall Antarctic quota at 16,000 Blue Whale units. This figure was loosely based on the large average figures from years before, including the heyday of the great slaughter, which, because of the subsequent killing, were grossly misleading, especially regarding the remaining number of Blues and Humpbacks. That set the ominous pattern for the next twenty years. I told Tisala how this disastrous position had arisen.

In a political decision in 1950, the IWC voted not to come within the ambit of the United Nations, as earlier proposed. Thus, any possible 'interference' by any non-whaling nations was removed. The Commission became a closed society of whalers running whaling for their own commercial profit. But the International Whaling Convention setting up the Commission had given them a cloak of respectability. The result was that national governments regarded the IWC as the body responsible for regulating whaling. For the next fateful twenty years they left them to it. It was like appointing serial murderers to be guardians of public safety.

I discovered that the underlying Convention itself was seriously flawed. The rules on the management of whaling were laid down in the Schedule to the Convention. And the Commission had the power to change it without reference to the Convention's signatory governments. At their first meeting in 1949, the Commission lifted the previous Convention ban on hunting Humpbacks in Antarctic sanctuary areas. This set the precedent. Despite frequent warnings from their own scientists that 'stocks' were in danger, the whaling members gave themselves the benefit of the doubt in setting the quotas. Whenever the evidence for the extent of falling numbers was not absolutely conclusive (which it never was because there was no method of counting the whales in the seas), caution was deferred to making current profits.

Tisala had enquired why endangered species, such as his own, were not more protected, even if only to ensure sufficient numbers for killing in later years. But now we knew the reasons for the continued deliberate priority targeting of Blues: their size and value under the Blue Whale unit quotas. Oil from a Blue Whale was the equivalent to that of five Sperm Whales or six Sei Whales, and involved only one catch. Those ratios, together with whalers' total indifference to the extinction of any one species meant that everyone still went first for Blue Whales.

Tisala wanted to know why the scientists, whom I confirmed knew the position with increasing clarity as each year went by, did not prevail upon the national whaling members to stop the over-killing which must inevitably lead to the collapse of their 'industry'. He said this word in a strange way as if he found it beyond belief that such genocide should merely be regarded as an industrial by-product, and that human governments should allow such a thing.

I told him that it was clear from the records that the scientists had made recommendations to the contrary. But they were up against rules which were framed to protect whalers' interests. The right of individual members to object to and override any quota proposal of the Commission became notorious. Tisala asked why such a rule existed in the first place. I told him that without it some of the nations would not otherwise have joined. The United States had insisted on the inclusion of the opt-out rule to safeguard what they then viewed as their own commercial interests. The dubious honour of being the first to use this self-seeking exemption fell to the French at the very first meeting in 1949. They objected to a proposed restriction on the use of factory ships. Similarly, in 1951, Australia objected to proposed restrictions on Sperm Whales being treated at land stations, because that would have affected Australian whaling profits. Of course, the nations that hunted exclusively at sea were happy to pass that proposal as it was irrelevant to them. The use to which the quota objection rule was put in latter years, especially by the Norwegians, Russians and Japanese became appalling for its ruthless exploitation, promoting the continuing genocide of some species, and most alarmingly of all, the Blues. That, I told Tisala, is how it has continued. The Commission has fiddled round the edges, occasionally moving or marginally shortening the hunting season or setting up inadequate so-called 'protected areas'. But always the principle applied that each national whaling fleet voted so that nothing should seriously interfere with their own killing.

As more nations were entering whaling, there was increasing pressure on each nation's 'share'. They each sought to maximise their 'take' by deliberately catching Blues before making up the quota by taking the still comparatively numerous Fin Whales. As these in turn began to decline, they supplemented the catch with Sperm Whales, the remnant of the Humpbacks and then the smaller Sei Whales. For a few years, they managed in this way to sustain the main bulk of whale catches. But they were heedless of the approaching extinction of the Blues and Humpbacks.

In 1952, for the first time, despite the determined efforts of the whalers, the quota had not been reached. There were not enough whales left. In alarm the scientific committee at last recommended a drop in the quota from 16,000 to 14,000 Blue Whale units. But the Commission rejected this and set the overall quota at 15,500. Moreover, they rejected any idea of quota by separate species.

I reported to Tisala that by 1954 there should have been better news for the Blue Whales. In that year, the scientists were so alarmed that they recommended a complete ban on hunting Blues in the North Atlantic, the North Pacific and the Southern Oceans outside Antarctica. To the surprise of some, the recommendation was adopted.

But the only two nations that relied on hunting Blues in the North Atlantic were Denmark and Iceland. Both objected, so the North Atlantic ban was a dead letter. Similarly, the only whaling nations that hunted Blues in the North Pacific were the United States, Japan, the USSR and Canada. All of them objected: the formal ban was therefore in effect null and void. As a publicity exercise, the Commission could say to the outside world that they had passed these bans. It gave the impression of responsible action. But it was a complete and cruel deception, further demonstrated by the Commission's refusal to pass the proposed ban on killing Blues in the Southern Oceans, and their refusal to lower the Antarctic quota for the following year.

'So, during these years, all round the world one by one, we were all being killed,' said Tisala heavily. He sighed, remembering. I could sense the weight of his sadness.

'And all to provide what are now inessential products or trivial luxury goods at the behest of a group of men who are cruel, greedy and deceitful; and this is facilitated by the inaction of governments and the indifference of the rest of mankind. For this our society and wisdom, the achievement of our creation in the oceans, is to disappear.'

He thought for a moment and then said: 'If men will do that to us, what will they not do to lesser species across the world?' He saw the enormity of the task: to engage and change the minds of men. And added: 'This will not happen voluntarily among the ignorant, selfish and wicked, but only if they are restrained by the more enlightened part of mankind.' He mused silently and then added: 'But first finish your account of these last few years.'

I said, 'That hunting season – 1954-55 – the total number of Blue Whales killed fell again, but only because they couldn't find enough of you, although they still hunted for you everywhere. The next year the scientists, in the face of the falling figures, recommended a limit of 1,250 Blue Whales to be taken in the Antarctic. They commented that "the Blue Whales' powers of recovery might already be found to be largely lost, even if they received total protection".'

Tisala said: 'So they knew. What was the Commission's response this time?'

'Breathtakingly devious. Because the actual catch had again fallen below the quota, they decided, on the recommendation of the scientists, to open the limited part of the Antarctic that had previously declared a sanctuary to Blue Whales; the specious argument being that this would relieve the pressure on whale populations elsewhere.'

'That was the season that they killed Sayli and our unborn child.' He breathed out and made a slight sound, as if he were reliving the pain of it.

Then he said, with something in his tone of quiet anger, 'Didn't the scientists know that their whaling masters would grasp this recommendation while ignoring the accompanying recommendation to limit numbers?' I was about to answer when he said, 'You will tell me the scientists thought, as it seems they often do, that their specialist knowledge would put them in charge of its use.'

'If they did, they deluded themselves, or were covertly complicit for political reasons. You understand us all too well, and you are right. And at the same session of the Commission, the whaling nations also refused to accept their scientists' suggestions that separate quotas for Blues and Humpbacks should be set; they rescinded the ban on hunting North Pacific Blues; and, although they trimmed the actual total whaling quota by a small amount, this was only because they knew they would not find enough whales to reach that target anyway. This is also why they passed a further nominal reduction by 500 units in the quota for the year after. But even this token gesture was too much for the member countries that then represented the great bulk of the whaling industry. Formal objections were entered by Norway, Britain, the USA, the USSR, Japan, the Netherlands and Panama. Thus the small drop in the total Antarctic quota set by the Commission for 1956-57 did not apply to a single nation that actually had a whaling fleet in Antarctica.'

Tisala said quietly, 'It ought to be unbelievable.'

'We do not need to go on – '

'I wish to know. It is my task to know.'

So I had to tell him how the misery has gone on. Each year, the Commission has voted down, or its affected members have objected to, any serious curtailment of their slaughter. In 1958 – only five years before the time when we were speaking – another marginal drop in the Antarctic quota was passed, but objected to once again by every single Antarctic whaling country. Among the Blues the result was the death of over another 1,000 in Antarctica alone that season – a catastrophe leaving few remaining Blues.

'They all know there is an impending crisis,' I said, 'and part of it surfaced the next year. Really, the stage had been reached when internal rivalry for a profitable share of the whales available had become uncontainable. Norway and the Netherlands left the Commission. They would now be bound by none of its rules, such as they were. Japan too threatened to leave. The Commission, to persuade them not to, and to placate remaining members, hastily passed a number of indefensible proposals. Despite the plight of the whales, the hunting season was both extended and brought forward. They knew, for the scientists had pointed it out, that this would result in an increase in deaths of pregnant females. The Antarctic quota was actually increased. The effect was, adding in the quotas Norway and the Netherlands set for themselves, that three years ago – the 1959-60 season – the overall quota was higher than any previously set since the Second World War. The Commission had come a full circle: its own survival was seen as more important than the aims stated in the Convention to "protect all species of whale from further over-fishing".'

'So "fishing" was embedded in the Convention,' said Tisala.

'Fishing or whaling – it was greed, profits and genocide by whatever name,' I said.

'Is it not obvious even to them that we are nearly finished and their industry must soon collapse,' asked Tisala. 'They must know, from the evidence of their own eyes that there were scarcely any old whales left and that they were killing children and pregnant mothers.'

'Oh, yes. On their own figures, four years ago over half the Blue Whales killed were what they termed "immature".'

'Our children,' said Tisala. 'They intend to finish us.'

I said in some desperation: 'The truth is, despite their protestations to the contrary, they simply do not care – any whale will do – but Blues are best – to reach their target and support their profits.' I drew breath and stated the stark reality: 'The dreadful position is that there will be enough whales of other species left to enable whaling to survive enough years to ensure the extinction of your kind.'

That was a very low point. Tisala was silent in thought. After a silence so long I became aware of the lapping water of the inlet, Tisala said: 'Now I am going out to sea.'

And afterwards, when I thought of it, I began to despair. There's not enough time – they will be overwhelmed – finished – how do we stop it: How? And images of beautiful Blues being destroyed, explosions of red blood disfiguring the seas kept recurring in my mind by day, and in my dreams by night.

When we resumed Tisala said: 'It will come down to a question of timing.'

And continued calmly, 'Now we know more, our evasive actions may give us a few seasons. In that time, you, David, and those who can help, must urgently seek to change minds.'

And sometimes the news seemed to be marginally better. It was clear there was disquiet within the Commission, and mounting criticism from the outside world was concerning them. Occasional anti-whaling articles had appeared in the press, and were now becoming more frequent and insistent.

I reported further developments: 'They are at last becoming sensitive to criticism, but their response does not augur well. They have decided that reports of the Commission meetings should no longer be publicly available and nor should quotations from them permitted in the Press. They intend to cloak their future activities. They know their industry must collapse, but are trying to gain another few years without interference, which would give them additional returns on their existing investments. A couple of years ago they set up another scientific committee – "to investigate stocks and make recommendations".'

'Was this not always the scientists' function?'

'Yes, but another committee looks like fresh action and buys them time. Still, they are at last clearly worried about the future. This new committee – the Committee of the Three Scientists – has recommended that the Antarctic season for hunting Blues should be shortened and certain Antarctic areas closed altogether. But these proposals are a grossly inadequate response to their own conclusion that any real recovery of Blue Whale stock now requires a period of total protection in the Antarctic.'

'The idea is at least a start,' said Tisala, who always sought some sign of hope. 'They have given proof they know that wrong is being perpetrated, and that exposes them to pressure.'

'Yes, but they were only suggesting a period of two or three years protection: just enough time for your few remaining adults to have a single child. Hopelessly inadequate – they would all be slaughtered within a season.' I became angry. 'Spineless folly among the scientists – they have the knowledge, but refuse to take up any wider responsibilities.' No doubt,' I added, 'as they are employed by the Commission they feel the need to preserve their jobs; and doubtless will argue that they must keep their jobs to provide at least some restraint on the members; and that any more radical proposals would have been rejected outright. But their proposals were rejected anyway. If the scientists had any real sense of responsibility – even for the long term future of their bloody "industry" – let alone any higher aspirations – they would have spoken up in completely different terms.'

'So what did the Commission decide next?'

'They refused to grant any protection at all to you Blue Whales, and merely put back the opening of the hunting season by a few days. It made no real difference at all – in the preceding years the technology of the hunting ships had improved considerably – they can kill more of you in a shorter time providing they can find the victims. Anyway, once again all the whaling nations affected lodged formal objections: Japan, the UK, the USSR and Norway (who rejoined the Commission just in time to lodge their objection). Again, the result was that the shortened hunting season applied to not a single nation with a whaling fleet in Antarctica.'

'It is dismaying,' said Tisala quietly.

'Huh! Do you know what else the Commission did? They abolished the Antarctic quota altogether for the 1960-61 season – just two years ago.'

'With terrible results for us. What figures did they admit to?'

I said, 'The official figures are just over 1,700 Blues killed – of which over 70 percent were immature.'

'I know we lost many of our remaining children,' said Tisala, 'but I do not understand the figure – it is impossible – there were not so many of us.'

When I investigated the figures further, it seemed that for a few years the numbers had included the killing of so-called Pygmy Blue Whales. These were smaller cousins of the Blues, who frequented the Indian Ocean and never came so far south as the Antarctic waters proper. Because that was area of the Southern Oceans least visited by the Blues and Fins, the Pygmies had for a number of years avoided the main slaughter. Now they in turn were being decimated, largely by the Japanese. And outrageously, the inclusion of their numbers enabled the Commission to argue that there must be more Blue Whales left than in reality there were.

Tisala said: 'From soundings that I had gathered in two years ago, I believe our worldwide numbers then were below 3,000. And in these last two years we have lost a half of those – we are less than 1,500. I fear that I have come too late.'

I did not say so, but I thought blackly that his conclusion might prove true, for I knew from the last Commission meeting, held in London just a year before this conversation that the news was bad. Although the scientists had at last become sufficiently alarmed and bold enough to propose the first really radical drop in quota ever – to between 5 and 7,000 Blue Whale units, the Commission obdurately resolved to leave the quota unchanged at 15,000. And there were no proposals whatever to provide any protection for the tiny numbers of remaining Blues. The cold truth dawned on me. So far as the Commission and the whaling nations were concerned, Blue Whales could be hunted to extinction: they saw no point in trying to protect them any more, because their scarcity had made them commercially unimportant.

I felt horribly oppressed. The great darkness was engulfing us. I almost believed that in another two or three years, the greatest animal ever to live in our planet, perhaps in the knowable universe, would be finished, gone for ever.

CHAPTER 27

The Struggle

That was the dire position reached in 1963, two years after Tisala first spoke to us. Humanity's feeble attempts to regulate the inhumane practice of whaling had almost totally failed. The result was the death and destruction of wonderful individuals, the devastation and ripping apart of whole families and societies, and the imminent extinction of the magnificent Blue Whales. For my part, I could scarcely believe the repulsiveness of the whaling industry, and long before these revelations were complete, Ellie and I had become determined to help save the whales. We began our campaign in earnest.

But the International Whaling Commission did not of course itself hunt whales. That was done by the commercial whaling fleets of its member countries. What had been happening in the whaling industry was this. The massive pre-war dominance of the Norwegian fleets in the 1930s was at first only in any way rivalled by the British and, in the late 1930s, by the Japanese. After the Second World War, for 15 years, the Norwegians again dominated the slaughter. The British, and on a lesser scale, the Dutch, sought to rebuild their whaling fleet, but the British never regained even half of its pre-war size, and by the end of the 1950s it was dwindling. But meanwhile, the Japanese became increasingly dominant, followed by a new whaling power, the Soviet Union. By about 1960, the year Tisala came to me, the Japanese overtook the Norwegians as the owners of the largest whaling fleet. And soon after, the Soviet fleet was on a par with Norway's. Other nations, in the face of increasing scarcity of the great whales, gradually dropped out of the Antarctic hunting.

By the time of my campaigning involvement I was able to report to Tisala that, in the Antarctic at least, South Africa and Panama had ceased to hunt, the British were down to one factory ship, and the Dutch appeared to be about to sell their remaining factory ship. But these ships were not disappearing. The Dutch, the British and even the Norwegians were selling their factory ships to the Japanese. The threat to whales was shifting not diminishing. And the Russians were building. Although the number of factory ships after the Second World War never became quite as numerous as before, the factory ships then built were huge and with vast capacity for processing harpooned whales. The Soviets had recently produced the two biggest whaling ships ever seen in the world – in 1959 and 1961. And increased capacity was accompanied by bigger, faster and more numerous catcher vessels to hunt down and kill the remaining whales of all species. And to recover their investment costs both Japan and the Soviet Union sought to do everything they could to twist and bend the regulations of the IWC to their advantage; and where they could not, to flout them. Thus, they kept their whaling enterprises going, to the endless agony of the whales, and brought the Blues to the edge of extinction.

I did not then know how much of the next two years we should spend campaigning against this grotesque activity. That battle came to dominate the lives of our little group, but most of all, Ellie's and mine.

We knew we held a unique key: our knowledge of Tisala and his kind, the gentle, wise giants of the oceans; with mankind the most intelligent animal in the planet. But the question of whether and how such knowledge might be used perplexed and worried me constantly. On the one hand, I was bubbling over with excitement and ideas: surely the whalers – or at any rate their scientists – would have their views transformed by what I could reveal. And if, despite all reason, they would not listen, press and public support might be enlisted, governments might legislate, and whaling at last be stopped in its tracks.

But on the other hand, I knew from the earlier history how implacably the organised whaling industry would fight to retain its slaughterhold on profits. If I told them about Tisala and the advanced nature of Blue Whales they would demand proof and scientific 'testing', under their control, by which they would mean the opportunity to discredit my claims. To counter this, I would be obliged to reveal the location and workings of Inis Cuan. And that I dreaded. They would solemnly pronounce that, as the world's main whale research institution, they had never previously found convincing evidence of whale linguistic ability. (Though they had never researched the matter, and as every one of the thousands of whales their scientists had investigated was already dead, such a conclusion might have been anticipated.) They would take months to make a formal response, saying they needed time to evaluate my evidence. They would talk of setting up a special committee, and delay it by wrangling over its terms of reference. Members would use the ploy of threatening to leave the Commission, to prevent which the Commission would suggest a special conference… in the spring, or autumn, this year, next year… And then we would smilingly be told there were organisational difficulties. And all the time, whales would continue to be killed – perhaps with renewed urgency, for the whalers would feel the tide turning against them. It might all be too late for the Blue Whales. I imagined Tisala as the last Blue Whale left to swim alone in the oceans for a few years – for I refused to imagine this wonderful animal being killed by a foul harpoon. I pictured him, by some skill or wisdom, surviving. But in the back of my mind I knew the reality.

Our little group – me, Ellie, Robert, Eric, and Guinevere – discussed the alternative option of revealing our findings to the government. Surely, our argument ran, the government would protect our work, protect the whales. But this notion soon evaporated when we considered the long years of government indifference. Initially, there would be sympathy, but when it came to action, various difficulties would arise: we would have to understand this was the Commission's area of responsibility; there was the structure of the industry and unemployment to consider; there was the problem of parliamentary time; and we realised, did we not, that we were asking for an international treaty. We began to realise the government might not even be benign. They might demand – might even impose – not just access, but control, 'in the national interest,' of our sanctuary at Inis Cuan. And what of the military? The Ministry of Defence would be interested – worldwide cetacean communication, they would say, could be vital to increase national security in the Cold War balance of terror. But despite all these fears, I argued that the terminal crisis for the Blue whales demanded that immediate action – and risks – be taken. And so late into the evening round the kitchen table on Eilean Mòr as night and the arguments closed in about us, the debate went backwards and forwards.

In the end, Tisala settled the argument. 'All you fear is probably true,' he said. 'If the whalers knew of this haven, they would track me going north and hunt me down. They would seek to destroy me, the living evidence of our intelligence.'

One night when I could not sleep I saw a lone whaling ship in the North Atlantic mist, tracking a single Blue Whale. He used every turn and stratagem to escape his persecutors. He most urgently did not want to die, for this whale carried in his mind whole worlds of precious knowledge that his pursuers neither dreamed of nor comprehended. If he could evade them long enough they might give up the chase, or be seen by another ship and sheer off, for what they were doing was illegal – forbidden even by their own community and regulations. But he knew that with their powerful engines and their sonar, the whalers in the end would run him to exhaustion. In my mind's eye I saw them hunt him down. And flinched with horror as the loathsome harpoon struck him, and again as the heavy grenade exploded within him, and the sea erupted in an ineradicable red stain, and darkness fell on the eyes of the ocean. Afterwards, if challenged, the whalers would say it was a terrible mistake; that unfortunately an inexperienced harpooner had taken a Blue Whale for another sort.

Tisala said one day: 'I must stay alive to be of wider use. I cannot yet fulfil my task.' Even then I did not immediately understand that he was thinking beyond saving his own kind to the reformation of mankind and the preservation of the Earth.

So it was agreed in the end that I would not make any immediate disclosure about Tisala. We would pursue our cause in other ways. Initially I was to direct my campaigning efforts at the British whaling industry, the IWC and its Scientific Committee. As it happened, the 1963 IWC meeting was due to be held in London. I wrote to the British representatives and was eventually granted a meeting with them.

Before my first meeting I was nervous, but determined, and armed myself with all the up to date information and statistics to back up my own knowledge. The figures cried out against the continued hunting of the Blue Whales, and the other great whales. But I knew that to persuade them they would have to be given a viable alternative.

To start with I was quite well received in a public relations sort of way. They wanted to indulge this unknown young biologist intent on cetacean research. But their welcome was too cheerfully fulsome for the business in hand: it felt a specious sincerity. Their large comfortable boardroom made me uneasy, for I knew on what it was built.

'Yes Mr Somerset, tell us about your ideas. We always like to listen to academics, though we have to take a practical line ourselves.'

But as I suggested there might be possible new ways of tracking whales through voice and song research I could tell from their glances at each other round the table that they were becoming interested. The idea of listening to whales – their songs, clicks and whistles – to learn about whale society appeared to be entirely novel to them. But they listened attentively. A whiff of self-interested advantage was in the air. But when I eventually suggested that such studies would require a total moratorium on Blue Whale hunting, so their number and social structure could recover, I was met with stony faces.

Outwardly, I was given assurances of their concern. They pointed out that they had provided much of the information on whaling now in the public domain – information and statistics, on stocks, whales taken, estimates of remaining populations, and so on. They claimed credit for efforts to persuade non-member countries to abide by certain restrictions, thought they did not say this was to preserve a bigger share of whales. Much play was made of their scientists' endeavours to study the life cycle of the main species (which they cheerfully acknowledged was done by dissecting and analysing whales which they themselves killed). Their aim – and their scientists' researches were well advanced – was to establish the holy grail of the whale fishery: the magic goal of MSY – Maximum Sustainable Yield. The 'harvesting' should be such as would ensure the long term continuance of the industry. In other words, how many whales they could kill in a season without adversely affecting the numbers available for killing in subsequent seasons. And though their holy grail too was fictitious, this supposedly scientific endeavour cloaked their activities in feigned respectability for many years. But while they accumulated data and statistics, the basis upon which any commercially realistic MSY might have been established was being rapidly destroyed by their members' annual plunder.

That whaling itself was horrible appeared never seriously to have entered their heads, let alone troubled their consciences. And when I confronted them with the suffering and cruelty involved, they fell back on the argument that whales were a natural resource available for exploitation for the benefit of men. One or two laughed rather uncomfortably about the cruelty involved, but they assured me the industry was working on that. They thought that with powerful modern boats the killing rate was quicker, for the whales could be run down to exhaustion more rapidly, and exhausted whales made easier targets, so accurate harpooning is more likely than in earlier days. I reminded them that the explosive harpoon remained much the same, but they said they were working on that too. Electric harpoons were mentioned, but until those were perfected they would have to rely on the heavy explosive harpoon, which had its advantages as it was cheaper. For smaller whales the cold (non-explosive) harpoon held much hope: there was not much left of a little Minke Whale if hit by a great explosive harpoon, but a cold harpoon left more of the whale intact, which helped the whale-meat market, though the killing time could unfortunately be longer.

I did not know it then, but the electric harpoon was never to be perfected, and was quietly abandoned, and it was to be many years before the cruel cold harpoon was finally banned; which has left whaling to this day with the hideous monstrosity invented in the 1890s. The cruelty of any whaling continues unabated.

But to save the Blues without giving myself away, I found myself coolly discussing renewed hunting in due course, when their numbers recovered. And I pressed only for restraint in hunting Humpbacks and other species; for I knew that an appeal to end all whaling would be wholly counterproductive.

I hated myself for employing such arguments when all I wanted was to stop the killing forever. But I found myself compromising, and talking calmly about 'the percentages of immature Blue Whales taken,' when my brain said to me, you are talking about the genocide of Tisala's children. I began to hate these people.

I was not an experienced campaigner, but quickly learned that anything other than an appeal to their self-interest was futile. At one stage when I got carried away and argued that the nobility of the creatures should ensure their protection, I was smilingly told that young men sometimes tended to take a romantic view, but that they were obliged to take the hard scientific view. But when I said I thought that was a misuse of the word 'scientific' the smiling stopped. They intended to kill whales while they could. I argued for alternatives, such as whale watching – almost unheard of in those days – but this was dismissed as commercially insignificant. Killing was a much better prospect. We reached an impasse. But it was decided they would like another meeting. And in the meantime they dismissed me with, 'You had better talk to our scientists,' the implication being that they would straighten up my thinking while investigating my ideas on song and call research. I left the meeting baffled and depressed.

But they did not alter my thinking. Among the scientists, when I met them, I found some sympathy and concern, and I discovered they were constantly trimming their own arguments, assessments and worst fears to meet what they knew would be the intransigent commercial attitude of the representatives of their member nations.

My arguments sent them back to their data. They considered and even once or twice modified their models, their variables and what I knew to be sometimes their guesswork. The truth was that, while the evidence of gross over-whaling was clear and obvious, their information had sufficient gaps and unknowns in the detail to provide the members of the Commission with just sufficient excuses to vote down their scientists' recommendations year after year. I took with me an analysis of their own figures, showing a more alarming reading of the situation than their own conclusions. This was based on my knowledge from Tisala that the rate of reproduction amongst the Blues was less than the scientists supposed, and that the critical point, when survivors were so few among the scattered remnants that extinction became inevitable, was frighteningly close.

I argued for the desperately needed abolition of the Blue Whale unit, and the introduction of species quotas, with a nil quote for Blue Whales. I urged them that scientists had a wider duty, to prevent the extinction of this species in particular, and the other endangered great whales.

The fundamental reason the Commission overrode their scientists' recommendations was that the whaling nations did not care: whales were a free resource, which they would plunder to the end. Their public words did not, but their actions, said: we will kill and take profit while we can.

So arguments were turned on their heads; more hard won sanctuaries were reopened as whales grew scarcer elsewhere, to 'lessen the pressure' on those whales outside the sanctuaries. The resulting plight of the Blues and the Humpbacks was deliberately ignored. The important aim was to keep up the overall level of whales killed. Once, they gave the lie to their solemn talk of 'sustainable whaling' by producing an economic model showing that more profit would accrue if catches were kept at a maximum for a few more years, even if that led inevitably to the wiping out of whales worldwide and the certain eventual collapse of the industry. For otherwise they would be faced with wasting assets and a less profitable gradual decline.

At my second meeting with the IWC representatives I argued for a total ban on taking Blues throughout the world, on the basis of their near extinction, and thus their commercial irrelevance; and that, if they became extinct, the IWC would be open to such public opprobrium that the whole future of the whaling industry might be put in jeopardy.

By their reactions, the Commission spokesmen made clear they thought nothing of public opinion. They were dismissive of public interest in, and understanding of, the whaling industry. They regarded themselves as the experts, who could see off any opposition. But I argued on.

I raised the much talked of 'observer scheme'. The idea was that observers from other nations should go on each other's whaling boats to prevent breaches of rules. The observer scheme had initially been argued for in the 1950s by the Norwegians, which surprised me given their ghastly record until I realised that, as the country with the biggest whaling fleet, Norway had most to lose by others cheating. So now, when Japan had started to support the observer scheme, I was no longer surprised: now with the largest whaling fleet, they had most to gain from compliance among competitors.

I raised the issue of dishonesty: opposition to my approach began to stiffen. I knew from Tisala what had long been the subject of rumour and accusation between whalers – that flouting of the quotas and restrictions took place. Over the years Blues had been secretly killed in covert disregard of the protection the world innocently thought was in place. When I had relayed to Tisala the times and areas of the supposed protection, he had estimated that, in the last two years alone, at least two hundred Blue Whales had died illegally. I knew this for a certainty. Since the entire worldwide population was down to less than 1,500, this continuing illegal murder constituted a deadly threat. I did not mention the source of my knowledge, but when I raised these issues with the Commission, they blustered and said they believed all their members were honourable. It was a feeble show, for I knew in private they accused each other.

None of them cared a thing for the Blue Whales themselves; nor for the idea that they were acting in wilful disregard of the wonderful intricacy of the world's ecology. The two emerging whaling powers – Soviet Russia and Japan – were apparently without ethics in this area. For the Soviets, confounding capitalists in the interests of the enlightened Soviet proletariat was both justifiable and laudable; and the Japanese, similarly lacking ethics, though masked by their formal politeness, in reality believed that foreigners were inferior and had no business to be interfering in Japanese whaling. They were now well embarked on the shameful course of trickery and deceit in whaling which has subsequently damaged their reputation as a civilised nation.

Our second meeting was getting nowhere. My every suggestion was blocked and parried. My desperation rose. I said I thought there would be a public backlash against the industry's cruelty as it became more widely known. 'But it won't – the public doesn't see or care, and besides, as you know, we are researching improvements.'

'But getting nowhere, so they may argue. And people's perception may change.' Then I took a deep breath and said: 'Do you think the public would find acceptable, as a method of farming, the slaughter of cows by chasing them round the fields until they were exhausted, and then shooting them at twenty or thirty yards with a bullet, supposed to explode their lungs or heart, which might or might not be accurate?'

'An absurd analogy,' smiled the chairman. His face smiled but his eyes did not. His eyes were watching closely.

'Only, of course, if there was no other way,' said one of his colleagues. But there was a ripple of trouble around the room. And in their eyes and shifting comments I knew they began to see me as an enemy.

At one point we got onto employment in the whaling industry. They argued the old convenient lie beloved of many heinous industries – that they had a duty to their employees to minimise present unemployment; though their greed was rapidly ensuring the demise of whaling employment. I told them, if they rated profit above the indifference to the truth before them, that they would hurry to extinction the greatest creatures in creation before they could be properly studied. I was accused of being unhelpful and aggressive. And eventually I overstepped the mark out of frustration at their intransigence and asked if they applied their employment argument to the employees at Auschwitz, Dachau and Stalin's Gulags. I was called an intemperate young man and the barriers came down against me.

The chairman said, 'I don't think we can help you further. You may wish to speak again with our scientists. They will explain our approach. We are guided by them.' My second and final dismissal. He was coldly hostile. I looked at the speaker across the table. He was well fed, smartly suited and very assured. I wondered if my eyes told him how I despised him. I thought, you bloody liar! One of their scientists had confided to me, 'It takes years for them to accept even part of our watered-down advice.'

I left the meeting trembling – angry and dismayed. And realised I had denied myself any further influence with them. Afterwards, my interventions in that meeting pleased me more than they should have done. I felt an excitement, a pride, in having spiked their corporate humbug and hypocrisy. But my mind said, and what do you think you have achieved? And much later I was told that the minutes of the meeting made no mention of those exchanges except to say that 'there was discussion on humane methods of hunting'. The surface of reasonableness was to be maintained. But I afterwards learned too, that my words had shaken some of them, and I suppose might have added to the British withdrawal from whaling that was then taking place. I conferred with Robert, who was down in London awaiting the outcome. He listened to my angry report. We quickly concluded that our arguments would not prevail in such a body at least for some years. He said: 'You must stay calm and work on the scientists: they seem to be splitting from their masters. That is the way to pressurise the Commission.'

So, a few days later, back with the scientists, I argued calmly that if a total ban on hunting Blues was not forthcoming, the season should anyway be shortened. I knew they were concerned about this, and the linked issue of killing pregnant females, and urged them to press this more strongly upon their political masters.

I asked to see their charts and records showing in detail where the fleets had been hunting in recent years and in which weeks of the season, and argued in sustainable yield terms for protective measures for mothers and calves. But I had another motive. In the guise of interested biologist, I was also a spy. Given an extra week or two by shorter hunting seasons, Blue Whales can swim considerable distances. They had to go to the feeding grounds if they were not to starve, but they could also vary the places and times to seek to avoid the factory ships and their merciless catcher boats. The information I gleaned was afterwards disseminated by Tisala to Blue Whales across the oceans. For the first time, they were acquiring advance knowledge and could plan avoidance.

At times during some of those meetings, I began to be encouraged. On occasions, to my delight, some of the arguments appeared to carry weight with the scientists, who indicated they were thinking along similar lines. But Tisala was less sanguine than I, and under his steady questioning, my initial optimism was often turned to doubt and apprehension. For we knew well enough that whatever the scientists might say, the Commission members had a long history of disregarding scientific recommendations.

We now knew, and as Robert said, we should probably have known before, that effective restrictions on whaling, let alone its cessation, would not take place without a change in political attitudes. We turned to lobbying others.

After the bitter disappointment of the 1963 IWC meeting, the fact that the dire predictions of the scientists had been broadly vindicated in the following season raised some hope that the 1964 meeting, again in London, would bring improvements. But despite the scientists' bolder recommendations, the members of the Commission remained intransigent. The changes they did agree were again largely illusory. In the North Atlantic, the ban on hunting Blues and Humpbacks was extended for five years, this time with the acquiescence of Denmark and Iceland, though it did them little credit, for they knew there were scarcely any such whales left. The major whaling nations were happy to pass the proposal for none of them anyway bothered to hunt in the region. But when a similar attempt was made to prevent the taking of Blues in the Antarctic, objections were lodged by all whaling nations affected: Norway, the United Kingdom, the Soviet Union, and, most importantly of all, Japan – Japan whose 'share' of the Antarctic whaling industry was now more than half the total. The ban was therefore wholly ineffective. Moreover, because of disagreements between the Soviet Union and Japan no quota limits at all were set on Antarctic catches for the following season. Despite all efforts the slaughter was set to continue.

I gave warning to Tisala that then the Japanese alone would have seven large factory ships and over a hundred powerful catchers in the Antarctic. The Blues were so reduced that it was imperative that they should somehow escape the hunters if the final act of genocide were to be avoided. For the Blue Whales the season of 1964-65 looked like the point of no return.

CHAPTER 28

A Glimmer of Dawn

For two years now, from our base in Inis Cuan, Tisala had been sending messages and information into the whale world. As the intelligence spread, a significant number of families made the long journey from the Southern Oceans to the North Atlantic, and some to the North Pacific. Most took evasive action while remaining in the south. The news of what had happened each hunting season took several months to reach us. Each season we waited in trepidation.

But while we waited, life on Inis Cuan went on. Tisala's seasonal visits were always a triumph and a relief. Though we were much concerned with the anti-whaling campaign, the centre of everything was still on his learning. This proceeded at a pace which continued to awe us. Each time he departed from the island, we were fearful for his future. As I increasingly appreciated the scope of his achievement, and then his wisdom, my fear mounted: to lose him would be to lose a being of unique value in the world.

I remember one day walking with Ellie along the cliffs of Inis Cuan when we were discussing these things. Penny was on my back in the carry frame and Will was toddling along with us holding Ellie's hand. The island then was part of our lives, and we were part of it. It was a sunny day in late summer. We stopped to watch butterflies, and when they fluttered away, followed them to new resting places. We named and recognised the flowers that grew everywhere, and the birds – the little ones flitting between rocks and bushes, the bigger ones soaring around us on the updraft from the cliffs. The island worked its magic. This, I thought, is how life should be.

But when I looked out across the sea, I was always aware that beyond the horizon in the furthest oceans the last of the Blue Whales were facing their grim struggle for survival. With Tisala's knowledge and own calculations, and by mentally deducting the old and very young, I had concluded that there were not many over 800 Blues through whom new generations could be born. Split between male and female, and by groupings in the separate oceans, the numbers in the separate locations were down to a few dozen, except in Antarctica, where they were in the low hundreds. But only a few groups needed to be hunted down in the North Pacific and Atlantic for them to be eliminated. And we knew that although more numerous, the southern groups, because of the numbers of factory and whaling ships in Antarctica, had the balance tipped even further against them. We estimated that, if the deaths this season were over 500, the end might be unavoidable. At the very moment of mankind's discovery of the Blue Whales' true wonder, the whalers might send them to oblivion, and the Earth lose its greatest creation. As we walked on the island with our young family Ellie and I waited with intense apprehension.

It was not until our following spring – the Antarctic autumn – that we knew what had happened. That season the Antarctic summer had been bad. The weather hindered the whalers. When Tisala returned he reported that he knew of only twenty deaths. He said there may have been others of whom he had not heard. Later, after the Northern Hemisphere summer, there were four known deaths in the North Atlantic. The numbers overall seemed miraculously small. We felt a joyful sense of relief and even some speculative optimism. Only two years previously, the mortality had been nearly a thousand – about a third of the then population. But now it seemed that only forty or fifty had died. Tisala's assessment was sober. 'There are very few of us left for them to find and we do not yet know what has happened in the North Pacific.' But he thought that their evasive actions must have played some part. (We afterwards learned there had been twelve deaths in the North Pacific.)

Some while before that, word filtered through from one of the IWC scientists that the huge Japanese fleet had, so they said, failed to take a single Blue Whale in the Antarctic. I said to Tisala, 'We know they have almost certainly lied, unless the Russians and Norwegians took them all, but even if it is not completely true, it is still astonishing. They claim not a single Blue Whale.' I felt a surge of hope.

Tisala recognised the significance of it at once: 'Perhaps now the Commission will ban the hunting of Blues in the Southern Oceans, for they must believe that if they do not, they may never find Blue Whales again.' But when I thought about it, I became worried for that very reason. The Norwegians, Russians and Japanese might still oppose a ban to allow them to kill any Blues they found next season, to have one last bite of profits.

So it was with happiness and excitement that I was able to relay to Tisala the eventual outcome of the IWC's 1965 meeting. The absence of a single acknowledged Blue Whale catch in Antarctica where only thirty years before, at the start of the Great Death, whalers had slaughtered 30,000 in a season shook even the whalers to the core. A ban was at last imposed on taking Blue Whales in the Antarctic and a five-year ban in the North Pacific. But fears of breaches of the bans were not allayed: the observer scheme remained blocked. When Tisala asked about restrictions on other species, I had to tell him that the former Antarctic sanctuary had not been reinstated and other suggested protective measures had been voted down. Nevertheless, this year did mark, for the Blue Whales at least, a turning point at the very edge of their total destruction.

There remained much misery to come in the history of whaling, but for the Blues – for the first time since the 1920s – it began to look as if eventual extinction might be avoided. Two years later, in 1967, in the face of almost total worldwide absence of sightings of Blues, the IWC shamefacedly extended the protection from Antarctica to whole of the southern hemisphere. And in those years another great change had begun. The public in many countries were awakening to the revoltingness of the killing perpetrated by the whalers, who found themselves on the defensive for their careless genocide. Increasingly, they went in fear of bad publicity, public opinion and the threat of legislation. At the very brink, the spotlight of knowledge was being shone into their cruel and bloody business.

Those months were a high point – when I came to believe my friendship with Tisala might be helping save these magnificent beings, who had had swum the oceans for millions of years; that they might after all survive the devastating onslaught of humans. And sometimes my whole body – stomach, torso, face and fists – contracted and shook with the joy of it, and being a part of it. For, if the Blue Whales could survive the next few years, we could see the possibility of a great change coming in the world's attitude to whaling.

Our lives had become so bound up with the struggle that the prospect of this change was reflected in our family life. I found myself released from a great tension and laughed and played tumble games with the children with a carefree joy that had too often been missing. And in these times, Ellie's eyes told me she loved me more than ever. I was then a happy man.

In the following summer, 1968, we had a family holiday on the French Mediterranean coast. We stayed in a little old-fashioned family hotel just up from a small sandy beach. Will and Penny took to the warm sea and spent hours in and out of the water. Ellie and I took turns supervising, she a neat figure in her bikini, the whole family gradually changing from the pale-bodied English who had arrived, to a more healthy-looking brown, marred only by a number of mosquito bites on arms and legs. We spent much of each day outside, except for lunch and early afternoon, the hottest time of day, and once when Ellie had a bad headache – 'Too much sun,' she said – and she retired to bed feeling unwell.

Up from the beach you went in through an arch into the basement of the hotel – a bare concrete room with two backless wooden benches. The regime, run by a formidable matriarch, Madame Lequesne, demanded children's shoes off, brushing sand off feet and No Sand In The Hotel. There were brushes in the corner to sweep out any sand before it was carried upstairs. Madame was usually on guard in the marble-floored lobby above, keeping a beady eye open for young offenders, some of whom were sometimes shooed downstairs again to brush off properly. She always wore a black dress set off by bright red lipstick, applied a little too high on the top lip. The children were in awe of her. But one evening I went into the bar and saw Will, aged five, perched on the top of a tall stool next to the bar with a large glass of green liquid in front of him, and looking mighty pleased. Madame Lequesne pretended not to know anything about it, but a little smile played round her mouth, and I saw her wink at Will.

One day we went into the market in the nearby local town just down the coast – a pretty fishing port. The busy market square was shaded by plane trees and full of dappled sunlight. The children loved exploring the different stalls with the strange and familiar fruit and vegetables piled high, the fish stalls with their fishy smell and exotic sea creatures set out in melting ice, the spice and olive stalls and those with brightly painted pottery and cloth. At one end of the square stood a large church. Its door opened and from it came the sound of beautiful singing. Drawn, we went in, eyes adjusting to the dark interior, lit in places by devotional candles. There was no sign of a choir, and apart from a few old women sitting or at prayer the impressively large building was empty. The recorded music stopped, and there was silence. Will caught his mother's hand and leaning towards her asked in a serious whisper 'Is this God's house?'

'Yes.'

Will peered round the dark emptiness. 'I suppose God's out.'

I caught Ellie's eye and we tried not to laugh.

In the evenings sometimes we ate together on the outdoor terrace overlooking the sea but on some nights the kids ate earlier and were tucked up in bed leaving us to dine together. On one such evening, Will and Penny were in bed and Ellie was reading them a story when I went in. 'We should go down in a minute, darling.'

'Ssh! Dad!' said Will, 'We haven't finished.'

I signalled my apologies and sat on the bed. Ellie was reading the Noah's Ark story. At the end a thoughtful-looking Will asked, 'Mummy, why did God drown all the animals? *They* hadn't been naughty.'

'Perhaps to show how angry he was with the humans, who had been very naughty,' said Ellie. She paused. 'But I agree, it does seem unfair on the animals.'

'It was silly of God to make mosquitoes,' said Penny, scratching her arm.

'Anyway, Noah shouldn't have allowed them on the Ark,' said Will.

'I expect they hid,' said Penny, solemnly.

Downstairs over dinner, Ellie said, 'It's a dreadful story when you think about it. What is the justification?'

'I think, to emphasise how good God was to Noah and his family. But, even if you treat it as a myth, it seems a strange way to achieve that: God destroying nearly the whole of his own creation to make a point. Man and God treating the animal world as a plaything. A very bad lesson. And a fictional, and therefore untrue, account we have been shackled with ever since.'

'You mean in the light of evolution?'

I nodded. 'And cosmology and advances in theological history. Ideas that are changing the world. Salut.' We sipped our wine and watched the sunset.

It was a happy and precious holiday.

CHAPTER 29

On Evolution

As an adjunct to the history of whaling, Ellie, Tisala and I had discussed any number of topics – ship-building, nation states, wars, geography, economics, the industrial revolution, population growth and the like. On every topic, I realised Tisala was patiently observing and linking areas of knowledge. He always wanted to go to the reason for things, and the fundamentals of them. Throughout his learning, he questioned and ordered, slowly creating a coherent whole. It was astonishing to me to observe a being whose species had developed over millions of years in the unchanging environment of the sea, assimilating things almost wholly outside his previous experience. It was as if somehow his mind was prepared for the task of understanding and illuminating everything that intelligent men had struggled with over the centuries.

Perhaps most of all he delighted in knowledge discovered in the history and advance of science, which in our lifetimes was continuing all round us and at an accelerated pace. Tisala constantly asked for information on the latest theories and discoveries. Robert Thompson supplied most of the physics, I provided biology and palaeobiology, and we shared the chemistry. The history of life on Earth and that of the wider universe was being revealed at an astonishing rate – down the scale through microphysics and microbiology and up the scale to the most immense concepts of space and time probed by astronomers and astrophysicists. Tisala was intensely excited by it all.

I argued that in fifty years time, the scientific view would be commonplace, accepted by educated people throughout the world. But Tisala said that, although our race had done wonderful things and extended knowledge into unheard-of realms, this learning was the province of relatively few. The continued behaviour of the many, including some seen as leaders, belies that advance. He feared that we will continue to kill each other in future wars – wars for resources or land, interspersed with tribal wars and their near relations, national and religious wars – and will continue to destroy the surface of the Earth in the name of economic growth. He said that although an increasing scattering of us humans have knowledge which could begin to curtail these evils, such knowledge will not inform the choices of electorates or the programmes of autocrats until the level of learning is transformed; and that in fifty years time, though many will have abandoned both religious and political ideologies, much of mankind will still be subservient to one or other of the mass religions or ethnic nationalisms. And only a smallish percentage of humans will have any better idea of the nature of the world and universe they live in than the people who set out in the name of greedy commerce to exploit and destroy whales; and who now do so for other available resources, such as forests, minerals, oil, and anything edible or burnable, very often with less constraint than their ignorant yet wiser, more awe-inspired ancestors of earlier times.

He feared that this destructive blindness of belief combined with the ferocious instincts of humans will be hard to overcome. 'But overcome they must be, or the whole Earth will be damaged, and much in it destroyed. It can only be achieved,' Tisala concluded, 'by the spread of better ideas, for with knowledge comes both the means and motivation to behave more wisely.'

Part of the problem, he thought, is the sheer extent of knowledge, and the divisions between areas of knowledge. The scientists promulgate their science, but often in specialist confines and too often not the morality of its use; nor do they apply their knowledge to a reassessment of outside areas such as nationalism, racism and religion. The religious interpret the world only in terms of their own beliefs and assumptions, however contradictory. The politicians interpret the world through the close-focussed lens of immediate expediency, and their actions are too often a trail of mismatches with real needs and opportunities. In short, the starting places all vary, or are incompatible, and too little connects.

'Let us instead consider a new ground of consensus, one that may serve all humans of goodwill – the cumulative evidence gathered worldwide by generations of science-educated people of all persuasions. We can start before the beginning of the cosmos, and although this still borders on the unknown, the old creation myths of man can now be replaced by a version of the real creation story.'

The finding I taught Tisala was this: the scientific story of the evolving universe, as far as we then understood it. That in the beginning there was energy, the early form of which is not known, and which lies beyond present understanding of the laws of time and space. Afterwards, in its earliest identifiable form, men have called it electromagnetic energy. This may have existed before space and time. Nobody knows. But for the purposes of our universe, which is enough to be going on with, energy first materialised when it took the form of matter after space and time were created. Matter has mass, and decays, and therefore necessarily requires space and time to exist; and light cannot exist without space and time, for it can exist only as it travels though them. It will be found that space and time, light and matter are all forms of stored energy. As you approach the border between energy and matter, which scientists have done when they peer into ever-smaller sub-atomic particles, they find no definite boundary, energy and matter eventually partaking of each other's characteristics. The smallest particles of particles will appear not to be particles but energy without mass.

'These things,' said Tisala, 'are on the edge of knowledge by their nature, and we have to hold our understanding in suspension. But from the beginning of the known universe onwards, your species has very remarkably and with great skill put much of the story together: there is a wonderful logic and coherence in the understanding you have unfolded.'

I had laid out the story to Tisala as best I could, given the new knowledge that was all the time coming in. I recount it here (amended in a few particulars since) because, towards the end of his life, Tisala said I should do so, for he knew then I would try to write this book, and hoped it might reach some of his unknown friends – 'the bank and office clerks, computer operators, teachers, house daughters, farming people, workers and artisans: any with lively minds, in Europe, the Middle East, Western Asia, the Indian sub-continent, the East, China, Japan, in Oceania and the Americas, North and South.' And when he listed them, I could sense his compassion, his wish to love all humanity in the world.

He understood the accumulated evidence showing how, at the cosmic bursting into birth of the known universe, matter in the forms of the first elements, hydrogen and helium, came into being about 14 billion years ago. How from these elementary clouds and swirls of gas, there followed the formation of the first gaseous galaxies and stars. When by the force of their own gravity, the matter in stars was sufficiently condensed they became nuclear reactors and from that took place the evolution of chemistry. Over billions of years the elements and chemicals of the universe began to form in the burning and exploding destruction of stars, creating from simple elements more complicated ones. Some of these like carbon and oxygen had extraordinary properties; they then combined with other elements, eventually to form elaborate molecules. And then, about five billion years ago, how a medium-sized star in our own galaxy – the Sun – was formed from the gravitational pull of the coalescing hydrogen, helium and debris of exploded former stars. And circling round this new sun were other bits of gas and debris, which in turn coalesced under their own gravity, the far flung outer ones to form large gaseous spheres – the planets Saturn and Jupiter – and the inner ones with their heavier elements as molten rocky planets. Nearest to our Sun was Mercury, then Venus, and then our own planet, Earth, just far enough out from the Sun to maintain water-based life. I told him how the Earth grew by accretion, its increasing size and gravity attracting further rock and debris from the coldness of space; how there was much ice bound up in such debris, all of which plummeted into the growing sphere; how the increase of this enlarged ball of rock, metals, ice and gas led to pressures within that melted the rocks into a slow molten liquid; and how the planet was bombarded and pock-marked by a rain of meteorites that sank into its seething surface, further enriching the new planet chemically.

Tisala intervened, having placed himself in imagination beyond the Earth to consider how and why the Earth should spin: 'I suppose that if the main bulk of debris lay in belts in response to the Sun's gravity, when it began to coalesce, and fall into Earth's local gravity it was mainly coming from particular angles and perhaps that tended to nudge the forming sphere into a spin. The spin created night and day, and the variant tilt the seasons, and pre-determined much about the life that was to develop on Earth, including giving us the strange regenerative cycle of sleep.'

'Yes, for all I know.' I said. 'But what is certain is that when the Earth was formed, stars continued – and continue – to be born across the billennia and live and die throughout the universe. Creation itself still continues. And the reason we've not been aware of it is that space is so vast that even the nearest stars in our own galaxy are so far away we see only tiny pinpricks of light. Our inadequate eyes altogether fall short of anything more distant. It was only with telescopes and an understanding of radio waves that the truth could be uncovered. The only star the fierce reality of which we had any inkling was the Sun, which we now know burned in a steady state for five billion years before man evolved on Earth. Without the heat and light of the Sun nothing of man or whales or any other form of life would have arisen in the Earth.'

I resumed and told him the creation story pieced together by scientific endeavour. How gradually over the first few hundred million years, the heavier elements sank by gravity to the centre of the spinning globe, forming its core, and the lighter elements tended to rise to the surface. How some of lighter gases were too light to be retained by the planet's gravity and drifted off into space. How some of the heavier gases remained above the molten surface, pulled down sufficiently by gravity to form an atmosphere of choking, unbreathable gases, mainly carbon dioxide and nitrogen. How gradually the surface of the planet cooled and formed a crust that afterwards became the continents; and how meanwhile one of the lighter components after the gases, water, escaped from the interior to the surface and, in the heat, turned into steam and water vapour, rose into the atmosphere, and on cooling turned to rain and returned to Earth, so gradually cooling the surface further, and allowing the water to gather, and lie there. So formed the crust, and the oceans and the early lifeless landmasses. And gradually the crust thickened, and the molten interior spilled out less frequently. Until now only the occasional movements in the Earth's crust lead to volcanic outbursts.

When I looked across the inlet, I could see outcrops of ancient pink rock, crouched and worn, lying all about us, and over towards Eileen Mòr and the other islands, slabs of overlying volcanic rocks. I said to Tisala: 'The remnants of some of the oldest rocks in the world are here in these islands – you swim among them. They are older than life itself?' And being present amid such colossal ancientness with a sentient member of a species far older than mankind filled me with a deep and silent awe. I said eventually, 'we know the age of all the parts of the world's crust. All round the world people look at rocks and hills and mountains, but few understand what they see.'

Then I told him how, about 3,800 million years ago, some of the chemistry involving carbon became so intricate that at some point it spontaneously divided, chemical combinations of molecules for the first time on Earth splitting and growing again, multiplying within themselves. These chemical structures thus slipped into the replication of themselves, forming new chemical arrangements, and forming new entities endowed with what we now call life, entities with the ability to reproduce themselves. Thus out of combinations of chemistry arose life. And those first forms of life were microscopic bacteria. We think they came out of the volcanic hot water of the early seas. They lived only in the water, and the land was barren.

I outlined how increasingly the outer surface of the planet cooled, and with it the oceans. How the hot water bacteria, with infinite slowness over hundreds of millions of years, adapted to their cooler environment and began to use an outside source, the Sun's energy, to break down carbon dioxide in the atmosphere so they could use – feed on – the carbon thereby freed; and how they thereby released tiny amounts of oxygen – two parts for every carbon part they freed – into the atmosphere. And as the bacteria over countless eons spread in billions and trillions through the oceans which covered much of the planet, their little tiny exhalations of oxygen began to change the composition of the atmosphere, preparing the way for a new form of life. And as they did so, the bacteria themselves developed. The mechanism was the banding together in co-operation of several single forms of bacteria to form larger and more complicated ones. At some stage, about 3,000 million years ago – 800 million years after the first known appearance of bacterial life – there was another vital development. Another of our arbitrary borderlines was crossed: from these enhanced bacteria, organisms more like tiny plantlife developed, and from these ocean-living algae. Microscopic plant-life had arrived. From these simple one-celled plants, more complicated multicellular plants evolved. And then eventually, over vast periods of time, some of the more developed plants began to show the characteristics of what would become called animals.

The animal-like plants at some unseen point slipped undetected over the next line, becoming creatures that might be called animals, though still retaining many characteristics of plants. At an early stage, these primitive plants and animals had found ways to reproduce themselves, no longer simply by splitting, but by first fusing with another of their kind, and then splitting so that the new entity carried a double parental inheritance. So, perhaps 2,800 million years ago, the first sort of binary sexual reproduction was born, and with it a crucially enriched opportunity for reproduction passed on by those components we now call genes.

Tisala said: 'When I take my mind down to microscopic level I wonder if in these far off times the faint glimmer of sentience among the molecules and cells was to be seen: the sensing that they needed to join others to develop, and having done so, that their entity was as big as fulfilled its purpose, so that to grow again it first had to divide; that, and perhaps the Sun's warmth that relaxed the membranes of the cells so that they divided but did not disrupt themselves.'

'Nobody yet knows,' I said, 'but it's possible'.

Tisala said: 'But to extend knowledge you must first create an idea, and then test it to see if it is true or not. You see, you are turning me into a scientist. But go on.'

I recounted that after millions of years, when plants and animal-life had developed sufficiently specialised cells and organelles within themselves, the method of sexual reproduction began to change. The parent, instead of itself joining and splitting, pushed out new entities – patterns of itself – from within its own structure, without the need to split itself any longer. So came the generations that filled the seas with new life.

And with the burgeoning of sexual reproduction, plant and animal life was set to grow. The microscopic early life had given way to the tiny, and the tiny in turn grew in size and complexity. This process went on with immense slowness. For more than 2,000 million years, down to about 800 million years ago, all plants and animals were soft bodied, and all lived exclusively in the seas. Except for bacteria at the splashy edge, the land mass was arid and lifeless.

During this long, long period, the prolific and increasingly larger forms of animal life (but only a few of plant form) turned predatory.

Their forbears had used cell membranes to enclose animal cells, so that all the cells remained and co-operated as the new enlarged animal. Their descendants, now larger free-floating animals (some were like prototypes of small jellyfish) or rock-attached, like sea anemones or sea lilies, ingested small passing animals and plants, so breaking them down and using their chemicals for their own fuel. At some unseen point, feeding off the living had arrived.

Then between about 600-500 million years ago, the pace of development began to accelerate dramatically. Animals with harder outside cells were eaten less often and so survived to pass on their characteristics. So gradually across countless generations (by utilising the hard chemical calcium) those creatures developed harder exteriors: protective casing or shells. Within 100 million years, there were numerous defensively equipped small animals. And some animals, like sponges, grew bits of calcified internal structure. Some worm-like creatures, to develop control of their movements, grew a chord of nerves along their increasing lengths. Other species of chordates arose, and within another 100 million years, the chords of nerves of some became protected by bone: the vertebrates had arrived in the seas. And from them descended the early forms of fish.

'But not of whales,' said Tisala. 'You have told me that we come much later.'

'Yes, and by a strange route.' I said.

I told him how much else had happened first. How about the time of the first fish, perhaps 500 million years ago, another great change took place in the history of the Earth: sea plant spores gained a footing ashore, and plants first greened the edges of the land. So the plants crept ashore, by the margins of the seas, into the brackish bays and mudbanks and up the rivers into fresh water. Some plants adapted in the still waters of lakes and lagoons by growing longer stems to reach above the water for the Sun's power to photosynthesise food from the atmospheric gases, which we call air; such stems becoming stiffer and stronger to stand in the thin air. The leaves adapted too, developing a waxy exterior to retain water in the cells, and pores in the waxy surface to act like breathing valves. And here was the beginning of trees. So, from the first creeping shore plants evolved ferns and swamp trees. Eventually some of their descendants grew away from the water altogether, and became forest trees, forebears of all the trees that beautify the Earth. And all that took 300 million years. But it was still a strange deep green, for as yet there were no flowers or grasses.

In the meantime, and parallel, when there were plants on the land to eat, animal life came up out of the seas and followed them onto the land, up the rivers and creeks, into the marshes and lakes. The cased and segmented creatures of the sea crept out to take advantage of the growing, sun-nourished plants. These were the arthropods whose fossils we have found – the forebears of our mites, insects and scorpions and they began to adapt to life on the land. And then came certain fish – first using their fore fins as props, nibbling the green plants, and returning to the water; but gradually evolving stronger fin bones and bent-angled flippers; which in turn developed into limbs, and feet to tread the Earth. From scales developed scaly skin to protect their water-retaining flesh from drying out. Out of the water they began to breathe air to obtain oxygen, and so, like lung-fish, over time developed lungs: internal oxygen-abstracting organs which gradually replaced their water-and-oxygen-sifting gills, which were not built to work in the dry air. And from some of these former fish descended and developed all the land vertebrates of the future, every last one of them with four legs.

And so came the first amphibians, creatures of sea and land, some of the descendants of which still happily exist as amphibians – frogs, newts and turtles.

'Turtles,' said Tisala, 'another ancient and peaceable animal you men are carelessly destroying. But go on with your account.'

I described how, to stay on land, in the thin air, the bones of animals had to grow bigger and stronger, as the stems of plants had done, for extra weight must be carried by the body in such conditions. And so from the amphibians came the reptiles, some of them part water loving, like crocodiles. But then came wholly land-based reptiles, among them dinosaurs and snakes. And competition for food became more mobile and fierce. And because the air is less dense than water, sight improved, which both protected animals and extended their hunting range.

Tisala raised questions throughout my account – for instance that snakes do not have four legs. I told him the fossils show their forebears did. But snakes found their wriggling movement in hot dry places used less energy than walking, and so their legs fell into disuse, shrank and eventually disappeared.

'So the poor biblical snake who was blamed for so much was not at the beginning of the story at all,' said Tisala.

'A long way from it – probably a mere 200 million years ago – though millions of years before men appeared on Earth.'

I resumed my account. There were other developments too. In the age of reptiles, some dinosaurs grew feathers – fluff – to keep warm, for the land, unlike the sea, could be bitterly cold: and over millions of years, some, adapting their bone structures and enlarging their feathers found another use for them: feathered light forelimbs became wing-like and helped escape, and mobility. So, in due time, the creatures gained flight and eventually birdhood. Every modern bird has dinosaurs as forebears.

Others of the four-legged creatures developed in their own ways. Some, instead of laying large numbers of eggs that had to take their chance, developed their young internally, which, particularly among bigger animals, was more efficient and meant they could suckle them and look after their young enabling the period of the young's development to be increased. So out of the reptiles came first the mammals, only about 200 million years ago. Strange creatures to us, having both reptilian and mammalian characteristics, but developing over 100 million years towards our more familiar groups of mammals.

I told him too of land animals that afterwards adapted their four-legged inheritance – such as those that developed the use of their forelimbs for handling things, like kangaroos, squirrels, monkeys and, much later, men.

The members of one species, four-legged, and probably dog sized and furry, perhaps after the dark days of the great meteorite destruction about 65 million years ago, found it advantageous to go back to the sea. They looked for food in the shallows, and began to swim again. In time they became increasingly aquatic. These were Tisala's ancestors, and those of all whales and dolphins. So, over several millions of years, their front legs became again two flippers, and their back legs trailed behind and were drawn up into their more streamlined body (the residual bones remaining within them to this day). Their tails flattened out and extended as they themselves grew, and they adapted but retained their lungs. So that in some 20 million years they became what they are – the great whales, the dolphins, the porpoises.

As was fitting, Tisala questioned me closely about his own ancestry and their aquatic adaptations, which we explored in detail. I will not repeat that here, but will finish the creation story of science.

Before the ancestors of whales returned to the sea, flowering plants had developed on the land. From the first simple flowers, which were little more than coloured leaves, there emerged the eventual range of exotic blooms. They evolved in tandem with new insect life, as foes and collaborators: flowers are to attract insect pollinators of their seeds, by which they grow and reproduce – hence the enticing gorgeous blooms, nectar and perfume. But insects also attack and eat many plants – hence their defence of aromatic oils, and sometimes poison.

But only after the whales return to the sea did the most important flowering plants on Earth become widespread: grasses. They spread as a result of climate change with the establishment and growth of the great ice sheet in Antarctica and its lesser equivalent in the Arctic. The latitude on land between the cold northern forests, and the hot equatorial jungles was gradually filled by grasslands. Very importantly and unlike most plants, grass grows from the bottom, so can encourage but survive constant grazing. With grass came the rise of ruminant mammals, cows, camels and deer. Grass, after oceanic algae, became the most important basis of the food chain on Earth, including, I said to Tisala, man's; not only because we eat cattle and sheep, but more directly; for wheat and rice and other grains are developed grasses.

The mammals that remained on land during the following millions of years, like the flowering plants, underwent a spectacular display of new development. As in former ages, many thousands of forms and species did not survive, but those that did were the increasingly familiar forebears of all the animals and flowers that teem in the world today.

Among them, about 25 million years ago, when whales had become whales, was a species of small furry four-legged mammal that lived in the forest. Little is known of these animals in the next 15 million years or so – what intermediate forms they took – but from them eventually came the line of animals we call primates: monkeys and apes, who increasingly altered their four-legged stance into a two-legged one. Among the apes were the ancestors of orang-utans, gorillas, chimpanzees, and man-apes. The man-apes and chimpanzees split from their common ancestors, it is becoming clearer, as recently as 7 million years ago. The man-ape species we have called hominids, though the genesis of these species is not yet known and settled, for fossil findings are relatively few. But more links in development from apes to men are as we speak being discovered. Beings recognisable as some form of men – by now upright walkers with larger brains – are distinguishable about two million years ago. From some of these the form of present intelligent man appears to have emerged – surprisingly recently – perhaps within the last 200,000 years.

Tisala said: 'And so you came, spreading, it is thought, out of Africa, nearly unseen until you emerged out of the caves of the ice ages into the woods of Europe, the grasslands of the Middle East and Western Asia, and into the light of history.'

When I had concluded this liturgy of evolution, I said, 'That, as I understand it, is the picture provided by the accumulated evidence provided by our geologists, palaeontologists, biologists and chemists. That is the picture of creation accumulated from 200 years of studies of the fossil record of the surviving parts of the Earth's crust (for much of it has subducted back into the molten interior of the Earth), and of many thousands of studies of the planet's chemical and living biological record. The main outline is clear, though no doubt there will be additions and corrections, sifting events and details as knowledge advances. Understanding the genetic codes will unravel more, altering and enlarging understanding.'

Tisala said: 'But already what emerges is a wonderful body of knowledge, bearing the hallmark of truth, for whenever it is added to or further understood, it becomes more clear and certain.'

And in the silence that followed, I looked at Ellie, who had been listening. I felt an excitement, almost an ecstasy, at comprehending and being part of this discovered reality, and alive with intimations of further wonder. And I was proud of being teacher to the greatest mammal in the world.

Then Tisala continued: 'But it means that all your earlier poetic or symbolic creation stories, despite their charm, stand exposed as fiction, and one insufficient to guide man wisely in the world. Yet on these stories you have built your belief systems. And without belief in the stories, will you humans change for the better, or worse?'

'For the better,' said Ellie. 'We will. With goodwill and knowledge, I really think we can.'

She was lovely in her optimism.

CHAPTER 30

The Coming of Darkness

Sometimes light and sometimes darkness comes from expected quarters. The next spring, during our stay on Inis Cuan, just after Penny's fourth birthday – Guinevere made her a chocolate cake with a hollow chocolate elephant on top flanked by four white candles – Ellie had a worse than usual headache. It went away but two days later came back and was even worse. It lifted again, but by the end of the week she had a third and more violent attack. I put Ellie in bed and cooked supper for us. Ellie didn't eat. I began to be frightened, but tried to be reassuring and said we must go over to Eilean Mòr in the morning to ring her father for a medical opinion. Later that evening I suddenly realised that despite her initial protestations she was almost completely incapacitated. Ellie had a bad night. I slept intermittently, but the darkness seemed to stretch ahead for endless hours.

The next morning she had partly recovered. We packed up a few things and I took her and the children across in the boat to Eric and Guinevere's. The water was calm, but I went at half sped to minimise any jolting. When we arrived, she walked gingerly into the house as if she was afraid of jarring her head. She sank into a chair and was glad to hold Guinevere's hand when she tried to explain how she felt.

I rang Edmund and described what had happened. He asked some questions. 'You had better get to her a doctor and a hospital for some tests as soon as possible – immediately.'

'What do you think?'

'I don't know – it doesn't sound like meningitis but I don't like the sound of it.' I remember his short pause. 'Don't say so to Ellie. Let me have a word.'

Father and daughter spoke, Ellie in some distress. But he said something that seemed to relieve her.

Eric and Guinevere were wonderful. Guinevere telephoned their doctor on the mainland. 'Is that you, Charlie?' I heard the beginning of the conversation through the open doorway but she turned or lowered her voice and I strained to catch the words. Ellie was suffering. I was frightened and wanted her in hospital, and prayed there would be no obstacles. Guinevere came back in. Dr. Henderson would meet us off the boat and would ring the hospital. Eric organised transport. Guinevere would look after the children. At one point Ellie seemed a little better and apologised for all the trouble. Guinevere ticked her off for talking nonsense.

We made the journey to the mainland by late afternoon and were met by Dr. Henderson who drove us straight to the hospital. Ellie held my hand. Hers was slippery with sweat.

Dr. Henderson said: 'We'll run some tests on you, young lady, and keep you in for observation. I expect you'll be fine.'

I smiled at her to show my confidence but felt sick with apprehension.

And she wasn't fine. When the results came back a very subdued Dr. Henderson said to me, 'I'm afraid I have to tell you your wife has a large tumour in the brain. I don't know if its operable – the surgeon is looking at the x-rays now.'

I asked what it meant.

'If they cannot operate, she may not have long to live.'

I felt the cold creeping up me. And when the surgeon spoke to me, I was numb. The tumour was in an advanced state, lodged deep near the medulla at the base of the brain, and was not operable. It was difficult to say, but she might live only a few weeks.

Initially I did not accept the verdict – or that nothing could be done, and argued with the surgeon. But every possibility I raised – surgery, drugs, the new radioactive treatment, a second opinion, London specialist units – was quietly ruled out. Trephining and occipital treatment were impossible because of the tumour's position; no drug could specifically reach the site, unlike the drugs for lymphatic cancer; irradiation would have to penetrate too far – even if possible, a massive dose would be needed, and would destroy too much vital healthy brain tissue; there was no magic a second opinion or London could perform.

I looked at the surgeon in growing horror, as each hope was eliminated. Who was this man calmly passing a sentence of death on my carefree beautiful Ellie?

'You can... Nothing?'

He shook his head and said he was very sorry. He must have heard the disbelieving revulsion in my voice, but he was a kind man and a good doctor and knew that my questioning of his opinion arose from my desperation. He patiently led me through it again, steering me towards his conclusion, and with Dr. Henderson explained the x-rays. I stared at the blackish smudge the size of a small apple and begun to hate the foul alien crouched in her beautiful head. This smudge – this lump – was to end Ellie's life – it was ridiculous – outrageous – and I became deeply angry. But it changed nothing. Slowly they brought me to accept the reality. I felt myself being led out of one world into another, colder place.

The next two days passed in a slow blur. Ellie insisted on being told the truth. So she too learned that she was dying. She was very distressed and tearful, though she fought hard to be calm. The white painted hospital bed for some reason reminded me of wartime. To start with, she could not believe that she was going to depart from the world, that the future – her future – was almost in the past, and that she was leaving us.

But when Ellie thought of our children or me, she seemed to summon up a determined acceptance. She gave me all sorts of instructions about the children, trying her best to mother them to the last. I could see as she was fighting and exhausting herself, and sometimes she shook uncontrollably.

By the end of each day, I too was drained. But the nights were worse. I was staying at a little guesthouse near the hospital, and slept badly, and woke every time with a sickening lurch in my stomach remembering where I was and why. An angular shadow hung over me on the ceiling of that room and I stared at it in horror when the shelter of sleep was torn away.

On the third day, in an interval when her racking headache retreated, she felt a little better, and a pool of calm was created. She suddenly said, 'I wish we were back on Inis Cuan.' I could see her remembering. 'What is happening with Tisala?'

'He's gone out to sea for a few days.'

'I am disrupting the work – the whole... Everything.'

'Come on, darling.'

But she wanted to know, to be reassured: 'You must keep on – you and Tisala – promise me.'

I made an indeterminate gesture.

'You must!' she said. 'I know how important it is. It is your work. It is for the whales and the world.'

I said hopelessly, 'I promise I will. But Ellie – ' and I looked at her in despair. There was a silence.

Then she said, 'We must tell Will and Penny. We will have to make arrangements for them.'

The children were coming over the next day with Guinevere. We spoke of our flat in Battersea – perhaps selling it and buying a small house near her parents or my mother, and what might happen to the children when schooling started. We spoke too of their grandparents, and later on Susan, who might help to provide homes or places to stay when I had to be in the islands. She wanted the children to be with me as much as possible – including time in the islands.

'That is a gift your children should have.'

I noticed the 'your' with a jolt. She was preparing me for her absence.

I said: 'Guinevere will insist on them staying with her.'

'Dear Guinevere.' Ellie leant back on her pillows and shut her eyes with a little smile.

The next afternoon Guinevere arrived with the children. When Ellie saw them, she could not keep back her tears as she hugged them. She tried to brighten up and spoke to them. And from her attention to their chatter, I could think for a moment that nothing had changed. Penny wanted Ellie to mend her doll's dress which had a hole in it. But she could not cope. She handed the doll to me – 'Let Daddy look.'

And while Penny asked her mother more childish questions, I poked desolately at the hole trying vainly to close it up.

'Why are you crying, Daddy?' asked Will.

'Well, Mummy is very ill, and I'm… I'm very sad.' I looked at Ellie beseechingly, asking her with my eye not to leave us.

And then I was ashamed – as if I were the one suffering, not she; and because I was asking her to do what she had no power to do, what she could not do – live. But she knew it was out of love for her, and my dread of losing her. I saw the love in her eyes and the glimmer of a smile.

She held her hand out for mine. 'My poor love.'

I stroked her hand – suntanned, so young and healthy looking to the wrist but then her arm was pale. In the Hebrides even in summer you usually wear long sleeves. The decoration on the short sleeve of her nightie was blue.

She seemed relieved to see the children, and though she said nothing, I guessed that she had been afraid she might not see them again.

A day later, Penelope, Edmund and Philip arrived. We were all distraught, but tried not to show it to Ellie. She was comforted by their presence. Edmund spoke to the surgeon and Dr. Henderson. When he came back in and saw me looking at him questioningly he shook his head.

At one stage I heard Ellie say to Penelope, 'Sorry about this, Mum.'

'Don't be absurd, dear.' The habit of educated, practical management of life prevailed. But then her, 'Oh, Ellie!' and her haunted look gave away her mother's misery and dread of losing a child. Loss was in everyone's eyes.

Philip said to me, 'I can't believe – is she really going to die?' Dismay was in his face. He was very upset though he tried hard not to be. It struck me watching them together that, as I was losing my wife and married life, he was losing his sibling life. Afterwards I took him along the waterfront and we drank beer and talked.

In the following days we took turns to sit by her bedside, and to look after the children. But as the days went by, attempts at encouragement and cheerfulness gave way to more silent vigils.

One day Eric arrived with a message for Ellie from Tisala. He consulted his piece of paper and read, 'From the sea, I think of you with love. My first land daughter is always with me as I listen to your gentle voice.'

When she heard 'daughter' Ellie smiled and said, 'He is a silly.'

Eric resumed, 'Be at peace with your life and hold onto love, and the love of those who love you.' Eric cleared his throat.

Ellie said quietly: 'Tell him I love him too, and bless him very much.'

Ellie was in hospital nearly three weeks, with a few better intervals, but increasing pain and distress, which they treated with increasingly large amounts of painkiller. And so she gradually withdrew from us.

Near the end, when I was alone with her, she said, 'I don't think

I can hold on much longer. I want to say goodbye to everyone. Say goodbye to Tisala for me. Send him my love and ask him please forgive us. Tell him that you and he must guide and look after each other.' She paused, and I could see the tears welling – 'but I shall not be there... and the children...' She broke down in bitter sobs. I took her in my arms.

'Ssh, ssh – remember what Tisala said – you will always be with us.'

'Ssh ssh' – and I thought of the calming syllable used down the ages, in the caves by mothers to little children when wolves howled or mammoths trumpeted outside and men were out fighting for the survival of them all. 'Ssh ssh' is the lapping of little waves on a quiet shore when all is well. I felt the calmness returning to her, and holding her, I somehow felt strong.

A little later looking at me she said, 'My darling David. I don't want to leave you, or any of... It's so hard.' Then she said, 'Please bring in the others.'

Then everyone in turn went in to say goodbye. Eric and Guinevere came out in tears and suddenly looked very frail themselves. Penelope, Edmund and Philip – all in tears. I think we were all in tears. We hugged one another for comfort.

I took Will and Penny in, and Ellie spoke with them and fondled them and stroked their heads.

After a little I said, 'You must say goodbye to Mummy now.' They were so young. I think they thought it was like a longer form of saying goodnight, which after their kisses and final words from Ellie, I perhaps compounded by saying, 'Now Mummy must go to sleep.'

Then Ellie and I said our own goodbyes, but she wanted me to stay with her. Soon the pain returned and they gave her morphine. She slept, and died two hours later. It was just three weeks after the first diagnosis. It was a terrible time.

CHAPTER 31

Alone

In the days following Ellie's death my mind kept asking, again and again, why did Ellie have to die? What was the purpose of her death? What use was she in heaven? I must have blurted something of this out to the vicar because I remember him saying in a kindly voice, 'David, it is not for us to question the plans and designs of God, though sometimes we may not understand them. But you may be sure that Ellie is this day with Christ in paradise.'

I recognised his use of the words of Christ to the murderer hanging on the cross next to him, but they brought me no comfort – rather unease and disturbance. My childhood religion said it was true, but a newer voice said it is not true; she died because she had the horrible bad luck to have an inoperable tumour, which is a matter of defective biology. And what would have happened to God's plan if it had been in an operable place, and successfully operated upon? Should I suppose she would have been saved, only to be taken by God in some substitute death? I thought of the advances of medical science, and the many tens of thousands of lives it has saved. That must frequently interfere with God's plans and intentions and oblige him to adopt other ways of taking people to heaven. Was that why Ellie's tumour was 'placed' in an inoperable position? I felt a sense of revulsion, for it seemed a sort of backward logic, with God acting as a semi-malevolent and threatening power. These thoughts flickered and went round in my head in between the misery, but went round unresolved.

One part of me wanted Ellie's ashes to be scattered on Inis Cuan, so that she would always be there in that beautiful wildness. But in the end I gave Ellie back to her childhood and her parents, to be where her home had been, where our children would hold their grandparents' hands when they put flowers on her grave, and be surrounded by love at their home.

The day before Ellie's funeral, when I was sitting quietly with Will and Penny on the sofa at Fieldbanks House, Penny asked the same question; 'But why did Mummy die?'

'Because God wanted her with him in heaven', said Will trying to make sense of it.

Quietly tearful, Penny said 'But I want my Mummy.'

'We do not always understand God's ways,' I said. 'It *is* very difficult to understand.' I meant, difficult to believe, but did not say so. I hugged them both long and tightly, gradually our warmth comforting each other in our loss. But I found I did not believe what children are taught. The comforting scenes of my childhood religion were falling away.

Ellie was buried in the churchyard of her Hampshire village church. At times, I struggled with tears. But I had duties to attend to in the service, children and family to support, greetings and condolences to accept, people to thank for their sympathy: the discharge of my Ellie's life. There were tears too from family and friends, and some of the women from the village who had watched her grow up.

The church stood on a slight rise. After the service, the families and close friends went down the flagstone path, down towards the fields, past the old gravestones – the names, the years spelt out, among the tombs the voices of nature gone. We laid Ellie to rest in the grass-covered earth. But standing by the graveside holding the children's hands, I knew the cold of death. Only their little hands gave mine a spot of warmth. I felt as though her half of me was torn away and I was bleeding into the ground. And afterwards I cried inwardly for a year, and often after that. And sometimes in the night, when I wake from a dream of Ellie, still do.

Soon after Ellie's funeral there came a time when my numbness and misery turned to bitterness and anger. It repulsed my being that one so young, so beautiful and gentle, should die of a malign anarchic growth in her brain, displacing the love and laughter of her mind and choking it off in pain and distress. Such a thing became to me grotesque.

One day when I said something of that to Tisala he spoke to me sternly: 'You have suffered a natural death. You have no need of bitterness. Nature is wonderful, but flawed. There are defective beings in nature, but we see little of them, for they die or they do not long survive except in sheltered places where they are hidden. So we are not much used to them. And your medical knowledge has raised hopes – you humans have begun to unravel the blind turnings of nature. But disease and deformity are part of life. Beyond the little pool of light cast on human affairs by your science, it will remain so. Yet that truth is as nothing besides the astonishing, teeming abundance of perfection in the natural world. Look around you, recognise how much is good and perfect, and then remember that where there is life there must be death: that is the necessary condition of life, for otherwise there could be no change, no advancement, no emergence of consciousness, no one and nothing that could create or comprehend language and love. And to some, death will come early by natural causes. Do not therefore give way to bitterness. To be bitter is to cripple your survival, and damage those around you. You have children. Ellie lives in them – be grateful. And she will live in your mind, and the minds of those who love her. Your duty and fortune is to survive. You must flourish where you can, loving as much as you are able, and destroying as little as possible. It is your duty to do so because you have inherited life at a high level and it is for you to raise it higher where you can, and not impede other lives that touch on yours from the same opportunity.' He had never spoken to me in such a formal way before, or with such authority.

But he said it in such a way that I felt he was leading me out of a dark place, enabling me to acknowledge and accept my great loss as part of nature. He did not mention, or need to, the contrast with his own losses. I knew he saw in his mind each generation of his family – his grandparents, Saba and Siana, his father, Tarba, his mother, Sayli his wife and his children, his uncles, aunts, brothers and sisters, his cousins, nieces, and nephews – and all the unnamed thousands and thousands who had been unwontedly slaughtered; many in their childhood, some even deprived of their chance of birth, dying inside their mothers as they were killed, for fashion, or lubricating oil, or soap. The relentless genocide had continued over four generations – a hundred years of outrageous human greed and barbarity, until now there was left only the last handful of his noble species.

And yet he was not bitter: his mind was calm and rational and evinced love and wisdom at every turn.

Here, I realised with a surge of joy, was a love free of the imaginatively seductive supernatural and its darker face, superstition. Here I was not required to 'worship' or 'submit to' the jealous God of the Jews, or 'surrender' myself to a risen Christ, or to follow the convolutions and beliefs of the religion constructed around his life that had so entangled my mind in my school days when I wanted to believe that God is love, but found a vast train of baggage in scripture, doctrines, dogma and church teaching: religious beliefs distorting a desire for love of higher things. Later, enquiring into the Hindu and Buddhist interpretations of God or life, I had found that they too required the burden of impossible impedimenta, each seeking to build particular religious experiences into a comprehensive world view from an inadequate base of knowledge. And in all religions, when the questioning became too close, and could not answer what did not fit, or lay beyond, people were told, God's plan is hidden, it is a mystery, or, your reward will be in heaven, or, we are not meant to understand but just believe; though all believe in different things that cannot stand together.

But here was a love without any of that, boundless and free, at one, not at variance with the ideals of the honoured thinkers of mankind – the better ethics of Christ, Mohammed, and their God-free fellow thinkers, Buddha and Confucius; and numerous men and women of goodwill across the ages. Here was steadfast forgiveness, generosity and love of neighbours – found to be in all life on Earth. So Tisala took me out of any bitterness or self-pity. This glimpse of a new philosophy determined me to use my life for Ellie, for Tisala, for our children and all the inheritors of the world. And he was right; Ellie did live in my mind, and spoke to me and laughed, and in a new way accompanied me in life.

Tisala said, 'Remember her with pleasure to your children.' So I learned to speak of her quite openly in every day occurrences when the children were with me; but most of all in the freedom of Inis Cuan. This was our place, where, perhaps because of fewness of the people, or because memories were little overlaid, somehow I felt – and I think the children did too – that there we remained a family, and she was about us. So I learned why it is good to talk about the dead with the bereaved, for the dead do not leave the truly bereaved, who take comfort and pleasure in finding them living in others' minds.

But it came to me constantly in little incidences after she died, that she had physically gone forever. When I took a shirt out of the drawer that she had put there, I remembered with a pang the way she had of folding clothes, neatly, carefully, giving a shirt a little pat as she finished, as if she would impart a touch of love to the garment. Initially, I found these reminders very hard, and missed her constantly. But as time went on, I looked forward to finding her touches, and though inevitably they became fewer as months stretched into years, they became not sad but precious.

Sometimes, even years later, Tisala used to recall whole sentences or more of what Ellie had said and I had half forgotten, but recognised. He knew I loved to hear her voice in her words and see her in my mind again.

He said to me once: 'If only you humans remembered and did not forget, half the wisdom of each generation would not be lost, and half the world's trouble would not arise.'

Another time, when he had raised a memory of Ellie, I laughed: 'I think you were in love with her yourself.'

He said, 'I love you both.' He did not live in the past – he brought the love of past life into the present. And then I knew that I loved him – that he had nurtured in me a wider, deeper feeling, beyond the close bond of a man and a woman, or parent and child, the love searched for by the wise down the ages, the love that resides in the understanding of wisdom.

But after Ellie died, I began my lonely years. It is hard to raise children, and sometimes of course there was anger, resentment, cross words and tiredness; but most of all when the children were with me, whether on the island, in London, or at their grandparent's, or with my mother, or with Eric and Guinevere, I delighted in their company and the work of bringing them up. I was often surrounded by friends and family. We had many happy and laughter-filled times. But in between, underlying all, lay the burden, the dull physical ache, of loneliness.

CHAPTER 32

Will and Penny

In the end, I kept the flat in Battersea. I was able to get a job part-time as a researcher at the Natural History Museum. It did not pay much, but with my income from Aunt Jane's remaining money, enough to enable us to survive and for me to continue what had become the hub of my life, my work with Tisala on Inis Cuan, and what flowed from it.

Although I loved taking Will and Penny to the islands, I soon found the children were a distraction from work – constant supervision was necessary, and difficult, in such a place. So, initially, they tended to stay with Guinevere and Eric, who treated them like their own grandchildren. When Will was a little boy, he followed Eric round all day, like a lamb its mother. Eric built small model ships out of matchsticks. 'Eric's very clever,' announced Will, 'even though he's got a funny thumb.'

But Eric and Guinevere were both now in their early seventies, and I was reluctant to impose too much on their goodwill. Besides, the truth was I breathed more freely when the children were not there, at least during the precious weeks each spring and summer when Tisala returned.

So early on another pattern emerged: family support. My sister Susan and I were always close. Susan had married soon after Ellie and me, and was living just down the road from us in Battersea. Her husband, Giles, a solicitor, worked in the city. Their children were nearly the same age as ours. 'The kids,' she called all of them. She offered to have mine to live with them for those weeks when I went to the islands.

Extraordinarily, when I look back on the start of this arrangement, neither Susan nor virtually anyone else knew about Tisala. But the children did. And although they knew it was our secret, I was always afraid of them innocently blurting something out. So I confided in Susan, trusting her completely. She could keep an ear on the children's conversations. She could disarm any slip jokingly, saying we had a family story about a whale. I was afraid rumours might reach the wrong ears in London, for the conductivity of rumours in a big city is astonishing – 'Heard an odd thing about whales the other day...' And so might Tisala be put in danger. Susan asked if she could tell Giles, and I agreed reluctantly. I was always apprehensive when the circle of people who knew of Tisala increased, but comforted myself with the thought that a keen legal brain might one day be helpful.

'Solicitors are a better bet than most,' Giles said smiling. 'We are privy to all sorts of secrets. The working of our profession and standing depends on trust.'

'So why,' I asked smiling, 'do people widely regard lawyers as crooks?'

'They don't and shouldn't, but in the modern age, the cheap press will have it so. Makes me mad. Of course, there are cases of abuse. But if governments promote distrust of professionals in legislation, and newspapers condemn the whole profession for the crimes of a few, they'll do great damage to society – damage, they'll find, not easily rectified.'

He sometimes got quite hot in defence of the law – 'As it should be. There are, of course, various idiocies in it. And there, the problem is often the politicians. Everybody knows that without good law, no society can function properly, let alone a complicated one like ours.'

When schooling started, Susan took on the school run as well as all the unending tasks of caring for an enlarged household for weeks at a time. The four children got on pretty well, though I occasionally heard of upsets. Penny and her cousin Sophie became close friends. To start with, Will and his cousin Simon were wary of each other, but later when they found sport in common, they became good friends.

In the holidays, the children regularly used to stay with my mother. She proved to be a popular and devoted grandmother taking on again the role of teacher of the young.

'Granny's quite strict isn't she, Daddy?' said five year old Penny one day.

'Yes – she wants you to be brought up properly, so you know how to behave. Very good for you.' I pressed her nose with my finger and she wrinkled her face, but could not suppress a smile.

I realised anew my mother's skill with children. She chatted easily to them, explaining the world through household events. She read them stories. The old sofa became again the snug ship for voyaging into new worlds. We went out into the fields and woods. I showed them the haunts of my childhood and taught them the countryside things I had learned – down by the river, across the meadows and up in the grassy hills – still almost untouched, though the village itself was growing – infilling here and there, a little cul-de-sac development down Back Lane, and everywhere more cars.

Similarly, they always loved their visits to their grandparents down at Salisbury. The drive down would be full of excited chatter and giggles about whether the piece of string would any longer be able to hold Granny's gardening mac together, or whether Grandpa would let Will taste the sherry again. (He had been found teaching Will to distinguish sherries by getting him to stick his finger down the bottlenecks and licking; Will had pronounced the dry one 'filthy', but liked the sweet one.) There were hugs and kisses on arrival, running up to their bedroom and exploring the house and garden. In summer there were rides with Grandpa on the sit-on mower – Penny hanging on tensely, Penelope calling out, 'Edmund, do be careful'. And Will, when it was his turn, twisting the steering wheel this way and that, his face suffused with excitement; but being taught to drive in a straight line so as to produce the ordered stripes of an English lawn, which would so pass into the minds of another generation.

And there was going to bed, and Will, on the landing standing in the middle of the old Persian rug folding his arms and pronouncing, 'Fly to the mountains of the south!' which he had from one of his books.

As it happened, I had been exploring with Tisala the history of the Persian civilisation. 'This rug's from Persia – Iran,' I said, 'look at the lovely colours and patterns – some are made in the town, and some in the tents of nomads in the desert. Feel the fineness of the knots.' And we knelt down and felt the rug and looked under the corner to see how it was done.

So I was made to tell them in bed all about Persia and the great palace of Persepolis with its carving of men and bulls and horses, and how it was lost – buried in the shifting sands of the desert; and of the rose gardens of Shiraz, where the poets wrote, watered by the engineering miracle of the qanats running for miles underground from the mountains; and how the river, so wide the ancient bridge has nine spans, runs down into the shimmering salt desert, and is swallowed up in the ground and disappears; and the coming of Islam, and the beautiful mosques of Isfahan, the unbelievably blue and turquoise walls rising round the graceful courtyards, the shaped domes of blue or yellow and their flowing patterns of miraculous symmetry, built by a wise and tolerant ruler, Shah Abbas the Great, not distaining craftsmen from Europe; Isfahan the beautiful, its gardens and the tree-lined streets green and cool with flowing water, though set in the desert and surrounded by desert mountains, purple in the evening light.

'And that,' I said finishing, 'is where the rug on the landing came from. Now bed.' But they chorused protest, and would not let me go until I had told them more – of the great bazaar in Tehran, and the piles of jewels that underwrite the currency; and the winding road leading up the mountains to the pass and high Mount Damavand – a snowy peak above the desert – and on the other side, the sudden green-clad jungle slopes plunging down to the shining Caspian Sea. And it was only when we got to the sea that somehow a resolution was reached, and sleepy heads allowed me to tuck them in.

But always at Fieldbanks House I was aware of Ellie's voice and image, remembered clearly, but just out of reach in the light of ordinary day. And sometimes sleep came with difficulty. And it was another sea that held the other sustaining purpose, and the fulfilment, if it could be achieved, of my broken life.

And whenever I headed north to Inis Cuan, my spirit rejoiced in an upward surge of optimism. For though in human terms I was lonely – the cottage was empty without Ellie or the children – being with Tisala, talking and working methodically through the areas of knowledge of mankind, gave me a cumulative sense of excitement. In that way five years passed, with Tisala returning to the islands every spring and autumn on his migrations to the Arctic and the tropics. And increasingly I realised that here was a being able to process the whole gamut of knowledge, sift out the valuable from the dross and make sense of a thousand jumbled topics. So often the complexity and sheer bulk of the material, often badly or obscurely written or presented, defeated men's minds. But Tisala's capacious mind seemed to master everything.

But to start with, often arising from my own dark loneliness, compounded by my scrutiny on Tisala's behalf of man and his often-appalling hatreds and actions, I felt oppressed and gloomy for the future. I was afraid for the remaining – pathetically few – Blue Whales. But also afraid when I thought of our most dreadful century – of the wars and civil slaughters, the millions killed and the fearful march of weapons – for poor humanity and the fragile world. Yet when I observed his greatness of mind, and the undertaking he put it to, I felt humbled and privileged.

And as time went on – five years from Ellie's death in some ways passed quickly – and Tisala steadily addressed wider areas of knowledge, I found a new and wonderful view of the world emerging. But that only came after much questioning and dismantling of the structures and detritus of human beliefs and attitudes accumulated over millennia. And very often I stumbled most in those areas where, paradoxically, good resided, such as religion and philosophy. So the day came when I said to Tisala, 'But what about God?'

CHAPTER 33

On the Origins of Belief

Tisala had by then given much thought to the religions of men, and the God who stood behind them. He thought it true that you cannot logically disprove the existence of an omnipotent God; though no more can you prove it. Nor, he thought, can you absolutely disprove the existence of any number of earlier gods – the bird-headed god of Egypt, the Roman god of nature, Pan, or the child-eating Aztec god – but as you move away in time and place from the locality of these gods into the light of wider knowledge, the possibility of their existence becomes more and more remote; belief in them becomes first bizarre, then irrational, then virtually impossible.

He said the idea that God must be man-like rests, in addition to his maleness, on two strange assumptions: that humanity is the only serious intelligence that exists or will exist and is therefore god-like; and that there is only one inhabited world in all the universe. He argued that both assumptions would be shown to be wrong. If other forms of intelligent life are found to have evolved in the universe (as we would wholly expect from the myriad forms of life that have come and gone on Earth and the colossal numbers of likely worlds scattered through the billions of galaxies), then such intelligence would find absurd the idea that God, if he exists at all, is like the ape-man from Earth.

'And then consider the probability that other intelligent life has developed in the universe and is more intelligent, and more morally advanced than man. It is logically impossible for them to believe that God is like a man. It would be the same as men arguing that God is like a monkey, or us whales believing that a God of the whole universe is like a primitive fish. Such ideas are wrong by the nature of the ideas themselves when looked at in the light of reason. The lesser cannot be God of the greater.'

He held that, as the pre-origins of the universe are still unknown, the possibility of an omnipotent 'Prime Mover' God must logically exist. But that logical possibility did not equate with, or in any way require, such an actual outcome. Any God who might exist would have to be both infinite and remote, for any God who created the universe must be able to contemplate it as an entity in all its astonishing detail and vastness. Any 'Prime Mover' must be outside those dimensions. 'Is not the likelihood of such a "Being" existing, whether or not being credited with human characteristics, infinitesimally small? We are left with the possibility of some sort of spirit – a spirit, that pervades the universe, and to which all life aspires.'

He went on, 'You tell me many theologians now accept that "the old man in the sky" concept of God is not to be taken literally, but metaphorically; that is to say, it is fictitious; though I understand the church authorities are not keen to pass this teaching on to their congregations. But with what do they replace Him?'

I said: 'They say it is a mystery, but that there exists some form of background reality, a ground of being, which is beyond human power to describe, but is God. But I've noticed that when they talk of God being active in the world – as they do, for without such activity the existence of God would be meaningless – they slip back into imaging a humanised deity. They do this because, if they rely on scripture for their vision, they have no real alternative, and they still want their God to be like man.'

'Don't these theologians turn reality round?' asked Tisala. 'They say that man made in the image of God means that man has the characteristics of God – love, tenderness, mercy and so on; that human emotions are god-like. But it might as easily be concluded that they have invented the process, and that man, in common with other species, has developed from lower forms of life, and has slowly acquired some better characteristics which are from within himself and not from any external source or power. And that all life may so develop.'

To Tisala the whole idea of serious supernatural religious belief was unexpected, especially among intelligent beings. The world whales lived in was simple and beautiful; and it was self-evident to them that the higher things of life – their consciousness and delight in it, their sense of social cohesion and unity echoing and linked round the oceans of the world, their songs, their kindnesses, their love of others, the spirit of life itself – all came out of their own development and not from any external source.

'We Blue Whales saw that we had developed beyond the stressful fights of lower life for survival, for we were in the happy position of being frightened of nothing. We knew that thunder and lightning, and electric charges that we saw in some fish, were natural phenomena, as was the magnetism we used in our navigation. It never occurred to us to be frightened of such things, or attribute them to 'the gods'.

He questioned me on a common thread and claim in religions, that God is exclusively responsive to human needs.

And I thought, it is true, when you know the history of time and space and life on Earth, that the likelihood of any form of personal God shrinks almost beyond possible reason. After the first moments of the known universe – across the stupendous expanding fury of light and darkness – we can be sure – we largely know the detail of how – it could and did occur with no evidence of, and no need for, any form of divine creation.

'But I can understand the reasons,' said Tisala, 'why the history of the way the world evolved is not more widely accepted. For many it requires much un-learning, especially of religious and cultural teaching, which you humans find particularly hard to discard even when irrational, owing to the power of ideas over your imaginations. And understanding such development requires a shift in timescales that humans seem to find difficult. You are used to living within a short time horizon.

'A human child thinks his grandmother aged 60 is very old; adults think a house of 300 years is very old; a country that has kings who go back 1,000 years has a long history; back 2,000 years you are in the time of the ancients; and 6,000 years ago you are at the very dawn of civilisation, before most creation myths, and before your present religions were thought of. Yet all that history is as yesterday. You have to re-run all that time again ten times, to get back to early man, and multiply all that a hundred times to reach the prototypes of man, and double all of that again to the time when the lineage of man split from the apes. And all of the time we have so far computed is not one quarter of the time we whales have swum in the sea. Yet, in the history of life on Earth, even that is still in modern times. Look at the geological time scale: the whole of your recorded civilisation is little more than a one-millionth part of the Earth's history. But most of humanity seems unaware of this knowledge.

He observed that the history of the evolution of life demands imagining a scale of time almost beyond imagining. Moreover it is complicated in its detail, and it is as yet incomplete. It is therefore easy to misrepresent or misunderstand. It requires the acquisition of knowledge, not a simple leap of faith. And that, for the great majority of humanity in the urgent business of day-to-day living, seems difficult, remote and of little consequence. By contrast, religion only requires a leap of faith to give an immediate emotional reward, or even to deliver eternal life, which, with its glimpse of thrones flanked by angels, or its paradise gardens, seems desirable, and therefore requires little effort to believe. He said, 'You humans find it alluring and exciting to think you are loved by an all-powerful God. In your own mind it alters and makes significant your place in the world. But have you not often believed in God because much seems inexplicable in the world, and you sought some safe haven?'

In sum, he thought religious belief is a coming into the shelter of an imposed system, where you surrender your mind to a claimed authority, though the imposition is made attractive by the promise of rewards.

'Don't you think,' I asked, 'we could instead follow the sciences, so far as they take us?'

Tisala said that science is not a religion but is a gradual uncovering, by trial and error, of reality. It is the accretion of true knowledge, which explains reality and replaces earlier ideas and misconceptions. So science is of inestimable value as a measure or yardstick of what, both in religion and outside it, is no longer tenable. He thought that, in religion, it is the supernatural elements that have led mankind into so many of the difficulties arising out of religious belief.

'Yes,' I said, 'science works differently. We don't 'believe' in electricity. But the light bulb works, as do a thousand other things explained by science. If they weren't true they wouldn't work.

'Even that overstates your advance. You use things you may only partially understand, like radio waves for broadcasting, as men used the tides long before they understood what caused them. Science finds that the supernatural is not true. But scientific knowledge says little about how you should behave. Science can be used for good or ill. Many of your weapons, and for us your harpoons, would have been better never invented. It is abundantly clear that science on its own is not enough; you need a moral dimension as well.'

But reverting to religion he said: 'If you know nothing of the course of evolution, let alone the chemical and neurological workings of the brain, the truth you can tell is a limited truth, and one likely to be mixed with many untruths. Without that knowledge, I can see why in history men believed their various religions. Your minds are developed in nature to eliminate fears and unknowns where you can; such are disturbing, and you crave the comfort of certainty. So you have always found the existence of gods or God a ready remedy for fear and ignorance.'

'But belief in the existence of God raises a mass of new unknowns and unknowables. A burden which has to be carried, and too often distracts mankind from more fruitful living, as men are weighed down by the tangled requirements of their various and incompatible religions. It creates a whole alternative world, which I think will turn out to be illusory, a construction of fertile misapplied imagination.

'And I have learned,' said Tisala, 'that when men have sought to establish such values as love and harmony, the attractiveness of their message has often been swamped by the clamour of the human world, or by the drive for hierarchy and power of formalised religion. In religion, but not only in religion, narrow conviction wedded to power seems always to have brought conflict.'

He thought such conflicts arise also from the physical nature of life on land, with its fearful deprivations and dangers, and possibilities of weapons, wealth and power. In the oceans, he observed, Blue Whales are all equal and free, and none is above another, except in kindness and wisdom as leaders of their family. 'Imagine the absurdity of a Blue Whale seeking to raise armies against his fellows, or own part of the ocean. What men need, since your societies cannot be rid of power, is wisdom wedded to control of power. Wisdom is the right application of knowledge, and the beginning of wisdom is love. Many of you, it seems, have sought to be free of power – have withdrawn – holy men and women, meditators, hermits, and many a quiet private person; but ultimately you are subject to the exercise of power from without. In some ages time passes peacefully, but others have brought persecution and destruction. Many have tried to enlarge their freedom from external power by using wealth – indeed that is the preferred method, it seems, in your present societies; but that leads us from religion in to economics, and brings its own difficulties.'

Sometimes Tisala's linking of new areas left me trailing in his wake; but also in admiration, for I knew with increasing confidence that he could unify what commonly remained separate. I can still see myself during the breaks in these conversations sitting on the rocks overlooking our much-loved inlet of the sea, like the earlier boy I more dimly remember on a yellow-lichened rock by the seaside, but now no longer without a father-figure, and discovering new worlds quietly with this beautiful slate-blue wonder of creation.

And as he spoke, I saw more clearly that the passing of religions from the world might make it a lighter, brighter place – the nightmare baggage of the past, of phantasmagoric fears and beliefs, the guilt, the divisive righteousness, the distorted fanaticisms, might be laid down, and men, who like Blue Whales can rise above much of the struggle to survive, may espouse the good and smile at life in the Earth.

But when I expressed such view to Tisala he said, 'Yes, but if men are to do without religions they urgently need the better morals and ethics often endorsed by them. So men must find and adopt by consent a commonly acceptable code of morals and ethics to govern their behaviour, and restrain the use of power, both of individuals and of states. And in part at least, I understand your religions have moved towards ethical advance. So let us explore further.'

CHAPTER 34

On Religions

Tisala argued that the founders and followers of religion seek the truth. So the religions must be looked at closely in their own terms to see how and why in practice they have produced much that is wrong and bad, as well as much that is good. 'And men are in need of good.'

He thought that religion resulted in a system of belief based on a leap of faith – a series of assertions that God exists, that he created everything in the universe and that he speaks to men. A leap, to minds outside that tradition, that is an open invitation to error.

Tisala thought religion at its best is a system of knowledge attempting to explain, order and improve the behaviour of men. But it was an attempt to shortcut the long and difficult process of finding the truth from the observable and verifiable in the world. The shortcut was for the religious mind to start and conclude with the presumed final creation and to say: 'Look at the wonderful world: it can only have been made by the gods,' or later, 'by an omnipotent God'. And each religion claimed this had been revealed to them exclusively, by nature, the scriptures, the prophets, or God himself, according to their various tales. Tisala said, 'But the trouble with revelation and the faith arising from it is that it is often not amenable to reason, is next to superstition and is often indistinguishable from it. Faith is a determined belief in conjecture.'

But he did not blame the proponents of religion for their attempted shortcut: indeed, he thought it was inevitable. The knowledge necessary to discover the wider truths did not exist in earlier times; and in the meantime, people had great need of an ethical framework by which to order themselves and society. And it seems that the attempt to create ethical rules and structures was from the beginning intertwined with supernatural and divine elements which, with their rewards, and punishments for disobedience, sought to lend authority to the ethical behaviour required by men.

Tisala said, 'Is not the pattern of priestly religion, from before the Nile gods and onwards this: they assert that their religion is true, and every other religion must be wrong; and not only every other religion, but every other attempt to discover truth another way, as many found, such as the early explorers of science, even when showing church doctrines to be absurd?'

'Do you not thus set up,' asked Tisala, 'a destructive cycle, where religions fiercely seek to preserve and often to spread their own assertive beliefs? And there follows your history of religious wars, crusades, persecutions, and executions; where what should have been good becomes a fearful evil.'

He had thought why this should happen, and concluded it is partly to do with power. He instanced the roles of power and hierarchy in the Roman Catholic Church. Here, a simple claim to stand in the footsteps of the apostles of Christ became a cloak for the power and hierarchy for which the church acquired a taste in the days when the Christianised Roman Empire bestrode the world.

'A taste,' I remarked, 'they have arguably retained ever since.'

I recalled the history. When the power of the derelict medieval Roman church was challenged in the Reformation, it reformed itself by a counter-reformation to preserve its power and authority. Where the Church subsequently gained influence, as in Central and South America and parts of Africa, it led to distortions in the emergence of those societies. For the Church was seeking to impose, by authority, a whole straitjacket of revealed belief on widely different societies at a time when gradually many of its asserted beliefs were being shown to be based on error.

Tisala thought there was a great difficulty in seeking to improve mankind and our societies with dominant authoritarian religions in place, because what needed to change was the viewpoint of the entrenched religion itself. He said: 'It seems it is the same in all religions where power resides; and the more complete the religion, such as Islam, which imposes detailed God-revealed cultural and social laws as well as religious ones, the more difficult is reasonable reform.'

'I am afraid,' I said, 'that where authority is put before the advancement of ethics, error, oppression and bloodshed has often followed.'

Tisala thought that history showed this to be true of all closed systems, both religious, but also secular such as fascists, communists and racists; who had upheld their beliefs and systems by every means at their disposal, including propaganda, war, torture and murder, and in the case of most religions adding the threat of eternal torment in hell. Where death by burning, or stoning, or now by bombs, is held to be just or righteous, or cleansing, or to save souls, that, said Tisala, is instantly recognisable as power – religious or secular – exercised in the cause of ignorance and evil.

And beyond that, such fanaticism is everywhere hallmarked by sometimes bizarre notions of narrow belief, each wrapped in its little cocoon of certainty.

In the east, he noted that the great religions were not for the most part imperial structures, though in modern times, Japan had disastrously started to follow that route. Hinduism is more amorphous, supporting a multitude of Gods. It is noticeable, he said, that for the most part Hinduism has lost its characteristic tolerance only when faced with a monotheistic warrior religion. He thought it significant that Buddhism established a system of spiritual enlightenment without the belief in any god or supernatural being at all. He noted too that one of the older civilisations, China, was sometimes guided by a moral secular philosophy which was not a religion at all: the task was attempted by philosophy.

'But on your religions, the question I come to,' said Tisala, 'is whether and how they can embrace new discovered truth without it destroying themselves.'

He thought that they continue to survive largely because of the tradition of past belief, their integration into the social fabric of their societies and the reluctance of people to lose such succour. They have valuable ethics and social values to teach, but their reliance on supernatural events, and their assertion of divine authority as their ground of justification is, he thought, a delusion which, in the coming century of greatly increased and multi-sourced communication, will more and more come to be seen as such.

'Indeed, from what you tell me, great numbers of nominally religious people do not truly believe, but more or less accept outwardly what they are taught without troubling to challenge it, at least until experience teaches them otherwise.'

'But you think we still need our religions?'

'I think that without religion much good in the world would not have arisen. It is an endeavour to reach higher things: the admirable striving of men for the better; but because of the imaginative viciousness of your species, the solutions adopted were too often misguided and frequently appalling, such as the continuous human sacrifices of the Aztecs.'

'But,' I protested, 'that was a very primitive religion.'

He made a dismissive sound. And I thought of the line of other religions which had indulged at some stage in human sacrifice – Egyptian, Jewish, African, Chinese, Japanese – and no doubt others. He said: 'The Aztec part of the human race, and their religion, flourished only a few hundred years ago. They illustrate the danger of religion without adequate philosophy and ethics.

He argued that the idea of sacrifices to the gods, which permeates our religions, arises from our own natures. In all human society there is hierarchy. Among men, the kings, the powerful in whatever guise, demand submission and tribute; the weak seek appeasement and protection by giving gifts and offerings. In religion, these ideas were transferred to the gods, who were seen as powerful and who needed to be thanked or placated: from little domestic offerings of corn or salt at house altars to large ritual sacrifices worthy of temple deities. The more powerful the deity, the more notable the sacrifice – pigeons, goats, calves, bulls, humans. But why God should have been thought to want such sacrifices was not understandable to him, other than as a desire for an acknowledgement of kingship, which he thought clearly a human and not a god-like desire. For an omnipotent God to desire sacrifices of creatures from other creatures seemed misconceived. No true God could either need or require such things.

'Which is why,' he said, 'I find the central Christian idea of sacrifice so disquieting.'

For the Christians had the arresting idea of reversing the sacrifice. It was Christ – the son of God – who made the sacrifice for men. But why God should be thought to have needed or required such a sacrifice perplexed Tisala.

'That has often baffled me,' I said. 'The much stated but little explained idea that Christ died once for all sins.'

'It is explicable only if you believe in the "fall of man" and "original sin", as set out in the story of Adam and Eve whereby all humans born thereafter supposedly become sinful. And bizarrely, whether or not you take the story literally, Christianity requires a belief in the substance of the doctrine, because the whole purpose and rationale of Christ's death and resurrection was to reverse the fall of man and thereby save and redeem mankind. But isn't the doctrine, like the story, a fiction?

'Take away the story, which you told me all serious theologians now concede is metaphorical – in other words literally untrue – and you have to find a "real" mechanism whereby all generations of humanity are born universally "sinful", which is itself a form of supernatural assertion.' Tisala paused and then said: 'Where is this mechanism? It seems to me that it does not exist. The more obvious explanation is that humans are mammals that have developed with some nasty behaviour, and become both better and worse along the way.'

He thought the theological position very strange, and even stranger when, 300 years after Christ's death, the Christian religion adopted another doctrine, which became a belief, that Christ was himself God: the result of which appears to be that God sacrificed himself to himself to satisfy His own demands for atonement of breaches of His own laws, which breaches were anyway within His power simply to forgive. Tisala asked, 'Should we not conclude this is so contrary to reason as to demonstrate it untrue?'

He found also that the doctrine of the Trinity – three persons in one – which is presented as a deep mystery, gave great difficulty. Parts of the Jesus story require him to be a man, wholly a man, for there to be any rational explanation of things he is reported to have done or said or felt; but in other parts, as the early Christians developed his story after his death, it is necessary for him to be the Son of God; and in parts, as for the later elevation of his story into a world religion, he is required to be God himself. This last step is necessary, because if Jesus is left merely as the Son of God it diminishes him in the order of the universe; and since Christians wish to hold that theirs is the ultimate religion, it cannot be so diminished.

This set me to thinking about Christ's death: he fulfilled voluntarily (albeit reluctantly) God's plans and arrangements for his death. And in one sense, as he was claimed to be not only the Son of God, but God, he fulfilled his own plans and arrangements. But it can also be argued that he therefore knew he was not really going to die (or only briefly), but come to life again everlastingly. Tisala said, not without sympathy, that the more likely reality behind the gospel stories is that Jesus, if the statements attributed to him are true, was a deluded religious reformer. He believed in the intervention of his God; who, if there *is* no personal God, of necessity remained silent. Jesus had a profound knowledge of human ethics and needs, but in this case was misled by his strong sense of religious calling.

Similarly, with the much claimed unique sacrifice of his life to redeem the sins of the whole world both before and after his own time, it may be argued that, as he knew that after three days he would be alive again for billions of years, for all eternity (indeed, that was the whole object of the exercise – to abolish death), it was perhaps not as much of a sacrifice as the church has preached. Tisala again concluded that all these doctrines are so against reason that they do demonstrate their own untruth.

He thought Islam avoided all these difficulties because Mohammed, and afterwards his followers, presented his status as only a prophet and interpreter of God's word. In this Islam was much less ambitious than Christianity. But it nevertheless claimed the prize of being the only true universal religion by promoting Mohammed as the final, ultimate prophet and interpreter of God. Therefore, although only a man, his words were treated as the definitive unchangeable words of God.

That Christianity is therefore in error is something Muslims long ago concluded, though they themselves then substituted another faith – that is to say belief in another conjecture – to the effect that the God of the whole universe should have spoken exclusively to an unlettered middle-aged Arab, who needed authority to fight his campaigns in a pagan and fractious part of the Arabian peninsular; and that what he was told happened to be helpful to him, and coincided with conditions obtaining in that time and place. People of all other religions, and those who have moved beyond religion, have long ago concluded this claim to uniqueness was also untrue, a mistaken belief. There now exist much better and more verifiable ways of explaining the world.

In sum, Tisala concluded that as part of a way of living Christ's startlingly advanced ethics and many of Mohammed's rules had much to recommend them; but much of the rest, as elaborated by their followers, is misconception, some of it with cruel results.

Again I felt a burden shift, and the world under the sun seemed a freer place. I remembered the teaching of sermons in my boyhood that seemed to leave unanswered the questions they raised: how did Christ 'save' sinners two thousand years later, and in countries where they had never heard of him, and if he did not, why not? Why, in the Noah's ark story, as a child as young as Will could ask, did he drown all the animals, who were blameless? Why, in Christ's parable of the talents, was one person sent to hell and eternal torment not even for any dishonesty, but because he had not invested the money well? And many more, raising serious questions and anomalies: because if God and Christ are shown to be subject to the defective ethics of the Jews of those times, they could not in any proper sense be universally divine. But I thought too of the country church of my childhood with its cross on the altar, and us village children bringing up autumn produce – apples and potatoes in shoe boxes lined with blue paper, and bunches of carrots, the tops soon wilting, and jars of jam or pickle. I had told Tisala of our pretty medieval church, decorated with autumn foliage and berries. I wondered if these were relics of sacrifices.

But Tisala said: 'An awareness of a need to be thankful is good, whether or not you believe in God; besides, those are not sacrifices but charitable gifts. And if they rose originally from the idea of sacrifice, love applied to a wrong may transmute it into a good.'

Where ethics – the pursuit of the good through reason and love – were addressed by our higher religions, he thought they had much wisdom to offer, as in Buddhism, which is widely praised and followed for much of its ethical content. He thought it perhaps more a philosophy than a religion, because, despite not having any supernatural element, it is a thought system, but proceeds like a religion by unverifiable imaginative assertion, which becomes structuralised as doctrinal belief. Conversely, he observed that most ethical philosophy traditionally takes as its yardstick the application of reason in its thought, as did Confucius and the Greek philosophers.

He concluded that most of our higher religions are a conflation of philosophy and religion, the one influencing the other. Thus, pagan Greek ethics were widely adopted and interpreted into Christianity by the gospel writers and early Christians; and Confucianism was eventually given a more religious turn by the addition of ideas from Taoism and Buddhism.

'The history of your religions can be read as a constant working out of a dilemma: the promotion of the religious and supernatural, vying with the promotion of the good and ethical. But the unhappy tendency is for the supernatural element to grow and be elaborated as the religious structure becomes more formalised, while the ethics of living tend to become secondary.'

I saw down the centuries priests laying out their vestments for the next ritual; and then raising funds for richer vestments, and for greater, more beautiful buildings. And, though it is part of the problem, the result is undeniably magnificent: the spirit of man offered to the supposed spirit of God. I wondered how the priests of Egypt felt looking out from their gorgeous temples to the growing indifference of their people. A shift in the shoreline of faith involves decay and death.

Tisala resumed his train of thought: that although religion can foster much good teaching of higher ethics, the problem in practice is the burden of religiosity – the religion itself becomes its own object. As to the truth of religious tenets, it seems that most of them cannot be, for the 'truths' of each religion contradict those of other religions. If Christ is God, then by definition much of Judaism, Islam, Buddhism and Hinduism must necessarily be untrue. But if Islam's Allah is truly God, then Christ cannot be, nor the half-recognised God of the Jews nor the Gods of the Hindus or other religions. And if the Buddhists' belief that there is no such being as God is true, then God-based religions must be untrue.

That the religions try to live together is understandable, not least because they declare much ethical common ground, such as the requirement to love or behave well towards others. But in their purely religious terms they are mutually incompatible and all of them except one therefore must be untrue; and that one is false to everyone else. And he saw that this conflict continues within religions. He noted with dismay that every major religion has its splits and rival beliefs, often murderously enforced. Among Jews false prophets and idol worshippers were persecuted and punished – Moses, we are told, killed 3,000 fellow Jews for breach of the newly delivered Ten

Commandments; among Muslims there were, and are, centuries-long blood feuds between Sunni and Shia; and the whole history of Christians is permeated with division: the Arian and other heresies to do with the status of Christ, the Orthodox East and the Catholic West, Roman Catholic and Protestant, and many fragmented intolerances.

He took, for example, the argument over the Roman Catholic Christians' belief that in the Eucharist, the bread and wine actually become the body and blood of Jesus. If this is the truth, then the Protestant Christians' belief that it is purely symbolic must be wrong, and vice versa. This belief, called transubstantiation, only became the doctrine of the Roman Church in 1215, twelve centuries after the death of Christ. Up until that time, no one – none of the apostles, none of the saints during the first twelve hundred years of that Church's existence, nor any of the first 200 or so popes – believed as official policy that the bread and wine actually became the body and blood of Christ, for the simple reason that the idea had not then been imposed. The idea arose from wording in the Bible originating in Corinthians and Mark, neither of which require the belief, which may be seen as an unnecessary add-on. But by the seventeenth century, four hundred years after the concept was installed, it was so passionately held that it was one of the main causes of the bitter Europe-wide wars of religion, known as the Thirty Years War.

'And what was achieved by these wars between Christians?' asked Tisala.

I was forced to admit that the religious issues remained wholly unresolved, though two or three million people had died (very roughly speaking, for no one really counted), and much of the groundwork was laid for three centuries of nationalistic enmity between the French and the Germans, culminating in the two world wars of our own advanced century.

Tisala said: 'Thus the poison spread out of religion into the wider realms of race, national and economic power. Did not it occur to anyone to ask if it mattered at all what was believed?'

I answered: 'The trouble was that the full authority of the Roman Church has been put behind such beliefs. If you seek to reverse such doctrines, the church has to admit serious error, something they rarely feel able to do as it undermines their whole authority.'

He said: 'But such accretions and decorations of religious belief are doctrines which are nothing to do with anything Christ himself taught, nor what any reading of his fundamental message could consider essential.'

He observed that having invented this strange idea of bread and water turning into flesh and blood, they heightened its significance by the use of art. I had shown him examples of the extravagant gold and jewel-encrusted monstrances the Church had made to house the transformable bread and show it to the people, so increasing the wonder and awe of poor and humble believers, and thereby their belief; though the priests themselves must often doubt whether such transformation takes place, and engage in difficult semantics to justify their practice to themselves.

Tisala said: 'Is not a like case the status of Mary, mother of Christ?'

I had told him that she was always a respected figure, but 400 years after her death, respect was turned into a doctrine – the exaltation of Mary. And so began the practise of intercession to Mary. She became a way to God, seen as gentle and feminine, useful in an all-male, and eventually celibate, priesthood. So a strong cultural movement in religious art arose in the Middle Ages – Mary and the saints appearing with increasing frequency in pictorial form. The saints had similarly, but later, in about 1000 AD, been turned by the doctrine of canonisation of dead saints into an exclusively Church-appointed Roman Catholic hierarchy. So, in the case of Mary, the way was prepared for latter-day doctrines – the immaculate conception in the middle of the nineteenth century; Mary declared to be the Mother of God (not merely Christ) in 1931; the doctrine of the assumption of the uncorrupted body of Mary to heaven after her death, adopted in 1950; and the declaration that Mary is the Mother of the Church in 1965. And in the meantime, the Church gave credence to such things as tears and blood and even miracles issuing from statues of the virgin in grottos.

I said, 'When you know the history it is hard not to conclude that these things build on each other. They acquire the hallmarks of a cult. The holy Roman Church of latter-day beliefs. I suppose it helps to keep ignorant populations enthralled to the power of the church.'

Tisala said: 'Do they not ask, in the light of wider knowledge, whether the beliefs are mistaken, misleading and will be unsustainable?'

He thought that the more complete and authoritarian the religions are, the more they are in danger of collapse. Some of the Protestant Churches, who have applied more reason to their religion, like Locke in England, or the Quakers, have simplified and reduced what they are required to believe. Protestant theologians have increasingly faced up to fundamental biblical difficulties. Tisala said: 'Though their churches appear less certain, they may be more capable of flexible reform and so last longer. The more a church insists on belief in accretions and decorations, the more likely its followers will eventually say: "This is too much. This is nonsense". And once they question the rightness of authority in part, they will question it further.'

'And I suppose,' I said, 'the churches are afraid that any backing off will empty out their religion. For instance if the apostolic succession may not be true and doesn't matter, or the virgin birth, why not the miracles of Christ, or his physical resurrection, or the existence of heaven and hell? You are left with a religion that is irrevocably changed. And if you go far enough you come to the question, "Does God exist?"'

'You do,' said Tisala. 'They are right to be frightened, for there is no logical stopping place. The reason is that truth is indivisible; it is true or untrue; and it is difficult to conclude it is anything but untrue. And you have told me how they answered these challenges.'

I had told him how in the past they lashed out at such ideas. To keep their structure intact and their adherents bound to it, such things were pronounced wicked heresies, and their proponents condemned to death and everlasting torment. For centuries, they burned people to try and persuade them to recant and join their holy Church, but if they would not, the torture went on because it was intolerable to them that people should hold views contrary to their own beliefs. The Roman Catholic Inquisition burned alive 30,000 people, nearly all fellow Christians, because they believed things the Church taught they should not believe. And only slowly over the centuries did they retreat from such compulsory fanaticism.

'If I hadn't seen the bloodiness of human whaling and learnt your histories I would find it difficult to believe that men could be so ignorantly cruel,' said Tisala. 'I understand they excused themselves by claiming they did it to save souls. But it was a terrible religious perversion of love, and a failure of toleration, mercy and reason; qualities that should be the mark of any advanced religion or ethical society; and so much needed in your world.

'Their supernatural beliefs have entrapped them. If they do not change, religions among the educated will increasingly dwindle away; but if they do change, they cannot survive in their present form. It will be hard to be a church leader, except among the backward, many of whom will be persuaded to accept the old dogmatic certainties.'

Yet he concluded that there is a common purpose available to mankind, whether you believe any religion or none. He said: 'If belief is treated as private, there is no great difficulty, at least with advanced theology. Both advanced theologians and secular humanist thinkers wish the world well. Both want higher forms of love and reason to overcome what the religions call sin, what others call animal behaviour, and what both call evil when a conscious being deliberately chooses the bad. What matters supremely is an attitude of love and reason, and action resulting from it. That is what your world needs.'

I said: 'And the problem with much of the religious part of the equation is that the enlightened theologians count for little besides the theocratic insistence on conformity and orthodoxy of powerful religious authorities.'

But he thought they have an even more fundamental difficulty: that religions have over the centuries been protected because the great bulk of humankind has believed that God – of one sort or another – exists. Tisala was intrigued by this – why this should be, the effect it has had on human society and what will happen now the assumption is for the first time being widely questioned.

And I remembered that Ellie, who had been in on most of these earlier conversations, had been quiet as we sat on the rocks by the inlet, and then said, 'My love, where do you think all this will lead?'

'I don't know, but I think we must follow it.'

'Yes.' And she had replied to her own question, 'I think, and I hope, to the truth.'

'So,' Tisala said, 'let us explore the genesis of belief in God.'

CHAPTER 35

Against Exclusivity

'If you start, as you have in the past, from the assumption that God exists,' Tisala said, 'many things follow.'

He said it was easy to see why the Bible, for instance, should then be believed to be the word of God. It may be admitted in informed times that it was written by men, but it can still be seen as the word of God by most believers: it arrives in a complete volume, out of the past, mysteriously, like words scored into tablets of stone. People forget that it was written as many separate scrolls and books, some of them several hundred years apart, each set down by scribes in desert communities or towns, with drafts, amendments, and rejected pieces; and re-written and altered by succeeding generations, complete with misinterpretations, (not least, because early Hebrews before about 600 BC used no vowels, so like-spelt words were muddled). The result was that the Jewish Old Testament was not all written and fixed in its present form until shortly before the birth of Christ, and the Christian form of it not until about 300 AD. That too, Tisala said, seems to be soon forgotten, as are the centuries-long and acrimonious squabbles as to what should be included or excluded from the Christians' own New Testament. And in time a general aura of holiness settled over the whole book, which is kissed, held up and revered.

Tisala said: 'ABus, for many, having assumed the existence of God, the Book does indeed become his infallible word.'

But that, he found, raises a problem: incorporated into the Bible are strange views and fanaticisms, rules suitable for particular times, but not others, rudimentary knowledge, ignorant and primitive ethics, such as human and animal sacrifices, and vengeance. And all of it is supposedly fixed for all time as being the Word of God, not challengeable or changeable by any agency, whether reason, experience, new knowledge, common sense or wisdom. This he thought has had dire consequences.

He found the same difficulty arose 600 years later with the Qur'an, which accepts parts of the Bible as God-inspired, but disregards and alters much, and denies the main claim of Christianity: that Christ was divine, the son of God, and God himself. And the Qur'an, instead of the Bible, is claimed to be the true final, immutable and complete Word of God.

'So there exist two such versions, each denied by the other. And the Qur'an, like the Bible before it, when produced in a beautifully calligraphied form inlaid with gold, became unquestionable.

'These religions are creations,' said Tisala, 'that will take much unravelling.'

He went on to observe that Christianity was fortunate and unfortunate. Though Christ was literate, the teaching he gave was oral, and in ethics confined to general principles. Not for him the imposition of a whole set of strict cultural and social laws through religion. I said that indeed a reading of the earliest Christian documents – before the later Gospels – arguably showed Christ's main intent was partial reform of Judaic ethics and religion to free it from the stifling effect of Judaic theocratic law. The result was that scholars and wise men should have been freer to advance enlightened society.

But Tisala observed that Christianity had then come into the hands of one of the most tortuous religious minds that ever existed: 'That convoluted zealot, Paul'. Paul, the self-proclaimed apostle, whose skilful but perverse writings led the way for the transformation of Christ's original teaching. As we had studied the New Testament it had become abundantly clear that the adoption of Pauline doctrines gave rise to beliefs of which Christ himself had never dreamed. And that these were afterwards taken up, and the narrative of Christ's ministry additionally enhanced, by the Gospel writers. Hence, to accompany Christ's subsequently perceived divinity, his angelically attended birth. Hence also many reported signs and portents such as the 'finding' of prophecies about Christ in old Jewish biblical texts; which 'prophecies' in turn blithely assume and impose as truth on believers the fanciful conception of prophecy itself, with its unquestioning but impossible foreknowledge of future time.

Tisala said, 'In the known universe we know of nothing – no evidence, no mechanism, nothing at all – to support the idea of people being able to foretell the future. Is it not reasonable to conclude that there is no such thing, but only the deluded misconnections of those who come after?' If scholars really face these problems, he thought, they will end rejecting considerable passages of the Bible. He quoted the saying: 'Study prophecies when they have become histories.'

'But,' I said, 'Christ himself quoted prophecies.'

Tisala said: 'Some are attributed to him in the New Testament, thirty or fifty years after his death by writers coming out of a tradition of prophetic belief. They may be rightly or wrongly attributed, but if Christ did say them, does it not demonstrate again that he could not be divine – for he would otherwise know they were untrue? It would also show him less wise than one would like to suppose; an outcome anyway indicated by the fairly numerous and fearsome statements attributed to him on the judgement and hellfire awaiting those who did not comply with his conception of repentance.'

In such ways the new religion became saddled with what I now perceived as impossible theologies. Tisala said prophecy is an example of predestination; it seemed to him to be an attempt by believers to guarantee order in this world and their passage into the next – an idea which to his mind was based on a delusion. He supposed the idea grew out of the Jewish belief that they are the chosen race. Transferred to Christians it became: 'As through Christ we are specially singled out, the chosen elect, God will not abandon us, and we will go to heaven.'

Tisala commented, 'yet when they have suffered a tragic accident or death, or when something has occurred that seems wrong or inexplicable, many will accept such a fate and say, "It is the will of God", thereby attributing to their God actions or acquiescence which, if they existed, would often be moral outrages against any true God-like behaviour. Fatalism is a sign of weak thought.'

In my delving into the history of religions sometimes Tisala's enquiries puzzled me. But while he was infinitely patient with my floundering among the history books and texts, he always kept me at it, and gradually I found my viewpoint changing.

'It is necessary to look at the history,' he said, 'but always remember, the purpose is to enable you humans to deal with the legacy.' And somehow, out of the bewildering plethora of materials and writings, he always had the capacity to draw the essence of things together.

'An underlying problem,' said Tisala one day, 'is that of exclusivity combined with force.' He quoted Christ's assertion that 'I am the way, the truth, and the life; and no one comes to God but by me.' He had enquired carefully of me about this and noted that it is a sentence which in truth may – we do not know – have been invented and put in the mouth of Christ by a creative evangelist as long as seventy years after his death, for it only appears in the Gospel of John. But on it is built the exclusive truth of the Christian religion, as interpreted by the victorious church. And that, with the doctrine, adopted three hundred years after Christ's death, that Christ was a member of the Holy Trinity – one and the same as God, and the spirit of God (a view that neither Christ nor the original apostles or first Christians had apparently heard of) – is the source of the combination of exclusivity and authority that fuelled two millennia of Christian power in Europe and the world.

This resulted in a Christianity promoting its views too often by force – persecution, wars, crusades, executions and burnings; the curse of exclusive self-righteousness. Unbelievers were seen not only as wrong, but evil, often pernicious, filled with the devil, and therefore legitimately to be destroyed. This curse of exclusivity turned Christians, under the guise of seeking conversion and salvation, into savage persecutors, fervent and murderous.

'But the distortion of exclusive rightness appears to have a similar effect in parts of the Muslim world.

He saw that some Muslims, in the name of the unique rightness of Islam, have killed each other and non-believers for the sake of disputed rules, and to stage holy wars; though it seemed to him there is nothing holy about war. By such a doctrine people make Allah a cruel and ruthless God, which he thought an offence against Allah's perceived mercy and higher nature. Tisala argued that an enlightened understanding of Allah increasingly would exclude holy war, except in its higher sense of overcoming the bad in oneself.

Sometimes in those discussions, Tisala would pause, and I came to recognise that this often indicated his mind was turning to other areas.

He said: 'But this lethal combination of exclusivity and force is not confined to religion. It is a recurring pattern in human affairs. We have seen that where men have thought themselves as a unique Godlike creation, they have abused their fellow animals.'

I thought of the long sad list of human-led exterminations, like the four million North American buffalo, wiped out in a mere three years of careless killing; and killing with them the way of life of the plains Indians.

He did not need to remind me how whales, among many animals, have cause to abhor the destructive force of men, employed for their own casual convenience, confident in their God-given knowledge that man is supreme on Earth, and that all nature is put there for his exploitation. It was whalers from the nations of the reformed Christian religion – the Norwegians, Icelanders, Dutch, Americans and British – who began the genocide of whales. But Tisala pointed out that non-Christian traditions are no better: the whaling records of the godless Soviet Union and the ancestor-worshipping, race-exclusive Japanese have subsequently superseded the Christian whalers. And the Japanese, Norwegians and some others were still continuing the killing, though the evidence of cruelty and the threat to many species has long been overwhelmingly obvious. Any form of wider responsibility or care seems as nothing to them beside their self-regard and remorseless self-interest.

But Tisala continued on his wider tack: 'And between men, it seems that any race or society which seeks to set itself exclusively above anyone else comes to practise evil.'

He cited the Jews, whose history we had studied. As is well known they were taught to believe they were the chosen race. Under the Lord's promise and covenant, as delivered through their leaders, they thereby justified to themselves many evil acts, not least the claiming and ethnic cleansing of the 'Promised Land' by Joshua, including the wholesale slaughter of women and children. All entirely justified because their God – the only true God – had promised the land to them, or so their leaders told them. Indeed, in recording these matters in their scriptures, the Jews attributed the glory, but also shifted the responsibility, to their God; a strategy afterwards copied by other religions. The Lord of Hosts smote the enemies of God's people. And, testifying to the enduring power of ideas, many Jews believed down the centuries, and to Tisala's surprise I reported that some still believe, that they are the chosen race, so conferring on themselves a supposed exclusivity and right of action that condemns all other people to inferiority.

I said: 'That, and their blind self-righteousness, with their ferocious but strangely primitive set of morals – an eye for an eye, a tooth for a tooth – an attitude which will bring further calamity upon themselves and others, for it will provoke a bitter counter-response.

Tisala thought this claim and practice of Jewish superiority, and the resentment it brought was what turned into hatred across the centuries. It was their insistence on their separateness as the chosen people of God which ran contrary to the clear knowledge amongst Christians that they were exclusively right, and amongst Muslims that they were.

I said: 'And there was the question in Christianised Europe of the responsibility of the Jews for the death of Jesus.'

'That is different', said Tisala, 'and Christianity bears a separate responsibility for that part of anti-Semitism.' Down the centuries the Jews have stood indicted by a monstrous absurdity which Christians allowed to thrive, namely that because a few hundred citizens of Jerusalem in about 30 AD may have called for a man's death, that is a reason for despising and reviling several million latter-day Jews.

Tisala concluded that the Jews made an untrue claim of exclusivity, and were met in return by untrue claims. It is a pattern that other ethnic minorities and their host countries need to avoid. It is now the business of communities everywhere to expose all such claims in the light of history, reason and emerging biology; and act to create more harmony in the world.

He saw that in the history of humanity – right up to the present time – the same errors of principle have widely occurred. He considered the Germans, a people of civilised poetry and music, but with a malnourished democracy, who succumbed to the Nazi Regime and its dangerous doctrine of exclusivity: the dogma of the master race, which led to appalling use of force against whole nations and groups, including in grim irony, the Jews. So world war and genocide brought death to millions, and eventually retribution and ruin on the whole German nation.

'The idea of a chosen race or a master race is fraudulent, and very dangerous when combined with economic and military power. It was a terrible fulfilment,' observed Tisala, 'strangely paralleled by the Japanese, who, I recall, had long known and were taught that they were the exclusively superior race. It was an ignorant world view.'

While informing Tisala, I had learned that Japanese exclusivity was both racial and religious. It is established that the Japanese islands were inhabited by a mixture of peoples originally from Mongolia and Korea. But the descendants of these people came to think of themselves as a separate special race, the Japanese. Their native Shinto religion fatally combined weak ethics with ancestor worship, which led to a form of racism, despite their mixed ethnic origins; though Buddhism for a long while ameliorated the trend. In the days of Japan's geographical seclusion, in the seventeenth and eighteenth centuries, when the sword was still the main weapon and was wielded by the fractious feudal Shoguns rather than the nominal Emperor, such aberrations caused only limited, and internal, damage.

But, after the fall of the Shoguns and the reinstallation of the Emperor from 1868, Japanese nationalism adopted a form of state Shintoism under which the Emperor was declared divine, and school books re-written to claim an unbroken line of divine Emperors since the foundation of Japan by the sun-goddess, from whom the Emperors were said, absurdly, to be descended; and under whom national unity and authority were to be established while industrialisation took place.

And with twentieth century armaments and military mentality, this concept became a disaster. Any people beyond Japan's shores were regarded not only as inferior, but deserving of Japanese exploitation. Their class of militarily-inclined rulers had this impression reinforced by their conquest of Taiwan in 1895, by defeating a chronically inefficient Russian Navy in 1905, occupying Korea in 1910 and Manchuria in 1931-32 by when their pride, and contempt for Chinese life, led them to appalling atrocities.

Tisala said: 'So two supposedly master races, Germany and Japan, incongruously became confederates in ambition to conquer less deserving elements of mankind, whom they regarded as sub-human, and treated with cruel barbarism.'

I said: 'As they were also killing you whales, for oil for nitroglycerine to arm their own doomed immoral aggression.'

'Such is the folly, but also the strength, of bad ideas when combined with force,' said Tisala.

He paused again. 'But it is clear that many other people among the human races have suffered the delusions of exclusivity in some form. I understand the Chinese long thought they were the only civilised people, though it seems they were content to know nothing of anywhere else. The English, at least for a time, saw superiority as a God-given right; and I have the impression that some Frenchmen somehow still retain such a view of themselves.'

'Yes,' I said, 'although God's part in it has long been diminished.'

Tisala went on: 'And from what you say, the Americans are showing a similar arrogance. Perhaps they too easily confuse excellence with power, thinking themselves superior on the basis of having the richest economy the most powerful military and the largest consumption of the world's resources in history; so, like other nations who have gone before them, deluding themselves.'

He said: 'The idea of exclusive superiority is a product of ignorance and false pride. Reduce ignorance, and you diminish false pride. Among nations, freedom, knowledge, tolerance and debate need be used to disarm the peddlers of exclusiveness.' I had a strange feeling in Tisala's mind a strategy was forming.

'But,' he said, 'then there is this problem: the potential for development of a better humanity has been taken hostage and subverted to the use of those in power.'

But before I could ask him what he meant he said:

'But that is for another day. Now I'm going out to sea.'

This became a habit of his when he had reached a pausing point in examining the frenetic world of mankind. There was a place not far from Inis Cuan where there were great underwater towers of rock and deep trenches, though at the surface all you could see was a scattering of rocks. We called it The Sump. A place where no boats came and where Tisala delighted to dive and rise among the rocky sentinels, in the calm world of the sea, and where we believed he was safe.

On that day, because it was sunny and calm with just a light breeze from the west, Eric and I decided to take the boat out to The Sump. Very occasionally, at low tide, and if the conditions were just right, you could land on the central group of rocks if you knew the channels in. It was less than an hour off low tide and The Sump rocks were near their maximum exposure as we approached. There was even broken water near the Little Sump – a group of rocks lying just to the south-west – which rarely showed themselves except at the lowest equinoctial tides. We wove and nudged out way carefully through the right channels. We put ashore on the dark, algae-covered rocks, with their scattering of lighter barnacle encrustations. Eric and I clambered the few feet to the top and looked for Tisala. But what we saw was a sailing boat, not far off. We had been concentrating on the passage in and had not seen it. 'It's coming this way!' said Eric, after a few seconds.

'We must warn Tisala.'

'Yes, but where is he?' We gazed everywhere, but the sea was empty.

I cursed myself for not having told Tisala we might come out: he would not be looking for us. 'He must be about – if he surfaces near there, the secret will be out. A Blue Whale in these waters would be news everywhere.'

'What on earth are they doing? They're heading straight for the Little Sump,' said Eric.

'They've probably seen us, and think it's okay.'

'I hope they've got proper charts.'

'Where the hell is Tisala?' I looked around, heart in throat, and back at the boat. It was only a few hundred yards off, and coming on. Then, on the far side of the rocks, quite close, but heading round towards the boat, I saw Tisala rise slowly. I shouted out, 'Tisala! Look out! Boat!' and pointed my arm in the direction of the boat. He slid below the water. I was not sure if he had seen or heard, but he did not appear again for two or three minutes. Then I saw a glimpse of him a bit further off, low in the water, and only for a few moments – not the length of him, nor his dorsal fin. I knew he had rolled slightly, raising his line of vision to look before the water closed over him.

'He's seen us, and he'll have been able to see the boat from there.'

'Thank God!' said Eric. 'But those idiots are still coming towards the rocks.'

We gesticulated, pointing towards the danger, and at last they saw their position and changed course away. One of them stood up in the cockpit and waved – a sort of thank-you – as they headed away eastwards.

We were quiet in the boat on the way back, cross with ourselves for not having been vigilant enough; a mistake we would try hard not to make again.

'Unusual for any boat to come there at all,' said Eric. 'More boats, nowadays.'

I returned towards shore with an undefined feeling of unease and urgency. That was our first warning.

CHAPTER 36

On Power and Hell

When we resumed our discussion I asked, 'What did you mean about the use and subversion of power?'

Tisala said he was recalling, for instance, the history of the Christian Church in Rome. What had much troubled him was the extent to which the original simple teaching of Christ could be so diverted by the theology and rules of the Church to produce the complicated structure of wealth and political power that emerged. By the Middle Ages the Church had become a vast and powerful bureaucracy imposing detailed legislation: a legal system much more than divine religious body, with courts and rules and laws and heresies – the very thing its founder had rebelled against in the old Jewish religion.

And as it grew, the system became more corrupt. A succession of Popes had abused their power, living in great luxury off the wealth levied form the faithful; supposedly celibate Popes appointed their own illegitimate children and other family members as cardinals, some while still teenagers; and pursued power in politics, diplomacy and war. Too often heresy equated with merely opposing the wrongful practises and pronouncements of the papacy, and too often official torture and execution followed. Tisala noted this coincided with the Church's monopoly of religious power in Western Europe.

As Popes, under the explicit constraints of Christian ethics, often betrayed their founder and trust, Tisala concluded it was hardly surprising that other rulers and leaders when they achieve power, widely perpetrate evil. 'To reduce the evil of authoritarian power is one of the great tasks facing you humans.'

He found it hardly surprising that, when the medieval Roman Church was corrupt, its mechanism for pardon was also corrupt: it cynically peddled and sold pardons for sins, however bad, in return for cash payments. Forgiveness by proxy was also encouraged – pardons being available for long dead relatives in return for sufficient cash payments. Tisala said, 'So, for money the Church licensed sinning,' said Tisala. 'Little wonder the Protestant reformers rose in revolt.'

But Tisala thought the more serious error is in the Church and the priests. They have built a system in which their pleasure in exercising supposed power and authority to forgive overrides their commitment to wider moral good. Even in their own religious terms, it is better to leave forgiveness to God; and the day they do so will be when they have overcome this aspect of love of power.

Religiously, by the Reformation, the Roman Church was in a decayed state, defending indefensible practices and fundamental errors about the nature of the universe. It censored new learning and ruthlessly condemned its proponents, including such as Bruno, who was burned alive, and Galileo. In the ferment caused by the new scientific and geographical discoveries, and scholarly dissention calling for new Biblical interpretation, the papacy saw its monopoly of doctrinal dictat, the source of its power, disappearing. Printing presses and vernacular translations of the Bible allowed people to read and question the church's teaching and law. In response, Pope Paul III, in 1545, sought to preserve the Church's authority by pronouncing that 'Tradition' (meaning that which is authorised by the Church) was of equal validity with biblical teaching. Tisala commented that here was a valuable mechanism that could have led to a reinterpretation of the Bible to rid it of myths, fables, inadequate ethics, and a whole cluttered encrustation of unwisely accumulated beliefs and practices. But instead he feared it was often used, when it was used religiously at all, to reinforce them and to promulgate further doctrinal impositions, such as the cult of Mary.

Even more unhappily, Tisala saw that the power to promote 'Tradition' to a required part of church belief was used politically, to bolster the power and influence of the Roman Church. He thought it no accident that the declaration of papal infallibility was made in 1870, in the very last days of the papacy as a territorial power ruling its own states. As it became clear that the Papal States would be lost to the emerging Italian nation, the papacy – the Pope and Curia – sought a countervailing accretion of 'spiritual' power. Despite dismayed opposition within the Church, the doctrinal infallibility of the Pope was pronounced, pressed through by beleaguered cardinals and a Pope who had previously shown no knowledge of his own infallibility. It seemed a clever stratagem. It entrenched a powerful weapon for the enforcement of the papal will.

But Tisala said: 'It was also dangerous, both for the Church itself and for the wider world. Wrongful or foolish use of such authoritarian power could cause great damage and undermine or even destroy the authority that wields it.' He thought the consequences of the doctrine would return to haunt the Church, for it placed authority above reason.

Tisala understood that the rationale used to justify it was based on the infallibility of Christ, which was conferred on him unofficially, within about eighty years after his death, by virtue of his acclamation as Son of God; though this was officially recognised only in 325 AD at Nicea, amid much opposition from some of the early churches, at the behest of the non-believing skilful emperor of Rome, Constantine. And it was only a century after this formal adoption at Nicea, which included Constantine's forward-looking description of Christ as 'consubstantial' with the Father, that Christ became recognised, not merely as the Son of God, but as God himself. At the Council of Chalcedon, in 451 AD, following many bitter disputes over what became heretical beliefs about his status (as to whether he was merely a man or a prophet, or was the Son of God), an ambitious reason-contorting Trinitarian definition of Christ was reached. He was pronounced co-equal with, and one and the same as, God and the Holy Spirit; as a result of which, Christ, now being God, was invested with a wholly infallible infallibility.

The papacy declared that infallibility, at least in doctrinal matters, passed to the bishops of Rome by way of the biblical statement whereby Christ appointed Peter as the foundation of the Church, and then by the doctrine of apostolic succession whereby the Popes somehow inherited the by-then-supposed infallibility of Peter; though both claims are unsurprisingly disbelieved by nearly everyone else. The apostles, including Peter, were humble men, and had no such pretensions.

Tisala found extraordinary how, nevertheless, nearly two thousand years later, the Church having long claimed Peter as the first Pope, the nineteenth century papacy then claimed that Christ's infallibility came down through Peter and the line of over three hundred popes; though 'came down', when considered, must mean intervention by God and endowment on each pope in turn, for in reality there was no 'line' but a disparate and often disputatious series of papal elections. One pope had no less than three reigns because of various intervening papal disputes; and for forty years, during the Great Schism, there were two popes, one elected at Avignon, and one at Rome, both contenders claiming to be the rightful successor to Peter.

'I suppose,' said Tisala, 'that if the question of doctrinal infallibility had arisen earlier both would have strongly denied the infallibility of the other.'

'Yes,' I said, 'they each tried to raise an army against the other, to fight it out.'

Tisala sighed, and observed that none of three hundred previous Popes had apparently realised that they were doctrinally infallible, which he found scarcely surprising, given their many imperfect performances in office.

I said: 'But apparently, in 1870, Pope Pius IX discovered this inherited papal power, which his successors have gratefully accepted. They have used it, among other things, to try to control the procreative lives of the faithful, and increase their number in an attempt to garner more souls for God.'

Tisala found this very strange. He thought that, if God were to exist, he must do so as a higher being. Such a God would not count people like coins – the greater number the more exciting the tally. That is the mentality of man in operation; that is pride of possession, like a miser counting his money, a tyrant his soldiers, and here a church the number of its souls, though this last presented as for the glory of God. But he noted it was the poor who suffer the most from these notions, which are imposed using the lately acquired power of papal infallibility. The poor from whom the priests thereby withhold the means of control of their fertility: the crowded impoverished communities, misled into further impoverishing themselves, and bringing more suffering on all their children. The richer, educated faithful disregard the papal injunctions, for they are no longer susceptible to the threats of hell, and the Church turns a blind eye, or issues absolutions.

He said: 'You have told me that most human beings are born, live and die in ignorance and wretched poverty. Where is the glory of God in that?' He thought the Church should abandon the claim to papal, or any other human infallibility, for many of them must know it is not true, and has led to such terrible wrongs.

He saw how much conduct on Earth is influenced by the expectation of heaven. If belief in heaven did not exist, the Church's position on many things would have to change completely, for it is the promise of heaven by which they justify the existence of the impoverished masses. 'You will remember that we Blue Whales believe in no afterlife or heaven, and when our society was whole, voluntarily took steps to ensure our numbers did not increase beyond the good of our world. No God, if he existed, would want maximum numbers, but would want higher beings, engaged in developing moral and spirit-filled lives; for that I think is the whole true purpose of all religious construction.'

Tisala noted too that infallibility was attributed to Mohammed's sayings, not only in the Qur'an but in what his followers wrote down in the Hadith. This gave rise to the power exercised over the faithful ever since by the clerical authorities, who assumed the right of final interpretation. It is parallel, but logically inconsistent, with the infallibility claimed much later by the Popes in the Roman Church.

This reminded Tisala of another 'bible' of infallibility – of great influence in our own century – Das Kapital; though I said it was read by few except believers, and understood by fewer of them. He doubted if Marxism was capable of being understood, at least in relation to the real world, for he thought it a tortuous fantasy, based on a partial misunderstanding of its two main subjects, history and economics, and devoid of any wider balancing philosophy. Yet it sent half the world off in a wrong and terrible direction.

But Tisala recalled that Marx was idealistically sincere and concerned for most of mankind; though, like many men pursuing an ideal world, he too easily contemplated conflict. And the nature of his book undoubtedly gave those who came after him the opportunity to unleash evil on the world.

Tisala said, 'The writers of books must take every care they can; but those who follow bear a large responsibility of interpretation and action, and all influential books need wise interpretation.'

One day, when we were talking of religion, he said he was amazed that people of our intelligence, knowledge and ingenuity should still widely believe in the Devil – Satan – evil supposedly embodied in and directed against humans by an external supernatural person.

Tisala recognised that many people, at least in parts of the world, appear no longer really to believe this; but that even among these, there was ample evidence of a jumble of lazy thinking, leaving a residual part-belief that emerges to distort the prospect of a better or truer view. He thought one consequence of belief in such a supernatural Devil is that people tempted to be or do evil are relieved of their personal responsibility. There exists, the Churches argue, a powerful force inciting them to evil, and humans, taught that they are sinful weak creatures, are likely to succumb. The focus is removed from evildoers onto a fantastic world of demons and lurking subterranean forces, built up to emphasise the salvation on offer from the Church. The Church claimed authority to forgive, pardon and absolve. Tisala saw the intended good – wiping the slate clean, so relieving the individual from the fear of hell and divine retaliation, But he asked, 'Wasn't this only necessitated because of the Church's primitive view of the nature of God as a purveyor of hell-fire justice, picked up from Judaism?'

The larger point he thought is this: the existence of 'the Devil' or 'Satan' as a supernatural being gives rise to a need for a whole balancing religious force. He saw how the Devil enters the world through the Bible, by the extraordinary notion of the fall of man, in the story of Adam and Eve. It astonished him that for many hundreds of years religious humans have believed literally that all the pain and evil in the world was caused by the disobedience of two mere humans 'in the garden of Eden'. This belief requires that God, in punishment for their eating one apple against his command, demanded the setting in train over thousands of years, the suffering and death by disease, famine, war and murder of untold millions of his children, whom it is simultaneously claimed he loves. Tisala thought it as bizarre an idea as could be conceived by any mind with the power of thought.

And it was an idea that disregarded the suffering, pain and death in the animal kingdom for millions of years before men appeared on Earth; an idea which had some excuse before such things were known, but not since.

He thought that, in the light of the increasing knowledge of the natural world, the earlier, cruder, forms of belief arising from the doctrine of Satan and the fall should have become unbelievable. So he expected images of hell, with fiery pits and demons in eager attendance, to have given way to more subtle forms of hell, such as absence from God. He saw how Purgatory and more lenient forms of punishment had been promoted, at least for the elect or unfortunate, as an escape route from the moral dilemma caused by having an omnipotent, all-loving God, who dispensed damnation and eternal torture. Tisala thought that now men have at least a better idea of the age of life on Earth – three thousand million years – any reflection must bring the realisation that eternal punishment would be so out of proportion to any possible sin that no God who retained even the smallest element of love or mercy could morally impose such a penalty; and it must therefore be a misconception.

I said: 'A misconception I fear still promoted in some quarters by the threatening pronouncements of religions, whose authorities sometimes have a deep interest in maintaining hell for disciplinary purposes; that is to say, though ostensibly for their believers' benefit, actually to maintain their power over them.'

He was initially surprised, following the gentler, loving concept of God taught by Christ, that the unremitting fierceness of the Christian image of hell had developed as it had, with many still apparently deemed deserving of eternal punishment. And he was discouraged to find that plenty of later reformed parts of religion took up the same dreadful vision. He questioned whether humans really needed such a threat to keep them from evil; and he concluded that for the most part the evil were evil anyway, and it was the good who suffered the anguished terrors of threatened damnation. He was appalled by the idea of mental torture and fear of eternal torment in hell that must have afflicted the lives of millions of humans across the centuries. And he pondered what misery could have been saved if the biblical authors had only thought differently, more enlighteningly.

Tisala believed that probably, though many among the under-educated still believe in such a hell, more retain a hope of heaven, for the rewards and pleasures of an afterlife seem generally desirable. But he wondered too how long this would and could continue.

For Tisala thought it true that the weakening of the grip of hell on men's minds results also in weakening the power of heaven. Where death meant the certainty of going to either heaven or hell, the desirability of heaven was much promoted by the extreme undesirability of hell; and similarly, heaven must be desired most by those whose lives are torment on Earth, full of misery and suffering.

But Tisala observed that Christianity had itself made progress. The Roman Church developed Purgatory as a crude first step, but even then the relief it gave was reserved only for that church's repentant members. And then, regrettably, Rome stopped and has not yet moved further. More advanced were the many in the Anglican Church, and some other reformed churches, who have tacitly and by degrees dismantled the fearful concept of hell. They have preferred to believe that, somehow, despite the various biblical statements, including those attributed to Christ, the loving God would circumvent the fires and agonies of hell in favour, if not of outright abolition, at least of amelioration – hell then seen simply as the absence of God. Perhaps after all not so unlike the Greek burial-chamber subterranean world. He thought the next step for religions would be to construct a belief that an all-loving God would 'somehow' reach even into that world, and abolish torment; and that, in the end, everyone should be 'saved'. He concluded that eventually such reasoning would lead to the realisation that the whole concept of hell is misconceived and untrue.

He regarded such a process as the rise of a higher moral judgement, reason and sympathy overcoming faith misplaced in a supposedly immutable book. 'So we can be rid of your Hell. There is enough trouble in the development of life in Earth without concocting such a fantasy. You humans have been greatly foolish to have indulged in such so long, and should remove it from your religions and your minds.

So much of our religions now seemed to me untrue that I wondered how much longer they would survive.

Tisala said: 'You have shown me that they have always been replaced – many have gone, and none of your present ones is much older than three thousand years, which is a small fraction of man's existence. But there is a dilemma of timing, for I have learned plenty enough of what your godless regimes have inflicted on the world. You still seem to need religions as a bar on your worst instincts. But in the meantime, the problem with religions is this: the good in them is needed, but to get it followers are obliged to take up and perpetuate what I am forced to conclude is a dangerously wrong view of reality and the world, from which much evil has flowed. The advance required, as mankind increasingly knows, is by willing persuasion of minds to accept higher good and reject unreason. And that when religious beliefs are rejected, people should hold on to and enhance the morals and restraints that religion and philosophy have fostered.'

As to who really believed what, he thought it is clear that many who attend churches, mosques and temples have in reality mixed minds of beliefs, often partial or vague and unformed, but who find other reasons for loyalty. Men are by nature social animals, and derive pleasure from being part of a community where they are accepted as belonging. Sometimes when belief is arrived at by the thrilling discovery of inclusive faith, together with personal acceptance by a great being, called God, it is often at an emotional moment, in conversion meetings, or troubled times in the converts' lives. Suddenly the world's terrors and uncertainties are removed – for example, by giving your life to Jesus, and an all-loving Father, or by accepting Allah and his messenger Mohammad – Islam and its whole system – the convert may think every problem of existence is resolved. Sometimes, less exaltedly, religion comes from family background, joining in the life of church, mosque or temple, with the attraction for many humans of hierarchy, ritual and ceremony; and music, worship and sometimes, moral teaching. Tisala concluded that the survival of religious practices is readily understandable.

'But none of this makes it true,' I said.

'No, but at the time it gives the believers real and perhaps much needed relief or lift,' said Tisala. 'It is an escape route that has served many.' But he remarked that where later disenchantment with belief advances far enough, those props will not be enough. Sometimes the cause of loss of faith is trauma, which faces previous believers with the contradiction – previously unexplained but not then requiring explanation – of an all-loving God and cruel or pointless death or destruction. Then the Church's explanation that "It's a divine mystery," or "It is the will of God," or "God does not want it to happen, but allows it in an evil world," becomes inadequate, and even repulsive.'

Tisala said, 'Faith and emotions are close partners in humans, but violation of the emotional trust can release suspended reason.' That is what happens, he thought, to thinking people as they learn of things that put them beyond accepting the full rigours of their religion, and afterwards larger and larger parts of it. The priests and believers then shake their heads and say, 'He has lost his faith.' They do not allow, even to themselves, that the person has found his faith misplaced and untrue. And their congregations are taught to protect themselves by regarding their former brother as cut off, a lost soul, or even a mortal sinner, and sometimes worthy of death, depending on the strictness of their own thought cage.

He recognised of course that lack of religious faith arises as well from the lure and availability of material pleasures; which is widespread among the very many uncommitted to formal religion. But much of that he thought a shallow response of people who soon enough find such pleasures delusionary, at least as a source of real happiness: 'For we know the nature of humanity is greater than that, and you have given plenty of evidence that many find a need for things of the spirit'.

Tisala said: 'What is needed is a new morality, one universally accepted. Much of it of course will not be new, but newly conceived and understood. Out of moral philosophy and the best morality of the old religions, and by reason and love applied to new knowledge will grow a new spirit and code of ethics, to guide men. They will be free from superstition and the supernatural, and the heavy burden of the past. So your great religions, unless they morally develop beyond themselves, having played their part in raising mankind, will fall into disuse, like the earlier religions long gone by; though groups and pockets of believers will survive for many years, clinging to their shrinking certainties and cults.'

Such were the discussions I had with Tisala in those years. As his mastery of history and the human condition advanced, his ability to strip away the confusing plethora of folly and delusion that crowd about the history of man's activities and beliefs delighted me. I felt as if I were being led into a better and more rational world, where reason, knowledge and goodwill might be applied to do good in the

Earth. And I found to my surprise, though I was brought up in the Christian religion, that I accepted with complete calmness the feeling of overwhelming probability that the God of my traditional religion does not exist. More than that, I found it exciting, welcome and uplifting.

But oddly enough we did not then explore further the concept of heaven. We were then more concerned with the hell of whaling.

In those days with Tisala, I often felt exhilarated and excited and eager to press on. But our time together each year always seemed short. And always underneath, as each season went by, and Tisala departed from Inis Cuan to the summer Arctic or winter tropics, I felt a dread of what might happen to him out in the open ocean where whales were still being hunted by the cruel unspeakable merchants of genocide, my fellow men.

CHAPTER 37

Whaling 1964-75

The news from the whaling front, in the years following my ejection from whaling circles, had been bad as well as good. After 1964, I had no longer sought to confront commercial whalers directly, but my continuing unofficial contacts with IWC scientists revealed that they were increasingly disillusioned by the continual rejection of their scientific advice. Every time the more conservation-minded scientists came up with research, which showed, yet again, that gross over-whaling was taking place, year after year they found their recommendations overruled by their masters, the whaling members of the IWC.

From Tisala I fed the scientists down in London a stream of ideas and suggestions: that they had overestimated the whales' reproductive rate, which was not just a question of numbers multiplied by gestation and nursing times, but was adversely affected by the destruction of their social nexus and the traumas of individual family losses; that it was possible to distinguish pregnant females if, before giving chase, the formation of a family or group was observed for a short period; that there should be much tighter rules governing distances and weather conditions for firing harpoons, which would reduce the incidence of 'struck and lost' and the length of agony for struck and mutilated whales. It was the hideous cruelty and destruction I hated, but to diminish them I argued dispassionately that it was inefficient: it required time-wasting and costly use of further harpoons, which caused loss of valuable whale products by splattering parts of the still living whales into the sea. (I once made this point to a Norwegian whale-ship owner. He considered for a moment and said, in excellent English, that he thought the percentage of loss was fairly small, and that the industry could bear it.)

These and other imperfections in the whaling industry, such as turning blind eyes to the killing of young whales and nursing mothers, would, I argued, be controlled by the imposition of a mandatory observer scheme; and that otherwise the whalers would run their whole industry into an early death by unrecorded overexploitation But my great fear was that it might survive long enough, by hunting the smaller whales, to exterminate the surviving remnants of several species of the great whales – first the most endangered Blues, then the Southern Rights, and then possibly the Humpbacks. I warned repeatedly that the whole scandal would be so great that the public would rise in revulsion against the entire industry, and would demand an end to it, and the shameful inertia of governments that allowed it. And to the scientists I increasingly pressed the argument that their moral duty as scientists was to stop the destruction. But some of them remained adamant that their role was merely technical, confined to measuring and monitoring to find the elusive sustainable yield for the industry.

To start with what small progress there was seemed pitifully inadequate in the face of looming catastrophe for the Blues. Then, as already recounted, a turning point was reached when pressure in the IWC resulted in the passing of their ban in 1965 on hunting Blue Whales in the Antarctic and North Pacific. But the Blue Whales had virtually disappeared. And so, two years later came the extension of protection to the whole of the Southern Hemisphere. It was desperately late in coming, but it was a source of great rejoicing in our little community on Eileen Mòr and Inis Cuan. Down in London amongst most of the scientists there was a sense of relief and achievement. And the change in feeling was gradually spreading through the more enlightened members of the Commission, and out into the wider world.

Not of course that whaling had ceased. Far from it. With the annihilation of the Blues, the whalers were busy decimating the Fin whales, and when their widespread destruction was advanced were to turn to the Sei, and would next hunt the Minke.

But in 1967 the Blues, the gentle wise giants of the ocean, were on the edge of extinction. Tisala told us of Blue Whale families split and huddled in small groups, attempting at all costs to avoid the remorseless whalers, yet needing to swim to the food-rich seas. The seas of paradise became the waters of death and destruction. For although the Norwegians, Russians and Japanese had not formally lodged objections to the Blue Whale protection, and were nominally bound by it, the reality was different.

The Norwegians, who all through the twentieth century were responsible for killing more Blue Whales than any other national whaling fleet, saw the heyday of profit was finally over and were at last reducing their fleet. After 1969 they abandoned commercial whaling for the great whales in Antarctica, and two years later abandoned it in the North Atlantic. They mercifully transferred their exploitation to a different sort of oil – that from the bed of the North Sea. But they continued to hunt smaller whales. So I remember clearly my feeling of relief when the news of cessation in the North Atlantic came through. A rogue whaler however, did remain a threat to Tisala and his kind. Former Norwegian whaling captains and senior harpooners began to appear on other whaling vessels under flags of convenience. And Norwegian whaling interests invested in Canadian whaling. The Canadians, more honest than some, admitted the killing of three Blue Whales in the late 1960s.

The focus of killing shifted to the Russians and Japanese, who both retained formidable whaling fleets. The Russians continued to hunt Blue Whales when they could find them, despite the IWC resolutions. They simply omitted any killed from their records and reports. This continued throughout the late 1960s and into the 1970s. Every year Tisala brought news of continued deaths. Blue Whales killed where none should have been, mainly in the Antarctic, but some in the North Pacific and other places where the Russians were not involved. Every death was now increasingly critical to the chances of survival of his kind. Our initial optimism was badly shaken. We had been hoping for news of new births at least holding their own, and perhaps increasing in relation to mortality. But for 1968, Tisala had assessed that the Blue Whale births of a hundred and sixty were outweighed by a total of nearly three hundred deaths, well over two hundred of them at the hands of whalers.

I remember my bitter anger when during her illness Ellie, who had insisted on being told, had been so distressed by one such setback. And I was glad that the last piece of news she had was of a group well known to Tisala in the North Atlantic who had three successful births and no losses. And it was in these years that the whales took increasingly effective evasive action, and even the lying Russians found their victims dwindling. After 1970 the killing of Blue Whales never exceeded fifty in any season, and after 1975 was in single figures. Amongst the misery of reported deaths, Tisala began to report a cautious note of hope.

As to the Japanese, having reluctantly accepted the protection of Blue Whales in Antarctica in 1965, and within months of my exhilaratingly running down to the shack in Inis Cuan to tell Tisala the good news, these same Japanese started to whale out of Peru and Chile. Neither of these two countries was a member of the IWC, and its resolutions protecting the Blue Whales did not therefore apply to them. Thus the whalers of those countries, and anyone else flying under their flag, could legally continue to hunt Blue Whales in their own territorial waters and all the international seas of the world. Thus, cynically, did the Japanese whalers seek to avoid their more public commitments under the IWC. The Japanese delegation compounded its hypocrisy the next year by publicity accepting the extension of Blue Whale protection to the whole of the Southern Hemisphere, while Japanese whaling continued under different colours.

With Robert Thompson's help I had been canvassing several members of Parliament, including a junior minister, and we wrote letters and articles to the press, a number of which were published. It was a small contribution, but to our delight we increasingly realised we were not alone – disquiet and calls for whale protection were beginning to appear in the whaling nations and more widely across the world. Our correspondence and information-sharing grew.

In 1971, almost too late to help the Blues, the observer scheme was finally passed and introduced. For the first time there was an outside check on the hunting record of each fleet, though there were suspicions as to what mutual arrangements were made between the Russians and Japanese in observing each other's activities. Almost too late again, the fateful Blue Whale unit was finally abolished the following year. Now at last scientists could recommend a quota setting for each species which took account of the crippled scarcity of the endangered species. And for the Blue Whales, the quota set, at least officially, was nil.

But on our islands there was little sense of triumph – more a sense of exhausted relief. Only slowly as time passed did we allow a more positive belief to grow that the greatest creature of all the

Earth's creations might after all survive the blind onslaught of men. A glimmer of hope was signalled back and forth between the two polar ends of the world in the journeying of Tisala and others of his kind.

But the old attitudes remained entrenched in parts of the IWC. In 1971, I received an agitated report from one of the scientists about the proceedings of an international whale conference held in Virginia, USA. There, a group of industry scientists reported that many whale populations had been so drastically reduced by commercial whaling that continued 'harvesting' as a separate venture was no longer economic. They finally admitted they did not know enough to produce a true picture of 'biologically sound harvesting'. I could scarcely believe their dismaying, unrepentant admission, following the long years of their organisation's destruction of the great whales throughout the world. All their years of confident assertion and detailed figures supporting the 'harvesting' of so many thousands of great whales were worthless. But the scientists had not finished. To improve their 'picture' they thought scientific analysis should be uncoupled from dependence on the capture of animals on the traditional whaling grounds.

In other words, they were proposing to search out the last remaining sheltered places for whales in the oceans, and their often-undiscovered breeding grounds, and expose them area by area, species by species, group by group, in the name of research, to justify further exploitation. They did accompany this with a call for 'proper management' of the 'stocks'. But they knew the dreadful reality of all previous whaling history and the morally bankrupt policies of the whalers. I said to Tisala that this must be one of the most flagrant examples of scientific dereliction of moral duty: to use their science in such circumstances without securing guarantees against abusive use to which it was certain to be put. Defending, but in reality condemning, themselves they added that no action had yet been taken to prevent the over-exploitation of the remaining unexploited stocks of Cetaceans, particularly the Antarctic Minke Whale. They followed this with the arousing affirmation that 'It is not enough to seek protection for a species only after its numbers have been so reduced as to threaten its existence.'

They added another popularity-seeking declaration, that whales should be 'useful' monitors of pollution in the oceans caused by heavy metals, pesticide residues, radio-nuclides, and other fallout products. By 'monitors' they meant that the whales would act like canaries down mines, ingesting these toxic substances; though in the case of whales they would first have be killed and cut up to see if indeed they had been sick and dying, which, if so, would enable the whaling industry to give a public-spirited warning to the world, while otherwise profitably using additional whale products. They added seductively that, because of the present impracticality of directly garnering the oceans' plankton, 'harvesting' of whales was by far the most effective way of tapping these resources. Ecological balance was nowhere mentioned, let alone any thought for the whales themselves. But their efforts for the public good did not stop with the larger whales. They noted that smaller whales, including the porpoises, represented 'a resource of major potential economic importance,' and that in the near future, 'porpoise hunting as an end in itself would become an important enterprise.'

'Harvesting' was a term under which they sought to neutralise their guilt and the ghastly sham and cruelty of their activities; though inadvertently it was an appropriate term for indicating the blanket mowing down of everything in their path. It was like dustbowl farming, but much worse, for the environment did not belong to them, they cared nothing for it, they planted nothing, and instead of corn they were cutting down beautiful sentient beings.

Left to itself, the whaling industry would not stop: under the pretended cloak of scientific management and public good they might destroy any remaining species of cetacean in the oceans.

But in the following year, 1972, the sun shone on the sea again. A great chance came for the anti-whaling groundswell to be heard. For some years, there had been growing in the civilised world a wider realisation and unease about the conduct of the whaling industry. Conservationists, marine biologists, some politicians and increasingly the scientists connected with whaling at last concluded that the member nations in the IWC would never regulate whaling properly of their own volition. They had destroyed species after species of the Great Whales and were now proceeding to 'harvest' yet more species, including the only remaining unhunted rorqual, the Minke Whale. But this time there would be no other unexploited species left in the oceans, except the porpoises and dolphins. A growing number of informed and alarmed people decided they must bring pressure to bear on the whalers by other means.

That year, the United Nations was to hold a Conference on the Human Environment at Stockholm, which was to discuss the future of other animal species. When it came to discussing whales, the anti-whaling groups persuaded the Conference to debate a sweeping moratorium for ten years on all commercial whaling. To those at the Conference who were in the wider realms of the environmental future of the world, the matter was obvious. In the debate and the surrounding discussions, the whaling nations were so taken aback by the weight of sentiment against them that in the end even the hardliners only dared to abstain. The Stockholm Conference voted fifty-three to nil in favour of the moratorium, with twelve abstentions. The result underlined the sad tragedy of the United Nations' previous decision in 1946 to hand over the future of the whales to the IWC. The error of that decision was further underlined when, two weeks after the UN conference vote in Stockholm, the IWC met for its own annual meeting.

At that meeting the British and the Americans, supported by the Mexicans and the Argentineans proposed an identical moratorium. The whaling nations, in the security of their own organisation, laughed at the proposed resolution, and it was thrown out. But it was a mistake to laugh, for it exposed their stance, and fed their opponents' determination. The resolution was presented at each of the following three annual meetings: in 1973, 1974 and 1975, but failed each time because a three-quarter majority was required under the rules for such a resolution. In these years, Australia, Canada, France and Panama joined the pro-moratorium countries.

The pressure was growing on the IWC. They felt forced to adopt new whaling management procedures to try to placate their critics. But like so much else the IWC had purported to do, it largely failed. The killing went on, and indeed the whalers sought new ways of circumventing the restrictions closing about them. The members of the Commission, each year setting controversial quotas to permit maximum profit, against the advice from their scientists, saw an opportunity. Taking advantage of provisions in the original Convention, they persuaded their governments to license increased scientific whaling for research. Whales killed for this purpose were counted in addition to the commercial quotas set. They thought 'scientific whaling' would demonstrate their commitment to proper husbandry while allowing them to kill extra whales. For the increased knowledge was to take place via autopsies. It was a disguised method of increasing their kill.

In the southern hemisphere, the ailing South African, Australian and New Zealand industries flagrantly used and abused this loophole to prop up their dwindling commerce. The New Zealand whalery nevertheless quickly collapsed, mercifully for the good reputation of that country. Years later, in the North Atlantic, the Norwegians, the Icelanders and the Danes were to use it, and most damaging of all, the Russians and Japanese were to use it on a worldwide basis.

In years subsequent to 1973, as the struggle to pass a moratorium on whaling grew, all sorts of subterfuges came to light. Japan started paying money to small non-whaling nations to persuade them to join the IWC and vote down the increasingly urgent attempts to restrict over-whaling. The Japanese entered trade and aid deals with some of these countries in return for whaling voting quota 'understandings'. Conversely, when conservation-minded small nations, such as St Lucia and Antigua in the West Indies, joined the IWC to seek to counteract the pro-whaling vote, the Japanese put trading and other penalties and pressures on them to seek to neutralise their votes. That the Japanese were behaving dishonestly became clear. They changed the names of whaling ships and companies to which they belonged to hide the fact that they were under Japanese ownership; they gave false information about their shipping interests abroad, for instance designating one ship as a shrimp trawler which was afterwards observed to have had a harpoon gun mounted in its bows. Information leaked out from crew members that there were Japanese interests where none was publicly acknowledged, including on occasions, the presence of Japanese meat traders on foreign ships. By various routes, whale meat appeared in Japan, some from South America marked 'produce of Spain'; some came from Icelandic or Norwegian whalers, transferred by sleight of hand through different entrepot ports.

In addition to whaling out of non-IWC whaling countries, Japanese whaling interests emerged in pirate whalers under all manner of disguises. One was the notorious pirate ship *Sierra* registered in Cyprus (a country which had no knowledge or interest in whaling).

This ship for several years hunted whales in the so-called protected areas, including the South Atlantic.

Most of the whales killed in these years were not Blue Whales, but sometimes they were. Tisala told me of a number of scattered deaths in Antarctica, up the Chilean and Peruvian Pacific coast, and in the Northern Pacific. On only a few occasions did these matters come to public knowledge – such as when a 'struck and lost' Blue Whale died and was washed up on a shore, as happened in Peru.

But from the early 1970s the anti-whaling members were roused. To counter the vote procuring activities led by the Japanese whaling interests, other non-whaling nations were persuaded to join the Commission and support the call for a moratorium. Some former whaling nations began to change sides. The balance was shifting inside the IWC.

And outside, a revolution was taking place. A few years previously, in 1969 the US Government had withdrawn the licensing for killing Pacific Grey whales. The Californian whaling industry, the last American whalers, collapsed in 1971, to be followed by the Canadian whalery, despite Norwegian investment. In 1972, to coincide with the Stockholm Conference, the Friends of the Earth produced its first whale campaign manual: the sordid slaughter record of the whaling industry, latterly in defiance of its own scientists, was being laid bare and the public informed of the complicit countries. And countries and companies receiving and trading in whale products were listed. A public boycott was called for. In 1973 a cross-section of public figures and organisations, including Prince Bernhard of the Netherlands and Prince Philip, Duke of Edinburgh, the World Wildlife Fund, the Royal Society for the Prevention of Cruelty to Animals, and many others, petitioned the IWC and the Japanese and Russian governments against whaling. In 1973 the British government was at last prepared officially to ban the import of most whale products.

In the same year, in the United States, the Save the Whale campaign began its worldwide advertising strategy of drawing public attention to the horrors of whaling. The public imagination began to be engaged. Never again would the whalers benefit from the widespread public ignorance and indifference of the first seventy years of the twentieth century, which had allowed their unscrupulous genocide to destroy whale populations across the world. In 1975, Greenpeace activists took their little boats and sought physically to disrupt Russian whaling off the American Pacific coast. Their resultant pictures and campaign caught and informed the changing public mood. In America, Congress passed legislation which for the first time could penalise whalers by applying potential sanctions in fishing and other trading areas. So gradually the greatest weakness of the International Whaling Convention itself – lack of any enforcement procedure – began to be addressed.

That was the background against which we had been continuing our work. These were heady days on Inis Cuan. But there were still more years of killing to come.

CHAPTER 38

The Russian Trawler

In those years my life rotated between London and the Hebrides. Bringing up Will and Penny was a full-time occupation, even with Susan's and sometimes my mother's support. It gave me deep satisfaction and pride, interspersed with occasional episodes of acute anxiety and frustration. When in London, I had plenty of work to do, and new learning to absorb, I told myself it was a full and happy life.

Yet whenever Tisala returned to Inis Cuan life seemed to take on a new purpose, another dimension. I was always elated that he had survived another season and tracked his way back across the ocean, and took delight in the renewal of our friendship and the continuation of our work.

My task of equipping his mind became all-pervasive. When I was engaged on this my sadness and loneliness without Ellie fell away, and I felt alive and vital. And when news of some advance against whaling came through, or when Tisala told me that some group of Blue Whales, previously feared for because of their silence, had after all made contact, I felt a strange and thrilling emotion. A spirit of unity was being created, growing, not only between whales and men, but revealing and advancing the underlying unity of living things. And sometimes it was as if the sea itself, through its deep channels of communication, was listening in to our endeavour and was part of it.

When the news was bad – of more deaths, or some hoped for advance against whaling blocked or reversed by the world's whalers, or the longed-for moratorium voted down again, I felt it viscerally. And always behind my eyes in the depth of my mind I heard the refrain, 'Too late. You may be too late'. And I would dispatch more anger-driven letters to address the latest backsliding or outrage.

In the late spring of 1975 we were waiting for the outcome of the moratorium vote at the annual IWC meeting. It seemed possible that this year the vote might be carried. The public anti-whaling campaign had been vociferous and well-informed and more nations were believed to be becoming supportive. So when Tisala returned, to the usual rejoicing, I was in a particularly buoyant mood. I felt the spring renewal even more personally than usual, in part because the previous winter back in London I had met a captivating young woman at a New Year's Eve party. In the weeks that followed we met several times and I began to wonder if, I began to ache with the hope that, my eight long years of widowerhood might be lifting. She was not the first. There had been two or three false starts over the previous years. One was perhaps frightened off because I was too anxious and serious. One failed where we were fast and furious, but where passion eventually was found incompatible with our commitment to our children – she had a little girl – and our respective lives. One was a friend, but despite a few flutters of possibilities and that instantly recognisable difference in glances at supper parties, one or other of us each time proved reluctant to take it beyond the point of friendship. But this time I felt things might be different, hence my buoyancy. And in addition, the kids were up with me on their Easter holidays, staying with Eric and Guinevere, and revelling in the activities of the islands, helping with jobs, walking and chatting, boating and fishing, which was a delight for me too in between my work with Tisala. Both Will and Penny wanted to see and talk with Tisala, and came over to Inis Cuan two or three times. But one day Will and Eric came over on their own, Will as excited as any eleven year old, hanging over the bow of the boat as Eric brought it in, watching the sea bed slope up, the colours change, and signalling with his hand where the strip of sandy bottom lay between the rocks. Will tied up and Eric clambered slowly out of the boat. He was nearly eighty and beginning to be old. But he loved Will and would do anything for him. Will gave him a hand to get ashore. He was always full of Eric's doings, recounting to me 'Grandpa Eric' did this or that, or what he said or told him; words of knowledge or shrewd insight, or outrageous stories recognised as such and loved, and the cause of constant laughter.

That morning Tisala had gone out to sea for a couple of hours. Afterwards Will had gone round the inlet to the headland to look for his return. I was quite confident of Will's ability to look after himself. I left him heading off and made Eric and myself some coffee. We sat chatting for a while in the sunshine outside the shack. Then I turned to finish some work in hand, and Eric said he would stroll up Spyglass Hill – the name Will and I had given the to the little hillock behind the shack.

A short time later I heard a shout.

'Dad!' – the urgency in the cry made me look up sharply. Will was approaching round the inlet, hurrying across the rocks. 'Dad! Something's happened!'

'What is it?'

'It's Tisala.' Will came up, his binoculars banging against his chest, and out of breath. 'Tisala' – he twisted round and pointed down the inlet – 'he was coming back in when he suddenly sheered off and headed away. He dived – a deep dive – he didn't come up – I lost him. I couldn't see him any more. Why did he do a deep dive? Why didn't he come in?'

'I don't know. Let's go up Spyglass. Eric's up there.' Apprehension gripped my chest.

We could see Eric sitting on a rock with his back towards us. We ran up the hill. As we climbed I looked seaward over my shoulder and saw coming round the headland of Eilean Mòr what looked like an ocean-going trawler, bows towards us. It looked like a big Russian trawler. Sometimes they came in the Hebridean waters, festooned in radio equipment and monitoring equipment: everyone up this coast knew that Russian trawlers meant cold war spy ships seeking information about Scottish based British nuclear submarines and their movements. I was not unduly alarmed, but shouted up to Eric and pointed at the boat. As we came towards him I saw him stand and look through his little brass telescope. I heard him exclaim 'Jesus Christ!' He never blasphemed. He lowered his glass and turned to me. I remember the deep line that plunged down his face and seemed to take his mouth with it. 'It's a whaler.'

I looked through the telescope. The boat was turning westward and slowly revealed its side view. There was the sneering raised bow and the squat ugly harpoon gun. I hardly noticed that it had too an unusual amount of what looked like radio masts and equipment. 'What the hell is a whaler doing here?' I said. We looked at each other.

'When did Tisala go out?' asked Eric.

'About two hours ago. He probably went out to The Sump. As he came back he must have seen the whaler. How far out was he Will, when he dived?'

'About half a mile.'

'He must have recognised the whaler and known it to have sonar, which – if it were on – would have spotted him coming into Inis Cuan. He would know the whaler could follow him in and we couldn't physically stop it. He would have been trapped.'

'They surely wouldn't harpoon him in the harbour,' said Eric, shocked.

'No. Outrageous – flagrant... Can't be sure. They might, you know. The sickening bastards. They mustn't find him.' The horror stared at me: Tisala in mortal danger – our haven – everything – might be destroyed.

I tried to remain calm and think what Tisala would have done. 'He's probably gone north close in to Inis Cuan, to keep land between him and the whaler. He might make a dash back to the Sump – the rocks and undersea ridges and columns would hide him and make it very difficult – dangerous even – for a boat to follow.'

'What's it doing now?' said Will, pointing. The whaler was turning its bow towards us, and coming on.

'God Almighty, I hope Tisala's not trying to come in now – their sonar may have picked him up.' We could see a man on the harpoon platform.

We searched the water anxiously with our glasses, but the sea was choppy and we could see nothing. 'He might be in close to the cliffs,' said Eric.

I looked at the still water of the inlet, but could see no familiar slight surge and flat upwelling puddle that would signal Tisala's arrival. The whaler was getting nearer. The man by the harpoon could now be seen doing something with the harpoon.

Suddenly I said: 'We must stop them coming in – if we sit the boat across the channel entrance they will have to sink us to get in. They won't do that.

'I've got my shotgun in the shack,' said Eric.

I ran down the hill, aware of Will close behind me. Eric came stumbling down after us. I arrived panting at the little jetty and jumped into the boat. 'Loose her off, Will.' He did – and made to jump on. 'No! No! Stay ashore.'

'No! I'm coming!' He jumped in and crouched in the bows, back towards me, before I could stop him. There wasn't time. I headed down the inlet at full throttle, but watching out for Tisala. I couldn't see any sign but knew he would come in under us. I slowed at the narrowest point of the channel and went broadside on near Eric's 'No Trespassing' board, which I noticed needed painting. I cursed that I had let it go – it didn't look very official.

I looked towards the outer entrance. If the whaler came in, it would appear round the outlying islet, only about a hundred yards from us.

'Will, get a fishing rod out.' He cast out across the channel.

'Good.'

'They won't bloody get past me,' he said fiercely.

We waited, gazing at the end of the islet, and occasionally glancing down below us, looking for a great dark shadow. I thought, if they come they may try to push past us – I'll have to block them. I wished Will wasn't in the boat. But then I thought, he can stand in the bows and wave like a windmill and shout. They won't run a child down. My mind said, what are you doing – this is grotesque – now Will is in danger. But I knew the whaler might appear at any second, and that I had to stay on station. No, they wouldn't dare run us down. Why should they anyway? They couldn't think a great whale would ever come into such a rock-bound place. Sonar, you fool. I prayed hard that Tisala would not appear. The notice: they might think they had strayed upon a secret government installation. Were they a spy-ship? – they will push in and investigate and afterwards say they had come in to make an engine repair. Then I was glad that our notice was weatherworn and rather amateur – they will think it's a private project. But what if Tisala appears? Stay out, stay out. So my jumble of thoughts ran.

The minutes went by. We saw Eric making his way along the rocks above us, shotgun in hand. When he was opposite us he indicated he would climb up to the ridge. From there he would get a view. He seemed to be painfully slow. I kept glancing towards the sea entrance. Still no trawler. We watched Eric struggle to the top and disappear. Total silence in the boat, the water lapping, and an agonising wait. My eyes flicked constantly between the skyline and the entrance of the inlet – if the whaler was coming in it must be close by now, though it would have slowed right down as it approached the islets and the rocks. Perhaps they had no local charts. Where was Eric?

'Dad,' asked Will in a low voice, 'why hasn't he signalled us?'
'Not sure.'

The skyline remained bare, as did the inlet entrance, just smallish waves coming round the corner into the approach. Then we heard what sounded like a cry or whoop and Eric reappeared waving his gun. He pointed repeatedly away from the inlet entrance.

'They've gone past,' I said to Will. Relief flooded through me.

We scrambled ashore and raced up to the ridge. Sure enough, there was the whaler, stern towards us heading away to the north, away from Inis Cuan and away from rocks which lay further to the west.

'Thank God,' I said.

'But where is Tisala?' asked Will.

'He'll be about,' I said, confidence returning. 'He'll probably keep out of the way for a while yet.' For some while we kept an eye on the whaler. It continued on its way northward and became a dot on the horizon. We trudged down to the boat.

We felt light-spirited and joked about holding the Russian Navy at bay with a fishing rod and an empty shotgun, and so released our fear and tension.

'If they'd seen a Scottish blunderbuss pointing at them, they'd have headed off,' said Eric with a touch of pride.

'They'd just have shot you,' said Will.

'D'you think they would?' he said, as if it hadn't occurred to him.

''Course,' said Will.

Eric let out an indignant 'Hmm,' but looked at the ground.

But the day went by and Tisala did not appear. Will spent hours on the cliff top and twice I went out to him with food and reassurance, though I was beginning to get anxious myself. It was not until early evening that I saw Will waving from down the inlet and pointing at the entrance. He came hurrying back. And then I saw the familiar surge and bow wave in the water, and a section of the great back breaking the surface and coming steadily towards us. The sight had never looked more serene and magnificent and the stresses of the day dissolved into happiness.

But underneath I was alarmed. This was the second and much more serious warning. Subsequently, we thought of and introduced various safeguards against the return of any Russian whaler or other intruders. After some debate, we repainted the warning notice. And after this, one of us always went up Spyglass with binoculars to scan the area before Tisala left the inlet for one of his breaks. I worried whether this incident was the first of a new more intrusive trend in cold war surveillance, or worse, that the visit of the whaler was just that: a whaler looking for whales. Had a spy-trawler's sonar previously picked up Tisala and recognised a large whale? Big as he was he was nothing like the size of a nuclear submarine. Was that why this whaler had appeared? Gradually however, as the days passed into weeks, and no further whalers appeared, I began to hope the incident was a one-off; that the visit of the whaler was coincidental, caused by who knows what Russian calculations or circumstances. But beyond immediate worries I knew that there was nothing we could do to protect Tisala once he left the islands for his seasonal migration to the Arctic or the south. And the imperative to make progress with our work beat in my mind.

Sometimes I marvelled at what had been achieved. When I looked back at the 1960s, from Tisala's earliest days with us – the painstaking learning of communication and language, the beginnings of wider education and learning – I was astonished, and the sun seemed to shine on many happy memories. Yet those early years had been darkened by the grim struggle for survival against the continuing genocide of the whalers, and the deaths closing in on Tisala's remaining family and kind. Then came Ellie's death, for me a huge and life-numbing loss, though she would have scorned to put her single death as anything beside the genocide of the whales. And always behind these killings and death loomed an even longer shadow – the threat of nuclear annihilation for the world, for in those days it seemed quite likely. Bristling America was just across the sea one way, and Russia, lurking behind the Baltic Sea, the other.

But it was from those same years – when the Blue Whales were at last largely protected – that the balance of my recollection began to shift gradually to a lighter and more optimistic view of the world's future. This change was influenced by our wonderful discovery – so far as I knew unique – of interspecies language. Human understanding of advanced animal minds had been revealed to be wildly inaccurate. This discovery brought to our lives a whole new sense of kinship and purpose.

My outlook was irrevocably changed. As a biologist I was obliged to look again quite differently at the animal kingdom. I soon found there were signals – evidence – all round us that many animals were in various degrees more highly developed than we humans had previously supposed. I began to compile cuttings and notes. From around the world there was a stream of incidents and reports about animal consciousness and intelligence. It soon became quite obvious that the reason they were not more widely recognised was human ignorance, strongly reinforced by the old presupposition that man was a separate godlike creation and animals were merely animals. Tisala said it seemed the growth of this outlook coincided with the agricultural settlement and urbanisation of man, which increasingly took educated people away from equal contact with the free-ranging animal world. So what had been recognised by our forebears – intuitive knowledge of natural kinship – was largely lost, though some of it was reflected in the fantasy spun into myths and stories.

This purblindness in men's minds had only gradually begun to lift with the public spread of scientific knowledge, and only recently with the ever-increasing awareness of biological advances from spectacular colour photography, in books, cinemas and on television.

Into this spreading realisation had come my startling knowledge from Tisala that Blue Whales, and so probably to some degree other whales and dolphins, have the physical capacity and consciousness for advanced thought and language. I knew too that by learning and adopting a pre-existing language, they could leapfrog the slow evolutionary creation of original language. It stared me in the face that we should regard and treat the higher animals as possessors of minds not so different from our own, and in some cases more well disposed.

So, though the loss of Ellie hung over my life in those years, gradually I came into a lighter world. Part was due to the softening edge of time, part to the resilience of human nature, and part to my comfort and delight in my growing children. I knew myself much blessed in their existence. And in the exhilaration of our work, the triumph and relief of the Blue Whales' survival, but above all in the wonder and purpose of my friendship with Tisala. In these years his pursuit of knowledge of humanity brought a new perspective of enlightenment and understanding into whole intractable areas of human activity and its effect on the world. To be part of this exploration gave me a sense of awe and privilege, and it created an extraordinary sense of hope for the future. Perhaps too much so; but that is what it felt like.

For instance, war is not a cheerful or hopeful subject, yet by the end, Tisala's enquiries into the origins of war taught me not to be overwhelmed by the increasing monstrousness of it – especially in our century. He taught that humanity was capable of mastering it. This may seem foolhardy given the continuance of wars in those years, and the ever-present threat of cataclysmic nuclear war between the communist East and capitalist West. But it is true, and I will try to set out how he did it.

CHAPTER 39

On War and Peace

We had often spoken of war. On some days the incongruity struck me forcibly: the great whale, lying alongside the rocky shore in the waters of our calm and peaceful sanctuary, exploring whether and how the planet in the hands of man could be saved from future wars. Yet even then I vividly sensed that this was a new hope: a capacious mind beyond the normal limitations of the human, ranging on the turmoil of our affairs.

These were the last years of America's war in Vietnam, which was featured widely in the media, but with little enlightenment. It was the beginning of the period when journalists, at least on television, with its need for pictorial images, seemed most interested in the minutiae – the explosion behind their hotel – and suchlike uninformative incidents of war. And there was the gradual realisation, both in the western democracies and the communist world, that warring governments of all kinds were involved in deluding themselves and lying about the true state of affairs.

The United States and the USSR, respectively in Vietnam and behind the Iron Curtain in Hungary and Prague, had betrayed the aspirations of their people. Nor were wars at that time confined to Cold War regions – in 1973 the third war between the Arabs and Israelis – Yom Kippur – had erupted. Within two years, just as the Vietnam War was finally concluding, countrywide and ghastly massacres began to take place in Laos and Cambodia. In the same years rebellions, insurrections and wars broke out in Uganda, Ethiopia and the newly freed Portuguese Africa – Angola and Mozambique: conflicts which were to develop into long, miserable years of civil war. And behind all these remained the louring threat of nuclear war between the two greatest military powers that had ever existed in the world.

Yet this was the peace, I had told Tisala, that 'we' had enjoyed since the Second World War. One day, when Tisala had obliged me to confront some of this unhappy history, and a few other contemporary peacetime wars and invasions, such as in Korea, Greece, Tibet, Cyprus, Algeria, Sudan, Kenya, Cuba, Malaya, Biafra, Pakistan, and so on, he said: 'To stop wars, the first step is to consider the causes of wars.'

He said he did not mean the particular circumstances of each war, often, but too late, exhaustively dealt with in our history books, and different each time, but their common underlying causes. He thought that if these are recognised and kept clearly in mind before the outbreak of any war, the prevention of such war is more likely.

He thought the origins of war were diverse but relatively simple. There were primeval wars, which include many modern wars. These arose out of insecurity and its counterpart – aggression – territorial, ethnic or cultural: the desire to conquer for riches, resources and land; and the converse fear of loss and subjugation when suffered by or imposed upon a population. To these basic elements were later added doctrinal aggression – religious, national and imperial, and then ideological, such as by fascism, communism and democracies. Often, he said, these conflate with more primitive forces: racial superiority allied to nationalism and political doctrine forming a particularly virulent mix. In the twentieth century world, that is what makes addressing the causes of war more intractable; that and the change in scale of warfare from the simple taking of outsiders' lands, animals and women, to the vast continental wars of nations, made greatly worse by the power of the nation state to raise money, and latterly to commandeer a nation's whole industrial output and populace.

Then, he said, there was the clear willingness of rulers to use war as an extension of national, religious or political policy, the heady exercise of power exacerbated by the development of the non-combative role of the rulers, diplomats and even generals: they plot and plan war on a huge scale, and in war-room comfort, never facing the battlefield dangers of their soldiers, whom they sent out in divisions and armies, like pieces on a chess board.

Then he cited the primordial willingness of men to fight: the rulers able to raise armies either for mercenary payment, or more nobly, but disastrously, by mass patriotism or indoctrination. He thought it clear that the growth in the scale of wars was caused also by the huge growth in human population, itself founded on economic and medical development; and by what he regarded as the evil of compulsory conscription, by which wars have been escalated to insane proportions, ensuring the virtual destruction of large numbers of the warring population on both sides. This willingness of men to fight was permitted and encouraged by the failure of rulers to negotiate and keep peace, the desire among them to win victories often outrunning all sense and reason.

I said, 'But where countries threaten their neighbours or tyrants of their own people, we are obliged to fight to survive.'

'Yes, often in the past, the nastiness or folly of humanity has made that step necessary. But for the future we are looking for ways – and they will only come step by step – where that seeming necessity can in many cases be overcome.'

He thought that where they can, people should refuse to fight, for ultimately war should *not* be the solution. It is a failure of humanity. Except for the deluded, nobody can like war. He could see that some like the prospect of it, at least at a distance, seeing it as a setting for their own male heroism. Such soldiers are useful for commanders to put in the front line, either to kill or be killed. He saw too that the proficient professional soldier does not like war, nor killing, except for the opportunity to serve and show bravery among colleagues so that he can look back with a sense of duty fulfilled, and relief at his own survival, which gives pleasure to his reminiscing. But hellish experience is why many others, often volunteers or conscripts, will never afterwards talk about it. Tisala argued that the people as a whole should refuse to fight. They should vote for governments that abolish conscription. They should oblige politicians to limit wars by relying on small, duty-motivated and honourable armies who are expected to, and will, obey the codes and conventions on the limitation of war, and be entitled to question and refuse to engage in immoral or illegal war. And war itself should be limited to necessary defence and enforcement of peaceful coexistence. Under these conditions the scourge of men's willingness to fight might be largely removed.

Tisala deplored the fatal availability of arms and the willingness to use them. He saw with dismay how over our history, the effectiveness and range of arms had increased under the skilled hands of the devisers of improved weaponry and armour. How hand to hand weapons, swords and axes, gave way to projectiles, spears and arrows, and they to shot and cannon balls. How the single laboriously loaded musket gave way to the longer-range repeater rifle. One man could then kill dozens. How that gave way to machine guns capable of firing six hundred bullets per minute; the heart-numbing endless lines of headstones, the war memorials and the shameful mass graves everywhere testifying to its efficiency. Bullets, shells, mines, conventional bombs, nuclear bombs and missiles: and with all these ingenious 'advances' the simple gave way to the more efficient. That is to say, it became easier to kill more people.

He observed that armourers had been succeeded by inventors and scientists, who had expanded the power of weaponry almost unimaginably in not much over a hundred years. These inventors and scientists, often patriotic, he deemed complicit in the spread of deadly arms around the world. For, he said, it is perfectly clear that once politicians and rulers have arms to sell they will find all sorts of justifications – such as defensive or doctrinal alliances and friendships – for doing so, though their real reason may be love of power or the rewards of commerce and employment. He was amazed to find how eagerly arms were supplied by governments, as well as private commercial salesmen, to dubious regimes that were unstable, primitive or murderous. Thus were they given the means to destroy their neighbours or their own peoples at their whim; and if nuclear weapons should in the future so spread, so would the power to destroy whole countries and civilisations in a few minutes of bloodshot madness.

But none of these things, Tisala thought, was the chief cause of war. What stood over and behind all these causes was the human imagination, developed in the body of an aggressive primate, exciting the adrenaline of the male animal, intoxicated by military uniforms in serried ranks, the hypnotic thump of marching feet, and visions of power, glory and empire. But he said it seems people who start wars under such influences only see the victory parades and not the horror and destruction of war. So paradoxically, the unifying cause of the worst wars is the failure or perversion of imagination. And unlike the 'advance' of weaponry, there appears to be no advance whatever in the control of the human imagination.

Patterns please the human mind and influence imagination. He saw this in the pleasure and wonder taken by humans in the structures of nature such as crystals in rock, ice or snow, or in children arranging collections of seashells, or in the symmetrical construction of ornaments or jewellery; but also in the façades of palaces or the parade ground patterns of marching soldiery or the formation of warships, tanks and aircraft. He thought the key is to distinguish the harmless and informative from the dangerously attractive, and remove the dangerous. He said people must learn to distrust shows of military power, and leaders who rejoice in such. 'Are they not unfit to govern in the future world?'

Tisala said, 'The human race must know itself to help itself.' He knew from the histories that the human animal with its wonderful but deadly imaginative capacity in the past everywhere saw 'empty' territory and fell under the spell of acquiring it. Of course, it was not empty, but the people there and their lives did not count. So dazzled by the vision of new lands or empire, the exploiter always marched in. Three thousand years ago the Israelites saw the Promised Land and took it as theirs, killing and displacing the then inhabitants; and teeter on the edge of doing it again. Alexander wished to civilise his conquered world; but bloody military conquest was uppermost, and he was not shy of destruction. Even as he recognised the wonder of Persia, he destroyed it.

'Ever since,' remarked Tisala, 'it has gone on, dismayingly. Let us simply look at the run-up to the present. He cited in the nineteenth century, the taking of 'empty' lands across the globe, such as the British consolidating their hold in India, Malaya, Singapore, Borneo and Hong-Kong, the Dutch in Indonesia, the French in the extensive territories of Indo-China, and North Africa. Similarly came the race for 'empty' Africa by the European powers – Britain, France, Holland, Belgium, Germany, Portugal – in the realisation that the 'empty' territories in the world were running out. Hence the likes of Cecil Rhodes and his vision of empire – pink on the map from Cairo to Cape Town. For that pink thousands of Africans died. For, though the empire-makers come with glory and often vision in their eyes, existing societies are disrupted and destroyed. So the British would 'civilise' and Christianise Africa, though there was first some opposition to quell, involving various inconvenient peoples from the Zulus to the Sudanese.

At this same time in the United States, the pioneers were heading west into another empty territory, and having to deal with another inconvenient population; but in that case they simply killed or otherwise got rid of most of them, which opened up the country very nicely for the white man, and soon the development of California was under way. Then, looking across the Pacific and seeing the European land seizures going on, America joined in and claimed Hawaii, other Pacific Islands and the Philippines over the heads of their native peoples.

Similarly there was the enclosure by Russian emperors of large parts of 'empty' Asia – in the greatest land mass in the world – out past the Caspian Sea, east to Mongolia and the Pacific and across into North America. The Russian Empire stretched from Finland to Alaska, all swathed in the flag of the two-headed Eagle, while the deaths and cries of the peoples in the way were silenced or ignored. The Russian empire-building only stopped when, in the south, it confronted the British, themselves probing north from India, and in the east met the Japanese. And the Emperor meanwhile lived in reflected glory and decadent opulence and ordered exquisite jewel-encrusted eggs for the Empress, who displayed them in a glass cupboard. And when this empire was overthrown it was replaced by worse: the Eagle gave way to what becomes a more sinister red flag raised with cries of freedom to the people, but smothering in an iron barbaric grip all it could command.

And opposite it rose the megalomania of Hitler for his Aryan Germany – hatred, the master race and lebensraum – ideas all seething together, bred by who knows what lurid images in his mind, twisted and distorted following the collapsed world-expansion of the first German Empire. Out of that German imaginative folly, as Hitler's own dreams of ruling Europe collapsed, Russia not only reclaimed the lands lost to Germany in 1918 at Brest-Litovsk but expanded further westwards than the Czars had ever dreamed. So half of Europe was 'liberated' or swallowed up. But their peoples awaited another day.

In the east, the Japanese followed the example of European and American powers. But whereas for the most part the western powers did it by trade and diplomacy, occasionally backed by force, in the case of Japan it was largely done by war and conquest: war unleashed by the disastrous imaginative mindset of the Japanese military. To the earlier victories and expansion of the late nineteenth and early twentieth centuries was added, after the First World War, an apparent reward for its growing power: Japan was ceded the trusteeship of the former German-Pacific territories. By the 1930s, with the victory over nationalist China, the annexation of Manchuria and the savage treatment meted out to the 'inferior' Chinese as in the mass pillage, rapes and murder at Nanking in 1938, the imaginations of the military minds that ran the Japanese were out of control. The hunger for resources and status to enable Japan to claim its rightful place in the world as the superior nation over all the western devils was to be solved by the establishment of a Japanese Pacific empire. This was to take in Indonesia and Borneo with their oilfields and extend southwards to Australia and New Zealand. New Zealand played a special part in the fantasy: the Japanese rulers saw it as an idyllic Japan South. It possessed a tiny population and productive land aplenty. Plans existed for a great replanting of New Zealand with Japanese people, the existing people to be removed as required for workforces elsewhere in the Empire, or forced into economic and political servitude, or simply eliminated. The Japanese military's treatment of the Chinese boded ill.

The flag, the rising sun, would extend across the Oceanic East and would flutter over a third of the world. Such was the folly of the perverted dreams of the Japanese military – something of which the ordinary Japanese population was largely unaware, except in the enhanced divinity to be accorded to the Emperor, the indications of power emanating from the Japanese elite and the swelling of a military economy. Japan was to have the biggest battleships in the world and the greatest aircraft-carrier fleet. And what were they for? An exercise in folly by the intoxicated imaginations and ambitions of a rigid and philosophically ignorant military caste, in which it seems they were the equal of their Nazi counterparts and allies.

I remember remarking that even the Führer had not been deified, that at least being beyond the range of plausibility in Germany. But when Tisala had finished his unflattering appraisal of humanity's war-fuelled activities, I saw clearly for the first time the pattern of disastrously flawed mindsets behind what are often taught to schoolchildren as proud patriotic exploits.

Tisala thought that what the peoples of the world must disown is this pursuit of aggrandisement. The first thing required is the universal recognition that the age of conquest and expansion has ceased. All the habitable world is occupied. Peace requires that all ambitions and problems, whether of history, border, race or religion should in future times be solved by negotiation and agreement and by the knowledge that transgression will be met by the withholding of friendship, assistance and trade agreements, by sanctions and in extreme cases the imposition of opposing force by international authority.

'But how,' I asked, 'can that be achieved? It hasn't happened so far, though we have had peace of a sort, and some international input.'

'We must consider that. The answer will not be easy. It will require a complete sea change of attitude both by your peoples and your governments. We will come to that, but in the meantime we should look at examples of what not to do, for they can be instructive.'

I had told him of the history of France as a great power. But he had seen their power, as he saw all powers, differently. What he had distilled was this: that after the failure of Napoleon in Europe there was little left but to deploy their nationalistic and cultural pride, some would say arrogance, in various colonies around the world. They fought wars to expand and keep their empire down the years – in North Africa and Indo-China until a few years ago, despite the strong contrary wishes of those populations. Even in the loss of empire they did not lose their pride in the supposed superiority of French power despite the need for third, fourth and fifth republics. So France became a nuclear power and arms salesman, thus retaining a certain amount of military influence by providing the means of death in a good number of wars, sometimes on both sides at once.

But this, Tisala insisted, was merely an example, and one very capable of reform. Many nations of the world either export arms, or having acquired them, distribute them to regions of strife, thus ensuring local arms races between militias, and years of destructive fighting, each political faction and ethnic group having its own little dream of homeland and power, which involves the clearing away of others, who have similar dreams. So homeland, justice, victory and freedom turn into conquest, power, revenge and subjugation; and always death to the innocents.

'Your history books and your world as we speak are full of it. How many wars, rebellions and uprising and massacres have there been since the end of your Second World War? The world is a busy place and often you scarcely hear of them, or you do not take them in, or you soon forget them, aided by those often in power and with whom you deal, who would rather you did forget or overlook them. But, though each conflict needs specific knowledge to solve it, we have seen the underlying principles are the same: insecurity, aggrandisement, revenge, greed and ownership of resources, all fired by imagination and with the will to fight and means of fighting all too readily to hand. You will have to apply your utmost wisdom, ingenuity, persuasion and generosity to those fundamental principles in the dangerous world you have made. Your wars will not stop otherwise.'

'You humans,' Tisala concluded, 'have arrived at a critical level of destructiveness. You threaten the future of the whole world. It is now urgent that you control your natures and wars to allow the world to return to its former assurance of continued existence.'

I said, 'We are the most intelligent beings in the planet; we will work it out.'

He breathed out slowly and I sensed that he looked at me compassionately, as if he knew he would have to lead me to an answer. Then I realised the hollowness of my reply. I thought of thousands of years of unending warfare and killing, and of the ominous future. It was all so vast and complicated. I felt fear, and then a revulsion against the murderous stupidity of our human warfare.

But when I heard the calmness and wisdom of Tisala, I felt a surge of hope and told him so.

He said quietly, 'If I live, I will do what I can to help.'

'Do you think wars can be abolished altogether?' I asked. And though I knew his answer, the wish when put to Tisala seemed for a moment to carry the possibility.

'We Blue Whales know no wars, and never have down many thousands of years. We do not have your nature, or the temptation of earthly wealth. But even among men I have noted a recurring urge to live a moral life, articulated down the ages by your philosophers, religious leaders, thinkers and often found among ordinary people when times are quiet: love your neighbour, do as you would be done by, know yourself. Many such sayings reflect your aspirations. And many of you hate war, yet your wars and atrocities persist and multiply. Your wars will not cease until the causes of wars are removed, and that, given the present misdeveloped state of your natures and imaginations, and the opportunities available, is perhaps impossible. But that "given" is what you must seek to change in the coming century. In the meantime what you must work for, and with sense and wisdom can achieve, is a great practical reduction in the incidence and destructiveness of war.'

He argued that all the causes of war need to be addressed worldwide by a Universal Treaty for the Control and Prevention of War. He thought the only sure way to secure universal compliance is to create a climate of opinion, in addition to a legal framework, across all nations whereby it becomes unthinkable for any nation, even those led by evil men, not to join, or afterwards to break, such obligations. This requires the worldwide acceptance by nation states, and other organisations, such as revolutionary forces or forces engaged in civil war, that their standing as civilised entities depends on their record of upholding the Treaty and the peace. It must become a matter of political necessity for all to do so and a matter of shame and rejection to breach it.

'That sounds fine, but how?' I asked. 'It's impossibly idealistic, and evil rulers by definition will behave evilly. We've had Conventions, and the United Nations doesn't work.'

'Hasn't, in the main, worked,' said Tisala. 'But the future is becoming different. And, in conventional war, unless you seriously set out to construct such a world you will continue in your old ways. And with modern weaponry, the result will be increasingly grim for millions of people caught up in wars, civil wars and the regimes of tyrants. To avoid this outcome you will need sustained argument and political determination; and increasing support by the peoples of the world.'

He thought such a Treaty should provide, for instance, for the unimpeded inspection of wartime hospitals and prisons, revisiting our existing Treaties in the light of experience and new international expectations. It should monitor compliance, in any case of war or civil war, with the Treaty terms, to include provisions for broadcasting breaches both internally and externally so that any state or organisation in breach will know it will be publicly exposed in the world and at home, giving rise to the opportunity for disapproval and opposition among its own followers and people. Other penalties would be added to the disapproval, such as the suspension of voting rights of governments in other international forums, and trade and financial penalties, including aid. And at the supply end, much stricter restraints on the supply of arms would need to be agreed as part of the Treaty, again with monitoring of all, and carrying serious consequences for any breach.

Such a voluntary agreement and interlocking of interests would create a sort of international union against arms and warfare.

It would require governments and peoples to accept constraints on their behaviour and internal affairs, for, he argued, the day of the absolute nation state should be over. Acceptance would be a test of the maturity, sincerity and wisdom of the country concerned. In democracies the people should demand that political parties seeking office will comply with such internationalism. For they will wish their country to stand high in the new world community of nations.

Tisala concluded: 'In such ways, with care and vigilance, humanity may advance, and seeing itself advance may expect and demand further similar advances from its leaders.'

It seemed wildly optimistic, yet somehow my optimism rose.

Then he said: 'But first of all you have a still more urgent challenge to face: you must survive and allow the world to survive the present and future over-riding threat of nuclear war.'

CHAPTER 40

The Nuclear Threat

We were talking at the seemingly irresolvable height of the Cold War. The ultimate catastrophe of all-out nuclear war between the United States and Soviet Union hung over the world. Their two systems of life appeared to be incompatible. War had thus far been avoided by the balance of nuclear terror, both sides being deterred by the belief that regardless of first strike, each would annihilate the other if war once started. Hence the frightening and frightened stalemate.

Tisala was appalled by this state of affairs and its threat to the life of the world. And as between the combatants, where use of weapons was so deadly that to use them meant self-destruction, war should no longer be a political option. The idea that war is an extension of policy by other means needed to be irrevocably banished. Tisala saw that it had triggered many wars, and catastrophically so, two World Wars. In a nuclear age it is a fearful doctrine, continuing the malign influence of the Prussian interpreter of Napoleon's wars, Carl von Clausewitz. It has led now to the logical absurdity of this superpower policy of mutually assured destruction: non-war preserved by threat of a war which would destroy civilisation and with it the purpose of such purported policy: to preserve the society and culture of the threatened and threatening powers. Tisala asked why the world did not see it as simply a colossal gamble imposed by the superpowers on the whole world, which must be urgently dismantled before some unforeseen chain of events tipped it over the edge, as nearly happened only a few years earlier, in the Cuba crisis.

That solution he thought would require a high degree of skilled leadership and trust if the parties were equals; but if one got ahead in the arms race, and became dominant, even greater leadership, for the stronger party would be tempted short-sightedly to use its advantage. The true leader, a leader of the world, which is what is required, would take the opportunity of his country's strength to rid the planet of this terrible threat. Tisala said that our whole history shows that all powers decline, so the wise power will use its strength to secure the best position in the wider interest while it has its strength. That would require unilaterally giving up some of its dominant power, and none but a great leader will achieve that, for he will be opposed by those of narrow vision, posing as patriots. And meantime non-war, depending on mutual terror, might last only so long as both sides believed it balanced.

Tisala saw that in arms races everybody sought to obtain an advantage over the current balance, hence atom bombs begat hydrogen bombs and hydrogen bombs begat cobalt and neutron bombs. The balance of terror became more terrifying at every new and ever more powerful development. 'For they may get to the point,' said Tisala, 'when one side feels it cannot balance the other side's latest advance, for technological or economic reasons. Then they may try another tack. 'For instance,' he said, 'suppose the United States were to develop a defensive system that they believed impregnable. In the wrong hands this might prove fatal, for their present fear and insecurity might turn to aggression and the use of power. If they had not by then explicitly rejected wars as an extension of policy, they might try to remove the Soviet threat by a massive pre-emptive strike; though it would be done in the name of defence. The Soviets conversely would try to circumvent the United States' defensive system and might conclude, if they came to believe that the system was not after all impregnable, or alternatively before it became so, that they should launch a massive pre-emptive strike while the opportunity existed; still in the name of defence, and to counter anticipated American aggression.'

He thought it obvious that there were a number of variations by which such a planet-destroying war could emerge. Ultimately, the only safe way to remove the threat was for both sides to disarm to the extent that neither was left with sufficient arms to annihilate the other or destroy the wider world by nuclear fallout.

He observed that we had missed our opportunities at the beginning of the nuclear age. The threat first grew from scientific ability combined with that old cause of war, fear. Fear that Germany, under its rogue Nazi regime, would acquire the atom bomb led the Americans to develop theirs. Then they used it as a matter of policy against Japan. Its impact on Soviet ambitions, and distrust of capitalist

America, led the Soviets to develop theirs. And once there were two, others would seek to follow. He found it sad but unsurprising, given the short-sighted folly of our nation state animosities and mentality, that early attempts to control nuclear force – I had told him of the first ever UN resolution, and the Baruch plan – failed completely in the face of great-power rivalry. So the nuclear arms race began, each side arming itself to a preposterous degree in the name of its own brand of doctrinal patriotism. Britain and France, playing at being great powers, acquired nuclear arms, first atom, then hydrogen, and so began a second nuclear threat to the world – proliferation.

I told Tisala that so far the race has seemed unstoppable, though a glimmer of faint reason, which was in reality more a mutual fear of atmospheric contamination, led to the first nuclear test ban treaty: the Moscow Treaty of 1963, which banned tests in the atmosphere, in space and under the sea; a ban which the next proliferators, the Chinese, together with the French, ignored for some years, so giving the lead to other would-be nuclear powers. The fears thus aroused led to the somewhat more promising Non-Proliferation Treaty. This interested Tisala very much. It rewarded the promise of signatory states not to acquire nuclear weapons with controlled access to the use of peaceful nuclear power. But I had to report to him that a number of states – some of those most likely to acquire nuclear weapons – were the very countries that did not sign the Treaty. That he thought was the real test. Though the Treaty had slowed proliferation, the result was ominous for the future.

Meanwhile the nuclear arms race between the existing two military superpowers continued. Only the first Strategic Arms Limitation Treaty, finally agreed in 1972, showed any progress away from potential catastrophe. In terms of weaponry available it was insignificant, but it was, said Tisala, at least a recognition of an urgent need.

He said, 'They are threatening to annihilate each other and destroy the Earth over a difference of method in achieving a human good.' He was amazed that they were not appalled by their own stance and condemned by the rest of the world. He thought it grotesquely immoral for them to consider annihilating each other's people, let alone releasing such destruction on the innocent world beyond their quarrel.

'Consider,' he said, 'if there were a nuclear war, and suppose some part of mankind survived the destruction and hideous nuclear aftermath. In an age otherwise notable for great achievement and advance, the politicians and military leaders responsible would rightly stand condemned in the eyes of the survivors as the perpetrators of the most stupid act of folly in the history of the world. Men would gaze in unbelief at their failure of imagination and political will to avoid such a result. Yet that is what you tell me the world now faces.'

He thought it an ultimate absurdity, some of it self-induced by their own propaganda. The minds of the leaders and military planners on both sides seemed to be full of distorted imagery arising out of ignorance, fear, aggression and power. He said: 'They may dress up in fine uniforms and delude themselves with smart analysis, but they are driven by the instincts of primitive warfare. And they have in their hands weapons of unspeakable power. Humanity urgently requires leaders who will put an end to this insanity.'

He thought the first thing to be disarmed is mistrust. He reasoned thus: trust is built out of understanding. Each must learn what is important to the other, for then the value of concessions can be gauged. All leaders act under constraints, and those too must be understood by their counterparts; for true leaders will make concessions in defiance of their constraints, but these must then be recognised and rewarded. Concessions should be matched by counter-concessions, and concessions viewed as strength and sincerity, unless proved otherwise. Above all, he said, the imaginative landscape must be changed. The carefully promoted propaganda must be dismantled, for it is a form of lying and prevents both understanding and trust, and strangely makes the enemy loom larger than in reality it is. A true leader will let the warm air of potential friendship blow across the political landscape and use it to establish a new climate. Imperceptively at first perhaps but then by bigger steps, trust is built, and then the nightmare of nuclear war may retreat and disarmament proceed.

Soon, if the leaders are wise, they will open up themselves and their countries to each other and co-operate in economic or cultural matters. For if propaganda is to be disarmed in the minds of a people, it must be replaced by a warmer, truer picture of the people and aspirations of the other land; that is a learning of years, and the sooner it is started, the sooner ultimate war becomes less likely; for it is common experience that when you have read about, visited and lived among a people as friends you fear them less and are the less willing to fight them. After a generation the politicians of both sides would find it much harder to go to war, and warmongers to be elected to or retain office.

'We must hope for such leaders one day in America and Russia,' I said.

'Not just hope,' said Tisala, 'All people must work for and demand such a change, scorning and exposing folly and the upholders of folly.

'But let us suppose, by way of encouragement to ourselves, that great-power nuclear disarmament becomes a reality, stage by stage, until the overarching threat of planetary destruction by nuclear blast and fallout is impossible because insufficient US and Soviet warheads exist.

'Do not then think that that solves all your problems. For the next thing you must prevent is nuclear proliferation. Where there are only two great nuclear powers, the danger may be containable until disarmament, but once others acquire nuclear weapons, the position becomes much more complicated.'

I said that, as he knew, we and the French had long had them.

He sighed, 'Yes, and your politicians argue that they are responsible and will never use them, except if attacked by the Soviets, and that it would be irresponsible to disarm unilaterally – it would be a neglect of their duty to defend their populations.'

I said defensively, 'Is it not a good argument?'

'No, it continues as policy the threat of cataclysmic war, and makes the mere possession of nuclear weapons a new obstacle to disarmament. Any state which happened to acquire them could argue the same.'

I wondered aloud if the British and French in justifying their nuclear capability show they do not trust the Americans to defend them, despite American promises concretely deployed under the NATO treaties. But he observed that other western European countries, some of whom are more imminently threatened, rely on American promises and conventional power. He could find no real reason why Britain and France should be different. On the contrary, possession of these weapons is arguably a great danger to them – it might make them first targets in any nuclear war.

Tisala concluded, 'It seems your governments play nuclear war games, hankering after their former status as great conventional powers, though it is against their own best interests, endangers their peoples, is a potentially disastrous example to other states, and thereby threatens future world peace beyond the cold war.

'Are not Clausewitzian political policy calculations once again triumphing over the underlying need to disarm the nuclear threat to the world? He thought it a policy that locks in future conflict and encourages other states to seek the key. And, though the nuclear powers will try to prevent proliferation, that without radical international reforms, they will fail.

'The good that could come of French and British nuclear possession lies in the influence they could have in promoting disarmament.' Some years later, when major American-Soviet disarmament talks made progress, the British and French exacerbated the position by refusing to include their own stockpiles in any resulting reduction. A great opportunity to avoid future proliferation was slipping away. Tisala thought there would be a period, maybe two or three decades, when it would be possible to stop nuclear proliferation, but that it would become increasingly difficult. We knew that already the Chinese had nuclear weapons, and it was rumoured that Israel and South Africa had or might soon have them.

Because nuclear weapons are initially difficult and expensive to make, it might be thought that at worst only a few, relatively wealthy and responsible countries might acquire them. But weapons would become cheaper and easier to make, and many nations would later have civil nuclear power, on the unimpeachable argument of providing electricity and a higher standard of living for their population; and the nuclear powers, for financial return, would help other 'responsible' nations to acquire a peaceful capability. He foresaw that, failing control, within a few decades nuclear power would be acquired by irresponsible states, where the leaders would have urgent need, in their imaginations, of nuclear arms against their enemies. For on the evidence of our history, he feared that many who attain power would be reckless, vainglorious or evil. He questioned whether the Americans would always be able or willing to go to war to overthrow such rulers. And he thought the use of nuclear weapons would often not be open to the Americans, as exterminating large parts of any such countries' population would be unthinkable.

So they would be obliged instead to wage conventional wars in distant countries, which would soon become unacceptable to their own people, as had recently happened in Vietnam. But after some years he thought they would forget, and under a new president there might be another intervention or two, until another setback and resultant domestic opposition rendered such policies impossible for another period.

And if in the meantime, no overall control of nuclear weapons is achieved, he foresaw that in the twenty-first century people looking back at the twentieth century – the most violent century in the history of mankind – might see the many years of peace between its set-piece wars as a strangely attractive and desirable time.

For he thought we had not recognised a new level of danger, below that of irresponsible states: maverick organisations, groups with their own bizarre or fanatical agendas who would kill and maim for some imaginary goal seething in their minds to the exclusion of all other views, reason or compassion, and not least endangering their own people, whom their lurid plans could expose to retaliation and destruction. And among the worst he said would be this combination: nuclear-armed politico-religious extremists. I laughed and said that it was too far-fetched and that I couldn't conceive of it happening. But Tisala said that failure to foresee it was a poor defender of peace. Then I thought of Israel, given their land by God and backed by fire from heaven, otherwise called nuclear weapons; and of their near compatriots, the groups of Arabs burning with fear, desperation, and the zeal of hate, those old causes of war. And I wondered to Tisala if people are condemned to future death and destruction, because their leaders continue to think of war as an extension of policy. He said: 'That is a curse which you humans must throw off. And you need to find new methods to control warfare, for your attempts to date have had limited success.'

He had considered the history of our modern innovations to limit war. He said we humans may see the dangers and wish to avoid them, but often fail to do so. He recalled, for instance, the Hague convention of 1899 to prohibit the launching of projectiles and explosives from balloons or by other methods. Our desire to stop bombing, particularly of civilian targets and populations, was apparent even before the invention of the aeroplane. But it was of no effect whatever in any number of subsequent theatres of war, and in the unlimited bombing, so far as the technology of the day allowed, of hundreds of cities and their civilian populations in the Second World War. He recalled too that the Geneva Convention of 1925 outlawed the development or use of biological and chemical weapons but that I had told him that thereafter more than a hundred countries, including many signatories, have subsequently indulged, and are indulging, in precisely those experiments and production.

'And yet you tell me,' he said, 'that in relation to nuclear weapons there will be no proliferation?' I did not answer, and after a short silence he said, 'Without disarmament and worldwide control, your record predicts that proliferation is certain. And with proliferation the peace of the world will quietly pass into the hands of some of the most undesirable and dangerous people. Your statesmen have little time.'

After one of these discussions, I remember walking along the rocky shore, thinking about it all. It was a sunny day, the sea lapping quietly, the seabirds mewing. I came across a butterfly, caught in a spider's web on a thistle, intermittently flapping its way to destruction. Very carefully, I disentangled it. On my hand it opened and closed its wings, as if testing its survival, before fluttering away. And that I thought, is it – the prevention of war depends on the control of power by a higher, better organised, power. And I felt again the strange contrast between the unseen but stark threat of terrible wars and the peace around me – a peace that ultimately all common humanity wants.

CHAPTER 41

Eric and Family

While these debates were going on things were slowly changing on the islands. The local community was ageing with the years. Jimmy MacLeod's father had died aged eighty-five the year before. I had been in London when he was buried among the MacLeods in the tiny island cemetery on Eilean Mòr. Eric and Guinevere, though fit, were themselves now old. When I had first come to the islands I had, with the viewpoint of youth, thought Eric old, though he was then only sixty-two. His age for me therefore had a sort of timeless quality as it advanced across the years. Jimmy MacLeod, whom I had taken as being middle-aged when we first met, had in fact been in his early thirties and seemed little changed, though now in his late forties. He had never married. In the early years he had had a sweetheart who lived on the Great Island. He had courted her for four or five years, but she would not come to live on Eilean Mòr and in the end he would not leave the island. The seeming timelessness of life on the island contrasted strongly with the changes I saw in Will and Penny, who seemed to be growing up with astonishing speed.

When Will was thirteen – in the summer of 1977 – Eric had a heart attack. He and Will were coming up to the house from setting pots for crabs when Eric gave a surprised grunt, screwed his face up, tried to grab his shoulder and then his chest with his right hand, doubled forward and collapsed. Will dropped to his knees, tried to hold him, couldn't, and laid him down. He looked towards the house and shouted, 'Granny Gwen!'

She heard the frightened shout and knew something bad had happened. When she came hurrying out, she saw Will running towards her – 'Ring the doctor! Grandpa's had... I think he's had a heart... quick!'

'Will, ring Dr. Henderson. You must get them to come immediately – the helicopter – go!' She pushed him towards the house and ran down towards Eric. The first spasm had passed. His face was calmer, but his eyes were bewildered. She took off her apron and put it under his head. He tried to speak – 'Ssh – yes, it's all right, my love. We're getting the air ambulance.'

Will got through, the system worked and the islands helicopter was alerted. When he came out of the house he shouted down to Guinevere, 'They're coming.'

'Will,' she called, 'blankets!'

Will reappeared and brought down an armful of rugs. Eric's chest was rising and falling gently. They made him as comfortable as they could and awaited the helicopter, anxiously watching Eric for more signs.

The first I knew of it all was at the end of the morning. I was at the shack on Inis Cuan, but was coming back to Eilean Mòr at lunchtime. When I reached the crossing point on Inis Cuan I saw Will on the other side waving his arms at me.

As I steered the boat in he called out, 'Eric's had a heart attack.'

No. Please No. Not Eric. A claw in my chest. 'Is he alive?'

'Yes.'

'Is he okay?'

'We haven't heard yet.'

When he told me what had happened I did not want to believe it. Eric the irrepressible struck down. As we hurried towards the house my heart raced and I felt that sickening fear again from ten years before – that churning dry-mouthed fear as we had taken Ellie to the boat. Ten years. Now mercifully there was a helicopter for emergencies. Eric was eighty and had aged noticeably in the last two or three years. But he was still the Eric who had embodied life at Eilean Mòr, and it was difficult to imagine the place without him. We knew perfectly well that both Eric and Guinevere were now of advanced age. They used to joke about it, and death – about popping their clogs, and which of them would go first. 'We might be in for a photo finish,' said Eric to Guinevere once, twinkling. And they would look at each other with love, bold and unfrightened.

Somehow, though, without thinking about it, my mind had put it all in the unspecified future. Eric went on from year to year doing little maintenance jobs and the physical work outside – keeping the boat, supervising the log supply (though Jimmy MacLeod and I did most of the sawing now), creosoting the shack – 'Filthy stuff,' said Eric, 'but an exhilarating smell'. And his little workshed was full of everything needed – tools, paint, roofing felt, zinc dipped nails and screws, graded and labelled in tobacco tins, and the rest of it. But this year he had sent Will up on the corrugated iron roof of the outsheds with the red oxide paint. Guinevere fussed around and Eric reassured her. 'He is perfectly all right. The boy is as light as a feather – Oi, Will, you're not supposed to be painting your jeans,' and Will had laughed and tried not to spill the paint.

And of course Eric and Guinevere welcomed us on the islands year after year as season followed season. We must have everything we need. Inis Cuan was my fiefdom as long as I needed it. Eric was fiercely proud of what was going on: 'This is an adventure of the spirit, the like of which I never thought to see.' He discussed at length the way Tisala's wisdom was illuminating the folly of mankind's history and conduct. Although he repeatedly came up against knowledge and conclusions that were beyond his previous philosophy and familiarity, he did not flinch from the ideas. And sometimes when he did not understand, or thought something needed further explanation, he would come down to the shack and talk to Tisala. 'The thing is, old chap, you were saying...' And Tisala would answer his questions, doubts and objections with the utmost gravity and courtesy.

But now suddenly all was changed. The stalwart Eric of the years had gone down. I prayed that it would only be minor and he would make a recovery, for I loved the man and I knew despite the jokes how it would be with Guinevere if he should go.

And behind lay the thought of what would happen on the islands. Guinevere might not be able to keep the place going on her own, even with Jimmy's help, and ours. The future would depend on what their daughter Mary wanted to do. I knew that Eric and Guinevere had left the islands to their only child, for Eric had discussed it with me. He had considered giving me a formal lease of Inis Cuan, but I gathered that the lawyers and Mary had been doubtful about it because various complications might arise, and the estate needed both islands to be viable. Mary had expressed her willingness to continue our informal arrangements as long as I wanted them. Yet I knew in the back of my mind that sometimes circumstances can arise that change earlier intentions.

But as we approached the house, all that was nothing in the immediate anxiousness for Eric. Penny ran out of the house and threw herself into my arms, burying her head. We went in. The news was good – Eric had survived. The helicopter had arrived with Dr. Henderson who had given him a rapid examination, injected him with a blood-thinning agent and given some comfort to Guinevere: Eric had had a pummelling, but he was a tough man and Charlie Henderson thought he would be all right. But Guinevere had thought Charlie looked grim; and there was the danger of a further episode. They would whip him into hospital quickly and telephone back. When I arrived the call still had not come. For an anxious hour we waited and talked in a desultory way. Then the phone rang. Guinevere answered, 'Hello Charlie.' She listened. 'Yes, Good.' She asked some questions, and we all listened to the silences of Dr. Henderson's replies. Guinevere said, 'Yes, we'll come over tomorrow.' She thanked him profusely and rang off. She sounded relieved. She reported what he had said – Eric was definitely a toughy. He was more comfortable now. No, there was no immediate danger – they were monitoring him – and a good night would help him. Guinevere rang Mary in Vancouver, and gave her the news. Yes of course she would come – at once – as soon as possible. She would get on to the travel agents immediately. There was a flurry of consultation at the other end. At this short notice her husband Tom had a problem with business commitments. He could follow on a few days later, if need be.

Though the news from the hospital was a relief, it was a sombre group who went through the evening, trying to talk in level voices, doing things that had to be done, and sitting at supper round the kitchen table. More than once my eye went to Eric's empty chair with its scruffy little flat red cushion, and I involuntarily wondered whether it would see him again. When we were washing up, and out of Guinevere's earshot, Will asked me anxiously, 'Will he really be all right, do you think, Dad?'

'I hope so, Will – yes, the doctor thinks so... but we must see.' And I saw in his eyes the fear of losing Grandpa Eric, as he had lost his mother. The rebuilt certainty of his childhood years might now have to endure another tremor.

The next day we went over to the mainland, and into the hospital, along a corridor with its hollow feel and sounds and vaguely clean smells – the strange harbinger of changing lives. Eric was sitting up in bed, feeling a bit feeble, but very pleased to see everyone. The prognosis was good – Dr. Henderson said he was very pleased with his patient. I could sense Guinevere's relief, both at the news, and being physically close to Eric again. There was some low key chatting and little laughter, then we left Eric with Guinevere to be together.

The following day, after another visit, when Eric had visibly improved, I went back to the island. Guinevere and the children remained, staying with friends. I was anxious to get back to Inis Cuan. I knew Tisala would be wondering what had happened, for I should have been back two days earlier. When I arrived he said he had spent most of the time at sea, twice coming back to see whether I had returned. He heard the news with sadness, but calmness. He was pleased to hear that Eric's mind was whole, and he was expected to recover.

'His time may be approaching,' he said, 'but let us hope it is not yet.' For the second time he sent a message of love and affection from the sea to a stricken member of the race who had destroyed his own world. He said: 'We should think kindly of our bodies which have sustained us so many years. Tell him to remember what he has escaped, and be grateful. And remind him to rest his mind on those he loves, and who love him, for that will support his spirit and healing.'

When I passed this on to Eric, he smiled and said, 'Tell him I'll do my best to obey orders.'

Mary and her daughter arrived in London from Vancouver, and telephoned. I took Guinevere to the station to meet the train. Because the news of Eric was so good, it had been decided that the daughter, Susannah, would take the opportunity to stay two or three days with the family of a close girlfriend of hers in London before coming on up. Mary's son Grenville could not come – he was at college and had his exams at the end of the month, but was sorry not to be here.

'He's just fine,' said Mary in answer to Guinevere's enquiry, 'but *very* busy.' Later she explained to me, 'He's just twenty, and looks like he's going to follow his father into engineering.' She spoke with an English accent, but with an indication of Scottish and Canadian influence. I could see something of Guinevere's purposefulness in her, and Eric's twinkle. When she smiled the skin around her eyes was quite wrinkled for someone in her early forties, as I supposed her to be – only a few years older than me – but her smile was broad and warm. I recalled her from a previous visit, but seemed now to see a new person. That night I peered at the mirror. The young man I expected to see was a bit older than I had thought. But not too bad for thirty-nine.

Two days later, Will and I went to the station to collect Susannah. 'I expect you remember her,' said Mary. I had a recollection of a pretty twelve year old. 'Anyway, you will easily recognise her. She'll be wearing a green top and has dark brown hair with a pigtail.' We had time to spare before the train was due and so went across the road to the local hotel. After a few minutes, I became aware that Will was looking at someone who had come into the room. It was a girl in a red t-shirt, who walked across the room without seeing us and looked out of the window. She was about sixteen, and beautiful; but though her features were lovely, it was the grace of her movements and the stillness of her face that gave her a startling beauty. I saw the young barman and one or two others look up. She was wholly unaware of the effect she caused, which was itself enchanting, lending an aura to her presence, a shimmer of wonder round her person.

I saw she had a pigtail, but her hair, though dark, caught gold in the light.

'Dad, is that her?' asked Will in an urgent low voice. I saw with amusement that he was transfixed.

'Shouldn't be, but may be. Go and ask her.'

'No, you do it.'

'Go on!'

Will reluctantly went up to her 'Excuse me.' He hesitated. 'What's your name?' She looked at him slowly, and it seemed for a moment as if a whole world hung on her answer before she said in a soft Canadian accent, 'Susannah.'

Will smiled shyly. 'Hello, we've come to collect you.' He looked over to me. 'Dad, it's her!' and his face spread into a wonderful smile.

We introduced ourselves, though she knew all about us. We thought we remembered each other from before – it was four or five years ago. We collected her luggage. She seemed a lovely girl, pleasant and chatty. Yes, she had had some lunch. As we went to the hospital, she wanted to know how her grandpa was and what had happened. Will told her, and of his part in it, and blushed a little. We said he was doing well, which was confirmed by the visit. In the ward she went up to Eric and hugged him.

'Hello, Grandpa, how are you?'

'Fine.' He looked at her. 'My dear, how lovely to see you. Sorry about being bed-ridden. Rather silly of me.'

We had a few words, then left them to catch up.

Afterwards, we went down to the ferry to cross onto the Great Island. Guinevere had gone over with Mary the day before. At the other end we picked up the truck and I drove across to the little ferry. Jimmy MacLeod met us there. It was a sunny early evening and the water calm across to Eilean Mòr. And so we arrived and went up to the house where there were kisses and hugs all round. 'Oh, Susannah, dear, it's lovely to see you!' said Guinevere, first hugging her and then holding her at arm's length to look at her. 'My!' – she too registering the evident metamorphosis.

That night as I lay in bed, I could not sleep properly but drifted in and out. I thought and dreamed of Ellie – the young Ellie I had loved on sight – and I was stirred and troubled. The subconscious tensions of years gave way and my heart cried for my lost Ellie and I felt a surge of love, from all those years before. And when sleep deserted me my whole loss returned and was overwhelming. And the imperative of animal emotion which had risen and fallen more mildly in two or three subsequent relationships, threatened to swamp me in agitated unhappiness.

In the days that followed, Eric made a rapid recovery. Within a week, he was back on the island, everyone making a great fuss of him. Soon Mary took him on her arm for little walks outside the house. I was back on Inis Cuan for most of the time, for Tisala was almost due to leave for the Arctic summer, and there was much to do. Will came over two or three times but seemed happy to stay on Eilean Mòr more than usual. Susannah, as well as helping her grandmother and grandfather, spent time with Will and Penny. She seemed to like their company. Not having younger siblings of her own, she took to looking after Penny like an elder sister. But with Will I sensed an awareness between two young people of a different attraction. Will seemed alternatively pleased and confused, and Susannah uncertain. She clearly liked him, but wasn't sure how to treat him when sometimes he looked at her. I saw these first stirrings and smiled to myself. There may be an unbridgeable gap between a sixteen-year-old girl and a thirteen-year-old boy; but the thought struck me that when he was a strapping twenty year old, she would be only twenty-three. Now, he was slightly under her height, then he would probably stand several inches taller than she.

In the evenings, talking with Mary and Guinevere, they clarified in my mind the pattern of previous visits. Over the years the whole family had come only twice, but Mary and the children had been more often, and of course Eric and Guinevere had also visited Vancouver. In the early days, I had not really taken very much notice: they were expected family visits and did not involve me. Besides, most of them had fallen in times when I was away from the islands. We worked out that we had only met Mary and the children a couple of times, and never her husband, though Mary herself had been over again only a year ago when I had been in London.

I remembered their visit of five years previously, because up to that point, Eric had not told Mary about Tisala, and before their arrival he had discussed with me the idea of confiding in her. He had clearly wanted to do so. He was looking to the future and thought she ought to know. The islands would one day belong to her and her husband and he wanted to make sure she understood the importance of my work and to make sure she would support its continuance. He told me he had put a sealed letter with his will, setting out in the clearest terms his unalterable wish that the work with Tisala would be continued to its end and that arrangements to allow this were of paramount concern to him. Guinevere too had signed the letter. Eric had told Mary all about Tisala alone with Guinevere one evening. She was spellbound. She thought it fantastic, and was amazed that all this time she never had any idea. They had explained that she had been such a long way away, and it was vital that Tisala should remain undiscovered. She was immediately supportive of the whole endeavour. 'I knew she'd be all right,' Eric had said when he recounted the conversation to me. There was a hint of relief in his pride. 'And I've impressed on her the absolute need for secrecy.'

One evening when I went back to Eilean Mòr for supper, Mary and I went for a short walk along the shore. She was well informed about the anti-whaling campaign in North America. And she told me what she had said to her husband about Tisala five years before. She had felt in a dilemma: she did not keep things from her husband, and wanted to share her knowledge with him; but she realised that secrecy was vital and reasoned that there was no real need for him to know and that he would expect her to honour the confidentiality with which she had been entrusted. In the end she had generalised, telling him that some biologists from London were making a study of whales off the Scottish coast, had located a rather unusual visitor which they were studying and that it was extremely important that no news came out about this, so that the studies might continue undisturbed. He apparently had some interest in whales, which he had seen travelling up the Canadian west coast, but he did not enquire further. He had not mentioned anything about it since, and she rather imagined he had long forgotten about it.

From time to time I became anxious about the slowly widening circle who knew about Tisala, so her stay reassured me. It was more worrying when the knowledge spread in an unscheduled way or by accident.

Shortly before Mary and Susannah were due to return to Vancouver, we were gathered in Eric and Guinevere's sitting room having coffee. Twice in the proceeding days, Susannah had expressed an interest in coming over to Inis Cuan to see the island. She knew I was working over there and promised she wouldn't get in the way. Twice excuses were made as to why she shouldn't come – no, not even to the island. Now she tried again. She knew Will was going and that this was the last day she could join us. I made further excuses. I saw her looking at me and thought she resented being kept off her grandparents' island by an outsider, though Guinevere also stepped in to shoulder some of the blame, saying she was hoping Susannah would spend the last whole day with her. Penny, who had become fond of Susannah's company and their activity together piped up, 'Let's not go – it's boring – Dad just spends all the time talking to that silly old whale.' She heard Will suck in his breath and she trailed off realising her remark had created a sudden pool of silence. She said, looking up at me defensively. 'But they're on the island too.' Susannah looked from one to the other of us. She looked to her mother for guidance and saw her mother looking at me. She looked down and blushed. She sensed she was the odd one out: that she, not the younger children, was the one excluded from something strange and important. Something that if she knew would change her perception of her grandparents and their island home.

It flashed through my mind to make light of the incident and merely repeat my usual explanation about studying animal communications. But I somehow felt she would not believe me – Penny's fateful words had been too specific and she would know it was untrue. And I found I did not want to lie to her, but to trust her, this schoolgirl from North America.

'Well, perhaps I had better tell Susannah all about it.' Turning to her, I said, 'Everyone else here knows, but it's vital that you never tell anyone outside this room about it. It must be absolutely confidential. I must ask you to promise me that.'

She had been looking at me solemnly but looked at her mother. Mary nodded encouragingly.

'I promise.'

'I was not going to tell you this time, because you were only here for a few days and what I am going to tell carries a very great responsibility.' She nodded, watching me again with solemn eyes. I was glad I had said 'this time', though it was unplanned. I could see relief in her face that her exclusion had been nothing to do with her personal worth, the sense of which, especially in the young, is so often vulnerable.

And so in outline I told her of the history of Tisala, how we had met and everything that had developed over the years.

She was a model of concentration and I noticed again her aura of stillness. She asked a few questions – one about the beginning, when I was a student, about Tisala and his family, about Ellie and one about Will when he was a little boy. And when I answered that, she smiled at him. At the end, I impressed on her that she was one of the few people in the world to know of our breakthrough – the linking of minds of others in the animal kingdom and finding there a whole world of rationality, kindness and concern; and that it was a matter, literally, of life and death and that she must never ever say anything to anyone outside about it.

Her mother said, 'Susannah dear, there is another thing: your father doesn't know about this. That is how secret it is.' She wanted to know when her mother knew, and seemed impressed by her mother's five years of apparently unaffected daily life despite the great confidence she carried.

Thinking about the incident that night, I found myself glad that Susannah knew. Yet doubt nagged me and my inner voice said: reckless optimist. And then I felt irresponsible, and wondered if I had been swayed merely by her attractiveness. I began to resent Susannah, as if she had been imposed on me, and felt dismayed that I had been so stupid as not to re-warn Penny that Susannah was not in the know; and guilty too of neglecting poor Penny. And for the rest of our stay I took care to include Penny in everything and laugh and play with her, for I felt the sting of her reproach.

But the next day Susannah seemed delightful and sensible and it was clear a visit to Inis Cuan could not be denied. Mary, who had never seen Tisala, decided to stay behind, saying her remaining time with her parents was short.

We crossed over to Inis Cuan and walked over to the inlet. Will was jabbering away, telling Susannah about this or that aspect of Tisala's life here and amongst the Arctic icebergs, giving Blue Whale dimensions and scornfully comparing the lesser measures of dinosaurs. Penny butted in from time to time to tell Susannah about baby whales, and that they sang songs, 'All day long.'

When we arrived, Tisala was out at sea. Susannah looked around and I felt her sense of wonder and suppressed excitement. I showed her around the shack, and explained the equipment, which she seemed readily to understand. Will proudly showed her round outside and recounted our clash with the Soviet Navy. A shadow of concern passed across her face, and she glanced at Will and then at me.

A little later Will pointed down the inlet, 'Here he is.' Susannah stared. Will said, 'Look at the bow wave – his dorsal fin is sixty feet behind it.' A sliding section of back broke the water and – 'There!' said Will as the fin appeared.

'Oh my!' She turned to us, clearly elated and awed, her eyes shining, and smiled.

When Tisala had berthed I introduced her to him over the link saying she was granddaughter of Eric and Guinevere. He already knew she was from Canada, and they exchanged greetings. Her initial awe soon gave way to interested engagement with this great being and soon he was answering her questions about Blue whales in the North Pacific. We had work scheduled for that day, and she stayed and listened in for an hour or so, before Penny and Will dragged her off to view the rest of that part of the island and the sea cliffs.

On the way back across the isle that evening she was quite quiet, but when I asked her, she said she had had a wonderful day. I stayed on Inis Cuan. The kids took the boat across the stretch of water to Eilean Mòr, Will at the helm. I watched them and returned a wave when they landed, and went back to the inlet.

The following day was the last day of Mary and Susannah's stay. I went over in the evening to join the group. With Eric restored, though feeling as he admitted, 'A bit knocked about', the party was transformed from the acute anxiousness of the start of the visit. But Guinevere and Mary, from their occasional admonitions to the whisky-sipping and unrepentant, joking Eric, showed their underlying concern.

The next morning, after making a great fuss over Eric, who was now pottering about quite happily, Mary and Susannah said their goodbyes. Poor Eric had difficulty holding his composure at their departure, and we all had the same thought though nobody expressed it.

When they had gone, Will seemed listless and out of sorts for a few days. Trying to cheer him up, I asked if he liked Susannah.

'She's all right,' he said looking away and in a tone that didn't encourage further questioning.

'I thought she was very nice. Maybe you should keep in touch and write her a letter.'

'Suppose I could.' He seemed to lighten up a bit, but then made a slight face and added, 'She probably wouldn't want to write.'

But she did write, in reply to his letter, which was mainly stories about Grandpa Eric and jokes he had made. She would love to come over again and see everyone before too long. This, and a bit more time, soon restored Will to his more cheerful self. But shortly afterwards I was plunged into apprehension by my own post.

CHAPTER 42

Illicit Whaling and the Moratorium

Within two days I received two separate reports of whaling that should not have been happening: unofficial and pirate killings. It added unwelcome confirmation of a persistent lethal practice.

We knew pirate whaling existed: it was a form of mercenary activity. A whaler would be registered under the flag of some non-whaling nation, and then proceed to whale on behalf of another country – often an International Whaling Commission member who did not wish to be publicly associated with, or accountable for such activity. In addition there was unofficial whaling: straightforward malpractice by an IWC member – not declaring the correct numbers or species of whales killed. The motive was the same: to appear to be a responsible country to the world, while hypocritically ensuring they retained the coveted whale products.

The Blue Whales should now have been safe, under the measures reluctantly passed by the IWC in the preceding years. We tried to gather information on known losses from the whales (often months after the event), and plot them against information gleaned from the remaining whaling nations about their fleets and hunting movements. Officially, no one admitted to killing Blue Whales. But someone was. In Antarctic seas, suspicion pointed most often at the whalers of the Soviet Union. Years later, after the fall of the Communist regime, the new Russian government admitted, to its credit, that the old figures had been falsified, and published revised figures confirming their guilt. The Japanese were also at first implicated in the Antarctic, as they were in some deaths in the North Pacific. Other nations, including Iceland and Norway, were suspects in the North Atlantic. But by the mid 1970s, losses were remarkably reduced, and in the years between 1975 and 1982, none of Tisala's own family was lost, which was a source of comfort and hope. And in those same years, the total of Blue Whale deaths from hunting known to Tisala was only – *only* – twenty.

Gradually, the killing had become more nearly balanced with the new and surviving births among the remnants of the Blue Whales. By the end of the 1970s, the first small and slow increase among them outmatched the total hunting and natural losses for the first time since the early twentieth century, other than the brief respite in the peace of the Second World War. By the end of the 1970s, most of the dismaying news related to the killing of other species. The poor Fin Whales, though their numbers were much reduced by the catastrophic 1960s, still suffered substantial slaughter, as did the Sei Whales.

But although the whalers were repeating their old pattern of destruction of one species after another, the world of whaling was finally changing. In the 1970s, following the Stockholm Conference with public pressure now growing against whaling around the world, I was able to report to Tisala a string of small victories. In Britain, the Ministry of Defence abandoned the use of whale oil. A widening spectrum of various companies – shoe and leather companies, which used whale oil in tanning, engineering companies and manufacturers of linoleum, soap and margarine – backed by a number of trade unions – announced that they would no longer use whale products.

By such individual decisions, strengthened at last by some government action – the United Kingdom banned the import of most whale products in 1973 – gradually the whalers' markets began to shrink, and with that shrinkage the viability of their cruel activity. The industry increasingly found the spotlight of public information on them. There were now substitutes for all whale products. Gradually, out of public pressure, legislation, economic self-interest and occasionally goodwill, the use of whale products diminished.

By this time, conservationists and a wider public were again pressing for a total moratorium on commercial whaling, and a number of the former whaling members in the IWC, now including in the forefront America, Britain and Australia, were actively pursuing a moratorium. We also learned with delight that members of the American Senate were putting forward amending legislation to provide possible economic and trading penalties against countries continuing to exploit whales and whale products. The American President was given power under the amendments to halt fishing imports from any such country concerned; and the US Commerce

Department was given powers to retaliate against infractions by halving and then abolishing misbehaving countries' right to fish in United States water. There now existed, for the first time, the means to coerce the whalers and put pressure on their governments; which means had been tragically lacking under the rules of the IWC.

In 1978 came the news that in Australia the Royal Commission Report of Sir Sydney Frost, an Australian judge, had concluded that all whaling was indefensible. The Australian Government acted on it. Australia's own remnant industry was halted, and this former whaling nation became the first in the world to oppose whaling in principle. This raised the prospect, and took the battle, from merely seeking a moratorium on commercial whaling (with the implication that it could re-start when 'stocks' recovered), to an outright permanent cessation of the barbarous hunting of sentient fellow mammals. But though it was a new beacon it was so far a lone one in a still hostile world.

Nevertheless, Tisala at once grasped its significance and the astonishing change in attitude it represented. And more good news followed. In 1979 the Seychelles, which had recently become independent from Britain, joined the IWC as an anti-whaling nation. In the same year the nations bordering the Indian Ocean unanimously agreed to designate the whole Indian Ocean as a sanctuary from whaling.

But still, in the IWC, the whaling nations continued ruthlessly to exploit the inadequate rules. The Japanese continued to be two-faced. In 1978 the Japanese government tried to neutralise pro-moratorium Panama by secretly threatening to cancel important orders for Panamanian sugar. The Japanese practise of bribes and threats to small nations continued.

In public they argued against any moratorium on 'reasonable scientific' grounds; though their interpretation of statistics was to most scientists a travesty. Meanwhile, they covertly did all they could to sustain the trade in whale products. At the end of the 1970s several of their stratagems were revealed. Among the pirate whaling ships, the infamous *Sierra*, was shown to be owned by Norwegians operated by South Africans but to be under Japanese supervision. This was a catcher converted to provide factory ship facilities. In the early 1970s it was catching nearly five hundred whales a year, wholly indiscriminate as to the species it killed. It sold the resultant oil to Norway, and meat to Japan. This underhand trade was exposed in 1979 to the embarrassment of those countries, for it gave the lie to their public protestations that their pursuit of whaling was guided solely by scientific criteria. But it was only one of a whole number of undercover operations by them to circumvent the growing pressure for restrictions on whaling. When threatened by US fishing sanctions for continuing to exploit and import whale products, Japan announced new laws forbidding the import of whale products from countries who were not members of the IWC. But their legislation deliberately allowed whale products to pass from non-members to members, and thus be imported legitimately into Japan; which was their intention from the outset. The legislation was a tactical sham. And then Japan persuaded non-member nations – South Korea, Spain, Peru, all of whom were whaling to supply the Japanese market – to join the IWC. Their imports again therefore became 'allowed'.

The cruelty and dishonesty of the remaining whaling nations and their flagrant disregard of both persuasive and legal attempts to control activities resulted in counter-violence. Some conservationists took the law into their own hands. We heard that a breakaway conservationist group had used its ship the *Sea Shepherd* deliberately to ram the Japanese-inspired pirate whaler *Sierra*, causing extensive damage and thereby removing it from whaling for six months of repairs in Lisbon. And shortly after that the group attacked and sank the *Sierra* in the harbour, without loss of life. In the same year, 1980, the group sank two Spanish whalers.

I brought news of these happenings to Tisala, reporting them rather triumphantly.

'I know it's illegal, but they got what they deserved and I can't say I'm sorry.'

'You should be,' said Tisala. 'A bad thing has been removed but at cost of violence; and the difficulty is that where violence is used whenever a person or group feels justified by the strength of their feelings, the result is anarchy and terrorism. But that such actions have been felt necessary is an indictment of the mentality and irresponsibility of whalers; and also of governments and international bodies, which have failed to create the consensus and legal framework they should. And that is a perennial human problem, for enlightened active political leadership is scarce and has to wait years for the pressure of public opinion to catch up and persuade politicians to act. That is what should change.'

Meanwhile, because the rules of the IWC laid down that a moratorium on whaling would require a three-quarters majority, it meant that by 1980 the whalers, now led by Japan, had a block of member countries, including also the Soviet Union, Norway, Iceland, Brazil and Chile, which could outvote the more numerous non-whaling countries. The 1980 attempt to pass a moratorium was therefore defeated. And the victorious whalers went on, yet again, to vote themselves quotas in excess of those recommended by their beleaguered scientists. But despite the will to kill, the 1980 season saw a further collapse in the killing. The whalers could find and take 'only' something over three thousand of all species combined. History was repeating itself.

But there was good news too: later on Tisala said he knew of no deaths that year amongst Blue Whales. In 1981 the conservationists and non-whaling members, which included Mexico and France, sought to neutralise the additional pro-whaling membership by encouraging other non-whaling nations to join: China, India, Jamaica, St Lucia, St Vincent, Costa Rica and Uruguay either joined or already supported the moratorium. And in 1980 the rest of the European Union, following Britain's lead, agreed to ban all whale products.

Our sense of excitement was mounting over this running battle, and on Inis Cuan I gave an optimistic assessment to Tisala for 1982 on the moratorium vote. On paper the result would not directly affect the Blue Whales, who were supposedly already protected by the earlier IWC resolutions, and now further protected because most of the previously non-IWC whaling nations (who had not therefore been bound) became bound by joining the IWC. But we hoped that a moratorium, as well as dramatically assisting the other species, would reduce the chances of Blue Whale kills by Japanese – backed by pirate or other irregular operations.

Yet as so often in the past, anticipation of advance was matched by further disappointments. As the pressure against whalers grew, they redoubled their efforts to preserve their remaining markets by other means. The scientific whaling argument now began to be raised in earnest. Everyone knew that scientific research whaling allowed killing over and above any diminution or ban on commercial whaling. Thus another loophole in the Convention was being exploited. It was to become a longstanding cause of future contention, but I did not then guess the extent of it.

Of more immediate concern, late in 1981, was this: I learned with dismay that the Danes had reversed their position and were now issuing scientific whaling licenses for the hunting of Fin Whales (previously protected since 1976) around the Faeroes. This alarmed me: Fin whales are next to Blues in size and importance, and sufficiently close in looks to Blues for 'mistakes' to be made: and Tisala's arctic journeys took him not far from the Faeroes. And in the following year, under the guise of the scientific mantle, Iceland too was allowed a quota of Fin Whales pending the coming into force of any moratorium. The danger to Tisala in the north had reappeared.

So it was with a muted sense of celebration that we finally heard the longed-for news that at the annual meeting in 1982 the anti-whaling members of the IWC succeeded in passing a general moratorium on commercial whaling. And the muted nature of it was reinforced because the compromise to get it passed was that the moratorium would only be effective in the 1985-86 Antarctic season – three or four years away. Moreover, it was to be reassessed by 1990. Worse still, the two largest whaling nations in the world, Japan and the Soviet Union, as well as Norway and Peru used their right of objection to the moratorium so that it was not binding on them at all. They seemed impervious to any argument, including the observation of the Antiguan delegate that 'There is no humane method of continuing this needless form of industry'. They were determined to get their many pounds of flesh regardless of the cruel moral and environmental indictment they thereby passed on themselves.

But while the whalers were still finding ways to kill the remaining few great whales, Tisala was applying his mind to another problem that humanity at large was ironically inflicting on the world: the spiralling increase of our own species.

CHAPTER 43

On Population

One day, Tisala said: 'The biggest problem and the biggest opportunity the world faces is the nature of humanity; and if human nature is the problem, human numbers exacerbate it dangerously.' He was amazed how little we seem to have applied our minds to such perceptions in the way we live in and use the world and the effect we have on it.

For two years, among his other demands for information, he had been pursuing knowledge about human population and a line of thought that I had sometimes been aware of, but had not focused upon. We had constantly discussed aspects of human nature and condition, but though we had often bumped into the underlying issue of population growth and its consequences, I now found Tisala had concluded it was perhaps the most critical factor for the future of the world.

I had told him that when modern man emerged out of the mists of the past, perhaps only a hundred thousand years ago, it is believed he came out of Africa, probably olive-skinned. Those who had stayed or went back into Africa became dark under that continent's sun. But most spread out into Europe and Asia and obtained a middle colouring, except those who went to the pale north. He thought that my information on this process was unsatisfactory and sketchy and likely to change in the light of fuller knowledge. The truth was that we did not then really know the detailed history. But even then it seemed likely that for long pre-historical periods the whole of humanity might have comprised only some tens of thousands of beings, and even at later stages – say thirty thousand years ago – perhaps only a few hundred thousand. It was likely that the early perils of existence and mortality were such, and the growth-time of children so long that the survival of the species was a close run thing. Other species of hominids had not survived. I told him that according to evolutionary theory it was over these millennia that mankind acquired the continuous all-seasons sexual capabilities and inclinations of our kind: we had need of them to survive as a species. But it is those same capabilities and inclinations that have had such dramatic demographic and economic results in more modern times.

Tisala said he understood that as recently as the end of the last ice-age, about twelve thousand years ago, when modern man and his societies began their astonishing development, our estimate of world population was perhaps between two and four million. By the rise of the great civilisations in the Middle East five thousand years ago, the estimates were about twelve to fifteen million, and by Roman times, two thousand years ago, and with rather more certainty, perhaps two hundred million, in some places grouped into little towns and cities, but mainly scattered across the five continental land masses.

This astonishing increase was in stark contrast to those of his own kind. He reminded me that the Blue Whales had for many thousands of years reached and maintained the population level optimum for their society. It matched their environment and their food supply so they were free to exercise and develop their happy consciousness in a world of plenty. He acknowledged that the Blue Whales had been a fortunate group, though they had partly made their own good fortune. 'We determined to remain a stable number – about three hundred thousand – perhaps the same number as men thirty thousand years ago. And, unlike men, we remained broadly the same numbers, until you started to slaughter us.

He returned to the history of mankind. He remembered that, though our numbers had increased by Roman times, compared with the modern world our then numbers were small. But he noted that we had already developed the majority of our great civilisations – in Sumeria, Egypt, Babylon, Persia, Greece, Rome, the Indus valley and China. He said, 'I conclude that it is not great numbers that lead to great civilisations among men, but a level of economics, social advancement and stability to enable your minds to flourish.'

He thought humanity does not need its great numbers; indeed that they are a threat to each other and the planet. I confirmed that since Roman times, despite high mortality, and with some fluctuations, our population has increased, slowly at first, but then with gathering pace. By a thousand years ago there were perhaps 300 million humans, and by the sixteenth century our numbers reached 500 million. Since when we have multiplied with ever increasing speed.

Some time early in the nineteenth century mankind slipped past the billion mark – one thousand million humans. We spawned our way into the billions, apparently with little regard to the consequences, and less concern or restraint. Our procreation was literally out of control: hundreds of millions of individual sexual decisions prompted by biological urges and taken by people without overall knowledge of the trend in their own country, much less beyond their local horizon.

'And even now,' Tisala said, 'when you have the means of communication across the world, it hardly touches billions who need to understand, and nothing seems to stop your procreative activity.' He contrasted this with the deep sound-channel communications of his kind, linking knowledge of their world throughout the oceans, forming a unity of understanding and using it accordingly. He said, 'We knew the oceans were full of other creatures, and being of prodigious size ourselves that we should limit our own population. But you humans, despite your intelligence, have done no such thing. You have pressed on blindly, exploiting ever more widely the land and the sea, and displacing all other creatures at your whim.'

We concluded the litany of numbers. 'By 1900, after you had begun to hunt my kind to provide the wants of your population, human numbers had risen by an extra 500 million in a hundred years. By 1950 even this colossal increase was dwarfed again: by another billion. The human population then stood at two and a half billion. And you tell me that by the year 2000, your population will surpass six billion. Three billion – three thousand million – *extra* humans in fifty years, which will then mean an *extra* one hundred million every year.

'The same each year,' he remarked, 'as half the population of the whole world in Roman times. And considerably more than the seventy million killed or who died of disease or starvation in the ten years of your two terrible World Wars.' He pointed out that I was born into a world of two billion humans, and if I live to be eighty will then be one of about eight billion humans.

These were not at all bad estimates for the time. In fact the world's population passed the six thousand million mark just the other year – in 1998. And two years later had grown again by a further 200 million: more in two years than the whole population of Britain,

France and Germany put together. So the *increase* of over a hundred million people a year was realised at the same time.

Even back then in the 1970s Tisala was greatly surprised that at least the leaders of the world's countries were not alarmed by what was happening – it was quite clear that the pace of population increase was out of all proportion to anything that had previously happened in the history of the planet and would have fundamental consequences.

I said, 'It does sound alarming, but there are probably ways we can work out the problem.'

'Are you not complacent?' said Tisala. 'Perhaps because you cannot properly comprehend such figures? You take what I fear is too often the human view: and it may be a fateful error for the world.' He said in one sense we are victims of the limitation of our species – we are a local territorial animal and cannot for the most part think beyond that. Men do not think they inhabit the world – but only the little patch of it which they occupy. So 6,000 million or 8,000 million in the world means little to anyone.

I tried to defend our shortsightedness. 'Some of us are aware of our numbers, but it's true we don't know what to do about it, apart from contraception.' And I remembered from my boyhood Aunt Jane's remark that she would be cremated because if everyone was buried there would soon not be room for the living. Since when the world population has more than doubled.

Tisala said that every child should learn world figures and the figures for their own country's increase over the last hundred years, and projections for the next 50 years. They should learn also of the success of those in more stable places. Thus those in countries increasing fastest would become aware of their situation, and be more able to choose differently.

He could see plainly the reasons why the increase had continued: first our biological urges, enlarged by cultural traditions including rights of individual sexual freedom, often without balancing social responsibilities; and then in medical life-saving advances and in exercising our agricultural ingenuity, for in broad terms, except for a few million here and there, we have so far managed to feed our surging population.

But to do so men have increasingly commandeered the environment, driving out native vegetation and animals to make way for domesticated animals and crops. And we have procured a vast increase in agricultural productivity by our farming skills – improving nature and output by cross-breeding animals and plants and feeding chemicals into the earth. 'So much effort and ingenuity to feed a population that should largely not be there.'

He understood that millions had faced dreadful deaths from starvation in recurring famines and hundreds of millions just held on to life at subsistence levels; but nevertheless the bulk of the population did survive, and not only survived, but continued its headlong increase.

In terms of individual histories he thought mankind had imposed on itself an appalling prospect for a long-lived species. He wondered if the starving were driven to curse their longevity and the long – continued suffering it brings, though nature mercifully tends to shorten such lives. Yet he observed that continuing life was their instinctive escape route, so they procreate, and hope. He thought it a miserable and heartrending existence, especially for a conscious, intelligent animal.

Tisala said he had already seen too many pictures and heard too many reports of pathetic, starving men, women and children, and the hope of life, displayed in brightly coloured clothes, betrayed in the blowing dust of despair or the biting cold of grey poverty. But too few apparently say: 'We must cease to have so many children.' So they follow their inbuilt animal instinct to outdo death and fulfil their innate function to pass on life, though in terms of humanity it is no longer needed and is instead a looming disaster.

I said: 'But the result is, the more people there are, the more people there will be'

'Yes,' said Tisala, 'with weighty consequences.'

He thought it had happened partly because it was nobody's problem. What does an extra three of four billion by 2050 mean, when you have a European or North American home, or a nicely appointed home in any place, commute to work daily by car or train, and fly to sunny or cultural holiday destinations? Similarly, what does it mean when your horizons are bounded by the edge of your shanty town and the acquisition of a piece of rusty corrugated iron for a roof, or by poor village fields and gathering branches to frame a shelter?

He wondered that we were not taught the history of our own land.

He asked how many living in England knew that only four hundred years ago the great metropolis of London only just spread southward over the river to Southwark, and northwards to Moorgate half a mile from the river, beyond which all was countryside; that eastwards beyond the shipping clustered below London Bridge were uninhabited marshes and mudbanks of the sprawling Thames; that coming out of London to the west, people saw fine country houses with gardens like the old Somerset House, and the country village of Charing Cross, before they came to another village, the political centre of England, at Westminster. Further out in the countryside were the villages of Kensington and Chelsea and beyond them the country retreat of the Bishop of London at Fulham. The total population of Shakespeare's London, including the outlying parts, was about a hundred and fifty thousand souls. Shakespeare's London – home, inspiration and busy workplace of the great playwright – was then by population one half of one percent of what the population of Tokyo-Yokohama is now. And the population of all England – the green and sceptred isle – was then about five million, or about one quarter of the twenty million or more each of Mexico City, Tokyo, New York, Seoul, Sao Paulo, or Mumbai; with twenty other urban areas not far behind with populations of between ten and twenty million each.

Tisala used to gaze – he said with a mixture of awe and fascinated horror – at pictures of night-time Tokyo and New York: the great towering blocks and heaped up buildings with their millions of pinprick window lights rising out of the plunging black canyons they created. He asked if the inhabitants of such places become frightened when they see all this and think of the astonishing continuous ingenuity needed to maintain such a structure in working order. At that time I laughed and reassured him, confident in our abilities.

He merely reiterated that all people should be taught the world's and their own demographic histories, and found it very strange that such were not an essential part of their curriculum from an early age, for rapid population growth profoundly affects the future of all people. He thought those born into huge urban agglomerations, or depressed rural areas needed to know how and why that had come about, and what other possibilities there might be. But he understood that ignorance, and the fiercely upheld impositions of sexual and social norms and practices in different societies, often excluded the wider view. And the more we looked at these matters, the more uneasy I became.

I had found world population figures relatively easy to come by, but when Tisala asked me to compile a table of some national historical population figures, it proved difficult, and in some cases impossible. Sometimes it was because the extent or boundaries of a country had changed, or a new political entity arisen; but mainly it seemed because no one at the time had thought to compile such figures systematically, and either they did not exist or were buried piecemeal in records beyond my capacity to search out. But with considerable labour I put together a table of sorts. It was incomplete, but startling.

I found, for instance that the population of Egypt in 1900 was under ten million, virtually all confined to the fertile strip of the Nile. Tisala cast his mind back over the history of Egypt and asked how many people were there when the pyramids and temples of the old kingdoms were built along the banks of the great river. Historians estimated perhaps half a million. By 1950 the numbers had risen to twenty million, and before the century was out would rise to over sixty million. And Cairo would swell from one to fifteen million in the same century. And beyond that? And the Nile itself no longer flowed with the old certainty of life-sustaining nutrients.

He asked after Iran, a country of which he seemed fond, beautiful but parched, where wealth was water running in its gardens. In 1950 fourteen million, in 2000 perhaps 70 million. All to be watered, housed and fed. He understood oil can buy many things. But when the oil runs dry? He thought the people in India, Pakistan and Bangladesh – each individual person – should know that when the Taj Mahal was built (by 1648) the population of the whole subcontinent was 100 million; in 1900 perhaps 250 million; in 2000 most likely over 1,250 million. And fifty years beyond that – who knows – perhaps 2,000 million. 'Do they think how they are living, and will live, in that old land?'

So we peered into the future. Wherever we looked, there were burgeoning population increases. In some countries – Nigeria, Mexico, Brazil, the Philippines – estimates of quadrupled populations within the last fifty years of our century were predicted. In other countries less, but nearly always the figures were relentlessly upward. Biggest of all was China. That old civilisation – for most of its two thousand years of existence less than a hundred million people – was now the colossus of the world, approaching 1,400 million. Tisala thought it no accident that the two countries which had recently attempted some control of population growth were China and India, both with vast multiplying populations and frightened governments; the one draconian, but with some limited success; the other free but ineffectual.

Tisala's enquiries made me piece together the rapidly moving picture of humanity's increase, marching – perhaps trampling – into the future. And I felt more starkly a growing disquiet for the world.

Often, looking around me, I contrasted those great heaving cities with our simple life on Inis Cuan.

I knew the island remained unspoilt because it was not under pressure from a human population. The land, more than two square miles, in reality was poor and rocky, in nature beautiful but only capable of supporting a family or two. I knew that much of the rural world works, and will only work, while humanity is sparse: otherwise we will destroy not only its beauty but its capacity to bear us. And all around me I felt the preciousness of every blade of grass and sprig of heather, and every little stunted tree.

There were daffodils on Eileen Mór but none on Inis Cuan. That autumn, Jimmy MacLeod and I planted three sack fulls of yellow daffodils on Inis Cuan, some round the little crofting cottage, but most in the inlet near the shack, stretching away where the soil allowed. It felt like an offering to the future, marking the spot where much good had come about.

Jimmy knew instinctively where to plant. We didn't speak much, except for the work. 'That little bank there' he said. 'They'll wave to those,' – he indicated across to where we'd planted others. Scattered wild plantings, according to the ground.

'Here, Jimmy?'

'Ay.' He stood up, straightening his back. 'We'll start them off, but they'll fend for themselves. They'll appear where it's to their liking.'

And I saw them spreading into the future, beyond our time.

CHAPTER 44

Human Numbers and Restraint

One day, when I had been brooding about the consequences of the now inescapable growing flood of humanity, I said to Tisala, 'What is the point of all these human lives on Earth?'

He said, 'You have asked a question humans rarely seem to ask. To each individual, life is everything, for without it there is nothing, and once an individual gains consciousness of life it is not lightly given up. But looked at from the outside the truth seems to be that too many of those lives have little point beyond mere existence and struggling to reach reproduction, and are pitiful.'

'You humans think a fish in the sea is a fish in the sea. If it lives to adulthood and spawns it has fulfilled all its potential; and even if killed young, at least it feeds others and has been what it should, a fish swimming in the sea. But I say, you have not understood the nature of fish, for they too have the beginnings of society. You say a Blue Whale is a magnificent sight, but I say a lone Blue Whale merely swimming in the sea may be a forlorn sight. We Blue Whales cannot truly be ourselves without our society, our pleasurable knowledge and love of our families and our songs, our joy, our kindness to each other, and our communications and linking of minds around the globe. We pay a price for being born a higher form of life with conscious possibilities: the tragedy and trauma of failure to blossom, or of destruction, are proportionately the greater. And you humans have built for yourselves an infinitely complicated potential. Your position is wonderful and terrible.'

He saw that many humans – millions – lived their lives in misery and never rose out of ignorance and poverty to the fuller potential of human life. For many – the starving, diseased and pain ridden – he thought that death must come as a relief, even young death. He recognised fully that an individual, except in extremes of pain or trauma, will choose life, though it may not be a free choice but an instinct to survive; which in humans seems often to extend to the savage killing of other humans to ensure self survival, something wholly unknown among his kind.

He said: 'In fifty thousand years, no Blue Whale has killed another. Nor have we allowed any of our kind to starve: we were aware of our numbers and adjusted our reproduction over the years to meet conditions in the oceans. But you humans, priding yourselves as the highest form of life, outbreed your lands and breed yourselves into armies and kill each other by the million.' He sighed. 'So many humans fighting and killing; yet so many millions cruelly treated by life and death.'

As he spoke, I felt his sense of waste and anger, for he thought it should not be like that; that humans should be able to master themselves. I say 'anger' but I think he did not feel anger as humans do – he had too serene a mind. But it was an affront to everything that gives rise to serenity and he described an emotion I learned to recognise in him – a mixture of painful sorrow and dislike. For, from within the whale world he had acquired a strong morality. Much later, I concluded it came from the profound sense of balance in his mind which gave rise to his insistent urge to solve such problems.

But then a thought arose unbidden in my mind: 'Are you saying it would be better if many were unborn?' I asked with some trepidation, for the thought felt brutal and callous – only one step away from wishing death, or at least the prevention of existence – on millions of my fellow human beings. But the more I thought, the more I felt it was the right question, and that having faced it was like passing out of a prison yard, previously circled inescapably; out of the gate of an old impasse into a country of new hope.

He had spoken previously of the 'strange belief' that gives the motive for multiplying lives on Earth to be for the pleasure of God, so as to furnish a place called heaven with risen dead. 'I understand,' said Tisala, 'that the followers of this religion argue that all life is precious. But that is not an argument for increasing life when much suffering will result, but rather one for preserving and enhancing the lives which you have.' He thought that by encouraging the creation of new additional life into great poverty and suffering, such people used their strange belief to betray the poor, all to gain more souls and bodies for a hoped-for heaven, after the living have tried and failed to sustain themselves on Earth.

We live, he thought, not by the will of any God, but as long as our bodies will support us. He thought we should all enjoy what life we can. But it would be better to live as humans should, before death comes.

'Yes.' I said. 'The best life we can, while we can.' I thought of Ellie, and her reluctant but calm acceptance of death. She knew from her childhood Christianity of belief in an afterlife, but I knew she did not expect it or rely on it for comfort; her life here on Earth was everything she knew. She had lived and loved and laughed, and said goodbye. Sadness at leaving life early? Oh yes, and the sadness of her loss for those left behind. But for her life was wonderful – happy and fulfilled.

'You were thinking of Ellie?' he said, though I don't know how he knew.

'Yes. Her happy life, but how in the end, her body couldn't cope with the tumours. She didn't wish to die, but I don't think she was afraid.'

'Death is not to be feared, except as avoidable and untimely loss of life. The young too can have wisdom from the quality of their lives. Hers made Ellie unafraid. She knew it was her time and that it could not be avoided.'

He commented that our concept of the 'grim reaper' shows we properly value life. But death itself, he thought, is not grim. At the end of a long life sometimes the body fails before the mind, or the body outruns the life – the constructive life of mind, memory and personality – which flickers and decays as it goes down. But beyond that he thought we should look to death for relief and release, and that death was then to be welcomed without any attempt to attain immortality by belief in heaven.

He noted that another form of heaven – nirvana – was viewed and had been developed by Hindus and Buddhists as an escape from their own doctrine of reincarnation of life, seen as a bondage of the cycle of birth, death and rebirth. He understood they saw this as dissolution of the individual and primarily as a release from suffering, though some went further to see it as seeking a generalised bliss. Like other religions, he thought that Buddhists used theirs as a balm in this life. A precursor form of release, they say, is by meditation and moral discipline. But when they claim it leads to the extinction of all earthly distractions and all ignorance, Tisala thought it a delusion. And though the semblance of detachment can be summoned up for a while, and is certainly more pleasing than many human activities, he viewed it as a strategy for use along the way of life, but not for life itself. 'For we not only live in the Earth, but are of it, to the last atom of our nails and hair, and ignorance is not dispelled by moral thought without knowledge. And knowledge, for humans, is attained with difficulty by engaging with the complicated world.' And he noted that notwithstanding their doctrine of escape from birth and rebirth, nothing in the religions of India has saved them from producing one of the biggest the most rapid increases in population in the world; while their secular government with its praiseworthy aim of social improvement has been left trailing in the slipstream of the nation's life. He thought it sad and moving for so many to live and die blighting the lives of each other.

To my question, 'Would many be better unborn?' he answered, 'It is clear much measurable suffering would be avoided.' He observed that if, say, half the human population of the world in 1900 were starving and disease-ridden, that would be some 750 million people. If half in 2000 were so suffering, 3,000 million would be. Within one short century more than an additional two billion people living in misery and suffering, hourly, daily across the weeks and months, many for years before their gallant bodies fail.

'You humans seem to think only so far: that it is wretched to live and starve in poor lands, too hot or too cold, without adequate shelter, food and water. But you then readily accept it as if it were some natural pre-ordained order; which with your abilities it is not and should not be.'

While he applauded our sense of compassion and need to act to alleviate crises when calamities strike, he thought we had done extraordinarily little about the causes of overpopulation that give rise to so vast a scale of misery. He noted that, speaking broadly, only richer people voluntarily limited their reproduction to give themselves ease and pleasant surroundings. For the rest, they breed and multiply in profusion, spreading and passing on their desperate existence. So they are forced to live in arid wastelands and raise a few ears of corn or goats against tomorrow's famine, or chance life in the inundated deltas or earthquake zones, or build shanty hovels in the margins of society, in the mudslide hills, or derelict and rundown parts of hopeless cities, and spend life scavenging among refuse. He understood that cities attract the poor with the hope of gaining wealth, but, when I showed him pictures of these places, it disturbed and moved him greatly.

Yet he saw that the poor do not themselves seek limitation of reproduction, thinking that large families will reduce their fear of incapacity and feebleness in later years. So they seek instead to chase the material glitter they glimpse beyond them, but which their cycle of poverty denies them.

'You think we shall see more and greater natural calamities in future years?' I asked gloomily.

'Yes, I fear it is certain,' he said, 'but many will be man-assisted natural calamities caused by the pressure of human numbers perched or huddled in places where they should not be.'

He thought this would give rise to something else that should not be: better off people, and governments, indifferent to, and even coming close to wishing for, catastrophes to remove the problems they may otherwise have to confront.

I protested – 'We would never... We value all human life.' I said.

'Who is 'we'?' he asked. 'Does my friend David speak for all humanity? You humans like to think you value life, but I see that often it is not true.' Given the morality of men, he thought the way was open for terrible events and even amongst the good, neglect was a counsel of moral despair. 'You humans have created this population dilemma, and together you must find ways out of it.'

As he learned more he became increasingly scathing about the long inaction of our governments in the face of population crisis. He saw in it covert indifference to potential catastrophe. Once he asked if slums were used as a method of containing large numbers of a population in defined areas so that they could effectively be forgotten by the better-off parts of the population. He understood that governments had competing priorities, but many were trivial or short term; and government indifference became guilt when indulging in more pleasurable pursuits such as lavishing resources on armed forces or impressive government buildings, and other such diversions, or favoured partisan projects, as civil war or commandeering wealth for a favoured few at the cost of the many, and thereby too often destroying or removing from use in the economy the means to create the real solution: a long enough peace and a sufficient standard of living to enable education to take root and spread through a whole generation and into the next. He was amazed how the educative solution had been so widely ignored. He wondered at the casualness of governments leaving their people blind, deaf and dumb, which is what he thought illiteracy in our complicated world must be. Thus people have become a threat both to themselves and the wider world, imprisoned by their poverty, ignorance and animal fecundity.

And Tisala saw in our history that many governments had encouraged population growth. Rulers thought power and empire lay in numbers. Kings, emperors and tyrants would be greater figures if they had larger populations to provide tax and wealth, and larger armies to foster territorial expansion. And in more modern times, larger industrial workforces to pump out wealth, which is another source of power, to secure their position in the rival nationalities and economic systems in the world. And that they seemed to be reckless and blind as to where their pursuit would lead. He found it astonishing when I confirmed that even then – in the late 1970s – when the problem of overpopulation was plain to see, individual governments should bribe their people by benefits and tax incentives to produce more babies for short term reasons of economic management.

He saw that 'growth' is the great cry and panacea of our materialistic world. And that 'growth' is thought to require a bigger and bigger workforce, though when those workers get old and need pensions and care, a bigger workforce again will be needed, so compounding the ever-upward pressure. And our economists, with rare exceptions, do not ask where the ever-increasing numbers will lead the world. He found they have come to regard themselves as technicians, and such wider questions as beyond their remit. He noted that Adam Smith, when he revolutionised the understanding of economics, was at base a moral philosopher, a qualification lamentably lacking from some of his modern successors.

I had long previously introduced him to the economists: those men who had sought to grapple with the working of trade, commerce, production, price, money – the whole realm of political economy, and all the means whereby men have sought to acquire and create wealth and win ease and comfort. Sometimes I noticed, when he came across important new figures and ideas, he seemed to pick up the feel and spirit of that time. 'Acquaint me with Mr Ricardo,' he said, as if he were entering a coffee house to be introduced to a potential intellectual friend. And he made me take him through the classical economists and their communist counterparts, through to the modern age of Keynes.

Always he seemed to be able to see where things were going. He reminded me that, in the early days of trade – say in China in the east, and among the Venetians, Dutch and English in the west, the creation of wealth was to benefit relatively tiny populations. Then, he continued, the better understanding and exploitation of economics unleashed in the eighteenth century by Adam Smith, Ricardo, the fathers of modern economics, and their successors, coinciding with the agrarian, industrial and scientific revolutions that transformed first the West and then the world at a time when the world's population was increasing by magnitudes previously undreamed of in the whole history of the planet. I concurred, and said, 'Wants and markets have been created for a huge range of products often not thought of in earlier times, that are now demanded as of right by a voracious consumer public.' The list of products made from the bodies of whales that I had described to him now lay clearly explained as a small part of the overall picture. In the space of three hundred years, or a mere ten generations, human impact on the world was transformed utterly.

And that impact I now saw was only the beginning. Even in my own short lifetime so much had changed. I remembered the Mediterranean world of student travels with my friends. Cars were then infinitely fewer in number, even in great cities like Rome and Athens. At Ephesus, where travellers came, but tourists and coaches were unknown, we found a ruined city abandoned eighteen hundred years ago, where the gods of the Greek and Roman world met Christian history. Untouched, as if it were yesterday. The Greek islands and the long coasts of Turkey were almost empty of hotels, with simple accommodation in timeless fishing villages. But now, I know, every bit of shoreline optimistically described as beach is being pressed into the service of tourist developments. At the wonderful city of Constantine, you came in through the ancient city walls shortly after open countryside, not the miles of suburbs that now stretch out. Istanbul, with no bridge across the Bosphorus, and the traffic intermittent, mainly dolmuses and buses. We wandered the empty streets in the heat of the day, the old city sleeping, not much changed in a thousand years.

And in that remembering, I saw differently the advancing impact of economic demand allied to our swelling numbers; and that all the centuries up to that point reached only the beginning of much greater changes now being seen across the wider world.

CHAPTER 45

Economic Resources

'And that,' said Tisala, 'is the looming problem: not just your numbers, but those billions seeking more and more in economic terms.'

He thought enough harm was done in ancient days when only the kings and emperors had the wealth to ornament their palaces; even then those few rapaciously exploited all available economic sources and fought and killed to get them. But now there will be 6 billion and in another generation 8 billion, grouped in jealous states, all aspiring to higher levels of living; all pursuing an increased share in the world's resources to create wealth and comfort for their part of the human race.

At first he had imagined that our governments were planning a co-ordinated and moderate approach, for he thought the leaders of *Homo sapiens* could be expected to show foresight and judgement. This was an opinion he was obliged to revise as his knowledge of human governments increased.

Tisala was amazed and silenced when he discovered that the paramount priority of most governments is to stay in power; that next they prized national defence, usually arming at great expense against their neighbours; and that governing with a view of long-term preservation of our wider civilisation was hardly practised.

'Did not Athens fall because the Athenians in their heyday extended their luxurious wants and therefore their trade commitments? For then they were obliged to build proud navies to defend it all, which led them into ruinous wars, and, having planted vineyards in place of wheat, came to rely on grain surplus shipped from the Black Sea, which proved a fatal instability and error.'

And he remembered those Romans whose Roman-British correspondence I had shown him, writing to each other in the third century of the Common Era, who could not conceive an end to their settled way of life, and thought Roman civilisation irreversible. Within a hundred years that empire was hollowed out to defend its swollen boundaries, and then destroyed.

But now he thought the threat to civilisation was not just to one country or region, but global. The provision of wealth and comfort for all the human race – while disregarding the doubling and doubling again of our population in the last sixty years of our century, and the prospect of many more again in the next generation – he thought the most colossally ambitious undertaking mankind has yet conceived. And on that premise ill-conceived, neither achievable nor in its effect on the world desirable; though he had no doubt, given our ingenuity, that we would see it a surprising distance down that road. But we would find our numbers and the costs and problems mounting against us, and we would become entangled in many dilemmas.

He said, 'You want to abolish poverty and to save millions of children's lives in poor countries from malaria, water-borne diseases, and starvation. But you will not be successful if you only save babies' lives but let them die at three, or five, or nine. You have to provide the means of sustainable life support to keep on saving them until the children can become useful human beings. Otherwise you will have failed. But when you save children's lives you must feed, house and educate them, and when they grow up, provide work to support them and transport to work, and in turn house their new families. And none of these things would be needed if they had not lived. By saving lives you will make a dangerously crowded world more crowded, and raise demand yet higher for exploitation of the world's resources by man. Yet you must save children. That is one dilemma.'

He understood the process of wealth creation, and thought we seemed strangely blind to the scale and the difficulties of abolishing poverty while apparently accepting as inevitable a further limitless rise in our numbers. And he puzzled that our governments and economists only ever seemed to focus on the creation of wealth, not its preservation, or its destruction (which is very simple – misinvest, knock down a house, crush a car, wear out clothes, eat food). Nor did they seem to count the underlying cost of using up the inheritance of our finite star-born world. He thought it obvious that our soaring numbers and demands would create a juggernaut of complicated living much of which, sooner or later, would be unsustainable and collapse; and that we could destabilise the whole environment of the world, bringing untold tragedy to ourselves and life on Earth.

'Let us look, for example,' he said, 'at America.'

He understood the broad story of America: how Europeans fled the divisions, constraints and enforced poverty of old Europe. How they came to the new world, the land of freedom, opportunity and boundless plenty, unless you were African. How, after independence, no foreign power threatened them. How they were therefore free to purchase, fight for and develop their own world, and did so, expanding into the great continent to the west. The rest of the world could almost be forgotten. They forged a new identity – American: adopting their own accents, the stars and stripes, patriotism by conformity in schools, and later in jeans and sneakers, and all the close-knit cultural ties – movies, music, parochial journalism – and sustaining all, the economic rewards of being Americans. So was formed America, where many people believe their country is the world, or at least the only part really worth belonging to. And I recalled reports of how few modern American children could locate even the most well known places outside America on the map. Tisala thought the founding fathers should have included 'the pursuit of learning' in their Declaration, as it would have encouraged many more Americans to face outwards, with great benefit in the world.

This story of America is well known. The result: on the one hand a certain magnificence – the confidence and ability to stand for good; and on the other a materialistic hubris, ignorance and delusions of uniqueness which Tisala thought could do terrible damage if not quickly unlearned in the coming decades.

He wanted to be an admirer of this brave new world – started in hope both of religious and secular liberty – but found instead a chilling record of slavery and exploitation of the blacks and savage destruction of the native people, accompanied by much destruction in nature, not least by whalers in the eighteenth and nineteenth centuries. But amongst it all he looked for and found elements of the better and more noble: belief in liberty, slavers turned emancipators, sacrifices in war made to fight evil, the pursuit of civil rights and remedies, and now a whaling nation turned conservationist.

But as to population, what did he find in this new world of humanity? By 1800 it was a land of four million inhabitants in the settled eastern part, with perhaps a further million or so native inhabitants in the then wide unclaimed expanse of the mid-West and the Pacific coast. America, that seeded transplant of Europe and Africa, by 1900, despite the near elimination of the native inhabitants, a nation of 75 million; by 2000 expected to be about 270 million; and by 2050 an estimated 380 million.

'Do they not find it extraordinary,' asked Tisala, 'that they expect to *increase* by over 100 million in the first fifty years of the new century?' An *increase* of more than their entire nation in 1900, well after the advent of their becoming the greatest industrial power in the world. Or, as he put it, the nation who, after they had fought the Second World War, numbered 150 million, *increasing* by another 230 million by 2050. So all those famous cities – New York, Washington, Boston, Philadelphia, Pittsburgh, Cincinnati, St Louis, Atlanta, Miami, Houston, Los Angeles, San Francisco, Seattle, and all the rest will have to be replicated and built again in their entirety, and half again, merely to house their extra people.

He saw that it would be disguised: beyond the wealthy downtown tower blocks of high-rise commerce, beyond the decay of slums and ghettos, suburbs and developments would spread from existing cities, extending urban freeways, roads, concrete, fences, wires, and buildings everywhere, and underground, water and sewage pipes, drains and cables, spreading like the tentacles of a fungus, the capillaries of urban sprawl. Los Angeles would be three hundred miles across, backing into dusty hills and fire-hazard woods and squeezed along the ocean front, some parts handsome, many not. And no one living in one section or area would face the full reality of the huge agglomerations created by human multiplication.

'And that,' said Tisala, 'is only the start of the cost of your modern civilisation. It is not static but a growing entity, consuming power and energy, and being fed and kept alive by copious incoming transfusions for consumption – fresh water, oil, gas, electricity, food, trees, plants, animals and fish, metals, wood, rubbers, plastics, cloth, wood, paper – a thousand things taken or made from the chemistry of the earth. How it is all to be provided?'

I said, 'They think their growth economy will provide all answers. America is the richest and greatest economic power the world has ever seen.'

'As Rome once was,' said Tisala, 'before they over-exploited and turned to desert the wheat lands of the empire in North Africa, and so assisted in destroying themselves.'

'True,' I said, 'but we are now much better equipped.' I argued that our ingenuity had set us free. We had engineered solution after solution – our agricultural revolution had fed teeming millions more then had been supposed possible by Malthus, one of the first to warn of the consequences of population growth. Our industrial, technological and now electrical revolutions kept us ahead, created wealth, and would lead us to further advances. 'Look,' I cited, 'at the prospect of cheap modern power.'

'I grant,' said Tisala, 'that your record is astonishing. But don't you think, though it has worked in the short term, by which I mean say two hundred years, that it may have masked the long-term consequences of your attitudes?'

Too often, he thought, we credited our ingenuity with solving problems when it might be better seen as postponing them, and often thereby compounding them, while using up irreplaceable capital. For he found nowhere in our economic exploitation any convincing consideration accounting for our using up the world's resources.

I conceded that we used what we found, or could buy, and hoped that before it ran out we would find more, or substitutes. But I remembered how the lead and tin, mined in my own west of England by Romans for the roofs of Rome, had gone now – worked out, finished – leaving only tussock-covered mounds of spoil, and dripping mine shafts in rocky places.

At one point I delegated Tisala's enquiries on the depletion of metals to Robert Thompson. He reported shortages of some – cadmium, mercury, cobalt and antimony.

'Locally?' I asked.

'No,' he said, 'I mean worldwide. The stuff is running out.'

I felt a little jolt, as when you hear an ice sheet crack, though afterwards everything looks the same.

Tisala considered our so far thoughtless waste of precious elements so short-sighted he was left incredulous at the paradox of our scientific cleverness, and our apparent stupidity – our complete failure to limit our population and conserve resources. He anticipated that under pressure of scarcity and increased cost we would improve our record. He understood from Robert that we were beginning to conserve metals, and re-use them; and that the sixty-eight metals known so far in the universe could yield many new alloys to our metallurgists. But now he learned that we knew some metals would disappear; that sometimes years of research on hypothesised alloys would fail; that sometimes substitutes would not be found; that as more alternatives were used up there might be less to turn to; that easily accessible resources, even where more plentiful, would be exhausted; and that the cost and energy required to release and process remaining supplies would inexorably rise.

And all this at a coming time when energy demands – electricity and the rest – would have soared, dwarfing our present day consumption. For he saw that all the world would want what the rich nations now had: televisions, cars, fridges, air conditioning and the like – all the panoply of industrial consumption.

And overall, pushed by our swelling numbers, the result would be an acceleration in the despoliation of the Earth, and the exhaustion of its riches.

'Like oil,' I said.

We had only a few years before, in the mid 1970s, come up against the first major warning after the industrialised world's unprecedented economic growth since 1945: the realisation that the oil so confidently being extracted from the ground was indeed finite; the resultant massive price rise sending a jolt through the world economy. The economic optimism of the western world felt a tremor, like the first warning of an earthquake previously thought far off.

I argued that higher prices will stimulate exploration and supply.

Tisala said, 'For a while – twenty years, forty years? – but in the longer run you are simply speeding up depletion.'

But I said we would adapt: cut down oil use by making more efficient cars, insulate homes to conserve heat, and so on. He thought, given the scale of our multiplying numbers, that would be tinkering at the edges, pushing back the crises for a little while, but little else. Yes, we would find new oil fields and stretch it out for longer – who knows: fifty or sixty years, maybe?

'But always at your back you'll hear your increased numbers hurrying near.'

He enjoyed language play, like a dolphin in new seas. But I recognised he had linked human numbers and death.

Oil led us to petrol and cars. He wanted figures, and made me, for example, come up with the number of cars in America, the great economic powerhouse: in 1950 nearly 50 million; over 200 million expected by 2000; and perhaps by 2050, 320 million.

When I reported this, I was startled by the scale of increase. But he said that the resources being used, and the energy in manufacture will not of course in 2050 be simply over six times that of 1950. The average life expectancy of cars being short, all these cars would have to be replaced every few years.

'Work out,' he said, 'the number of cars built and destroyed in America in that hundred years; not much over the life span of a long-lived human. And calculate the destruction of wealth and loss of scarce metals involved. And think how much fuel has been used, too much of it, you tell me, trivially.' He saw today's wasteful pleasures being paid for tomorrow, and the 380 million Americans of 2050 condemning their parents and grandparents for their wasteful short-sighted greed; and condemning their complacent governments who failed to take remedial action because they forgot the ordinary rules of economics do apply to America, or would not face the popular outcry that effective action would entail.

I said, 'And they do not yet see themselves as the greatest exploiters of world resources and producers of pollutants that the world has ever seen.'

'So far,' said Tisala. But I did not then pick up his double meaning.

He returned to the motor car and asked what would happen if the Chinese turn into Americans in habit? Perhaps 1,400 million Chinese by 2050, demanding pro-rata 1,000 million cars, and the fuel and highways to run them? Add India – perhaps as many again. And then in the rest of the world?

'You humans inflict these problems on yourselves because no-one beforehand properly *imagines* that number of cars.'

'And all the servicing back-up that goes with them,' I said, thinking of all the showrooms, petrol stations, garages and scrap yards of England, with our mere 12 million cars.

And cars are a small part of general industrialisation. Tisala had continually questioned me about pollution: 'We have seen some of it spreading out from the continents over the oceans.'

America I told him, with one twentieth of the world's population, produced one quarter of the pollution.

'And if all the world industrialises like America, what then?'

He feared for the delicate balance of many forms of life, even the growth of grass, the forests and the gardens of the sea, upon which all life ultimately depends. He questioned even then whether the exhaust from men's economic exploitation was not affecting the climate. If you looked, damage was visible, and more predictable. But it was uncertainly understood. Initially I had said the idea was fanciful, but said it with less confidence, as in the 1970s and 1980s slowly the information and the realisations trickled in. The whales, in his lifetime, had noticed uneasily the shrinking at the edges of the polar pack ice, changes to the pattern of krill abundance and other signs. But in the early days I laughed, and made light of our impact, saying it was probably normal weather cycles.

Too many people in the world, I knew. But our ruinous pillage and pollution of the Earth was still half hidden by our ignorance. Now Tisala is gone, and much is clearer and I am ashamed for humanity. Too many people, and too much suffering. But we cannot welcome death, once there is conscious life, even in general. And in individuals death always jolts our lives. Soon in my life there was to be one person less. And, as with Ellie, it was a person I dearly loved.

CHAPTER 46

A Visit to the Tropics

In December 1979, when Will was fifteen and Penny fourteen, we flew out of the English winter towards the sunshine of the tropics. We flew in a 707 – the new wonder of jet age travel – to a then fairly unvisited group of islands. For the first time in all these years I was to meet Tisala in his southern haunts.

The reasons for not previously going are simple – such a trip was difficult and not cheap to organise – the necessary equipment had to be shipped out and then transported to the outlying islands. I needed help but it was vital that the breeding areas of the Atlantic Blue Whale should remain secret. Will now was old enough to act as my assistant: no outsider would be needed. And to make it worthwhile, the children had to be taken out of school.

In explaining it to their head teachers, I gave out that it was a family expedition and that as a biologist I hoped to monitor behavioural aspects of dolphins, which would be educational. Our real purpose had of course to be kept secret. We had therefore to meet Tisala at an uninhabited location, yet one that we could get to with the equipment. As I had worked out the possibilities, the expense mounted. After the main flight, we had to take a small aeroplane to an outlying island. This was to be our base. With considerable difficulty I had arranged the charter of an inboard fishing boat which had to be brought over from a neighbouring larger island. And about three miles to the north, on the very edge of all the islands beyond which the continental shelf dropped into the deep, there were two small uninhabited islands, one with a sheltered bay and beach on the leeward side backed by palm trees and a low hill, the other hardly more than a large rock, but with a great sandy spit running to the west of it. Here was to be our rendezvous with Tisala, only a few hundred miles further south from his main summer cruising ground for that year.

We arrived on the main island on the 19th December, stepping out of the jet into the hot moist air, and transferred to the outlying island the same day after carefully stowing the equipment on the little plane. As we took off, Will and Penny peered excitedly out of the windows at the exotic but somehow ragged scattering of palm trees and shanty buildings. Less than half an hour later we saw a little island emerge from the astonishingly blue sea, and came in at an angle to meet the airstrip.

There was less evidence of human impact – a few small white buildings set in a flat area close to the shore, with green-clad hills behind. Beyond at one end we could see the cluster of glinting white and red roofs of the island's only township – village really – perched around the small curved bay, its harbour.

'This is more what I imagined,' said Will.

The landing was surprisingly smooth. We were met by a pickup truck and drove the short distance straight to the harbour, liaised with the harbour master, located the boat and supervised the transfer of the equipment and some of our kit. I was anxious that nothing should go wrong now, and spoke sharply to the boat boys when one or two of the boxes were carelessly handled. For I knew this expedition might not be repeatable, and that we could not afford equipment breakages. We had few spare parts. My plans were dependent on everything working. With that job done, we went up to the guest house, which was set in trees along the shore a short way beyond the harbour.

It was a simple, rather run-down affair, with pretty but flimsy mosquito outer doors, but all we needed, and the kids thought it wonderful. It gave out down a few wooden steps onto a beautiful white beach, with palm trees leaning as palm trees should. We began to enjoy ourselves, and the different experience of tropical islands, and their friendly smiling inhabitants.

The next day, Will and I set up and tested the equipment in the boat. To my huge relief everything was in order. We had four days to wait. We spent three days lazing and enjoying the island, in and out of the sea all day, snorkelling and beachcombing. There were two other families staying at the guesthouse – a retired English couple and a young Dutch couple with two little girls, who, other than polite exchanges, initially kept themselves to themselves. Not very interesting, I thought, for my two. But Penny made friends with the Dutch family and enjoyed helping, and playing on the beach with the little girls. Will made friends with two of the boat boys and went fishing with them, coming back with all sorts of information on island things.

On the due day we prepared to set off for the outermost island. We loaded water, food and our personal gear, and tied a little tender behind us. One of the boat boys, Carlos, wanted to come, but I said no. I saw him look at Will for help, but Will shook his head.

'We have work to do,' I said.

'I work,' he pleaded.

'Scientific work – very special.'

'Carlos, it's not possible,' said Will, 'but we'll fish another day soon.'

Carlos pushed his lips out, but seemed reluctantly to accept this compensated refusal. When we were ready, as he untied the mooring rope and tossed it to Will, he said, 'Okay, we fish soon.'

As we set off on our three-mile crossing I felt tense anticipation and rising excitement. As always, there was something about outlying islands, existing where two worlds meet. And this was a special meeting. But as we approached the two tiny islands the breeze got up and the sea became choppy. The boat began to dip and lurch, and spray flew.

'Shut that hatch', I called to Will, who went forward on the deck to do so, getting wet with another flying shower, and laughing.

'Getting breezy!'

'We'll manage,' laughed Will, looking forward eagerly. I could sense his own excitement as we approached these tiny tropical islands for our meeting with Tisala – thousands of miles from where we last saw the great whale slipping out of the inlet at Inis Cuan.

'Will we be able to land?' asked Penny.

'Oh yes, I think so. Yes – the wind is off shore – round the other side should be okay.'

I had selected this place months before, poring over a large scale map and a gazetteer of anchorages. And it was fine. We rounded a rocky corner, entering sheltered water. The previous motion was left behind and the boat slid gently towards the shore. We dropped anchor in thirty feet of calm water in the little bay, quite close in, for it shelved deeply down just below us, as the colour showed. I scanned the sea, checking for other boats, but we were alone. No boats – good. But no sign of Tisala either. It was eleven in the morning – we had arranged to meet from midday on. We went ashore in the tender. The island looked idyllic, and we spent some minutes enjoying the beach and splashing in the water's edge. The vegetation beyond a fringe of palm trees looked impenetrable and where the dense green gave way to the white beach, there was a debris of dead foliage.

At the end of the bay was a rocky outcrop about thirty feet high which would make a good vantage point. Afterwards we called it Spyglass South. Will took first turn to watch, sitting up there under his straw hat with his elbows on his knees, periodically searching the sea with his binoculars. Penny and I walked along the beach, exploring the little bay and admiring the shells we found. But we kept within sight of Will. Noon came and went. I looked up at Will frequently.

'We'll leave him a bit longer,' I said to Penny.

'You want him to see Tisala first, don't you?' smiled Penny, taking my arm.

'Well, he'd love that, but it's your turn next.'

'Look, Dad!'

I saw Will was standing stock-still binoculars trained out to sea. He turned to us and raised his arm, holding the binoculars high, and let out a great whoop. He started to scramble down from the rocks. We started running for the boat. Will came up. We pulled the tender out to the boat and clambered aboard. I turned the equipment on and sent out a message, confirming it was us.

I peered out. About a hundred yards off I saw the great slate back slowly wheeling before the dorsal fin rose out of the sea and sank in turn, as he came slowly towards us.

The speakers crackled slightly.

'Hello, David, everyone!' The familiar voice came across on the equipment.

'Tisala – wonderful! How are you? Yes, we are fine.'

We exchanged our usual greetings. But it seemed to me that his normal pleasure at our meeting had an extra air of anticipation in it. He stopped just short of the boat, on the deeper seaward side. We spent some minutes catching up on the details of his journey. No, he had encountered neither difficulties nor anything untoward on the last part of his passage and had been seen by no ship. He had been cruising about in this area for two days since his arrival, familiarising himself with the undersea topography.

When I looked back into the cockpit, I saw Penny and Will in their swimming gear and putting on flippers. Will had his snorkel mask perched on the top of his head.

'Dad, we're going to swim with Tisala.'

'You're not, you know.' His face fell.

'Dad, we've been planning it.'

'For goodness sake, Will, have you forgotten how big he is? He's not just a humpback. I know he's gentle, but an inadvertent flick with his wings could knock you under, or you could be sucked down – never mind getting anywhere near his flukes.'

But Will was determined and argued on. 'Look,' he said, pointing at Tisala, 'he's completely motionless. If you tell him we're there it'll be fine.'

In the end I spoke to Tisala. 'The kids want to come in and swim with you, but I don't think it's sensible.' How deep is the instinctive fear of loss when you have once suffered its misery.

But Tisala said, 'Let them come in. I will look after them.' So, after further assurances of care from all of them, in the end I gave way.

Tisala gave instructions for them to swim to his giant wings and clamber on – he would hold them out.

'Very careful as you pass his eyes,' I said. 'Not too close.'

They jumped into the sea, bobbed up to adjust their masks, and swam towards him. As they approached he slowly raised his great head so that the prow of his lower jaw stood about two feet high out of the water with runnels of water at first cascading from it, but subsiding to trickles off the great lid of his mouth. He watched them coming, and I saw him spread his pale, white-edged wings sideways just under the surface nearly at right angles to his body, the outer half curving back.

A grown Blue Whale's wings are eight feet long and at the thickest part, where it joins the body, the front edge is almost nine inches thick. The wings become thinner towards the outer end and the backwards edge, very like the wings of an aircraft, and with a not dissimilar function.

Will, treading water as he came opposite Tisala's eye, said something to him. Then he reached for the front of the wing Tisala held out for him, and twisting round pushed himself up, so he ended up sitting on the wing, facing forwards. Penny on the other side was more cautious and paddled to the tip of his other wing and held on.

I called to her, 'Climb on from the front – you can sit.'

She worked her way along the front edge and as she began to raise herself to climb up Tisala dipped his wing and she was lifted on, twisting round to sit as he raised his wing again. For a few moments they sat there. I saw Will and then Penny lift their masks. Over the speaker I heard Tisala say, 'Tell them to hold on.'

'Hold on!' I shouted.

And there they sat, hands trying to grip the front edge of the wing, arms straight and angled out by their sides, acting as struts; my two much-loved youngsters riding on the sea-wings of the greatest being the world has ever seen, like something out of an ancient myth, when magic invested the minds of men with all manner of wonderful possibilities and tales.

I saw the water stir behind Tisala as he gently flexed the most powerful set of muscles ever developed – for the measured upthrust of his flukes – and slowly he moved forward. There was a little shriek from Penny, but she hung on. I ducked down to the equipment and spoke to Tisala. He would take them in a circle past the boat, looping round the bay and back again. I shouted this to the kids.

Will stuck his legs out in front – the water splashing up against the soles of his feet as if he were water skiing.

'Tell him to go faster, Dad,' he called.

'No – You'll come off.'

If they had gone at any speed at all, both would have been swept off their precarious perches. It surprised me as it was that Tisala was able to swim keeping his wings at the surface of the water. He seemed to be at a slight upward angle, the front of his head out of the water pushing a bow wave before it, the wings swivelled to be horizontal, the rest of his length and his flukes down in the water. They made a slow loop around the bay, like a stately royal progress, then back towards the boat and slowly stopped. I watched as Tisala slowly subsided and the kids floated off into the water spluttering and laughing. The huge whale sank gently away below them, but so delicately did he move that there was hardly a ripple on the surface. As the kids swam for the boat, he surfaced again a little way off. They clambered aboard, and I laughed as they jabbered away excitedly.

'Fantastic!'

'Difficult to stay on.'

'But he seemed to ride up, then there was less pull.'

'His skin isn't slippery at all.'

'It has a sort of sweet smell.'

'Not like his breath – cor!' Will made a face and waved his hand in front of it as dispersing the pungent odour.

And so on. But gradually the realisation of a more profound part of the experience came through.

'Has anyone ever done that before?' Will asked.

I said: 'In all the whale stories I've ever read, from the ancient world to now, I've never heard so. And it seems highly unlikely. There wasn't a bridge, language or otherwise, between men and such great whales. You are the first.' We all smiled as the thought established itself.

'Cor,' said Will again, but this time exhaling slowly with the wonder of it. 'It's magic!'

'And you tried to stop us,' said Penny looking at me reproachfully.

'Yes. Well I… Okay. Sorry about that – you were right.' They did not need my explanation.

They wanted to go in again. But this time Tisala said, 'No, not today – another day perhaps.' They pleaded, but he was firm.

Will asked me, and then Tisala, if we could fix a rope round the base of his wing and over the top of the other wing, to give a handhold. After a pause Tisala suggested it should be thought about for another day.

'But today,' he said, 'I have an important request to make of you and your sister.' They looked expectantly at each other. 'Tomorrow I should like each of you to speak to me of four things – something informative, something sad, something exciting and something funny.' And in addition he asked that they should each recite a short rhyming poem.

These strange requests were unexpected and rather puzzled the children, but they promised to prepare something.

'He's never asked anything like that before,' Will said afterwards. 'I wonder why?'

'I haven't got any poems here,' said Penny.

'But I have,' I said, smiling at her, for I knew what was required. And to encourage them said I'd prepare something too.

For most of the rest of the day Tisala and I updated each other on whaling matters – he passing information about the Blue Whale world. The news was good. Though nominally the Blue Whales had been protected now for some years, up until that time Tisala had reported deaths by hunting amongst the Blues, mainly at the hands of covert killings by the Russian Antarctic whalers. But for the last year or two, the numbers were in single figures. And this was the first year when he knew of none at all. The horror of the slaughter and the sickening dread of extinction did seem to be receding.

But I had to report that the international struggle within whaling continued – over the inhumanity, the species hunted, and quotas. That was the time when we had heard of the shameful dishonesty of some whaling nations which went on – how the Japanese had now been found trying to bribe the conservationist Seychelles with the promise of aid which came, for whales, with deadly conditions attached, and how the hypocrisy of Japanese whaling was exposed when the purchase of whale meat from pirate operations outside the IWC was revealed.

So we caught up. But the dominant feature of our exchange was the optimistic tone we found ourselves using in relation to Tisala's own family and the gradual rebuilding of the lives of the Blue Whales in the oceans of the world.

We were still talking when Will dropped into the little cabin. Tisala was saying, 'Yes, tomorrow.'

'Tomorrow what?' asked Will.

'We're going to meet here again tomorrow,' I said. 'But now we must get back to the main island.' It was late afternoon and I did not want to be caught by the sudden early nightfall of the tropics. We left the bay together, but in different directions. I steered our boat back round the island, while we saw Tisala heading out for the deep.

That evening back on our island and as soon as we were alone after our meal, Penny and Will could talk of nothing except their day and their magical ride on Tisala's wings. And even when they eventually lapsed into silence I could see from the light in their eyes and their faraway looks that they were back riding in the sea, reliving the experience. Such vividness is given to children, memories that last as long as the mind survives, when later things are long forgotten.

I imagined Penny, who might be the last of us, eighty years on, perhaps an old wrinkled woman lying in a nursing-home bed, smiling to herself as she remembered the past and riding again on the wings of the great whale, and the nurses, who would not yet be born for sixty years, saying to each other, 'Sweet old thing, she's slipping away'.

We prepared our pieces for the next day, and though the kids were tired they both wanted to please Tisala.

'I can't do funny,' Penny said. But with a bit of teasing and banter we were all soon laughing. And with the help of some rehearsal and suggestions the requested elements were put together, and verses from poems chosen.

'I wonder why he wants all this?' asked Penny.

'He always has good reasons,' said Will.

'We'll see tomorrow,' I said.

And we did. We arrived at the bay by mid morning and cast anchor about half an hour before our planned meeting time. The kids swam from the boat and dried off in the sun. I had been watching out, but Will, standing on the deck saw Tisala first.

'Here he comes,' he announced. Then suddenly his voice changed. 'Dad! There's another one – there's two! No, three!'

We all jumped up.

'Four!'

'Five!'

In line aslant, Tisala leading, followed closely on his left by another, and behind them three more, came five Blue Whales.

As on the first times I had ever met Tisala, I was overwhelmed by a surge of exaltation, which screwed my face up with sheer elation.

'Just look at that,' I said recovering.

'The fourth one is very small,' said Will, now with his binoculars.

'She's a baby – six weeks old.'

'You knew?'

'Yes. But until yesterday it wasn't certain they would all come, so I thought it best to be a surprise. I didn't want to promise what might not happen.'

His momentary doubt was dispelled.

'Majestic,' he grinned.

'Who are they?' asked Penny.

'Tisala's family,' said Will.

I nodded. 'Come, we all need to be introduced.'

The whales had stopped, the back ones drifting up towards Tisala. We stood on deck, so they could see us clearly, and each introduced ourselves enunciating our names clearly and bidding them welcome. Then I ducked into the little cabin and we got onto the equipment.

'Hello David. You see we have come as I hoped.'

I said: 'Welcome, Tisala my dear friend, welcome back. And welcome Saba, Tarba, Yéni and little Nessini. Thank you for your journey to see us.' Tisala was making a rapid series of sounds. The whale closest to Tisala was his son Saba, named after his great grandfather. Next to him, his son Tarba, Tisala's grandson.

I said to Will, 'Tarba's eight – a Blue Whale teenager.'

Then came Yéni, Tisala's niece. She was a wonderful sight – bigger even than Tisala, as the mature females are amongst the Blue Whales. Keeping very close to her was her baby Nessini – she looked tiny besides her mother, but was longer than our twenty-five foot boat. It was her family who Saba had swum with when he was young.

The newcomers could not of course understand our language but when Tisala and I were talking I had the impression that they were listening intently, following the sound patterns.

After a while Tisala said, 'Now may we hear from Will, please.'

He sent out more rapid whale-sound signals. I looked out of the boat. All five whales were lying without movement in the water, heads towards us.

Will came to the speaker and gave his four sketches. He spoke of school, which was largely informational; of his sadness at the death of so many of Tisala's family; of his enthusiasm and excitement at swimming with Tisala; and he joked about learning to swim.

Then Penny made her contributions, telling them how and why we wore clothes and putting some on to show them. She abandoned her next prepared piece, relying on the spur of the moment on her excitement at meeting them all; but becoming sad in recounting the decline and death of her hamster. She struggled with the lighter element, but managed to make herself laugh.

Tisala said, 'You have done very well. Now we should like to hear your poem. Please read it steadily.' She was all concentration at the microphone and read her three verses clearly and with some charm. Tisala asked her to repeat it, which she did. At the end there was a slight movement in the water from the whales.

Then Will read his, holding the rhythm, and giving slight emphasis to the rhyme without being asked. He said he would read it again.

When he had finished there was again a stirring in the water, as if they recognised that something was complete. Tisala gave off a stream of sounds, as if he were commenting, or adding a reminder. He seemed well pleased and thanked the children for their efforts. Penny said she would go on deck and sing the whales some songs.

Will said to me: 'I know what this is about. Tisala wants his family to recognise our voices, and the different tone we use if we are excited, or sad and so on.'

'And the poems?'

'The poems I'm not sure about.'

'Those verses will act as a sort of code or password. The other whales do not now understand English, but Tisala says they will hold the sound patterns of the verses in their minds for ever. At any future meeting they will recognise who is speaking to them.'

'But...' and I saw the realisation slowly awakening in his mind. He looked at me with a grave seriousness.

I said: 'One day Tisala will be gone, and I also, Will. None of us knows how long he has. I pray we shall finish our work, but we don't know. It haunts me that it might be lost. If I die, you are one of my trustees to get our knowledge into the world. Robert and others will help. But up to now if Tisala were to die, there would have been nothing possible beyond what is already done. Now there is at least the possibility of continuation.'

'That's why we came here isn't it?'

'Tisala and Yéni would not allow the young to travel in a group to Inis Cuan. It is too risky – too much off their safest route, too near busy shipping, and too landlocked for such a group. The answer was to come here. It seemed wise when we planned it. But now I'm more aware, as Tisala pointed out, that we are imposing on you younger generation a great responsibility.'

Will thought for a moment. 'Perhaps it is more an opportunity. We needed to meet to have a chance to continue what you and Tisala have been doing.' His eyes smiled at me. 'Anyway, I'd love to be involved and I bet Tarba and the others would too.' Then he became serious again. 'But I don't know how it would work out. The thing is, Dad, for you and Tisala to stay alive. I have thought about that before.' He added: 'It would take years to get the others to where you are now.'

And behind the factual statement I glimpsed the deep dull pain and irreplaceable loss of his mother's death, and his young knowledge that I too was mortal.

But afterwards the strange thing was that my misgivings at burdening Will – for I guessed that it might fall on him more than Penny – from that moment fell away. Though what would be would be, our insurance policy was in place, and I was more than ever filled with determination to see our work come to fruition. Of course, in a sense it would never be finished but I believed we could change attitudes in the world, and buoyed up by this belief, that nothing catastrophic would intervene.

I became aware that Penny had stopped singing.

'Look,' said Will, 'they are waiting for us. We must go to them – and that means – swimming!'

So we called out that we were coming in, changed, and dropped into the warm blue sea. As we swam carefully in among the gentle giants, they hardly moved and we spoke to them all individually, taking our masks off so they could see us clearly close-to and match face to voice. I noticed Will speaking especially to Saba and Tarba. We all made a fuss of the twenty-five foot baby, who was curious and friendly, emitting a series of little squeaks, but keeping close to her mother. It was extraordinary to think she had been born only six weeks before.

When their absolute stillness and care with us was clear, I made a point of patting and stroking each of them to establish a physical closeness, talking welcomingly as I did so, and called to the kids to do the same. Thus in an hour those strangers from the deep became our friends who we knew by name and could recognise by their various singular characteristics. Later I made notes recording it all, Will and Penny chiming in with various things they had noticed, or said to the whales.

Afterwards, when we had dried off on deck, I went below. Tisala had asked me to play some music for them. I spoke to him and heard him relaying a message. And then across that little bay on the slight afternoon breeze floated some of mankind's most beautiful and tranquil music. And the stillness of its reception was broken only at the end by the stirring of flukes in the water and a ripple of response, which I thought reflected the ripples in their minds.

For four days we sailed each morning to the little island. On two days we did see some dolphins, and so had something to talk about when asked in the guesthouse. Each day we were met by the flotilla of whales. And each day, for a while, we joined them in the water. We watched Yéni suckling her daughter – strands of rich milk hanging in the water before dissolving into a bluish blur. Newborn Blues drink many gallons of milk a day, and grow with astonishing speed. They are born about twenty feet long and by seven months (the end of the nursing period) are fifty feet long.

Tarba and Saba particularly spent hours listening to Tisala and me talking. And I spent time with them going back to the beginning of learning our language – not that there was time for them to make any real progress, but to give them an inkling of how it might be done.

Will was desperately keen to ask Tisala for another ride, but for two days he said nothing as we went about discussions and tasks he knew that Tisala and I were anxious to complete.

Finally he asked me if Tisala had mentioned it, but I said he had not.

'I'll ask him,' said Will, 'but I don't want to use a rope.' I inclined my head questioningly. 'Well I thought about it and it didn't seem right. He's too free for that. And I thought – what if he had to swim away with the rope still attached? It would be a sort of handicap – maybe even a dangerous one if he got hunted. It might be like a prisoner's shackles – he should never have that.'

Afterwards, when he asked Tisala, he repeated this to him. Tisala listened to him.

'You have thought well.' I could tell from his tone that he was pleased. Yes, he would be glad to give Will and Penny another ride. And so they sat on the surface-cutting eight foot wings of the great Blue Whale again, and tisurfed slowly across the bay and back. But this time they were escorted, one on each side, by Saba and Tarba who watched the whole proceedings closely until they were deposited near the boat, and bobbed up shouting, 'Thanks Tisala! Great!' before swimming to the boat. 'Thank you!'

The next day Tisala asked Penny and Will if they would like a different ride. 'You could sit astride behind my fin, and put a loop over it to hold on to – it would catch in the nick in the front of my fin.'

'Wouldn't it hurt you?' asked Penny.

'No, no – it is old scar tissue. But the ride may be undulating.'

The Blue Whale's fin is small – a mere fifteen or eighteen inches high and set far back where his body tapers towards his flukes. The depth of the body at that point is about five feet, not round, but steep-sided and fish-like in section, and not much wider than a horse's back.

Will swam towards Tisala's dorsal fin, and Tisala sank slowly to meet him, the tip of his fin just showing above the surface. Will reached it, held on, looped a ring of nylon rope over it and slid astride. Tisala rose slightly, his long back flat and just clear of the water, the whole dorsal fin visible, and all glinting in the sunshine. Will perched there, a small figure on that great back, like a boy in the distant beyond, holding onto the rope ring and gripping Tisala's sides with his legs. About eight feet behind him the great flukes stirred the water, and slowly they moved forward. And then with a slight undulating motion Tisala slid through the sea, which began to stream past Will, pulling at his legs and causing a small turbulence where normally there was none to mark the passage of a whale. I saw Will fold his legs back at the knee, raising his feet like a jockey on a racehorse, to lessen the pull of the water. But unlike a horse rider, who rides with control on a broken and trained animal, Will had placed himself entirely in the trust of the largest and freest being on Earth: who in the natural world had no rivals or enemies, the wise incomparable colossus of the oceans.

Saba and Tarba had again joined the party as escorts, tisurfing as they circled the bay, sending out a stream of sounds – whistles, squeaks and deeper notes. And so this image and demonstration of trust and friendship between two worlds of parallel creation was fixed in the memories of all our group. And afterwards, in the days that followed, Will rode on Tarba and Penny on Nessini, using rubber rings over their fins to help hold on.

So the bonds were strengthened and the voices of the young reached out to each other in the sea, and from the boat across the airwaves and through the water, for it seemed that all wanted to build knowledge and love of each other.

And on several days, when we had swum with them in the morning, the whales insistently wanted to hear more music. So, in the quiet of noon, when the breeze dropped, we released through the air and water in the amphitheatre of the little bay that floating and cascading architecture of sound which perhaps tells most nearly of the heavenly propensities of man. They listened in profound stillness which told the wonder in their responses. And at those times it seemed that all creatures could be one.

When the Blue Whales arrived, I had recognised Saba immediately and had laughed with the pleasure of it. He was strikingly like Tisala, and echoed some of his markings. He had too some of the lighter colouring of his mother, and I soon recognised from earlier descriptions of Sayli his mother's quality of gracefulness. But now I knew him, most of all he gave the feeling – he had about him the hallmark – of his father's determined strength and serenity. Some of this was reproduced in Tarba. He was a beautiful whale. I may have been influenced by his family association but it may have been also because he was young and full of promise, for his cousin Nessini gave me the same feeling: she was perfect in form and surpassingly, breathtakingly, graceful. But they made me realise anew that the years were passing for Tisala. His body now had those imperfections and blemishes acquired over the many thousands of miles he had travelled, and the vicissitudes of life he had encountered.

And then, too quickly, it was the last day, when Tisala and the others were to leave us. He and I discussed a few last outstanding matters for an hour or so. Then we spoke of future arrangements.

He asked that Penny and Will should recite their verses once more. When we were ready, he called in Yéni, who had moved a little way off and was showing the signs of restlessness I knew so well before a large whale sets off on a long journey; no doubt a mother with a very young child the more so. Nessini came with her, keeping close as usual.

When we were gathered, the children spoke their verses again. But this time the basis of their understanding had changed – they were not reciting verses, but sharing them with friends. And their words and voices seemed to carry a new feeling and meaning. Then we said our farewells and thanked them all for coming.

And we called out their names as they left – first crossing in front of the boat as if reluctant to leave: 'Goodbye Tisala, goodbye.'

'Goodbye Saba – Tarba.'

'Goodbye Yéni.'

'Goodbye little Nessini, safe journey.'

'Tisala – safe journey to you. Swim safely! See you at Inis Cuan.'

'We should escort them in the boat,' said Will as they slowly turned seaward, led by Tisala.

'No,' I said, 'we must let them go. We could only follow for a mile or two, and the engine would be disruptive. Besides, Nessini has to learn to become wary of engines.'

'It's so stupid,' said Will, 'the greatest animals in the world being nearly wiped out – just as we find out how wonderful they really are – by the cruel greed of whalers. It's dreadful – a shame on us as humans.'

He climbed onto the little stump of a mast to prolong his glimpses of them. Suddenly, and simultaneously, two great pairs of flukes rose out of the water. 'It's Tarba and Saba,' he laughed. 'They knew we'd like that!'

And even more I was pleased that we took it as normal that we could recognise each whale from their individual characteristics.

When they had gone the little island looked lovely but somewhat desolate. We went ashore for a swim and walk along the beach. Penny and Will climbed Spyglass South, but called down that they could see nothing. They stayed up there for a few minutes and I guessed they were fixing the place in their memories and saying goodbye. But I think we all felt a little empty, and the island too.

Although we had two days left we did not want to go out to the island again, but stayed in the guest house and swam and fished from there, and took the boat on a trip, with a local boatman guide, round part of the coast. Carlos came too, and was very pleased to be included, smiling and laughing all day long. On the day we left, Will gave him one of his shirts, which he promptly put on. And he gave Penny a beautiful shell.

And when we arrived back in England, it was still the middle of winter.

CHAPTER 47

Music

At home in London I wrote up my notes from our meetings in the tropics and went over the events in my mind. Tisala had always been interested in our music, for in the whales' world, their own songs are of great importance. I knew that he had wanted his family to hear our music. He had asked, as I knew he would, for some of our most uplifting music.

The Blue Whales use their songs for all manner of social purposes: as a means of recognition, co-operation and affection between family members; over longer ranges between groups; as a comfort to the very young (as we use lullabies), and to the distressed; in playing and lightheartedness; and in courting. But in some ways the most developed, arising out of these courting love songs, are what they called 'life songs'. For Blue Whales are monogamous and become partners for life. The love songs of youth develop into these celebratory life songs which grow in length and complexity over the years and become, in the most advanced instances, veritable song symphonies.

I asked him about other species of whale, for although I had heard sound sequences from other whales, some of a few minutes duration, I had never heard anything like the song symphonies he had described. He said that the other species are still in the shallows of music-making and that the Blue Whales alone had developed these higher functions, by some little understood mechanism or trigger of evolution, though he thought it was to do with feeding-back effects of sound into mental ability, as consciousness and the mind enlarged.

I said, 'But if advanced songs exist only among you Blue Whales, the seas must be largely silent again. Our whaling has nearly destroyed your creation.'

'Yes, although it is also true that we sing our life songs intimately to our loves close by, at volumes that do not travel far.'

He thought music was one of the best accomplishments of

mankind. From reed whistles to the most sublime constructions, he saw that music has released in man feelings of joy and spirit. Yet he found it double edged. He questioned me on the connection between music and emotion, and the use we put it to, as it arose out of practical beginnings and functions. But with us he saw music also used for darker purposes: much of our earlier music was associated with war, primitive drum beats used to stimulate adrenaline and aggression, and the sound of clashing metal transferred into percussion and brass instruments. Trumpets – the clear callers of the angels – were appropriated to support the blare and clang of war. And when our war music became more sophisticated, it became more sinister, the dangerous conflation of marching drum, brass and stirring tunes.

He thought it significant that the medieval Christians, to whom music was an important pathway to God, had labelled their major mode the modus lascivius. I laughed, saying they had some strange killjoy ideas. But Tisala said he thought they were right to be wary of it in sacred music, the whole tone of which, with its drifting minor modes or keys, as in Gregorian chants, was to reach out for a rarefied spirituality. The modus lascivius – the devil's tune – was left for more physical things both sensuous and sensual; and more deadly applications like swirling military marches, engendering thrill and confidence, intoxicating and herding young men to join up as surely as the Pied Piper entranced the rats. Through pomp and emotion, marches promise heroism and pride, and deliver horror and destruction.

Tisala said, calling up echoes:

> 'Into the river deep and wide,
> Poured the armies, where they died.
> And the name of the river was called death,
> And hope and salvation were nowhere to be found.'

'It is a sad use of the power of music. Do they not think towards what they are marching?' He sighed. He knew the outcome: pro patria, music used to swell territorial and cultural pride, and bestow bravery. He saw that, as men were anyway going to fight and die (for their commanders often did not know how to avoid war, and often did not wish to), the uniforms, flags and emotional surge enabled the troops to face their destiny with bravery; but he thought it a wretched expedient, and one that made less avoidable and more deadly the incompetence of statesmen and generals, and war itself.

And I realised that it was not only in marches, but in other popular forms that the modus lascivius ensnared us, as in the European swagger before 1914, with the Austro-Hungarian empire waltzing its way to oblivion; a route followed by many others, more or less in tune.

As an aside from music he thought our artists too deserved censure. Their work too often glorified war: in the foreground the heroic general on his horse surrounded by glittering aides; the thousands of ordinary soldiers represented in tiny straight lines marching in a receding, pleasant and still ordered landscape decorated but then hidden by cannonades of smoke. So distance and subterfuge drew a veil over the ghastly reality. Even the dying, nicely filling out the foreground corners, are depicted as noble and gallant – veterans throwing out saluting arms towards their heroic general; though he doesn't see them, for his mind is on victory and glory. The sort of picture, thought Tisala, that excites schoolboys and nurtures in them the desire to join armed forces and wield weapons; that is to say, to kill their fellow humans. And he noted that, for the most part, pictures are not painted and displayed of the other half of the scene: the losing army's panic and destruction, the slaughter of men and horses, and generals intent on escape; though the horrors of our twentieth century wars had brought something of a revolution to depictions of war, which he thought a hopeful sign of revulsion from it. But he thought a still better sign would be that no such depictions were needed.

'Given how you humans conduct yourselves,' said Tisala, 'it is perhaps understandable that the paintings hung on regimental walls should disguise the truth, for it would otherwise be a constant and unsettling reminder to many of the men dining there as to how, at the whim of their politicians, particularly patriotic or righteous ones, they may be called to kill and be killed.'

He thought it should be obligatory for paintings and photographs of the full degradation, savagery, muck, blood and mutilation of war to hang in the council chambers of all who contemplate or who have the ordering of war, and like means of death. And that the pictures should not hang behind their heads but in front of their eyes, except when they themselves are photographed making solemn pronouncements about the need for war, and the inevitable victory of their just cause, as when they address their nations on television; and that their deeply suspect stage-managed settings of calm power, their backdrop of classical pillars and gilt and neatly draped flags, should be forbidden, and be replaced by depictions of the reality and charnel houses of war.

'That way,' said Tisala, 'from the outset, politicians would have to justify the reality of war, acknowledging that they are sending their countrymen and many of the so-called enemy to unspecified deaths.'

'My God!' I said involuntarily, 'That would stop half the wars!'

'You think so? But it might make, and mark, a change in perception.'

Tisala loved much of our classical music, but he thought the course of twentieth century western classical music revealing. After the early blaze of Mahler, Elgar and Sibelius, composers had tried to break the mould by abandoning keys in favour of a wider but more diffuse tonality. Much of it reflected the terrible wars, dislocation and noise of the century. It could be read as a bleak warning from the composers to humanity; but, if little listened to, a warning that will go unheeded. And though the mind can adjust to the inimical in music, he wondered if the experiment was not a false lead, going beyond the real benefit of music into an inaccessible mathematical exploration of sound outside the biological scope and reward of its listeners.

He thought the proper task of great composers is to overcome and transmute the trauma and disharmony of the age. He cited, for instance, Beethoven boldly using C major for the triumph of freedom in Leonora, yet with distant harmonies sustained and shimmering in the spaces beyond the main body of notes, like the tail of a great comet streaming behind its spectacular head; whereas twentieth century composers often seemed hardly to dare to use any major key at all.

He thought it interesting that he encountered no such difficulties with eastern music with which he found an underlying affinity, for he thought, like their own song systems, they were strongly social in their tenor. It was music developed to support and enhance living. Its base was peace – not war – tunes and rhythms that relieved the hardship of life or added the excitement of festival or dance.

But he was most interested in what could be achieved in the higher reaches of music. We discussed what came to be known to us as 'Ellie's question' from her original inquiry, asked years before, but remembered by Tisala and pondered over since. And when it was periodically raised, he would recall what Ellie had said, or would extrapolate what she might have thought, as if she were part of the continuing discussions. Tisala used commonly to speak of things said by members of his family – Sayli, or his grandfather, Saba – as if they had been talking and swim-flying together a day or two previously. For that with Blue Whales, having no physical props, is how they keep in their lives those they love.

Ellie had asked how you explain the expression of love or moral force or sense of the spiritual in music. Was it intrinsic to the music – in it before it was written – or was it in the composer and transposed into the music? I had sought to find the source of emotional significance in the keys. Everyone knows sadness is found in minor keys, but no one that I could discover really explained why.

Tisala suggested some elements. First, he thought the tension in sound that makes great music is intrinsic – it is in the nature and intervals of sound vibrations. But the composer must find it out and express it by juxtaposition of his notes and harmonies. And second, the listener must receive and interpret the sounds in his mind and feelings in accordance with the only instrument he has to do this, his biologically built brain and nervous system. And he thought it clear that the result depended first on the mind's chemical and electromagnetic properties.

He thought the reason classical composers are so widely held to have written some of the most uplifting music was their constant awareness of the heartbeat and voice of humanity. This, I had discovered, is recognised among musicians as the underlying rhythmic vitality – the pulse of life – that also sustains the melodic song. And he thought its musical validity was common not only to humans but to a greater or lesser degree among many related animals, clearly extending well back into lower mammalian life, and, he expected, to more distant cousinage than that. Tisala said he thought what happened was something like this: that the dissonance and tension in wonderful music, for instance in Mozart, worked because it is a daring variation from the norm of harmonies. But if dissonance is taken too far, it becomes the norm itself and the language of music is contorted, eventually into meaningless sound. This is because tonalities and harmonies that resonate in our brains directly relate to their physical structure and the way our bodies and hearing systems have developed and been constructed. But conversely, what our minds hear as beautiful music are combinations of sound that activate and link the electromagnetic pathways in the brain. As words when expressed give rise to thought, which leads to new ideas, so music gives rise to emotions resulting in feelings of love, exultation or nobility. Hence, he thought, the perceived moral force in Beethoven.

'This,' he said, 'I recognise at once from our own higher songs – what we call our symphonies of the sea, reverberating through the deep sound channels of the oceans girdling the Earth. Their higher purpose – to uplift and unify us all – is well recognised and loved; which is why we Blue Whales never use our songs for any threat or aggression.' He thought the use of music was a call to higher things among those who can hear; and that the best music gives rise to noble and sublime emotions released by the beauty of the sounds playing on and opening our minds.

Thus it can induce a calm expectation and clarity or an ecstasy, like an orgasm of the mind. But he thought that, though orgasm is a wonderful thing, perhaps in proper context the culmination of bodily function and expression, it has never yet given rise to a great thought. And here he found a puzzle: music, and thought expressed in words, used wholly different systems, yet we combine them.

Yet he thought it clear that words and music can work wonders together – for instance in our oratorios or sacred music, where words and music can more easily be reconciled because no action is required, or in the better operas where the necessary compromises to allow the musical emotions to flow can triumph over the difficulties of form.

I said I supposed another attempt at compromise was ballet, where the different nature of words and music is overcome by eliminating the words, which are replaced by the allied language of movement and gesture to carry the story forward. But perhaps that may also be its limitation: for all the heightening of emotion through music and visual staging, the expression of thought and feeling through silent movement was ultimately restrictive. The result, except at high points sometimes demotes ballet to entertainment. But Ellie, who loved ballet, used to argue that, *because* the power of music was combined with wordless movement, ballet portrayed human pathos and yearning in a way no other art form can equal.

Nevertheless, Tisala saw linked importance in sublimity in music and the development of thought through words. Suppose, he argued, the power of the brain is heightened, so new thoughts and ideas can be created. Then we achieve a wonderful effect: the co-evolving of our minds by music and words.

'I expect,' he said, 'that Einstein and Shakespeare listened to music.'

I said, 'Yes, Einstein played the violin and there's evidence for Shakespeare in the plays.'

'Let us speculate a little and say the evidence is in the rhythm of Shakespeare's lines, his leaping imagination and connection of words. And that the same is true of the Greeks. Evidence of the quality of Greek music abounds in the clarity of thought of the Greek philosophers. You tell me Greek music is lost, but if your scholars rediscovered it, I anticipate they would find it of a pure quality. A harp, a lyre, a flute or a few strings can unlock much in music. Thus perhaps have minds and spirits been enhanced.'

He concluded, coming back to the influence of music itself, that our best music demonstrated a power of the spirit – the desire and will to reach out and seek to raise our whole beings – nature, intellect and spirit – a heartening revelation to Tisala, who first knew mankind through our cruel savagery as hunters.

And I wondered whether these great Blue Whales are so endowed by nature in their minds and auditory faculties that, though they write no symphonies nor construct instruments, they can perhaps know more than we do of the true and exalted possibilities of music.

Each season when Tisala left Inis Cuan, he took with him in his capacious mind large swathes of memorised music to the polar or equatorial latitudes. He said he had no difficulty in 'playing back' quite lengthy passages silently in his head. And sometimes in the arctic or in the subtropics other sea creatures might hear the thundered melodic notes from Sorastro's dark and placid depths. But even this in our world spelled danger.

At the height of the Cold War, the US Navy reported to Washington that the Soviet fleet had a signalling system involving musical notation. This intelligence reached us through a physicist friend of Robert's, who knew the American ambassador. I spent two anxious months awaiting Tisala's return and praying that neither the Americans nor

Russians would investigate and track him down. So for some years that music ceased in the oceans and the creatures of the deep heard it no more, silenced by the dangerous folly of men.

CHAPTER 48

Eric

A year after the visit to the tropics, in the spring before Tisala returned, Eric had a heart attack in what he called the alphabet factory – the outbuilding where he had produced the painted letters all those years before to help Tisala master the English language. In later years this workshop was a favourite place of his, where he pottered and did odd maintenance and repair jobs. One morning in late March he did not come back to the house for his morning coffee. Guinevere eventually found him. There was no prior warning – she said he had been perfectly cheerful that morning. His death must have been sudden and quick, and this time there was no reprieve. He was eighty-two.

Guinevere rang me that evening – she had tried earlier. I had been in the Museum. We spoke for two or three minutes. I was stunned, not wanting to believe what she told me, but trying to muster help. Support and arrangements were required. She was okay. Yes – she had spoken to Mary. She and Tom were coming. She didn't know about the children – it was a long way for a funeral. Would I please let Robert Thompson and Ellie's parents and my mother know? No, they should not come up – too old and too far. No, no, she quite understood. Yes, of course I was coming up. She would be grateful. Will and Penny would come too. When we had hung up I felt a numb sense of loss. I went over in my mind what must be done and thought about the implications for the future. I made the various telephone calls, passing on the sad news, and talking it into acceptability.

Later I thought of Guinevere on the island and the coming funeral. I found myself hoping that Mary's family would come. We had seen them once since Eric's first heart attack.

That was in the summer before our trip to the tropics, when Mary, with Susannah and Grenville, had come over for a fortnight. Three days in London and the rest in the islands, where our visits overlapped by a week. This was the only time I had met Grenville. Contrary to my expectations, he had been charming – articulate and cheerful. He was much bound up with his life in Vancouver, about which he talked at length. In his mind the West Coast of Canada was a complete world. And much of it, from his account, seemed idyllic, which perhaps explained his lack of great interest in anywhere else. On that visit I found myself unexpectedly pleased to see Susannah again. She was no longer a young girl but signalled the threshold of womanhood. She had just completed her first year at college. She and Will appeared fond of each other, though I did not see any obvious signs of romantic attachment developing. Once or twice I thought Susannah a bit withdrawn, as if she were keeping her distance from him. And yet I saw in various little ways her affection for him. One evening she ironed his shirt, as Will watched. She had a serious mouth, not sullen, but firmly set as she worked. I thought again how beautiful she was. Once, when she looked up at me, it was with an arresting directness made more startling by the green-blue of her eyes set against her dark hair. When she finished, she smiled at Will, and it was unexpected, like the sunlight sweeping across cloud-chased mountains.

In between times, on two or three days, I had been working over on Inis Cuan. One afternoon I was surprised to see Will and Susannah walking towards the shack. I looked anxiously for Grenville, as he did not know about the inlet or the shack, and nothing of Tisala.

'Where's Grenville?' I said coming out to meet them. Will explained:

'We went for a walk – Grenville didn't want to come. We came in this direction and met Jimmy who had the big boat by the jetty unloading some fence posts. He took us across.' Inside the shack, she was very interested in everything, asking questions, looking at my bookshelf and fingering folders as she did so. But there was something reserved about her, as if she didn't want to trespass or impose herself, and when I had answered her questions and she had taken everything in, she suggested to Will they should walk along the cliffs.

I said 'You'll have to come back with me in the little boat.'

'What time are you going?' asked Will.

'Half four.'

'Longer than that,' said Will. 'Five?'

'Half five,' I said, not wishing to spoil their day. They seemed to enjoy each other's company and were always laughing together.

Two years had passed since then. As we headed north for the funeral I found in myself a strange mix of emotions: sadness at Eric's passing and apprehension for Guinevere and the future: Eric had been the lynchpin at the centre of that island world. But a sense of excitement too at the coming gathering and the extra awareness of being alive that comes with the death of one who has lived a full life.

A week later on a mild morning with glimmers of sunlight, Eric left his home for the last time. The two undertakers' men in black, Jimmy MacLeod and I carried the coffin out of the house and placed it on the handcart. Jimmy pushed the cart with the coffin cushioned by blankets to stop it rattling. I went on the front corner, one hand on the coffin to steady it, a funeral man similarly positioned on the other side. We walked down the drive, through the thin line of daffodils, a few just showing yellow, but mainly still in bud as if furled in sorrow for Eric, who would not see them again. Along from the drive parallel to the foreshore ran the remains of an old track. It passed the place where once a short line of crofting cottages had stood – reduced now to foundation outlines of three or four dwellings a foot or so high amid the grass and bracken. A little further on, where the track petered out, was the island cemetery, a patch of raised ground surrounded by a low stone wall and backed by a few birch trees. The wall was in relatively good repair – cared for by Eric and Jimmy. Inside the wall some of the grass had become tussocky, but some was short and green, kept lawn-like by the rabbits. There were a few weathered headstones and two newer ones of the MacLeod family, but most of the graves were now unmarked. Jimmy had dug a grave and I wondered briefly how Guinevere had chosen the spot. Afterwards I learned that there was a plan, kept folded in the MacLeod family Bible, and that Eric had chosen the place. He wanted to be 'In where he belonged,' Guinevere recounted afterwards.

We gathered round the grave. The service was led by the minister from the Great Island. He was an old friend of Eric's, despite their theological differences, and his short address had touches of wry humour that relieved the solemnity of the set words. Guinevere stood with her arm linked through Mary's. Her husband Tom stood on her other side in a black coat, and next to him stood Susannah, now a young woman, radiating health and beauty, and a little tearful. I glanced at Will. He was pale and near to tears. I looked down at Penny who was holding my hand. She was wiping her eye with the base of her thumb. I put my arm round her and she leant against me. The function of tears, I thought, is to unite people. The little ceremony drew towards its close. In summer, I knew there would be a delicate counterpane of yellow and purple wild flowers in there, taking no notice of the boundary walls. And even then I felt glad of the notion, for Eric would be covered and watched over by the island and would become a part of it. 'Rest in peace', said the clergyman. Yes, in peace, I thought. Goodbye Eric – goodbye, my dear old friend and mentor. The peaty earth accepted him quietly.

Afterwards we walked back to the house, about twenty of us in all, in little changing groups as we each greeted those we had not previously spoken to. There were a few old friends from the islands and mainland. I knew or had met all of them at one time or another.

I found myself walking with Dr. Henderson. 'He's a lucky man, David – no long decrepitude. But Guinevere will find it difficult.'

'Yes. At least it's spring. I'll come up for longer.'

'Good. We'll all keep an eye on her.'

Mary and Guinevere had laid on a buffet lunch for everyone. 'A proper bunfight,' Eric had once said, 'with plenty of refreshment, and none of your black ties.' And soon there was a quiet buzz of chatter and laughter, reminiscences and catching up. I saw Will and Susannah talking, and noticed he stood a couple of inches taller than her. I could not hear what they were saying. Mary and Tom came across to me. She looked strikingly well and calm, though she was anxious about Guinevere. Tom looked a bit puffy and unwell.

'Fine man, Eric,' he said. 'I was very fond of him. Full of great stories; and a great fisherman I believe.' As we spoke, Tom told me of his work. He clearly worked very long hours and was devoted to Mary. It was a bad time to leave his business, but – 'No question' – he had insisted on accompanying her over here. With his easy charm, I came to like him. Later I noticed he made no great effort to talk to other people, and gave the impression that he felt he did not quite belong here. And I realised again with a little kick of happiness that all this was a centre of my life. And then the sadness of Eric gone swept over me again. But at that moment Aunt Jane stood at my shoulder. Perhaps she came then because I was more alone again, but also to remind me how fortunate I was.

Near me I overheard Will ask Guinevere, 'Does Susannah have a boyfriend at college, Gran?'

'Lots,' said Susannah who had come up behind him, 'but none as handsome as you.' She smiled at him mischievously.

'I bet you do too,' he said, laughing. 'Cow.' She laughed back.

'Now, you two,' said Guinevere, looking at them fondly. 'Will, please take some more wine round. Charlie Henderson's glass is empty again. And Susannah, dear, there is more food still in the kitchen.'

So the wake continued until some of the guests reluctantly saw it was time to leave and head towards the boat. Jimmy MacLeod was to ferry them back towards the Great Island for their various onward connections or journeys home. Sad goodbyes were said, comfort and thanks were given, and quiet fell on the house on Eilean Mòr.

The next day the concerns of normal living slowly began to return.

'You can't expect a third year college girl to be a nun,' I said to Will, when Susannah came up in conversation.

'I know *that*, Dad,' said Will, a bit irritated. He paused. 'But she's still a cow.' So I knew it touched him.

'And what about Angela?' I said, referring to his school friend, who he'd shown a keen interest in lately.

'That's different.' But he couldn't quite suppress a smile. 'Well, sort of.'

Afterwards I thought about Will and Susannah and wondered what pleasant imaginings of Will's across the months had been displaced by the present reality; and whether it was reality, and of any lasting importance. Had he envisaged her – the image of a lovely, absent girl – as his princess, who he could mould and remodel in his mind's eye as he pleased? And what was the drawing power of such enthralment when put in the balance with kissing a girlfriend in her untidy single-bedded teenage room before supper while her mother was downstairs cooking a meal for him? The idealised image may be more powerful and enduring, as many romantics know, but may as well as delight bring danger of delusion. For love of a princess to bear fruit, it and she must be transferred into reality. But the school-friend is already there, though as well as her sexual proximity, so are her shortcomings. I thought, the role of imagination in love is to bestow on the one loved an aura, woven of images and feelings that may sustain the passage of the years and the adjustments of lives. We must have the vision, but measure it soberly in the daylight. 'Cow,' Will had said. I smiled thinly, envisaging the exchange, and then thought of Eric and Guinevere in their kitchen, bantering away as usual.

In the two days after the funeral there was much discussion. We went for walks, but on both days turned right at the foot of the drive, away from the cemetery. Penny whispered to me, 'She'll want to go on her own when the grass has grown.' I looked at her. Wounds in Guinevere and the earth accepted and understood. 'Yes, I think you're right.'

Guinevere had every intention of staying on the island. The question only arose obliquely. Jimmy MacLeod thought they could cope. Eric had not been very active latterly, so they largely already managed. One afternoon I spoke at length to Jimmy. He was fine, and would deal with the continuing upkeep and maintenance – fencing, repairs, paintwork, logs, the boat supplies and all the rest. I said he would need some help. 'Och, but you'll want to work on Inis Cuan.' I said I would come up more often, and do some of the two-man jobs with him. He was a stalwart man, but though outwardly he did not look that much changed from his younger self of twenty years before, he was now himself in his fifties. He lived as he had always done in his parents' cottage. His mother was well, though since the death of her husband she was showing her age.

We had talked about the future in general terms on previous occasions. But somehow with Eric there, the past had continued safely in to the present and on foreseeably. Now the disturbance of change, perhaps of an end, was nearer. I spoke to Guinevere. I knew it was an absolute assumption in any arrangement that Jimmy and his mother would be fully looked after. 'I've been thinking about that, as you can imagine,' she said. 'Jimmy will see me out. I don't know how long I'll be able to stay. Mary would love to keep the islands, but thinks that one day she may eventually have to sell up. She'll not be able to run things from Canada, and Tom will never live over here.'

The future I had always blanked out crept closer. Guinevere put her hand on my arm. 'But I hope I'll be here a few more years, and

Mary won't sell unless she has to.' To tease me, she added, 'But you'd better get on with your work.' She was perfectly at home with the idea of death, including her own.

My work formed a part of several conversations on these walks, when Tom was not present, for he still didn't know about Tisala. As soon as she found the opportunity, Susannah wanted to know how Tisala was – and about the latest work. I said that we were currently exploring theories of education, feeding in the new ideas on evolutionary neurology that were coming in – mainly from America. She questioned me closely and searchingly. At the end then she said, lightly, 'Pity you didn't get to this a bit sooner – I could have done with some neurological spark in my economics statistics.' She looked at me sideways with a hint of sly humour.

Will asked Susannah what her college life was like. He was about to apply to Universities here. He seemed interested in exploring the comparison. She loved college. Among other things she was studying English and North American literature, but was going to major in economics. There was some discussion about the merit of subjects, and the range of activities available. She had been taking part in the college anti-whaling campaign. They were promoting whale watching as an alternative. She had been whale-watching herself with some of the boys from her class – following the Humpback migration up the West Coast. No, she had not seen them breaching, but she had seen them smacking the water with their flippers. The name of one of her companions – George – came up a couple of times. 'George, is a delightful young man. I think you're very fond of him,' said Mary innocently, and oblivious to the effect of her remark. It transpired Susannah had brought him home a couple of times. I counted four paces of silence before Will said, 'I bet you didn't ride on their flippers.'

'No.' She laughed across at him.

'Oh yes,' said Mary, 'tell us about your trip.' She had heard something of it from Guinevere. And soon Penny and Will were recounting animatedly all the details, describing the islands, the arrival of the whales and the rides on Tisala.

'I was scared,' said Penny. 'He's so big – huge. I liked it more on Nessini – she's much smaller.'

'Well, all credit to you for doing it,' said Susannah, catching Penny by the hand and swinging it.

'I loved it,' said Will. 'It was like – well, it felt as if I belonged in the sea. We and whales became somehow like inheritors of the Earth and sea together. As if we were a sort of new unity. Like the lions lying down with lambs, but much better, because we can talk and understand.'

'Oh my, the philosopher!' said Susannah. And looking at him affectionately said slowly, 'Well you are the luckiest young man in the world.' She glanced at me, and then she looked at the ground, as if she'd said too much.

We stopped and turned to let Tom and Guinevere catch up. As they reached us Tom said, 'What are you guys talking about?' Mary dissembled discreetly. 'Oh, their tropics trip – it sounds lovely – and college, and exams. Will has his school leaving exams coming up next year and Penny her – intermediates.'

'O levels,' said Penny. There was more talk of academic subjects and possible future jobs and careers. Will was considering economics, so they talked of that, Tom enthusiastically advocating it for an understanding of the modern world, and to earn a dollar.

So the force of Eric's death was softened for a while by such concerns and activities, and ongoing life re-established. But Eric had died in school term-time, and Penny and Will had to go back. Three days after the funeral, we made ready to depart. Mary and her family were staying a few more days to be with Guinevere before their flight back. I was due up again for the new season in less than a month, and would try to come up some days early.

'I shall be perfectly all right,' said Guinevere robustly. 'There's lots to do.'

When we said our goodbyes, Mary had a tear in her eye. 'Bless you, David. Thank you so much for your support. I can't tell you – ' I shook my head, trying to find the words – 'Nothing – it's absolutely – you know how I feel about them – it's like one of my own family. Eric was wonderful to me – they've both been... just unbelievable.' We embraced. I realised I had become very fond of Mary.

Susannah came up. 'Goodbye Susannah.' I hugged her. She put her arms round me tightly, 'David, I'm so glad you're here.' I caught something about it – a subdued urgency.

'So am I. Don't worry – you're so far away – I'll look after her.'

'I know.' She was near to tears. 'Bye.'

When I kissed Guinevere goodbye we promised to telephone regularly – 'And immediately if you want anything.'

'Yes, dear, I will. But I don't want to be a nuisance – '

'And I don't want any of that nonsense.' She smiled her surrender gratefully.

Penny said her goodbyes to everyone. I saw Will go up to Susannah. He gave her a kiss on the cheek, 'See you. Safe journey.'

'Yes, Will. Bye. Look after yourself.' She gave him a kiss, but their eyes did not meet and they both turned away.

I wondered afterwards about not finding the words to express what Eric and Guinevere were to me. 'Unbelievable,' I had said, meaning I suppose beyond what was previously thought to be rationally believable, but is now found not so; an example, of unimagined kindness and generosity across the years. Yet not inexplicably beyond reason, but merely a previously limited concept of what is reasonable. So I thought, on the good side of humanity we may develop by seeing acts and examples of 'unbelievable' kindness or generosity or love, which inspire us to imitate them, thus gradually improving and civilising ourselves. As happens among the followers of many religious persons, at least until the religion itself outgrows its ethical message and demands doctrinal dominance, which often unleashes bigotry. I was reminded of Voltaire, that implacable critic of formal religion, whom I was sure would have extended his attack to later political forms of dogmatic belief, as Marxism and Fascism, and national or super-power invincibility: 'Those who can make you believe absurdities can make you commit atrocities.' History is strewn with the truth of that observation.

So, I thought, perhaps one day religions will be seen like Father Christmas – to be enjoyed and benefited from but no longer believed. Maybe we should believe rather in the humanity that underlies the idea of generosity and love attributed to St Nicholas, sifting religions for the better ethics of their founders, while recognising the higher possibilities of man.

Tisala said later when I raised this with him: 'It will be found true and important that experiencing the good and desiring to imitate it enlarges the consciousness. But when will you humans learn that the sensitivities required are not humanity's alone but are universal in the animal world? We all seek to rise above the cruel elements of the development of life. These aspirations, sometimes rudimentary, but in greater or lesser degree, are present in and desired by all animals.'

And I thought of the Blue Whales developing themselves in the freedom of the oceans, entirely without any of the evil imagination that taints us. The Blue Whales, as I now knew, leaders with ourselves, of the rising animal kingdom, but being brutally slaughtered by a small part of humanity.

But Tisala said, 'Look at your domestic dogs: the recent descendants of savage carnivorous pack-hunters, but now bred for good nature and temperament, treated and fed well. The result? – love, loyalty and playfulness, and, as those who live with dogs know, with increasing elements of consciousness and understanding of speech. But, in that setting, subservient to man and dependent on him.'

He observed that we humans have come much further, and are subservient to no animal, except ourselves. And though those in authority have promoted subservience to God, it will be found an illusory idea. And it is domination which needs to be challenged, in individuals by goodness, and in society, by the rule of law; both of which should embody the best ethics man can devise.

And that was the way with Tisala's mind – one line of thought slipped over into another, and new areas were linked and lit up. He saw that in our societies the rule of good law was imperative. He argued that it is by carefully balanced law that we humans should decide on the degree of discipline and ultimately enforcement which will be required to control and moderate the behaviour of the human animal while efforts are made to improve it by other means; including the teaching of ethics, and true education, which is not to be confused with academic schooling. And behind the law must stand acceptable morality, for it is that which gives the law its legitimacy and therefore its lasting authority to be obeyed. He said that majorities in Parliament and law-giving assemblies, and the law they create, are only proximate authority: a law passed without the backing of legitimate morality will not last: it will rankle and do damage to the body politic until the sore is removed. 'It is why, if you have wise judges, judge-made law is often better than legislation – it seeks to apply the form of morality known as justice in individual cases, so far as it can do so within the given framework of legislation and the experience and wisdom of the judges. That is why your judges must be both independent and be an elite of wide education, capability and incorruptibility.'

'People may see that as elitist,' I said. 'And people in modern democracies increasingly do not like "elites".'

Sometimes with Tisala I thought I was being drawn into a vortex of thought beyond my capacity to assimilate or order. Tisala's answer was this: in our complicated societies what was disliked were pretended elites and undeserved privilege. He thought false elites should be ridiculed out of their pretensions by reason and laughter. But they should not be confused with real elites. A real and valuable elite is not of 'class' or background, but of education, wisdom, morality, skill and honesty. But 'class', in the sense of exclusivity, or undeserved privilege, or disdain for others, is the negation of what true 'class' should mean among humans. He thought some of our societies had managed these things better than others. He recalled that in Egypt, when its old gods had died, and when it had absorbed Coptic Christianity and the coming of Greek, Islamic and secular elements, there had evolved out of this diversity an egalitarian acceptance in society: a person might be regarded as of gentle class by virtue of the quality of behaviour – kindness and civility – regardless of background wealth, landholding or occupation. In this, a street cleaner could sit equal with a ruler. He thought this was also true to some degree – he had gleaned it from our histories, here a little, there somewhat more – in many of our societies. And in an enlightened society, it is recognised and nurtured as a precious attribute. Yet at the same time people had to be wise and generous enough to accept and encourage the development of true elites, for they are the leaders and advancers of our societies. He thought this was widely understood and appreciated, though sometimes in a confused way.

'Like all those popularity polls,' I said, 'to find the greatest national figure, brainiest person, best dancer, sportsperson, song, film, novel.'

'Yes, the best, always the best: what you humans seek is the top quality – the elite of people and achievement that push the boundaries forward. Everyone, you tell me, wants to see and admire the best actor, ballerina, footballer, pop band; and in these examples it is easy because as entertainers they directly feed the public's feeling of wellbeing. But a wise society will value and cherish as much or more those who sustain the working framework and fabric of society, including its best statesmen, politicians and judges.' He observed at this point that where individuals are grouped together because they work locally and quietly there is a danger that their contribution will be underestimated: the best surgeons, nurses, lawyers, teachers, engineers or plumbers, and so on. Elites in an enlightened society are cherished as the top continuum of widespread competence, of service to society, to which all can aspire. He observed that we still use the term 'first class' as a term of approval and distinction, as for fruit, like apples at a market. In that sense 'real class', he concluded, despite the attempted Marxist damnation of the word, is a distinction too useful to loose to prejudice.

In a wise society those who are kind and civil sit equal, the street cleaner with the ruler, white with black, rich with poor, old with young. He thought civility, which is kindness dressed in fine clothes, both in behaviour and language, was a key to the proper survival of human societies, and that too many of our peoples had neither element sufficiently; which turned him once more to education.

And I remembered Eric again. When he came up against a problem that perplexed him, he used to say cheerfully, 'The key to progress is education, and I have as yet acquired little. Let us consult the oracle.' The oracle might be Tisala or Guinevere, a dictionary, encyclopaedia, or some tatty manual, whoever or whatever might have knowledge and illuminate the matter. Eric, right up to the end, like Aunt Jane, always wanted to learn. Now he had gone from us, but he had left his legacy of kindness and humour and his enthusiasm to do and to learn.

CHAPTER 49

On Education

In the months and seasons after Eric's death, Tisala increasingly turned to the subject of learning itself, and human education. He was perplexed by how knowledgeable we were, yet how ignorant and destructive. He remarked that as we are the planet's primary animal and for better or worse responsible for much that happens here, human education becomes of paramount importance.

Tisala found my early answers on education disjointed, even chaotic, despite my best efforts; answers which out of my own ignorance were largely confined to English models, with some limited reference to European and American practice. But he concluded that this chaos was also a real reflection of our too often counter-productive education systems. He found much in our schooling systems to admire, but given the knowledge we possess, much foolish and wasteful. He was initially surprised by this, considering the vital interest there must be to our species in providing the best education possible for our children.

We seemed to address our educational systems piecemeal, and plunged into changing the provision of schooling without first seeking to understand either the way our brains enable us to learn, or the object of it all, beyond general political ideas such as 'raising standards' or 'equipping our young to get jobs'. He thought those things were better valued as results, not the objects or the proper purpose of education. It puzzled him how we start in the middle, or near the end, and jostle backwards and forwards amongst reforms as the whims of politics, educational fashion and finance dictate.

We reform school structures, or exams, or curricula, as particular problems emerge, only to find – often years later – that we have merely changed the problems; often because all the change and disruption has been bureaucratically imposed to suit a theoretical system and does not win the mind of the children or teachers, without whose assent no system will succeed. Nevertheless he thought it remarkable, and owing to the inbuilt curiosity of children and the dedication of the better teachers, how much learning is imparted and imbibed. But overall he found the result was frequently a sad tale of opportunity wasted, lives unfulfilled and the ruin of hope. And beyond the blighting of individual lives lay the cumulative blighting of human societies. He observed how each generation has much to learn and re-learn, for otherwise the wisdom of one generation may be lost, or swamped, and the regression of the many may overthrow the advances of the few. He once said: 'I have learned how your civilisations, in dislocated times, decline and die.'

He found astonishing the idea that our politicians, 'To whom for some reason you have delegated the setting of educational policy and the administration of education,' can think that our children will be educated simply by being confined in schools between five and sixteen, or eighteen, or even twenty-one, for those who go to college.

'A lifetime for education is scarcely enough, as your thinkers have always known: but that span at least you must use. It is little enough scope to learn and pass on what you can. To start with an assumption that education is the same as schooling for a dozen years, makes failure certain. For schooling is not education, nor school years even the main learning years.'

He knew that our sciences increasingly show us the most important learning years are pre-school. But that vital fact seems largely unaddressed by human educational systems. And, at the senior end of school education, he asked why our politicians do not consider this: if education is confined to schooling, it is over and starts to become out of date almost before a person's adult life has begun, if indeed some of it was not out of date when taught. And of this 'education' perhaps three-quarters is afterwards forgotten.

He questioned whether our young people must not then go out to work, on the land, in factories, or in offices, in a world unrecognisable from their schooling, and often little understood. And he questioned whether that is not a danger to our societies, especially democratic ones. He saw that the burden of responsibility for enlightening people then falls on our much vaunted communications – newspapers, television and now the internet – and is not one they bear well.

Despite these strictures he saw that the links between education and economics are strong. The desirability of a minimum standard of living for all is clear, though threatened by the colossal increase in human numbers. He questioned the easily expressed optimism in some quarters that starvation and poverty would be quickly overcome. 'In the whole of history that has never been achieved.' And he thought we are making our task vastly more difficult by our strange pursuit of maximum wealth for every individual – a goal now becoming universally adopted.

For he viewed with dismay our histories and the relentless selfishness of great nation states, their policies and wars of economic conquest, their trade wars, barriers and special interests; the feebleness of will of leaders positioned to lead; the corruption, incompetence and indifference, political and economic, of many regimes; and, internally, the hostility of leaders to many of their own people, seen as being in the wrong tribe, race, religion, class or other disentitling group.

He was dismayed too by the misdirected dedication with which so many appear to spend their lives pursuing the allure and trivia of consumer compulsion, to the exclusion of much else in their lives; pitiful attachment to fads and fashions that scarcely outlast the hopes that bought them.

He could perfectly well see, and applauded, the attraction and pursuit of things desired as a way out of poverty, and as a measure and mark of betterment. But in its more extreme manifestations, particularly in the Western World, he thought the clamour for material things was like a feeding frenzy of a different sort: one which our excited imaginations have promoted into psychological necessity, though in reality not a necessity at all. Collectively, it is an urge by which our aggressive pursuits and our colossal numbers may half destroy the world. For wealth of that sort brings exploitation and waste. He found difficult to believe our casual and profligate use and burning of resources for fleeting wants and pleasures, which we threw aside next day in the pursuit of newer and brighter toys.

'It seems this wild chase diverts you from learning and the pursuit of higher things, sometimes for many years, sometimes for a lifetime, while the numbers and the follies of mankind multiply.'

I quoted: 'Getting and spending we lay waste our powers.'

It is true that 'getting' can bring satisfaction and even periods of happiness when successful. The 'spending' he observed was the meal after the hunt – and brings relatively brief moments of satisfaction and pleasure. But if relied upon for happiness will sate and delude. For, if that is the whole of life, all that has been achieved is mere survival, though dressed in material trappings. Then there is no individual development or advance. And among higher animals, as the phrase recognises, there is a higher calling. He admired the ingenuity and energy put to producing wealth, to the comfort of themselves and others, but pitied those with distorted and enslaved lives.

Tisala said once: 'If men behave well they can have the freedom of gods; but everywhere it seems they live in chains, first to economic necessity, and then success. In the realms of happiness money is a currency of little value. You humans have evolved to need fulfilment in other respects of your humanity, as has long been known among your wise.'

He was not of course suggesting the abandonment of economic activity – in our world he saw it is vital and may largely banish poverty. But he saw developing economies straining to chase developed ones, which then responded by straining to maximise their leads. It was the how and why and extent of it that he questioned, especially in the West in terms of need, but everywhere in terms of numbers, exploitation and pollution. He thought that, beyond a certain level, people, for their own happiness, as well as the good continuance of the world, need to limit their economic activities and augment a better balance in their lives by nurturing the other powers they have. He was aware that many individual people see this, but that at a social and international level it has so far, even when glimpsed as a coming necessity, proved impossible to do. He thought our greatest hope lies in the emergence of true internationalisation among nation states, and the pursuit of true education among individuals. And that one would not come without the other.

Then I saw where Tisala's thought was leading.

This approach was a vital part of the public aim of education, yet nothing to do with schooling. Tisala said, 'At a later stage such ideas need to be reflected in schooling and higher study so that they enter the mainstream of thought.'

But he saw these things on no syllabus or curriculum. I realised he had merely been clarifying the objects and surveying the context in and for which education might be used.

Tisala said, 'So now we need to go back to the beginning.'

I asked, 'But if education starts, as you say it does, before schooling, where should we begin?'

Tisala answered, 'With what is known about how you humans learn. For then you will have an understanding and a basis of measure to put against particular education policies.'

I will try to put down the essence of his thinking from my notes. He started from what I had told him about our knowledge of the human brain. We now know that much of the creation of the brain, and its ability to function at higher levels, takes place after birth. At birth the human brain is only forty percent of its final size, which is nature's adaptive solution to the narrowness of the human birth canal in comparison to eventual brain and skull size. This is an adaptation thought to be unique, certainly in degree. And, with the outside stimuli that help to form the brain after birth, it has led to man's privileged position in the animal world, though at the cost of a long and highly dependent infancy. The complexity of the human brain's cortex, and its ability to function at higher level, depends on these outside stimuli to develop and connect the capacity which is there by the courtesy of the genes and the mechanism of the skull's moveable and expandable bone plates.

We know also that human babies respond to outside stimuli from an early age, indeed even before birth, and long before they are capable of independent physical activity. Given this physiological condition it is of the utmost importance to provide babies with that which will most develop and satisfy them. First is the security and loving ambience created by the mother with her child. Beyond that the single most important influence is language.

He thought presciently that if the brain's activity could be seen, as afterwards became increasingly possible with the development of brain scans, the vital importance of a loving and articulate parent would become obvious. Much depended on the ability of the mother to create a feeling of wellbeing associated with learning in the infant's mind and to stimulate his or her inborn curiosity, the brain's predisposition to learn. It starts with the mother's loving gurgles and moves through the organised sound of words into the miracle of language. In the recognition of words and the use of them around the young child, the language is transferred to it, and much of the future of that child is set in train.

Concurrent with the child's initial experience of language, is its learning in two other vital areas: the physical and the social. The physical and social first come together on the mother's breast. Exploration of the physical world continues, first through the experience of bodily functions, and then by outside contact – initially close-to tactile experiences, as clutching a parent's finger, but afterwards by experiencing qualities like hot or cold or sharp or soft. So gradually the child comes into the world of physical things, such as objects or toys to cuddle, but also of separateness and danger.

And within two years, a child who can hardly walk comes, almost miraculously it seems, into the possession of language. The building of words and syntax from mama, dada, food and wants is extended as the world comes into view: home, tree, dog, bicycle; then, if they are lucky, perhaps picture books combined with words; and suddenly the whole world stretches out before the child. Tisala thought the mechanism of language learning will become better understood through new neurological knowledge. But it is already clear that by the age of about four a great deal of a child's linguistic ability – and with it the ability to think – has been developed, or long-term restrictions placed on it. He concluded therefore that the greatest opportunity in a child's initial education depends on having attentive and articulate parents. Parents who themselves can hardly speak whole sentences, or do not trouble to do so, are a liability to their children, and on a wider view, to society. He thought this would not be easy to remedy, for those parents were themselves likely to be victims of verbal poverty. It falls, he said, to the wider community to repair that grave disadvantage before the start of academic schooling. He was accordingly very surprised that in England we imposed formal schooling on our children from the age of four or five, when clearly quite often the linguistic and therefore mental basis for it to flourish did not exist.

As with the verbal, so too the social. The child's horizons first take in other family members – fathers, siblings, grannies. The lucky child is indulged and makes agreeable family bonds; but later finds its wants and demands come up against the separate views and requirements of others. So begins the compromise of social living: deferring demand, co-operation, sharing and the awareness that self is not the only self. Such learning, needs careful guidance, explanation and discipline by the parent and others if it is not to be traumatic or turn into frustrated belligerence; which is where, he concluded, so much personal and social antagonism among humans arises.

In reality, initial education continually combines these elements – the physical, verbal and social. Imperceptibly these three elements come together as the complications of human living are experienced by the child. Here are the opportunities for delight and upset, playing and falling out, in a widening circle, first with siblings, then in wider groupings, as playgroups and nursery friends. So the early concepts of balance arise and are sought – give and take, tolerance, fairness, right and wrong, the restraint of force. Ethics emerge and their intrinsic value begins to be understood and applied. The degree of achievement of social and physical balance is critical for the wellbeing of the individual, and cumulatively of society.

'That is how,' said Tisala, 'in good conditions, you humans begin to acquire education. And you will note that all this has happened though we haven't yet got your child to school, or subject to any supernatural religious instruction.'

The pattern of our acquisition of education did not surprise him for it reflects a more universal practice. Blue Whales similarly surround their newborn with love – the protective, wholly dependable touch, guidance and presence of the mother. So too the lactating link, in their case without substitute, essential for life; but with it also, the emotional food, reinforced by the mother's sounds and songs and language. And then the baby whale becomes aware that beyond its mother are other members of the group – the father, siblings, aunts and cousins – the beginnings of their social nexus.

So he found it is, in various degrees, among many animals, though language itself is scarce, and mainly rudimentary. It is the advance of language that distinguishes the most advanced species. It is the great enabler. Language, he suggested, grows out of consciousness and imagination, the ability to picture things in the mind: to which words add form that may be communicated and thus triggers further thoughts, ideas and the application of reason. The power of language to formulate thought propels the mind in an upward growth. But this development of language has never existed in a vacuum. It arises in and is grafted onto a whole world of physical animal instincts and reactions. And though it may be used to modify them, the use to which language is put is also much modified by them. 'Now that your science is enabling you to recognise your evolutionary past, your language is freeing you from blind dependence on it. A great opportunity lies in the ability of man to mould his own higher evolution.' And he thought that from one angle education was much about such modification of our inherited influences. But in this, from our murderous cruelty and aggression, he thought we were as yet not much advanced; and that language too is capable of much destructive misuse.

I asked him what he meant.

He thought, for instance, that the role ascribed to Satan in Judaism and its later offshoots, Christianity and Islam, may be seen as an early but primitive and burdensome attempt to recognise the dilemma posed by human savagery and evil. 'Burdensome,' he said 'when those religious metaphorical inventions were imposed as literal truths.' And he remarked that he found it extraordinary that these primitive notions still survived in our societies; and that unless they were defused by being shown to be untrue they would still cause much trouble in the world.

But such aberrant use of language to forge ideas was not of course confined to religion: he found it throughout human society, for instance as in justifications for slavery, in class and racial prejudices, and so too in political ideologies such as Communism and Nazism. And at a more individual level, socially, use of words can enhance the power of the bully, the criminal and the disputatious. He thought language was perhaps one of the most wonderful things to evolve out of life on our planet, but that it carried dangers too.

He said our task was to use language to advance our more ethical and constructive natures. There, he pointed out, the religions of the world have often contributed greatly to the betterment of mankind, and in reformed religions may still do so; as have secular thinkers and philosophers from many times and places, as Socrates and Confucius, in developing their codes of ethics and conduct; to which he added the efforts of lawmakers in building civil societies reflecting ideas such as freedom, justice, tolerance and the rule of law.

'Now,' he said, 'your societies are spawning knowledge, change and advances at such a rate that *everyone* must also take on new responsibilities to apply ethics and good conduct.' He instanced the urgent need for scientists to integrate ethical responsibility as humans into their work. Much evil, he thought, has come from their frequent past failure to do so, for beyond their science are those who use and exploit scientific discoveries dubiously, as industrialists, arms dealers, militias, governments, drug barons and suchlike. If they in turn are to become responsible, or be stopped, the culture of responsibility must spread more widely. Ultimately, individuals must take up more responsibility. To do so they must be aware, and to be aware they need knowledge, and to have knowledge they need sufficient education.

'So,' said Tisala quietly, 'it is education and the adoption of good ideas that has to overcome, not only some of your now misplaced animal drives, but the imaginative and verbal superstructure that propelled men from mere savagery into fanaticism, barbarism and evil.'

'The aim of education should be to enlarge your understanding of yourselves and the world; to acquire knowledge and apply it to how and why you think and behave, and should think and behave. Education should seek in each new generation to consolidate and spread a common consensus to enhance the good and diminish the bad. And the need is widespread and urgent.'

CHAPTER 50

Aspects of Learning

Tisala thought that the nature of education might be illuminated by looking at different aspects of learning, which for convenience he divided education into three. The first he described as natural learning, the second as practical and the third as academic.

'Do not think,' he warned, 'that each of these can be treated in isolation. They constantly interconnect and merge. But in order to understand the whole it may be useful to look at the component parts. For it seems to me to explain why sometimes too much of your educational effort appears to be either wasted or ineffectual.'

He said our notion of schooling is mainly academic; and because the first two aspects are so neglected – left largely to chance and coincidental acquisition – the academic itself is made lopsided and less effective.

By the first aspect, natural learning, he meant such things as come from nature, from biological inheritance. This 'natural' element should permeate all through education. In the future our growing knowledge of ourselves and our brains, our genes, our neurology, our inherited characteristics, such as our innate ability to learn language, will improve our approach to education. But the natural learning of children extends beyond that base. In the family, in the home, in the school, in the locality and eventually in the wider world, the emotional, ethical and social connections already spoken of cry out to be developed to promote love and kindness, and the expression of them fostered and socialised into helpfulness, as in manners and courtesy.

Playground fairness should transmute into justice. He noted with interest how our 'rules' in games become elevated for adults into 'the laws' of the game, and domestic rules, in the wider contexts of restraint within society, become laws, and above that, the rule of law. He understood that, at all levels, in the complicated minutiae of our lives, these aims will be difficult to achieve, and perhaps never achieved completely; but that he thought must be our constant and conscious aim and endeavour.

But, Tisala thought, the first natural aspect concerns the physical development of the body. Since all animals rely on their bodies as the sole means they have of sustaining life, he thought it obvious that our bodies should be properly developed and exercised, and that we should rejoice in health and strength. For this permits everything else: the pleasures of the mind depend on having a sufficiently healthy body, as anyone who has lost it knows. He spoke of their own great seasonal migrations, when they swam magnificently together in the unity and intercommunication they had created and carried with them. Here was the power of the body in evolved balance with its conscious intellect. This was life itself.

He thought our neglect of our own physical prowess, replaced but not compensated for by our exaggerated spectator regard for sporting heroes, was retrograde to the balance and happiness of people's lives, and in the long run would be the cause of many ills and discontents. Not least, it must unbalance our being, and place an unwarranted burden on our minds alone to produce happiness. He noted without surprise that when people were free of compulsory education they often developed an interest in their own bodily fitness to revert to a better balance and accommodation with themselves; though too often it was late on, driven by awareness of impending loss, or was already remedial, or was cosmetic.

Another great natural competence that humans need to master is skill at language, especially within three years of birth. First, then, we should concentrate on our children's ability to comprehend their own language and to speak it, to enhance the power of thought itself, and the ability to communicate. And those abilities depend markedly in the first instance on the quality of talk and vocabulary the child hears around it. That is how deprived homes produce deprived children. He saw that in our complicated world, verbal poverty is a lifetime handicap, may be more limiting than relative economic poverty, and is often largely responsible for it. As he explored into primary and then later education, it became clear that this wonderful initial natural ability required the careful addition of conscious input and practice.

'Its extension into the skills of reading and writing is a practical matter, as is a more advanced comprehension of the language. Everyone can themselves learn more words and how to use them. Therein lies understanding. People may help themselves by putting themselves in the way of better talk by seeking out those better equipped, by listening to radio and television, by reading, and conversation in good books, where available. Many thus take the chance to escape from the limitations of their childhood or the narrow currency of localised languages and regional accents where they are so strong as to amount to a language barrier or prison, unusable beyond their own locality.

So over the years, practical linguistics should deal with the growth of vocabulary and power of expression, and through them arrive at conversation, discussion, debate, and speaking in public; each capable of higher development by the application of practice and experience; and further acquired by crossing over into an academic context of learning and conscious further mastery of language, including written skills. And now, in our modern world, we must also master the means of electronically extended speech and writing as with the telephone and computer. Tisala was fascinated by the burgeoning spread of our ability to communicate, but wondered how we would put it to best use.

But as well as competence in bodily health and language he recognised other natural competences. Such were the understanding and use of emotions and feelings, including in proper context the sexual aspect of our lives; which senses he found in our education little taught, or left to chance experience, at least until the onset of trouble, when it is late and difficult to remedy. He said this should be a pervasive aspect of attention in our education through its different stages.

Then he turned to his second element of learning, the practical. Tisala said it was obvious that mankind had a burning need to feel competent and at home in the physical world. Inventions and innovations made society more complicated: life supposedly made easier for the individual, yet for many, more difficult to master. He thought that much social disruption – disaffection, hopelessness, cheating, laziness and crime – arose from failures in this.

He saw that there is a pressing need to understand and master many different practical skills, where our ever-increasing division of labour brings with it a spreading incompetence in more and more areas of life. He remarked once that fish swimming in the sea have no feeling of incompetence, for they are wholly adapted to their environment; and that incompetence is the penalty we humans pay for 'progress', moving us out of our natural world, if such is not continually accompanied by successful education. He thought that if people repeatedly feel incompetent they will feel unhappy. And if people are unhappy, all the wealth and technical advances of our societies will not compensate the individuals in it for their loss, or society perhaps for its consequences.

So he came to place great importance on the second, practical element, in successful education. He concluded that the beginnings of it must lie in the home. The initiation into social and economic competence is found by giving the child tasks about the home. These should be real tasks, gauged within ability and motivation, which in turn increases both. Subsequently this should be done also in their first schools, and not as an optional matter but an essential. Parents and teachers who deny their children such tasks, even out of indulgence, deny them one of the fundamentals of good education. He saw that in our simple societies and among wiser adults this is often widely understood, at least intuitively, and achieved. Everyone knows that children, properly encouraged, delight in helping and that is the foundation of their practical skills in the real world. The pleasures of co-operating and competence result in feeling of happiness, fleeting perhaps, but repeatable. And if substantially repeated, resulting in sustainable periods of happiness and the knowledge of how to reproduce the process in their lives.

Tisala saw that there is a great range of practical skills that humans need to acquire, some essential, others desirable. The question of academic narrowness of education that we impose on our children concerned him greatly. Its counterpart was an increasing likelihood of practical incompetence in other fields, with its life-sapping drawbacks.

He saw perfectly clearly that the economics of our societies resulted in the ever increasing division of labour – specialisation – in people's employment. He thought the solution was to ensure a wide range of prior competence in basic personal accomplishments. All children should be taught and acquire a range of skills according to individual inclination, ability and the needs and practices of the society concerned: for instance, elements and practice of cultivation and gardening, mending of clothes, kites and bicycles, the pursuit of domestic crafts and cookery, home maintenance, decorating, carpentry, electrical skills, word processing and communication skills and so on. In short, a groundwork of confident ability, and for some, of later trade apprenticeships.

He saw this solution would require radical changes to our present educational systems. Many of the new skills would need to be learned outside the classroom, in society at large, in a range of different venues and experiences, and sometimes by importing trade and occupational skills into the classroom. The narrow monopoly of politicians, schools and teachers over the lives of adolescents should be broken and replaced by a wide range of co-operative learning and doing. He saw that there would be logistical and professional objections but thought that after adjustment the lot of teachers and children alike would improve. Above all, children would be released from the prison of academic grind, where appropriate, into the real world of practical skills and experience. Those who are now forced to sit discontentedly in schools often for a decade or more, understanding little, gaining less, hardly able to read or write coherently, causing stress and frustration to their teachers, disrupting fellow pupils' attempts to learn, and leaving school hostile to further learning, inarticulate and ignorant – those children would be set free. Teachers too would be released from the grind of teaching disaffected prisoners in their classrooms, and free to be guides of willing and fruitful endeavour.

But before these children leave school, Tisala thought it essential that they should have been well versed in matters of ethical, emotional and sexual education: natural learning merged with practical. And for some of this learning, skills from outside the classroom would be required.

Only then did Tisala come to the third aspect of education – the academic. He said that in humans the beginning seems to be a love of stories – tales of people, nature, events and ideas, which can lead to a love of learning pleasing to our emerging minds. He observed that minds can usually distinguish between fairy tales and truth; but that the fantastical can obscure reality and take years of unlearning. Hence, he thought, the classical Greek idea of strict supervision of children's stories, an idea largely abandoned, with unmeasured consequences, both in our religions and in our television age.

I remembered my childhood story-telling evenings when Susan and I snuggled up safely on the sofa with our mother in the warm sitting room of our little cottage full of bookcases. And I marvelled at her selection and her skill in demarking the borderlands of stories and reality, and the lessons to be drawn. One of Cicero's remarks came to me: "A room without books is like a body without a soul." And I wondered what the dominance of bad television in bookless homes was doing to the new generation.

Tisala thought that now we are beginning to understand biologically – neurologically – how our children learn, our teaching and learning should improve. It was clear that our educators had for a long time known how to promote effective learning from a teaching standpoint; but it seems that much down the years is periodically forgotten or neglected by new generations. A first requirement – a fundamental principle known to the Greeks, and to Romans such as Quintilian – is that teaching, if good learning is to follow, needs to fit the child's capacity, and proceed at different rates for different children. Teachers must get to know the ability and aptitude of each child. But teachers facing over-sized classes cannot find this out or respond adequately to individual needs, such as those arising from difficult backgrounds.

'Why then,' asked Tisala, 'do you so often commence schooling with the largest classes?' He saw that this must mean that too much primary educational effort is ineffectual and wasted. Frustrated teachers then fall back on teaching 'what children of that age should know'. Insufficiently prepared pupils are swamped, and their learning road half destroyed from the outset, with repercussions for the whole school system and in various degrees lifelong disadvantage for the pupils.

The second requirement, Tisala argued, again long known from Classical times and reaffirmed in Renaissance times by Comenius and others since, is that the most effective learning requires encouragement and praise to nurture motivation; and its opposite is coercion and compulsion, and teachers who practise these, imposing rote learning and enforced repetitious exercises, "drumming it in", and imposing exam swotting by promoting the fear of failure. In passing he noted, in a modern echo, that 'driving up' standards was not an educational phrase, but a sure sign of ministerial incomprehension and incompetence. He remarked that Plato was right to regard the Minister of Education as the most important official in the State, who should spend half his life preparing for the responsibility; but that the post is too often regarded by politicians as a staging post to higher office, and given to unprepared loyalists as a political convenience.

He thought people should reject any educational system that forces teaching on children who are ill-placed to learn and compounds the wrong by imposing obligatory subject matter on them that is irrelevant to their lives. For instance, he thought it absurd to spend years teaching all children one of many foreign languages, usually that of a neighbouring state or by some historical connection. In the case of England the politically imposed language has traditionally been French, imposed on all children between the ages of nine and fifteen. Foreign language teaching starting therefore about two years after neurological evidence shows that a child's natural linguistic ability to learn a whole language by absorption has evaporated in the light of growing consciousness. And so classrooms full of reluctant school children are condemned to spend six long wasteful years as they pass from childhood into adulthood, misusing and frustrating the most complicated organ in the known universe, and foregoing other vital education, to learn sufficient French to say 'good day' and buy bread in a small part of Europe; which accomplishment they can learn in a week when motivated by going there; but which otherwise few of them will ever use.

He was not belittling the learning of languages as such – far from it. Clearly, to know another culture through its language is enjoyable, valuable and breaks down nationalistic isolations. But to impose it flatly on a whole nation of schoolchildren, nearly all of whom would never master or need such language, was a sign of political wishful thinking, missed opportunity and an abuse of power.

He remarked that, historically, the earlier languages of the world, though fascinating, with their local characteristics and qualities, were sometimes linguistically limited, inadequate for housing the vast knowledge and complexities now progressively emerging in the human world. The better the tool of language, the more easy the route to knowledge and its transmission, which in turn can lead to good actions and greater co-operation in the world. The prize, Tisala thought, was immense.

To him as an outside observer this all seemed clear, but he saw few signs of its widespread understanding, let alone concerted action on it by governments and peoples, who were largely still wedded to their familiar systems and usage. 'I understand of course,' he said, 'that language gives you part of your identity, and that will continue, for life will still mostly be lived at a local level. But that identity should no longer circumscribe and limit. You each need an additional new identity as citizens of the Earth, and a universal language goes far towards establishing that, as increasing numbers of you are experiencing.'

'For now that you have discovered mankind is really one people – black and white, yellow and brown, all equal, and now you can travel and communicate easily throughout the globe, the world needs to learn one language – a common world language. And the one that crosses the most linguistic barriers and unites the most people happens to be English.' He saw that once it might have been Latin, and later Spanish; and now perhaps Mandarin or Hindi, but although they are spoken by vast numbers they are largely confined to one part of the world.

'The English language is both complicated and rich and can be the barrier-breaking language of the world; it has the vocabulary needed for a global language, though no doubt it will itself be modified as it is adopted as the common language of humanity.' He thought it possible that within three or four generations the world will largely learn that the route to a universal language is for the young of the planet to learn English from birth, as they do their own tongue, so utilising the marvellous predisposition of the evolved human brain to master language. This will demand the most radical change: one of the greatest educational challenges to be largely accomplished before the onset of schooling. But a change of huge importance; a change allowing people to join an exciting world, and more easily trade and communicate within it, for a universal language gives its people citizenship of the world.

As he so often did Tisala followed a subject into new channels, and out into new seas. He remarked once that 'the first language of understanding is instinct and behaviour in nature; the second language is language; the third language is history; and the fourth language is ethics. These are the languages that you humans need to understand.'

History he defined as that which has been and which explains and illuminates the present. It includes the glittering half-explored evolution of chemistry in the universe, and from it the emergence of life and all that has flowed from that down to the present. 'Without good history, how can you understand the present, or the coming future?' History should not be confused with the self-important propaganda of nation states and national histories, which too often illustrate the aggressive vanity or political bias of the tellers. 'History that does not rigorously seek out the truth is dangerous. You humans often seem to forget,' he said, 'that histories are satisfactory in proportion to their nearness to the truth.'

He believed that from better understanding may come a better future.

I said, 'Unfortunately many humans seem to find history most interesting at the level of heroic stories and drama – hence the abiding interest in kings and queens, tyrants, wars and conquests; or, in more academic histories, a consideration of minutiae and details of passing importance, while the real lessons of history go too much untold.'

'The importance of history as a language of understanding lies in right selection. For there is too much history, and now you are recording so much, its growth, like your population, is multiplying out of all proportion.'

We discussed what should be taught in schools. The story of our own particular land should be of interest, but within the scope and context of world events and civilisations, not studying the detail of past events for the sake of unachievable completeness. The study of history should enable humans to become citizens of the world.

What to select? Tisala said, 'Sufficient narrative and facts to arrive at understanding.' The birds-eye view (he noted the limitation of our own perspective) he considered a vital and skilful question of selection. Thus the map of historical understanding and curiosity is laid. The history teacher handles the golden language of the world's heritage. He thought a boring history teacher was inexcusable. Everything important that has been created, or come about in the passing of time, is part of history. To turn the young away from that is to exclude them from any possibility of understanding the world they live in, and will help to shape.

My own schoolteacher's words came back to me – that success in school is for the pupils to leave knowing they are ignorant and with an abiding urge to do something about it. Then the prospect of a lifetime's pleasurable and useful learning opens up.

We explored many aspects of education, which he thought should be much concerned with the development of abilities and skills, and perhaps above all to arouse the love of knowledge necessary for a lifetime's journey into self education. Knowledge itself should be gradually acquired, level by level.

'At what age', asked Tisala, 'do you start teaching children about the soil?'

I laughed and said I couldn't imagine such a topic was ever taught.

'But I understand', he said, 'that after water it is perhaps the most important component of life for you humans.' In the wide lands of Africa and India and all rural places, he thought the children should learn about their soil – how it is formed, made fertile, and maintained. And learn in history how the annual fertile floods of the Tigris and Euphrates assisted the development of civilisation, and how that of the Nile, bringing mud which transformed the desert into the Egyptian world, has sustained it for 5,000 years. And that where there are no great rivers the existing soil is precious and fragile: not many seasons can undo the soil, and once you have depleted the soil you create a dust bowl, irreversible without the difficult application of much greater resources. And that in dry places, the wind blowing the swirling dust up and away is not merely a passing misery – dust in the eye rims, in clothes, in the huts – but that it is dangerous. The chances of survival are blowing in the wind. For the legacy of poor land is starvation. If the land dies the plants too will die, and then the animals and the people.

So, for our children, the knowledge of how to prevent that is vital. And the realisation that, in part, prevention is by reform of the dust bowls of education, which are avoided by cultivating the fertile minds of children with skills and useful knowledge.

One example that we discussed – for, say, for seven to nine year olds – concerned the need to acquire a map of knowledge. A few statistics – the biggest and most important crops in the world; and their own most important ones whether they be potatoes, corn, rice, olives, oranges, bananas, cocoa; and their status in the world. Then our nine year olds have the start of an economic framework of the world and their place in it. Then they may learn that Americans farm vast prairies for corn and wheat. And that there and elsewhere in the world, developed industrialised agriculture scientifically applied has grown with spectacular success. In such places they can afford to nurture the land with chemical fertilisers to maintain the soil, producing sustainable crops year after year, and can sell the surplus to feed the world, if it can be bought and transported. So the map unfolds, with questions, answers, enquiry and deduction, giving them the flexibility to apply informed thinking to the world they find, but always within their scope.

But later they should find that behind the economics of large scale modern farming stands the question: how many people are to be fed from the areas of cultivatable soils spread patchily across the usable land surface of the Earth, even where there is available sufficient water? The great prairies of the temperate regions and the rice fields and terraces of the East depend on the rain and underground water. And what if the weather and storage patterns should alter? 'As their knowledge grows, so should their care and caution for future conduct and life.'

I remember writing to Robert Thompson at this time. 'If you give Tisala education for a topic he asks about soil, water and people, and shortly you get geology, geography, climatology, agriculture, world resources, transport, economics, finance, population control, the environment, and politics.'

In learning, he argued, facts illuminated by understanding become knowledge, but knowledge requires experience to become wisdom. Elements of wisdom can be found by the young quite early in the realms of natural and practical learning, for experience is fundamental to it; but wisdom lies largely beyond the remit of academic schooling, for its knowledge must be built on by later experience. In the long process of academic learning, knowledge that cannot yet be used has to be accumulated. It is therefore vital that sustaining motivation is developed. Tisala argued this is best done by creating and nurturing a sense of understanding and purpose.

Once when we had reached a pausing point Tisala said, 'Your true teachers are very, *very* important people.' We plunged back into education. I have several notebooks dealing with his assessment of primary, secondary and tertiary education, and its organisation. There is much in them that I believe could be distilled with great advantage. But that is for another place. In applying such reforms he thought the first principle was to evolve, and not revolutionise. 'With few exceptions you move by adjusting the present by manageable degrees so as to secure the willing and successful participation of the children, teachers and the public. For learning is in the heart of the pupils, and in their mentors and not in any system of education however grandly imposed.' That approach he thought would help promote balance and happy usefulness in many lives.

But while education is vital to human life, he thought it also urgently needed to be enlarged beyond concern for our own species to a new appreciation of the natural world of which we are part. He found scattered signs of this amongst those who observe and care for the natural world; in some who recognise the numinous or spiritual; and in some who under the pressure of our increasing numbers and consumption of resources, understand the need for the preservation of the planet. But for the most part he saw the shadow of humanity remorselessly stretching across the continents, and through the seas and oceans.

I said that we were now more aware of our dominance, and its effects.

Tisala asked, 'But enough?' I remembered and quoted H. G. Wells: 'History becomes more and more a race between education and catastrophe.' And that was said before most of the threats of catastrophe which we can now see, arose.

'Which is winning?' questioned Tisala. 'Education or catastrophe? The urgent need for the best education of humanity is a vast undertaking. It will call for a world-wide shift in priorities. It includes the schooling of your children, but starts well before that and goes far beyond. It is the key responsibility of individuals, families, communities and governments, for without it even survival itself is thrown in doubt. But with it you can transform the future of the world.'

Tisala said that the remedy to the world's troubles lies partly in right action. He reminded me that the fourth language of understanding is ethics, which is philosophy in action. 'The right application of ethics, and ethical properties, such as love, can transform the world. Ethics tells you how and why you should proceed in your discoveries and actions, which will become part of unfolding history, and which will encompass the planet's future, and stretch out into the nearby universe. Fortunately, your ability to go beyond the Earth is much less than your ability to see and understand. So, provided you do not first destroy the world, you will be able to reflect on outer space without endangering it.' But we did not then see the pollution of inner space that was just beginning.

This then is something of what Tisala said. I have omitted much, but have tried to indicate the sweep of his thought. And certainly ever afterwards I have found the pronouncements of educational officialdom, and especially government ministers, woefully inadequate, for they never address the whole picture. But at that time, after Eric's death, I too had other things to address and soon our life in the islands was to be further shaken and changed by events.

CHAPTER 51

Guinevere's Grief, and Susannah

When Eric died, Guinevere lived through her grief. On some days, when his absence struck her badly, she told me she became gloomy. And if she allowed herself to start thinking of her own mortality, she became frightened, not of death, but of her ability to cope physically on the island if her body or its functions should start to fail. She did not talk about it much, but now and then, if we were talking late, it would surface. She was not afraid of admitting openly to these thoughts, and faced her fears that way. This was a period when I was working long hours with Tisala on several aspects of humanity's attempts at civilisation. On two occasions when I reported to Tisala that she seemed particularly low he said, 'You must stop work and go back to her.'

She knew the years were running out for her also, but was stoical. One day she said, 'Fortunately David, we live in the present where we belong. We can eye the future with a certain wary smile.' She was doggedly pleased to be alive and in possession of her health and mind. She tried to live in the past only briefly, and then recalling incidences of Eric and their life together that gave her pleasure. She would come up with some recollection and laugh. Then she would say, 'We were so fortunate.' And she still found their lives together a source of wonderment and content. I often had the feeling, as she placed a vase of flowers on the kitchen table and finished arranging them, or did something that Eric would have noticed, that she was living happily. She managed to turn his absence into a positive presence, perhaps enjoying hearing echoes of Eric's approving comments.

But for the most part she focused her life solidly in the present. She took a keen interest in the estate, and regarded it as her privilege and pleasant duty to keep it up together, with Jimmy MacLeod's steady help. She spent long hours at her tasks that might have daunted many a younger woman. She did not regard it as work, but as her life.

And always she wanted to know the latest of Tisala's interests and ideas. Her own input and questioning was shrewd and acute. On the question of education she had much constructive practical insight into children's ways. She argued that of course the mother knows best the child's state of development, because she is habitually with the child and is motivated by love, which picks up signals no carer will consistently do.

I said, 'What if the mother herself is little more than a child, and is the victim of a deprived background, emotionally, linguistically, socially and educationally – ground down by poverty or abuse? The ability of such a mother to give a whole fruitful education is beyond the natural impulse to motherhood. How do the ignorant mothers of children in rural poverty or in the slums educate their young?'

'Yes, of course that is a terrible position. But properly educated women, with their motherly instincts, are better placed than so called experts, certainly in the earlier years, and very often later, to devise sensible education. And anyway educators are not in such control as they think they are. Be warned,' she said, warming to her theme, 'by the coming second generation of social dislocation. And beware the third.'

I smiled at her passion. 'You watch,' she said, wagging her finger at me, but smiling in spite of herself.

She was not well versed in the social traumas of many of the children of modern society. She came from a world where it was realistically assumed that the parent unconditionally loved the child; which to her meant steadfastly guiding the child to be brought up properly, and where the child in return would love the parent on a lifelong basis. This was reflected in her talk of friends' children, whom she regarded as her friends too, and frequently had the compliment returned. She kept up a steady correspondence with her friends, and the arrival of letters in the neat handwriting of her generation were a source of much pleasure to her. She would lay the envelope on the kitchen table, creating an anticipatory delay of expectation by doing some job and then making a coffee before carefully opening it. She used the back of envelopes for lists and did not like them torn open roughly.

In her replies, she sketched simple images of life on the islands, jumping from one matter to another in a jumble of sentences; but the overall effect was somehow charmingly coherent. I have one of her letters to me from this period, when I was in London. She wrote: 'We eventually found the cow hobbling and looking somewhat puzzled. It had put its hoof through a bucket and was carrying it about like a doubtful fashion statement, but more painful than that – she was cut about above her fetlock, silly creature. Jimmy coaxed it off her. He is so good with them. He had to go to the mainland so he got a replacement on the way back, and a new spade. There was a drama at the ferry. It was a bit rough, and the wind wrong as they came in. They got the mooring rope on but the wind caught the bow, strained the hawser 'til it squeezed out all the water. The Captain saw the warning and shouted at the deck hand, but he couldn't do anything. It snapped with a great crack. They had to pull out and abandon landing 'til they could fix a new one. The sheep looked rather sick, poor things, so did Mrs Cullen, apparently. Jimmy said, anyway she shouldn't have been away shopping with Joshua ill at home. He fell and hit his head – very nasty. Suspected fracture of the cheekbone, but isn't. Whisky, I suspect, from Dr. H's little joke. Did you read that article? You didn't comment. If they don't treat the fence posts properly, they rot in ten years and ruin the farmers. They can't afford to re-fence everything.'

Her own troubles and infirmities were treated with understated irony and humour, but those of others, when required, openly, and with much sympathy and kindness. The successes and difficulties of younger members of her friends' families were always of great interest and comment. So she kept herself in touch and well informed and this made her seem much younger than her years. Most of all she kept up a constant correspondence with Mary, which I think developed more after Eric's death, perhaps in compensation. Mary was very good, relaying the goings-on in Vancouver. Her family was close and in touch, though thousands of miles away.

In the spring, about a year after Eric died, I came up to the house one day. Guinevere met me waving a letter. She was full of the latest news from Mary. 'Dear Susannah is coming to see me in the summer. Isn't that lovely?'

'Yes, that will be wonderful for you.'

But I thought of Will. He was coming up to help me. Their visits would coincide. We chatted about other bits of the news. Then she paused, coming back to the visits. 'Will still has a girlfriend doesn't he?' she asked.

'Yes, but... So far they are still together.'

'Mary says Susannah is trying to decide whether her young man is for her in the long term. She is very young. I hope she is not precipitous.'

I felt a tightness in my throat. 'You mean she may get married?'

'Well nowadays you can't tell, but I think so, though Mary isn't very clear. One of her student friends.'

I wondered if Guinevere wanted me to know about Susannah's relationship so as to protect Will from false expectations and being hurt. I felt strangely uneasy, but we went on to talk of other things. Later I tried to put thoughts of the visit out of my mind. This was not difficult because at that time I was working hard supplying information to the anti-whaling campaign. For although the moratorium was passed, it was not yet implemented, and there were whalers intent on pillaging what they could before the ban came into force in 1985-6. And as always I was trying to keep abreast of Tisala's pursuit of knowledge.

He was then ranging across an ever-growing spectrum. But somehow increasingly he seemed to be able to draw everything together. No one in those days seemed to have as coherent an overview of our emerging world. Under Tisala's analysis and synthesis many of these subjects seem to me to be linked together: men's animal natures, the multiplication of human numbers, our imaginative delusions, nuclear or biological war and economic exploitation. They were driving our world. We began to see it: with the advance of modern knowledge and communication, the world was shrinking. The old idea was of empires stretching unlimited round a vast globe to far-flung places. English minds had dreamt of an empire upon which the sun never set. German minds had constructed a latter-day European empire to match the Japanese delusion of a somehow borderless Pacific empire. All these had been swept away in the Second World War and replaced by a closer – a few hours flying time – understanding of the world, but where all the aggression of the previous disastrous history of humanity remained as strong and dangerous as ever. And behind that change of view slowly arose another: the issue that emerged and coalesced from Tisala's enquiries concerned the whole future of this unique and beautiful orb circling the sun. All hung together in the balance. And against the world's driving imperatives we had only our attempts at wisdom, which comes from reason, knowledge, goodwill, ethics, love and education.

Yet not many years later, towards the close of the century, the trend was to seem clearer, the outcome worse, and the remedies more urgent. We seemed to solve problems: the cold war and its threat of nuclear devastation, only to realise later that the problem has not been solved but merely deferred. And worse, that the best chance of nuclear containment and disarmament has been missed. Economically, growth now brings a more pleasant life to many, but masks its unsustainability in the face of uncontrolled increases in humanity's numbers, and the clamour for wealth of unreformed nation states. So overwhelming is that drive that the balance and survival of the natural world itself is now at risk. Early on we were aware of glimpses of the future danger of climate change; but the ominous truth that a threat to the world was being forged that would belittle even the danger of nuclear war was not understood. Now we look at the world's nearly two million different species of animals and many millions more of plants and wonder how many will survive. And whether whales and men will be among them.

But in 1982 the Cold War still existed and climate change was more speculative. There were enough problems to work on, and some of these things were then further off.

In between all this, after long sessions of talk with Tisala and when I had made my notes for the day, I would sit in the quiet of the evening on the rocks overlooking the inlet, when he had gone out to sea. Then my thoughts turned to the present, and Guinevere and the gathering of our little group. I found myself looking forward to Susannah's visit. Will was coming up for three weeks in the middle of August, after a holiday in Greece with some of his university friends. I knew he was juggling loyalty to the work with Tisala and me with the development of interests and friendships in his own life. But he insisted on coming up, and though I did not press him, his help would be welcome, as well as his company. The need for secrecy was a recurring problem. It was difficult to explain to his friends why it was always impossible for them to come and visit. The protection of the whole undertaking was sacrosanct. Will knew and accepted this. Indeed he insisted upon it more fiercely than even I.

When I spoke to Will about it on the telephone he said 'Angela will have to put up with it. She will be with us in Crete.'

'I didn't know that.'

'Yes, she's coming.'

'You mustn't mislead her.'

'What do you mean? Dad, she's my girlfriend.'

'About your intentions.'

'What about them?' He sounded irritated. 'You seem to know more about them than I do. Give over, Dad. I don't know what you mean. I'm not marrying her.'

Initially I was taken aback by this rebuke. But afterwards, to my surprise, felt almost pleased. We got on to other things – kit and money needed for Crete, and things he could bring up here. Towards the end of the conversation I mentioned that Susannah would be visiting Guinevere. He seemed pleased.

Spring turned into early summer. In my weeks with Tisala we had covered good ground. He departed from Inis Cuan, on his way north to the feeding grounds. As he slipped down the inlet I followed him out. When he was ready he circled, his head raised, watching as we said our goodbyes. I stood and raised my arm. And then he turned and plunged, the great flukes rising out of the water. Then he was gone on his long journey north.

I spent a week with Guinevere and did some jobs for her before heading back to London, and more research work. I was due to collect Penny from Susan. For years Susan and her family had provided a secure and welcoming home for Penny in the weeks I was away in the islands. But always we enjoyed our return home, and now I found myself looking forward to being with her for the summer. My teenage daughter was beginning to assert her independence, which I watched with a mix of pleasure and concern. And, in between the inevitable occasions of difference of view and the stresses of adjustment, we were perhaps closer than ever.

I returned to the islands in mid August, to find Guinevere remarkably content, busy about the demesne and looking forward to Susannah's visit at the end of the week. After a couple of days I went over to Inis Cuan to prepare for Tisala's expected arrival. I spent time checking the equipment, making a small repair to the boat and doing maintenance jobs on the shack. On the day of Susannah's arrival I kept out of the way and continued working.

The next afternoon I crossed back to Eilean Mòr. The water was calm, but I was not. The familiar little jetty came into view. But this time it felt different, with a sense of expectation and apprehension. Will was due within the week. We would find out how Susannah stood with her boyfriend. I came into the kitchen. 'Ah, here he is.' said Guinevere. Susannah was standing by the table and smiled broadly. I thought how beautiful she was.

'Hello Susannah, lovely to see you.'

'Hello, David.' She moved round the table towards me. We hugged briefly. Momentarily warmth and softness. I became aware that my heart was thumping. But I no longer knew whether the thump was on behalf of Will. Afterwards I chided my stupidity.

We chatted as Guinevere got ready to dish up supper. Guinevere said, 'David, cork please.' I read 'Haute-Côte du Beaune'. Eric always drank French wine, though he used to claim that the two best wine regions in France weren't really French at all. Bordeaux and Aquitaine ought to have belonged to England, but we foolishly lost them despite the Treaty of Troys, and the Burgundians should have stayed independent. And wherever he retold this line he used to end with, 'But we won't tell the French.'

So, we talked. How was Susannah? Fine. What about the degree? – all done – last semester finished in May followed by the final part of exams. Course work as predicted – very pleased – but final results awaited. Then what? Six months economist's internship in a big company with forestry and paper-making interests in British Columbia. We chatted about Grenville and her father, business, and real estate in Vancouver. I heard but hardly took it in. Instead I saw her eyes, her face sometimes envisaging her in Vancouver but now here, close by, with a hint of a smile picked up at the corners of her mouth. She answered enough to satisfy immediate curiosity and social convention. But she was more eager to talk about life and goings on here and in London. She had clearly been talking at length with Guinevere, as a number of references to recent events revealed. She dabbed a finger on the table to pick up a crumb. 'How's Will?'

'Fine, loving university. Just been in Crete with friends. He is coming up next week so you will be able to quiz him yourself.'

She looked down momentarily. 'With his girlfriend?'

'In Crete? – Yes.'

'And Penny?' She looked up. She wanted to know all about how Penny was doing, what she was enjoying at school, her activities, what clothes and music she was into. I was able to report she was sparkling and coming through her teenage years with remarkably little angst so far; and that we got great pleasure in each other's company.

'She is very sorry not to be coming up this holiday. She is going on holiday to France with a girlfriend and her family.'

'Yes I heard.' She seemed disappointed. 'I was so looking forward to seeing her.'

When Guinevere was out of the room she asked me anxiously how she really was. With the odd caveat I was able to be truthfully reassuring.

'But I'm a bit concerned – '

'More later,' she said as we heard Guinevere coming back.

She wanted to know about the latest work with Tisala.

I outlined it briefly. 'But you don't want – '

'Yes I do.'

'Now you'll get him started,' smiled Guinevere.

So I told her how he had been looking at education and how I had been struggling to bring to him so vast and amorphous a subject. 'But the extraordinary thing is, his mind seems to be able to see the fundamentals quite clearly. Sometimes I see glimpses, as if behind all the sprawling opaque burden of educational provision there lies, if we could but analyse it, a transparent simplicity which, properly applied, could improve so many lives.'

Susannah said: 'Politicians talk in terms of systems, but every child needs their own education.' She had plenty of ideas for educational reform from her own recent education. And so the talk of education flowed from human nature via schooling and the environment into learning, and then into economics and society. She became deeply engrossed in Tisala's assessment of the aim and future of education. She came from a spacious new world where optimism and the possibilities of economic growth were so far thought of as boundless.

We talked through the meal and coffee and nightcaps and at last reached a pause. Susannah sounded exhilarated. 'It's truly fascinating. And what is he looking at now?'

'For a year he has been asking about ethics, and also international affairs. I'm beginning to see what further synthesis he is heading for. But sometimes he asks things that have no apparent bearing.'

'But I bet they do.'

'Yes, I bet so too.'

And so we talked further into the night until in the end Guinevere said 'As much as I love you, my eyelids are coming down and I am going to bed, and I think you should too. Susannah still has jet-lag to adjust to.'

'I'm sorry,' I said.

'Oh no!' But her smile was wan. 'I'm a bit pooped.'

'And I have to get back to Inis Cuan in the morning.'

'Yes, and we have lots to do here,' said Guinevere patting Susannah on the hand. I saw then that Susannah did look tired, and now somehow weighed down. And when she looked at me I sensed a silent question but I did not know what. And when we said our good-nights I felt awkward and confused. Afterwards, and before I fell asleep, I realised with a little kick in the stomach that I had failed to find out about her boyfriend.

The next morning I left early and spent the next two days working in and around the shack, and consulting some of the books and information I had brought with me. But I found myself edgy and sometimes distracted in my work. I kept returning to Susannah's unknown involvement with her boyfriend until I became angry with myself – it was nothing to do with me and there was probably nothing in my idea of Will and Susannah.

And soon I lost myself again in work. Tisala was due back at any day, and there was much to anticipate. But then everything changed.

CHAPTER 52

The Terrible Event

As it happened, the day Tisala returned Susannah had come over to Inis Cuan. She had been keen to come. I had initially felt irritated by the prospect of intrusion into my domain but eventually admitted to myself that it was in truth also because with it came unsettling and disturbing issues. And I found myself pleased that she was so interested in our great undertaking.

I was as usual excited and animated by the prospect of Tisala's return. My anticipation probably showed. She laughed and said the atmosphere was contagious. She was excited too. In between periods of lookout I checked over bits of the equipment again, quite unnecessarily.

'Look,' she pointed, 'here he is.' And at the far end of the inlet was the familiar shape and low bow wave coming slowly towards us. We went out of the shack and stood on the rocks above his berthing place. I felt again the old sense of excitement and joy at his arrival. We watched for a few seconds. He seemed to be coming very slowly. And as we watched I knew there was something different, and my sense of joy began to give way to apprehension. Was the bow wave smaller, or the way he held himself in the water unusual, or was it his movement? – it seemed constrained. In those long seconds I could not work it out, but slowly I knew there was something wrong. And as he came close I saw near the surface a long whitish streak along the top of his left side, made greenish in the water. And in nearly the same instant I saw the red, livid and horrible, and flowing from it a plume of darkness spreading out behind him.

'God almighty, he's wounded – there's a great slash at the top of his flank.' I heard Susannah's intake of breath and was aware of her startled glance.

I could now see the extent of the gash – it was seven or more feet long, towards the middle hanging open horribly. Then I thought I caught a glimpse of another wound below it. As he came to a halt at the berthing place below the shack, the black plume of blood behind him caught up and swelled into a dark cloud around his left side as the blood welled from his wound.

'We've got to stop the bleeding.' I saw Susannah look at me, frightened.

'David, it's huge.'

'We've got to hold the wound together. Strap it somehow, if it's an artery… I don't think it's an artery – it's not pumping.' But how much blood has he lost, and how long has he been like this?

'I must speak with Tisala.' I leapt back into the shack, switched on and spoke to Tisala. He was weary and in pain.

'Two days ago – '

'Two days!' – even whale blood does not congeal quickly in water.

'Yes, south of the Faeroes of all places – a single whaling vessel surprised me.'

'Bastards! The bloody, bloody bastards.'

'David, you must try to close the wound.'

The wound ran back from just in front of his wing, about two feet above it, and slightly downwards. It was now difficult to see the extent of it because of the blood clouding the water but allowing for foreshortening in the water I realised it must be fully eight or nine feet long. From the shallow angle of the wound I thought they must have fired from a considerable distance – much too far to be sure of success. A maverick outfit, probably Icelandic or disaffected Norwegian under the orders of some criminal self-righteous, ignorant sea captain. I felt loathing rise up inside me at the catastrophic evil men can so casually inflict. Commercial whalers who care nothing for the destruction and long agonies they cause. It might even have been a laughing pot-shot – what the hell were they doing south of the Faeroes? – but result was a terrible, unique destruction and my anger turned to fear – Tisala the wise giant of the deep, the irreplaceable – and then I felt the panic arise within me – our work, we haven't finished our work – if he dies now everything will fall apart – I will be left alone, alone again, to try to put together what I – no I can't – my surge of panic grew. Tisala, this wonderful being and his greatness would be gone – the Tisala I love would be gone. And I realised fiercely how much I loved him.

These thoughts tumbled thrtough my mind in seconds but

immediately after, as I looked at him lying in the water – I knew he had to come here to me. And in place of my fear and momentary panic there grew a grim determination that he should not die, and an implacable calm resolve.

I knew what must be done. 'I am coming to inspect. I will use your wing. Can you lift yourself a bit?'

'Yes.'

We tersely agreed the signals.

I grabbed a face mask off the hook, went out onto the rocks, kicked off my shoes and jeans and jumped into the sea. I swam the few paces to him and scrambled onto his wing. It was still submerged but he swivelled it horizontally and backwards along his body to form a platform. As he did so he raised his front half slightly in the water – the top end of the wound came clear and I squatted down ankle deep in the water. But as he came up the supporting weight of water was removed and I saw with horror the wound began to sag further open exposing the whitish blubber. Instantly the blood welled red. He seemed to realise this too and subsided gently again. I couldn't see the whole length of the slash but I had seen for an instance the second gouge below the first. To my relief it was only two or three feet long. I pulled on my face mask and slid off his wing into the sea. He moved his wing outwards away from his body. I took a deep breath and went under. By keeping my face close to him I could just follow the wound on its downwards slant through the murk of blood. Two breaths later I knew the main wound ran almost to the first of his grooves – I could feel the ribbing a few fingers widths apart a short distance below the end of the wound.

I came up through the cold water and turned towards the rocks. As I swam ashore a plan formed clearly in my mind. Susannah was standing white-faced on the rocks: 'How bad is it?' She was nearly in tears.

'Bad – its nine feet long, but I am sure no artery is cut, thank God. There is a smaller wound underneath, not so deep and bleeding less. The first thing is to support the wound and stop it sagging open. Then we must sew it up.'

She looked at me aghast and whispered, 'How?'

'The climbing rope and fishing line.'

We keep Will's climbing rope hanging up in the shack. 120 feet.

I worked it out rapidly. About 32 feet around his body. 'It should go round three times. Immediately behind his wing – then underneath and round again two feet further back, and then again. I will need your help. You will have to push the wound closed as I tighten the rope.'

I suddenly thought what I was asking. 'You will have to stand on his wing. Can you do that?'

Rapid nod of her head. 'Yes.'

'I will speak to Tisala.'

In the shack I sat at the equipment, dripping wet. 'Towel, Susannah.' I indicated towards the backroom, and noticed for the first time that I was shivering. The Hebridean Sea even at the end of summer is very cold to humans. She brought a towel and I dried the worst of the wet and noticed the towel was stained with diluted blood. 'Thanks.'

I reported my findings to Tisala and spoke of my plan. I felt Susannah put a rug around my shoulders.

'Are you in much pain?'

'Yes, considerable, and the salt burns.'

I told him about my plan with the rope. 'It will be painful.'

'Yes, but you must do it, I have lost much blood already.'

He would try and roll in the water to bring the wound up to the surface. It might stay open less. We would try and close the wound sufficiently to be able to sew it with a fishing line. We could then see the lower cut more easily too.

I cursed that Will's wet suit was still up at Guinevere's, and thought of getting it. Two hours or more. Too long.

'Right, we have to try it.'

I told Susannah to get in the boat.

'The water is freezing. This may take some time. Try and keep dry.'

I threw the climbing rope into the boat and pushed off across the few feet to Tisala. He had already moved his wing to the platform position. Susannah climbed on. I tied one end of the rope around my waist, unwound some length into the water and gave the coil to her.

'Make sure it plays out and get it tight against the back of his wing – here.' I indicated.

'I'm going to dive underneath and throw the rope over the top. Bring it round about two feet along and then I will repeat. It should reach three times round. Watch out when Tisala rolls or you'll come off.'

She nodded silently. I crouched in the bow and then roll-dived to get some momentum and swam down under the great bulk of Tisala, then up towards the lighter water on the other side. I came up, drew breath and untied the end of the rope, pulling it in after me until I had enough coiled to throw over his back. Susannah's head appeared above his back.

'Rope coming. Watch out!' Up it went. Susannah grabbed it and pulled it over.

I swam towards his tail – the great flukes lay near the surface but I ducked underneath before them – under the four feet of his draft at the narrowest point – and swam back along his side of the boat. I found the loose end of the rope and double half-hitched the rope through itself and then secured it.

'Ready? He's going to roll.'

I thumped Tisala three times. Tisala slowly rolled. Susannah found herself leaning perilously over the top of him but she hung on and scrambled back. As she did so his wounded flank came out of the water and lay exposed on the surface. It was a ruinous sight ghastly to behold. Susannah was kneeling at one end.

'Push the edges together.'

She moved in and shoved. Her hands and clothes became smeared with blood. I fought to tighten the rope, bracing my legs against Tisala's side.

'More. Push. Push!'

The gaping wound narrowed by an inch or two.

'Again! More – good.'

So we worked, repeating the process. Three times the rope was passed under the huge body. Three times Tisala rolled and maintained his position to aid us. Three times we tightened and shoved and pushed, and the horrible sagging wound like a rift valley, a foot across at the widest point, gradually closed. It was ugly and open and still bled. But by the end the rope roughly held the gaping wound together. And never once did Tisala flinch.

I felt a surge of relief. I had hardly noticed the cold but then it hit me – numb and shuddering and my teeth chattering uncontrollably. Susannah was pale, shivering and covered in blood. When Tisala had rolled back she had managed to stay on Tisala's wing, but the water sloshing about had soaked the legs of her jeans. I pushed the boat alongside and helped her in. We made for the shore.

As we entered the shack I said, 'Get out of those clothes. There are some dry things and thick jerseys in the back room.'

I found some dry clothes for myself and while she was changing, stripped, dried myself and put them on. Gradually my shivering came under control. I was desperately anxious to speak to Tisala. And afraid. What pain had we inflicted on him on top of the trauma he had suffered in the last two days?

Over the equipment I said to Tisala, 'Are you okay?' There was a momentary silence. Then as if he was coming back from a great distance he said, 'Yes, I think so.'

'Did it cause great pain?'

'Yes, but I am glad of it, for the pain is the condition of reaching new life.'

And for some reason I thought of Marcus Aurelius, nodding approval. And then, for the first time, allowed myself to believe that he might not die.

'We've got the rope round three times – it has pulled the wound together.'

'Thank you, David.'

He sounded exhausted but he said 'What about the second wound?'

I told him its extent and that we had got a rope across it.

'Now I must try to sew the wounds.' I explained my plan.

'Yes,' he said, 'You must do it.'

I searched the oddments box and found, stuck through a roll of cloth, a large canvas-stitching bodkin.

'Boil this, please Susannah. Careful, don't drop it – it is the only one.' I gave her the needle. 'And these scissors.' In the box there was a ball of waxed string and in the bag next to the tool box a square of adhesive canvas intended for minor boat repairs. I cut the square into strips. From Will's fishing line I took a considerable length of the green nylon, tied a knot in the end and cut and prepared several additional lengths. It was for sea fishing and was fairly substantial. I took a small piece of card, cut nicks in it and wound the line round it in separate pieces, wedging the ends. I went out to the peat bog a little way behind the shack, and collected a large bagful of sphagnum moss.

Back in the shack Susannah brought the needle and the scissors through in a saucepan.

'We must wash our hands. Then wipe the line with disinfectant – there's some Dettol on the shelf. Cotton wool's in that packet there.' Susannah found the Dettol, but the bottle was nearly empty.

We washed like surgeons. Blood poisoning, I thought as I did so. Beyond our present efforts, even if successful, I knew lay that risk, but dismissed it with a mental shrug. This urgent business first, or we may not even get to that.

'We'll use the sphagnum moss – it has iodine – it is all we have.'

'You could anchor the stitches with a button.'

'Yes – good idea – the bigger the better.' I indicated the bedroom. 'Use my pyjama top – cut them off.' She did so and we threaded one on each length of line, knotting it firmly at the bottom.

There was a clean shirt in the drawer. I wrapped the card and bodkin, the scissors and the ball of string in it and rolled them up carefully.

'What's the string for?' asked Susannah.

'The line may pull through the flesh.'

'Susannah, I need you to hold the wound together as I sew. Can you do that?' She nodded, but I saw fear in her eyes.

I spoke to Tisala again and said we were ready. I asked if he could roll again to bring his flank to the surface, and this time maintain his position for sufficient time for me to work on the wounds. He said he could hold that position for perhaps half an hour – maybe less – but then he would have to roll back to breath. We arranged signals.

We had put our wet clothes out on the rocks to dry. They were still sodden but had warmed up a bit. My shirt was cold to the touch, clammy and heavy and I dragged it on with difficulty. Susannah got into her ruined jeans.

In the boat, I pulled across to Tisala, Susannah clutching the precious rolled-up shirt and the bag of sphagnum moss. I climbed up onto Tisala's wing, which he held out as before, and I secured the boat's rope round his wing base. 'Shirt.' She gave it to me. I helped her up onto Tisala's wing and pushed the boat away.

My fist thumped Tisala three times, and, as we crouched down, slowly he rolled, his rising wing tipping us into a crawling position. On the top side of his flank, we avoided the great gash which now laid on the surface of the water. It was a horrible sight, but I was relieved to see that the rope prevented the wound from sagging open along its length. The second gash looked more manageable. I set to work, pushing the bodkin through his living flesh remorselessly.

'Push, Susannah.' She tried to bring two sides of the great gash together in front of my stitching. The bodkin was slippery with blood and difficult to pull through. Each time I wiped my fingers on my shirt to improve the grip, my fingertips became tacky with drying blood and each time the bodkin went through again it was wet and slippery. It was slow work and rudimentary. To start with I was oblivious to how hard I was gripping the bodkin to get it through, but gradually became aware my fingers were becoming sore and painful. Progress seemed to be pitifully slow. Desperation rose within me – my efforts seemed so puny and the task colossal – and then I could not see what I was doing properly and realised it was tears. I tried to wipe my eyes with my wrist.

I heard Susannah say, 'You're doing fine, David.' Then suddenly I felt a surge of anger at the outrage of this grotesque wound, and stuck the needle in savagely and pulled the line through, and again and again. Then my rage subsided, and I went on. The fishing line was holding.

Tisala angled his wing. It was the signal for him to roll back. I stopped sewing and calmly stuck the needle in his flesh. As he very slowly rolled, we crawled up his back and slid our feet down onto his waiting wing. He subsided a bit more and we were knee deep in water as his blowhole came clear and he exhaled forcibly with a loud shwoosh! – spray rising twenty feet and the unique pungent smell of whale drifting across us. He inhaled and then repeated the cycle two or three times. I listened for sounds of weakness or irregularity, but it sounded full and steady. After a few minutes he gave the signal and again rolled sideways and we scrambled back to continue our work.

So I became a whale surgeon and Susannah my nurse. For two hours we worked, suspending the work every twenty minutes or so when Tisala rolled. Slowly my irregular line of stitches zigzagged their way down the great gash. Susannah dabbed on the sphagnum moss. I fought to get under each part of the rope as we came to it and carry on. But each time it was another stage. The bottom end of the wound was difficult – we were both exhausted, and there was less room to work where Tisala's body tapered slightly. But finally the great gash was done and the end tied. Then we turned to the smaller wound. It was a mere three feet long and the edges were closer – perhaps I was getting better – it seemed easier. Towards the end I could sense Susannah's exhaustion – she hardly had the energy to push the edges of flesh together any more. I saw she was in tears – frustration and desperation at the feebleness to which exhaustion had reduced her efforts.

'Just a bit more – we're nearly there. You're brilliant.' She did her best to push with her remaining strength but the tears slowly trickled down her face. Then that too was done.

'Now the strips.' The exposed skin was drying, and I used the shirt to help. I tore the backing off the adhesive strips and applied them at intervals across the wound with a couple across the smaller gash. They seemed to take and stick, but I didn't know how long they would last in the water.

I looked at my handiwork. It was crude, but it seemed to be holding. The bleeding was much reduced. I thumped Tisala again and by slow degrees he rolled one final time till we stood on his wing. I pulled in the boat. Cold and exhausted we fell into it and went ashore, leaving the great whale recumbent in the water. He did not move at all.

As we clambered ashore we were stiff with cold, bloodstained and frozen. Going into the shack, I immediately went to the equipment to speak to Tisala, saying over my shoulder, 'Susannah, kettle and hot drinks.' But when I glanced around Susannah was sitting on the floor, her back against the wall. She was shaking violently. I felt a strange and overpowering emotion, like a dam bursting after years of slowly accumulating pressures.

'Here,' I took her a large blanket. 'Get up.' She hardly could, but I lifted her up, wrapped the blanket around her and without thinking, held her tight in an enveloping hug.

'Bless you, Susannah – you were wonderful.'

'Sorry,' she said, still shaking uncontrollably, 'I can't help it.'

The eyes that met were of two new people, searching. I sat her down in a chair, went to the back and put on the kettle. I was in a ferment. My hands were shaking – the cold, the release from stress; but my inner self smiled at me and I knew there was another cause, which I suppressed violently. Wars on two fronts are folly.

'Susannah, I must speak to Tisala.' She nodded. I looked out of the window. He lay motionless. I felt suddenly drained, and beyond that frightened. The phrase 'the coming crisis' came into mind and stabbed me. Was he in shock? Had our efforts traumatised him too far? Was he dying anyway?

'Tisala, can you hear me? How are you?' I waited. The silence lengthened. 'Tisala, can you speak? – I need – '

In a crackle I heard 'Yes, David I can hear you. I'm all right but that was painful. It's easing a little now. Is the wound holding?'

'Yes, I think so. Only careful movements – the less the better.'

'Yes. I am very tired. If the pain subsides enough I shall try to sleep.' He paused, and said quietly as if from a long way off: 'David: the blessing of life on you both, and thank you. I hope your world and mine will remember this day with grateful thanks. If I live, I will owe you my life.'

'You *must* live, Tisala. You must not leave us. We need you to live, beyond – beyond anything I can say.'

'If your rope and stitching hold and I don't develop blood poisoning, thanks to you I have a good chance. Nature is strong and I am bending my mind to that determination. Now I must rest.'

I knew that Blue Whales have sometimes recovered from terrible harpoon injuries and believe that determination to live can help recovery even from the most horrendous wounds, if vital organs are not destroyed. They had long ago found, he had told me, that the expectation of recovery and a concentration of will can physically assist the body's chemistry. I marvelled that they had known intuitively what science has only recently confirmed, and I as a biologist believed, that the brain itself is a chemical and electrical construction of biology and can influence the body's healing response.

His remark had released in me a great wave of relief and exhaustion. With Susannah's help I had done what I could, and knew it was no longer in my hands. He was engaged in saving himself. And with that remark he somehow took the responsibility from me. And Susannah had been – wonderful. I looked around but she was not there. I went through and found her curled up in the bed fast asleep. Very quietly I went back to the main room. Early evening light was coming through the window. I went outside and sat on the rocks and watched Tisala, praying for his recovery. Once he stirred slightly. It was too late to take Susannah back to Guinevere's. Besides we could not leave Tisala tonight. We must stay. Food. We had not eaten for hours. I went in and made a meal of bread and tinned sausages. Perhaps the smell of cooking woke Susannah – she came through looking dishevelled. I thought she had never looked more beautiful. My defences were crumbling but they held on tensely. No, not now. She doesn't want… not now. Perhaps not ever.

As we served and ate the food we talked quietly. It was late. I would have to stay. Of course I must stay – it was unthinkable to leave Tisala, and she was not up to going back on her own. She hoped Guinevere would not be worried. It was settled that I would take her back in the morning and would then return again to be with Tisala. I made up a bed on the floor in the main room. Then I went out to Tisala in the boat before the light faded to inspect his wound. The long wound was all holding together, and bleeding was reduced to a little seepage. I could not see the lower wound but thought it best not to disturb him. Back at the shack I spoke once more to Tisala. The pain was less. He would try to sleep.

Susannah was finishing the washing up when I rejoined her. We did not speak much but I tried to thank her and tell her how indispensable she had been. She said she was grateful to have been there and able to assist – it was a great privilege. I protested, 'Susannah, it would have been impossible without you – I don't know how – it's so important.' We fell silent with our own thoughts and imaginings on the terrible event that confronted us. I tried to think beyond it, but always came back to the dark present. My mind and feelings revolted at the idea that he might yet die. We wondered aloud how Tisala really was, but it was a desolate exchange for we simply did not know and would have to wait. We spoke of a few practical things – but a great tiredness asserted itself before it was even properly dark. We got ready for bed. Susannah emerged from the bedroom in a pair of my pyjamas and a thick sweater. She had taken the trouble to comb her hair. I smiled at her. 'Good night, you wonderful girl.'

'Good night, David.' She reached up, the lightest of kisses on my cheek.

I wanted to go on thinking of Susannah but had no sooner put my head down on my makeshift bed than I was asleep. I slept heavily at first, but woke in the night with a start, thought of Tisala and was instantly wide awake. Getting up quietly I looked out of the shack.

There was enough light to make out the flat top of Tisala's head and back above the dark water of the inlet. There was no movement. I very quietly switched on the equipment and listened. For several minutes there was nothing. Then I heard the long faint sound of Tisala inhaling. I made a slight noise in my throat. If he were awake he would hear. There was no response. The great whale was sleeping.

CHAPTER 53

Aftermath

Next morning I woke early with a kick in the stomach as I remembered the horrors of Tisala's gaping wound. I got up silently and looked out. It was just light. He lay in the water, but then stirred slightly, sending little ripples across the surface. I went quietly to the equipment. He was awake, but yes, he had slept and the pain was reduced to a dull throb.

Susannah was still asleep. I dressed and went out. It was a fine September morning, a little cool in the early autumn air. I rode the boat out to Tisala and inspected the wound so far as I could without asking him to move. Our surgery seemed to be holding and to my relief there were only little wisps of bleeding.

On my return Susannah was up and making breakfast. She looked up with a silent question. 'He's okay so far'.

'Oh, I'm so glad.' She spoke softly with an emphasis on the last two words. She looked serious and relieved rather than glad. Over breakfast we spoke further. She must return to Guinevere, who would be uneasy about her unexplained absence. I told Tisala over the equipment that Susannah must be taken back to Eilean Mòr, so he would be alone for a few hours.

'Yes, of course. Tell her' – and even he seemed for a second unable to find his words – 'tell her I am profoundly grateful and thankful for all she did.' His voice felt strained, and I wondered if he was in more pain than he was letting on.

When I passed on his words, my feelings of pride in her made my own voice sound unfamiliar. And I did not want her to go back at all. She too seemed reluctant. We both said it was because of leaving Tisala in his plight, but I was aware of the hope of other reasons.

A few things were packed in the rucksack, and we set off. As we walked across the island leaving Tisala behind, I was haunted by the fear of his death and some of my underlying anguish came through.

Susannah did her best to reassure me. We spoke of Tisala's chances, trying to be optimistic. Gradually my turmoil sank and I noticed that the sun was warm. In the boat, and as we had walked up towards the house we said little but I remember every detail of that short journey and how I stole looks at Susannah and did not know what to do or feel when once or twice our eyes met.

Guinevere was relieved to see us and said she knew there would be an explanation. She was dismayed at our somewhat disjointed account of the hideous injuries that Tisala had suffered. We recounted our attempts to staunch the bleeding. I was anxious to return to Tisala, and didn't stay long. First, I made a telephone call to Will.

He was desperately upset by the news, and came near to tears. He loved Tisala as a combination of grandfather, and friend. When I had explained the severity of the wounds there was a moment's silence.

'Dad, he's not going to die is he?'

'No, I don't think so.'

'I'll come up at once.'

'I don't know how much more we can do.'

'Well, I'm coming up. Tell him to hang on and do nothing stupid until I come.' Determination and love mastering fear. I promised to give the message.

When we had finished, I said to Guinevere and Susannah, 'Will's coming up on the overnight train.' Susannah looked pleased. It was arranged they would come over to Inis Cuan with Will when he arrived – probably the next afternoon.

Then I rang a senior vet I knew at London Zoo who dealt with marine animals, and asked him about slash wounds in seals and dolphins and whether nylon fishing sutures could be left in safely. His preliminary view was 'probably', but there was some risk, and better to take them out if feasible. He thought nothing could really be done about possible infection.

On my way back across Inis Cuan my turmoil of thoughts and feelings returned but became more ordered as I approached the inlet and peered anxiously towards the water. Tisala came into view behind the roof of the shack. He was in the same position. I called across the water to him before going into the shack and speaking. He was calm, but pleased by my return. Only then did it strike me how much he had placed himself in my care, trussed up in a rope in a small inlet. He was pleased at Will's message. 'He is helping me already.' Afterwards he said it was well known that, as with determination, knowledge of love can touch off a healing response in the one loved by what he now thought were electro-magnetic impulses, releasing chemical properties in the body.

So began a series of anxious days and nights spent monitoring Tisala's condition. He stayed in the inlet. He said he felt little pain when he was immobile, and so long as he only moved very gently. But I knew he was concentrating his mind, resting and willing himself to heal. When I asked him he said the healing properties are released by nature. 'Attitude influences recovery: an ancient form of antibiotics.'

Afterwards he told me what had happened. He had heard a boat coming from behind him, but it seemed to be on a course that would take it past him at some distance. He was off his guard. He was a long way south of any normal whaling waters. Moreover the ban on Blue Whale hunting had been firmly in place in the North Atlantic for a number of years and the only danger had been rogue whaling ships technically hunting other species a thousand miles further north. No Blue Whale had been killed in the North Atlantic for several years. So when the boat had come quite near he thought it coincidental and was unprepared for any attack. Too late he heard the engines change and saw the activated whaler and the bow harpoon gun manned. As they fired, he twisted and plunged to the right but felt the searing slice of the harpoon head as it snaked past him. Mercifully the glancing impact did not detonate the warhead. His great bulk plunged straight into a deep vertical dive.

Whether it was the sight of his colossal flukes and the realisation that they had fired at a Blue Whale, or some other factor, he did not know, but when he surfaced again ten minutes later the whaler was a mile away and did not appear to be in pursuit. He exhaled very slowly and gently so as not to make a spout and dived again more shallowly without raising his flukes above the water, changing direction as he did so and dreading to hear the engines of a kill-intent whaler bearing down on him. But each time it was further off. Eventually he began to believe they would not come after him. Then, after the adrenalin rush of survival reaction, the pain of his wound began to assert itself. He knew his vital organs had not been hit, and the harpoon had missed his wing so he could swim. But it had raked across the top of his flank and he realised the wound was long and dangerous and that blood must be streaming from it. He did not know if he had been fatally wounded, but decided to head for the shelter of Inis Cuan, and help. How the second wound had been inflicted remained unclear – perhaps a sideways gouge of the massive harpoon.

As I watched the great whale lying horribly injured in the water I felt bitter dismay, and anger against the whalers. This magnificent being had survived all the years of slaughter and genocide inflicted on his family and the whole Blue Whale population, but now had received a possibly fatal wound from the illegal greed of one small whaling vessel. And this was the summer when the International Whaling Commission had finally passed a resolution for a complete moratorium on commercial whaling.

Although the Blues were already supposed to be fully protected, it marked a great shift in the perception of whaling as a whole, and held out hope of a longer term cessation of this cruel ecological disaster. But within weeks of that advance, this: Tisala's ruin and near destruction. If he died his death would be through the cruelty and ignorance of men; the cutting down of a precious life, a unique ambassador to a better world.

The next morning I inspected his wounds from the boat, fearing to find signs of infection, but the wounds remained clean, although I could not see the lower one very clearly through the water.

Will arrived at the shack that afternoon. Slightly to my surprise he came alone. Susannah had come across to Inis Cuan with him but had taken the boat back leaving him to walk over the island to the inlet. 'She thought she should stay with Guinevere, and didn't want to be in the way here.'

I felt a pulse of disappointment. 'She could've come – didn't you – '

'They'll come the day after tomorrow.' He was much more immediately concerned with Tisala. They spoke over the equipment, Will probing how he felt. He could do nothing, but his presence and words seemed to me somehow to increase Tisala's prospects of survival. There was something reassuring in Will's youthful expectation and urging of recovery.

He wanted to inspect the wounds. He had brought his wet suit over, and climbed into it.

We paddled the boat gently out to Tisala. When we came up

against his flank I could see Will's dismay at the extent of the great slash – he exclaimed quietly. He ran his hand gently alongside Tisala's wounded side as if his touch would help him. He dropped into the water, face mask on, to inspect the lower end of the great cut and the smaller wound below it. He surfaced at the side of the boat. 'I think it's okay.' He scrambled back in. I patted Tisala's side as if to indicate encouragement. When we had returned to the shack Will spoke to Tisala trying to muster reassurance, but his voice betrayed his disquiet.

Tisala said, 'You are very kind, Will.' Then, quite clearly, 'I am not going to die. This is not yet my time.' Will and I looked at each other and Will smiled. It was as if other things were moving in the world.

That evening over supper Will wanted to know everything about the attack and what had followed. We spoke too of the future and for the first time about what would happen to our knowledge and what was to be done if Tisala died.

And eventually we got onto other things.

'How do you find Susannah?'

'She's great. We get on really well.' She'd asked him about Angela, and he'd said that he sort of loved her. It became clear that Will had ceased to think of Susannah, to whatever extent he ever had, in a romantic light. I felt a strange feeling, the turning of events, familiar but new, like watching the sun coming up on a summer's morning.

'She's still got a boyfriend too.' Silence, and a long chill returning.

'How do you know?'

'She told me. They had a semi split-up a few months ago but I think it's back on.'

So when Guinevere and Susannah came over again a shift had occurred. I found her more beautiful than ever, but now as I allowed myself to dare to want her, to love her, my initial sense of release became uncertainty and an enhanced fear of rejection. But it mingled with a growing sense of it being right, despite the odds.

Outwardly little had changed. But there was a new lightness on Inis Cuan now that we believed Tisala would recover. Susannah said admiring but teasing things about me as a surgeon. Guinevere said we had both done a wonderful job but it was early days, too early to be sure. There was caution, but pleasure and warmth.

About two days later when Guinevere and Susannah came over

for another visit, and only a week after the surgery on Tisala, there were clear signs of the wounds healing, and still no visible signs of infection, to my immense relief. The wounds were raw-looking but the irregular line of congealed blood looked black and clean. The big wound had held together along its entire length. Tisala had begun to change his position in the inlet almost as if he were restless at his enforced inactivity. He said as much in answer to my question. I took it as a good sign.

Day by day my spirits began to rise. Will's seriousness began to lift. The sense of tension slowly relaxing was reflected in the tone of our conversation and the return of laughter. As Tisala began to recover he insisted that we begin work again. His active mind was not content to wait further on his bodily repairs.

But when Susannah and Guinevere came over again they brought an unwelcome telephone message for Will. Angela's grandfather had died. The funeral would take place in four days time. Will said at once he thought he should go. But I could sense his dilemma. He fiercely wanted to stay with Tisala, and he loved being up in the islands with Guinevere. But here was a call.

'How well did you know him?' I asked.

'Not that well, but Angela was very fond of him.' And that was it; he wanted to be with her. The 'sort of love' was perhaps stronger than he knew and drawing him towards a new family. I said there was not much more he could physically do for Tisala at present; healing time was what was required. He made me promise if he went, to let him know immediately of any deterioration. He could come up again after the funeral. But we knew the university term was due to start in a fortnight or so, and the chances were that he would not be back. He would be sorry not to see more of Guinevere and Susannah, but he was more concerned about not being there to help me with Tisala.

Will spoke at some length to Tisala before reluctantly packing his rucksack. He left for Eilean Mòr with Guinevere and Susannah to start his journey south. I always loved having Will with me on the island, and more so in some ways each year. Normally I would have been very disappointed by his early departure. But now I found myself almost secretly pleased, for I knew that Susannah's departure was only two weeks away. Two short weeks.

But only a few days later, when Susannah had come over on her own, I had other issues on my mind. Tisala's healing was such that after consultation with him I had decided to remove the rope. I was initially apprehensive as to whether without that binding the healing would hold together with just the fishing line stitching. But I was also concerned that the tissue should not heal around the rope beginning to incorporate it, like barbed wire on a tree trunk, so that removal might tear away the re-forming tissue and reopen the wound. The tight loops around his body were also beginning to chafe and hurt Tisala, impeding his assessment of movement. He thought the rope had done its job.

So when Susannah arrived, after brief discussions, she was plunged into the next stage of the operation. We took the boat out, and came gently alongside Tisala, Susannah holding the boat up against his wing, between his wing and flank. He rolled a few degrees. With some difficulty and the help of a penknife spike I undid the end of the tight wet rope and lifted it carefully where it first passed over the wound. It came away cleanly, leaving a little livid scar. I threw the rope end over the top of him, pulling it in through the water under him. In removing the second loop, some skin came away and a little ooze of blood appeared. I cursed, but it was very slight and I was not much concerned. Susannah was watching anxiously. I shook my head, 'It'll be okay.' We repeated the unwinding. The last loop came away cleanly and I threw it over the top of him and pulled it in. I patted Tisala three times, and Susannah manoeuvred the boat carefully away a few feet where he could see us. We watched Tisala make careful small flexing movements, lifting his left wing gently two or three times. I went into the water to inspect. Through my mask I could see the great wound. It was holding along its whole length. I felt a kick of exhilaration and on surfacing called out to him that it was good.

Afterwards, back on the equipment in the shack, I reported with cautious optimism to Tisala. He was pleased and thankful to be free of the rope but said the wound must be given more time – another week or longer – before he tried any greater or more testing movements.

So then Susannah and I had time together. Her visits without Guinevere continued, but she returned to her each evening. And though she now came on her own and seemed to want to, she insisted that the work with Tisala went on, and remained reserved as I went about the daily routines. Tisala and I had begun to resume our discussions. She joined us, listening intently, and gradually became engaged with questions and observations.

In between, in our own time, sitting on the rocks, or walking, or over meals, we spoke of Guinevere and families and things here on the island, in London and Vancouver. We spoke of her views and mine on a scattering but increasing range of topics. I began to hope it was exploratory on her side, as it was on mine. One day she agreed that next time she would stay a couple of nights, 'to save the journey and be more helpful'. I treasured the days when Susannah was with me. On the nights she stayed, as before, we slept in separate rooms. This close apartness only intensified my growing feelings, but I hesitated to show them. And hers were hard to read.

Yet in one field she seemed to allow herself to become closer: in the care of Tisala. She was as anxious for him as I was myself, and in this common bond we grew towards each other. And when she took the fishing-line stitches out of Tisala she was the chief nurse, and I the assistant. In the days before we did this, Tisala had slowly increased his movements, including some partial rolling and swimming gently round the inlet. He reported that he felt sore and tender, but otherwise good. My further inspections confirmed continued healing along the scar tissue.

Three and a half weeks after we had put in the stitches we clambered again from the boat onto Tisala's wing. He rolled a little to bring the line of the wounds onto the surface and we crawled onto his flank, avoiding the wounds. Susannah knelt and set to work. She cut and snipped with close attention, occasionally saying, 'Pull that bit through,' or 'hold that' or 'pass me some sphagnum moss.' As before we had a bag of this ready to dab in the open points of bleeding. She worked as gently as if she were tending a slash in the side of her own child. And in my love for her I thought that her breathing on his flank was like the breath of a healing angel. My stitching was irregular, zigzagging, and sometimes doubling over, and occasionally knotted – done in crisis and with little thought for eventual removal. The tear by the rope had congealed and formed a new scab. Length by length, she drew out the line. It took her an hour of careful work. But eventually it was done and only occasional tiny pin pricks of blood to show for it.

After that, day by day Tisala grew stronger. He said he felt as if his freedom was becoming his own again. Within a week he took himself cautiously out to sea, and after another week he was exercising daily. He said he used the exhilarating experience to build his recovery further. In between times we continued our work. He was anxious to return to it. His near-escape seemed to add a sense of urgency, although he always proceeded calmly.

But the time came when we began to think of his winter migration. He said he would make the southerly winter journey slowly, and stay in the intermediate wintering waters, so as to avoid the traditional longer migration. He was conscious that he had lost an important part of his strength and knew he must conserve his reserves over the winter, and for the long journey north next spring, for he would eat little until the following Arctic summer.

Wonderful though Tisala's recovery was, each day also brought nearer the departure first of Susannah and then Tisala himself. Each day my underlying agitation increased. I knew we were at an important phase of work, but found it hard to keep at it, both when Susannah was with us and when she was over on Eilean Mòr with Guinevere. In a few days she would be flying back to her life in Vancouver. I did not tell Tisala of my feelings for Susannah, but I think he picked it up from things said and the inflection in my voice when she was mentioned. He became additionally kind and considerate towards her, and openly showed his own affection for her.

On the last visit before her departure she came with Guinevere. I guessed with a sinking feeling that she did not want to be on her own with me. But she seemed keen to come over always insisting that they must not interfere with the ongoing work. I was left in a state of unhappy doubt and puzzlement. Although there were signs of fondness for me I was afraid she believed her future life lay back home in Canada, and I became more reserved in my attitude towards her.

But when she said farewell to Tisala, she became upset and tearful, and she let me hold her close against me before recovering herself. On the day she left I went over to Eilean Mòr. When we said our own goodbyes I was aware of emotion on both sides, but we mostly confined our words to exchanges of goodwill and relief at the outcome of Tisala's ordeal, and for me gratitude and thanks for all her help. We agreed to stay in touch, and I hugged her closely, but felt a strong sense of impending loss.

Guinevere said afterwards, 'She's a lovely girl, David. My granddaughter Susannah.' She said it with fond pride, but I looked at her and felt an outsider.

Two days later I felt torn again, bidding godspeed to Tisala.

'Go very carefully, and look after yourself.'

'I will, so far as I can. And you too.'

But when he swam slowly down the inlet, I didn't know if I would ever see him again, and felt bereft and alone standing on the shore.

CHAPTER 54

London, 1983 and Ethics

Down in London, I waited anxiously for Tisala's migratory return. As I looked through the window at the winter scene, the springtime tilt of the Earth, releasing the annual wonder of warmth and light to the northern hemisphere, seemed an age away. Perhaps it was the heavy cloud cover, and the cold that year, but I fretted at it impatiently and waited anxiously for the return of light and life, and with them, Tisala.

People say London is a wonderful city, full of the glories of mankind, but that year it seemed increasingly unreal. I became oppressed by its great mass, bound up in its complicated daily routines and myriads of idle practicalities, its corolla of depressed run-down areas rising and falling with the building and decay of bricks, and beyond that the endless miles of suburbs stretching out, creeping across the land. My early admiration of the engineering wonder and advance of its railway systems now seemed part of its decay. The graffiti was on the walls.

And beyond in the distant sea I thought of Tisala's mind moving in the wider context of the future of man on Earth as our beautiful planet swept silently through space, on its great ellipse round the sun. I knew he would try to return early, for even if his healing had continued without relapse, the whole episode of his terrible wounds would have taken its physical toll. He would need to return to the Arctic feeding grounds to replenish his strength as soon as he could. Always I felt the nagging fear: had he suffered delayed trauma, or succumbed to infection, and was the long migration a great burden – perhaps too great a burden – on such a whale, now approaching sixty years of age?

I had wanted to fly south to rendezvous in the warm Atlantic to check how he was, but he had dissuaded me. He would survive, or he would not, and such a visit would change nothing. He had said, 'It is kind of you to be anxious, but I should like you to think of other things, for much will depend on you.'

He wanted me to continue our work in the winter months and said that if I spent time and money travelling south I should be distracted and the work would not progress. He stressed the importance of the current state of our work. His mind was absolutely steady, but I glimpsed in his insistence his recognition of time pressing, as the waters closed behind his flukes each season. Besides, he said, to mollify me, he was not sure how far south he would go, or be able to, depending on the mending of his wounds; and he did not want to arrange a meeting which he might not keep – that would be a bad outcome: a long and wasted journey away from my family and work, and perhaps leaving me alarmed as to what had happened. It would be of no benefit to anyone.

So I spent the winter at home in London with Penny. Will was away at university. But Penny was studying for her 'A' levels. She was a good student and teenage rebelliousness now seemed to have passed. We enjoyed each other's company. We shared the domestic routines – I cooked most of the time, and she largely coped with the washing and ironing. She was turning from a pretty child into a beautiful young woman. In many things she reminded me of Ellie.

My part-time job at the museum continued. At that time I was working as part of a small team linking the evolutionary descent of Indian and African elephants. Doubtless, we added something to the sum of knowledge, but sometimes I fretted at the time expended and argued with my colleagues that we would do better to be actively concerned in ensuring that the dwindling number of both species should survive the onslaught of man. Conservation was a term now spoken of, yet everywhere I turned, the story of the whales seemed to some degree to be repeated. But I was pleased to have the job for the income, and enjoyed the company of my fellow biologists.

In between times I delved as much as I could into the subject and history of ethics, and related matters that Tisala had enquired about. During these researches I would envisage future conversations with him, trying to anticipate his questions. Then my mind often went south to the warm Atlantic of the lower latitudes, and I would see the great shape glittering in the sunlit waters of the Mid-Atlantic Ridge as he rested, and willed the strength of nature to heal his grievous wound. For that is what I wanted to believe.

However, as often, my mind travelled to Vancouver and saw

Susannah going about her life and work, and waiting for the spring when she might come over again. For that too was what I wanted to believe. But then I imagined her talking and laughing with the young men, and suppressed and partially denied the love growing within me – telling myself that it was foolishness, and the next I would hear would be of her engagement.

She had said she would like to hear from me and asked for reports of any news. So I had an excuse as well as a reason to write. I found in the whaling records one or two tales of remarkable recovery from harpoon wounds among whales which I relayed to Susannah with comments purporting to show a confidence not always felt. And sometimes in the hours before morning, a lurking fear of Tisala's death would wake and haunt me and I would lie in bed sleepless waiting for the daylight to release me. By day those fears could be banished.

So we began to write, and in our exchange of letters I found comfort and happiness. But they were not love letters. On my side I would not write one for I did not know she would consider such a thing, and feared that a declaration might result in the end of the relationship so delicately grown. And I preserved the secret hope that, if she were free and came again in spring, she might then find something to love in me, though I was twice her age. So I wrote of loving things – family incidences, Penny's growing up, Will's academic progress and of Tisala's love and aspirations for the world. And in our exchange of letters – for as the winter went on the letters became a steadier trickle – I looked for signs of what I dared to hope was a warmth and spontaneity that spoke of things unsaid.

Will came home in the Christmas holidays. He and Penny laughed and chatted and argued, forming a changing and more adult friendship. The unity of my family gave me great pleasure amongst the coming and going of friends, and our kitchen meals and discussions. We went to the theatre and a Christmas musical. Angela came and a girlfriend of Penny's. We spent Christmas Day with Susan and her family. Giles as always was a generous host, and though becoming pompous with the years and seniority in his firm, unendingly good-natured. The four cousins had become close friends, full of banter and the exchange of enthusiasms and worries, teenage minds darting everywhere accompanied by doubtful diction and teenage exclamations. Susan's Christmas dinner had echoes of our own childhood – little traditions

I remembered: always red and gold crackers, and the same old blue sauce boat garlanded with bay leaves.

I wondered how long such festivities have lit up the inside of winter homes, and how many past generations would recognise parts of the twelve days of Christmas, putting off the end of the festivities and the hard part of winter.

So arrived the new year, 1983. But for three more months we would not know if Tisala had survived his injuries. We waited and fervently hoped.

In the year before the attack on Tisala's life we had discussed mankind's attempts to evolve and apply moral codes by which to conduct and improve human life. Tisala said he saw in our histories many instances of the dissemination of good ideas followed by a pattern of success, often linked to the spread of good law, which, like the better religious values, made attempts to produce a basis of agreement and compliance with a moral code. But he saw too that periods of success were often followed by periods of decline, with law and religion used to oppress. He had followed the rise and fall of countries, empires, civilisations, religions and the flux of movement of different people across the continents. Yet, despite the swirling chaos of history and the common pattern of recurring collapse, he saw too there was always a residue – a legacy of ideas found good, admired, revised and passed on, to be built into a new society. Among religions, the nearest thing to the emergence of a world system of morals had come with Christianity in the West, Islam in the Middle East, and Buddhism in the East.

He had trawled too through the words and lives of the philosophers who have added thoughts and ideas to the morality of their times; and which have been absorbed in religion, law and conduct to the benefit and ethical advance of our societies.

He found much to admire in the two great legal systems produced in the western world, the Roman and the English, despite the cruelties and defects of their earlier days, for both have grown and spread into the modern world, and proved capable of reform and improvement. He thought it clear that without such systems our modern societies across the world could not be sustained.

But he thought the law on its own, even in moderate hands, would not be sufficient: 'For it is asked to deal with such a colossal range of wants in your complicated societies, that it's in danger of losing its ethical base. And in religion you have conspicuously failed to live up to the best standards, and have widely adopted worse. You have often failed your Gods or God, and now you are discovering anew, as many have done of past religions, that they have failed you. Are they not an extension of yourselves? Do supernatural religions therefore offer a false hope? If you decide to live in the world without God, as many of you have, and more I think will, you will dispel that great shadow of the past. But you will urgently require a better code of ethics and a more complete consensus on conduct to live successfully together, if the wars and murderous dislocations of the twentieth century are not to be surpassed in the coming century.'

In looking for a new future, Tisala had said we should first look into our past, for much good ethical material is lying to hand. He thought the emergence of moral law – codes of conduct – among humans must have come about by slow accretion as such conduct was found advantageous or desirable. Much of the process seems lost in the past. But he was surprised that we appeared to know so little about it, or to care. Perhaps it was because if the moral code is believed to be God-given, we don't look further. The story of Moses – with the code handed down complete on tablets of stone dictated by God – which permeates Judaism, Christianity and Islam, precluded much curiosity. The moral code sprang fully formed out of the mouth of God, as interpreted by Moses and picked up by Mohammed.

But Tisala asked what really happened, and that involved me in much research over many months. The result was startling, at least to me. He expected that there would prove to be an intelligible history of ethics over at least the last 100,000 years of human development, but I found little that predated our relatively recent acquisition of writing. Even our early writing appears to be lost, except for some fragments on baked clay, or carved into stone. So it is only when we get to Sumer and Egypt, about 4,000 years ago that parts of the story emerge coherently. And only then by the chance rediscovery of a block of black diorite stone eight feet high and inscribed with 3,654 lines of writing in 44 columns, found by the French at Susa in Babylon in 1902. 'Only twenty odd years before my birth?' asked

Tisala, surprised.

'Yes, and it seems to be the first substantially complete moral and legal code of the human race to have survived.'

'If that is all you can offer me, let us look at that first.'

So I told Tisala of Hammurabi, a Semitic king who extended the old Babylonian Empire, running from the former Sumer near the Persian Gulf to include Iraq and much of modern Syria in the northwest. On his incised black column of stone the King depicts himself as receiving this, his moral and legal code, from the Sun God. Tisala said, 'No-one believes, I think, in that Sun God anymore, so we can ascribe the code to Hammurabi himself without causing upset or offence.'

Here was a detailed set of laws based on a moral code of what was right and wrong. Tisala questioned me closely on the date. I said it was more modern than originally thought. Hammurabi's reign, as now believed, is given as 1728–1686 BC. He promulgated his code of laws towards the end of his reign, when he had extended his empire. Here suddenly is a picture of a complete society in an advanced state of civilisation. Provision is made for central government and local administration, for professional men, priests, lawyers, doctors, businessmen, tradesman, artisans, farmers, brickmakers, builders, carpenters, tailors, merchants, boatmen and slaves. The well-to-do and the slaves are alike considered, regulated and protected. The rights and duties of officers and constables are laid out, and those of the Royal or public messengers, who ran a kind of postal system. Agriculture, rents, tithes, division of crops, the position of tenants and landlords are all carefully detailed; as in domestic affairs are marriage, divorce and adultery. Here the law of restitution is set out, and that of retaliation regulated and circumscribed. Here is the penalty of an eye for an eye, a tooth for a tooth. Here even is the injunction to rest on the seventh day. And here is a morality that would be repeated, sometimes almost line for line and word for word, when 500 years later Moses went up Mt. Sinai to be given his code of laws by the Hebrew God.

The penal code of Hammurabi is harsh. For violence and crime there is a long series of offences punishable by death, as are many non-violent crimes. But throughout there is a detailed attempt to balance the duties and rights of victims and perpetrators – to achieve in short 'justice' as then conceived. But Tisala said, 'It may look like ferocious justice, but what had gone before?' And he remarked that there had been plenty of regimes in modern times much less concerned with justice. He thought it clear that the code was built on precursor systems. 'You could not have the city states of Sumer and early Babylon – Ur, Agada, Lasa, Susa and Urak – existing as you have told me they did, like their Egyptian counterparts for 1,000 years and more before this time, without a moral code embedded in the rule of law.'

But in this code there is an advance. Tisala was intrigued by Hammurabi's preamble and conclusion to his code: 'I Hammurabi, the excellent prince, the worshipper of my God, decreed justice for the land, for witness, plaintiff and defendant; to destroy the wickedness of the strong and not to oppose the weak, and to give justice to the orphan and the widow. In my heart I carried the people like a real father. Like unto the Sun God, I promulgated. I established law and justice in the land and made happy the human race in those days.'

Then Tisala asked, 'And who were his people, whom he made happy?'

'A complicated mix of many amongst the Semitic tribes of the fertile crescent, who afterwards became Jews and Arabs.'

But Tisala was not content with this. 'Look at their languages, then and later,' he instructed, 'for that will tell us.' And the answer included Akkadian, Babylonian, Syrian, Hebrew, Moabite, Phoenician, Aramaic, Palestinian, Samaritan, Old Arabic, Punic, Modern Arabic and Israeli Hebrew.

Tisala said, 'You tell me some of these people became and are even now bitter enemies. Do they not know they are the same people? Your languages divide and promote exclusivity, which often breeds contempt and hate; but morals and laws should unite.'

He wanted to know what happened eventually. I gave him the information, but the synthesis was his. Though Hammurabi's Babylonian kingdom was eventually replaced by the Assyrian, the ideas he codified survived amongst the various people who lived and travelled in and around the fertile crescent; that area where man learned the arts and skills of civilisation, along the curving line of hills and mountains of western Asia that run now through the borders of Iran and Iraq, and Turkey and Syria in the north, curving away southwards to modern Lebanon, Palestine and Israel. These marked the limits of the rainfall, and therefore plenty, except below the hills in the easily travelled and well irrigated plains of the Tigris and Euphrates. But otherwise beyond lay the great deserts. Tisala said, 'You are telling me that the growth and sustaining of your ethics depended first on water, and perhaps not God.

'Perhaps now,' he said, 'the genesis of the Ten Commandments becomes clearer.' And he laid out the early history of the Jews, but not as I had previously heard Bible stories as a child – stories assumed to be of great but unspecified antiquity, coming out of a holy, majestic book before history existed, where one accepted readily that miracles and magic abounded, God sat on mountain tops and spoke out of thunder clouds and fire to individual men, and angels and demons were present and moved among the lives of men.

Tisala instead applied his mind to the historical facts, so far as I had been able to supply them. Over two years or more I had given him history, stories, myths and archaeological discoveries, and answered his questions, which often seemed random at the time. But it all came back from him in a unified understanding.

He said he sought to set out the truth as he had it so far, though doubtless further study would modify and improve understanding. New discoveries would be made, and he thought there must be material scattered already in repositories in the Middle East, or in the basements of museums and libraries, whose significance had been overlooked, or forgotten, and awaited an enlightened eye, and consolidation with the accumulated evidence of the past. He was intrigued by the possibilities of the tools of modern science, atomic dating and the whole new input of biological evidence which was then just becoming available through DNA.

The story he pieced together was this. The Hebrew tribes that later became the Jews absorbed the moral and legal advances of the Babylonian lands as they travelled through them as nomads; though being nomads they had little use for the detailed regulations of urban behaviour, and their adoption of these had to await nearly a thousand years. Their own tradition symbolises and personifies those travels in Abraham and his descendants, who lived after Hammurabi, in their journey from Ur near the Persian Gulf through Iraq, Syria and Southern Turkey over perhaps a period of a hundred years. They came round the Fertile Crescent, turning south from Haran and through what would become Lebanon and Israel – the land of the Canaanites, where the Babylonian influence of Hammurabi and his successors was widespread. To the south and east lay the deserts. After the land of Canaan the fertile land ran out. They had been through the best, but further to the south lay another best: Egypt. And so some of them went to the land of Goshen, in the Nile delta, where they lived among and mixed with the Hyksos, an earlier Semitic arrival, who had made good and came to rule that lower kingdom of Egypt. Here, in about 1600 BC, is set the biblical story of Joseph. Here the wandering tribes found the advantages of settlement. About 200 years later the Hyksos were expelled by the Egyptians, who re-established their earlier rule up the eastern Mediterranean coast. But the Hebrews of the biblical group stayed in Egypt for another 400 years, until the reign of an oppressive pharaoh, probably Rameses II, who built a new capital for himself in lower Egypt, in Piramesse in the Nile delta. At this point a leader called Moses arose among this group of Hebrews, who decided to re-emigrate back across the Sinai Desert to the land of the Canaanites, the nearest land of fertile promise. They regarded their departure from Egypt as a heroic escape. 'And as you humans do, they afterwards invested the story with supernatural and colourful deeds and happenings, with plagues from God, with parting seas and pillars of fire.'

But what interested Tisala was the moral code they had acquired and took with them. He questioned me closely on the date of Moses' exodus from Egypt. I reported that the scholarly consensus said about 1200 BC, five hundred years after Hammurabi's code. During the four hundred or so years the Hebrews had been in Egypt, they had held to the laws and morals they had brought with them from the old Babylonian kingdom. 'That they had done so probably means,' said Tisala, 'that, following the examples and influence of the Babylonians and the Egyptians, the Hebrews had by now evolved their own script; so their records had begun.' And they had begun too, to develop their earlier ideas of God. It seems they never adopted the pantheon of the Egyptian gods, but they did absorb the ideas of their times. He quoted the prayer of supplicants to Osiris, whose judgement the Egyptians had to pass on death before they could enter the fields of paradise; which were located somewhere vaguely beyond The Nile, or sometimes in the Milky Way: 'Behold, I did no evil thing. I did not do that which the God abominates. I allowed no one to hunger. I did not murder. I did not commit command to murder. I caused no man misery. I did not commit adultery. I did not diminish the food in the temples, or the grain in the weight of balances or divert the running irrigation waters.'

He noted that much is cast in the negative – the attitude is one of self-justification, and fear of offending Osiris and so being kept out of the heavenly fields. And the God's authority was wielded with both threats and tempting rewards for the hereafter, and not for virtue's own sake. 'And sadly,' said Tisala, 'these attitudes have reappeared with bad effect in the code later provided by Moses.'

He asked how many people left Egypt with Moses. But it seems that history is silent. Perhaps it was a few hundred, perhaps a thousand or two. I discovered that we know from the archaeology of scattered trade records and settlements that groups of Hebrews and other peoples often moved between Egypt and the lands to the north, and that this two-way traffic continued long after the group led by Moses had left Egypt. But Tisala thought this was nevertheless a small but historic movement, because of the influence, which the written record of it had in the world. He argued that Moses must quickly have seen, in the difficulties and fractiousness of their journey, that greater unity was required if they were to remain a unified and effective group of people. This is clear from the eventual later telling of the event in Exodus. So arose the first codifying of their morals and laws. As Hammurabi before him had used the Sun God to promulgate his code, Moses spoke of a powerful monotheistic development of the idea of God, to put forward a moral and legal code that such a God might be expected to hand down.

Tisala said: 'So God was formed in the image of the code. And because the code was often harsh, so too were made the characteristics of that God. Interpreted repressively, cruelty was to echo down three thousand years of religion, for Moses did not aim at the happiness of the people, but at their obedience. It was a retrograde mistake in the emergence of human morality. It was one Hammurabi had largely avoided, and seven hundred years later Confucius was to avoid, in his case by explicitly rejecting any supernatural elements in the conduct of human behaviour.'

But Moses wished first to establish the authority of God. For Moses was wise enough to know that people in superstitious times are ultimately more likely to believe in a thing if its authority derives from some all-powerful source, greater in the hierarchy of men's minds than a mere mortal; a lesson afterwards followed by Christ and later still by Mohammed. The first thing for Moses to do therefore was to promote God as all-powerful, which needs imaginative and dramatic input. Hence the miraculous events of leaving Egypt. So too in the deserts of Sinai God spoke to Moses alone through clouds and fire and thunder on the mountain top. It is recorded that the Hebrews cowered further off down the mountain, so none of them saw God or heard him speak, except for a few in a later version, but were willing to believe that Moses did. And that God with his finger burnt the Ten Commandments into tablets of stone and dictated, in direct quotation to Moses, long passages of the more detailed supporting laws that ran to several chapters of what eventually became the Scriptures. Tisala thought it remarkable that these transparent unlikelihoods were retained, initially through oral tradition, and then in earlier writings before emerging some three hundred years later in the book of Exodus in its present form.

In the Ten Commandments themselves Tisala noted first that although they contain some moral precepts they are presented as commandments – the demands of an all-powerful authority. The first three are negative prohibitions. They are used to establish and maintain the authority of Jehovah, and banish any rivals:

'You shall have no other Gods before me.'

'You shall not make any graven image or any likeness of anything that is in the heaven above or the Earth beneath.'

'You shall not take the name of the Lord your God in vain.'

And these commandments were accompanied by threats – God is made to say he 'will not hold him guiltless who takes his name in vain,' and the degree of punishment goes beyond that of a human legal code, where death is the ultimate sanction. Here, God is made to state that he is a jealous God visiting the iniquities of the father upon the children to the third and fourth generation.

'Where is justice, or the happiness of the people?' asked Tisala.

The fourth commandment reproduces the Babylonian provision of the seventh day for rest. In passing Tisala noticed that this reappears in Genesis, which scholars have found was written after Exodus; indeed, in its present form, long after. Then comes the only other positive command: 'Honour your father and mother' and here Tisala noted that threat is replaced by reward – 'so your days may be long'; though a sensitive soul could read threat into the implied alternative of short days.

The remaining five commandments are, once again, strongly negative prohibitions:

'You shall not kill.'

'You shall not commit adultery.'

'You shall not steal.'

'You shall not bear false witness.'

'You shall not covet your neighbours' possessions, including his wife and servants.'

Tisala said, 'So your ancestors were in such a raw state that the believed creator of the universe had either to threaten or bribe them to obtain obedience. It does not augur well for the behaviour of men on Earth.'

The fierce insistence of Moses on obedience to an unseen authority to hold his people together found an ominous echo eighteen hundred years later in Mohammed. So, to the already overwhelming power accorded to God was added the mentality of a military conqueror; a legacy, Tisala reminded me, that Muslim scholars have wrestled with ever since, and now, with modern firepower, have more urgently to solve.

Reverting to the Ten Commandments Tisala noted that there was nowhere here the injunction to 'love' God, or your neighbour. 'That as I understand it,' said Tisala, 'had to wait seven hundred years and two further developments.' The first was the telling of the Ten Commandments in Deuteronomy. About three hundred years after Moses, the form of Exodus was settled. Another three hundred years after that the present text of Deuteronomy was settled. Here the Ten Commandments were retold – largely unchanged, though with some glosses. But the chapters of Mosaic Law that followed had progressed. No longer were they regulations suitable for a nomadic people, but for urban dwellers of some civilisation. The harshness of the code largely remained, but here and there it was ameliorated by something more nearly of humane justice. And here was the commandment to love

God with all your heart, soul and might.

The second stage is recorded in Leviticus. This book, Tisala noted, has another complicated genesis, being an amalgamation of various earlier writings, but not gathered and collated in their present form until perhaps a hundred years after Deuteronomy. Much of its law is new and more priestly, often with strange social, sacrificial and ceremonial regulation; but is now a dead letter, except amongst its small persistent remnant of adherents. But what interested Tisala was its advance in moral teaching. In a reworking of the Ten Commandments, and among the negative injunctions, is found, although still put in the mouth of Moses and God, a duty of insistence on truthfulness, on justice and mercy, and of kindness to the poor and strangers, to the weak and slaves, and even to the 'lower' animals. Here was the command to love your neighbour, although the neighbour intended is clearly the local Hebrew neighbour, rather than any wider understanding. Many of the peoples, who the incoming Hebrews from Egypt under Moses' foreign successor, Joshua fought and sought to displace, were excluded from this concept of neighbourliness. And the people of Samaria, who were people transplanted from the Babylonian empire into Palestine and Israel, but separated from the Hebrews by language and religious differences, were accordingly looked down on and resented as interlopers. Another five hundred years were to pass before an Aramaic speaking Jewish teacher was to tell the story of the good Samaritan and through his followers, to universalise the concept of good neighbours; though the lesson ironically remains to be learned in the area where it started.

'You must think,' I said to Tisala, 'we are a pretty backward lot, to take seven hundred years to make a few advances.'

'You were ignorant, and your imaginations prey to fanciful creations. You were divided by language, territory, culture and conflicting superstitions. And unhappily it seems that many of you still are.'

What surprised him was that the Ten Commandments apparently continued to be regarded as the immutable word of God through so many subsequent centuries, for he thought they are manifestly inadequate as an enlightened exemplar of behaviour, not least because of the attitude attributed to God. 'Such,' he remarked, 'is the double-edged persuasion of faith.'

For what happened afterwards, he thought, was both better and worse. The ferocity of parts of the code of Hammurabi and Moses was ameliorated by developing Judaism, and more dramatically by the ethical teaching of Christ, elements of which were later adopted and newly applied by Mohammed. But ideas such as redemption and mercy were horribly tangled up in the later Jewish, Christian and Islamic ideas of eternal punishment in hell, which were an aberration flowing from the fatal religious insistence of obedience and submission to an authoritarian God.

What interested Tisala was that despite everything the religious peoples developed their moral and ethical codes, broadly improving them. 'You can say, as devout believers have always said, that this shows the wisdom of God percolating through to man. But if you ask why you need God in all this the answer is: only because your existing beliefs in God demand it. Otherwise you can conclude that the centuries of human living and experience led to the slowly improving ideas, which was elsewhere the case, as in classical Greece, in Confucian China and the Buddha's India.'

This was the state and direction of Tisala's discussions with me at the time he received his terrible wounds. I knew he regarded the development of higher ethics – how man may accept and live by the good – as a key to the future happiness and survival of the world; and that his exploration of our ethics was tantalisingly unfinished in his capacious mind.

As the time for his return to Inis Cuan approached my nagging fear for his wellbeing increased. My preparations to go back to the islands were haunted by forboding. I went up two weeks earlier than usual, anticipating his need for an earlier return to the feeding grounds to regain strength. I spent the first two days with Guinevere. The March weather was dull and cold, the tail end of winter. She knew I was keen to cross over to Inis Cuan, and insisted I should. Though I had jobs to do, each day seemed to drag and I found myself constantly gazing down the inlet. I tried not to think of days ominously passing. But the water of the inlet remained undisturbed.

On the fifth day looking out from the shack, I suddenly caught my breath. There – no – yes! – the black glint of his back in the water, and then the great shape coming slowly up the inlet. He had survived! I felt again the thrill, the burst of wonder, that surged out of months of suppressed anxiety.

We had long spoken with the words and tones of greatest friendship, but now there was an even greater affection in our reunion. He was tired and subdued, but was calm and rational. First, I inspected his wounds. They were wonderfully healed, though leaving hideous scars. Yet even they were beginning to fade down some of their length. But I noticed other changes. After the winter, when he had eaten little for six months, living off the replete blubber of the previous summer, he was as usual thinner. But this time I became aware that the streamlining effect had turned to a muscular atrophy. There were dimples and ripples in his skin, like a slightly deflated balloon, as if the great structure of sinews and vigour within had shrunk and diminished. He too was aware of his condition and knew he must not stay long but must make the journey to the Arctic feeding grounds. 'I will need to swim more slowly than usual,' he said, 'so I must not delay.'

Yet in the days that followed he turned his mind again to his self imposed task: exploring the phenomenon of man. And his mind seemed not to have been dimmed or affected by his terrible experience; on the contrary, his sense of logic and reason and his will to explore and construct seemed keener and more balanced than ever. I came to think afterwards that his escape from death only enhanced the concentration in his mind.

CHAPTER 55

On the Origin of Christianity

So after he had returned that spring, Tisala turned his attention to the origins of Christianity. I had spent much of my winter in London deep in books exploring this at his request.

The Christianity I had been brought up in, was presented as a single whole truth, one glorious story from Adam and Eve through parts of the Jewish Old Testament to the culmination of a detailed divine plan in the life and revelation of Jesus. But previously, when I had started to recount it like this to Tisala, he had stopped me. He wanted to know the sources and history of the writings that make up the patchwork of the New Testament.

Under his insistent questioning and my subsequent research over many months, I found a different story; found with difficulty because of my preconceived ideas, and the scale and intractability of the material. But gradually this different story took shape. I discovered too that scholars have widely known the thrust of this altered knowledge with increasing particularity over the last hundred years or so as biblical scholarship advanced. It takes a bold mind to upset the final word of God as taught in one's childhood and believed by the faithful of a whole culture. And although the history of the development of the New Testament was now much better known, it seemed at the time that the knowledge revealed had not been unified, or new conclusions drawn.

Tisala once said 'Out of Moses came forth Jesus.' All was not sweetness. Amid the bold ethical advances in Jesus' teaching he found also a pervasive dark side to his teaching with the old recurring threat of judgement and eternal punishment and the demand for exclusive obedience, some of which led to terrible events across history, and which for a very long time held sway within his churches; and in some quarters still does. Tisala observed that it was to the credit of Christianity that most of the churches eventually developed the teaching of the more advanced ethics put forward by Jesus, although these ethics were themselves subservient to the main thrust of Christ's own teaching about the Kingdom as recorded in the four gospels. And he found that Christians had the same problem as the Muslims after them – the word of God (which therefore had to be believed) was trapped in the form given to it at a time of superstitious beliefs and uninformed thinking.

Tisala found that a reading of the earliest gospel, Mark, unencumbered by images and stories in the later gospels, shows Jesus as a man driven by reforming zeal against the Jewish religious establishment, especially the Pharisees and the scribes (lawyers), whose religion had become all ceremony, and where the observance of detailed letter of the law had overcome its original purpose, often hypocritically. In Jesus' eyes they were misleading God's people. Tisala thought it ironic that the Pharisees were so heavily criticised, for it was they who believed in the already existing idea of resurrection at the last judgement, while the Sadducees, who were much less criticised by Jesus, held that belief in any afterlife and in angels was wholly untrue.

Tisala was interested that for Jesus 'the enemy' was the Jewish establishment, whom he found corrupt, and that he hardly mentions or criticised the Roman occupiers, at least before his trial by Pilate. Indeed, Jesus praises a faithful centurion, and teaches that Caesar should be paid what is due to him. He thought the explanation lay in Jesus' own religion, which he found was not at all Christianity as it afterwards became. He believed in the Kingdom of God on Earth, that the initial stages would come about by reforming the Jewish religion to promote better behaviour and that this would take place within and under the rule of Rome, for the Romans did not interfere much with the practice of Jewish religion. And that, in the coming of the final Kingdom of God, which he believed was imminent, and its accompanying judgement, all wielders of temporal power would in addition to becoming irrelevant be judged and found wanting. So Jesus had no interest in opposing or overthrowing the Romans; which disappointed many Jews, who awaited a Messiah who would restore both the temporal and spiritual power of the now mythical golden age of David and Solomon.

Instead Jesus sought reform by doing good and demanding that people should behave better – here he had radical improving ideas

– and that this practical 'repentance' would usher in the Kingdom of God on Earth, and was beginning to do so. But his demands for reform were backed up repeatedly with the same ferocious and often repeated Mosaic threats of doom for backsliders, and the promise of reward in heaven for 'believers'; though what his hearers believed in was necessarily different from the 'belief' eventually constructed for Christianity. During the three years of Jesus' ministry time was short, for he and his followers believed that theirs was the last generation and then would follow an apocalyptic day of judgement when the majority – 'the non-believers' – would be sent to hell and everlasting torment. 'How,' asked Tisala, 'can such beliefs be attributed to an all-loving God?'

He explained further. Mark's gospel is historically the earliest and closest to Jesus of the existing gospels, though it is clear there were earlier oral and written stories, now lost. Mark's viewpoint is that of an intelligent, naturally devout, but otherwise straightforward mind. This supports the scholarly consensus that the author was John Mark, Peter's assistant, who wrote down the stories he heard from Peter when he was in Rome towards the end of Peter's life (about 65 AD), and when John Mark recognised that the living link of Peter with Jesus would soon be gone. Here is set out the simple belief that Jesus would bring in 'the Kingdom of God,' promised from Old Testament days. This was to be done by cleansing the Jewish law – hence the barrage of criticism against its keepers, the Pharisees and the scribes. Hence also the great importance of repentances and the healing miracles in this book as a demonstration of the new kingdom. Illness was then seen almost exclusively as a result of evil – the work of demons which should be cast out, which Jesus in these stories repeatedly did. The modern knowledge that disease and deformity is caused by biologically aggressive bacteria, viruses and genetic defects, was nowhere understood, and not at all by Jesus or his followers.

Tisala was initially puzzled however by the absence of almost the whole of Jesus' ethical teaching from Mark's gospel – there is he noted hardly anything of the moral precepts and the Sermon on the Mount of the later gospels. He concluded that the original disciples, led by Peter, were so bound up with the idea of the imminent coming of the final kingdom that mere reform by good behaviour was a matter of less importance than of telling and recording the stories of miraculous healings by casting out of devils as 'proof' of the coming Kingdom.

He came to the view that the truth glimpsed in this early gospel had become obscured and overlaid by the later supernatural myths. And Tisala noted that the other synoptic gospels (those dealing with the narrative of Jesus' life) were written later – Luke's gospel in around 75 AD and Matthew's in about 85 AD – over half a century after Jesus' death. The time lag, it appeared, made a decisive difference. Luke extensively draws on Mark, and about half of Matthew is taken directly from Mark. Yet both gospels are quite different from Mark, and are filled out with material from unknown sources, both oral and written, and display a wholly different mindset.

Tisala knew that by the time these two gospels were written the expected coming of the Kingdom in the first generation's lifetime had not after all occurred. Both Jesus and his original followers had been mistaken. The imminent end and Judgement Day of earliest belief and certainty had not happened. So belief slips away from the idea of the Kingdom of God on Earth as envisaged in Mark's gospel and transfers the expectation in these two new gospels to the future 'Kingdom of God in Heaven'. By the time of Matthew, this shift, and accordingly the aim of the Christian writers, had altered. There was to be a waiting period before the Kingdom of Heaven arrived. Therefore, in the meantime, they must prepare for the second coming; and that involved repentance by reformed behaviour. The emphasis had changed, and Jesus' ethical teaching acquired a new emphasis. So here, in Luke and Matthew, are found for the first time fifty or more years after Jesus' death the beatitudes (blessings), though they are a strange comfort for the weak and the oppressed (only making sense in the context of the coming heavenly kingdom). And, much more importantly therefore, here for the first time are the Sermons in the Plain and on the Mount, which scholars agree are a compilation and summary of ethical teachings attributed to Jesus. It was these advances in moral teachings that Tisala found the most compelling in the whole Christian story. And much else obscured them.

Thus he noted other important changes of aim in these two gospels. The original portrait of Jesus in Peter's recollection, written down in John Mark's gospel, clearly shows that he was initially regarded (and regarded himself) as having the credentials of a Rabbi teacher, a devout Jew, 'a son of God' and something of a moral prophet, a bringer of better things, 'a son of man'. The phrase was taken up by Jesus to refer to himself. It came from the Book of Daniel: 'One like a son of man came with the clouds of heaven'. This book had been written at a time of Jewish persecution less than 200 years previously, when the Jews were looking for a national saviour. In terms of scriptural writing it was modern. The Jews were waiting for something to happen. It was an obvious choice of title for Jesus to take, and he apparently used it very extensively of himself: it occurs eighty times in the Gospels.

Only as Christianity evolved was it considered that these appellations were not enough. The first additional idea was that of the 'Messiah' expected by some Jewish beliefs. Their idea of the 'Messiah', 'the Christ', was mainly one of a temporal great king who would restore the kingdom and banish foreigners. For the little golden age of David and Solomon, much magnified in the Jewish imagination by its loss, had fallen apart into two warring mini-kingdoms of Israel and Judah after the death of Solomon. It had never, in the nine hundred years before Jesus' time, been reunited. And in the meantime, both kingdoms had repeatedly been conquered and resettled by different peoples, the Egyptians, the Babylonians, the Assyrians, the Sumerians, the Persians and now the Romans. That is why some Jews looked to Jesus to overthrow the Romans, and were disappointed by his lack of any such intention. Over the previous centuries various candidate kings for Messiahship, including Hezekiah and Judas Maccabaeus, were hailed, but had all failed. None had been able to unite the qualities of prophet and man of God with those of successful temporal kingship. The idea of Messiahship was at Jesus' time still hedged about with these Jewish limitations on the idea.

And that is where it might have ended. Tisala observed that Mark's gospel – Peter's account – originally ends without Peter, or anyone else, having *seen* Jesus risen from the dead. There is only a message from a 'young man' sitting in the tomb that Jesus has risen and will go to Galilee before Peter and the others and meet them there. And the events of the very early church after Jesus' death show that, in the hands of Peter and the Jerusalem Christians alone, Jesus' ministry would probably have resulted in no more than a reformed sect of the Jewish religion. It was clear that Jesus was to be no temporal king. The whole idea of the Christian 'Messiah' was invented later and differently.

Tisala was intrigued how the spreading belief that Christ had risen from the dead changed everything. The first evidence of this is in Paul's writings, and in the glosses tacked onto the end of Mark's gospel some years later by an unknown author. By the time of the gospels of Luke and Matthew the aim of the scripture writers was to 'prove' Jesus' credentials as 'the Messiah' – now seen as a solely spiritual leader whose kingdom was the Kingdom of God in heaven. It was a huge leap from the historical Jesus. These gospels, Luke's perhaps written in Greece and Matthew's written in the Romano-Greek city of Ephesus, were heavily influenced by Paul's development of Christianity as a new and quite different religion. The missionary work of Paul and others had by now been stretched out into the gentile world of the Roman Empire of the eastern half of the Mediterranean. And Jesus was being universalised as a spiritual Messiah, 'the Christ', 'the' Son of God. And more than that, God himself was being universalised – revealed not only as the God of the Jews but 'the God of all mankind'. As part of the establishment of the credentials of this newly enhanced version of Jesus as 'the Christ' in the gospels of Luke and Matthew there appear, for the first time, the miraculous birth stories of Jesus.

I asked Tisala, 'Are you saying these were a deliberate fabrication?'

'We do not need to think that.'

He thought it clear that the climate of widespread belief in spirits, which later ages might call gullibility, provides the background. But he thought we have to ask why these stories did not appear earlier. They are not referred to in any of the earlier writings – Mark's gospel, and Paul's many epistles, are completely silent. Nor are they referred to by Jesus anywhere – in the whole of the New Testament there is no suggestion that Jesus ever mentioned or even knew about these stories of his own birth.

Tisala concluded that the miraculous birth stories of Jesus, like many other examples of stories embedded in mankind's religions, were an imaginative overreach; but the result was falsification. 'Stars stopping over stables, and angels ascending and descending from the heavens: only people ignorant of any understanding of astronomy could write, and believe, such things. Now it has to be explained by scholars as metaphorical, in other words, symbolic fiction.'

Tisala asked, 'What is the origin of these stories? Is not the obvious source of the birth stories, Mary, Jesus' mother, the only person present throughout?

'It is speculation' he continued, 'but the non-appearance of any of the birth stories until Luke's gospel in about 75-80 AD – about fifty years after Jesus' death – probably means that they did not exist until after the death of Jesus. After his death, amid the excitement of the disciples and Jesus' circle over the believed resurrection, very likely they would cast around for early signs of Jesus' extraordinary qualifications.'

I said, 'You mean they would consult Mary, and she, turning over her reflections on her son's apparent transformation might have said that he was a child from God? And not wishing to be more specific, or admit any pre-marriage liaison, might have said that an angel visited her. For if we say virgin births are impossible, we have to account for the actual birth some other way.'

'Something like that beginning is likely to be true,' said Tisala. 'I understand that virgin birth stories had wide existing currency in those times, and that there are other examples of virgin birth stories before this one.'

So, perhaps spread by the enthusiasm of the disciples and developing groups of believers, including the gospel writers and evangelists, the stories began to circulate, and as they do among humans became enlarged and embroidered over perhaps a thirty or forty year period. Quite long enough for the material to emerge as the fully-fledged miraculous birth stories eventually written down by Luke and Matthew.

'And I suppose', I said, 'some time during the period before the appearance of these birth story gospels, Mary almost certainly died. If we assume she was say, twenty – nearly a teenage mum – at the time of Jesus' birth in about 5 BC (the original dates are known to be wrong by five or six years), she would have been a hundred years old when Luke's gospel was written. We do not know when she died, but it is much more likely that she died twenty or thirty years before this, and so could not contradict the increasingly elaborate birth stories that emerged in Luke. And Matthew of course was ten years after that. So the stories passed unchallenged into the scriptures.'

Tisala thought it interesting that there are other stories that may have also come from Mary, again probably after Jesus' death. And they similarly only emerge much later: he cited the story of the twelve-year-old Jesus in the temple at Jerusalem. This is found only in Luke's gospel, and as he remarked, is told from Mary and Joseph's point of view – Jesus was missing, and they went looking for him. So probably the story did not come from Jesus himself, and again there is no indication anywhere that he mentioned or even remembered the incident. Likewise in the story of the first miracle, turning the water into wine at Cana. Mary is the essential witness. But this story appears in none of the earlier writing, and not even in Luke and Matthew, but only about seventy years after the event – about two generations after Jesus' death, during the period of his growing glorification by the early Christians – in the gospel of St. John.

So too the only miracle attributed to Jesus after his death, the miracle of the draught of fishes, which enlarges the resurrection story. And though Peter is at the centre of the incident it does not appear in Peter's account – Mark's gospel – not even in the later addendum to it – nor anywhere in Paul, nor even in Luke or Matthew; but only years later in John's gospel. And who was John? We do not know. Nobody knows. Christian scholars widely agree that, writing his Gospel two generations later, he could not be the apostle John, but they have never yet been able to discover who he was. Yet much Christian theology and many of the most famous passages purporting to be Christ's own speech are found exclusively in his Gospel. And I came to realise many of these things only because of Tisala's patient questioning.

When considering St. John's gospel, Tisala observed that none of the birth stories of Jesus appear in it, though it was written later than either Luke or Matthew. The reason, he thought was that by then the miraculous and supernatural had already permeated Christian thinking and did not need repeating. This text instead amply demonstrates that John was fixed on the vision of Jesus as 'the' Son of God and the saviour of the world, and on the way to becoming God himself. He noted also that John had little to say about the ethics of Jesus – the Sermon on the Mount and such teaching is missing from his scheme, though so too is much of the earlier hell-fire teaching. In its place is the detailed sacrificial coming of the holy spirit. Tisala observed that this is put in the mouth of Jesus over no less than three chapters of direct quotation, again purporting to be Christ's own speech, at the last supper, expressed in words sometimes of Paul-like convolution, and indeed written in the shadow of Paul's writings.

Hardly a word of it appears in Mark, Luke or Matthew, though they had all earlier recounted the last supper itself.

In the fifty years from Paul's missions to the writing of St. John's gospel all is changed: a new religion is forged, another uniquely true religion; and though it is undoubtedly correct that the new religion tried to improve the behaviour of men, in the hands of authority it was to be enforced by many a war over two thousand years.

Tisala sighed, 'You see how much baggage there is accompanying Jesus' ethics – his basic call for a change in human hearts.'

And that, he remarked, is before you consider such texts as the Book of Revelation, where the imaginative but lurid concepts of heaven and hell are developed in a bizarre treatise, whose authority and value was long argued over by the early Christians; and which in a more rational world Tisala thought would never have been admitted to the canon of holy scripture.

I said, 'You mean it sent Christianity further in the wrong direction?'

'The imaginations of men were bent towards holy superstition.'

And I saw the history of the Christian churches dressed in fantastic clothes both intellectually and literally, symbolised by Revelation's throne of God, a throne echoed down the ages by those – the cathedrae – of the bishops, who built great churches round them, all to the greater glory of God; though incidentally the robed and bejewelled prelates were mightily elevated.

Yet it is now widely accepted by many Christian scholars that the Book of Revelation is more symbolic fiction, and like the birth stories and miracles, factually untrue. Yet all these were for nearly 2,000 years taught and believed as literal truth – gospel truth – and so sustained belief in Christianity. If taught literally, they have become unbelievable, except to entranced believers cocooned within the story itself. That is why Muslims and those of other non-Christian religions do not believe in the miraculous birth story of Jesus, nor in what that belief helped to support: that Jesus, a first century Aramaic Jew, was by all the signs and wonders marked out as 'the' Son of God, and eventually revealed to be God himself. They say such beliefs are simply mistaken.

'But similarly,' said Tisala 'I understand that Christians and other non-Muslim religions see at once that miraculous stories from Islam, if taken literally, are also unbelievable.'

For there is a similar process in the strange and supernatural world of The Qur'an. He cited for instance the night flight of Mohammed to Jerusalem, which occurred, we are told by tradition, when Mohammed was about fifty, in the middle of his attempted reforms and military conquests. Like Moses in the Sinai Desert, struggling to hold together and discipline his groups of Hebrews, Mohammed was struggling to impose his will and thinking on the inhabitants of Mecca, the ruling Quyrash people, many of whom opposed him.

In the seventeenth Surah of the Qur'an, The Night Journey, are set out a re-telling and echo of the Ten Commandments and parts of the Mosaic Law, similarly backed up by threats of hell against non-believers. Moses enlisted God to his cause by going up the mountain to him, and coming back with the Ten Commandments and the detailed Law. Mohammed, more modestly, enlisted the help of all the major prophets of God for his endeavours. It is revealed in the sayings attributed to Mohammed that he was awoken and received a message from the Angel Gabriel, in the Qur'an known as Jibreel, and told to mount a winged mule-like creature and fly to the Temple of Solomon in Jerusalem. He did so and arrived at the site of the Temple, although the temple itself had been destroyed by then. There he met the prophets from earlier ages – Adam, Moses, Abraham, Isaac, Ishmael and Jesus. And here the Angel Gabriel asked him to choose wine or milk to drink. He chose milk, with long-term cultural consequences. Much more significantly, here he was confirmed as the last Prophet, who was being given the final words of God for mankind. No doubt emboldened and inspired by this he sought still higher authority. So the Angel Gabriel then carried him up in the sky and showed him the gates of heaven. Here he received the commands of God, Allah, that he and his followers must pray fifty times a day, every day. But Mohammed, having consulted with the other great law giver, Moses, begged Allah to reduce it to five times, which Allah in his mercy agreed. Mohammed descended from heaven and completed his night's journey by flying the 600 miles from Jerusalem back to Mecca on the winged animal.

Tisala enquired if this story, like its Christian counterparts, did not emerge for a number of years, and whether it was written down after Mohammed's death, he himself not being able to write. He thought it would be interesting to learn from Islamic scholars how soon this story emerged, and what use was made of it in promoting this new religion.

Meanwhile the historical Mohammed, over the following two years, cultivated converts and allies in the rival town of Medina before launching a successful war against the Quyrash for Mecca; and afterwards militarily extended his power and influence by further conquest in the wider Arab world. Tisala commented that faith does not spread by military conquest, for faith comes through the conquest of individual minds. But military conquest may of course facilitate the spread of faith, especially where the faith is not only a matter of private belief, but is a public religion much concerned with a whole way of life, embracing social laws and culture.

'But no wonder,' said Tisala, 'they built that beautiful Dome of the Rock Mosque on the site in Jerusalem.' He thought the placing of the Dome there was also a salute to the Jewish prophets, though the Jews have been slow to see it as such, for they seem blinded by territorial possessiveness.

Tisala enquired whether Muslims believed the story literally, or whether it was quoted as metaphoric, in other words purely symbolic; and if so what they think it symbolises. He remarked that, like the Christian stories, they seem to have used it to help secure belief in the Prophet; and even if their scholars accept, in the light of reason, that it is symbolic, in other words historically untrue, it is still used to support the beliefs that the story engendered.

By these enquiries Tisala shed what was for me new light on the religions of the world. I began to understand how, on the one hand, Christians had come to believe that Christ was 'the' Son of God, and therefore the only way to God; and how the Muslims had come to believe all that mistaken, and that Mohammed was the final arbiter of God's word; and how other religions formed their own exclusive beliefs.

'I suppose,' I said, 'you can go round it with all the ecumenical soft words you like, yet have to conclude that nothing can reconcile those incompatible beliefs. The strange thing is, they are all symbolic stories anyway.'

'You must reach your own conclusions,' said Tisala. 'The beliefs cannot be reconciled, but lives can be. You humans can constructively decide to let others live their own beliefs and you yours in peace together; which is a tolerance that your histories show has sometimes and for some periods been achieved, but is always likely to break down, too often in war. This is true not only between religions, but between different sects and divisions of the same religion.'

And he remarked that all these religious stories were worth nothing without the peaceful tolerance – goodwill and charity – of humans towards each other and their fellow creatures; which God, Allah and Jehovah in their more advanced projections would undoubtedly be found to agree with, for he thought they come from the minds of good men.

'It seems that all religions have brought much trouble with them, as we have seen from your histories – wars and killings, persecutions. A religion that pursues or allows those things proves itself deeply flawed, for such things should not happen in a more rational world.'

He found the direction of reform obvious. All men of goodwill, of all religions and none, should talk and agree, not on beliefs, which may be privately held, but on moral actions which are publicly undertaken. For then they must consider and apply higher ethics, which is the common link of all religions and enlightened human endeavour. The true task is to produce a universal ethic that all accept and live by, in peace with those who believe other creeds than their own.

And that universal ethic, even in his emaciated state, was what Tisala was working out in his mind that spring.

But that was not the only thing on his mind. When he had been at Inis Cuan a week he told me that he would leave in three days time, for he was to meet Tarba, his grandson, who was coming to escort him to the Arctic. I knew that Tisala was very fond of Tarba and regarded him highly. He was lively and intelligent.

'They all know what I am seeking to do and that it is important that I live a few years more. Tarba wishes to protect me.'

I said, 'How? What could he do?' But then I knew the answer. Put himself in danger to distract attention from Tisala.

'He would risk that?'

'I could not dissuade him, and his mother and the others would not. Now let us return to work.'

We did so, but I found myself very subdued, and in between times over the next two days I often thought of the brave young Blue Whale swimming just to the north of us.

'Is he your – ' I was going to say 'heir' but the word stuck. 'Would he ever come in here?'

'He has promised me he will do so, but only if I am killed before my time. He wishes to be what he is, a whale of the deep oceans. He will start his own family soon, and his chosen love awaits him. They plan to go to the southern ocean. There we are trying to rebuild our ruined society.'

I suddenly found myself asking, 'Tisala, will you find another wife yourself?'

'My task is here.' He paused, 'But you, David, are still young enough. And should do so.'

'You know – ?'

'Yes, I do.' He said no more, but somehow I knew at once he gave it his blessing.

Two days later I waved Tisala goodbye. As he moved slowly down the inlet I called after him, 'Look after yourself. Give Tarba my best wishes – and thank him.' Then as he moved away I prayed to myself, please look after yourselves and both of you keep safe.

I spent three days staying with Guinevere, doing various jobs. And in the evenings we talked about many things long into the night. Three days after that, back in London, I reserved a last-minute place on a biology conference in Vancouver, and, following a telephone call to Susannah, booked a flight.

CHAPTER 56

Vancouver

The conference was on various scientific aspects of the cetaceans, but the main focus was on whales, and I knew that representatives of the whaling industry would be attending. During the conference I put up at the Hotel Vancouver in the centre of the city. The sessions seemed to drag. There were introductory talks I did not need, which left me impatient. There were reports on research, but the findings seemed marginal, and sometimes were inaccurate. But I couldn't divulge to my fellow biologists what I already knew, and was confined to arguing, 'What if new evidence were one day to show...' There was little perceptive response or even the allowance of hypothetical speculation at all. Scientists could be very pedestrian, especially those whose research was funded by whaling interests.

But the whole atmosphere of the conference was radically different from earlier ones. The people with the light in their eyes were now the anti-whalers. Pro-whalers now found themselves in the minority, their aggressive confidence diminished and their defensiveness increased in a way that would have been quite absent a few years earlier. Their culpable indifference to the whaling genocide could no longer be maintained or excused. Awareness of their expulsion from the central consensus on whaling had shaken them, and they were left with what seemed increasingly peripheral arguments as to when and under what conditions whaling might be re-introduced after the moratorium.

On the second evening I left the conference, having been invited to Mary and Tom's home for the evening. Susannah's home. I found my heart beating like a student's as I walked across the open approach to the house and rang the door bell. Mary opened the door with Tom standing behind.

'Dav-id!' She opened her arms and we kissed. 'Come in – welcome!'
'Hello Tom.'

'Hi, David: good to see you.' He shook hands warmly.

'Grenville!' Mary called up the open stairway, 'David's here.' He came down.

'Hello Grenville, how are you doing?'

'Okay thanks David, nice to see you.'

But Susannah wasn't there.

'She'll be coming by later,' said Mary. 'She had a work assignment, but she's re-arranged.'

The bell rang again. Another couple arrived, and an attractive woman on her own.

'Meet our good friends, Gilbert and Rose-Mary, and this is Christobel.' Our names were repeated to each other in the North American manner.

'Rose-Mary, Gilbert, this is David. David, Christobel. Christobel, David.'

'How d'you do.'

'Hello.'

Then questions about my journey and visit.

'Yes, easy journey thank you. The conference? Yes – well, actually pretty boring really unless you're into it.'

'Fine hotel.'

'Yes, and convenient.'

And so introductory talk merged into visitor's talk. But underneath, for me, tension. Where is Susannah? All through drinks, where is Susannah?

Yet I was pleased by the anticipation of her coming, and in the meantime found myself enjoying my welcome and the home where she had lived. These were the people and furnishings and pictures that she had seen all her life. Here were the photographs, proudly framed and smiling – Susannah and her family – Susannah as a little girl, another as a high school graduate and the formal set piece of college graduation.

We sat at the table and started supper. Still no Susannah, but talk and laughter.

'I've come to see how you all live, and to explore Grenville's earthly paradise.'

'Do you like what you see so far?', asked Gilbert rhetorically. 'We are very proud of this city.'

'Well,' said Rose-Mary –

'Oh no, Honey, I'm not saying it's perfect but – ' and he launched into a eulogy.

'We'll take you on a drive tomorrow,' said Mary.

'You should see Stanley Park.' said Grenville, and various sights were discussed.

'I would like to show you our art gallery,' said Christobel, who was looking at me rather too much.

'You are very kind,' I said. But felt that things were slipping away from me, and declined two or three of the suggestions, claiming conference commitments. Escape, but half imprisoning myself.

And then she came. Unexpectedly, through the dark doorway, smiling. My beautiful Susannah.

There were greetings all round, and she took a place at the table. Mary dished her out a plate of food, and the talk went on.

I watched the light in her hair and the concentration in her face. Our eyes met, briefly, more than once in between the conversations, and for longer when she asked me about Guinevere and the island. Mary chimed in with anecdotes about her mother and Eric, and Susannah recounted impressions from her recent visit. I gave a veiled account of my work on the island, and then looking Susannah in the eyes said, 'Susannah was a great help on a biological matter that had run into grave difficulties – a wonderful help.'

She coloured slightly. 'I did what I could.'

Shamelessly I fended off supplementary questions from round the table.

'David goes up to the Hebrides twice a year,' explained Mary. 'Now that is a heavenly place.'

'If you forget the midges,' said Susannah smiling at me in mockery, 'and the rain.' But for a moment her eyes belied her words, as if she had really said, 'We know a place, an isle in the sea, where paradise is found.'

'The islands are lovely.' And I said my bit.

Gilbert came back on the theme of nature, riding in on the glories to be seen in the Canadian west – the forests, mountains and rivers. I imagined him in a canoe, wearing a red tartan lumber jacket, and a beaver-skin hat, too big, coming down over his forehead.

'Sounds wonderful.'

'Yes it surely is.'

'I shall have to come back and see it all.' I warmed to his enthusiasm. Friendship all round me, and happiness inside.

But the upshot was that with the conference (I did have some commitments), a tour of the city with Mary, Susannah and Grenville, and a sightseeing boat trip with Mary and Christobel (Susannah had to be at work), Susannah and I were not going to have much opportunity to speak on our own. The thought nagged me: perhaps she did not want to.

But I found out much about her Canadian life during our exchanges on the tour. We drove across the Lion Gate Bridge, high over the Burrand Inlet, the sea away to the left. In between sights and landmarks, we chatted – city life, Canadian attitudes, and work. When she spoke she was animated and involved. She clearly enjoyed her job, relating it to wider economic issues.

'Your father's influence?' I said.

'Dad? – yes.' She laughed.

Grenville said, 'She wants to become a top company director. Watch out, Mr Chairman!'

'That's what you know. Anyway, why not? I'd get you in order.'

But sometimes she seemed almost dismissive of her role at work, and the economic treadmill reality of a modern corporate career. And then her serious look descended on her.

We drove out beyond the city's residential area, and up into the mountains – 'The Coast Range,' Mary said – to a restaurant for lunch. There were fine views back to the city. At lunch part of the social fabric of their lives emerged, friends and activities were talked of, provincial politics and Captain Cook. It somehow pleased me that Captain Cook had turned up again. In 1778 the discoverer of Tisala's Antarctica, and half the oceanic world, had sailed up The Sound between the mainland and Vancouver Island. And somehow in my imagination Susannah and I were further linked like a prophecy. That's how it's done, I thought. Oh yes, 'Study prophecies when they are become history.' One of Cook's officers, Captain George Vancouver, who explored further up the coast, gave his name to the settlement city previously known as Grandville.

'I'm not sure where Grenville came in,' said Susannah, smiling sideways at Grenville. 'Spelling's always been a problem.'

Grenville's girlfriend took centre stage for half the desert course. To start with she sounded charming, but she wouldn't go away. And the clock kept on ticking. She became irritating. She was banished, came back, and was finally banished again. My unasked question, 'And what of Susannah's love life?' simmered all through it, my heart thumping in a mixture of anticipation and dread. Later, I told myself.

In the afternoon as we drove back into town, I asked Susannah if she would show me Stanley Park. She would be delighted. Mary dropped us off.

We walked through the park.

'Do you like the folks out here?'

'I like them very much. Everyone has a wonderful exuberance and energy – you make us look a bit sluggish.' We walked a few paces. 'And I've been so pleased to see your home and where you've lived.'

'I still do.'

'Yes.' Pause. 'Susannah, are you coming over to see Guinevere in the spring? – I would love to take you round some of London. You could stay at the flat. Show you my home.'

'I would very much like to come.' She paused. 'But Mum has asked me to come with her.'

'You could both come and stay. It would please me very much.'

I looked at her. Her eyes answered me steadily, but with an underlying apprehension of something looming, something large. And I sensed almost a fear.

A little later she said: 'Christobel said she wanted to go to London.' I wondered where this was leading. After a few paces she said, 'Do you like her?'

'Yes, but she's a little bit haunted.'

'She's divorced.'

'Yes, your mother told me. I hear she has had a sad time, but is coming out of it. Good luck to her. She suggested my showing her something of London too, but she must have other people she knows there. Anyway, I trust it wouldn't clash with your visit. Much more important.' I said it lightly, but to tell her the truth, and added more urgently – 'Please do come, Susannah.'

A little smile, 'Yes, of course I will. And I am looking forward to seeing Grandma again. And Tisala. And the spring and – oh you know – everything.'

But I saw that she hedged round mentioning me, and we arrived at the Planetarium overlooking the water across to the city.

In the end I did not ask her about her boyfriend, and she didn't volunteer. I thought, there's no point – it's hopelessly clumsy. Either she likes you, and when she comes over again things will develop, or they will not. If she loves another, she loves another. You cannot press her now – so young and beautiful a woman – you'll just repulse her. I heard Tisala's voice: 'The right question is, will she come to love you? You will know soon enough if it is a false hope. Free spirits in time come to know their counterparts.'

And then, too soon, it was departure to the airport and heading home – home, yes – but away from Susannah. High over the Atlantic and the Greenland icecap and then across Tisala's route to the Happy Islands in the Arctic north I thought about the visit – the incidents, conversations, nuances – and found myself happy in the main, and yet in the painful uncertainty of unresolved love.

During the long hours of the flight a hundred thoughts revolved in my mind and feelings swelled and sank. I found myself observing my own happiness, and the half-felt unhappiness that flitted through me, like a plane through clouds with the dark Earth beneath. And I began to consider how happiness came and went, seemingly dependent on mood, on certainties, or the lack of them, and wondered what Tisala would make of the concept.

I was so glad to have seen Susannah in her other life. And now she also knew me in that context. Our worlds were linked. Vancouver, instead of being an unknown world where I had no place, was a city where I had been, felt at home, and liked. Perhaps likes follow desires. But what *would* follow was uncertain. I had warned myself against pressing her too fast, but alternately regretted my reticence and commended my own restraint. Yet in her 'everything' I found hope, and hope sustained me.

But beneath my first layers of thought I was aware that a dilemma lurked. Eric and Guinevere had already given me so much. Was I misusing their open generosity by seeking their young granddaughter? And another awareness lay behind: would the family think I was influenced by a wish to possess the Islands? It seemed unlikely that Mary, or Grenville, would ever come to live there. But if Susannah…

And then in my head I heard quite plainly what Tisala would have said. 'David, examine yourself: do you seek ownership of the Islands – is that your underlying desire? If so, you should forget Susannah for you would betray her future happiness, and eventually your own.'

'No Tisala, the answer is no. What I really seek is to love Susannah, and to have her love. To give her my love and find again the wholeness lost with Ellie's death.'

'Then you are free to seek her love. And you shouldn't let the question of ownership deter you. For what is the ownership of Islands? Above and beyond the responsibility, the trust you already exercise, title is almost nothing, just a licence to access. An owner merely borrows a label for a while. The islands are already in your bloodstream, part of your freedom, and nothing can ever dislodge the past twenty years.'

And I recalled what he had said not long before when we were discussing the future. 'Possession is the downfall of man. You humans must unlearn your terrible lust to possess, for beyond proper needs it is a bringer of trouble, and is often the enemy of happiness. I speak both of your own individual lives and public society at large. How many wars and heaps of dead have resulted from the greed of kings and rulers to possess? How is the world pillaged to satisfy your urge to own and consume? And now you are so numerous, and still increasing, the need to change is urgent. You are blundering into unknown territory, but do not see the consequences.'

And so I went and saw and tried to prepare a way for the future. I knew with full certainty that I wanted to marry Susannah, if she would have me. But *that* I did not know.

CHAPTER 57

London and Susannah

June in The Hebrides is a particularly beautiful month – the tilt of the Earth brings sunlight and long days. All the landscape and its life seems to respond, open and bloom. Colours are intensified, even among the lowly lichens – white and bright yellow – and the rich green mosses. After Tisala's departure for the arctic summer I usually went south to London, and very often missed the best months in the islands. Sometimes I had stayed up, or returned, to help Eric and Guinevere, or to carry out some piece of research. And this year I hoped that Susannah was coming, and that we would go to the islands in the summer.

After Vancouver we corresponded. My letters continued to be restrained about us, for that felt right, but I wrote openly about other enthusiasms and feelings. In the intervening weeks a new calm had come over me and I was no longer afraid of losing her. I knew myself for a happy man: blessed with children, friends, money – not much, but enough – a home, the islands, and a life full with the privilege of working with Tisala – a purpose and task I loved, and wondered at continually. And I wrote to her of all these things, seeking her views and opinions. And in her replies I found a warm, intelligent response. The arrival of her letters – instantly recognised – lying on the hall floor beneath the letter box, gave me a kick of pleasure.

At Easter Will came back to London from university. It was Penny's eighteenth birthday. We hired a local community hall, decked it out, got in a caterer, a quantity of drink and a disco. Thirty of her friends and Will's, stomped and celebrated the night away.

Penny was in her last year at school with 'A' levels looming. She spent long hours in her room revising. She had a place at Durham University for September, to read English, dependent on her results. Will, older and wiser by a full year, and now after two terms an acclimatised old hand at university, took time to help her run through her revision and test her on completed sections. It was a good family time – we went to exhibitions and pub lunches, and discussed friends, careers, art and politics. London is a congenial place from which to foster views of the world.

Half my mind was still in Vancouver, and I regaled Penny and Will with recollections of the visit, and I suppose most of all with what Susannah had said and done, on one occasion ending with:

'Well, they were all very kind and Susannah was lovely. We had a great time.'

Will said: 'Good. I think she's smashing, Dad.'

'Yes... well, I have always been very fond of her.'

He caught my eye and smiled. My son looking out for me. The change of roles surprised and pleased me.

'Why don't you marry her?' asked Penny with startling directness. 'We'd approve, wouldn't we Will?'

'Course.'

'Thank you,' I said, startled, and half laughing it off. 'She's only twenty-three, on another continent, and surrounded by young college men.'

'Poor Dad.' said Penny, putting her hand on mine and kissing my forehead. 'You're not really old. Just a bit. And you're better than them. Anyway, Susannah likes you.'

My correspondence and telephone calls with Susannah intensified, becoming more personal and intimate, but wider and deeper in other ways too. It gave me intense pleasure openly to share with her my work with Tisala. She knew, she knew! Sometimes I walked around my room clenching my fists in excitement. She had been there at the critical moment and had helped Tisala to survive. She and I together. My angel-nurse, who had held Tisala's gaping side in her hands regardless of the pouring blood and the gore and the freezing water, and had persevered long after she was numb with cold. I remember her dishevelled hair and blood-smeared face, frozen hands and body, teeth chattering uncontrollably despite being wrapped in a blanket. I loved her then, and wanted to love her forever.

My dam of marital loneliness, held up stoically over the years since Ellie's death, felt as if it might break, like ice in spring, and the river flow again. But above all, I told myself, what I wanted was her happiness. And if our distances apart – miles, ages, culture – were not to be bridged by an over-arching love, then so be it: she must find her happiness with another man, and I would pick up my task again, and rely again on what was already mine. But I hoped with a burning hope.

One day in late May, in reply to my invitation by letter, we spoke on the telephone. With my heart thumping I heard her say, yes, she would love to stay in London for a few days before she went north to the islands to see Guinevere. She hoped very much I would come up too. No, Mary was not after all coming. She might fly over later in the summer. There was a little silence. Then we spoke of mutual pleasure in the trip, and arrangements to be made.

And afterwards, delirium, until a voice inside me said such intense pleasure – happiness – is dangerous and may not last. But with triumphant certainty I scorned to be afraid – I would love this girl regardless. Twice I had found love. And by Ellie was greatly loved, beyond what any man could expect. And in Susannah I hoped... And if she does not love me, I'll love her anyway in my heart. For I had learned from Tisala that life should be a noble construction of what we are and what befalls us. We have a duty, a happy duty, to use the opportunities we have to endeavour to become the best we can. So ran my mind and feelings. High-flown, but deeply felt. And worthy of her.

So on the day of her arrival I was agitated and calm, and laughed at the coming of my fate. I had spent two days tidying the flat in a frenzy of anticipation. Vacuumed the whole place, dusted the shelves, and all the ornaments that were sometimes missed; polished Aunt Jane's silver candlesticks, turned cushions over, plumped them, filed paperwork away, straightened books, bought flowers. Two vases. Just to welcome her. Not too showy. One for her room. Made up the bed in Penny's room. Took down the big pop-band poster – the lead singer looked too young and handsome. Only a kid. But the poster left a horrid tidemark on the wall. The poster went back up again. What a fool you are: either she will love you or she won't. You will have to suffer the consequences, again, of giving your heart. Yes, but I wish to do so. Whatever the consequences? Yes.

We met at Heathrow. This beautiful young woman and I. She came walking out through customs into the arrivals concourse. There again was that aura of loveliness but now in me there was a surging love and physical desire.

Our eyes met and smiled. She came up to me. We kissed on both cheeks.

'Susannah, lovely to see you. Welcome.'

'You too David.'

'Here, give me your case. The car's in the multi-storey.'

Stop-start conversations – the journey, the traffic, even the weather: wanting to come closer but adjusting to years of absence to get there. We drove into London, catching up on families and goings on. Yes, Will was back at university – another few weeks before the summer vacation. Penny was in France with some of her class, post exams. Yes, she thought they went well.

We crossed the river in warm afternoon sunshine, and came home to Battersea. I opened the door of the flat and ushered her in, dumping her case in the little hall. We went through. She said, looking round with a smile, 'So this is where you live. It's bigger than I thought.'

'It's – well, we're very fortunate. Some of it needs redecorating.'

'It's lovely.'

'Yes. Well, it's our home. The kids have nearly left now.'

We did a quick conducted tour. 'Will's room is a shambles. Boys.' But she wanted to see it.

'If you would like to sleep in Penny's room.'

'She wouldn't mind?'

'No, not at all. Here.'

'Oh yes, this is Penny's room.' She looked round as if it were familiar and smiled. The handsome young man on the wall grinned at me. Drug addict.

'Flowers too.' she laughed, and I caught something of excitement in her face.

So began five whirlwind days. We explored the capital – the sights and sounds of London, the architecture, the hubbub, the parks, the peace, the river, the museums, the galleries. We saw and admired, we walked and talked, explained and commented, ate out and ate in.

We went to Westminster Abbey. As we went in the north door she said 'Here we go – History, with a capital H.' And inside, 'Oh my.'

A jumble of white marble edifices and memorials. The statesmen of England still vying with each other for space and prominence among half forgotten noblemen and worthies. And further on, the earlier brightly painted tombs of Tudor and Jacobean England. But rising above them all, the soaring Gothic masterpiece of medieval building.

'Look up, Susannah.'

'How *did* they do it?'

'With belief in God, and wooden scaffolding. And taxes.'

And, in the inner sanctum, more restrained than the marble monuments, the shrine of Edward the Confessor, saint and Saxon king before the coming of the Normans a thousand years ago; and round the horseshoe apse of the great Church the plain stone tombs of a line of English kings: Henry III, Edward I, the law giver, Edward III. I whispered histories as we went, though some of the less famous were unfamiliar and we had to read the little plaques. And beyond them in the linen-fold intricacy of their chapel, the Tudor monarchs, Henry VII, and Elizabeth of England herself.

Susannah spent a long time in Poets Corner and told me things I did not know about several of our poets. And afterwards we walked past the end of the Houses of Parliament, through the Victoria Tower Gardens and sat on a bench looking out across the Thames to Lambeth Palace before walking along The Embankment to The Tate. I wanted to show her Turner and Cotman – the sublime in nature, and their light-pouring skies. She wanted me to look at the freshness of the Impressionists. We walked through the large galleries of the eighteenth century enlightenment.

'Their marble monuments may be a bit much, but their real memorials are their ideas. Do you know...' and I launched off, ending, '...Look at their faces, not their wigs. They ushered in the modern world, but it didn't conform to their precepts.'

And so we explored parts of London, that great agglomeration of human endeavour.

But the real exploration of those five days was of ourselves. And by the third evening I knew my feelings were returned. And that we were becoming lovers. Back home that evening, Susannah insisted on cooking.

'A treat,' she said. 'At least it's meant to be.'

The candlesticks went on the table, the Côte de Beaune came out. The cooking progressed among smells and sizzles, and tremors of excitement. Eventually we were ready. We left the great world outside.

'Eric's favourite,' I said, pouring her the wine. We reminisced, remembering various scenes with Eric and Guinevere.

'This,' indicating my plate because I had a mouthful, 'is delicious.'

'You're most welcome. I hoped you'd like it.'

'You can come again. In fact, I don't think I'm going to let you go. Makes my cooking look inadequate.' She smiled, but with a trace of uncertainty.

'Oh, everyday cooking.' She shook her head in mock sympathy.

So we talked. We spoke of happenings in our lives, and of our families, and the people we loved, edging closer to the centre of our own lives, and our eyes met more and more.

Now was my Rubicon, dangerous, but most decidedly to be crossed.

'Susannah.' I took her hand, and felt a small returning pressure. 'You know I have fallen in love with you. I love you very much.'

Our eyes held each other. Her eyes were large and serious.

'Oh, David.' Then she said, very softly, as if she was reaching out, 'Oh, my love. I love you too, I always have done.'

'Please will you marry me?'

'Yes, yes I will.'

We kissed gently and gazed at each other.

We forgot the pudding, which was nearly burnt, but was rescued just in time amid happy laughter. Afterwards, sitting on the sofa, we found ourselves gazing again at each other in a sort of wonderment.

'I can hardly believe it.'

She smiled and laid her head on my chest. And then everything flooded over me. Susannah, Susannah. She had entered my soul from the beginning. From the first day when Will and I had met this beautiful creature in the Station Hotel, when the world had stopped; and begun anew. She had come disguised in my mind as a young girl, and as a friend for my children. I was used to being alone, and always had other cares and concerns in the forefront of my mind – Eric's illness, Guinevere, the future, the kids' happiness, my work with Tisala, his safety and the protection of our base, and the whaling campaign. Then slowly, with her visits over the years the impediments had been reduced as the pretty girl became a beautiful young woman.

'Do you remember, on your first visit, when Eric was ill recovering after his heart-attack, I thought of you as an elder sister for the kids –

you were so sweet with them – big sisterly.'

'Why sisterly?' She looked down. 'It could have been motherly. Those poor motherless kids.'

'But Will and you... I thought – '

'I loved Will because he is your son. And Penny. I wanted to look after them for you.' She paused. 'But it caught me out too. At first I thought you were very serious and a bit grizzled. And I was surprised because I had heard all about you from Gran. And she always spoke of you as a young man.'

I made to protest – 'A *very* young man.' She screwed her face up in pleasure – 'A hero prince, certainly under thirty.'

'Susannah, I am a dozen years beyond that.'

'Thirteen,' she said and squirmed away from me, laughing. 'My maths isn't that bad.' She fingered the button on my shirt. 'But I gradually found I loved you anyway.'

'When did you – '

'I think it started from the beginning of that first visit. When I met you and your children and Tisala in the islands. It was a revelation – a completely new world to me. You stirred my imagination. When I went back to Canada it made our life in Vancouver seem, well – flat and very ordinary. And when I thought about you and your work with Tisala my longings were crystallised and magnified. My grandparent's islands were transformed: I had found romantic excitement and a whole new vista of knowledge.

'In part of course I found knowledge and romance at college. But always in my mind there was Eileen Mòr, Inis Cuan – and you. And as time passed and boyfriends came and went, and I saw you again on our visits, the impossibility of loving you diminished. Somehow I grew towards you in age.'

Her words to Will after Eric's funeral came back to me, 'You are the luckiest young man in the world.' So, even then.

'But I couldn't read your response. So I kept my feelings hidden. And I was wary of them – they were overwhelming and I was afraid you wouldn't see me like that, or that they were unrealistic or might burn out. But they didn't... And the distance, and – '

'Ssh.' I held her close, and said: 'And I thought I had no business to love someone so young and beautiful as you, and who you were – their granddaughter.'

She said: 'And then at Tisala's terrible wounding, I knew. To me you were beyond words, wonderful – how you went about saving Tisala's life. I knew I wanted to marry you. But I didn't know how, and was afraid you would think me still too young. So I waited, and was scared that you would find someone else. But you didn't.' She kissed me lightly.

'I didn't want anyone else, Susannah. And once I knew that you and Will weren't... then I began to love you freely. And long for you. How I have longed for you to be my wife.'

She said: 'And when you came over to Vancouver, then I hoped, and watched and saw. So when you asked me to come here...' She paused. 'I think Mum knew. She said, "Perhaps you should go over on your own this time."' We smiled at each other and laughed.

And at the end of the evening Penny's bed remained unoccupied. Our trials and lives apart had been long enough.

CHAPTER 58

On Inis Cuan Again

Two days later we took the train north to the islands. We had a fair amount of luggage between us, partly because Mary had sent some things over for Guinevere and I had one case half-full of books, mainly for Tisala.

We had decided not to announce our intentions to Guinevere immediately, but to enjoy our new relationship for the first two or three weeks on the island without the formal acknowledgement of a public engagement. Now we had found each other, we found too how each had been longing for the other, and we wanted time together to make up the gaps of the past.

'It will give us time to adjust.' The old caution stirred faintly within me. But seemed absent from the mind of the confident New-World young woman I loved.

'She'll spot it anyway, I'll bet.' said Susannah laughing.

When we arrived, as the boat approached the little jetty on Eilean Mòr, we were chatting with Jimmy MacLeod and could see Guinevere coming down to meet us. We clambered out of the boat joking with Jimmy about the amount of baggage. Guinevere welcomed us warmly as always. Back in her kitchen we started swapping news – from Vancouver, London and the islands, so far apart yet so closely associated.

We spent three days with Guinevere – a mixture of pure holiday and dealing with jobs about the house and outbuildings. We weeded and tidied up the house's little courtyard – there were a few thistles and grasses along the line of the outbuildings, something that Eric would have dealt with. But the sheltered sunny patch of hollyhocks was still there, though not yet in flower. Susannah weeded round them carefully. Perhaps our love was obvious from the delight we both took in each other's company, but if it was, Guinevere said nothing in those first days.

One afternoon Susannah said to Guinevere: 'Gran, let's take a picnic and walk up to the top of the island.'

'Oh, I think – no – you two go. I think I'll stay behind.' Her eyes were alive and full of pleasure. I knew she doted on Susannah. 'It's a little far for me now, dear.'

But she wouldn't hear of a shorter walk either, so Susannah and I set off together. We wound our way in the sunshine up and across the high bogs of Eilean Mòr. And at the summit stopped and gazed lazily at the views before descending down to the far coast, always drawn to the water's edge and the perfection of the shoreline. Contentment as well as peace came dropping slow. It was one of those sunny days when freedom and happiness seemed unendingly intertwined with the beauty of the landscape, and the great ocean shimmering all beyond.

The next day we completed preparations for going over to Inis Cuan for a few days. The pile of kit grew – food, sundry supplies, extra bedding for the cottage, tools and materials for maintenance on the shack, books, papers, videos for use with Tisala.

Whenever I crossed to Inis Cuan – however often – it was with a soaring sense of happiness. I had sat in the boat with Susannah previously, watching her beauty. But this time it was different. It was something to do with the peace of a soul that knows it is coming home, but now joined with another. Two souls in this earthly paradise together.

We stayed in the crofting cottage, cleaned it and turned out the contents to air in readiness for the coming season. And after a couple of days we went over to the inlet at Cala Bearn and spent a week in the shack. There were jobs to be done. We wood-stained the windward side of the shack. There was a roof leak in the main room, and I clambered up to deal with the repair. We cleaned and generally made ready the interior. Susannah found a blanket still smeared with Tisala's blood which she washed and pummelled and hung out to dry. Sometimes we took time off and walked the cliffs. And all the time, in between jobs and eating, sleeping and making love, we talked, exploring and sharing things from our earlier years; and ideas, feelings, opinions, and our future together. We sank deeper into each other's lives.

So that by the time we returned to Guinevere on Eilean Mòr, we were ready for the world. And this time it was different again as we approached the house. I felt the exhilaration of momentous commitment.

'Come in, come in!' said Guinevere appearing at the door. We sat in the kitchen, the kettle on for coffee.

'Well, how did you get on over there – all well?'

'Yes, it was fine.' I paused, and then went sailing proudly in. 'Guinevere... Susannah and I have something to tell you.' Even then, for an instant, a little edge. Susannah held my hand. 'We want to get married.' We looked at each other, and back to Guinevere.

'My darling children. Oh! how wonderful! I can't tell... David... Susannah, dear...Oh!... Eric would have been so delighted.'

She smiled at us almost in tears, looking from one to the other in a sort of disbelieving happiness.

'Have you told Mary?'

'We haven't told anyone else yet.'

'I'm sure she'll be delighted too.' Guinevere on our side, whatever else. As always.

'You must ring her. And your mother too.' She hesitated: 'And Will and Penny?' She looked at me.

I smiled, 'I think they know.'

'And... oh well!'

So the phone was soon busy. Penny and Will were lovely – the kindness of their reactions, and what they said both to me and Susannah, brought tears to my eyes. Well-wishes poured in as our news spread. And if there was initial reserve in some quarters, I felt and saw nothing of it. Perhaps among some of Susannah's family and friends our age gap was a talking point, or her going to live in London, but acceptance and kindness were the norm.

That summer marked an unfolding happiness for us both. And for me the gift of a new balance and contentment that I knew had been missing in my widower years. My memory of those weeks is bathed in constant sunlight, and though June in the islands was fine, the weather records otherwise show an average sort of year.

We stayed with Guinevere and on Inis Cuan for another fortnight. We walked everywhere on the islands, perhaps subconsciously creating a new sense of knowing them as a shared experience. But we were busy too. Jimmy MacLeod wanted my help with a new gate and some fencing. We sank a shaft for the gatepost, with some difficulty and much sweat.

Susannah helped Guinevere in various domestic tasks. One day they sorted through a chest of drawers and Guinevere insisted on giving her some beautiful family table-linen, including a large damask table cloth.

'We'll never carry it all!'

'Take it in dribs and drabs. It's more use in London than here.'

One day I took Susannah in the boat, circumnavigating Inis Cuan, stopping off here and there to show her favourite places. We came back towards the inlet past the rocks to the islet. I used those landmarks to describe the seabed and the underwater features and passage so vital for Tisala, for I wanted her to know, to share; and in case of future need. The day was flat calm and we landed on the islet, a tiny kingdom even complete with butterflies – Small Whites, one of the Fritillaries, and Small Blues.

But in the evenings, in more domestic surroundings, we turned to talk of wedding preparations. We were to be married in late October, quietly in London, after Tisala's autumn migration south. Guinevere would travel to London, but she did not want to undertake the journey to Vancouver. We would then go to Vancouver for a celebration party and our honeymoon. In the meantime Susannah was to return to Canada at the end of her four-week trip. She had much to do before Vancouver ceased to be her home. But she allowed herself only six weeks. She wanted to come back to London for a period before we returned to the islands for Tisala's autumn visit. And when we came to leave the islands, it was unwillingly, with a sense of events parting us again.

So when Susannah left me at the airport, I felt the ups and downs of happiness, the fleeting emptiness of being alone again, the complicated skein and play of human emotions that ebbed and flowed through those days. The flat in Battersea seemed strangely barren in a way it had not been before; yet there were new and cherished memories, and sometimes it felt as if she was still with me. When we spoke by phone, distance was nothing, but afterwards she was a continent and an ocean away.

But underlying the momentary downs was the deep happiness of my life then. This love, this trust, this fruition, added to the whole point and exhilaration of my existence. To my surprise it even enhanced my already greatly rewarding work. And now Penny in particular would have a mother figure, and one of whom both she and Will were already fond.

Susannah was supposed to be busy preparing for her move to England – dealing with her possessions, termination of employment, tax, and a hundred other things, as well as seeing friends and helping Mary arrange a reception party. But when we spoke by telephone, which we did almost daily, among all these things she wanted to know and engage with my work. She knew Tisala was exploring ethics.

And when she came back to London before our autumn move north she joined in with an intense intent. She had decided views on political and economic issues, but had not studied formal philosophy or biology. She read and questioned me on the works and material Tisala was considering. She had much to learn but was not afraid to let me see when she did not know something.

'Formal ethics may not be my territory,' she said, smiling at me, 'but I know something about happiness.'

And so did I. And from my long training with Tisala, I sought to comprehend the basis of these feelings. For assuredly at this point life felt wonderful. Instinct and my years told me it was built on an already existing basis, but my reason struggled to account for its emergence through love.

CHAPTER 59

On Happiness

So when three months later Tisala said: 'The explanation of happiness is relatively simple,' I laughed.

'Yes?'

'But bedevilled by you poor humans in false starts, lack of knowledge and failure of thought.'

'Explain, please, Tisala.' said Susannah, who was keyed up with anticipation from my earlier accounts of Tisala's discussions. Now at last she was part of it.

So he did. One false start, he thought, was the idea that happiness was a gift of the gods, and afterwards God, in his various forms; a notion that led to a tangle of mistaken ideas.

One was that those people who believed they were made in the image of an all-loving God expected a 'right' to happiness. All they had to do was to behave according to God's rules (though these would be discovered to be different, according to which religion is involved) and they would be rewarded with happiness, perhaps on Earth and, in a perfect form, in heaven.

Tisala said, 'As you know, I have found no reason to believe in God, and compelling reasons not to believe. So, as people do find happiness in their earthly life, it is reasonable to conclude it comes from other sources.

'Let that be our hypothesis. Then it follows, and becomes immediately clear, that happiness cannot be a gift of God, and there can be no such thing as a God-given "right" to happiness. We must therefore look for other explanations.'

Tisala thought that another result of attributing the source of happiness to God lay in the distortion it caused. For instance, that Thomas Aquinas' 'ultimate' happiness (seeing God in heaven) thereby downgrades other forms of happiness, such as those derived from the senses and from the exercise of moral goodness. In this Aquinas largely followed Aristotle, although Aristotle's idea of 'supreme' happiness lay, not in seeing God, but in the exercise of reason. This he thought brought men nearest to the attributes of the gods. Aristotle, though championing reason, thus retained a genuflection to the supernatural – to the Greek gods, 'who everyone now accepts were purely imaginary'.

Christians moved the fulfilment of happiness out into heaven, further away from mankind, leaving behind on Earth its difficult reflection, religious love of God. The same had been done by most supernatural religions which have come and gone among the civilisations of mankind.

I asked: 'You think heaven is an imaginary place, or state?'

'I would be surprised if it were not so.'

I said, 'If heaven is only an imaginary place or state, ultimate happiness has been promised to us for no purpose whatsoever, and many people deceived.'

Tisala said, 'It must be hard for the humans to love the idea of a disembodied God, especially one who is believed to preside over all manner of perplexing and horrible events on Earth.' And to set up 'ultimate' or 'supreme' happiness as goals he thought anyway a mistake. 'They do not exist and you humans thereby, in chasing a mirage, misunderstand and undervalue the sources and instances of true happiness.'

A second false start lay not in religion, but in philosophy. The trouble here lay, not in handing everything over to God, but in handing it over to reason supported by insufficient knowledge. He acknowledged, of course, that our wisest philosophers had arrived at many valuable insights. But their systems mainly rest on metaphysics mixed with reason, for lack of scientific knowledge. (He surmised the reason why Aristotle's ethics had endured so long was that he, above all the classical philosophers, was closest in many ways to common sense and acute observation of the physical world, though he got much wrong.)

He thought this flawed method was true up to modern times. I had told him of the English philosopher Bertrand Russell (who was a mathematician, but crucially knew little chemistry or biological science). He cited Russell's book *The Conquest of Happiness*, and remarked that the warlike title showed he did not understand the origins of happiness; which verdict he thought confirmed by its contents: largely confined to a – useful – discussion of instances of what happiness is not, and by the application of a sort of modern, rationalised but nonetheless defective metaphysics.

'Metaphysics,' said Tisala on another occasion, 'seems to have been the attempts of your philosophers and early scientists to work out matters from first principles before they understood the first principles of matter.'

It was a ramshackle imaginative superstructure leading nowhere, like alchemy, and though shot through occasionally with insights, tending to the abstruse and occult.

'I have waded through your metaphysics,' said Tisala. 'It is what happens when good minds attend on fantasy.'

'It tangled me up all right.' said Susannah.

'Which is why,' I said laughing, 'French intellectuals are in such a mess.'

Tisala asked: 'Is your traditional metaphysics a useful vehicle for arriving at anything, except confusion?'

I smiled, seeing the struggle of years to find value in the contents of much metaphysics being swept away as an unnecessary and misleading endeavour. 'You mean it's an obsolete prototype?'

'Perhaps one less piece of baggage for you.' said Tisala, making his smiling sound.

He thought any new metaphysics, if it is to be useful at all, must constantly measure itself against scientific knowledge. It may extend beyond science – reasoned hypothesis enlarges the possibility of knowledge – but it must not be in contradiction of science. And since much of science is uncertain – it awaits the next improved explanation – nor can metaphysics be certain. He concluded that metaphysics conducted on any other basis is likely to be futile.

The trouble with the old philosophical approach to happiness was the need the philosophers felt to start from and build a purely rational scheme. He instanced Aristotle again who imposes his scheme by definitions. This leads to divisions, sub-divisions, exceptions and ultimately contortions. Thus he says happiness is 'the good.' which is an activity of the soul, which is itself divided into two parts, rational and irrational. Then the irrational is divided into vegetative (found even in plants) and appetite, which is found in all animals. But then, he doubles back and says the appetite may be part rational when the good it seeks is 'approved' by reason. Tisala remarked that Aristotle's observation is often more accurate than his categories, which are in neat square blocks. And this same error he found true of many of the western philosophers, Descartes, Berkeley, Kant and others.

'I do not want to go far chasing down that channel, for it is based on divisions concocted in a man's brains, not in reality. The natural world, of which you are a living part, does not work like that.'

He said our human knowledge had taught him that things often develop by accretion, in graduations and by degrees with infinite slowness: as with emergence of life itself from the stardust of the universe, evolving from the first microscopic plant life across three billion years, to us – *Homo sapiens*.

'Named,' Tisala remarked, 'in premature aspiration.'

Tisala understood that each and every one of these species, as we now know, evolved out of their predecessors. And within a species, male and female, orientation, sexual drive – all too on sliding scales according to biological makeup. And in all these things the passing-over moment into any different classification is hard to see or define at the borders. It is a single ever-branching procession of life, still growing, and never in logical square blocks.

He concluded: 'And no-one knows what wonders of formation are yet to come, what higher beings, better than men or whales, if they are given their time. Likewise, I think we shall find that happiness is not a supernatural gift, nor to be conquered, nor prescribed by reason, but is a capability that has arisen by degrees out of the developing forms of life.'

In the West, philosophers tried to apply pure logic, though most of them were still tangled up with their ideas of divinity. But at the same time men were deluded by the idea that man alone had reason. He quoted, but I forget where from, 'Reason more than anything else is man.'

'Which we now also know,' I said, 'is not true.' I thought of Tisala's powers of mind, and kindly wisdom, and was awed. And saw that *our* reason is trammelled up with many lower animal attributes. But equally, that reason must be burgeoning everywhere in the natural world, and I wondered if it might emerge in less troubled forms than it does among humans.

Tisala assented but, going on, added: 'In criticising Western philosophy I'm not implying that Eastern philosophy is better: mostly it is not: and where in the eastern traditions the anchor of reason gives way to mere speculative beliefs, it soon becomes indistinguishable from superstition. In the East they have tended to lean to the mystical, very often accompanied by a withdrawal from life to attain favourable circumstances. The mystical has often risen out of ignorance as a substitute for knowledge; and withdrawal from life for most, who must earn their food and shelter, is difficult or impossible.'

He concluded that reason remains the mechanism of advance. It is not the use of reason itself that is wrong, it is the lack of real knowledge to which to apply reason that has caused the difficulties and errors.

He said you could see it clearly in Descartes, and at an extreme in poor Nietzsche. Nietzsche, who by elevating unscientifically one characteristic of the human animal – 'the will to power' – into an abstract absolute, grossly distorted his vision; and by applying warped reason to his distortion, he distorted reality further (which others later used with evil consequences), and outlawed himself from any hope of happiness. It was an exercise in malign metaphysics.

'And that is why your philosophers have made little advance in ethics over 2,000 years: entrenched misunderstanding of the source and nature of ethics, and lack of scientific knowledge. The classical philosophers, and ethical innovators, such as the Buddha and Christ, had taken ethics nearly as far as they could be developed within such misunderstanding and ignorance.

'But now, because of advances in real knowledge, your philosophers, provided they understand at least chemistry and biology and the history of them, are much better placed to make a synthesis of the elements that lead to happiness. That in turn will have a profound effect on ethics. I mean the code you should live by; improvement in which will help you to achieve better living, and happiness. Many of the mistakes of the past, in the light of your new knowledge, can be jettisoned entirely. If you are wise enough, the way is open for spectacular advances.

'Do you think,' he asked, 'that we have sufficiently eliminated the false trails, and may now set out in a less encumbered way the origins and meaning of happiness?'

Susannah had been making notes. She looked at me, her eyes smiling.

Tisala thought happiness – the ability to feel happy – began to develop in all living organisms as they evolved in nature. Like all elements of developed life happiness starts more humbly and rises on a sliding scale.

In the structure of plants, having sufficient water and sunlight gives rise to an ability to react: the plant stands up and opens or turns towards the sunlight.

'But happiness?' I said. 'Surely fanciful?'

'No, not happiness, but it is the beginning. If you have taught me truly, and I think you have, it will be found not fanciful when you know a little more. Next you have plant-like animals and then, a few steps further on, animals with rudimentary nervous systems such as the sensory feeling of touch, or ease, say, after ingesting food. Happiness will be found to derive first from simple pleasures developed deep in our animal past giving us the use and pleasure of the senses. We would not call that happiness but it is the origin of a sense of wellbeing and contentment. And you will note the characteristics that allow it: an organisation working as it ought in a benign set of circumstances. These are the early conditions of rudimentary happiness: the biological working of a nervous system and the electrical and chemical components of impulses in the brain. Later, in higher animals, we will come to say that these generate emotions. And among a range of emotions eventually floats happiness.'

He said, 'Consider a step higher up the ladder: a lion lying in the grassland basking pleasurably in the sun. Here you have a conscious mind. The lion knows it is basking in the sun, and moves to the shade when that gives more pleasure. You can argue as to whether he is merely content, or whether he is happy, but if you add another dimension: the power of conscious reflection, the balance changes. If the lion thinks, I am a lion in my prime and this is a perfect day, you would tend to credit him with happiness rather than mere contentment.

'The way you humans use the word happiness to describe your condition applies to many more animals than you like to think. I know of my own experience that we Blue Whales and other whales and dolphins, can be happy, and be properly so called.

'Take what you have described to me: a dog that welcomes its mistress home: its chemical and nervous system and its brain react to create emotion. It is at a level of consciousness both to feel its pleasure and to know (which augments the feeling, perhaps into happiness) that it is loved by a creature of a different species.

'You have mainly been very ignorant about your fellow animals, being blinded by your delusions of uniqueness.

Such, he argued, will be found to be the origins of happiness in humans: they are the same biological elements found at various levels of development throughout the plant and animal kingdoms. And we higher animals therefore contain and retain lower level contentments and pleasures as well as achieving what we call happiness.

Tisala said: 'Now you can see, perhaps more clearly, why I conclude that there is no God-given right to happiness. It does not accord with reality. Your advance in knowledge makes demonstrable what we always intuitively believed.'

But I queried whether there was such a 'right' arising from any other source.

'No,' said Tisala, 'it is a delusion in those terms. If you search for happiness as a right you chase an illusion that does not exist. If you demand happiness you will not find it. Look instead in the right place. Contentment, and beyond it happiness, comes when the balance of existence is right. At some point contentment slips over into happiness. For happiness comes as a consequence. It is a consequence that flows through biological channels, but can be variously gained and released: in part by personal disposition, both genetic and acquired by nurture; in part by habit (the practice of happiness); and by right living. You may earn and give yourself happiness by good and reasonable conduct of your own life; or you may too, as many of you seem to do, destroy your own chances of such.'

He remarked on two limitations on human happiness. The first he said is temporal – the duration of happiness. With such biological origins, and dependence on nervous systems and chemical balances in the body, you would not expect to find happiness to be a permanent state. It is impermanent – often fleeting; a matter, he said, you humans know all too well from experience in your tumultuous world and your alternately frightened and aggressive reactions to it. He noticed without surprise that a number of our philosophers, such as the Buddha and Epicurus, have concluded that happiness is best nurtured in tranquillity.

I could not help contrasting the shortness and interrupted nature of human happiness with that of whales – better developed and more sustained. I knew they had learned to spend long periods of their lives in a state of conscious serenity and happy social communication in their fearless free ranging of the oceans. That is, before the cruel stupidity of whaling.

This thought reinforced his second observation on the limitations of human happiness, which he said is circumstantial. Because we humans live in the thin gaseous atmosphere on pieces of the Earth's crust that stick out above the main habitat, the oceans, and being largely immobile, we are prey to the imbalance of climates found there. Our ability to live happily is in part circumscribed by weather and the availability of water, food and shelter; to which we have added social obstacles, as fighting, wars, slavery, careers and such like. Our facility for happiness had to develop when variable circumstances were favourable; and often they were not. In addition we, like many carnivorous hunting animals, have inherited not only our sexual urge to survive, but our strongly aggressive drives and their counterparts, frustration, depression, timidity and fear. And when these are ascendant, happiness is hard to nurture, or is displaced. It may still be found in niches of our lives – little patches of happiness lighting up small respites even in the most appalling circumstances. For the propensity to seek happiness is now built into the nature of men, as it is in whales and other of our fellow higher animals.

'You will know how lives may be dominated by external circumstances. We will come to that, but I am here speaking of times when they are relatively benign; though a wise person may impose his mind even on adverse circumstances which would destroy the happiness of others, and so retain happiness or at least contentment. Your Socrates at his death was such a one. I think such strength among wiser humans is not uncommon.

'But having sought to clarify what happiness is, and what gives rise to it, and what can disrupt or destroy it on a personal level, we must acknowledge its public dimension. You can hope and expect – and direct – your laws and the behaviour of other people to be such as allow and facilitate each of you the freedom to order your lives with better opportunities of happiness. And there we come to the area of public moral conduct, and in your society the necessity and desirability of enshrining some of it at least in law to achieve discipline among your fractious people. And there too, in the public sphere, if the law is bad, arises the evil of political or national tyranny, which can destroy the potential happiness of millions of individuals.'

Tisala said: 'So let us take stock. We think the ability to feel happiness is a physical emotion provided for and arising out of our evolutionary biological development. We say that even the most 'spiritual' ecstasies of happiness depend on these physical capabilities. The most exalted romantic or religious loves use the same physical base: they borrow the emotional mechanism from our evolutionary past. The feeling itself arises from a state of mind – from which an emotional surge is released – literally triggered by electromagnetic and chemical changes in the brain that are felt as happiness. But we know too that happiness may be displaced by either internal or external circumstances: by things that are incompatible with the emotion of happiness, such as fear: for instance, and among humans, by ill health, unemployment or a failing marriage, with their underlying fears of pain, poverty and rejection. And fear of life itself ending suddenly, as by fatal disease or battle or social violence or plane crash.'

He remarked once: 'Your mechanical transport has alleviated your immobility, but for some has imposed the heavy tax of untimely death.'

Tisala noted here what everyone knows, that happiness can also be destroyed by the pursuit of pleasure. For there can be pleasures both physical and mental, such as overeating or drinking, exploitative sex, use of drugs, pleasure in aggression or violence, foolhardy activities dicing with risks of bodily injuries, the consequences of which as soon as the sensation of pleasure is past, far from bringing happiness, exile it, and often bring its opposite, misery.

'And the reason why this is so is because such things put a life out of its true balance. That is the effect of not distinguishing right from wrong, wisdom from folly. A life in disarray does not bring happiness.'

Tisala said he took it as self-evident that happiness is a desirable state, for he noted that it only emerged, after its simpler precursors, pleasure and contentment, as a development in higher-conscious animals. But he said it is a mistake to pursue happiness all of the time.

I asked him to explain.

'What children you are!' he said smilingly. 'Do not become unhappy because you are not always happy. You do not need to be. When you rest you want sleep, not happiness; and sometimes contentment and pleasure are enough. And the crossover moment between these three, as we have seen, is difficult to define or recognise. They are on the same spectrum. Yet with skill and judgement the more exalted forms of happiness can be increasingly enjoyed on many occasions, and highlights prolonged.

'The question to ask is, what brings this state of mind? For if we know that, we can do much to release happiness within ourselves. There are many triggers of happiness; some are scarcely more than pleasures, perhaps momentarily passing over into flashes of happiness, like the awareness of beauty in a flower or face, or in the fortunes of a game, or in a social contact made. But these like many we could think of are examples of fleeting happiness that may not outlast the hour. The happiness we should cultivate, as many wise humans have known, is of a more enduring sort. And there are more general grounds that make it or its recurrence more likely and more sustained.

'The emotion or feeling of happiness is likely to be released when the mind and body are both pleased with the state of their existence; then you may become happy to the extent that you think you understand the world or feel you have a measure of control within and over your life, or when it is in equilibrium with its surroundings and your fellow beings.'

I said, 'But if you say you can be happy when you think you understand the world, it follows you can be happy when your understanding is wrong. "When ignorance is bliss, 'tis folly to be wise".'

Tisala said: 'An understandable, but a short-focused saying. The problem comes when ignorance is no longer bliss. And worse, your ignorance in the meantime may have inflicted much damage in the world. But the saying has point. The Egyptians could happily worship their gods (despite much fear in their worship, as in later religions), though their beliefs were entirely untrue. The difficulty comes when you find the world does not accord with the religion you are taught (for it is from teaching that belief comes), and when you find your faith untrue. This, in your world of open and increasing communication, will happen more rapidly in the future. And many who lay aside religion, and with it some of its ideals and social structure, tend to fall into lower forms of behaviour, and by bad example teach their children to regress. That is how civilisations decline, if there is not a new and better idea of life to follow.'

He saw consumerism in the West in that light – an uneasy doomed attempt to shore up individual happiness by the pursuit of individual plenty.

'But half of North Americans want to be millionaires,' said Susannah. 'That is what they pursue in their lives.'

'I fear you may be right, and not just North Americans. And if you humans are greedy about acquiring great wealth, you will become both aggressive and miserable, for aggression is an enemy of happiness, both for the aggressor and victim. And there will always be others who will outdo you. A child absorbed in floating sticks in a stream can be happier and see greater fleets than a distracted millionaire on his yacht. It is not the wealth that guarantees happiness, though wealth properly viewed and used frees a person from the constraints of poverty and may enable him to put his life in better order. His happiness will depend more on his state of mind, and that will be influenced by the balance of his life and conduct. Millionaires are people who, like everybody, want to be accepted by their fellows. Sometimes they are so misled they think they can buy acceptance, and even respect and love, and feel it the more badly when they cannot. But respect and love come differently, through right personality and conduct. Too often they think wealth an automatic passport to happiness and forget our old observation that money cannot buy it. Wealth can then become a handicap, for having acquired it they think they should be happy, and if they are not they feel failure more than a poorer person. And when wealth is used as a form of force, it leads directly to unhappiness.'

I said: 'But the world wants to follow the American dream of wealth – '

'For *every* human?' intervened Susannah. 'It is a false dream, and one which is economically unsustainable.'

Tisala said: 'And beyond a point undesirable anyway. Moreover its growing destructive industrial process is beginning to unbalance the world, the climate patterns, and the gaseous mantle of the Earth upon which all life depends. Your growing billions of people would do well to ponder deeply on the nature of happiness, and adopt a changed course that may avoid this future fate. Your human ability to gain happiness may just have evolved far enough to rescue you from yourselves. Let us hope so.'

CHAPTER 60

A Wedding

I

In October that year – 1983 – Susannah and I were married in our local church in Battersea, for that still seemed the right place.

Our families gathered round. Will and Penny, of course. My mother, still sprightly, came up and stayed with Susan, Giles and her grandchildren. I asked Edmund and Penelope but they thought 'the upheaval' as Edmund put it too much and asked us to visit them afterwards. Mary, Tom and Grenville came over from Canada, making it an excuse to have a few days holiday. Guinevere came down and stayed across the river in the hotel where we had the reception, which somehow grew from the original quiet intention. I laughingly suggested a new collective noun for a gathering of old friends: an insistence of friends; but it made me grateful for the pattern of our lives.

Penny was our bridesmaid – lovely in a pale creamy-yellow dress, and looking after Susannah as if they had been friends from birth. And when I turned to see Susannah approaching up the isle on her father's arm I felt a tightening in my chest. Susannah, coming to give her young life to me in love, willingly, fully, perhaps forever, and I trembled at her beauty and brave self-knowledge. This beloved young woman who was enabling me to feel whole again. And I determined to give her children, and happiness all the days of her life, so far as it was in my power. And the question of the extent of my power did not then arise.

Will was my best man. He ran the day like an old hand, and reminded me what to do and when to do it. Afterwards at the reception he made a short but fluent speech. His assurance surprised me. He made something, speaking for Penny and himself, of my characteristics, and spoke about Susannah and me from across the years. His words were entertaining, but unexpectedly moving in their kindness. My children made me very proud that day, but Susannah proudest of all.

A week later we flew to Canada. When we arrived at Mary's home – Susannah's childhood home – I was almost nervous.

Mary said, smiling, 'Now I will have to be a mother-in-law contemporary and – I – am – *delighted* to be...' and she gave me a long emotional hug.

Mary and Tom held a splendid party for us at their home. And Tom with his 'son-in-law David' introduction made me feel like an Olympian. More and more people came, young and old, all with smiling white teeth and an outpouring of welcome and goodwill even more overwhelming than the rising hubbub of voices. Susannah introduced me in the enthusiastic North American manner to those of her friends I hadn't met previously. I found myself forging or renewing links with everyone in the same easy way, and we made well-intended but sometimes extravagant promises of mutual visits for the future.

And then we had a fortnight's honeymoon in the silence and grandeur of the Canadian Rockies, part of the time seeing the well known sights, but staying five nights in a log cabin on a lakeside reached up several miles of unmade track. We had the use of a canoe and an outside barbecue. The canoe was called *Minnehaha*.

When we took the canoe out, one of my abiding memories is laughter together on the still, black water. And then listening to the silence, and the great awed quietness of the fir trees and mountains all around us, and the dab of our paddles. That and being snug in our cabin at night, coming together in love on the big bed in the corner, lit by the glow of our wood stove; and afterwards lying curled up gently in each other's arms, naked in our warmth and happiness.

We read *Hiawatha* out loud to each other, but never finished it, stopping at the fulfilment of the lovers' courtship. For our own always drew us back to each other.

And the days were long and slow, and all too short, before we headed homeward.

So we began our marriage. For a period, we had life to ourselves. We lived in the London flat. Apart from some wonderfully chaotic and happy weeks in the vacs, Will and Penny were away at university. Susannah got a job working a three-day week for an economics magazine, researching and writing articles. Three days was good because she could sometimes work four or five by arrangement, and concertina the extra days off into longer holiday periods in the spring and autumn. She became my invaluable helper with Tisala in the islands, which were already in some ways our first home.

And for Tisala and the whales of the world, those years of the early 1980s were pivotal. The moratorium on commercial whaling, voted for in 1982, the summer of Tisala's near fatal encounter with the illegal whalers, was still not due to be implemented for another two years after our marriage.

I carefully checked the North Atlantic whaling records: in the year Tisala received his hideous wounds no whaler reported striking a Blue Whale, by mistake or otherwise. I did not expect anything different: the Blues were ostensibly protected and any such admission at that time would have been particularly damaging to the whalers' rearguard action to continue whaling.

In the North Atlantic, Norway and the Danish Faeroes kept up the hunting of the other species. Norway had objected to the moratorium, so legally, if not morally, could continue to kill whales. Fin, Sei and Minke Whales were their publicly intended victims. But whenever the poor Fin Whales were hunted I was always anxious for Blues.

In the southern oceans the Japanese and Russian fleets were the unpredictable danger. But even here, whole seasons now went by without any reports of Blue Whale losses. Although we did not know it until later, the once huge Russian kill was rapidly declining as numbers of all species ran low, and their whole whaling fleet was falling into decay.

And all across the world people and the whales waited for the moratorium to come in. This was the background to a period of great fruitfulness in my work with Tisala. His capacious and generous mind seemed constantly employed in understanding and mastering the workings and grievous dislocations of the human world.

The following March, when Tisala had returned to the cool but sunny promise of the Hebridean spring, I one day asked him for his views on the meaning of life. He asked what I meant.

'Why we are put here, or why we are here.'

He thought the question very strange. He said, 'There is no such thing as "the meaning of life" – the idea itself is wrongly conceived. But there is plenty in life which is full of meaning, and what gives it "meaning" in the sense you use it, is value; an idea we must consider further.

'For my part', he continued, 'I have come from a tradition with a philosophy of life that accepts there is no such thing as the supernatural. Consequently, I have no difficulty with the idea that I live while I am here and cease to exist when dead. If you are afraid of not existing after death, I think you are afraid of reality. And you have no need to be, for those are the terms which enable us to enjoy life in the first place. To invent scenes of immortality is almost certainly to seek refuge in delusion; and delusion if it progresses far enough subverts or even dislodges reason, and distorts lives.

'We may make a reservation for the possibility that something of our spirits – the spirit we have developed through our consciousness – may survive, or may pass into something different – though your Buddhists and Hindus have concluded the opposite – that the idea of nirvana is oblivion. We cannot state that some form of survival is theoretically impossible, for our knowledge is not sufficient; but it is unimportant to our lives: it will happen or it will not, and so far no mechanism for it has remotely been shown to exist; and increases in other knowledge make it less likely.

'And far from making life pointless, this conviction reinforces the natural feeling of all animals, including humans, that this life is what we have and know we have. We should therefore enlarge and cultivate our understanding of it and our opportunities for happiness in it while we can. That is why it is a crime to take life, especially unjustly or unnecessarily, for with life you take nearly everything.

'Let us clear the way. The idea that you are "put here" presupposes that there is someone – I take it you mean God – to do the "putting". This immediately gives rise to a host of difficulties: why are so many (of every species that has ever existed) only nearly "put here"? Billions upon billions of seeds and eggs have started out, but withered and died. Among all species of mammals, including man, there have been countless millions of naturally aborted foetuses, and those who suffer death at birth, or those who shortly after birth are preyed upon and devoured, or become sick and die, or are malformed and cannot long survive. It would be an inexplicably strange way for an all-loving, all-powerful, life-giving creator God to behave.

'But if you conclude there is no God, all these difficulties are immediately resolved and the original question itself is seemingly meaningless. No-one "put" us here. There is no person or power that exists, or ever has existed which could do so.

'And your question "Why are we here?" becomes simple to answer. Immediately, it is because our parents came together in sexual intercourse on a certain day so that just one unique egg and sperm were joined and grew. Beyond that you can follow the trail backwards to your grandparents and earlier fore-bearers and ancestors. And beyond that the chain goes back to the development of your species, and beyond that to earlier forms of life, and so on back to the start of life and beyond that again to the formation of the planets and stars and the universe itself. That is why you are here, because of what has happened over fourteen billion years. At the latest part of that tremendous natural creation we are here because we were born and have survived.

'That is enough. To me the knowledge you have shown to me, which your species has painstakingly and cumulatively put together, is vastly more wonderful than all the strange myths and stories invented in your previous imaginings. It has about it a rising clarity of truth, evidenced by thousands of reason-based and demonstrable known events, cross-checked and understood by cause and effect and falling into a cumulative and explicable pattern of development. You humans have unravelled a more wonderful and astonishing explanation of natural creation than anything an imagination could conceive. For those of you – and may it spread to all – who have the chance to acquire true knowledge, it awaits your discovery, if you will but consider the evidence and abandon contrary ignorance. And, for the better future of the world, I hope you will conclude that you have a moral duty to do so.'

So said Tisala. In the silence that followed I remember thinking with a quiet ecstatic joy, as I looked across our calm haven, that Guinevere's island – the Island of the Sea – was for Susannah and me at that moment the most beautiful and important place on Earth. For here was being worked out in our own lives something remarkable in the history of life. I knew Susannah felt it too from the way she looked at me with her deepest eyes. That night we made love with the intent to bring a child into the world.

CHAPTER 61

On Meaning and Value in Life

When we resumed our discussions a day or so later Tisala said:

'So let us consider now what gives life meaning. And that entails exploring what gives it value. It seems commonly supposed among you humans that producing happiness is what makes a thing valuable. But it is the reverse of this, for we found that happiness is an emotional consequence derived from good things that we identified as giving rise to it. It is not the happiness that bestows value. It is the thing of value that bestows happiness. Happiness is the result, the outcome, of doing or being something that you recognise as being valuable; that in some part fulfils your aspiration to higher humanity, and is found most completely perhaps by fulfilment in a nobly balanced life. And that is why, without that higher balance, happiness's lower manifestations of contentment and pleasure can be a distraction or contrary influence. Contentment can lead merely to sloth, and pleasure to dissipation. So we should focus, not on the happiness engendered, but behind it to see where value arises.

'The usefulness of happiness is that, being pleasurable, but a greater good than mere pleasure, it encourages further thought and behaviour that gives rise to itself, so promoting the doing of valuable things: a state badly needed in the human world.'

Tisala put forward a number of areas where value is found.

The first is in our bodies and health, which, though obvious, he said we appeared too often to overlook or take for granted: ask anyone suffering from lacerations, amputations or other wounds, or anyone suffering from a painful disease, or who becomes blind or deaf. The bodily destruction of value and thereby happiness by fighting and wars, and other self-inflicted misery continually dismayed him. For health is perhaps the most valuable thing we have, and the enjoyment of a healthy body gives irreplaceable value in life, and an easy route to happiness.

The second is in relationships whether personal, as in friendship or love, or social, such as work or community related, which give rise to one of the most important areas of value. Of course, in reality social and personal relationships overlap and merge, as perhaps pre-eminently and most valuably in family relationships.

He thought it clear that man, though aggressive and quarrelsome, is a gregarious animal, who values – and should value greatly – a form of society where he belongs and can be useful. Such conditions increase the personal and social value of a life, and contain and diminish belligerent attitudes. Among the many mechanisms of relationships he cited the bonding effect of human humour and laughter, which he thought was developed in nature for this purpose; and that we only had to look at the converse of happy relations, breakdown and hatred, to realise the value of sociable attributes and characteristics.

The third area he marked out, strongly linked to the second, is that of moral and ethical conduct, altruism, and spiritual care, which the wise among us have rightly identified as essential endeavours to give value and therefore happiness in human life. In the individual sphere, good thought and conduct contributes much to a fulfilled and balanced life. And in a social context these attributes, of which he thought kindness a foremost example, can transform the workings of society. But what is needful here are commonly accepted standards and assumptions. And that, in a world where previously separate societies now mix and live together through the enormous advances in communication and travel, is one of humanity's biggest challenges.

'To that,' he said, 'I shall return shortly.'

Tisala's fourth area was knowledge. He thought the world of knowledge perhaps the most wonderful thing about humanity. But for knowledge to deliver its true value it must be available and transferable. Our understanding of the physical world and the workings of those parts of it we label biology, chemistry, physics and maths, together with the whole superstructure of society and civilisation – arts and architecture, political and social institutions, economics, medicine, engineering and the rest: he thought all of this the most awesome achievement of our more enlightened people. Our advance owes much to finding out and applying knowledge.

And on the obverse side, the consequences of our previous lack of knowledge have been gradually diminished: the dark and bloody times of superstition – tribal, ritualistic and religious; the inability or failure to understand so many things, from illness and disease within our bodies, outwards to all the world.

But, inexorably in our human world, with knowledge came too the misuse of knowledge, very often by those who also abuse influence and power. 'And to that I must also return,' he said.

His fifth value area was that of skills acquired by individuals. He was intrigued by the sheer multiplicity of physical skills and practices among humans. Many are among valuable everyday things, as in the many aspects of home-making and cultivation, or in other occupational training and careers. Some are in particular activities like music, art, sport or pastimes. He thought it plainly obvious but often under-recognised that such things add a sense of value to the individual's life and accordingly trigger pleasure, contentment and happiness, both fulfilling and encouraging people further.

'And the downside?' I asked, for I knew there would be one.

'Among particular things there is the danger of imbalance. People who devote their lives to a monoculture and afterwards find failure, or that their devotion is passed over or discounted, have paid too high a price in terms of their fuller human purpose.' He cited narrowly focussed sportsmen whose lives are ruined by a career-ending injury, or artists who after years of burning obsessional activity one day stare at their canvas and know that in their hands paint is just paint, and face self-destruction. 'When the magic in the mind that buoys up the endeavour fades or is extinguished, you need your wider and deeper humanity.

'I see it is a dilemma, for to achieve excellence you must focus on the thing, but it is a sad error among humans to destroy your life for it. You must consider the worth of your skills. For to acquire a high level of skills in a trivial endeavour is no mere investment in your life, but consumes part of your life and carries the cost of greater things foregone. And the telltale sign of this imbalance is success or failure leading to a life out of joint, as in financial profligacy or alcoholism, and to personal misery.

'Sometimes you should laugh at your earnestly acquired skills, for many of them lead to imbalanced ways of life like those of a snooker player who spends his life tapping balls across a table-top, or a juggler, or accountant, or a thousand others. For laughter brings perspective and humility and reminds you that the purpose of skills is to give value in your lives.'

These five areas he thought some of the main ones. But we should cultivate our awareness of the range of values everywhere present in our lives, and know that in reality they are not separate categories, but run together and merge.

'For instance a nurse may find value, and from it happiness, in her skill and knowledge, in her working relationships, some of which become personal friendships, and in moral and altruistic values arising out of her care for patients.' He paused, and with his smiling sound added, 'As we know, doctors and nurses sometimes fall in love.'

And I remembered the effect Susannah's care for him had had on me. Even when stricken with terrible wounds, he had finely observed.

'It is each person's privileged opportunity to educate themselves as well as possible throughout their lives. And to work out what is the proper and meaningful structure of their lives. For assuredly it is your higher pleasurable duty as a human, and is within the power of all individuals, by what you learn and do, to make your own life and through it those of others, more valuable.

'And that is one reason why untimely death, particularly of the young, is so upsetting: it strikes down this upward process. And if you believe it true that there is no afterlife, untimely death is sad, for it is final. And this should make you more careful of life, and an enemy of sudden death, whether by avoidable disease, or civil and doctrinal killings, or war and all the rest.'

He spoke of moral conduct and thought we should search it out both for its own sake and as adding value to life, and through it increased happiness on Earth. And to do so without any longer needing or relying on the possibility of something beyond – the idea of heavenly reward, or being burdened by the threat of punishment in hell. For although those ideas have sometimes comforted people or curbed their excesses, very often they have not, but instead have distorted human views and conduct of life as it should be. 'Does not belief in the supernatural separate you from reality and truth, and imprison your true spiritual freedom, which is philosophic love?'

He said the spirituality that religion responded to in its, to him, strange supernatural constructions was in reality our natural spirituality, present to some degree in various higher animals. Our capacity for this had increased as we evolved into consciousness, and could then be advanced by thought, training and deliberate habits. Love and goodness had been sought by us in our lives, for they lead to better and happier lives and help to free us from our lower animal traits. He saw spirituality as an enlightened state of consciousness, nourished by higher feelings and reason.

He thought the more we can cultivate these things, the more value in proportion our lives will have. When we say we have a purpose in life, we are saying we have found things of value that give life meaning. It is for all to increase this quality in their lives. 'I have looked at happiness first, and now value, and its consequential release of happiness,' said Tisala, 'as part of what may give you new insight, for we all need a worthwhile vision and aim. And since I understand many of you cannot now believe in heaven and the supernatural, these things may help you find new inspiration, so you will less often lose yourselves in the distractive troubles and small pleasures of life.'

But as part of this re-assessment he thought, both in the private and public domains, that the need for agreement on moral behaviour was startlingly clear.

He was surprised that we had not made a universal code in the light of new knowledge. And even more surprised that the world still relied on such codes as the Buddha's and the Judaic Ten Commandments, albeit improved by its own amendments in the Talmud and by the ethical teaching of Jesus of Nazareth.

These codes often antedated much new knowledge, or were law-based on then current ideas and expediency. They spawned rules imposed by Christian churches and Islam and many other religions, and often had not much to do with any system of moral conduct, but more with the social or political aims of leaders, or with supplications to the Gods or God and the perceived demand of deity for worship and obedience.

He thought that if you look at the old religious texts in this light you see that some well-known writings, such as The Lord's Prayer in Christianity, which answer these God-led requirements, have scarcely a reference to any moral or ethical matters. So that, when there is no longer a belief in that God, there is a dislocation in the conduct of men's lives.

He thought humans therefore needed the help of a universally accepted moral code. 'For the world is otherwise too complicated to manage.' He saw that the history of mankind is strewn with the consequences of the lack or breakdown of agreement on moral conduct. And he concluded that, if our higher humanity is to be more fulfilled and the worst excesses of our natures avoided, man, the social and herd animal, needs the greatest agreement he can get among his fellows as to both private and public conduct.

All this leads to the importance of moral codes that can be widely taught, accepted and acted upon. He saw valiant attempts made in many of our civilisations to promote or impose such codes, attempts which were often frustrated or made divisive or fragmented by being tied to the fortunes of a particular religion or culture, which in due course was likely to fail. Some have attempted universalisation, but usually either from within a religion or a philosophy or from self-interested motives, as in our codes for the conduct of war, which are then too often widely disregarded, except when convenient.

But now for the first time in history the whole world of humanity is sufficiently linked for there to be a new universal code of ethics and conduct. This should be a code of principles to be accepted and acted upon, and afterwards reflected in all societies, cultures and religions, and in national and international law so far as possible.

One day he said, 'You have taught me of the affairs and minds of men for twenty years. I offer you a code of moral principles. They are not wholly new, nor can they be, but perhaps they advance earlier codes.' And they came fully formed from his mind, and he gave them as follows:

1. In all things be and act as a trustee of the Earth.

2. Love all creatures who are worthy of no harm, and visit no cruelty or suffering on any.

3. Do not arbitrarily, carelessly, wastefully or without good cause destroy living creatures or plants, for life is precious.

4. Love all mankind, and your neighbour, who is everyone whom your actions affect; show respect and do kindness and good to them as you would wish done to yourself.

5. Love, honour and respect your father and mother, your

partner and your children as you would wish to be loved, honoured and respected by them.

6. Seek out, and live with, honesty, wisdom, love, justice, courage, restraint and hope.

7. Seek to give and receive value and happiness by developing your own better nature and qualities; and behave towards all sentient creatures so as to promote their chances of happiness in life.

8. Practice forgiveness and mercy until the enmity within you dissolves, and you earn yourself the gift of peace; and never deliver retaliation or revenge, for they will corrupt your spirit and life.

9. Always speak the truth, except where true kindness otherwise requires.

10. Always seek peace; meet tolerance with tolerance; and intolerance with wisdom and persuasion.

11. If you have a religion or other set of beliefs seek always to examine and improve it, and, apart from ceremony with fellow believers, believe your religion in private; and as against other religions or beliefs claim no exclusive rightness and allow others, being peaceable, to follow what they believe in as you would wish them to respect your beliefs likewise.

12. Do not kill or wound or physically harm another human, except in necessary, immediate and proportionate self-defence.

13. Do not steal; nor seek possession of that which belongs to another, except by free agreement.

14. Before bringing a new life into the world consider, accept and act upon your personal and wider responsibilities; and consider the long outcome you may place on any life so created.

15. Before consuming, or causing the use of, resources

consider the state and happiness of the world, and of your spirit, and act accordingly.

'You will see at once,' said Tisala, 'that these no longer put forward any demands from an authoritarian god or one concerned with procuring his own worship. For such demands are no longer believable by many, and so are not of universal or unifying use.

'This new Code of Ethics arises instead from insights of reason and love. It seeks to advance the spirit of life on Earth. These are precepts from what wisdom we have acquired; and being so are capable of improvement. Their aim is the good of all in the Earth. I give them to you as a gift from the ocean, for the learning you have given to me.'

When we had written them out I remember feeling – with a sense of awe – that we held in our hands a new inheritance for our planetary intellect, distilled from a mind, the mind of a Blue Whale, presently, but not in the future, unique in creation. Mankind was no longer intellectually alone. And here was a new code of advancement for all peoples. We came to call them 'The Universal Ethic' and often referred to them as 'The Tisalan Precepts'.

But my initial sense of euphoria was short-lived. For Tisala said that this was not enough. It was only one side of the work: the precepts were for people in their individual, social and religious lives. The next need was for a similar code in the public domain. For he saw the colossal damage industrialised man and modern warfare might inflict on the world, exacerbated by the threats of foolish or evil rulers.

'And that,' he said, 'Is the next difficult challenge to be overcome.'

As he spoke I turned to Susannah, and we looked at each other with a wild surmise. I felt a surge of hope, and for a moment I nearly believed Tisala could change mankind, which denotes my own foolishness.

And not least and most immediately because of the continuing threat to Tisala's life from the Norwegian and Icelandic whalers in the North Atlantic and Arctic, as we were soon reminded.

CHAPTER 62

Whaling: the 1980s and the Japanese

In those years the campaign against whaling was continuing. And in the islands we monitored the struggle with close attention. We knew that the great majority of whalers were now abiding by the rules giving absolute protection to the Blue Whales. But we knew also from Tisala's terrible wounds that it would only need one renegade or 'mistaken' killing for the disaster we dreaded most to happen. Every time Tisala left for the Arctic we knew he might be hunted and killed, that his awe-inspiring fund of knowledge, goodwill and wisdom might be savagely exploited by an illegal harpooner chasing nothing more than illicit profits. Remove profits, and the odds for the whales improve again. So we awaited the longed-for moratorium on commercial whaling. Each hunting season was impatiently ticked off, and the next anxiously awaited.

But at last the day came when the moratorium was implemented: from the Antarctic summer of October 1985 to March 1986, and the Arctic summer of 1986. It was to apply for five years, and then be reviewed. It was a reprieve, not a permanent cessation, but it was a vital advance.

On Inis Cuan we celebrated it as a great day for the survival of the whales, and for the slow civilisation of mankind. But we knew many difficulties and loopholes remained and that the whaling nations would continue to fight for their cruel rewards. And so they did. It was not long before we heard how the worst offending nations put up new stratagems.

At the centre of the web of dishonour – for that is how I had come to view it – sat Japan, the country with the largest whaling fleet in the world, and the Soviet Union. Both formally objected to the ban, which therefore did not apply to them, and continued to kill whales commercially both in the Northern Hemisphere and in the Antarctic, where they brazenly violated the world's sanctuary. But both also agreed they would not hunt the protected great whales. Their main target was now said to be Minke Whales, of which they admitted to killing over 5,500 in that first season of the moratorium.

Norway too, officially objected, and by the defective letter of the Convention law continued to hunt whales commercially, 'harvesting' nearly 400 Minke Whales in the first summer, 1986. Iceland and South Korea had both announced that they would give up commercial whaling, but immediately commence 'scientific' whaling. That first summer the Icelandic whalers killed over 130 whales 'for research', including over eighty of the great Fin Whales, near cousins of Tisala's Blues. I wrote angry letters to the Icelandic Government at this further destruction of the endangered Fin Whales by the abuse of the concept of scientific research.

The Icelandic Government remained silent.

It had been internationally accepted that to prevent covert trade, whale meat resulting from research should primarily be for local consumption. But the Icelandic and Norwegian public did not want it on that scale, and only a tiny percentage – some said five percent – was so used. And what happened to the many tons of whale-meat, the 'by-product' of this 'research'? It was discovered that the Japanese were facilitating the survival of these countries' remaining whaling industries by providing a secret whale-meat market. In 1986 whale-meat from the 'scientific' catches by Norway and Iceland was found being sent to Japan, some of it marked '1985', thus pretending to be whale-meat caught prior to the moratorium.

I said bitterly to Tisala, 'It carries the trademark deceit of whalers. And the research will be a charade. It is commercial whaling by any other name: and the stench is the same – lies, greed and hypocrisy.'

But the Icelandic whaling industry soon paid a penalty for its deviousness. At the end of 1986 conservationist saboteurs entered the main Icelandic whale processing plant and smashed the computers and other equipment with sledgehammers, unplugged the refrigeration on 2,000 tons of whale-meat. Then back in Reykjavik, they attacked two of Iceland's four whaling vessels by opening the stopcocks. The vessels sank, and with them, for the moment, sank the Icelanders' profits; and their costs rose.

And in these years the tide of public opinion and attitude was steadily moving against the whalers. A number of member countries in the IWC, following the Australian lead of 1978, now took the view that commercial whaling, certainly for most of the great whale species, should be permanently banned.

In 1987 the Russians, whose once huge fleet was much diminished and near the end of its useful life, ceased whaling in Antarctica. In the same year the Norwegians, who, though obdurate whalers, had perhaps tried hardest – albeit in their own interest – to come up with viable scientific knowledge to enable them to continue whaling, felt obliged to announce that they would abandon commercial whaling. But immediately replaced it with 'scientific' whaling.

And the next year, 1988, we learned that Japan, under trade pressure from the Americans, would also accept the moratorium; though in their case the replacement plans, for 'scientific' whaling, included the proposed annual killing of over 800 Minke Whales and 50 Sperm Whales, on a more or less permanent ongoing basis. The scale of it – which was almost the same as their previous commercial kill – said everything.

'It is surprising', said Tisala, 'how a country that takes its honour seriously can allow such a thing to be done in its name.'

I said, 'Yes, and the whalers are backed strenuously by the Japanese government.'

'And the Japanese people? Do they know what is being done, and how?'

But that I did not know, and found it difficult to answer, though I said they had a weak free press, with little discussion of these issues, and were a publicly conformist society.

And when the Scientific Committee of the IWC, which was now conservationist, in due course reviewed the results of the new 'research' by Japan, Norway, Iceland and South Korea, they found it variously defective, irrelevant, unusable and adding little or nothing to previous knowledge. The results were so predictable that in a strange way I found the confirmation the more depressing, for it confirmed also that, though whaling was supposedly reformed, the remaining whalers were not. The adoption of 'scientific' whaling was in most cases a stratagem to preserve their whaling fleets until the moratorium could be reviewed, and as they hoped, abolished, in 1990. And this desire was in turn driven largely by the Japanese whale-meat market.

Yet as we watched these developments, and quietly continued our work, we hoped that their enthusiasm for 'scientific' whaling would tail off in the wake of results that did not aid their cause, and as their ships aged; and as it became clearer that the non-whaling majority on the IWC would vote to retain the moratorium after 1990, and perhaps indefinitely.

The war, at least for the Great Whales, seemed almost to be won, but it was never a final victory, for it was a moratorium imposed by the votes of a whaling body, some of whose members, though a tiny self-interested fraction of humanity, wanted badly to reverse it. We knew that only when there was a permanent and accepted cessation would the long term future of Blues, Fins, Sei, Bowhead, Humpback, Right, Grey and Sperm Whales be safe from annihilation by men.

But meanwhile, the news over those years that came back from Tisala's family and wider contacts gradually improved. There were still pitifully few Blues left alive, but slowly their numbers were increasing. By the late 1980s we knew from our feedback that the Blue Whale population of the world had risen from the near-extinction numbers of about 1,600 to nearly 4,000 over the 25 year period. Slowly, and with relief, increased live births and then survival were being reported. Tisala's son Saba now had four children. All had survived to adulthood, unlike the decimated generations before them. One of them was Tarba, who we had met in the Tropics, named after Tisala's father.

And they in turn had begun the next generation. Tisala's first great-grandchild was born in 1980 and by the end of the 1980s he had five. Young Nessini, Tisala's great niece, who we had so fallen for in that visit to the Tropics, now had a baby daughter herself.

We knew now that, provided men never again hunted Blue Whales, the greatest beings ever to live on the planet would survive in their natural habitat. They would continue to add to the wonder of the world, and in Tisala and who knows what successors, we might find wisdom that might help save mankind from itself.

But their society was still fractured, a remnant of its former glory. Tisala thought that it would take a hundred years for a viable form of it to be restored. 'Beyond that,' he said 'we cannot see: we whales, left to ourselves, might in 200 years – if the balance of oceanic life is favourable – perhaps restore something like our former society.'

One day, when I was talking to Tisala about the iniquities of the Japanese whalers, I said: 'Nowadays, whenever there is bad news about whaling the name of Japan is always present.'

But Tisala startled me by saying: 'The poor Japanese.'

'The poor Japanese? – They kill whales everywhere they can, and to do so, lie, dissemble, bribe, cheat, deceive and falsify their science.'

But Tisala reprimanded me.

'You must distinguish. The whalers and the government are not the Japanese people.'

'But are not the people complicit? I've never heard of them protesting about what is done in their name.'

'In part, perhaps; but ask why. Here you have a secluded land, whose religion in world terms has always been weak in ethics, and whose society in the past has been cruel and rigidly hierarchical, with a tradition both of social subservience internally, and arrogance towards outsiders. This, as we know, was used in the nineteenth and twentieth centuries by the militarily inclined rulers of Japan while introducing western industrialisation. First they elevated the Emperor into a divinity, and then used loyalty to the Emperor and the traditions of subservience and arrogance to launch terrible, unprincipled military adventures, in the guise of deluded dreams of empire.

All that is true. But a hundred years ago, to the Japanese, Japan must have seemed like an almost endless world within a sea-girt world – beautiful and rugged terrain, exuberant vegetation, thousands of miles of coastline, islands lying beyond islands, seemingly forever – a vast area of land and sea scarcely ever travelled or seen from end to end by its people, virtually none of whom had contact with the outside world. In short, just the place to foster delusions of uniqueness and superiority; and unfortunately urged in that direction by the caste of mind of its rulers and the educational system they imposed. So was achieved the exclusion of free thought, and knowledge of different and better ways, which on any objective view had been discovered among a number of the more advanced sections of mankind elsewhere in the world.

'That is why. And this is why too, all may now change: education, television, bullet trains and aircraft, travel and the internet – all will show them irretrievably that they live in a modest and not always enviable chain of volcanic islands on an unstable part of the Pacific rim, and that, in the wider world, as well as bad, there is much good, some of it more advanced than in their own islands.'

Tisala continued: 'So I argue that it is the tiny but still arrogantly nationalistic Japanese whaling interests, backed by their government – which is complicit – who impose a moral degradation on Japan. They think they are defending a national interest. But what they do is to cut their people off from common humanity. It is not a question of doing what foreigners want, or following an alien culture. What is asked of the Japanese people is to join a universal ethic and attitude to life. The whalers damage the soul of Japan.'

I said: 'And there must be reformers in government who would help them negotiate a cessation. It would do more for the good reputation of Japan than anything else.'

Susannah said: 'Yes, and I bet their government could easily deal with remaining employment and compensation issues.' And afterwards she embarked on a program of research that showed conclusively that the economic and social cost of the cessation of whaling was derisorily small: all that prevented it was political will. Her paper was sent to the Japanese government, but was never publicly acknowledged.

But beyond these issues, Tisala's mind had already ranged more widely. For he hoped and trusted that one day, men would cease to hunt whales. But he had come to know too that the future of whales, with much other life, would also depend on man, not just as a hunter, but as a world-dominating species, who even now was changing the planet.

For in those days we were becoming increasingly aware of the threat posed by a mankind whose own numbers are out of control – growing billions requiring ever more food, resources, and energy; in the oceans scooping up the fish with ever larger nets, destroying stock after stock, treating as enemies any competitor animals in their natural habitat; and perhaps fatally unbalancing the food chains and ecosystems, so that the whole terrestrial and marine world may be plunged into a crisis of survival; these and other threats arising directly from the desire to feed, house and service our billions, with their insatiable demands, resulting in alarming exploitation, and large scale industrial pollution.

For, though the Earth is a rich and wonderful place, over these years Tisala saw the shadow of a dark future advancing over the horizon. It came out of the land, but threatened not only the land but the oceans; and over them both, the most delicate part of the Earth: the shimmering miraculous mix of gasses that make up the essential life-providing atmosphere, the air we breathe.

'You men, focussed largely on your own busy nation states and their growing economies, do not seem to see what is entirely obvious to an outsider; and your politicians resolutely do not want to see. All that is needed is to consider the simple arithmetic.'

He said that what we had told him, but not apparently understood, was this: that in, say, 1900 – only one lifetime ago – the industrialised world consisted of quite small parts of America, Britain, Germany, a few other European countries and Japan. Out of a then world population of about 1,600 million, the industrialised world, with its pull on resources and its pollution, was only about 100 million people.

By 2000 Tisala understood that out of a total population of 6 billion, the industrial urbanised population of the world would be, very roughly, 2 billion; and both growing more rapidly than at any previous time in history.

He said: 'If my son Saba survives a full lifetime, the population of the human world might be nine billion people or more – half as big again as it now is, but with a greater proportion of industrialisation: an industrial consuming population perhaps three times as big as now. Who knows what will happen if your population continues to grow and burn resources and pollute on the scale you are now doing. These things might prove too much for the ecological balance of the planet: they could precipitate fundamental change: of temperature, weather and seasons.'

In those days of the mid-1980s, even Tisala did not see clearly the speed of potential and catastrophic climate changes. For in our ignorance we did not give him the information which was then accumulating. And although he warned us of changes – warming in the Arctic and Antarctic pack ice – it was then in its early stages. But in general terms he foresaw what might be coming. And at the root of it all was the size of the human population and its relentlessly increasing demand for material consumption.

But these things, although then seen, seemed in a distant future. At the time Susannah and I had more immediate concerns.

CHAPTER 63

Families

Our hoped-for child did not arrive according to plan: the months went by without Susannah becoming pregnant, and anxiety crept into our rationalisations. And we felt the old insistent power of unborn babies drumming in our veins, and seeking entrance in the world.

But in the autumn of 1986 we found to our delight that she was expecting, and as all progressed well anxiety melted into happy anticipation. We prepared for the baby's arrival in June.

In the maternity ward after Susannah had been through six hours of painful labour, through the anxious peaks and troughs of agony and respite, I watched our daughter come into the world, leaving the haven of her mother's womb. First a dark patch appeared – the top of her head, pressing out between Susannah's widely parted legs, out from her heaving, pushing body, the swollen abdomen rising and falling with gasping cries of her efforts. The midwife, assisted by a nurse, had been calm and encouraging and now was full of praise as she eased the baby out. I watched, and once again thought it miraculous. Miraculous, like the birth of whales in the oceans; perhaps like all births, miraculous, yet everyday and universal.

Susannah, sweating and exhausted, held our baby close. But when she looked up she smiled at me in pure joy.

We called her Julie. As babies do, she changed our domestic life. The cries and gurgles, the whispered quiet, the smells, the warmth, the nursery colours, and the kicking and soon-smiling helpless tyrant, all transformed our house in Battersea.

But the larger pattern of our lives went on. We took her to Eileen Mòr that September, aged three months, where her great-grandmother doted on her, except when her crying persisted too long. Then Guinevere looked tired.

'She'll not remember me. I'm too old. But I'm delighted she's come.' She patted Susannah's hand and smiled at her.

'Of course she'll remember you', said Susannah, taken aback by her grandmother's bluntness. 'Don't be so silly, Gran.'

She smiled, accepting the reprimand.

'Yes, perhaps she will.' But she gazed out of the window with stretched old eyes, looking into the past.

Will came up to the islands as often as he could. He did a great deal to help me, especially in the period when Susannah was wrapped up with caring for the baby, and our working relations pleased me deeply. Angela had broken up with him, which caused him some misery, but slowly he found that he relished his freedom, and the excitement of new chases. When in the islands he had long conversations with Guinevere 'about life'. He learned much from her attitude to her own and earlier encounters and amorous experiences, about which she was quite open and straightforward. And she was always interested in his goings on and relationships, if sometimes disconcertingly perceptive and direct in her questions and comments.

'She's got an amazing perspective, Dad. Makes you think what you really think, and why. No flannel with Granny Gwen!'

He loved these talks and laughter with his honorary grandmother. Towards the end of her life they grew very close. 'My Will', she called him, proudly, and made it sound as if he were the most special young man in the world.

And the same was true on a larger scale in our talks with that other greatly honoured figure in his life – his philosopher friend, Tisala. Sometimes we held four-part conference talks, gathered round the equipment in the shack, in which Will, like Susannah and me, became wholly absorbed. And afterwards, when we were walking the island, or cooking, or sitting on the rocks by the harbour, the discussions would go on. At this time Tisala was exploring the wider reaches of public morality and politics.

But I noticed over the next two years that Guinevere was gradually sinking into a smaller world, forgetting things and facts, losing her wider interests, sometimes fretting over keeping up with her daily tasks and restricting her concerns to the welfare of those closest to her. Her letter-writing days were nearly gone, as were many of her friends. She wrote reminder notes to herself in an increasingly unsteady hand. But always she remained full of good humour and kindness.

At that time too Ellie's parents were beginning to show their age.

Over the years, I had continued to visit Edmund and Penelope with the children, but less as time went on. When they were teenagers and then students, they sometimes went down on their own. Occasionally Philip was there. We remained on good terms, but I felt less for him as the years went by and as he grew further away from Ellie. He had become an accountant and acquired many of the useful but limited preoccupations of that calling. And sometimes, if he said something disclosing a shallow attitude or with which I was out of sympathy, I found in myself a little flicker of resentment that he had lived and Ellie had not. It was no doubt unfair, but it was there, so I record it as an incident of animal behaviour. Susannah had already been down with me a couple of times. On the first visit, after our wedding, I had spent some of the weekend gardening with Edmund while Susannah had chatted with Penelope. But when we had a new child we somehow went less.

When Julie was two, we left her with Susan for the weekend and we went down to Fieldbanks House, with Will and Penny, who were always pleased to be with their grandparents. When we drove up Penelope and Edmund came out to greet us, and for a moment thirty years almost disappeared. Then the old excited tumult of arrival took over. But now Will and Penny towered over their grandparents, who were white-haired and frailer.

'Look out, Will,' laughed Penelope as he engulfed her in a hug, 'You'll knock me over.'

'Hi, Gran!'

'Grandpa!'

'David, Susannah. Come in.'

The rose on the front of the house was now enormous, but though magnificent had the feeling of unkemptness, with some stray branches blowing loose, and the deadheading neglected. Edmund saw me looking up at the rose.

'Too high,' he said. 'Can't cope. Anyway, the old girl won't let me up a ladder.' He looked at Penelope and said sideways to me, 'Don't always obey, though.'

There was a straggle of weeds along the edge of the gravel. But when we went through the house, the garden beyond was as neat and well cared for as ever, though now smaller: the bottom section had reverted to nature, and the paddock beyond was let out to a local farmer. Edmund now relied wholly on Tom Taylor, who had turned out to be a natural gardener.

'He knows the soil. It's patchy with the clay. If he says a plant will do well there, it does. If he shakes his head, it won't. He does everything now. Couldn't do without him.' Tom Taylor was now in his late fifties, and after his mother's death a few years before, had upped and married a village widow, to the pleasure of everyone, and his own happiness.

Penny and Will chatted intimately and at ease with their grandparents – health, news, relationships, careers. I saw Edmund looking proudly but wistfully at Penny. Sometimes both youngsters reminded me of Ellie – not only looks but a tone of voice, a glance or characteristic movement. And I saw her live again, passing into the lives of her children.

At their first meeting Penelope and Susannah had found they liked each other. And when Penelope saw how fond Will and Penny were of Susannah, that eased her heart. I watched with pleasure the warmth developing between them. Edmund, I think, did not see her as someone to whom he needed to relate closely, though he was always considerate and kind.

Not long after this visit, when I was telling Tisala about the family, he said, 'The pleasure we derive from family is a joy, but in humanity has become a problem too. You have created a huge difficulty for yourselves and the world by your vast numbers.

He thought it essential, for our own welfare as well as that of the world, to slow and then reverse the increase. And that this is best done by billions of individuals voluntarily deciding to have fewer children. The ways of achieving this are as many as there are many cross-currents of human desire and expectation to complicate the issue; yet essentially it is simple: it requires a conscious decision by each person to take control of their own life. And this in turn requires a certain level of education and achievement of individual thought and independence, sometimes in defiance of local customs.

He startled us by saying that a reduction by two thirds – from 6 billion to 2 billion – was a realistic long term aim. 'At any time in the history of the Earth up to the twentieth century, 2 billion would have seemed a colossal number.'

He thought we could learn that it is neither disastrous nor a form of failure to have less children, or even none at all. We should cultivate social acceptance and praise for such decisions. Then some will find their lives, and the contribution they may make, easier and better without the long commitment of child rearing. 'This has proved difficult for you humans to learn, because by biological chemistry and therefore also psychologically, like other animals you are largely geared to desire children; or at least the sex that results in them.

'But this urge and drive has outlasted its original reason and need for the survival of your species. Now the very success of the mechanism is counter-productive. It needs de-fusing. And it is clear that your modern contraception, freed from cultural and religious strictures and practice, and widely applied throughout the world, would do much to help break the mould by uncoupling sex from procreation.'

He said that dramatic change would come when it was recognised and accepted among the women of the world that, in general, two children, where they survive, can and will bring the joy of a complete family; and that larger numbers bring on the world a troublesome and even dangerous future. If that becomes the norm, among women of the world, and if they have sufficient control over their sex lives, he thought the future of the Earth, quite literally, could be transformed.

As to men, he thought the men in some cultures, and the uneducated, were a difficult part of the equation; a problem exacerbated because of the dominance of men in so many of our societies, demanding sex and not caring whether or not the women produce children, often many children. Among the poor it fuels hopelessness, among the rich it fuels pride and vanity in maleness, like the insistent dominance of rutting animals.

'Otherwise, what good do multiple children do a man? He increases the burden on the Earth and on himself and his wife, and raises up future growth in a numerous new generation. Rather, fathers should befriend each child and educate themselves, their wives and their children for happiness in their world. That is a more noble way.'

Tisala noted, of course, that a reduction in our numbers would over time also ease the pressure on resources. But he noted too that for the individual, finding happiness often leads to a decline in the desire for material goods; but many of these, like fancy clothes or cars or precious jewels, often acquired at great cost, have little fundamental value. He thought that they lead, not to happiness, but rather to a misleading sense of pride and false superiority. Often better things are free or abundant, like kindness or fresh bread, and render acquisitiveness useless, because they please our whole being, body and spirit.

But in the end Tisala remarked, individual reform alone is not enough: the political and industrial competition of nations needs to be reformed at national level, and by seeking international and global solutions. But that requires a wider view of focus and vision, and the will of nations to act in concert.

By such discussions, we arrived at politics.

CHAPTER 64

The Nation State, War and Peace

'The willingness of the nations to act in concert,' said Tisala, 'has been sorely missing in the modern human world.'

He saw that, though the nation state has in the past been a useful way to organise ourselves, it has always had major drawbacks, and with the accretion of economic and military power has grown ever more destructive and threatening.

'Who can think that the nation state, with its sacrosanct sovereignty and ability to make war on its neighbours or more distant states – any seen as crossing or impeding its "interests" – is in its traditional form any longer an adequate model?' But he did not advocate the abolition of countries – he found too much of value in them – but their modification and the development of alternative structures.

I had taught Tisala something of modern political history. As usual, when we discussed it, he summarised it with ease and clarity, in a new light. He said: 'Too much of your history is of wars. You are mesmerised by the drama and spectacle of war. Your endeavours to build peace are forgotten. We should therefore consider the history of peace or its failure, for if that is not understood it will be to the lasting cost of future generations.'

I had traced the emergence of the nation states in Europe in the sixteenth century, which may perhaps be taken as the beginning of the modern world. The dominant power to be contained and balanced was the Hapsburg power of Spain and Austria-Hungary. By the end of the seventeenth century and through the eighteenth century it was France, culminating in the European Alliances against the expansionary wars of Napoleon. Always one side saw containment, the other encirclement; which was which merely depended on who was dominant.

I had told him how our nations had proceeded by trying to achieve a balance of power: not of real national co-operation, but alliances of military pacts with a view of balancing enmities, and to contain alien power. And the reason it continually broke down was that each protagonist, when he thought he was strong enough, wanted to seize his advantage. Thus 'victories' were attained, though they usually provoked sufficient opposition for the end result to be counter-destruction, before a new balance was struck in the peace treaties. Foolishly imagined glory and power, but not the cost of it, was the traditional limit of that mind-set.

Accompanying and following these attempts to balance the steadily increasing power of the nation states came the era of land and empire grabbing: when nationally organised states took over other areas of the world where there was no such state-organised resistance.

Tisala said he understood that Spain and Portugal led the way in much of the New World; Britain in India and North America, clashing with France in these and other areas such as the West Indies. In Asia, in the nineteenth century, Russia expanded east and south across huge areas, with attempts to contain them by the British and French, and eventually, at the beginning of the twentieth century by the Japanese in the east, who were pursuing their own expansionist agenda and wars. Meanwhile, many colonising nations were pushing at the doors of old Imperial China. And in the New World, America was enlarging itself by purchase, war, internal expansion and colonisation into a continental and potentially a world power. Curiously, almost the last 'empty' place to be carved up was Africa, where the traditional powers of Britain, France, Portugal and The Netherlands were joined by the newly emergent and economically powerful Germany, and then Italy and Belgium.

And throughout this process, trade and imperial expansion went hand in hand; they fed off each other. From time to time throughout the history of these 400 years the balance of power broke down: that is the history of modern warfare. It did so disastrously in the Napoleonic wars. And, arising out of that traumatic experience, after an unstable but partly successful balancing act in the nineteenth century, in the catastrophic World Wars of the twentieth century.

'So now you have reached the frightening Cold War stand-off of national and ideological enmities. And round the skirts of this great threatening conflict are many nationalistic wars of independence, of states emerging from former empires; wars you tell me where the sovereignty of nation states is used by internal factions to crush opponents and to advance themselves to power.'

Thus states emerge in various forms of national, ethnic, economic and religious ideology, and potential enmity; and too often the nation state legitimises tyranny and evil. He said: 'It is clear and sad that so many new states behave like clones of their imperial parents and seek to extend their own influence and boundaries, and overrule their own minorities. The key is to establish by consent a unit that is viable and happy in itself, and able to grow more so.'

He could not initially understand why we had not made more progress away from national wars. 'Were there no attempts to restrict your warmongering?' I told him of earlier attempts to create more international structures, such as the terms of the Quadruple Alliance, the victors in 1815, who, after the destructive horrors of the Napoleonic Wars, agreed to meet thereafter on a fixed regular basis, 'For the consideration of measures most salutary for the repose and prosperity of nations and for the maintenance of the Peace of Europe'. But it was a mere alliance of the 'Great Powers' of the day. No other states were included, and there was no recourse to arbitration or international law. The 'Great Powers' were insufficiently advanced for that, as was shown by the abortive attempts by the Czar of Russia to broaden the alliance into one embracing all the signatory countries of the Treaty of Vienna, and to guarantee peace by international law. And in the next hundred years all was lost in the swelling tide of rivalry between nation states. The more I looked at history from Tisala's perspective, the more extraordinary and foolish it appeared to be.

But I found that there had been attempts to break the pattern, though often confined to the small print of our history books, and written off as 'failures'. After the jostling for position of Crimea and the Franco-Prussian War and in the comparative calm that followed, real advance was made in Europe: international co-operation and organisations were established in commercial, labour, cultural and scientific fields. But in politics and security the advance of arbitration, though increasingly used in international disputes – in nearly 300 cases between 1815 and 1914 – was confined to secondary matters. The greater use of such ideas was thwarted by the refusal of the 'Great Powers' to countenance any encroachment upon their complete sovereign independence.

I said, aware of the feebleness of the history of peace, that efforts had been made, particularly by another Czar of Russia, at the two Hague Peace Conferences in 1899 and 1907, to expand and regulate the application of international arbitration. The Czar, though well intentioned, had by the second Conference been made additionally aware of the ramshackle nature of his empire and its military weakness by Russia's naval defeat by Japan in 1904 and 1905. But no one else was as apprehensive as he, and the Conferences got no further than a pious declaration that 'restriction' on the 'heavy burden of arms procurement was extremely desirable for the increase of the material and moral welfare of mankind'.

In the years that followed, further attempts were made to include major military and security issues in arbitration. But despite the burden of the industrialised arms race on all the Powers, and its obvious dangers, all these attempts to achieve disarmament by such means failed totally. Ironically, treaties of arbitration were finally signed by the US, Britain and France in 1914. Germany refused, the Kaiser telling the American envoy romantically that he 'relied on his sword'; though he meant industrial power, artillery, machine guns and a malleably patriotic populace. And although it was the foolish German Emperor who said it, the others acted similarly.

Tisala said: 'So, in the pride and fear of states, their armies and nations grew towards the stupidity of a war which nearly destroyed Europe, and took the lives of 25 million people. So much for the "affairs of honour and vital interests of nation states". I have learned that whenever in your histories I hear "the honour and inviolate sovereignty" of nations being invoked, I know you will tell me that what followed was destruction.'

'Yes – what followed, the First World War, brought previously unimagined levels of destruction. It was so appalling it was dubbed "The War to End all Wars".'

'How did they think they were going to end all wars? They must have had wise aims, and a planned strategy to implement them – tell me of these.'

I read and searched, and found, dismayingly, the warring European leaders silent. The greatest war in history had no aims, except to defeat the enemy and not be conquered, and to sit amongst the winners at the Treaty party, arranging retribution and dividing up the territory of the losers. The phrase 'The War to End all Wars', and the desperate desire of people for it to be fulfilled, was empty rhetoric.

Tisala asked, 'Was it not a gross betrayal of the millions who died?'

Only in January 1918, as the war ground on in its fourth year, was a new voice and direction found, in America's President Wilson. His background qualification was as a lawyer and academic historian, which gave him an awareness of historical consequences and the requisite drafting skills. In his speech of Fourteen Points to Congress soon after America joined the War, in which he stated the aims of the war, he opened a new era and began to change the approach of nations. He sought open dealings between nations to remove the danger of secret pacts and understandings, so that powers would be disciplined by their public agreements. He advocated self-determination for all subject peoples, a wide measure of disarmament and equality of trade amongst all nations consenting to peace. His crowning idea was to form a 'general association of nations' to afford guarantees of political independence and territorial integrity to great and small states alike. Among nation states might was no longer to be right. The vehicle which was to change the world was the League of Nations: the first practical attempt to build an international organisation to promote world peace.

Tisala listened intently and questioned me closely.

I told him that it sought to provide an alternative to war between nations: to provide for the settlement of disputes by arbitration and consent, and for the use of collective force against aggressors. For the first time there would be a world body that would restrain the belligerence of nation states. Each member state, regardless of size or strength, was to have an equal vote. The League was to promote international law and was charged with running the international Court of Justice. Here was to be an attempt of all humanity to live in peace and harmony.

'But,' I added, 'it was a hopeless failure.'

Tisala made a disapproving sound. I recognised it at once, and in the silence that followed awaited my rebuke.

'Sometimes, David, you are as shortsighted as many of your politicians. Not a hopeless failure, but a political one. You humans should not dismiss such attempts as failures, or belittle them in your histories. From what you tell me your modern world has urgent need of such a concept. You must study why it failed, for that gives you a way forward. Besides, you are too dismissive: I understand the idea of self determination of peoples was eventually widely accepted, and the rights of small nations among large. Is that not so?'

I acknowledged that it was.

'So what went wrong?' asked Tisala. 'You were not ready to graft such a thing onto your existing world and attitudes, and the Great Powers would not give up their power?'

'Yes,' I said, 'you have surmised correctly.'

I recounted how The League was set up, not independently, but by, and incorporated into, the terms of the Treaty of Versailles imposed on the defeated Central Powers – Germany and the Austro-Hungarian Empire – at the end of the War. In the end this was the only way Wilson could persuade his recalcitrant European allies to accept it at all. The new League was therefore formed after, and too late to affect the terms of, the peace settlement which disastrously remained a Great Power affair.

It is well known how the Treaty itself was politically vindictive in the outdated manner of conquerors. Clemenceau's France demanded the severest retribution, although the French had not won the war, but had merely, with much help from Britain and allies from around the world, and latterly from America, not lost it. And though Germany had lost, it was itself untouched; the war had never reached German soil. Indeed, in Eastern Europe, following the collapse of the Russian Empire in 1917, the Germans were the victors, in possession of large swathes of previously Russian territories; and – in March 1918 – only months before the end, had shown their unreformed colours by imposing their own ruthlessly harsh territory-acquiring Treaty on an exhausted Russia. At Versailles these territories were stripped from Germany, as were its overseas colonial possessions. In some the principle of self-determination was applied, but some territories were distributed to the victors like prizes in a raffle. Germany's allies, the Austro-Hungarian and Turkish Empires had collapsed: they were dismembered into new nation states, largely based on ethnic principles, though the complications on the ground were often too much for simple map-making.

So were created both new nations and new dangers from transfers imposed on the losing combatants. For instance, Japan, although it had not fought, but because it was an ally of the victors, was handed German territories in China. The struggling reformers in republican China were ignored by the Western powers, as was the principle of self-determination, and the seeds of new conflict were thus scattered freely.

And the victorious powers, though insistent on divesting the losing powers both of their own territory and their possessions, had no truck with the idea of self-determination for their own territories and possessions. The British and French empires and the colonies of the other colonial powers would go blithely on as if nothing had happened.

'But it had,' said Tisala. 'The idea was out. However, was there great trouble before it advanced much further?'

'I hadn't thought of it like that, but yes.'

The real punishment imposed on Germany for the sin of imperial ambition was not territorial but economic. Dismembered, Austria-Hungary and the Ottoman Empire largely escaped. Monetary reparations were to force Germany to pay for the whole cost of the war. Not merely a king's or emperor's ransom, but the entire economic future of a large nation to be siphoned off over many years. This led, most immediately, to Germany's economic collapse in the early 1920s.

Tisala wanted to know how it was ever thought such reparations would work, and what arrangements were created for compliance and if need be, enforcement. Ultimately I could find him no answers, for there were none.

'It is the old spectre of men's imaginations betraying their reason. It is the small-minded, glittering idea of the spoils of war transmuted, by the colossal scale of the conflict and injury inflicted even on the victors, into retribution, revenge and repayment by damages.' Tisala thought it breathtakingly foolish.

I said that the Americans, and to some extent the British, tried to ameliorate the financial and economic penalties, which disregarded Germany's ability to pay. But they failed, so Treaty terms were demanded that did much to ensure further conflict, for the new German Republic was saddled with an impossible task, and its leaders with the opprobrium of complying.

Tisala said: 'So now tell me what I fear will be the sad history of the

League of Nations.'

And so I had to tell him how it failed. Of the powers that should have led it, the USA and Britain in effect withdrew. In a backlash against European and world involvement, and despite President Wilson's (sometimes self-righteous and inflexible) advocacy, the United States Congress refused to ratify – rejected – both the Peace Treaty and the League of Nations. America retreated into its own continent and its domestic affairs.

Tisala commented that Wilson's conception of the League should be held in due honour for its vision. 'You should spread such ideas,' he said. He thought that behind the failure of Congress lay the indifference or ignorance of the people. 'A democratic factor to which we shall be obliged to return.' He added: 'So, the then greatest democracy in the world refused a new role: it too would play the nationalistic game; and thereby bring on itself and the whole world much future trouble.'

I said that the British were guilty too. Although a member of the League, Britain was half-hearted, still thinking itself a victorious 'Great Power'. It refused to sign the fundamental Geneva Protocol for the internationalisation of peaceful settlement of disputes, an omission which brought one step closer the next round of war.

Early on the old Great Power mentality induced the victorious allies led by France to exclude from the remit of the League any revision of the Versailles Treaty. Thus half the League's purpose was excluded before it could begin. The League itself was crippled by the principle of unanimity in the Assembly and the Council: any power could veto any proposal. National sovereignty was to reign, except where the Powers might, and sometimes did, agree on minor matters, such as administering and mediating in smaller territories like Danzig, Macedonia and Lithuania.

The dangers of The Treaty and the missed opportunity of the League were gradually realised. Germany, the loser but unvanquished, began its traumatised slow recoil. Too little and too late some element of conciliation was offered to Germany – the American-chaired Dawes Plan, though upholding reparations, aimed at rescheduling them 'to take the question of "what Germany can pay" out of the field of speculation and put it in the field of practical demonstration'; and Germany was rehabilitated to the extent of being allowed to join the League. The German chancellor, Streseman, who made compromises to secure these advances was afterwards reviled at home by those stirring up a more fanatical nationalism.

I told Tisala that it was a Frenchman, Aristide Briand, who out of this unhappy scene sought to change the direction of international politics. On his initiative, in 1928, the French and the Americans made a treaty – The Kellog-Briand Pact for the 'renunciation of war as an instrument of national policy'. Within two years this act had been signed by most important nations including Soviet Russia. But the Pact forbade only wars of aggression and had no enforcement provisions. It was a declaration of hope but was not sufficient to turn the habits of nation states.

But Briand, a veteran politician who had struggled with the old methods of political conduct, and seen them fail, went further: he made prescient proposals for the unification of Europe.

'But nobody took them up? asked Tisala.

'Not a hope, at least at that time.'

And France, like an inadequate stable hand whipping a recalcitrant but powerful horse, built up German resentment, and did much to ensure an eventual violent reaction. For Germany had not outgrown its militarist past; on the contrary, worse was about to happen. The French tried to ensure peace by emasculating the German nation economically while imposing strict unilateral disarmament, though by this time they were mentally and militarily more shell-shocked and emasculated themselves. Their own fear and weakness showed in their next tactic: they built the Maginot Line – a concrete wall along the whole of their eastern frontier with Germany. It was like a bolster down a bed to prevent a rape: an indication of fear, an ineffectual response, and an invitation to an aggressor to climb round it.

Tisala thought it a sad acknowledgement of inadequate statesmanship. First, that it was a throwback to the mentality of the seventeenth century: Vauban's static line of massive stone fortifications. Second, he noted, you only have to glance at a map: there was nothing except for respect of international law and the honouring of neutral territory to prevent an attack round the end of the concrete wall, through Belgium. And the makers of Versailles had turned their back on the development of the real alternatives of friendship, co-operation and international law in favour, once again, of relying on their sword; which was now weak and blunted, and which anyway they lacked the desire to wield.

Tisala said: 'Concrete walls are a sure sign of failure, whether the Maginot Line, or, as others will find in the present time, the Berlin Wall, or in Belfast, or, conceptually, as you tell me the Americans now propose, in outer space. They solve little, and worse, by providing a temporary false sense of security they encourage both the neglect of real solutions, and countervailing reactions tending towards force to shift the silent violence imposed by concrete walls. Fear and politicians build walls. Statesmen remove the reason for them.' Israel had not at that time started to build its wall. Tisala said: 'Wisdom is a perishable commodity, and though it can be preserved on paper, it must be carried in other minds to be of use.'

We reverted to the inter-war years. I recounted how, during the 1920s, the ideas, procedures and actions of the League were gradually sidelined by a series of national and power-based interventions, acts, pacts and treaties. Streseman died and Briand died and the League's proposals on general disarmament, in 1932, which had been the rationale for disarming Germany at the end of the War, came too late. In the east, Japan had invaded Manchuria in 1931. The Great Powers did nothing and therefore the League was seen to be powerless. China was abandoned by the international community.

Meanwhile the economic progress of the world, often a cause of international co-operation, had been badly damaged by the financial collapse in America, with its worldwide repercussions.

And in the politics of national ambition, Hitler was edging towards power, and Stalin's Soviet Russia, kept outside the League, was rearming. Germany was similarly about to start, in defiance of the League and the Treaty. Hitler's and Japanese aggression were under way and Mussolini was about to follow. Once again the 'Great Powers' would not act, and therefore the League could not. The idealism of Wilson and those who had supported the League, the 'end all wars' mentality, and the efforts of some politicians in the inter-war years were almost exhausted. They were increasingly opposed by the inflexible pride, fear and wills of sovereign nations, some of which were now in the hands of dangerously minded leaders.

When I had finished recounting this part of mankind's progress Tisala exhaled and said, 'So your modern nation states were busy abandoning the brave idea of international community. Twenty-five million dead, and that was all your statesman could manage? It does not augur well. What happened next? Where were the British?'

'We were as ineffectual as the rest. Everyone was fearful of future war in Europe and many turned their backs on reality, though we were increasingly unable to hide from the growing reality of economic struggle and social malaise at home and the rebuilding of armed alliances abroad. By 1935, the Powers, some more quietly than others, including the British, were rearming.'

'The idea of the League had failed to tame the fears and ambitions of nation states?'

'Yes, and the League had to stand by helplessly when Italy invaded Abyssinia, and Germany became involved in the Spanish Civil War.'

'So then your peoples had to endure a second great war of nations, for I think it was nationalistic war dressed up in totalitarian rhetoric – German and Italian fascism, Japanese absolutism and Russian communism.'

'Yes, those nations all sought territorial expansion and the aggrandisement of empire; by duplicity if they could get it, but otherwise by other means – war.'

'It seems that five generations on, Von Clausewitz was still at their shoulders. And I fear he is still in men's minds, though he himself might be appalled by what has been unleashed.'

Thus we reached the Second World War.

'So this time forty-two million people died before the hallucinatory German dream failed, and with it the Japanese and Italian versions.'

'Yes', I said.

'So what did your statesmen attempt this time?'

He sent me back to the books. I realised he was searching for a different understanding for our future. And amidst all the troubles and destruction of our human history, I found encouragement.

CHAPTER 65

Hopes and Peace

One day Susannah found me poring over a pile of history books in the shack, as I tried to answer some of Tisala's questions.

'Why the Second World War?' she asked Tisala.

'To understand your modern world, peer into your future and to see if future wars may be avoided.'

I told him how our leaders tried to avoid the many mistakes of the end of the First World War. First, they considered aims. As early as August 1941, four months before the United States entered the war, Churchill and Roosevelt met secretly at sea off the coast of Newfoundland and drew up the short document known afterwards as the Atlantic Charter. It set out 'certain common principles' on which Britain and America based 'their hopes for a better future for the world'. It made clear that America and Britain, and afterwards other countries who endorsed it, would seek no aggrandisement territorial or other; that they respected the right of all peoples to self-determination; that they supported access to trade in raw materials on equal terms for all countries regardless of the conflict; that they wished to bring about the fullest collaboration between all nations in the economic field, and that they hoped for freedom from fear and want for all, with the disarmament of all aggressive nations, pending the establishment of a general security system.

Tisala said, 'So there were now to be no prizes in war, except for the defeat of evil and aggressive forces, and peace itself. The ideas are there, but how did it go on?'

I recounted that many of those who endorsed the Charter had, like Britain, mixed motives, and needed American support, but nevertheless eventually came to apply most of the principles set out. But Stalin, cynically, also endorsed it. He desperately wanted arms, materials and food from the allies; but otherwise had his own agenda.

Tisala thought it an act of statesmanship of Roosevelt and

Churchill to declare for self-determination for all – something he recalled none of the victors had even contemplated, in relation to their own possessions in 1918. And with the Charter's public and explicit rejection of future reparations and economic penalties against Germany, it was a landmark shift in international thinking.

Tisala said, 'Here is an example of a good use of power, for it must have helped establish ideas that might change the future for the better.'

And I marvelled how he could pick out, amongst all terrible events and destruction of a world war, those things that were necessary for the advance of peace and civilisation among the fractious nations formed by humanity.

But Tisala also found it extraordinary and appalling that, far from restricting warfare after the horrors of the Great War, this war was a greater War, not only more widespread militarily, but involving direct attacks on, and killing, huge numbers of civilians. For the first time whole cities and their inhabitants were deliberately to be targeted by mass bombing: London, Coventry, Plymouth, Hamburg, Dresden, Berlin. Worse and more destructive as the war went on, culminating in the obliteration of Hiroshima and Nagasaki. And this was aside from the horrors of the racial genocide and widespread atrocities of the war.

He made me search out the origins of renewed attempts to establish world peace and security – this time through the League's successor, the United Nations. I reported that in 1943 – before the outcome of the War was certain – the Allied Powers decided to draw up proposals for such an international organisation. The following year, at Dunbarton Oaks outside Washington, the United States, Britain, Russia and the Republic of China (then not communist) drew up proposals from which the Charter of the United Nations emerged at the San Francisco Conference, between April and June 1945. By then, encouragingly, delegations from fifty nations were present.

I told him of the UN Charter, and its six principal organs. How, this time, it was drawn up, signed and ratified before the peace treaties that ended the War; how it was to be more inclusive and better empowered; how the General Assembly of nations was to bring the world together; how the Security Council was entrusted with the function of world peace and security and was given the means and power to enforce its decisions to settle disputes and prevent aggression; and how the Economic and Social Council and the International Court of Justice were to promote economic fairness and development, and protect human rights. And how, as the Powers, sometimes reluctantly, shed their empires in the following decade or two, many new nations joined.

In some respects there was more realism. In 1948 the first Secretary-General of the United Nations, Mr Trygve Lie, a Norwegian lawyer, said that, 'It was not believed that the Great Powers would always act in unity and brotherhood together. What the founders of the UN did believe was that the UN would make it possible to keep disputes between both great and small powers within peaceful bounds, and that without the UN that could not be done.'

Tisala said, 'Now I must be like your schoolchildren and study the Charter.'

'We never studied it,' I said. 'I doubt whether any children study it.'

'Not even at senior schools?'

'No such idea has ever crossed the minds of our educationalists. They are too busy with the details of hundreds of pages of their national curriculum. The Charter is quite a long document,' I added defensively.

'But at least the content and main import of it?'

'A few university students doing international politics.'

'But how do the new generations learn what they need to learn?'

'I am afraid, very largely, they do not.'

'Yet you all hope for world peace and understanding? What foolishness you bring upon yourselves.'

Tisala thought people in democracies need to be familiar with the underlying principles of the important constitutional documents and commitments of their history. 'That is what leads them to know who and what they are, and what considerations should guide their leaders, so they can keep a democratic watch on what their leaders do, and hold them accountable. The time of wars between nations should be past.'

Tisala paused, and then asked, 'So what did happen?'

I told him how there were real hopes that the new body would bring worldwide pressure for the peaceful resolution of disputes. And indeed, there is a history of advances in international co-operation and peacekeeping to be told proudly. In various disputes and theatres of war the pressure of UN peacekeeping forces has added a new and hopeful dimension to the containment and resolution of conflict. It is not always successful, for national politics and reluctance to undertake international responsibilities have sometimes impinged.

'But nevertheless I can see humanity advancing.' said Tisala.

Yet he saw with that within the UN structure, despite the high hopes, the declared equality of all nations, and the more international and inclusive nature of the Charter as drafted, the Great Powers maintained control over their own interests and influence. Like the victor powers in 1918 the Permanent Members of the new Security Council, who were all victorious wartime allies – that was the basis of this membership – were not willing to give up their own sovereignty even in the name of international order and security. If they could work the UN by agreement they were willing to try it but otherwise they reserved their positions by granting themselves individual vetoes so that each of them could completely block international actions, whatever the views of all the other member states.

Tisala made me check the Charter.

I reported that the sentence that defines the limits of the Great Powers' political co-operation is in Article 27 of the Charter, when it deals with the voting, and therefore the power, apparently granted to the Security Council to impose peace by international co-operation. Decisions of the Security Council, except on procedural matters, 'shall be made by an affirmative vote of nine members *including the concurring votes of the permanent members*'.

'You are telling me that world co-operation can be frustrated simply by a single vote of any one of the permanent members: the United States, Britain, France, Russia or China?'

'Yes, in those eight words lies the world-paralysing veto.'

Tisala added wonderingly, 'It is absurd. But tell me what happened.'

One of the first results was that this veto was used by Stalin's Soviet Union, after a disagreement with America, to exclude wartime ex-enemies from membership of the UN, quite contrary to the earlier preamble of intention and the spirit of the Charter. And when in 1949 the Republic of China became a communist power, and formalised its solidarity with the Soviet Union by Treaty in 1950, the Security Council was immobilised by the global split of the Cold War. The Permanent Members of the Security Council each championed their own interests and form of government as paramount, and above the interests of international accord. And they have clung to them ever since. And the paralysis spread into the General Assembly, both sides using trade and aid to persuade existing and afterwards new members to take their side.

The attempt to circumvent dependence on the balance of power had been neutralised within the rules of the UN institution. Once again the bare power of individual states triumphed over international order.

Tisala said, 'And that I believe is still so?'

'Yes. And although much good has been done through the UN in economic and social fields and in lesser wars and disputes, its central aspiration has not been achieved. We have failed again, and this time our failure may have catastrophic results.'

'Now you are backed in the dangerous stalemate of the Cold War and the balance of nuclear terror that freezes the world?'

'We are.'

'That is the measure of your failure; the whole world stands in danger of nuclear catastrophe.'

'Yes. The lack of trust between America and Russia has grown into a huge nightmarish reality.'

'So you are back in the lurid half-lit land of the human imagination.'

I had told him of the strange dark mind of Stalin and his murderous distrust of everything and everyone, with the fear of hell all about and before him, allied to the old desire of conquest and domination. And how this stain spread in the minds of many in his apparatus, and their American political counterparts, who came to view 'the Communists' as a form of malign, cunning and powerful evil.

'Such is the power of human imagination bolstered by propaganda and failure to communicate. Wherever there is conflict in human affairs you invest it with the power of your imaginations and it serves you very ill, for you are all, in normal daylight, just humans. But the delusions of empire started again?'

I said: 'Yes, immediately. Stalin's badly savaged but victorious Russia advanced, though in the name of the Revolution, across Eastern Europe restoring and expanding the Russian Empire by obliterating a dozen independent countries against the wills of their peoples.'

'Thereby', Tisala interposed, 'the Russians set up their own hallucinatory dream?'

'You think it is illusory too?'

'Certainly it is. Throughout your histories, sooner or later, imposed empire always breaks down. The Czarist empire did, the Soviet will. Only the willing participation in union of free peoples can create a stable, war-free world. That is your aim and the enormity of your human task.'

I began to think the outlook too bleak and too complicated for humanity to save itself from nuclear destruction. But Tisala proceeded with the immense calm steadiness of his kind, searching and constructing.

He questioned me closely as to what had happened at the onset of the Cold War and what could have led to a different outcome. 'For the time may come when there is another opportunity to heal the world, and if you do not understand what happened last time you are more likely to miss the next opportunity.'

To start with there appeared to be no Soviet Cold War masterplan for Eastern Europe. But slowly across Europe the iron curtain came down. In Eastern Europe only Greece (with American help) and Yugoslavia escaped the Stalinist net.

In America, as after the First World War, there was a strong move in Congress to withdraw from Europe. But this time, critically, the American President, Truman, won over the Congress. Peace would be given a better chance. The Americans would stay in Europe. Communist advance from the east was to be met by resistance in the west. The immediate instance of this was in Greece, and aid in Turkey. The West in Europe was defined.

'So emerged the balanced terror of the Cold War – though the idea of mutual destruction has held their hands for nearly forty years?'

'Yes, and there are signs – in the recent arms talks – that both sides recognise the long-term folly of the position.'

Tisala said, 'Appallingly dangerous as it is, so long as they hold off from war it contains an opportunity: the UN – the international gathering of mankind – is like a house waiting for a long winter to end, so the shutters can be opened to welcome in the sunlight. It will require the nations to shed their nationalistic clothes, and put on those of common purpose and action. It awaits the confidence of statesmen to do so and complete the proper structure of this international house.'

The reforms required, he argued, include the removal of the veto and the re-modelling of the Security Council. 'There lies a great prize for the future of worldwide peace and civilisation.' He thought that under no circumstances should a veto be granted to any new Permanent Member of the Council. It would destroy the chance of any real reform, and with it the chance to create an effective world political authority. The challenge lies rather with the statesmen of the current Permanent Members to disclaim their privilege, which would be a definitive answer to those rising states seeking such privilege for themselves. 'But the world still waits?'

'Yes, still.' And I remember the long silence that followed.

I said, eventually: 'But outside the political structure, things went better.' And told him how economic co-operation had advanced, at least in the West, and increased on a scale never before achieved in the history of the world. And that, though with less certainty of outcome, has largely continued.

'Let us look at that,' said Tisala.

I recounted how in economic affairs there were revolutionary advances. The inter-war lessons had been learned – the terrible blunder of reparations, and the financial and economic catastrophes caused by national protectionism and the Great Depression were now recognised. Influenced by John Maynard Keynes, the English economist, the workings of economic systems were better understood. Co-ordinated economic activity and co-operative governmental inter-ventions were set to transform the world's economy. In July 1944, a month after the Allied invasion of Nazi-held Europe, the Americans and British met at Bretton Woods. A new international monetary system was created under their guidance. With it came the machinery to order and assist it – the International Monetary Fund and the World Bank – both run by the United Nations. But the nations faltered at the founding of the third full international organisation, which should have freed up world trade for the benefit of all peoples. Instead the nation states fought to retain their immediate trade advantages, so only a more limited agreement was reached, in 1947. (But without Soviet Russia, and so, by extension, Eastern Europe, to their great loss.) This was the General Agreement on Tariffs and Trade. For those who did join, the scope and benefit of world trade was gradually widened by patiently negotiated steps over the following decades.

In June 1947 the US Secretary of State, General George Marshall, put forward one of the most enlightened and generous economic schemes ever proposed and implemented: Marshall Aid – billions of dollars offered by the Americans to allies, neutrals and ex-enemies alike. It may be argued that the US had done very well out of the war in terms of industrial growth and accretion of capital, not least from Britain, who had spent enormous sums procuring American military and other supplies; and undoubtedly the Americans were also concerned to contain the advance of communism across Europe. Nevertheless, the billions of dollars the Americans poured into Marshall Aid for four years transformed the prospects for the economic future of Western Europe. Britain and France benefited most, but so did fourteen other nations, critically including the ex-enemy Germany.

To receive the aid the recipient countries had to undertake to increase production, expand trade and add their own financial contributions. Common economic co-operation was the criterion. These things were overseen by another new and valuable body, the Organisation for European Economic Co-operation, afterwards better known as the OECD. But once again politics loomed. Russia, suspicious of American designs, refused the offer of Marshall Aid both for itself and its new satellites. Eastern Europe was condemned to fifty years of comparative poverty. And the economic co-operation that might have ameliorated and eventually overcome the political distrust was frozen out, so cementing the East-West divide, and the threat, as a nuclear arms race developed, of a third world war of unbelievable horror.

But in the West, I told Tisala, this was the underlying economic organisation that ushered in the unprecedented economic boom of the second half of the twentieth century; and the now familiar modern world of supermarkets and shopping malls: vast halls of consumer choice, and other spectacular outpourings of inventions, goods and services. The world was moving from cotton, coal and peanuts to a world bonanza in exotic foodstuffs, fibres, electronic devices, energy and travel.

'And,' I said, 'this is still continuing. But the crucial history and influence that the development of global economic activity has for the betterment of the world is dangerously little understood, though people and nations across the world take its daily benefits as given in their lives.'

Tisala said: 'I understand it brought much pleasure and ease into millions and millions of human lives. But like so many human affairs, it is double edged and has brought with it the growing promise of future problems.' He meant in terms of resources used up and pollution released, and the looming consequences of both.

Tisala resumed: 'But go back to Western Europe. At least economically, I think you largely recovered from the worst folly of habitual European war-making; and have something of hope to tell me?'

CHAPTER 66

Europe – A New Beginning?

'Nowadays, when you think of Western Europe,' I said, 'you think of holidays.' I recalled the well-ordered countryside of France and Germany, and the architecture and culture of the great cities. But most of all we rained-on British love the beautiful weather and scenery – Switzerland, the Italian Lakes and round the shores of the Mediterranean.

Susannah and I had increasingly spent our summer breaks in these places. And now with Julie we had a small ambassador. Children open doors everywhere. New foods, laughter and understanding across a continent. And all at peace. Yes, of course there is another side, but it is nonetheless remarkable. What a transformation from the ruinous wars and catastrophes of the earlier part of the century.

'So,' asked Tisala when I had described this, 'how did you get this far?'

I told him how, after 1945, in Western Europe there was a new beginning. He seemed particularly interested in the growth of the European movement, and made me explore the pioneers in the nineteenth and early twentieth centuries. It was a tale of attempts at co-operative construction frustrated by the ambitions and actions of nation states.

'The point,' he said, 'is that they were looking for an alternative – a better form of political organisation for humanity than the aggressive nation state.'

But only after the death and destruction of the Second World War was there sufficient humility and will to co-operate.

'And there,' continued Tisala, 'I hope lay a turning point in history.'

The French, after several hundred years and the terrible losses of the Great War and the further morale shaking of the Second World War, were tired chasing or defending glory, and at last preferred peace. 'It was that, said Tisala, which will give the French their freedom.' But even then, as, with their old adversary, they led the formation of a New Europe, they were slow to learn the lessons of the divestment of empire – Indo-China and Algiers; and De Gaulle was to be Janus-faced. Germany lay divided and in ruins. The cost of militarism was plain, and was rejected. Germany too preferred peace and thereby gained her freedom.

The new signs were there. In September 1946, Churchill, attuned to this, in his speech in Zurich appealed for a 'kind of United States of Europe,' to be commenced with a partnership between the ancient enemies of France and Germany. He spoke of the future of the 'European family' depending upon the resolve of millions to do right instead of wrong. The idea of a new form of international unity had been raised. In May 1948, about 800 delegates from various European countries attended the Congress of Europe at The Hague. Churchill was chairman and stated: 'We must proclaim the mission and the design of a united Europe whose moral conception will win the respect and gratitude of mankind... a Europe where men and women of every country will think of being European as of belonging to their native land, and wherever they go in this wide domain will feel "Here I am at home".

And from that Congress grew the European Movement.

But in what followed, Eastern Europe would not take part. The advance of communist Soviet Russia, largely by its 'empire-building' actions excluded it.

'So did the British lead the way, politically, in Europe?' asked Tisala.

'Politically? No, the British mentality was still too insular.'

I recounted how the ruling Labour Party concentrated on internal reforms and turned its back on European integration, for the old nationalistic reasons. Its 1950 pamphlet *European Unity* stated flatly that it would contemplate negotiating 'no iota of sovereignty' in any form of European unity.

'The concept of pooling sovereignty in beneficial co-operation was beyond it?'

'Yes, though they were shedding British sovereignty in the Empire.' But the mentality of independent empire remained for a few years more. So, in Europe, Britain stood on the sidelines.

Tisala followed intently the determined attempts of the western

Europeans to prevent their long, sterile history of warfare, destruction and bitterness from ever repeating itself. He thought the names of the Frenchmen Jean Monnet and Robert Schumann, the Belgian Paul Henri Spaak, the Italian Alcide De Gasperi and the peaceful diligence of the German Chancellor Conrad Audenauer would be rightly honoured in the history of endeavours to harness and reform mankind's fierce territorial nationalism.

'We British did not see it like that,' I said.

'But the continental Europeans did. They led and gathered the willingness of their own peoples to try a different and perhaps more enlightened way.'

I had told him how they started in a modest but practical way with a treaty forming the European Coal and Steel Community in 1951, followed by a treaty to co-ordinate and regulate civil nuclear energy. And in 1957, with the Treaty of Rome, came the fuller economic union of the European Economic Community. Their immediate idea was to create a single internal market by adopting the benefits of co-operation. It necessitated some pooling of economic sovereignty – a bold step, putting the application of economic theory above the narrow nationalism that so bedevilled the earlier twentieth century.

Tisala said: 'But I can see its underlying idea also involved the abandonment of past nationalistic, imperial or totalitarian ambitions. Without that historic change it could not be done. And that was a giant advance, was it not?'

'Yes, I think so, but it was not always understood.'

At the centre of it, necessary to overcome and remove the history of terrible enmity, were France and Germany, supported by troubled Italy and the independent but small and anxious Benelux countries. And from that, buoyed up by economic success over the following years, slowly emerged the larger European Union.

I had been an enthusiast for this process, though without fully understanding its potential development, ever since my days of undergraduate debate. I told Tisala how the British under Macmillan began to change their minds. And that at the critical moment the country was led by a statesman with unusual vision and determination, Edward Heath, albeit one, like President Wilson in 1918, of a certain narrowness of character, whose administration was afterwards overwhelmed by domestic events. But he did enough, and enabled Britain to step out of its old declining world and into what we hoped was a brighter future. Others too saw this future: when Britain joined in 1973, so did Ireland and Denmark. These were the first of many additional countries to see in the European Community a new and better world.

'But the question of the nature of the union as it has since developed needs careful consideration.' said Tisala.

I nodded agreement. 'Yes, it does.'

However, by that time, though the emphasis was economic, the new liberal democracies' success gradually dispersed the remaining nationalistic fascist and communist attitudes and regimes in Europe. In Italy, France, Germany and Greece, because of the success of the European Community, those old national fanaticisms were marginalised. There was a movement into the more rational light of liberal democracy. Germany was accepted into the United Nations in 1973. In the next two years the old fascist regimes in Spain and Portugal disappeared with the passing of their respective dictators. Both made the changes necessary to allow entry, and by popular wish, joined the EU in 1983.

'Much of this,' said Tisala, 'is very recent – it has come about while I have been with you. It seems to me you have here the first really serious attempt to create a new way – the voluntary association of free nations to develop and civilise their nationhoods within the security and discipline of an interlinked and peaceful continent.

And though we did not then know it, within a year or two the old Cold War immutably frozen 'Eastern Bloc' would dissolve peacefully, and emerge again as free European countries, not least owing to the determined desire of their people to join the European Union, for which democracy is an entry requirement.

That membership should be aspired to by other countries became the best chance for achieving reform and responsible development. Not only had it transformed the relationship of the ancient war-waging powers of France, Germany and Britain, it also became the context in which the endemic sectarian violence in Ireland was overcome; it allowed Germany to unite, and the Czechs and Slovaks to separate peacefully; it was to transform the eastern European satellite countries of the communist Soviet Union; and it may finally overcome the murderous history of the Balkans.

'Is it not apparent to all that the incessant wars between neighbours of earlier centuries become increasingly impossible in such a structure? If the community is successful, war between member states will be a thing of the past. The scale of this achievement, and the economic and civilising rewards that come with it, are incalculable.'

'But still it seems not to be recognised in some quarters,' I said. 'Memories of the realities of war are short and every-day issues obscure the wider view.'

He understood the difficulties – I told him of the tense negotiating over differences and particular problems, and of the temptation by member nations, not always resisted, to press narrow self-interest too hard. But Tisala said that these arguments will diminish over the years as more areas of common policy by consent are established. Clearly, there is much wrong and backward within different member countries – religious, social, agrarian and industrial problems and prejudices, corruption and crime – but there always was: the European Union inherited the defects of the nation states. But he thought that there is much greater chance of diminishing these problems within the mutual help and discipline of the union than ever there would be in relying on the volatile decisions of individual nation states who might, as in the past, sometimes fall under feeble, chauvinistic or belligerent governments. He thought that Community compromise and co-operation, though often imperfect and accompanied by much wrangling, yet peaceful and cumulative, a better way. Areas of once sacrosanct sovereignty are found unnecessary in such a structure and among friends. Poorer nations find financial help, and all find greater economic opportunities, and in politics, the chance to resolve previously intractable problems.

'It seems to me,' he said, 'a development of breathtaking importance for the future civilised organisation of mankind. Is it not the greatest experiment in the voluntary international government of peoples in the history of the world? Imagine the world if there were such a union in the Indian sub-continent – India, Pakistan, Bangladesh, Burma, Nepal and perhaps wider still; or such a union in the Middle East, initiated perhaps round Egypt, Israel, Palestine and Jordan, but bringing in too Lebanon and Syria and in time, who knows what other nations. Those regions would emerge with benefits of security and economic and social advancement beyond anything dreamed of in their existing fractious and destructive world.'

He therefore thought it critical that the European endeavour be seen to work in the longer run. And there lay the next challenge. He saw that, because of the complicated societies we have created, a European structure that seeks to order and improve fairness and progress between different parts of them is bound to involve complicated and sometimes contentious rules; some of which will be found to be bureaucratic, inappropriate or even absurd. They need constantly to be simplified, reformed and where unnecessary or obsolete, repealed. But it has also enlarged and enhanced the level of living in the Union: a whole restrictive panoply of petty national control – visas, passports, currencies, medical assistance, limitations on rights to work – have been removed. Such reforms are transforming the lives of its inhabitants; and many are coming to recognise this. But the endeavour remains quite capable of breaking down, unless it carries the peoples with it. He thought it therefore of paramount importance that popular acceptance should be sought and won at every stage. 'That is the key,' he said.

'It will not be done by – and people rightly beware – politicians in a hurry seeking power and influence. If the European Union politicians go too far too fast, they may destroy the whole edifice. And that would be an incalculable tragedy.

'Yes, many of us fear the creation of a superstate.'

'People should be wary,' said Tisala. 'But they should also consider the structure of the Union of Europe as a means of eliminating war and securing the benefits of peace and prosperity.'

For it to flourish he thought it imperative both that the people were sufficiently informed to support the venture, and that politicians seeking power must be prevented from hijacking the European idea into any new version of a nationalist superstate. As to the first, he thought it clear that popular democracy may also be ignorant and unwise. It is likely there will be a strong residue of people amongst member states who look back to the past supposed national glory and fail to see changes desirable in the coming century; particularly so amongst those who cling to an obsolete idea of national independence in a world of increasing, and beneficial, inter-independence.

'And neither you nor the world can any longer afford constant wars and conflicts, which disrupt and destroy your peoples' lives and civilisations, and divert so much of your ingenuity and treasure into arms, and blood-soaked earth.'

'Nor will it be done by the minutiae of over-zealous bureaucracy. Rules for proper regulation are needed, but the balance of acceptability should ultimately be with the people. It is their union, and politicians and bureaucrats must serve it. If your politicians become statesmen and bring sufficient wisdom and reason to bear, they may remove many problems from the lives of your peoples; but I think they can only do so acting together in a commonly worked out framework, for together you have unprecedented experience, discipline and motivation, and alone you do not. It is for your peoples to decide how, whether and to what extent the interlinking should move towards integration.

'They may wish to work out over a generation or two the levels of confederation, and what you call subsidiarity – local autonomy – in different policy areas. And some will wish to travel faster and further than others. They are not to be frogmarched by politicians. They are rightly wary of setting up by mistake a new powerful version of a nation state. This union should be different and operate in a new way by a new light. The members and the people should know it, and insist on it, and become proud of it, as a new and hopeful departure. Then it will attract their growing loyalty and pride.'

'How is this to be done?'

'By education. The most important political priority of the European Union is to educate its diverse and different peoples in the inclusive partnership of belonging – feeling and knowing that, here, they belong. It will be a great and ongoing task. It has clearly started already: many people in Europe know in their hearts from their experience of the Union so far that they have found a good way – through all the arguments, difficulties and set-backs – they know they want this Union of nations to survive and grow. But it may not develop as the politicians have envisaged. They must be responsive to the worries and fears of their peoples; and the peoples must be given the opportunity, and take the trouble, to understand.

'No nation is an island entire unto itself.'

I smiled at Tisala's adaptation, and then at Susannah, who had come in from the shack's little kitchen with two mugs of coffee.

'That idea runs contrary to the human desire to be monarch of all we survey,' said Susannah, laughing.

'Now there is another issue,' said Tisala with his smiling sound.

That afternoon when Tisala had gone out to sea, Susannah, Julie and I went for a cliff-top walk. A favourite place was the low cliffs to the west of the inlet. Some way along there was an old deer path heading diagonally down and forming a rough way to the rocky shoreline. Just above it there was a little flat area – a table-like plateau – covered in soft sea-grass with a broken edge where you could sit and watch the sea coming and going to the rocks below. We sat, legs dangling, and watched a couple of seals in the water, and three more hauled out on a sloping slab, while seabirds wheeled and mewed above us.

I felt, as I often did on Inis Cuan, a fierce sense of belonging.

Susannah said, 'How I love this island. Just look at it.' Nature's mantle lay on everything to the last whorl of lichen minutely clothing the rocky base rising out of the sea.

'We are very, very fortunate.'

'Does it arouse your territorial instincts?' asked Susannah with a touch of mockery.

'No, we don't need to be monarch of all this. Yes, legally we have possession, but it is not that which matters – much more, that it allows us to live with a true sense of belonging.'

Later I thought of what Tisala had earlier said of idyllic Japan. Where a nation is geographically an island, as in Japan, the feeling of uniqueness can be strong. The proud Japanese retreated into isolation, with dire consequences both for themselves and for those they mistakenly assumed inferior to themselves. And still to this day it is symptomatic of at least the older Japanese that, as tourists, they do not for the most part engage with the world they visit. They take thousands of photographs of places as the trophies, and rush home and shut themselves into their little rooms to view their prizes. And what have they got? – pictures of their smiling selves posing amid a backdrop of famous places. They have captured their own captivity in their pictures. I said all this to Tisala. Susannah added, 'Now you mention it, I have seen it with the Japanese tourists in Vancouver: they always want to get in the best place in photographs, and sometimes don't mind disregarding others to get there. And it's true their smiles seem always aimed at their cameras.'

'Are you saying,' asked Tisala 'that they have travelled the world but for the most part have not engaged with it or its other peoples, and that their cameras are too often the instrument of their isolation?' He paused, then remarked: 'There will be many of whom it is not true. The true traveller wishes to engage with and understand the people and history he sees about him. And the means of this is observation, language, enquiry, contact, conversation, knowledge and the acquisition of experience. The young at least will learn how.' And I could tell he wanted them to, and to think well of them.

But he thought it true too that living on an island can lead to a greater awareness of what lies beyond. And reverting to Europe he said: 'You English may cherish your island set in a silver sea, but you were fortunate. You ranged abroad to other worlds both in your ships and in your minds. Shakespeare was in the Roman Empire – in Rome and Egypt; he was in the hub of the world's renewal, Renaissance Italy, in Padua, Verona and Mercantile Venice; and in Denmark, Scotland and Athens. Marlowe was in Germany with Faustus and Western Asia with Tamberlaine. And the common people of England in their playhouses went with them. Small wonder the age of exploration, trade, enlightenment and science opened up before them.'

He observed, 'The evolutionary cause of imagination is the usefulness of illuminating and linking realities. The expression of that realisation is what makes Shakespeare great. It needs to be the aim of statesmen. The dreaming up of fantasy, political fantasy, such as empire or patriotic superiority, is the counterbalancing danger.

'Now the young in modern Britain again need to know the complicated reality of the world. Too many of them, from what you tell me, are under-educated and are too bound up in the narrow confines and fashions of their own urban society. But the vitality of British young – like many elsewhere – may overcome these disadvantages, which includes the distrust of foreignness. Then they will be at home – as Churchill hoped – with their fellow Europeans in Continental Europe. There lies a secure future, if you people will accept and help to build it.'

Tisala thought that within the shelter of an EU – a voluntary grouping of peoples – we should expect not only that it will grow, but that it will change internally. Countries that were previously unitary, whether by conquest, imposed political settlement or merely the accidents and incidents of history, may wish to part. He cited Belgium: put together in 1837 from disparate parts of the former Spanish lowlands, the Belgians have struggled to be a nation. In the shelter of the EU structure, in 1971 their long-standing differences were partly resolved by semi-separating into three confederated areas under the Belgian crown. 'They have avoided war, and, by evolving internal solutions, have at least contained their animosities.'

In general terms, these are matters for people and their governments to work out. And eventually, when options are agreed, to be settled by careful localised plebiscite, like a better Schleswig-Holstein. Within the EU, the Belgians have so far avoided strife and civil war. We were, only a few years later, to witness the contrast in the fractured Balkan Yugoslavia, outside the EU.

Tisala resumed: 'If you gain international structure you gain peace and prosperity, and then you can negotiate adjustments internally. Perhaps this may be done within the British Isles by Scotland and even Ireland. Belonging to a greater structure, where much is already settled, makes adjustment infinitely easier: all are already friends, allies and economic partners. You have a choice, you humans: co-operation, or confrontation and strife.'

In this context Tisala thought two things should be considered. First, where there are differences and animosities much work must be done by all peaceful means to remove the prejudice and fears of the differing peoples. He contrasted the various examples of negotiated settlements – perhaps involving boundary changes, some movement of people, some compromise, compensation and economic support – with its antithesis of the horrors and destruction of war. And I thought of his extraordinary solution to the Israel-Palestine conflict: he had outlined an entire peace treaty.

Second, in settling matters people may wish to re-organise their countries within the union and come together in a different way. But no one should pursue separateness in the imagined guise of the old nation state. 'It is no longer enough, though nationalistic politicians are often the last to realise it.' On its own he thought national independence would be found too often to resolve little, provoke conflict, and be counter-productive of a better society.

He saw that these issues are often bedevilled by our concepts of ownership. 'Lapland' means the land where the Lapp people live, but if you transpose where the people live to the name of a state you assume ownership: as in Serbia 'belongs' to the Serbs; and then by extension, they claim greater Serbia. 'And in that possessiveness lies your trouble, for the Kosovans will say Kosova is ours. And there is your conflict, like the Irish in Ireland, Israelis in Palestine, and nations and separatists the world over. Possession is the downfall of man.'

'In the misappropriation of a name by force lies the start of half your wars. We have seen the role of inadequate imaginations, of reactionary politicians on the one side and revolutionaries or independence fighters on the other. They allow their dreams of the trappings of power and wealth as nation states – bright mirage models of their fantasies – to lead to force of arms and death.' Tisala sighed. 'So many wars destroying people.'

But the mind of this great being went beyond our trouble spots, and he said next, as if it were a natural progression, 'America is leased to the American people by history; and they should know that the lease carries obligations to humanity, and beyond to the wider estate of Earth, in which all life has legitimate interests.

'And Russia, China, India and Brazil, and all the countries of the globe are so leased, and their occupants should know it, and act accordingly. Properly considered, none of you *owns* the land within your boundaries, which merely demark the administrative divisions between groups of humans. Though as human animals you naturally become loyal to territory, and overlay that with elements of culture. They are temporary leaseholds carrying wider long term responsibilities.'

He thought that, even less, should any nation *own* part of the neighbouring seabed. Men cannot *own* the seabed, nor the waters over it, nor the life within it. The extension of land claims by encompassing island-dotted areas of sea or underwater ridges or continental shelves is a device and legal fiction countenanced by self-interested nations who hope to exploit and gain thereby. It is an unjustifiable form of colonialism affecting the denizens of the deep and the rest of humanity, and such claims are an invitation to future strife and conflict between men. I wondered what was coming next, and glanced at Susannah, who raised her eyebrows at me enquiringly.

'There is a nationhood of whales. We do not own, nor claim to own, the seas, but dwell there from the high latitudes to the Tropics. There we have our nationhood, Blue Whales, Humpbacks, Fins – the great whales. This is the boundaryless nationhood that is shared with the fish and other sea creatures, as you would say, internationally. And that internationalism should apply to men.'

He thought the seabed, beyond an immediate coastal band, should be held in trust for the world and administered by a reformed United Nations for the benefit of all, with a fair return for licensed development and use of undersea resources granted to developer-nations by international consent. The balance of such wealth and resources thereby released, he thought, should accrue for distribution among qualifying peoples and schemes worldwide. Here, he argued, was an instrument for the better use and regulation of resources, where governments must be willing to accept the terms and supervision of true international order and accountability; whereby the world would acquire by international agreement a wise system of benefit and removal of conflict. And the sea with its delicate balance of sea creatures and the great gardens of algae and plant life would receive consideration and protection.

He paused: 'For beyond national organisation lies love of the wider world. The whole European endeavour is but a stepping-stone. And this remodelling of the nation states is only part of the coming changes. Even your greatest nations should now know that the notion of total national independence is outdated and is neither possible nor desirable.

'You need the peace of international co-operation and the removal of national disputes and antagonisms. For you have now to confront greater issues – worldwide population excess, exhaustion of resources and destabilising climate change.

'You are trustees of the land, the oceans and the atmosphere. Your duty is to behave as trustees should, and to the extent you accept those restraints, so in proportion you may be regarded as wise and advanced. And up to now, for the most part, you can be regarded as neither wise nor advanced. For the most disruptive institution of mankind, wreaking havoc on the world is the organisation you call the nation state. But, because of the inadequacies of human society, that is the unit the world relies on to save the future, at least until such time as you can evolve effective consensual supra-national institutions.'

And I knew he was building such a structure in his mind.

CHAPTER 67

The Parliament of the World

'It seems,' said Tisala, 'that you have many half-working models of international co-operation, headed by the United Nations. But you need a more coherent unity. They need to be viewed together for their contribution to the state of wellbeing in the world – and not to be run as part of power politics or as self-interested exclusive clubs.'

I thought of many intergovernmental initiatives, such as the Group of Seven (afterwards Eight) leading industrial powers; and the Commonwealth and similar associations of nations arising out of historical, trade and cultural connections. And below that level many cross-border associations, friendships and subject-matter interest groups. I began to see how, in our complicated societies, all these form a balance and rein in the over-dominance of any one model or vehicle of statecraft. They are an opportunity for links and understanding between peoples. They flourish in the quiet business of living in harmony together. And I saw that superstates are neither needed nor desirable. On the contrary, they threaten everything. Tisala thought they should bring themselves into the sort of voluntary restraint now developing between nations in Europe.

Then, as he often did, he extended the scope of the argument. 'Beyond these matters we come to the wider reaches of international co-operation and dealings. The advance that would restrain nation states and persuade them to behave more wisely in accordance with world opinion. I mean the reform or rebirth of the United Nations into an effective and truly international body. There lies a great prize for the future of world civilisation.'

'But is it realistic?' I asked. 'You are trying to change the politicians who exercise this power.'

'Yes, and it is necessary; but the leaders themselves must come to see it as beneficial. The exercise of power is a pleasure that should carry a heavy duty of care; and the more enlightened the rulers the more aware of it they will be.'

Tisala argued that an effective world body needed effective powers of compliance to equip humanity with a true international parliament. Such was needed to prevent war and promote world disarmament, to the great benefit of all, including the superpowers, and all who carry the cost and burden of armament.

He thought no nation should have the right to wage war, except in emergency self-defence, without the sanction of the UN. The UN should become the international barrier against war, accepted by all nations, however mighty, as the sole sanctioner of legitimate necessary war. But that required a widespread shift in attitude.

And as Tisala explored the consequences of the UN Charter's reform, Susannah and I wrote down his projected ideas, and a newly shaped Charter emerged.

In political terms permanent membership of the Security Council would carry obligations as well as rights. It was no longer to be a club of the self-appointed 'Great Powers' reserving rights to themselves. The aims of any proposed war or military intervention and the means of attaining them would have to be set out beforehand within a resolution requesting UN authority for war. Cooling-off periods would be obligatory, giving the opportunity for alternative solutions. Nations, however powerful, that went to war without UN sanction would be held to account by a range of consequences. Then, as part of an overall reform, he proposed the abolition of the veto in the Security Council of the Permanent Members. In the new UN, emerging leading nations similarly would acquire no veto rights, nor would emerging unity groups, such as the European Union.

Part of the preamble read: 'It is recognised and agreed by all nations that it is not fitting, nor appropriate to the needs and security of the world, for any member state to have an individual veto over the decisions of the Security Council.'

The document was revolutionary.

'They will never give up their vetoes. Imagine what would happen to an American president who tried to give up the US veto?' said Susannah.

'Or the Russians and Chinese,' I added.

'Are you humans so foolish as to guarantee yourselves future wars and strife? And how will you otherwise overcome your international political paralysis?' He argued that power can be removed by many means, such as defeat in war, economic collapse, or by stalemate and inertia. Why not by exercise of statesmanship, which avoids the destruction of other means and promotes the benefits of new agreement? What if America led the abolition of the veto?

'If the American people are wise, they will support such a plan; and they will allow their president to do so. Because the time is coming when other nations will have to be admitted to permanent membership of the Security Council, or the UN will break down completely. And to give additional nation states vetoes would be to extend the present folly. The existing Permanent Members would preserve their own freedom and influence more surely by pooling their sovereignty in enhanced UN authority, and thereby acquiring, and granting the world, the means to enforce their collective determinations. And when, sometime in the twenty-first century, China is the greatest power, or India or some combination of powers not yet foreseen, the British, the French, the Russians, the Americans and even the Chinese themselves, will be glad that the veto no longer exists.'

He thought a chance for such reform would come at the end of the Cold War. The then dominant power would be in a powerful position to introduce such a reform. He foresaw the US as the sole superpower. He saw this as the likely outcome because the Soviet empire had the internal weaknesses of all propaganda-supported autocracies, despite its formidable exterior appearance. Then, he said, will be the moment, the opportunity, for the most radical international reforms since the Second World War.

He concluded in short that the world should turn its back on the ancient aspiration of imperialism, and learn to live without any new imperialism. A great danger, he said, might arise from the isolation of Russia, which ought to be welcomed and helped into a new and honourable position in the world. In later years he watched with dismay as the West began to cold-shoulder the new emerging Russia. He thought it absurd for America and Russia to be at enmity, and a gross failure of American leadership, given its pre-eminence. He considered it obvious that they should become the most co-operative of friendly nations, in economic and political reform and in the policing of the world's nuclear capacity.

At the time of these discussions he said: 'The world will need wise American presidents. A real danger to world peace will then lie in the narrow nationalistic views of the American people. And a great chance for peace lies now in their wider education. For the time will soon pass when the American people will have such an opportunity.' He thought reform in Europe and in a new Russia could do much to assist the right American decisions. 'But whether the statesmanship will exist is very difficult to see.'

Within astonishingly few years after these conversations, Gorbachev's recognition of the unsustainability of the then Soviet Union, his vision of ending the Cold War and his attempted half reforms, led him, and critically the Russian state, to accept the peaceful dismantling of the Soviet empire. America, for the moment, was left supreme; and with a unique opportunity to disarm, and lead world reform. But, as I write, the reform of the UN still awaits the arrival of wiser heads than those provided in the West in the aftermath of the Cold War, and far from disarming, military nuclear power and proliferation is advancing, and new potential enmities are being allowed to arise. The opportunity is slipping.

And Tisala is now gone from us.

CHAPTER 68

On Modern Whaling and the Future

On Inis Cuan our seasonal jobs went on – maintenance of the shack and boats, renewal of bits of electrical equipment and monitoring the steady flow of news and information about the world's whale populations and welfare. I spent more time helping Guinevere with little jobs she now found difficult to do. She had abandoned her vegetable patch, though she persuaded Jimmy MacLeod to continue to grow potatoes.

At the same time we watched with excited incredulity, like everyone else, the unfolding collapse of communism across Europe and the beginning of its end, as we thought, as a system everywhere.

But on the islands in 1990, the most immediate issue was the future of the whaling moratorium, and with it the future of the great whales. It was the year for the renewal or abandonment by the International Whaling Commission of worldwide protection from commercial whaling.

We had been involved, as had many others, in supplying information and arguments for the indefinite extension of the ban. With the somewhat sporadic help of the press, and a perceived shift in public support, governments had increasingly been convinced. Among member states opposed to commercial whaling, efforts had been made to recruit like-minded nations to the IWC. Certainly, they were given diplomatic help to join, but I believed they joined and voted because they thought it right to do so: the plight of the whales struck a widening chord throughout the world.

But whether that would be translated into sufficient votes at the IWC was another matter. My information was that a vote against a resumption of commercial whaling was anticipated. But it was well known that all sorts of attempts were being made to induce members to cast their votes for whaling. The meeting was held at Noordwijk in the Netherlands.

The voting figures when they came through established that the whaling nations had been unable to raise the votes they required. The moratorium was to be extended indefinitely.

The pulse of relief and sheer joy on Inis Cuan was electric. I hugged Susannah and spoke to Tisala in extravagant terms.

'That's it – whaling's had it. They'll never recover from this.'

Tisala was deeply pleased, and glad of the confirmation of concern among men.

It was another step in the struggle for natural welfare over narrow commercial interests. But he was cautious for we knew the whalers would use the legal weakness of the original 1946 Convention to continue to hunt and kill whales. And Tisala, looking further, said, 'One day not too far away, unless you humans change unexpectedly fast, you will be dealing with a crisis arising from the much bigger problem of overfishing, for a similar destruction of fish species would threaten the whole structure of marine life.'

But at that time we were most concerned with the future tactics of the whalers. The whaling nations complained that the wording of the original moratorium had been that of a temporary measure, pending finding more scientific evidence that might support a return to commercial whaling. That was true: the non-whaling nations had of necessity adopted the wording in order to establish the moratorium initially. But by 1990 it was clear that, despite the hopes of the whalers, what new evidence there was supported the anti-whalers. Of contrary hard evidence there was none, although there were the usual optimistic projections from the whalers. But everyone remembered the earlier history of self-interested and misleading figures and assumptions trotted out by the whalers year after year as they destroyed species after species of the whales. And this time it was not to be allowed.

And as I reported excitedly to Tisala the defeat of the whalers in 1990 was more significant than that. The world was advancing – the large majority of IWC members no longer saw it as a club for whalers trying to maximise the annual kill on a sustainable basis. The new philosophy was turning towards the idea of the IWC as the world body charged with the long term preservation of the whales. They were now recognised as a unique branch of the intelligent higher mammals and part of the Earth's complicated and precious ecosystem.

And for the next decade that view predominated. The 1990s were the best years for whales in the whole of our blood-splattered century. Former whaling nations who had done some of the greatest damage in earlier times – the USA, Britain, the Netherlands – had joined Australia and many others across the world in opposing whaling on principle.

Despite its original opposition to the moratorium Soviet Russia, one of the two great whaling industries of the previous forty years, had by now effectively abandoned Antarctic whaling. Four years later, in 1994, the new Russian government revealed what we had long known from Tisala, that the statistics of kills in the Antarctic under the old communist regime had been falsified to hide the killing of Blue and Fin Whales despite the Soviet Union's public agreement not to. There lay further evidence of the amount of damage and danger of extinction that scientists had long suspected. The scientists had to revise their figures: the position was worse than previously understood, and the extension of the moratorium the more necessary. That same year the IWC, led by the conservationist members, voted to extend the Antarctic sanctuary permanently south of the fortieth parallel.

But some countries still did not accept the cessation of whaling. The rearguard of whaling nations increasingly resorted to the loophole of killing for scientific research, for which they could set their own quotas. It was by this means that the three worst offenders, Japan, Norway and Iceland continued to kill whales to feed the commercial Japanese whalemeat market. It was a knowingly dishonest trade, and they tried to hide their activities. In 1993 the Norwegians were discovered sending whalemeat to Japan disguised as consignments of shrimps, and three years later as mackerel. In Iceland the whaling was centred around a single whaling company, and the purpose of its being – apart from a tiny domestic market – was profit from the Japanese meat market. In 1993 Norway, emboldened by the lack of consequences, quietly recommenced commercial whaling, allocating themselves a quota of 300 Minke Whales, which rose by 1998 to over 670 per annum. And as the Millennium approached, with all its hopes for the future, they all looked set to celebrate by raising the killing further.

One day, when we were discussing these issues, Tisala said: 'If the people of Japan, Norway and Iceland knew more of the true place in nature of whales they might persuade their governments to object to hunting us.'

I said: 'But they now know you are intelligent warm-blooded social mammals. And the history of the whalers' destruction and cruelty is there for all to see, if their publics will only look. It's a shameful indifference to wider sympathies and responsibilities.'

'I understand,' said Tisala, 'that governments don't like being told what to do, and they and their whalers immediately turn it into an affront against their independence, their sovereignty, and so seek public support – which tacitly or otherwise – they have so far received. But it should not be seen as a question of telling them what to do, but of persuading them not to wish to do it.'

I said: 'It doesn't help that both Norway and Iceland are outside the EU, and not therefore amenable to the give and take on sovereignty issues that now increasingly characterises the mainstream European nations. If they will not reform themselves, I think they should be subjected to economic consequences.'

For it remains true that whaling is destructive, cruel and wholly unnecessary, and it can be easily shown that, neither in Iceland nor Norway, is whaling in any way commercially important. Nor are they in any way dependent on whalemeat. A very small quantity of it is eaten, because available, but if it were not it would easily be replaced by fish farming or purpose-raised meat.

Iceland is a small country of only about 250,000 people living in a cold, difficult environment. As a result they cling to their special independence, though that sometimes renders them isolationist in their attitudes. The Icelandic economy has been dependent on three things, fishing, tourism, and now, what will become their greatest source of wealth, providing they don't become greedy, an outward-looking financial sector. Each of these three is vastly more important than whaling. Even within fishing, whaling is a small fraction of the business.

I said: 'All the Icelanders need to do is look at the figures. Within the tourism sector, whale watching is much more profitable than whaling. And this better source of revenue and reputation is put in jeopardy by the continuation of whaling. Some say as much as forty percent of the Icelandic tourist industry is directly related to the desire of tourists to watch whales in their natural environment. The fact that, round the corner, they are also killing whales is very much played down or actively hidden; which hypocrisy and deceit is largely kept from their visitors. Whaling has become an incubus inflicting serious harm on Iceland and its reputation in the world. If Iceland wished to secure its economic and cultural future it would voluntarily cease whaling immediately. Then the beauty to be found in Iceland could be rejoiced in free of the dark shadow of hypocrisy and deceit that now characterises Iceland for all who know the truth.'

Tisala said, with his smiling sound: 'So says my David.'

Over the years I suppose I had grown into Tisala's way of thinking, and subconsciously, his way of speech. And then I felt proud of that.

'Well, it's true – their reputation and economy is being put in jeopardy by a handful of obdurate whalers supported, so far, by their government. They still talk about "their" whales – the old god-given right to ownership and kill transferred to Icelandic whalers – miserable specimens of humanity.'

'Remember that righteous anger works best when it is moderate, and in support of reason. But yes, the better view is that we whales belong to the ecology of the oceans from the Arctic to the Tropics and that Iceland has no moral right to kill us on our migratory routes, or disrupt that ecology.'

'Yes, I say whales are not in any sense "theirs". They are an independent part of the world to be honoured and protected. There are strong reasons, including avoidance of cruelty, for not hunting any whales at all, but there is no justification of any sort for them ever again to hunt any of you great whales.'

The Icelanders are responsible for the most blatant outrage of recent years by their killing of nearly 300 of Tisala's cousins, the great Fin Whales 'for research', *after* the moratorium, between 1986 and 1999; the Fin Whale being a species high on the UN's list of endangered species. Such 'research' had no proper justification whatsoever. The Scientific Committee of the IWC repeatedly requested Iceland to cease this research. Their response? – to avoid its rules, they left the IWC in 1992. The slaughter of the Fin Whales dismayed Tisala more than any other recent infraction. It is legal only because of what have universally come to be regarded as the serious defects in the original Convention. I said: 'It may be legal but it is wholly dishonourable, and wrong. Why do they do it? It is pure bloody-minded butchery to exploit the Japanese meat market for a minimal sleazy profit. Shame on all Icelanders who support it.'

'And in Norway', said Tisala, 'I think the position is both better and worse.'

I told him that in Norway, as I understand it, the whalers are not supported by the bulk of popular opinion. Far from it. The whalers survive by a more insidious public indifference. Norway has a vastly long and indented coastline with thousands of islands. The whaling takes place in the north, away from the view of most people. Commercially some fishermen claim it as a necessary adjunct to fishing but it is neither necessary nor honourable, for it survives under cover of deceitful marketing of its products to Japan, even though the Norwegian whalers despise the Japanese as blubber eaters.

And although whalemeat is still sold in Norway, it is now an incidental addition to plentiful food. You will see it in the fish markets of Bergen and Oslo, usually packaged like salami, and it is available in some restaurants. But it is mostly regarded as a marginal food, like reindeer meat, a curiosity for tourists to try. Local people mostly deny eating it at all. It would help to end the horrible trade if tourists objected to its sale, and actively refused to eat it.

To a small extent, 'the fishing industry depends on whaling' argument put forward by Norway has a slight measure of truth for a few northern Norwegian fishermen. It would be much preferable for them if the viability of the fishing industry was dealt with by the better regulation of it. The local northern fishermen, who kill whales needlessly, are much more threatened by adverse trends in fishing – the large fishing boats advocated by their own government on grounds of economy, the use of Danish seine nets scooping up everything on the seabed and destroying the habitat, and foreign fishermen taking cod and other species out of northern waters. The Europeans could here contribute constructively. Such reforms would help the local inshore fishermen, who know their waters and the sustainability of the fish stock that frequent them.

Susannah said: 'Norway is a wealthy country with huge oil revenues for a tiny population. There would be no hardship and easy compensation if the government introduced a cessation of whaling. It could easily do it while protecting their fisherman. The Norwegians want friends but they will lose them while they kill whales.'

I said, with an underlying anger, 'There is now in Norway a conspiracy of silence as to the true nature of whaling. Oslo has a magnificent maritime museum in a large building spread across many rooms. In a small corner of one room there is one mounted harpoon gun and a few other items with small uninformative notices in Norwegian indicating the existence of whaling, mainly related to the distant history of sailing ships and Right Whales in the very early days. That is all. The biggest and most ferocious whaling fleet the world has ever seen, with its deadly armada of hunter killer ships and its array of factory ships, which dominated the twentieth century whaling scene and was largely responsible for the near extinction of several species of the great whale, has simply disappeared. It is not to be seen or heard or referred to. In Norwegian schoolbooks and history books it merits a mere passing reference or two. It is a form of holocaust denial and should shame all Norwegians, for it makes them complicit in the ignorant crimes carried out by their whalers. It is deeply unattractive, and taints the good name of Norway.'

When I had finished this outburst Tisala lay silent in the waters of the inlet, and for once did not counter-balance what I said.

I had been to Norway and likewise found that it is socially and commercially convenient for them to pretend not to see the truth of their own history and continuing part in the destruction of the whales. The whalers hide the sickening cruelty of it and promote a vague idea of Norwegian maritime culture, appealing to a form of national tradition. And nationalism, as we know, is useful in the control of loyalties.

'Their official fishing industry publications make much of its contribution and are highly informative, boasting of the three million tons or so of fish and seafood taken every year and of the more than 200 different species of fish and shellfish. Much useful information is given about many of the species, from the well-known – salmon, trout, mackerel, herring, sprat, cod, haddock, halibut, plaice, prawns – to the lesser known including red fish, tusk, wolf fish, cat fish, caplin, and various specified shellfish including sea urchins. But of whales? Never a mention. Oh yes, they know perfectly well what they are doing. Shame on Norway.

'The same deliberate "blind eye" evasion is everywhere in evidence in Norwegian tourist publicity: it extols the magnificence of nature, its great fiords and the islands and adorns its photographs with pretty smiling blonde girls. The young of Norway are delightful but their attractions have been recruited to support a dishonest cover-up. The tourist publicity for the Lofoten Islands and the Tromso Coast – the centre of whaling activity – even boasts of whale watching, and calls the whales 'magnificent creatures'. Sometimes it mentions whale research in the small print hinting at their concern for marine resources but never mentioning the unending slaughter of its practice. And of current whaling? Scarcely a word or any indication that it goes on. Why is the truth hidden? Because they rightly fear both public and tourist reactions. But the result is that modern Norway lives a lie. And all in subservience to a wholly unnecessary Japanese meat market. It is shameful.'

'We must endeavour so to persuade the Norwegians,' said Tisala.

And for the first time he sounded weary with the long years of struggle.

But he went on. 'And what of Japan? You tell me that without the Japanese whalemeat trade neither the Icelandic nor the Norwegian whaling industries would continue. Most of all we must persuade the Japanese.'

I said: 'Like those other two nations the Japanese have tended to regard the issue as one of defending their culture and independence. But in their case, the attempts to persuade them to stop whaling are also portrayed as a "western" imposition.'

He had enquired carefully about modern Japan. I had told him that after their defeat in the Second World War (which Tisala said they would gradually come to see as giving them their freedom to join the modern world) there were shortages, including that of meat. And in those times whalemeat arguably performed a function. But now, after the successful transformation of the Japanese economy, whalemeat is not needed. Indeed it seems it is not even much liked, so that the amount sold has fallen dramatically in recent years to the alarm of the whalers. With the shortsighted aid of the Fishing Ministry, they have sought to create new markets, targeting school meals, where pupils have to comply. This campaign is accompanied by attempts to influence children's minds by promoting a culture of whale eating dressed up as patriotic. Their children and students and their wider public are not informed of the dishonesty and dishonour of the history of whaling and the deceit it perpetrates to seek its own continuance.

Susannah said: 'What I find most abhorrent is their casual acceptance and deceitful masking of the savage cruelty and destruction their hunting continues to inflict on you. Their consciences seem to be missing.'

I said: 'The Japanese whalers claim, wishing to deceive their public, that their whaling techniques are much improved and are no longer cruel. We know this is wholly untrue. They still chase whales, sometimes for long periods, to exhaustion. The radar has certainly improved: the whales can no longer escape. They use bombs and grenades intended to explode inside whales which sometimes only half do their job and maim and cause agonising deaths. They have on occasions, on their own figures, conceded that up to forty percent of kills need a second harpoon. They do not say how many need three, or four, nor the number where they kill or maim but lose the whale. Nor have they any method of telling whether they are harpooning and exploding grenades in pregnant mothers carrying young whales about to be born. They do not know if they are killing old whales or young whales or key family members or what damage they thus do to families and societies; and neither do they care. All they see is meat and profit.'

'You are kind to care so much, and I find hope in that.'

'But each killing goes on just as in the terrible days of the 1920s and 1930s. In the death of an individual whale, nothing has changed. The whalers continually say they are advancing research on better techniques but evade the fact that they have been saying that for over a century with precious little result. They seek to disregard and to hide the cruelty, and where they cannot they seek to confuse the public with wrong or irrelevant claims. And the lie is evidenced by the history of the opposition of whalers, led by Japan, to observer schemes which could demonstrate the wrongness of their claims; and their determined efforts to ensure that any observers imposed on them are from like-minded whaling nations, who it may be supposed would be pleased to report that they saw no cruelty. And what do we find as the twentieth century closes? The Japanese are once again seeking to overthrow the observer schemes. Dishonour and shame on the Japanese.'

And while I was basking in the satisfaction of righteous indignation, Tisala was strangely quiet.

Then he said: 'But the Japanese have a refined sense of aesthetics, though we have seen from their religion and politics that their ethics have been weak and often seem not to link up with their aesthetics.'

He considered the Japanese garden: havens of peaceful contemplation with their quiet rocks and spreading cherry tree boughs and autumn-flaming acers. Such people, he thought, should not be bloodily whaling – causing screaming agony and plunging deaths. 'But the need of the Japanese to adopt a wider ethic is only a particular instance of the need of all humanity. Though it may seem to some that such ethics come from the west, in fact they come from a wide variety of sources across the world, and they have been improved by many peoples.'

'And by you,' I interjected, referring to his precepts.

'Another attempt,' he said. But went on, 'If the Japanese people would come to endorse these world ethics they would enter a lighter and more friendly world, and be welcomed in it.'

When he had finished speaking Tisala was quiet for a few moments, and then said:

'Where is the Emperor of Japan?'

I said: 'Silent in his palace.'

'And the high-collared kings of Norway, the Queen of Denmark and the president of Iceland, where are they?'

'All silent.'

'The Emperor could say, not because of any political pressure, but because he has concluded that whaling is wrong, that the Japanese culture should be accordingly adjusted. And he could let it be publicly known that it would please the Emperor if his government would rule and declare that imported whalemeat from Norway and Iceland are no longer welcome, and should be illegal. So too with the princes of the European whaling countries.'

His thought ranged wider.

'In your world the use and role of princes is to be the exemplar of their peoples' identity within a wider humanity, their ethical mentor and the enlarger of their consciousness, so as to promote what is good within a nation. It is indeed a high office, if it is not neglected or misused. Too many of your princes have thought the trappings were the thing; which is a measure of their failure. They should look after their country's soul. Why do these princes not let it be known that they view the continuation of whaling, and its inhumane and underhand methods, as a breach of trust not fitting for their country to perpetrate; that they disapprove of the degradation of their countries' and peoples' reputation at the behest of outdated traditions and self-serving commercial interests? For it besmirches the good name of their countries and taints their societies with cruelty and indifference.

'The Japanese, you have told me, have no long tradition of open and free debate or independent press. But now they have both. Let their Emperor and Empress lead the people. The Europeans have less excuse. All these princes could advance and enlighten their societies by their guidance and by enlisting the support of their people, above all the young. I have no doubt that the young of Japan, Norway, Iceland and Denmark have as much kindness, goodwill and beauty of mind as any other people on Earth. Let them express it in their views and actions, for the benefit of us whales, and for the enhancement of their own societies. The advance I hope to see is for the Norwegians, the Icelanders and the Japanese voluntarily to wish to join the non-whaling majority of nations in a more enlightened view. That would be a great day for us whales, and for humanity.'

Tisala continued, once more looking further, and said: 'Perhaps mankind at last is beginning to understand and undertake its true role. As the most dominant intelligent animal in the Earth it is by that fact the trustee for the whole. This privilege and responsibility far outweighs any mere national claims to sovereignty. No nation should have the right to violate or despoil the oceanic sanctuaries decreed on behalf of the world. If, in whaling, the law on this is defective, or where some seek to circumvent even that defective law by going outside the IWC, or by setting up their own regional authorities, it and they should be overridden by better law from the UN. And where that higher law is itself impeded by defective setting-up under nation state auspices, the UN itself must be reformed. Such reforms should lead to laws guided by higher ethics, the High Law of Mankind, and recognised as such. Then you will fashion a means to promote the good and restrain the bad globally. You may thereby save not merely us whales but many endangered species and environments. The time may come when your advance into enlightenment may serve to save the world and enable the wonderful experiment and experience of life in Earth to survive and continue on its upward course, with man no longer its destroyer, but its guardian and trustee.'

And when he had finished, Susannah said quietly, 'Now there is something.'

Tisala said: 'David, write it in your book. So that all may recognise and know what whalers have done and are doing. You cannot undo what is done, but you can change the perception of the past, and you can change the future.'

So I have tried to write to give Tisala's plea for life to the people of Japan, Norway and Iceland, whom he sought to understand and love. And, beyond anything to do with whaling, but with everything to do with the future of mankind and the Earth, to spread his gift of wisdom and love to all human kind.

CHAPTER 69

Guinevere and Heaven

In the following year, 1991, Guinevere died. She was eighty-seven. Like Eric, she died without leaving her beloved island. We were in London, but preparing to come up. She had a cold and cough, in the chill winds of March, which hung on. She said she was better, but it came back at her. The first we knew of any relapse was when she rang and said she had taken herself off to bed. When Susannah telephoned again in the evening she said she was feeling rotten. But she continued to protest that she would be fine. She promised to ring the doctor. Two hours later Susannah rang her again to hear the verdict. She hadn't rung the doctor. 'Young Dr. Murray'.

Susannah reported: 'She sounds terrible. Breathless. I'm ringing Dr. Murray.' Yes, he would get out there in the morning. Didn't want pneumonia developing.

But when Jimmy MacLeod called in early next morning, he found her dead in bed. At the funeral Dr. Murray said, 'I think she knew.'

The previous autumn she had made a point of coming over to Inis Cuan to see Tisala before he departed for the winter tropics. And she had told me cheerfully that she was ready to go too. The smell of urine and creeping decrepitude in the mainland nursing home was something she wanted to avoid if possible.

'I have lived here and I wish to die here if I can.' She had gazed round the inlet and indicated with her hand, 'Just look at this. I wish to be buried in this soil. What could be more peaceful and complete – beautiful?' She laughed. 'I am a child of nature. Christian by upbringing, but really just a human. You and Tisala have taught me a great deal – I bless the day when you and then he arrived. Then your poor lovely Ellie and now my Susannah...' She patted my hand and her old eyes set in a wrinkled sea smiled at me.

She went on: 'But the strange thing is, wherever Tisala's mind has led I had the feeling that underneath I had always known – felt –

something of the truth of what he says. He somehow brought clarity where before I had only fleetingly or dimly perceived. You know, David, I feel greatly privileged. I am so glad to have been able to play my part.' She held my hands. 'You must write your book. But I don't think I shall see it.'

When Tisala returned in the late spring, a few weeks after her funeral, he was saddened by the news. But afterwards he said, 'She lived a good life and is safe from suffering. She told me when she came to say goodbye that she was very tired and thought her time was near. She asked after my family and talked about her own, and about us both as great grandparents. She had said, "You whales are quicker than us – you'll get ahead by a couple of generations by the time we're finished."'

Tisala continued: 'I replied: "We are still pitifully few, but now we have new hope. And I have found such true friends – David, and everyone here. You have helped our world. And now we know we have many friends among wider humanity."

'She hoped we would always be welcome and safe in this place, but she did not know if it would last. She told me she was afraid that I had learned much of the precariousness of human affairs, but believed the next generations are better. I said I would hope to see her in the spring. But it was not to be. She was a kind, good human.'

We had buried her next to Eric in the little island cemetery. Mary was unwell, and in the end did not come over from Vancouver. So Susannah and Julie, the next two generations, led the little group of mourners. Susannah damp-eyed and brave, Julie pale and holding a little bunch of primroses, Guinevere's favourite flowers. On the way we had to hold the coffin down on the cart because it was so light, to stop it clattering and bouncing. 'Don't rattle my teeth out,' she had said one day, laughing. I smiled despite myself, and held on, and wanted to weep. Oh Guinevere. Guinevere and Eric, my steadfast, immovable friends. Now both gone. We were a smaller number gathered round the grave that time, poor Jimmy MacLeod in hopeless tears. Afterwards, up at the house, with tea and wine, we managed to raise smiles of remembrance for a lovely spirit.

For Jimmy MacLeod her going was the end of the life that he had known since boyhood. Now it was the turn of 'the young lady,' as he referred to Susannah. Outwardly, in the months that followed, nothing much changed in his occupation but he too was slowing up and without Guinevere's direction we gradually noticed that things began to be done less frequently and sometimes were left undone.

Mary inherited the islands from Guinevere, but visited infrequently, and left the occupation and running of them to Susannah and me. We spent half the year in London, though we went up to the islands as often as we could. The islands, like many similar outlying ones, became less habited. But when we were there the old spirit of the place seemed unchanged. Julie grew into a lively little girl, pretty like her mother. Like Will and Penny before her she loved playing on the foreshore and collecting shells, and accompanying us in the boat over to Inis Cuan and the inlet. And she too grew up with a great Blue Whale for a friend.

About a year after Guinevere's funeral I went to another – a full Christian funeral – in a great church. The service was all of love – love divine and human love – as was appropriate for the memory of the woman whose sad passing and life was being remembered and celebrated, with tributes recalling her personal, domestic and humorous qualities. The priest, in his address, solemnly recited as a certainty that God – the Christ-God – is in his heaven; that the soul whose body lay in the flower-covered coffin before us was gone to heaven, reunited with the loved ones who had gone before her; and that we could all be comforted accordingly, 'in the sure and certain hope of resurrection to eternal life.' I listened, but knew that I now believed none of it – that it was not true – though the mellow words, the beautiful service and the gathering of friends and families were indeed most comforting. There was no talk of sins, nor any mortal battle between good and evil – Satan himself had vanished from the Earth – no mention of Judgement, no hell, no eternal torment; nothing to disturb the attractive idea of reunions in heaven or the tranquil peace of the just, which for that moment we all perhaps counted ourselves among. We sat solemnly or sadly by inclination, but anyway well turned out, and warm in the pleasant knowledge of our own survival.

And it set me to thinking about heaven and the nature of love. As Susannah and I discussed these questions the complications seemed to multiply.

So I asked Tisala.

Tisala said: 'We think that love springs from animal emotions, which we have seen are the development of the faculties of the senses. An important element of this base is the urge to breed, and in higher animals to care for partner and young. So sexual attraction figures largely in love, though in the highest animals is often transmuted into a softer-edged and more imaginatively influenced amorous yearning and affection forming a new bond of union.

'But because of its origins, as you know, such attraction can often turn to purely physical desire or lust; or, if love, can be foolish or extreme. And does not obsessive or unwise love, for instance a hopeless unrequited love or an unsuitable infatuation, often bring ruin and destruction? The same is frequently and sadly true when love of country becomes unthinking chauvinism.

'Wise love needs reason to mediate with and balance it. Yet conversely in human affairs your reason is not unerring and is often best guided by a good love. This love, this higher manifestation, is emotion when tempered and combined with consciousness, reason and moral imagination. It has become a more elevated good, capable of achieving a remarkable transformation in the advance of life, and in the lives of individuals. It has added a wonderful dimension of value to those lives.'

'Our lives,' I said, and felt again the excitement of understanding, which Tisala so often evoked in me.

'Yes, our lives,' said Susannah as she lent over my shoulder listening intently. And I felt her breath on my neck and ear.

'You need therefore to recognise and know good love, as the Greeks recognised a form of it, agapē; though few of them practised it. Many other people have known some aspects of it, and amongst the religions many Christians and Buddhists have sought to emulate a related form of it; though the nature of their real and overriding human beliefs has often restricted its application and wider adoption in practice. The propensity to nurture that love is perhaps the most valuable quality of those inclined to religion, for it includes reverence for others, which is the foundation of much good love. But I have found evidence of it scattered widely in humanity of all sorts where your civilisations give it a chance to flourish. This higher form of love needs to permeate and spread among as wide a swathe of humanity as possible. And that presents a formidable challenge to you; yet one that many of you cheerfully and engagingly attempt. But I think divine love, though a noble concept, will be shown to be human love, magnified like other great loves, by the imagination.'

He spoke kindly and I envisaged love spreading round the world, pervading it like soundwaves through the oceans or radio waves through the ether and beyond. But as to whether love survives death, except among the living, he was very questioning.

Some years earlier we had discussed heaven. Guinevere had taken a keen interest, for she, like many, attached importance to the matter. She had said, 'Well, heaven is the lynchpin of our religion, but do we really believe it all?'

Tisala thought heaven an interesting concept. He knew that many images of God and heaven emerged from the varied religious beliefs cross-fertilised in the Middle East and eastern Mediterranean world, mainly in the two thousand years before the birth of Christ.

The result, when the Christian elements were added, was the monotheistic Judaic-Christian concept appropriate for an all-powerful God of the universe; but traditionally rendered, to be comprehensible to men, as a great robed and bearded patriarch sitting on a throne high in the clouds, surrounded by countless thousands of singing angels and worshippers, but who could descend to Earth and talk to men.

What puzzled Tisala was how these biblical images, reproduced countless times, have survived so long, for as soon as they are considered rationally many problems emerge. As in Christianity, that the second coming of Christ and the end of the world was believed to be imminent within months or at most a year or two. St Paul therefore had urgently to spread his message of the coming resurrection and heavenly order around the eastern Mediterranean in the short time remaining. Consequently he had some excuse for his inconsistencies and failure to address the problems of his inventiveness, such as bodies climbing out of graves on Judgement Day (a belief Tisala found deeply strange). But subsequent theologians with a much greater timeframe available seem not to have addressed it either, or not to have shared their results.

'And in more modern times, Tisala enquired, 'have not the problems increased? For instance, that when the true size and nature of the universe was discovered, there was no longer a place where heaven could physically be. Logically it has had to retreat, somehow, outside the boundaries of the universe. Yet the traditional Christian image of heaven serenely survives as a place where the familiar laws of physics are applied. There is light and sound – God seen in a bright white light, visible choirs of angels singing. Our images assume there must be time because music, as sound, is tonal vibrations spaced out in time. And if there is time, then heaven cannot be beyond or outside of time, as some apologists have argued. Our belief in heaven requires that life must exist there, whether it be in or out of the universe, for bodily parts are necessary – the congregation of the resurrected must have eyes to see and ears to hear. And although full bodily resurrection is apparently believed there seems to be little consideration of the consequences. Whether or not sexual or digestive parts are needed, is left silent in the Christian version, though clearly provided for in the Islamic version.

He observed that singing and music requires an atmosphere for breathing and the production of sound. But whether, where and how, the earthly mix of gases – oxygen, nitrogen, carbon dioxide and the rest – is available to enable the resurrected lungs to function is unaddressed. The Christian image of heaven simply assumes that somehow, somewhere, it all works, and works eternally.

And though this eternity seems to be locally envisaged within a timeframe, it is claimed the singing goes on everlastingly, which Tisala thought another difficulty. For he thought that heavenly music would be of such compelling beauty as to entrance the mind everlastingly, so rendering it benumbed and incapable of thought or even of worship; music heard as a ceaseless outpouring of love and joy, a sort of spiritual orgasm of ecstasy. But though the body is stated to be fully resurrected to enter heaven, the emotions are not. The negative ones – hate, envy, aggression – are unsurprisingly banished, but so too it seems are positive human emotions, such as delight, excitement and humour. The old requirements of hierarchy, reverence for superiors and dignity have exiled laughter from heaven. He thought it a strange invention, when we can laugh and smile on Earth.

I said: 'And presumably God would simultaneously have to deal with other matters, such as answering prayers or performing miracles or speaking to people on Earth, as is claimed he has always done. I've never understood how he is thought to answer prayers simultaneously to perhaps millions of different believers, all with different prayers; leaving aside the possibility of the same from a million other planets.'

And I, the human, found myself expecting the great whale to provide the answers.

'You are back to equating God as like with man,' said Tisala. He thought religious people would argue that God is able to do all these things at once and everlastingly, miraculously, for he is God and it is a deep mystery. But he thought that such argument is an invitation to the promotion of superstition. 'For do they not add, to stop further enquiry, that humans are not meant to understand these things, and if they try, that is the sin of pride, and the work of the devil? So, for believers, the system is made enquiry-proof. But it leaves them tied to an odd concept of God, and the church authorities dubiously free to require belief in any doctrine promulgated by them, however improbable in the light of increasing knowledge of our world.' And Tisala thought that ultimately this would satisfy no one, except those who have abandoned the search for truth.

'You don't think our enquiry is the sin of pride?' I asked.

'No – it is in the true spirit of earthly life. To develop our higher selves we must seek the truth.

'But you have raised another problem,' continued Tisala. 'For if God and heaven are distant, outside the universe, how do human prayers reach him instantly, and receive immediate answers? You have to postulate a wholly new form of communication that operates at millions of times the speed of light or radio waves – the fastest things known – which take billions of light years to cross the universe, outside which we are supposing God resides.

'An alternative is to postulate, for instance, that God is able to be present simultaneously wherever in the universe a prayer is raised. But how such a being might be thought to exist in reality is left wholly unexplained. Not impossible, but to me implausibly improbable.

'And if you come to that point you have travelled far beyond the realms of Christian beliefs in a God in heaven who resembles man, and intervenes personally, as believed for two thousand years; a belief shared, so far as can be ascertained, by Christ, who as Son of God might have been in a position to know, and as God should have been.'

He paused and I remember the water lap-lapping softly against the rocks and a shimmer passing over the surface, as if the sea were listening – partaking in – our talk. And my old understanding of heaven gave way to a new truth, and the old images became unreal and cracked, like decaying frescos of the religion that had relied on them.

Tisala enquired whether anyone had tried to measure the speed of thought, and was surprised when I replied that, so far as I knew, no one had. He said he would have expected thought, of which prayer is a form, to be an electromagnetic wave or impulse, or powered by one. In which case he anticipated the speed of thought would turn out to be confined to the already known maximum speed of electricity, which is a little less than the speed of light, and not therefore a mechanism or means of instantaneous transfer of prayers across the vast time-space of the universe. He acknowledged this might remain to be shown, but that in the meantime its plausibility was much greater than postulating an entirely arbitrary force – prayer – out of an imaginary wish at variance with, and outside the known electromagnetic spectrum, which otherwise largely explains the continuing working of the universe.

He said the reason that thought transfer appears to be instantaneous must be because it was only used locally, here on Earth where the natural speed of electricity meant that for all practical purposes it was instantaneous. Every heaven envisaged to be somewhere above the sky was in range. He was inclined to think that the locality of thought tended to demonstrate that thought and prayers arose out of the Earth; that their existence arose out of the evolution of life, which life included – relied upon – the utilisation of electromagnetic power. And I thought, the truth will be found to be that God is a concept which exists inside men's heads, for that is where he came into being.

He was surprised when I said Faraday had discovered electricity in the nineteenth century – the use of it, I meant. He mentioned electricity used for millions of years – for light in the bodies of ancient deep-sea fish, or electric shocks used for attack and defence, by eels, catfish and rays; the magnetic part of electromagnetism, used by many creatures – fish, reptiles, birds, mammals, including whales themselves, for navigational purposes; but above all the use of electrical impulses within the brains of animals and higher animals giving rise to consciousness and thought itself. Without it there would be no language, and these sentences would not be written.

But Tisala said concerning claims for heaven and resurrection, that further problems arise, which scripture-writers rarely seem to have considered.

He enquired about a person's age at resurrection. He thought the answer relatively easy where a person dies in their prime – a soldier or young adult killed or dying of an accident or unlucky early disease: they may be expected to be resurrected in the form of early adulthood at which they died.

He asked in what state a man is supposed to return, who once possessed character and powers but who died in a decayed state of old age, feeble and demented? Would his wife expect to meet him again in his dotage or prime, and if his mother died when he was a child would she expect him back as the child he was when she died?

And what of the millions of babies who died before their lives had really started and were undeveloped in body, mind or character? Are they supposed to come back as the adults they might have become, but whom none of their family would then recognise? And of what would their bodies be formed, if they died as babies but are resurrected as adults? For they are believed by many to arise from their graves or reconstituted ashes, and be recreated as living bodies. And if they return as babies, how can they worship God, or communicate with their families? Or are they everlastingly assigned to an uncomprehending babyhood in heaven? And what, similarly, of all the millions of foetuses and embryos aborted by nature down the ages, and now augmented by abortion by wish or need of their mothers?

And with modern understanding, he thought there is a further objection. It is part of the knowledge of mankind that the molecules that make up a body are, on death, by decay or cremation, distributed into other forms of chemistry – into escaping gases or as soil or ashes. They are then recycled into new life – gases being absorbed by new plants and animals, soil nutrients by plants, and plants and animals being eaten by other animals, including man. The constituents of the bodies of the dead are endlessly re-used in the formation of the living.

Thus it becomes physically impossible for bodies to reassemble on the day of judgement. Their constituent molecules and atoms have been used in countless bodies that would need them to be resurrected themselves, and the same materials will still be in use among the living.

Of course, some theologians have retreated in the face of such difficulties and argue that there is no physical or bodily resurrection, but only spiritual. But this is to swap one set of difficulties for others. It becomes necessary to argue, which the bolder of them do, that, from the evidence of much of the New Testament gospels and epistles, St Paul, the Apostles and Jesus himself misunderstood the position. And when theologians accept the timescale of the universe and the life in it revealed by science, as with honest assessment of evidence and in all reason they eventually will, then the end of the world and the Day of Judgement are likely to be postponed for thousands of millions of years, beyond the physical end of the universe, and the end of time. And that gives rise to a whole series of difficulties and increasing improbabilities not only within the interim but with the whole idea of resurrection.

Some less vigorous theologians are driven to postulate a parallel spiritual world coexisting with the known universe, where God and the faithful can happily slip from one to the other. But other than in our imaginative ideas, arising from the wish within men's brains, Tisala found no evidence at all for such a thing, and much contrary evidence in the one universe we do know.

So the questions and difficulties came. I had no answers, nor could I find any, except for the religious requirement to have faith regardless, even in the face of all known reason.

Tisala thought that implausibility is piled on implausibility, until it should be impossible to believe such things are true. He was obliged to conclude that the doctrine of resurrection can only be upheld by some form of miraculous magic, which he thought the spirit of reason quietly tells us does not, and should not, exist. He recalled that the purpose of all this speculated activity of resurrection is apparently to please a God who wishes all these forms of life to worship him; though why he should want such a self-aggrandising thing is nowhere explained or justified. The early Christians, St Paul and following him the gospel writers, who proclaimed resurrection were either ignorant of these difficulties, or in their enthusiasm for the rewards of resurrection disregarded them; as it appears do many of their latter-day followers.

I could see him contemplating the wide sea of history. And then he said, 'We whales have never felt the need for a heaven. We have had a different schooling. We have always accepted that our heaven is here in Earth. It is to be whales swimming in the wide oceans of the world, passing our lives in the pleasure of it all – the sunlight, the waters, our swim-flying freedom, our loves, travels, songs, our communications, our relationships and family building, our lives through the seasons and in our minds until our turn of years is over.

'And during our time, we delight in developing many forms of the rising spirit of the Earth, such as intellect and love, and contacting them in the minds of others. Our idea has always been that spirit emanates from within, arising out of the wonderful abundance of matter, which you have now explained in the evolution of chemistry, life, and consciousness. Our ethics develop from these and derive from the particular physical universe we inhabit. We have long known of the upward movement of the level of consciousness and reason in the higher animal kingdom. We know it amongst our own kind, and our cousins the dolphins and porpoises, and so expect it down the scale of consciousness and reason among the lower animals to the first stirrings of it among the plants. When we first came across men on the margins of the ocean world, we could see that they communicated and were intelligent; and when they sailed upon the ocean we welcomed them and moved gently among them. But ruin and misery were to follow. Mankind has nearly destroyed our heaven on Earth.'

'I can of course see why the belief in the supernatural arose,' said Tisala. 'It comes from the recognition of consciousness and reason outside their own minds. So the jump was made: if the spirit is outside me, it is outside in general. And so men, not understanding the natural world, created in imagination an external supernatural. Thus came the gods, and after them God, and heavens. But that these heavens have been fervently believed in for long periods is no evidence of their reality. The Egyptians believed in their Nile Gods for three thousand years.

Who now believes in them?

'And now,' he continued, 'if the old Christian image of God, bearded and robed in heaven, is discarded, believers need some other plausible heaven to support their faith.'

But he had not encountered any alternative Christian idea of heaven, except the often envisaged, but contextless meeting of dearly loved family members or friends. How this can come about, in what form, and in what setting, given the difficulties we had discussed, and the monolithic nature of the scene of heaven devised for the everlasting glorification of God, he found is left unexplored and unexplained. Some theologians faced with other such difficulties argue that – once again – heaven is not real, but metaphorical, not a place at all, but a state of being. Heaven is here envisaged as a sort of blinding light of unknowing, which he regarded as a negative version of imaginative delusion, the groping of imaginations for something beyond their reach, and untrue.

'But meantime,' I said, 'they have no image to replace that of "Heaven." and so continue to rely on the old images for the persuasion of the faithful, as well as to reassure themselves. They say, "We do not know – perhaps we cannot know; we just believe".'

Tisala said: 'In the sometimes sorry state of the human world, it may seem as well that people can so believe. But if untrue, it becomes a comfort based on falsehood, a refuge from reality that would be better faced: for the immediate comfort carries wider consequences.'

But, if the traditional view of heaven is no longer believable, he thought that people could nevertheless construct, in their imaginations, their own alternative heaven. True human fulfilment and ease in such a place as heaven might include a series of gardens, with special ones for family reunions, and some for sitting in and conversing quietly with friends. He saw English or Persian gardens according to taste, and no doubt for some, tropical gardens, woodland glades, or grassland meadows. And all with access up the mountain to the cloud-capped amphitheatre of heaven where angels sing. He said, despite the clouds there would be no damp or wind and rain, for the clouds are idealised to support the desired glory of heaven. Here God may come and go, leaving archangels in charge, as he visits the gardens of the faithful on the lower slopes and talks wisdom and love like a village Christ, or Mohammed, or Plato, Krishna, Buddha or

Confucius, as indeed those, his representatives, would do. In passing, he noted it was striking that none of these who has a heaven in their own teaching seems to fulfil such a role in their respective heavens. Perhaps because so relaxed and conversational a scene fitted ill with the dominating figure of an all-powerful God, or the reverence felt for some, like Christ, or Mohammed.

Tisala said: 'Such might be your new religious heaven, leaving aside the arrangements for sex and food and other pleasures. But the birds know this is not the real heaven. The real heaven is a world of limitless air and flight and endless birdsong filling blue skies where eagles have no appetites, but soar high in the ether of heaven eternally; and clouds hold no rain or snow and float among light breezes to make a scene of heavenly pleasure, above trees of everlasting fruit and berries, with no scarce seasons. But you humans would scornfully say, "This is fantasy," as you say of all ideas of heaven that are not your own. And if we whales were to construct a heaven, it would be a world of water, where no storms came, nor human hunting or pollution. We whales would move between the sunlit tropical seas, and the turquoise iceberg waters of our delight; and deep-sea trenches would echo to the sound of whale song and our words of love and wisdom. We would see our loves again and love without regard to population, for heaven would have a kind of unreal wonder, where there are no births and deaths, yet children come increasingly, but with never any crowding; and on a thought each whale could be whatever age he chooses for that moment; that moment which closes up and turns to other scenes miraculously, both in and out of time.

'But,' he said, making his smiling sound, 'in our kindness, we would allow green islands in our seas, with plentiful harps for the heavenly use of our poor land cousins; who would be pleased to make music for us. There would be separate islands for the other terrestrial animals, to preserve them from men. And it would be wise not to allow humans to come at all until they had proved themselves: when they understand that they must never kill or harm those below them, or damage the gardens of the sea or land; and must discharge the duty of trust that devolves on all advanced beings increasingly as they advance, actively to look after all others. Why then, even with your split tails, we might teach you to swim-fly properly.

'But you will see,' he said, becoming serious again, 'that each heaven we have constructed seems increasingly familiar: it resembles our planet, or what we might like it to be. For in the end, as beings of this world, our imaginations return, and should return, to a version of it. And the consequence, and the tragedy, of contemplating heaven as another and better world is the neglect or worse abuse of what we have, and do, here now in Earth – in the inner sanctum of the sea, or the precious delicate land, and under the outer fragile layer of atmosphere enwrapping us. For this is only the real world we know in all the universe, and beyond it. If men believed the only heaven that exists is that on Earth, the prospect for the world would be transformed. Within the constraints of the natural world, your clever species is capable of much and wonderful good.

'But it will not be done unless men learn to harness and control the still savage, greedy, evil-conscious animal within them. You have to overcome the drawbacks of your evolution by deliberately altering yourselves to rise above it. This is what your great religious founders and philosophers have long tried to do, despite the limitations of their knowledge. They knew too that one of the tools required is discipline, though they often applied it, or more commonly their followers did, in too negative and restrictive a mode. I can see this prospect, perhaps more clearly than you, for we Blue Whales in the oceans have been able to avoid much of the misery and exploitation of human development. We have experienced a fear-free, harmonious and beautiful world.'

And afterwards I thought – if there is no heaven, except potentially on Earth, then the whole thrust of most religions is mistaken: our father is not in heaven, there is no place, no state, to be resurrected to, nor any afterlife. The whole idea of Judgement Day, the Kingdom of God, and salvation in the next world collapses.

When I raised this with Tisala, he said, 'That must follow. But the consequences give rise to new hope and opportunity for better life on Earth. So we should look further at that, for isn't that the world we have been endeavouring to advance towards?

CHAPTER 70

Changing Beliefs

But shortly after this, our discussions were interrupted by Tisala's winter journey to the sub-tropics. After shutting down the shack and making the various caretaking arrangements with Jimmy MacLeod, Susannah and I went down to London for the winter.

We both noticed and enjoyed a more than usual awareness and delight in everything, even the downside and inconvenient things about life in London, seen and experienced every day, as well as the obvious enjoyment of family and friends and Christmas. Even when Julie got flu Susannah said, 'Well, it gives me the opportunity to nurse her,' but smilingly added, 'but I don't want two of you!' And we both related this enjoyment of life in the present back to our discussions with Tisala.

When he returned in the spring it became clear he had been thinking of wider issues, not only belief in heaven, but of religion itself, and what might follow.

He noted that though religions are mutually exclusive and contradictory, they have often been believed in some form by their own followers for long periods of time. He thought this longevity is sometimes seen by each religion as evidence of its own truth, but will eventually be seen as evidence of prolonged misunderstanding and error, like those many other religions, of various times and places stretching back in history, which have passed out of belief.

Without belief in its truth, a religion will fail, for logically no one can sustain belief in a religion they believe to be untrue. And with the great advance of human knowledge, better, truer ways of understanding the world have emerged and are available for all to study and evaluate.

He balanced this conclusion by observing that the great religions all, of course, contain much good ethics and teaching – an aspect that often makes them attractive and socially useful; but that good ethics do not *belong* to any religion. 'We have seen how ethics existed before any of your current religions.'

Having concluded that in their supernatural and exclusive elements all religions are untrue, Tisala said, 'The question arises as to whether or not one should say so, and set out reasons against religious belief, which may initially disturb or dismay the faithful, but may result in a more enlightened world.'

The first reason he gave to answer 'yes' was that truth has an intrinsic rightness and value that needs to be stated. The truth is the truth and anything that is not truth is untrue. Some say there are many truths, but that does not make many untrue things true.

He took an Egyptian example, when the ancient Egyptians slowly concluded that there was no pleasant duck-hunting afterlife such as their Pharaohs had dreamed of, and their preparations for it, if persisted in, would become an intellectual farce. So their religion slowly died, and the gods who guarded this afterlife died with them.

He thought it possible some might argue that the Egyptian concept of the after-life might after all be right. But he said that you can only test and judge that by going outside the limits of its tradition and mindset, measuring the beliefs against other ideas; which have cumulatively demonstrated that the Egyptian concept was mistaken, and is untrue. It became unbelievable because it was discovered to be untrue.

He asked: 'Does not the same logic follow for all religions that people conclude to be untrue?'

And he argued that, to rational beings, religions must become counter-productive if they mislead people and inhibit the growth of greater understanding. Therefore, there is a moral obligation arising out of our love of humanity to search out and make available the truth so far as we can find it. It is therefore wrong to withhold what ideas for advancement we have, because of the scruples of the religious. He made a saving for occasions when out of love towards an individual, it is right to withhold truth – at that time; but he said that is a matter of timing: it is never right to withhold what is conceived to be the truth in the long run, nor in general, for it is truth that enables us to grow as conscious ethical beings. 'Truth is our whole navigation in the sea of existence and without it we are ultimately lost.'

But in putting forward of new ideas and truths, which might

disturb those with pre-existing beliefs, he thought the likely benefits and results should be considered. In this for convenience Tisala took four groups of people, though he said in reality they are not mutually exclusive but overlap and merge.

The first group of people are those to whom any questioning of their belief is an affront, because they assert they *know* they are right. They take deep offence in the name of their god or God, often leading to conflict. This group throughout history has led persecutions, religious wars and holy wars. They become aroused to defend their religion at all costs. 'And you humans are good at finding that defence involves a need to attack.' The Christians did this in their aggressive phases – their persecution of alleged heretics, including torture and execution, the crusades, the inquisition, and so on. And some Muslims, perhaps because they feel their religion is under threat from 'western values' and 'globalisation', are currently in that state of self-righteous belligerence and sometimes violence. And this, he thought, is always a sure sign of a religion that has failed to develop the higher and more tolerant levels of ethics available to mankind.

'Such people,' said Tisala, 'are free to believe their beliefs if they can, but they are not entitled to force them on others or to punish different beliefs. And if they sanction punishments or outcomes of a lower ethical order, it demonstrates that their religion as practised is mistaken and in error. As the wise among them know, they then stand condemned as humans, and that failure demeans their own religion. For if there was a God, he would be the highest, most merciful being that is capable of existing. So I say that there is a need to illuminate the prejudice of beliefs as a first step to enlightenment. This group is in much need of better ideas and should therefore be made aware of them.'

The second group are those people of sincere flexible beliefs who love their gods or God and try to live up to the high principles of their religion. They try to follow their beliefs, and acknowledge the right of others to follow theirs. They are not the bringers of conflict, but rather of tolerance, so religions may live at peace together. Many live contentedly within these parameters and can view outside ideas without disturbance. These are often good people, who do much in their societies and are willing to develop their beliefs, being persuadable by goodwill and reason. There is no reason, therefore, to suppress alternative views. Rather, they should be widely considered.

Tisala viewed an alternative ideal and philosophy as greatly needed in our societies. 'Otherwise people may become disillusioned in a negative way when they lose their beliefs.' He thought the solution to the paradox of all religions believing themselves to be the truth is that any religion can only be viewed as uniquely right if seen from within its own mindset, doctrines and traditions. It becomes a self-fulfilling world. Step outside and all the icons and holy decorations begin to look like pieces of painted wood and plaster. If people have no alternative world view, then loss of faith can be destructive of their lives and conduct, as when undereducated people of simple prescribed faith migrate to cities and find that the world is not as they were taught, and in disillusion and want turn to crime and prostitution.

And, Tisala understood, people too often do not find good alternatives. In much of our current world more economic wealth, without better ideas as to its use, has led to a tawdry consumer culture that is often stigmatised as 'western' because it was first widespread there; although it seems to be coveted and adopted throughout the human world. That outcome is rightly decried for the hopeless inadequacy of its human vision.

'For all these reasons', said Tisala, 'even in this second and most deserving of religious groupings, it is right to put forward what some conceive to be unwarranted criticisms of their own religion; for it is done with a view of leading to better truths and understanding.'

The third group, which Tisala thought would prove to be by far the biggest group of believers, is that of partial or fragmentary belief in the religion. For instance those who hold simple childhood beliefs, and who later meet objections and questions in our complicated real world and are disillusioned. But he thought it clear that most in this group often held only partially defined beliefs anyway, and are ready to benefit their lives by coming to better beliefs. Moreover, what is 'belief' in a religion will depend on what a branch or sect or denomination of the religion a person belongs to. Within Christianity, or Islam or Judaism, there are quite different beliefs, some not at all believed by full believers in other sub-groups. Tisala observed that there can be no-one on Earth who believes in Christianity or Islam to the full extent of those beliefs as variously held by all the branches or sects at different times. And even what constitutes core beliefs varies surprisingly within religions. Many doubt or deny the existence of this or that – a personal god, the nature of the word of god, heaven, hell, eternal torment, miracles, resurrection, reincarnation, an after life, and any number of lesser beliefs; while many believe some but not others, often in different combinations. Many in this group acquiesce in their part-beliefs for social reasons, or do not trouble, in a busy and distracting world, to consider their beliefs, or the anomalies in what they believe, or don't really believe, or might believe if they thought about it.

The fourth group Tisala identified is that of no religious belief, or nearly none. In modern times this may be the biggest group of all, though some reject all specific religions but still retain the residual idea of the possibility of a deity, an unknown force or power behind the nature and start of the universe. But many in this group believe there is no such thing as a personal god, or religion.

There is a natural flow or migration between these identifiable groups, commonly, from belief to less belief, or to finding belief largely or wholly untrue. There is also a movement in the other direction. But this acquisition of religious belief is often instantaneous – not based on considering let alone understanding the full underlying theology – but on a leap in conjecture, or as a result of some vivid and immediate emotional experience which is given a religious explanation, especially among those with previously troubled lives.

Another exception to the more usual gradual migration between groups is found among violent extremists. These are often seen as implacably committed to their cause, but that impression arises because we hear much of their doings and opinions, but rarely those of disillusioned ex-fanatics. These don't often speak in public, perhaps for fear of reprisals, and when they do are frequently regarded as traitors and are rejected, or condemned as apostates, and sometimes even murdered or assassinated; which then tells us something about the true nature of some of their former co-religionists within this group.

'But they are important people', said Tisala 'for they mark a break from evil and the beginning of wisdom, but need the availability and support of new ideas and ideals to complete their transition. Some they may work out from their revulsion against cruelty, or as a new-found tolerance and kindness towards former enemies.

Tisala concluded therefore that for all groups of humans, putting forward an enlightened philosophy and world-view in the light of what truth has so far been gained from studying the world, is an urgent necessity. Such reflections may relieve and comfort millions of men and women in the varying groups of people within religions who have been confused, frightened or repressed by the claims and impositions of their religion or religious beliefs, or by those who purportedly claim to wield unanswerable or infallible rule-making authority in the name of that religion.' He thought such wielders of authority seek too often to block out and condemn other ideas, which are the only way by which the truth or otherwise of their own beliefs are properly tested and measurable. And coercion by authority indicates a fear of truth, and is a lower form of conduct than that which offers the freedom to accept reason and work out what is wise.

'Is it not true,' he asked, 'that freedom of thought and expression is the necessary condition for the growth and advance of wiser and truer world views? Anyone who seeks to deny you that tries to deny you the prospect of a better humanity.'

One day I asked Tisala what he thought would eventually happen to our religions.

'Ultimately, if you do not destroy the planet, but educate your peoples and manage to live with your greater knowledge more in harmony with yourselves and the world, the reasons you originally needed religion, and the religions themselves, will slowly fade away. But if you do not, or if you destroy your civilisation, or disrupt the very balance of the planet, then frightened people will cling to the remnants of religion, and out of that decay, knowledge and reason may be lost and a new dark age arise. And with it, who knows what strange and savage imagined faiths and beliefs?

'You can use imagination and conviction to postulate a better understanding of reality, but they should not be set up against reason. And that is what your religions largely do, when they set up faith by revelation and supposedly divine authority: they insist on it against reason. And that is why ultimately I think they will fail, as all your earlier religions have failed. For they offer an explanation of existence that, when measured against knowledge acquired through reason, will be found to be untrue; though internally, like a good fairy tale, they borrow coherent logic from the real world.

'You can say with increasing certainty that the religions of man have been an interim attempt to impose order and meaning on a then little-understood universe. The degree to which your understanding has now advanced is astonishing. You have enabled us to peer into much of the structure of the universe, from the sub-atomic to the swirling of countless billions of galaxies, and to look back across fourteen billion years of time and space, so that we can now see the nature of the universe and life within it across this large spectrum. But none of us can see the beginning or end, for our knowledge, and perhaps our minds, wonderful though they are, are not yet sufficiently advanced. And though such understanding facilitates wisdom, it does not of itself bring it.

'But is it not clear that what was long considered evidence of the activities of the gods, and then God, has been based on a misunderstanding of creation as it really is?

'Paradoxically, the upshot is that with the advancement of mankind's knowledge and understanding leading that of other animals, the creature that emerges with the nearest thing to god-like propensities here on Earth is that very flawed ape, yourselves. And the responsibility this gives you is to rise to the role and duty of trustees of creation before your original nature destroys it. It is a race upon which the future of the Earth depends. We whales, as one of the other advanced species of nature, will be able to watch and wish you well and perhaps help you in your task.

'You may recall that I said "Faith is a determined belief in conjecture". Now I say reason is greater than faith because through reason you can demonstrate the approach to truth, whereas by faith you can only guess at it. This is why all your faiths are different, while the laws of science are universally the same. Reason exists in everything in the universe. From the beginning it was so: there were reasons why the universe could expand into existence; there were reasons why hydrogen could evolve into helium, and so on into other elements; there were reasons why life could evolve from inorganic chemistry, and why higher life emerged from that. Everywhere there is a chain of reason. Without reason the universe as it is could no more exist than it can without time. Time is necessary dimension of existence. Reason is a process – the linking of causal reality. And it can only happen, like everything else, within time, at least in this universe.

Reason is universal. The origin of the occurrence of reason may not so far be known. Some may wish to call it divine, but I conclude it is nothing to do with any god or religion yet conceived.'

After this there was a silence. We went out and sat with Tisala by the water's edge and a breeze blew across the inlet making curved ripples on the surface. And I felt a click in the time of my own existence. I looked at Susannah, and she at me, but we said nothing.

He knew we had been listening to the silence for afterwards he said, 'Silence is a sea wherein movements and ideas in the mind may be connected. We whales make much use of silence. It surrounds and defines the sounds of the Earth. But you humans are invading that space too with your unending noise. You need to preserve and listen to the silence, for it enlarges awareness of life beyond your own.'

I remember that evening with vivid clarity, for in some ways it was a completion, and it was not far from the end.

CHAPTER 71

Final Days

The next four years passed at what seemed an ever-increasing speed. The seasons came and went. And with each we went up to live in the islands, like happy nomads, and each time Tisala returned from his ocean voyages.

In the freedom of the islands Julie grew into something of a tomboy. On Eileen Mòr, she struck up a great friendship with Jimmy MacLeod and was always badgering him to teach her the many practical things that he knew as part of island life. She loved coming over to the shack on Inis Cuan and helping me with the boats and other tasks – she enjoyed things that worked, re-oiling hinges or mechanical bits and pieces, and soon became proficient in a number of them. She was always demanding, 'Let me do it!' Susannah, with her Canadian view that women should engage with all possibilities, encouraged these traits. But when we were working with Tisala, Julie would happily scramble by herself among the rocks by the shore, or on the rocky rises behind the shack, examining the life to be found in the nooks and crannies. I watched in her the love and acute observation of the natural world that had been so important in my own childhood. She was always bringing things back for information – spiders' cocoons, birds' egg shells for identification, dead moths, and from the sea shore an unending supply of debris of marine life – her favourites were a range of small crab cases of different colours. She kept her treasures in a special box, except when they got too smelly. Very often she would make up little stories about them. She loved the books that we read to her, and I think invented all sorts of adventures in her own world.

One night I read her a story about the North American Indians – 'Red Indians'.

'You are not allowed to call them that, Daddy.'

'They were always Red Indians when I was a boy. Do you know why?' – I explained about the misunderstood size of the world and the undreamt-of continent of the Americas. 'I always wanted them to win, but they rarely did – they didn't have much chance, the poor Indians.'

'The cowboys had guns and were cruel.'

'Yes they were, and often ignorant and ruthless as well. But you see at that time people thought...' Another explanation –

'But Mummy's grandpa didn't...' And so on, the complexity of the human world unfolding.

But when Penny was married in the summer of 1993, Julie was transformed into one of three pretty bridesmaids and took great pleasure in her cream and green dress and posy, and the excitement of the whole occasion. Penny married into a farming family. Her husband, Michael, worked on the family farm in Wiltshire, not far from Edmund and Penelope, and she soon became happily absorbed in that life.

Will was married the next year, but my earlier worry that this might result in the loss of his assistance – which had become increasingly important – did not materialise. He moved to a new engineering company in Yorkshire – 200 miles nearer the islands – and negotiated a fortnight's unpaid leave in addition to his annual holiday. His wife, Claire, was a doctor, efficient but empathetic, one of those doctors in whom you would immediately have confidence. She joined a local practice in Yorkshire. Away from medicine her passion was painting, and she loved coming to the islands and trying to capture the landscape and the surrounding seas and skies. She soon became initiated into our Tisalan world and a welcome and valuable member of our little group. Their first child, David, was born two years later.

The year after Will's wedding, Mary came over from Canada. It was her first visit for three years. During it she raised with Susannah and me the question of the islands' future. We were sitting in the kitchen on Eileen Mòr, so often the council chamber in our lives, when she broached the subject. I remembered the first of such meetings, long ago with Eric and Guinevere, and myself as a student, at the start of everything. Immediately I felt a stab of apprehension – that this might be the end – and that she might wish to sell – might need to sell – though so far as we knew Tom's business affairs were fine. I knew we could never hope to buy the islands, but I had thought of ways and schemes to keep on at least Inis Cuan.

She said she had decided in her own mind that she did not want the continuing responsibility of ownership. She was pleased by how everything was working, but above all she wanted to secure the future. No, she did not want to sell, or want the money. She wanted us to run the island as before, but she proposed to place the island in trust to take it out of her estate. For us relief was followed by gratitude. After further discussions on the issues, and taking legal advice, a trust deed was drawn up and executed. It contained provisions and safeguards for the future so far as we could then see it. Susannah, Will and I became trustees, with Mary expressing the hope that in due course Julie might join us.

In the following months I grew into the idea of being a formal trustee of the islands, but found legal change made little difference to my attitude and outlook, for I had always felt myself a trustee. As always it was simply the islands themselves that mattered, and the preservation of our haven.

For years I had dreaded Tisala being killed. But that dread had mercifully lifted in later years with the protection of the Blue Whales, and its public acceptance by the remaining whaling nations. And with the passage of time our work had progressed. In those last years much was fulfilled. I have tried to incorporate the later conclusions into some of the discussions which took place over the years. Some parts were updated, but have not been reported and still lie in my notebooks. We watched new wars and killing, and new humanitarian disasters arise, and new threats of war and nuclear war emerging. We saw opportunities missed – of disarmament, of population strategies, and of resource and pollution management. But perhaps most dismaying of all was the gathering threat of possibly irreversible climate change, and its unquantifiable repercussions for the future of life in the Earth, within this miraculous shimmering sphere.

Tisala said: 'What is needful for humanity is intellectual and cultural evolution, consciously sought and used in harmony with your reason and increasing knowledge. You must understand and amend the nature of your biological evolution and your cultural limitations.

'It cannot be done with your old attitudes or religions. It needs a world view formed both by science and what may be called 'things of the spirit' – nothing to do with the supernatural, which I think will be found not to exist – but a spirit arising from within through higher consciousness. We see it, for instance, in the upward development reflected in advanced ethical and moral codes, both religious and secular, and in literature, poetry, music and art. It is a search for higher things in life, such as understanding and love.

'For many, your religions will be their starting point. But I fear they are blind alleys. No religion or system of thought can in the end stand against a greater truth.

He recalled that for thousands of years we humans had believed the world was flat. The evidence seemed compelling enough, yet it was completely untrue.

Tisala resumed: 'When we look at the material universe the question arises, where, how and why does 'spirit' arise? We have so far concluded, from the account given with increasing clarity by expanding scientific knowledge, that it comes from within, and is allowed by the process of evolution.

'But you will say that we must enquire further. For behind the development of the universe itself – its form, matter and the evolution of its chemical composition, and afterwards life – there lie other questions. Why should there be natural laws? Why the order of the chemical world and why the laws of gravity and conservation of energy? And why the logic of mathematics? Why should such things exist and where did they come from?

'Yet we should also ask why your second law of thermodynamics – that everything in the material universe tends towards disorder – should prevail. *Why* does the physics of the universe work that way? The only exceptions we see are for limited periods in local pockets of energy, such as, within our planet, borrowing energy from the sun to create and develop successive life. Perhaps overall, disorder – entropy – makes the universe like a firework, a rocket in the sky, that has to explode to reach its proper beauty, when the beauty can only exist within time and must decay to allow for the possibility of its own existence and for a new beauty to emerge. We may be near the full slow-motion glory of our universe's outward starburst. In a few billion years it may contract, or simply fade away, if all the energy in the universe becomes disordered. But if the law of conservation of energy is right, will another universe form? And will intelligent beings develop in that universe, as they have in this, to pose the same questions and ask if that is any evidence of a 'ground of spirit' reality? We can see the possibility that our universe may have come from a previous one, and another may, within the laws of physics, succeed ours. It seems to me that the end of our universe is most likely, not to usher in a purely spirit world, but a new material universe that we may hope will develop the attributes of things of the spirit, as we have here.

'But these things are little to do with any religion so far put forward: the religions proceed by myths and stories, the bulk of which we have seen are, in any literal sense, demonstrably untrue. They come from too limited and credulous a viewpoint. And where they are symbolic, they are not symbolic of any alternative reality, but only prove your powers of imagination. Your religions are inventions which try to account for awareness of a 'spiritual' dimension arising through consciousness. And it follows in that case,' said Tisala gently, 'that the term "God" and the idea of God are both obsolescent and should become obsolete. "God" is too limited a term. However you use it, it carries the shadow of anthropomorphic ideas – the idea of "an intelligence" allowing, creating, guiding or even intervening in the universe, depending on how many "human" attributes you believe God may have. May we still properly call things of the spirit "God"? I think the better answer is "no", for it distorts understanding.

'It may be suggested that "spirit" is the energy field from which the fundamental waves and particles and then matter emerged to form the universe we see around us. We can argue for such, but it may not be true. It may be wholly imaginary, a figment of educated imagination. Certainly, so far the evidence for such "spirit" in the universe has only been found in the advanced life of this world. And now we have the evolutionary explanation for that.

'And certainly, as I understand it, nothing like "spirit" has been found, for instance, in or around the electromagnetic spectrum; though you have identified many forms of energy: gamma rays, x-rays, ultra-violet and infra-red radiation, light, microwaves, radio and television waves. Nor has "spirit" been found in or around the forces: electromagnetism, gravity, or the weak and strong nuclear forces.' And then Tisala said, almost as an aside, 'And though I understand your scientists so far treat these two groups as separate, my intuition is that they will be found to be part of the same unity.

'My feeling is that things of the spirit, such as love, will be found not to pervade deep space or be any "ground of reality" underlying the universe. These things will only be found in life elsewhere locally in parts of the universe where advanced conscious and nervous systems have developed. Love, happiness and ethics, arise naturally – they are the jewels of such conscious nervous systems; as, on the way up, for instance, sight and sexual orgasm are jewels of developing physical systems.

'The things of the spirit are the language of conscious behaviour between higher sentient beings, and the logic of ethics is its grammar. I suspect,' said Tisala going off on one of his tangential links, 'that in the same way maths may be found to be a consequence of physics, not a fundamental reality, which describes but does not dictate its laws. Maths may turn out to be simply the language of physics, and its strong internal logic is its grammar. An idea,' remarked Tisala with a hint of playfulness, 'that may not much please the mathemagicians.

'And if we knew enough, the question of order found in the laws of nature, mathematics and chemistry, might so become explicable. At the moment,' said Tisala, with his smiling sound, 'perhaps we are still flat-earthers.'

'But for ourselves perhaps we can say this: the personal god of many religions, who is said to love but judges and intervenes in the world, we have found untrue. The supernatural in general has gone, likewise found untrue. There remains the possibility of some background intelligent or spiritual power "out there". But there is no place "out there" where it resides. Theologians stated it as "God", coming down to us in some wholly unknown way, though claimed as an existing reality. This is a possible hypothesis, but one as yet without evidence. We have concluded on the widespread evolutionary evidence and supporting scientific disciplines that what we call the "spirit" comes via life and consciousness, and that these things are internal – they have evolved from within – built up in the development of higher life forms.'

Tisala thought for a minute, and the silence grew. What he next said was this: 'In the end, whether the things of the spirit – love, wisdom, goodness – come to us externally from some divine spirit, or arise from within through the development of natural life, can remain open, and should not immediately matter, *Provided* mankind agrees on aiming for the highest level of tolerance, love, wisdom and goodness within both religious and secular teaching and practice.

'Where would that bring us? The world needs the antagonisms of religion and secular belief to be resolved and fall away. If all the religions and secular beliefs were to agree and strive to put into practice universal ethics there might open up a new prospect. One day perhaps, no more wars of religious or ideological certainty, no more Jihads, Crusades, fascist or communist force or coercion politics. In matters of race, and tribes – yellow, brown, white, black, Arab, Jew, African and all the others – no more genocide, no more exclusivity, no more exploitation of nationality. Instead, a new counterbalance might flourish, activated by love – of tolerance, mercy, justice, kindness and goodness, habitually used and built into your political reactions and constitutions, and actively sought and applied between individuals.' He paused. 'Such a prospect asks for much vision, but that is where you humans need to go, and need to wish to go.'

Then he said, 'Yes, of course we delight to enquire whether, behind the scientific and abstract principles we already see, is another dimension of reality which allows it to be as it is. That may be important to help understand the universe. But such enquiries should not distract from the urgent need to apply better ethics and reasoned reform within the world. For if you destroy the Earth, the possibility of ever knowing about greater things would be extinguished forever, and would be the ultimate tragedy for all life.'

That evening, which was near the time for Tisala's departure to the winter tropics, Susannah and I sat on the water's edge in the quiet of the evening, gazing across the turquoise and yellow surface of the inlet in the afterglow of the sunset. I thought how Tisalan ethics might make the world a better place, and how we might find the way to apply them.

But this time I had a sense of completeness that I had never felt before. That in Tisala's survival and ours, something important was coming to fruition.

And as I watched I thought in my mind's eye of Ellie, Will and Penny, Robert and Eric and Guinevere, Susannah and Julie – our group across the years. I looked at Susannah, who was deep in her own thought, and at her soft auburn-haired temple, which showed a few early strands of silver, like the first stars appearing in the sky. And I loved her the more, coming with me through life. She saw me looking at her and we smiled.

I think Tisala felt that completeness too. One day soon after he said, 'I have been, in my new life, above all creatures fortunate.'

We spoke, reminiscing about the contact we had tentatively made so many years ago, a time of critical anguish for the whole future of his kind. I shuddered when I thought of how carelessly we men had nearly destroyed this great wonder of life, the Blue Whales. Then we joked about our early attempts to communicate and laughed as we surveyed our survival and friendship. He said, 'I did not think, all those years ago, that a time would ever be when I would thank much of the human race for their understanding and forbearance. Now, that understanding and forbearance is needed, and urgently needed, in a far wider sphere in the whole demesne of this little Earth – our single precious garden.'

Tisala said, 'You humans are slow to learn. Your rulers and combatants are too often bad or misguided, and tolerant only of their own agendas, ambitions and cruelty. And your people and religions are still often mired in the foolishness of exclusive, militant or irrational beliefs. You laugh at your ancestors for believing thunder was the anger of the gods, but most of you have not yet cast off a whole range of other supernatural beliefs, nor understood that the natural world within the universe is even more astonishing than previously believed: wonderful beyond imagination.'

Yet within the same human affairs, Tisala found much of hope, much growth of knowledge, much kindness in daily living, and tolerance between cultures and nations. In short, a growing realisation in the world that it is one world, much smaller than previously conceived, that everyone is each other's neighbour, and that living in peace and tolerance together and addressing the common problems of the world are increasingly urgent necessities. His judgement was that, though within humanity's ability, success would depend on an unprecedented and disciplined flowering of knowledge, goodwill and co-operation over two or three generations, and the restraint and abandonment of mankind's worst follies: a sombre challenge requiring a wider understanding and optimism among people, and wisdom amongst statesmen.

In the following spring – the spring of 1998 – it happened that we were nearly all in the islands together. Susannah, Julie and I had come up in mid March. Will, Claire and their little David arrived two weeks later. We were expecting Tisala in a few days. We were staying at Eileen Mòr, Susannah presiding over the new generation, organising, advising, comforting children, delegating jobs, preparing meals with Claire and gathering everyone around. Will and I came in for lunch after each morning's work with Jimmy on fencing or clearing scrub. We were also working on the boats, and reviving the vegetable patch for Susannah. In the afternoons we worked on, or went for walks, or if it was raining, read, bodies propped up in various corners of the house, before we gathered again for the evening.

On a couple of the days I went over to Inis Cuan – the first time with Susannah and Julie, bringing out the bedding and food supplies and checking over the shack and equipment. On the second visit Will and I went over with Julie and we prepared for the coming season. Will sorted out a wiring problem on the equipment. We did various maintenance jobs on the shack. Will, closely watched by Julie, pushed his penknife into suspect areas of the wood. In a year or two, a few replacement planks would be needed. Meantime, we set to with the paint brushes, applying wood preserver heavily where bits of rot were discovered, soaking it in and watching the bubbles sizzling as it was absorbed.

The third of April was a sunny spring day, with a gentle south-westerly breeze. Tisala was due that day or the next. We all got up early, abandoned work, and went over to Inis Cuan, taking both boats. As always before, a lookout was kept for Tisala, Julie taking on the main role as Will had done in earlier years. But eventually she came down from spyglass hill, disappointed. 'Why isn't he here?'

'He may not come for a day or two,' I said.

'I know. He's late.'

Towards the end of the afternoon Will took her out in the boat. 'Julie, take a sun hat,' said Susannah. 'It's getting hot.' They set off down the inlet and out through the islets and rocks, into the sea beyond. Will had the fishing lines with him. They stayed out a couple of hours and caught three mackerel. But there was no sign of Tisala. He did not come the next day either. We gave each other various calm explanations, though he nearly always arrived within the predetermined three-day estimate, and I felt the old unease, a tightening of tension. And, for the first time, I felt a tiredness, a weariness with the human folly of whaling. But the end, when it came, did not come from that source.

The following day Julie was on the cliffs by the inlet entrance. I was in the shack checking some notes. My mobile rang.

'Dad! He's here! He's almost reached the outer rocks.'

'Well done, darling. Come on back.'

Once again I watched Tisala coming up the inlet. But there was something different. His approach was slower, less smoothly coordinated than in earlier years. I remembered noticing something the previous year – perhaps two – without, in the excitement of his arrival, registering the change. But this time when he came to a stop in his berthing place and we spoke over the equipment his voice seemed not as strong, older and more distant as if he were somehow withdrawing.

We talked of many things that spring. But more than usual about our families, his and mine. His now spread from the Arctic to the southern oceans. And he dwelt on his own world more frequently, and the painfully slow but unmistakeable recovery of the Blue Whales, and the even more gradual rebuilding of their decimated society. He seemed particularly well informed about the Blue Whales in the Antarctic and Pacific.

'Yes, in the last year or two some of our young adults have made more journeys between the hemispheres and oceans, and have passed word. It is the beginning of our greater strength and unity.'

He seemed deeply pleased; but relieved too that others were increasingly engaged in taking up the mantle of family leadership, and that liaison between the oceanic groups was gradually extending. Sometimes his reflections seemed to have an elegiac tone. He was not sad, but settled in his mind.

One day he said, 'I have lived to see a change that we did not think was possible in the fearful days of my youth. I have lived to see the threat of our extinction slowly receding, and our younger generations living. Together we have learned and been through much. Who would have thought such an alliance of nature would occur – and develop – so rapidly after so many generations of apartness.'

I knew it pleased him profoundly. And now he could believe that his kind might survive after all, and restore their world; and it relieved his sense of responsibility enormously. Yet it was as if this release had brought upon him an exhaustion from all those years.

That spring, towards the end of his time with us, he said: 'David, you know it is in our nature always to go on while we can. But I feel my time is coming. I may not come back from the icecap after the summer.'

And I saw his calm acceptance that his own life might soon be closing. At first I was dismayed. But he spoke quite calmly about it, and matters arising from it, and what would happen and what I must do. And I saw that he expected me to be wise and steady and stoical, and somehow he made me so.

I told Susannah and Will. Initial shock and dismay as we talked about it in hushed tones gave way to subdued concern.

Susannah eventually said, 'I couldn't bear him to be hunted down and harpooned. He will at least escape that. This is better – his natural span – but it has come too soon. Maybe he won't die yet.'

Will was more bitter, blaming the toll of unremitting alarms and stresses of the years of whaling, when first Tisala's grandparents and parents' generation were slaughtered, and then Sayli's and their children's generation, and his own terrible wounding.

'Yes, but consider what he has achieved despite all that.' And we marvelled again at the history of Tisala. So gradually we adjusted: the ongoing present we had known all these years would become the past.

One evening, when we had finished talking, Tisala said, 'Come out to sea with me and bring Susannah and Will and Julie. We will not be very long.'

I called out to the others, 'Tisala wants us to accompany him out in the boat.' We climbed in. Julie asking what was happening.

'We'll see.'

The day was overcast but flat calm. Claire, holding young David, waved us off. Tisala started off slowly down the inlet. I took the boat carefully alongside him and we went together until the narrows when I slowed and he went ahead out into the sea. We followed behind. He went out about half a mile and then stopped. I put the engine on 'idle', and then turned it off and we drifted silently. After a minute he started to swim in a widening circle round the boat. I wondered if he was reliving the past, and our first meeting, when I stood in the boat to welcome him. So, nearly forty years later, I stood in the boat saluting this great being, but now in the full knowledge of his greatness of spirit and achievement.

Will said quietly: ' I think this is part of his goodbye, Dad.'

Susannah held Julie. 'Remember this.'

'Look!' said Julie suddenly, pointing. The long slow back of another great whale surfaced a little way off and slid through the water to join Tisala.

'I think it's Tarba,' I said. The whale partly raised his head out of the water, looking at us, and made a short low sound.

'Yes,' said Will – look.' And we noted the markings of Tisala's grandson.

Seconds later a third blue back appeared near the others.

'I think this is a young one – she's smaller,' said Will.

'How do you know it's a she?' asked Julie.

'They always travel together. Anyway, it just feels like a female.' Afterwards we learned it was Tarba's youngest daughter, not yet three years old.

We all stood in the boat, holding each other occasionally for balance.

'Welcome the whales!' I called out. We all felt the old thrill anew. The whales were now almost motionless. Then the two newcomers very slowly approached our boat, and raised their heads and looked at us. We called out various greetings.

After a short while Tisala, after an exchange of sounds with Tarba, turned towards Inis Cuan. The other two whales slid away towards the open sea. The meeting was over. We followed Tisala back in. I held Susannah round the waist.

Will said, 'We forgot the poems.'

Afterwards, in the inlet back on the equipment, Tisala said 'Tarba and Sabisha, my great granddaughter, have come to take me to the feeding grounds, to the edge of the Arctic icefields. It is now further to go, and a long way for me.'

I asked: 'Will they first come into the inlet?'

'Yes, they know they will be welcome. Tarba will come. Sabisha is very young, but she will follow him.'

My heart knew now that Tisala was leaving us and did not expect to return. At first my mind had not accepted it. For three days and nights I had been intermittently overcome by a sort of panic – what remained undone, what questions to be discussed, what knowledge distilled? And underneath I felt a deep heavy sadness. Tisala was going. It was all going to end.

'Tomorrow I must leave you.'

'Yes, I know. You… You may return.'

'My dear friend, David.' I felt his love, and it comforted me even as his tone told me he would never come back.

That evening Will took Claire, David and Julie back to Eileen Mòr, promising to return with them in the morning. Susannah and I stayed on. Later that evening we spoke at length to Tisala. We went to bed far into the night, and very tired. Susannah folded me silently in her arms and we held each other.

The next day things were outwardly better – the others returned, there was talk, small jobs were done, food eaten and everyone wanted in turn to speak to Tisala. But in between, I felt the dull hopelessness of impending irreplaceable loss. Gradually, as the day went on, I grew calmer. I had known this day would come and prepared for it. Everything was now done and after the initial jolt I accepted it. And where the mind is steady, the feelings and emotions can follow.

In the afternoon Tisala said, 'They are coming.'

We saw two gentle bow waves coming up the inlet. We all stood on the rocks outside the shack and watched their approach. They came up to Tisala – who stirred slightly – and gently nudged him, turned and waited in the water.

I went into the shack and spoke to Tisala. He wanted us to speak to him with Tarba and Sabisha listening in.

I spoke first, then Susannah and Will, with Tisala responding as appropriate both to us and by strings of whale sounds to Tarba and Sabisha. He asked too for a reading of the poems – Will's, and with Julie reading Penny's.

He asked us to play two or three of his favourite passages of music. Tarba and Sabisha listened intently. Then he asked to hear the slow movement from Beethoven's last symphony. He had no need to hear it, for he carried the whole thing in his head, but nevertheless he liked to, as he had on previous occasions. I remember him saying once that this was music to accompany souls to their end in peace, and I knew he would carry it with him to his own end.

Will realised it too. He came back into the shack and said: 'Dad, you must speak to him last.'

I nodded. 'Yes.'

Then, after the music, in ones and twos everyone came in to say goodbye. Tisala seemed always to have the right words for each of us. And in and beneath the words were messages of care and love.

I was the last to speak with Tisala.

Then looking up I saw Tarba and Sabisha stir in the water. I believe they knew. I left the equipment switched on, and then went out on the rocks to join the others. Tarba went first with Sabisha close behind. But as they set off down the inlet Tisala circled and came back to the top end, coming past us again. As he did so he raised his head and watched us as we stood and waved and called to him. And then he shallow dived, for the inlet was only so deep, and his flukes came briefly clear of the water before he rose again.

Will was holding little David in his arms.

'Wave goodbye to Tisala.' His tiny hand waved.

Will looked at me and put an arm round my shoulders, still holding young David, who finding himself near my face held my nose in his hand and laughed. (Some years later, when he was eight, he told me he could remember waving goodbye to the great whale, Tisala. It was his first memory.)

Julie said, 'Is he really going?'

'Yes, love, I think he is.'

She called out, 'Bye Tisala.' She waved, but her arm slowly shrank back towards her chest and her fingers closed. Like us all, she stared after him. He swam slowly down the inlet for the last time, led by his escort.

Susannah held my hand and said, 'They will look after him now.' She was in tears. They went down towards the narrows, and the inlet was empty.

We never saw Tisala again.

So Tisala departed to the deep, his original domain. Somewhere out there, sometime that summer in the Arctic paradise, Tisala closed his eyes on life and took his long dive. He was about seventy-six years old. Old, but not a great age for a Blue Whale.

That spring before he left us, he had said: 'Our bodies have been lent to us by the food that developed and sustains us. Soon my body will be returned to the waters of the Earth and I shall be eaten and in turn sustain new life. My bones too will decay and release their goodness. Perhaps I shall eventually resurface in the form of algae to be eaten by the krill, and via them form the cells of new Blue Whales and other creatures.'

And I think knowledge of this ending and beginning pleased him.

CHAPTER 72

Valete

We stayed on the islands another week before Will, Claire and David departed. Before they went we spring-cleaned and began to close down the shack, and spent two days walking, talking, sometimes laughing between our sadder moments, and enjoying Inis Cuan. Will carried David in his rucksack, all along the shore and cliffs. I think we all gazed out to sea, but I sometimes felt as if we had withdrawn to the land and were seeing the islands and the sea differently.

Susannah, Julie and I stayed up another week on Eilean Mòr, attending to various tasks, before we too departed, for London.

In the autumn we went up to the islands again. There were numerous things that needed attention and I tried to be businesslike. But always I was drawn over to Inis Cuan, and went across nearly every day just in case. However, the early days of October went by and there was no sign of Tisala.

Then one day I saw again the bow wave of a Blue Whale coming up the inlet. For an instant my heart leapt – but almost at the same moment I knew it was not Tisala – the movement was different.

It was Tarba.

He had come to tell us by his return that Tisala would never return. He came to the berthing place, raised his head from the water and made a sound of greeting. I answered and then signalled I was going into the shack. I turned on the equipment and spoke to him for some minutes. He listened motionless. When we had finished he stirred and then carefully manoeuvring round the inlet as if he too were remembering.

He stayed for about an hour. Eventually he made sounds that signalled his departure. I got into the boat and went out to him. He waited and let me come alongside. I patted his side and called out a greeting before pulling away. He turned slowly and went down the inlet. And as he went an overwhelming determination formed in me that Tisala's history must be written.

My sadness at Tisala's going, and knowing that he went to his death, at first numbed my mind, and there was a great void at the loss of his company and with it half my way of life. Susannah was caring and protective towards me, as if I had lost a part of myself, which in a sense I had. She and the family were my anchor.

But I came to realise that in a sense Tisala was still with us. The inlet was empty, but everywhere I felt his presence, for he had left with us his great gift of love and wisdom for a better understanding of the world and its unity. And it comforted me that Blue Whales, the greatest living animal the world has ever seen, were living at peace in the Arctic and the Antarctic and the oceans of the world and that Tisala was remembered and loved in that world too. So I began to write.

I had of course long kept reams of notes as well as various scientific and general papers, and had provided for their safety in the event of my death, so the knowledge should not be lost. Some knowledge I would not release – such as the locations of the Blue Whales' breeding grounds – and some knowledge I might destroy, though that went hard, but we were trustees to the Blue Whales as well as having the knowledge of them. The world of unscrupulous men could still wreak havoc. There is as yet no effective international guardian – such as the United Nations may become – of the whales' world, and none with the authority and will to apply what should be the protective laws and powers of enforcement. When that day comes or when the Japanese, Norwegians, Icelanders and the remaining other whaling nations, enact and enforce both by law and by their public opinion the abandonment of whaling forever, then the world may benefit from the knowledge I and my fellow trustees hold, but not until then.

Yet I knew that the papers, and records, of themselves would not give a true picture of the wonder of Tisala. So, with Susannah's constant support and with her help and Will's, I have tried to set the story down. It has taken me six years, and more is now beyond me. I therefore put out into the world my greatly imperfect efforts, and hope for the willing assistance of my readers' minds and sympathies.

My great endeavour with Tisala is nearly done – though it will never be finished while I live. I have come back to a more ordinary – but full and happy – life with my wife and family. And somehow I found, though loving Tisala, I loved my family the more. We still spend part of each year on Eilean Mòr and Inis Cuan. It was strange at first – the empty inlet and knowing that Tisala would not return between the headlands, sliding through the water hardly disturbing it but for a little bow wave and the quiet agitated little whirlpool behind his flukes. I have never yet got over the habit of looking for his form among the waves outside in the sea. But I have settled now for living amidst the beauty of the place and the memories of what has been. I am trying to express myself better by writing poetry. For in a way the whole story of Tisala seems like a great epic in which the central figure is truth and the larger understanding of truth in the world.

Acknowledgements

I owe a great debt of thanks to a wide of range of people who helped me bring this book to fruition. Margaret, Jackie and Marilyn have been instrumental in transforming my almost illegible handwriting into type – thank you – without you, the manuscript would still be a stack of scrawled-on paper and backs of envelopes!

I am very grateful to all of my friends and family who read drafts of the novel: your comments and encouragement have all been invaluable in helping me improve the book. I would like to thank very much my editor and publisher, Toby at Blue Mark Books, for his patience and unstinting hard work over a long period.

But above all, I thank my wife, Sally, who has supported me in this rash adventure over more years than I care to count. Without her support it would never have been written.

Artwork Acknowledgements

The publishers and author are very grateful to Chris Lee for the cover concept and designing the front cover. Further examples of his work can be found at www.chrisleedrawing.co.uk

Cover concept and design by Chris Lee. Rear cover and jacket design by Blue Mark Books. Set in Bodoni Std Roman and Adobe Caslon Pro. Whale (front & spine) by Chris Lee; Sea by Chris Lee after a woodcut by Konen Uehara (1878-1940); Cuneiform courtesy of Richard Seward Newton; Harpoon guns (front) based on drawings from *Whalers No More* by W.G. Hagelund (Harbour Publishing Co. Ltd 1987); Dome (front) part of an 1859 drawing of the Capitol by Thomas Ustick Walter (1804-1887); Periodic table, atom, whaleboat and whale tail (rear) all copyright Blue Mark Books. All rights reserved.

While every effort has been made to trace the owners of copyright material produced on the jacket, the publishers would like to apologise for any omissions and would be pleased to incorporate any missing acknowledgements in future editions of the book.